The Rogue Queen

By

Rory McCauley-Hayman

This is a work of fiction. Names, characters, places, and incidents are either products of the author's imagination or used fictitiously. Any resemblance to actual events, locales, or persons, living or dead, is entirely coincidental.

Published by Rory McCauley-Hayman

ISBN: 978-1-970531-00-8

Cover design by Rory McCauley-Hayman

Cover art by Kiana Hayman [Hollyheart13]

Printed in the United States of America

Dear Reader,

This book was a gift to me when I started writing it, and I'm happy to share it with you in its physical form.

I've edited it as thoroughly as I can. Many of you may remember it in its original form, but this edition is a little different. Some scenes have been enhanced, others reduced, and a few descriptions expanded. Where it matters, though, it's still the same book many of you fell in love with.

Thank you for your continued support and for sharing your heart with me and my characters. I hope you enjoy this edition of my first novel.

Love,

Rory

To my family and friends — Thank you for loving me through every plot twist, character spiral, and "just one more chapter" writing binge. You kept me grounded while I lived in another world.

To my rogues — You fell in love with these chaotic characters right alongside me. Thanks for screaming in the comments, sending memes, and making me feel like I wasn't the only one emotionally compromised by fictional people.

Chapter 1: The Lost Pup

Warrick ran with the confidence of a young Alpha. His paws alighted on the ground as he skimmed through the woods. The wind whipped through his black and gray coat. Small animals scurried away as his large wolf ran freely through the forest.

This was his home, his land, and nothing could harm him here. He'd long left his friends behind, choosing to run at the full strength of an Alpha. He needed to clear his head.

He'd only just turned seventeen. They had a party and invited every unmated female in the pack. Warrick hoped to find his mate, but she wasn't in the pack. He'd have to wait for the next regional mate gathering. In the meantime, his Alpha training would start in earnest.

His parents expected him to be ready to take over the pack by the time he was twenty-five. Warrior training, management training, senior year of high school, extra-curricular activities, the pressure was immense. Everyone was watching him.

People compared him to his father. Pack members praised him or scolded him based on what his father would've done or what the Alpha of the Hunter's Moon Pack should have done. Warrick loved his pack, but he wanted to be seen for who he was, not what he would be or who he came from.

Hearing the babble of the stream in the near distance, Warrick decided to stop for a drink. The crickets and frogs quieted as he went past, resuming their songs after he'd gotten far enough away. He watched the water for a few moments. It soothed him.

The water was nice and cool, but after a couple of laps Warrick tasted blood. His wolf became agitated. He had to fix it. The health of the forest was his responsibility.

Warrick wandered upstream, looking for the source of the blood. Soon, he reached the area where the stream widened into a pond where he and his friends would usually swim. It was just deep enough for a fun time for the tall boys.

In the pale moonlight, he could see something floating. He shifted into his human form. On the shore, he ran his hand through his dark brown hair. The body was so small it looked like a child. His heart ached for the tiny human.

As Warrick waded out to the body, he heard a faint, struggling heartbeat. The kid wasn't dead! He moved faster, grabbing the little body and pulling it to him. It was a girl. The water made her hair dark and her little lips were blue from lack of air. The shadows of bruises played on her skin.

He took her to the shore of the pond and administered CPR. After a little while, she started coughing, and he pulled her to her side. A flood of water came from her lungs and stomach. Warrick rubbed her back as she retched, trying to clear everything out.

When she was done, he turned her to him. He smelled the scent of a rogue. It was coming from the girl. She was so close to death; her scent had faded. It didn't matter, though. She was small and weak. Not a threat to him or his pack.

Looking her over, Warrick found more cuts and bruises. Her clothing was stained and torn. This wasn't someone's cherished daughter. Her big eyes filled with tears.

"Pl… please… d-don't hurt me," she whispered in a raspy voice.

"I won't hurt you, pup. You're safe now. I'll keep you safe," he promised gently.

She started crying. It was a heartrending sound. All the pain she must have felt was in her sobs. Warrick rocked her and rubbed her back, telling her she was safe, trying to soothe her. Eventually, she faded into a hiccupping sleep.

Taking her home could be dangerous. Some wolves didn't care if a rogue was a child. They believed the only good rogue was a dead one. He decided to ask his father what to do. Alpha James was the smartest and strongest Alpha in the region.

'Dad, are you up?' Warrick asked through his link.

'Just heading to bed. Will you be back from your run soon?' his dad responded.

'I found a kid. She was nearly dead. I saved her, but I think she's an abandoned pup. She's not from our pack and she looks nearly starved,' he answered.

'Where are you? Is she awake? I'll be there shortly.'

'She's not awake. She started crying after I saved her and fell asleep.' Warrick gave his dad the location and waited.

About twenty minutes later, his father arrived with the pack doctor. Both men were just over six feet tall. Alpha James was thicker than Dr. Blair. Where the doctor was lighter in tone, with blond hair and pale blue eyes, Alpha James was much darker with chestnut hair and deep brown eyes. They were best friends, but opposite in almost every way.

Dr. Blair looked the girl over quickly. He shuddered thinking about what kind of monster could have hurt a child so badly. Tom turned to his Alpha with a worried expression.

"She's a rogue. There's no pack attachments on her, past or present. I'd guess she was born that way. She's weak right now; we could kill her easily if you choose, Alpha. What would you like me to do?" he asked.

He hated having to ask, but Tom knew he had to. Even though he knew his friend would never advocate killing a child. Rogue or otherwise.

"There's no crime a child this young could've committed, Tom. It's not her fault her parents were rogues. Let's take her in and get her healthy. Just because they did something wrong, doesn't mean we should," Alpha James said.

"Yes, Alpha. I'll take her to the van, Warrick."

"No. I'll carry her. I don't want to disturb her too much. This pup's been through a lot," Warrick replied.

His dad smiled at him. "Are you planning to put pants on or just walk around naked with a sleeping child in your arms?"

Warrick blushed. He was so focused on the girl that he hadn't thought about the fact he was naked. Dr. Blair helped him get a pair of shorts on and then led him to the van.

Alpha James was proud of his son. This was exactly the thoughtfulness and kindness he'd hoped to instill in his boys. He followed Dr. Blair and Warrick back to the van. Tom drove them to the pack hospital. They put the girl on a gurney upon arrival and wheeled her away.

"Nothing we can do from here. Dr. Blair will call us when she wakes up and we can ask her some questions. Good job, son." He patted Warrick on the back.

They got back in the van and drove to the pack house. It was only a few minutes away. Warrick leaned back against the headrest of the passenger's seat.

"I'm glad we could save her, Dad. I don't think her parents were taking very good care of her. What if we find out where she's from and it turns out they're bad? Can we keep her or do we return her?" Warrick asked.

"We'll have to assess the situation as it happens. Let's just get some rest and take care of what we can. I want to put you in charge of this situation. Do you think you can handle it?"

"Yeah. Can we have a couple warriors guard her so no one will hurt her just for being a rogue?" Warrick requested as they finally reached the Alpha's quarters.

"Sounds good. I'll put in the call. I don't think anyone in our pack would, but I understand where you're coming from." His father nodded.

"Thanks, Dad. Good night," he said and headed for his room.

James O'Connell watched as his son closed his door. If Warrick hadn't suggested it, he was planning to call in a couple warriors for the same reason. The boy had good instincts. The task would be an excellent exercise to start Warrick's Alpha training.

He went to his own bed after assigning a guard for the girl. Wendy would be happy to hear their son was a hero. She doted on the boys and always said what good men they'd grow into.

***

Two days later, Warrick got the call saying the girl had woken up. He'd been preparing questions and trying to plan for anything that could happen. If this was his first assignment, he was going to nail it.

Dr. Blair told him she was in and out of consciousness. She was weak from malnutrition and exhaustion. Warrick went to sit with her and try to talk whenever she was awake. The sooner Warrick settled the matter, the better.

When he reached the pack hospital, Diana, a nurse and Dr. Blair's mate met him. She took him to the girl's room. He saw two warriors standing guard and thanked them for their service before entering the room.

"We cleaned her up a little last night. Once she's up for longer, we'll get her a proper bath. Poor baby. She's been whimpering in her sleep," Diana said.

"Have you learned anything about her?" he asked.

"She's not offering any information when she's awake. There are cuts and bruises, which aren't healing as fast as they normally would. It looks like she's been whipped repeatedly. She has a silver burn on her neck as if someone put a collar on her. I don't know where her parents are, but, if they allowed this or did this, she shouldn't go back to them," she said solemnly.

The girl looked smaller, somehow. Warrick hadn't remembered her being so thin. Now there was light, he could see the silver burn. There was a bruise on her temple and more bruises on her wrists and arms. Some cuts on her arm looked pretty serious. He wondered who could want to hurt a little kid so badly.

"I'm gonna stay with her today. Is that okay?"

"Of course. Your father said you were in charge of her. I'll have the kitchen make you lunch later, but the Luna wants you home for dinner." Diana responded.

"I will be. Thank you, Diana," Warrick said as he sat by the girl's bed.

"No problem." She smiled and left the room.

***

It was another hour before the girl woke up again. Warrick saw her stir and put his phone away. She looked a little dazed, but not shocked about where she was. He saw her lick her lips and got up to pour her some water. Sitting her up, he helped her to drink and placed the cup on the table.

"Are you up to answering a few questions?" he asked.

She nodded slowly. Her eyes were wary, and she jumped at his movements. Warrick hoped he could help make her feel safe. As the future Alpha, he wanted to ensure the comfort and safety of everyone in his pack.

"My name is Warrick. What's yours?"

"B-Bellamy," she rasped.

"That sounds painful. Maybe we should wait on talking," he murmured.

She shook her head. "More water."

Warrick helped her to drink again. "Let me know when you need more or when you can't go on. Okay, Bella?"

"Amy. Please." She winced.

"Sorry, Amy. How old are you?" he continued.

"I think, twelve."

"You think?" Warrick asked.

"I remember six. No birthdays anymore. Counted Christmases."

"Where are your parents?"

"Dead. Hunters."

"When you were six?" he probed.

She nodded.

"Did the hunters take you? Is that why you're hurt like this?" Warrick questioned.

"No. I hid. CPS gave me to humans. I ran away. Tired. Sorry," Amy whispered.

He smiled. "Okay. Get some sleep. I'll wake you up for lunch. It'll probably be soup and Jell-O."

"Better than nothing… trust me." She laughed and grimaced at the pain.

Warrick chuckled and tucked the blankets around her. He mind-linked to Dr. Blair and Diana about her name and assumed age. Dr. Blair told him he'd thought she was closer to eight or nine, but malnutrition could've stunted her growth.

He contacted his future Beta, Marcus, to have him speak with his father about any murders in the area around six years ago that left a child survivor. It was a shot in the dark, but he hoped she came from a city or town nearby.

Chapter 2: An Uncertain Future

When Diana brought in lunch, she stopped to check Amy's vitals before waking her to eat. Warrick was right, it was chicken broth and jello. She sipped her soup. It would be a while before she had enough energy to heal any faster.

When she finished, she looked over at Warrick and nodded. She was ready for more questions. He thought about what information he would need.

"Do you remember your last name or your parents' names?"

She shook her head.

"Do you remember what city or town you lived in?"

She shook her head again.

"Why did you run away from the humans?" he asked.

"They didn't believe me about wolf. Said they were going to send me to a hospital. That I was delusional," she replied quietly.

"What happened after you left?"

"Stayed in parks. Ate from garbage. Lived in alleys. Stole clothes and food. Sometimes other rogues helped. Travelled with people. A witch took me home. Made me clean. Hurt me a lot. Fed me a little. Took blood for spells." Her eyes filled with tears. "Tried to sacrifice me."

"A dark witch. I'll let my father know to have patrols look out for her. Is that how you ended up in the pond?"

"Thought I was too weak. Didn't tie me up. Waited 'til she was doing something. Ran. Was so thirsty. Water was so cool. Wanted to die," she sobbed.

Warrick reached out and held her hand. She clung to him like he was the last solid thing on Earth. He couldn't imagine having to live like that. His parents had always been there, he'd always had food, and always been warm and safe.

"Do you want to join my pack, Amy? If we can't find anyone to take you, you can stay in the pack house with my family," Warrick offered.

"Please. I'll be good," she whimpered.

"I'll talk to my father. We'll look out for you. Do you know why your parents were rogues?"

"Mama rejected Alpha. Was in love with Papa," Amy replied. "Told to leave."

He smiled again. "Wow. They must have had a very strong love."

"How old?" She pointed to him.

"Seventeen. I *was* looking forward to meeting my mate, now I'm worried she might fall in love with someone before she meets me." Warrick chuckled.

She gripped his hand and looked warmly in his eyes. "Hope she doesn't."

"Thanks, Ames. You get some more sleep. We want you healed up as soon as possible." He patted her hand and stood to adjust the bed so she could lie down again.

A few hours later, his mother mind-linked him to come home for dinner. Warrick didn't want to just disappear, so he woke Amy a little and told her he was going home for the night, but she could have anyone call for him if she needed him. She gave him a sleepy smile and nodded.

***

When Warrick was out of the room, Bellamy sighed. Sleep was hard, and she'd been pretending in hopes he would leave. This was yet another twist in her already tangled life.

Losing her parents at such a young age was terrible. She still remembered them whispering their love for each other as they prepared to fight the hunters who were breaking into their house. From inside a large, decorative, wicker vase, Bellamy watched them fight for her life, for their lives, for the life of her little sister or brother still in her mama's tummy.

As she watched, the men cut them to pieces after shooting them. She vowed to train, find the hunters, and kill them. She'd been born a powerful rogue because of her parents' ranked blood. Through the years, Bellamy learned everything she could about fighting. She traveled with witches, vampires, other breeds of shifters, and even spent a year in a rogue collective.

After she finally found and killed the men last year, she let her guard down and ended up in the possession of that terrible witch. In the beginning, she was nice, but soon, she started giving Bellamy food laced with wolf's bane. Weakening her until she couldn't fight back. Putting that horrid collar on her like she was some mutt.

Bellamy shuddered. She hoped Warrick was telling the truth. More than anything, she wanted to feel safe again. She wanted someone to take care of her. She wanted to make friends and be happy. Bellamy prayed to the moon goddess.

"Please, let me have a home again," she whispered before exhaustion pulled her into a deep and troubled sleep.

***

When Warrick reached the packhouse, he was told he'd be having dinner in his father's office with his parents. It was strange, and he knew it was because they wanted privacy, probably to discuss what to do about their guest and her past. The offices were on the first floor of the house, and it didn't take long for him to get to his father's door.

"Close the door and come sit," his father instructed.

Warrick followed his Alpha's orders and sat at the empty spot around the small round table in the office's corner. Seated close as always, his parents nodded to him when he sat. He hoped his mate would want to sit as close to him as his mother always did to his father.

He gave his report on everything Amy told him. Warrick omitted the reason for her parents' banishment. If it was something illegal or violent, he would have told them. Breaking an Alpha's heart wasn't something they should be concerned about.

"Dr. Blair says she should be able to leave the hospital in a couple weeks. Her healing is slow, but they're pumping her full of fluids and all of her meals have added vitamins," Warrick told them.

"Good. The thing is… the witch has already started making incursions onto our land. She's looking for the girl and we've had patrols say they've scented her searching around the pond where you found her. The area smells like our pack because of how often we run there. We feel like it would be in the best interest of everyone if she were adopted out or sent to a rogue collective. Since you're in charge, I want you to make the decision on this. We can search for families in other packs who would be willing to take her in," Alpha James said.

"I told her she could stay here if I send her away… it would be like I was lying. I'm not saying you're wrong. The safety of our pack is important. I don't want to send her to a collective. She won't be able to protect herself. Is she able to stay at the hospital until she's better, or will it be too dangerous?"

He knew he had to think of the pack, which had about five hundred people, over one little girl. Even though he saved her, he knew he couldn't keep her safe against a witch. He just wasn't strong enough.

Warrick had always wanted a little sister and hoped to have one in Amy. She wouldn't have preconceived ideas about what an Alpha or future Alpha should do or how they should act. She'd just treat him like a normal brother. He could imagine her looking up to him and wanting him to protect her like a big brother should.

"We can keep her there for a few more days, maybe a week. Any longer, might not be safe," James answered solemnly.

"One person should be in charge of the decision. Mom, could you do it. No one else in the pack can know and I know you'll pick the best family for her," Warrick murmured in a strained voice.

"You got attached, didn't you?"

"I wanted her to be my little sister. I know how much Mom always wanted a daughter, but she got stuck with three boys. Amy's a little past the frilly dresses and hair bows stage, but I bet she'd let you dress her up any way you wanted." He chuckled.

"Thank you for thinking of me, sweetie. Right now, we have to think of her. I'll pick out the family who will give her the best life. Hopefully, it will be enough to make up for everything she had to suffer," his mom responded with a slight smile.

They finished their meal and Warrick went to his room to think of how he'd tell Amy she couldn't stay with them. She seemed smart. Her limited conversation had been rational and to the point. Maybe he could just tell her and it would be alright. He fell asleep with a lot weighing on his mind.

*****

Over the next couple of days, he visited often, but waited to tell Bellamy about having to move. Warrick wanted to make sure there was a family picked out and travel settled first. She was proving to be a very sweet girl.

Her stoic nature and polite attitude gained many fans around the pack hospital. She would have made a perfect Alpha's daughter. Something about the light in her eyes told people she was listening and caring, even if she wasn't responding much. And she was smart, too. Testing showed the only area she was lacking in was math.

Tyson, one of Warrick's younger brothers, visited Bellamy as well. He'd found she was great at fighting games. He brought a television and game console with him. She couldn't trash talk, because of her throat, but the top five high scores in his favorite game now read 'sukit'.

Through all of it, Bellamy waited. She could sense Warrick's nerves. Something was going on and she knew things would probably take a turn. Nothing in her life seemed to really work out. She'd always been looking for safety and stability.

Her whole life seemed to consist of loss and pain. The idea of living in a pack had given her hope. At least they weren't talking about sending her to a collective.

The year she spent in the Limb Torn collective was one of the best and the worst. Bellamy learned more about rogue born wolves, their laws, their traditions, and their abilities. But she hadn't found the security and safety she hoped to find. The leader, King Fuller, was a terrible, disgusting man who promised her to his son when she came of age.

Rogues believed females and males were equal in every way possible. It differed from pack wolves, who were often overly protective of their females. If this pack could accept her as an individual who didn't need to be attached to a male, she'd be thrilled. Bellamy knew she could be useful wherever she went, as long as the witch and King Fuller didn't get her again.

***

On the fifth day after he'd found her, Warrick rushed through his breakfast to get to the hospital as fast as he could. He didn't want Amy to feel alone for a single moment that she was with them. No matter what, she was his heart sister and he would always care for her.

He was right when he thought she'd see him and not his rank. Warrick vented to her about his stress and she listened while patting his hand. When she wrote responses, trying to reserve her voice, they were about what he felt and thought and not what he believed an Alpha would do.

"Warrick, come here for a second," his mother called out as he ran to the door.

"What's up, Mom?" he asked, changing his direction.

"I picked a family. It's a ranked family. They're very excited. They've always wanted a little girl but only had boys. She'll have four big brothers. It was the smallest family. They reminded me of why you wanted to take her in. She'll have a chance to find a decent mate when she's old enough, and she'll be well cared for." Luna Wendy smiled.

"Perfect, Mom. I hope those boys protect her like good brothers should. I'll let her know. How are we getting her to them?"

"We have several trucks and cars that leave every day. She'll be put into one leaving in the morning in three days. They'll meet another vehicle who will take her to a different town and so on until she gets to their pack. It'll have a lot of back tracking and misdirection, but we need to muddle the signal. After she's fully recovered, she'll join their pack," she explained.

"Got it. I'm gonna head out. See you later," he said with a wave.

At the hospital, Warrick entered Amy's room to see her awake and smiling. Someone had washed her hair. Now he knew it was actually a golden brown that looked like bronze. Her light brown eyes sparkled, and she looked a lot better.

"Wow, Ames. You're like a whole different person!"

"Dr. Blair said it was because of the vitamins. He said I might go home soon," she told him.

Her voice was so light and sweet. He hadn't expected it. More than anything, he wished he could have kept her. A precious little sister who sounded like an angel.

"I need to talk to you about that. Amy, the witch is looking for you. If we keep you here, she'll find you. My mom found a family in another pack. They really want you to come live with them. You'll have four big brothers to look out for you. As much as I'd rather have you for *my* little sister, I need to keep you safe," Warrick said softly.

"She's dangerous and powerful. It's not smart to keep me. I get it. I can't ask you to risk your lives for me." Amy looked resigned.

Warrick didn't like seeing her so sad. He wanted to see her happy. This was the best option for her. He knew she'd be happy in the long run.

"You know I wouldn't send you away if I had any other option, Ames. You're my heart sister. Just call me and I'll come running. I didn't save you just to have you get hurt again. You're meant for big things, kiddo." He smiled.

She returned his smile. He wondered if he looked sad, too. Warrick took off the necklace he was wearing. It was braided leather and had a carved white jade wolf's head pendant. He slipped it over her head.

"This is my promise to you. I'm always with you. The rest of the time you're here, I'm going to be here. I'll let my family know and I'll sleep right in this chair. We'll have every meal together. Just me and you, Ames," Warrick vowed.

Amy giggled. "Okay. Thank you, Ricky."

"*You* are the *only* one who gets to call me that," he said in a warning tone.

"You're the only one who gets to call me Ames." She winked.

Warrick snorted. "Weird kid."

Bellamy worried the new family might not want her as much as Warrick thought. She would try her best to convince them to keep her. She couldn't go back to living like she did before. Her survival depended on her finding a reason to live.

Chapter 3: Daylight Moon

[Bellamy]

It had been two days of travel since I left Warrick's pack. The people helping me would take me in one direction, then another, switching cars and drivers. I had no idea where I was or where I was going. I only knew I was getting away from the witch and that was enough for me.

I was on the last leg of my journey. The woman driving me was an ex-pack rogue who was friendly with the pack we were heading to. It was strange, but I figured it hadn't been the one that banished her, or she was from a destroyed pack.

Her name was Kate, and she was tall, willowy, and beautiful. She could be a model if she wanted.

As we drove, she made a little small talk. I generally tried not to give too much information. Ricky was the only person I'd ever told about my parents' exile. King Fuller was the only one other than him who knew. Well, Fuller and the Alpha who'd banished them.

"So, you're rogue born, right?" Kate asked, looking at me from the corner of her eye.

"Yes. I was born a year after my parents were exiled," I replied.

"I've only met a couple rogue born wolves. They don't like ex-pack rogues much." She laughed a little.

"You had different experiences and you're used to a different structure and culture. They get thrown off."

Kate smiled. "You're probably the nicest one I've met. I think you'll like being a pack wolf."

"It'll be good to have regular meals and a roof to sleep under. I just hope the parents they picked will be patient. It's hard going from one life to another," I told her quietly.

"They will be. I know they will. The Daylight Moon Pack is one of the top three packs in the region and they even help the rogues nearby if they need it."

"Cool." I nodded and stared out the window.

The city had faded into the countryside with fields of animals and crops butting up along the highway. My nerves were growing. I knew pack wolves knew little about rogue born wolves. I'd thought about downplaying my differences, but, in the end, I needed to grow stronger if I was going to protect myself. One day, Kyle would come for me, and I might have to fight him off.

I remembered the fight we'd had when I was eight. He was five years older than me and told me his father had given me to him. I was livid and told him I would deny him if I felt his wolf trying to influence mine. Kyle smacked me and said I would accept him or else.

Maybe he thought being raised by two ex-pack wolves would make me weak, but my papa had been the next in line to be head warrior in his pack and had trained me since I could walk. Bears, wolves, and vampires mentored me for the two years between when my parents died and when I ended up there. All of them taught me about fighting, at my request. I beat him soundly and told him I'd only mate with a male who didn't lose to me.

It had been big talk for a little girl. Once he was down and crying, I knew I didn't have long before his father would come after me. King Fuller inflicted well-known and terrible punishments. I ran.

My papa always told me, "Sometimes running is the best way to win a fight. Only the cocky and arrogant try to take on more than they know they can handle. It's better to live and plan than to fight and die."

"How do you deal with the idea of never having a mate?" Kate asked, pulling me out of my reverie.

"I don't understand."

"Rogue born wolves aren't given a mate by the moon goddess. You get heightened senses and stuff, but no perfect match. It seems lonely," she replied softly.

For all that I looked like I was much younger, and adults always ended up treating me as if I was much older after talking to me for a while. Probably the fact that I'd had to grow up faster. However, it could just be my intelligence. Papa had been really thoughtful and logical. It was good because Mama was really emotional and impulsive.

"It's another cultural difference. Being born a rogue is dangerous and we rarely have long life spans. The gift the goddess gives us is in being able to find a mate and create that bond ourselves. Our mate will either accept or deny the bond," I explained.

"If we reject a mate, we never get a second chance, our destined mate usually will, but we're mateless. Destined to find our own happiness and hope we can pick a mate as good as she did," Kate told me.

I knew this already. It was part of the story Mama would tell me. She'd refused the goddess' gift. Papa's mate died in a hunter attack on their pack the week after his seventeenth birthday. He would've had a second chance mate, but he was already in love with Mama. When her mate ended up being the Alpha, they were upset.

"A denial isn't the same as a rejection. Pack wolves reject something given, rogues deny a connection offered."

She pondered my words quietly. I enjoyed educating others on rogue traits, especially ex-pack rogues. The more they understood about their community members, the easier it would be to be friends. More than anything, I wanted people to be friendly. Fighting, wars, and deviousness all made me mad.

The fields bled into forest, and we started going up. I'd really been hoping for something like this. Playing in the trees was one of my favorite things about being alone. Running and hunting in the forest would be nice when I grew up. Things were looking pretty positive.

We talked about her mate search. She was an ex-pack child. One of her parents was exiled, taking the family with him. Kate was pack born but raised as a rogue. It was a tough situation.

She drove on for another thirty minutes, under two old pine trees which were slightly angled in an X over the road. I smiled. It was a border marker.

Soon, we slowed down and encountered a small gathering of people. There were several men who looked like warriors, three tall men standing in a half circle chatting, and a woman with four tall boys near a van. The woman had the same light brown hair as me. She was probably my new mom. Having the same coloring would be nice. It wouldn't be as obvious that I wasn't hers.

Kate stopped the car and turned it off before getting out and running around the car to open my door. I still had some healing to go, but I could manage a door. My nerves didn't exactly make me able to refuse when she told me she'd get it. I took her hand and exited the car.

We approached the group, who were now watching us closely, and I reached for my necklace, rubbing the little white wolf pendant. This was a terrible idea. I shouldn't have accepted. My stomach turned and tumbled. Kate patted my hand when a whimper escaped.

Way to look strong, Amy. I told myself.

"Hello, Alpha Moore." She smiled and called out.

One of the three tall men waved and started forward. He had blond hair, a thin build, and lithe muscles. Alpha Moore was only wearing shorts. As was one other man in the trio. The third man wore a gray polo shirt and blue jeans. He had dark brown hair and was bulkier than the Alpha.

"Hey, Katie! Is this Bellamy?" the Alpha asked.

"Yep. Safe and sound, as promised." Kate chuckled.

"Toby, get Katie some money for gas and her time. We appreciate you helping out."

"Happy to do it. She's a good kid." Kate winked as the other man in shorts handed her a thick envelope.

She let go of my hand and patted my head before trotting back to her car. I could feel my heart in my throat as I heard her turn around and drive away. We were at least three miles inside their border. I could outrun most people at full strength, but I wasn't anywhere near full strength yet.

The Alpha knelt down to talk to me. I hated being short. I was short for a wolf my age, heck; I was short for a human my age.

"Hi, Bellamy. We were told you like being called Amy, is that right?" he asked gently.

I nodded. Now that he was closer, I could see his light brown eyes. They were nice. He didn't look like he was bad in any way. I worked to calm myself.

"I'm Kieran Moore. I'm the Alpha of the Daylight Moon Pack. On my left is Tobin Franks, he's my Gamma. On my right is Daniel Carrington, my Beta," he explained.

The man on the left was shorter than the others, but not by much. He was the one who'd handed Kate the envelope. Similar to the Alpha, he was lean and had decent muscles. He had black hair and light blue eyes.

"I know this is a little scary, but I wanted to meet you. Your new mom wants you sworn into the pack as soon as possible. She's a bit mean." He winked.

I smiled a little, and they seemed to relax. For some reason, I was having trouble speaking. I'd never been too afraid to talk before. This was more like a disconnect between my brain and mouth. The man in jeans, Beta Daniel, knelt down.

"I'm your new dad. If you'll accept me. We want you to be safe. All we were told was your name and age, you were born a rogue, you were an orphan, and a witch was looking for you. Our pack is friendly with light witches who'll come tomorrow to get your aura cleaned of anything she could use to track you," Daniel informed me.

"Thank you," I whispered.

Thank the goddess! I thought I was mute.

He grinned. "Would you like to meet my wife and sons? She's been chattering in my head ever since we got to you."

I giggled. "Yes, please."

Chapter 4: A New Family

Daniel held out his hand, and I took it, following him back to the woman and boys. She was clasping her hands under her chin and bouncing with excitement. Though she wasn't as short as me, she was about five and a half feet tall, which made her the second shortest person on the road. She had a kind smile and a slight figure.

One boy whispered something to the other three, who hit him in a brotherly way. Not like they wanted to hurt him, but not like they were entirely playing. I'd seen Ricky and Ty doing that a lot. They were all varying mixes of their parents but had their father's solid build.

"Bellamy, this is my wife, Olive, and our sons, Galen is the oldest, then Hollis, Porter, and Bruce," he said, pointing out the boys who raised their hands at their names.

"That's a lot of boys," I murmured.

"It really is! I'm so happy you're here! You know Kieran's daughter is your age. I bet you'll be best friends!" Olive gushed.

"I'd like that."

It wasn't a lie. I'd love to have a friend, but pack wolves were particular about rogues. I fought not to wince as I remembered the rant Ricky's youngest brother, Rhys, went on about how dirty, violent, and useless rogues were. He was only a year older than me, so I forgave him for being a jerk. Thirteen-year-old boys held big ideas about the world, and pack boys sometimes acted arrogantly.

"Let's get you to the pack doctor for a check-up, then we'll show you your room. The fourth floor of the packhouse is split between the Gamma and Beta families, the fifth is for the Alpha family, the third is for guests, the second is offices and meeting rooms, and the first is general common areas. The boys will show you around tomorrow. I want you to eat and rest for the rest of the day," she said in a commanding voice.

It suddenly hit me. I was a Beta's daughter. Not a common wolf in a pack, but a member of the higher rank wolves. I'd been a little relieved about not joining Ricky's family when I found out he was the future Alpha. I didn't think I could manage to be a good Alpha's daughter. Could I really be good enough to be a Beta's daughter?

They pulled me along to the van, where I sat next to one of my new brothers. He was the youngest and had the same dark brown hair as his dad, but was about an inch taller than his mom. I jumped a little when he took my hand.

"Don't be afraid. We only eat redheads." He snickered.

"I'm allergic," I whispered. All the boys started laughing.

"She'll fit in great," one of the ones in the back said.

It was another ten minutes through the forest before the pack's town came into view. They had some little stores, a movie theater, a community pool, an elementary school, a middle school, a high school, and a library. I liked it. Olive told me the only humans who lived there were the ones mated to wolves, so we didn't need to keep it a secret.

After a quick stop for a check-up with the pack doctor, we continued on to park in front of an enormous house that overlooked the town. I was going to live in a mansion. My life had officially hit a peak. Getting out of the van, Olive and the boys led me into the house. It was immense.

They took me by the kitchen and introduced me to the omegas and other staff who worked there. The head of the kitchen introduced himself as Yuri and asked what my favorite foods were.

I just stared. A *favorite* food? I was just happy to eat.

"I… I don't know. Sorry," I murmured.

"We'll figure it out. You just tell me what you liked and what you didn't like after each meal," he said cheerfully.

I glanced around the room and saw pitying looks from the staff. It made me blush. No one had ever pitied me before. At least, not to my face. This whole thing was far more overwhelming than I thought it'd be. Olive and the boys took me out to the hall again.

"We usually have everyone use the back stairs. The front stairs are for guests, normally. There's an elevator over this way. Kieran's dad had it put in so his wife wouldn't have to walk all the way down the stairs when she was pregnant. Daisy, Bren, and I appreciated it when our times came." She laughed. "You boys take the stairs. I'll take Amy up."

They grumbled quietly and turned to a door, which I was guessing was the stairwell. Olive took me to the elevator, and we headed up to the fourth floor.

"I know, it's overwhelming. My family is one of the poorer ones in the pack. Imagine finding out my mate was the future Beta. I thought he'd reject me, for sure," she said.

"I can imagine. He wouldn't have, though. I've met ex-pack wolves. They all talked about how much they loved their mate at first sight. Even if they didn't know them before," I whispered.

It made what my mother did even worse. I'm all for true love and following your heart, but she'd broken someone else's heart terribly. The way she described it, she wasn't exactly gentle either.

Alphas tended to be aggressive and possessive, so I understood her need to completely shut him down. I just hated to think of the pain he must have gone through. I'd have kicked them out, too.

"You'll never have to worry about that. No male would reject the daughter of a Beta. When you find your mate, he'll accept you right away," Olive assured me.

I felt my face pale as all the blood in my body felt like it turned to ice. She panicked as I swayed on my feet. I was going to have to watch everyone find and claim mates. When I was seventeen, Kyle would look for me. Even if no one knew I was a rogue, he'd make sure they did. He wouldn't give up until I accepted him.

When the elevator doors opened, Daniel was standing there and picked me up. He carried me into an apartment, down the hall to a door that one of the boys opened, and set me on the bed. I was still panicking. The world felt distant, and I fought hard to find my way back. I told myself I would regain my composure and take control.

"What happened?" he asked.

"We were just talking and she went white as a sheet and started looking like she was going to faint. I don't know, maybe I said something wrong," Olive replied.

She sounded so scared and hurt. It instantly brought me back. I had to protect others. It was in my blood. She needed reassurance, and only I could give it successfully. I took a deep breath and held it for a few seconds before letting it out slowly.

"I'm sorry. I panicked. You didn't say anything wrong. You just don't understand what being rogue born means. I'd rather not explain this a lot, so do you think I could meet with everyone who needs to know as soon as possible? I'd like to do it before I'm too tired," I told them.

Daniel looked at Olive and then stared off into the middle distance. That's what mind-linking looked like sometimes. It seemed like he was just spacing out. I knew he had finished when he briefly closed his eyes before opening them and speaking to me.

"Rest for a while. I have Yuri working on a snack for you and we'll meet with Kieran, Tobin, Dr. Hale, and Clint. Clint's the head of the warriors."

"The future leadership should be there, too. It'll concern them. And the wives of all the head families. The Luna will need to know and her supports are your and Gamma Tobin's wives. They'll need to know how best to help you navigate," I said.

He chuckled. "You know a lot about pack wolves."

"I talked to ex-pack wolves whenever I could. I like knowing things."

"Are you going to tell us about your parents or your past?" the oldest boy asked.

He would be the new Beta when Daniel retired. That would be when the new Alpha took over. I wondered what this pack's rules were for it. With some, it was when they found their mate, with others it was when they felt ready. I guessed I'd find out.

"I'll tell you some things. I won't tell others. Unfortunately, I don't know what pack my parents came from, but even if I did, I'd like to not have my life as a pack wolf associated with theirs," I replied.

"Okay. We'll respect that. I'll be back in thirty minutes to take you to the meeting room. Explore your space or lay down, whatever feels right," Daniel said, and then they all left.

I looked around the room for the first time. Ricky had asked for my favorite colors. It was obvious he'd passed the information on to my new parents. They decorated the room in lavender, carnation pink, and forest green.

The hardwood floor had a large circular green rug and there was a purple flower rug in front of the door to the hall and one in front of another door. I crossed the room to look. It was a bathroom. My very own bathroom. The shower curtain had pink and purple dots in a pattern, the bath mats and hand towels were forest green, and there were two purple bath towels.

Returning to the bedroom, I looked in the dresser. There were all sorts of clothes, jeans, slacks, skirts, three different lengths of socks, different pajamas, and new underclothes. I hadn't worn underclothes in ages. The closet next to the dresser had dresses ranging from somber to frilly, t-shirts, blouses, tank tops, sweaters, and jackets. I'd regained a lot of the weight I'd lost and wondered if any of this would even fit me.

It wasn't that I was chubby; I was just practically a skeleton when they'd found me. With all the vitamins and stuffing me full of food for the past week, there were very few places where my bones were visible now. In the coming weeks, I'd probably gain more.

I returned to the bed and laid down on the pink comforter. The bed was so soft. I couldn't remember a time when I'd had anything like this bed. It was like a cloud.

Soon, there was a knock at the door. I jumped a little. The knock came again. Actual privacy. I nearly laughed. It wasn't funny, but relieving.

"Come in," I called out.

Daniel entered and smiled. I wondered at how easily this family smiled and laughed. My family had been like that. Ricky and Ty were, too. Maybe I could be as easygoing and cheerful, one day. Until then, I'd have to fake it.

"Everyone's ready and your snack is waiting. I'll carry you so you don't get too tired," he told me.

"Thank you. Umm… what do you want me to call you?" I asked.

"The boys call me Dad. You can if you want. Whatever makes you comfortable."

I sighed. "I'll let you know what I figure out."

He chuckled and picked me up, carrying me to the elevator and hitting the button for the second floor. Once we arrived, he walked down the long hallway to a room at the end.

"We had to use the lecture room. The boys all wanted to come, too. They want to support you and knowing about you helps. If you want, they can leave. We have the primary medical team, several elders, Kieran, Daisy, Bren, Tobin, Olive, Jason, Todd, and Clint. You let me know if you get overwhelmed and we can stop," he said softly.

"Okay," I whispered. I didn't know why we were being quiet, but I was okay with that.

Chapter 5: An Explanation and an Offer

When the door opened, we walked into a room with rows of chairs and tables. At the front was a podium, whiteboard, and a table with a bunch of different foods and fruits. My eyes widened at the food.

They didn't expect me to eat all of that, did they?

Next to the food table was another little table with a chair behind it. Daniel carried me there and put me in the chair. He moved to the food table and gathered a little of everything on a couple of plates, putting them in front of me. Then he nodded to the group and a few others came up to get plates. Thank goodness.

I picked through the plate directly in front of me. It was full of fruits. I noticed Yuri in the front row of seats with a notepad. Not weird at all… I picked up something green with a ring of little black dots and bit into it. I wrinkled my nose a little, but finished the entire piece. I didn't like the flavor.

After trying a few more things, some I knew and others I didn't, I looked up to see if people were ready. Most were lightly chatting, some were watching me, and others were concentrating on their food. Alpha Kieran saw me looking and cleared his throat, gaining everyone's attention.

"It looks like Bellamy's ready," he said. They all turned to me. "Go ahead."

"I'm trying to think of where to start. Both of my parents were pack wolves, almost everything I learned about being born a rogue, I learned during a year I spent in a rogue collective. A few other things I learned while traveling with others. Like, vampires prefer the taste of pack born wolves to rogue born wolves," I stated.

There was a low growl in the room at the mention of vampires. I knew the animosity wolves had with vampires. Talia, the vampire I'd traveled with for five months, was surprised at my lack of aggression. I fed her in exchange for information, training, and companionship.

"Did a vampire attack you?" Olive whispered.

"Yes, but not the one who told me that. She was my friend. We were together for five months. She taught me how to fight like a vampire," I explained.

This made the faces of Kieran, one elder, and Clint, to light up. Exactly like I'd hoped. Now, I had hope they would consider my training requests.

"Being rogue born means my senses are heightened more than a pack wolf's. You mostly get attacked by ex-pack wolves who are violent and unstable. Some ex-packs can't cope with being rogue and begin hurting themselves or others. It helps if they were banished with their mate," I told them.

"So, none of the rogues who've attacked have been rogue born?" a young man asked.

"Some might have. For the most part, they have no reason to attack. All they usually want is to live their lives. Unless a rogue King or rogue Queen orders it, they're pretty non-violent."

"A rogue King or Queen?" Kieran asked.

"Yes. They're an Alpha rogue born. Males and females are equal in rogue culture. You can see that difference in our mating rituals. When *you* turn seventeen, as a pack wolf, you can find your destined mate. They are given to you by the moon goddess and the males protect, while the females support. Rogue born wolves don't have destined mates." I saw Olive's hand cover her mouth.

"Instead, we pick our mate. We look for a person who'll match with our lives, strengths, weaknesses, and personalities. When we pick someone, their wolf, if they have one, is given our request. If they accept, we get to feel the stuff you do when you find your mate, if not, we move on and so does the other person. It's not a rejection, but a refusal. Since it doesn't anger the moon goddess, the person who denies the other can still find a mate," I explained.

The room was silent as they took the information in. Mates were important in werewolf society, no matter how they were born. Every young wolf was excited to find their other half. I hoped to find one when I was old enough, though it wasn't likely.

"When you're old enough, how will you find a mate?" a blonde woman asked.

I was guessing the woman was the Luna. She was sitting with Olive and another woman in the same pattern as their husbands. Luna in the middle, Beta female to the right, gamma female to the left.

"If I wanted a pack wolf, I'd look for an unmated male who had lost his mate and had no second chance mate. Alternately, I can look for a rogue born who has no prejudices. That's pretty hard to find. Otherwise, I'll just have to stay unmated. To request a mate who's already promised would make the goddess mad. I don't want to do that. Though… I guess I need to tell you… A rogue King may come looking for me after I turn seventeen. If I can't beat him in a fight, I'll have to be his mate," I told them with a blush.

"Explain," Kieran commanded.

"When was younger, I lived in a rogue collective. A bear I'd been traveling with took me there after we were attacked by vampires. The king, Mr. Fuller, said I could stay as long as I wanted. Once I was healed, I trained and learned more about being born rogue.

"One day, about a year later, Kyle, Mr. Fuller's son, also a rogue King, told me his father promised me to him when I turned seventeen. I told him I'd deny him. I refuse to be told who to mate with. He hit me and told me he'd beat me until I accepted him."

I took a deep breath. "He was thirteen, and I was eight, but I'd spent six months training with Stanton, the bear, five months with Talia, the vampire, the whole year I was training with the other rogue born warriors, and my father was a warrior who trained me since before I could walk. I beat Kyle up and ran away.

"He feels entitled to me. I told him I'd only mate with a male who didn't lose to me in a fight. Now, it's a requirement for me to find a mate. I can't have a rule that applies only to him. He must've turned seventeen in the last month because I've already gotten an offer from him and refused it. I don't have a wolf to pass the message, but I can still refuse."

"We'll protect you," one of my new brothers said. The others nodded in agreement, along with every other male in the room. They didn't understand. I sighed.

"You can't do that. I'm happy you all are willing, but I can't allow it. It'll make my wolf upset. I have to protect myself." I got nervous.

Telling them about Kyle made my stomach turn, but I didn't want them to be caught off-guard. This was the only way. I knew I had to tell them why they couldn't protect me. If they were going to be my pack, my family, I had to be honest.

"I'm a rogue Queen. I have to accept his challenge just as any Alpha would have to accept the challenge of a rival Alpha. If an Alpha challenged Alpha Kieran and everyone stepped up to protect him, he'd be seen as weak. For him it might mean losing his status, for me, it would mean losing my wolf or my life. I either have to fight him, or find a mate who's as strong as me," I said softly.

"You'd need an Alpha-blood mate," Kieran replied. "A son of an Alpha at least."

"That'll depend on her strength," Clint told him. "Once you're feeling better, we'll test you and see where you're at. I'll train you to the best of my ability."

"Thank you. I'll be happy to share what I learned while traveling." I smiled.

This seemed to please several of the men. They may not like being unable to protect me, but I could help them protect their pack. It would be enough.

"What about the witch who's tracking you?" Daniel asked.

"She needs to use my blood in a lot of complicated spells and then sacrifice me for the power she wants. Since I ran away, she has to start the ritual all over again," I told him.

"Can we protect you from her or is that going to hurt you, too?" Tobin asked.

"You can protect me from anything not wolf-related. I don't know that she'll keep looking after losing my trail. Once the light witches clean my aura, she'll probably give up and try to find another rogue born Alpha." I shrugged.

"Is there anything else that's important about you or rogue born wolves?" Alpha Kieran asked. "I don't want to keep you from your rest too long."

"There's little that's immediately important. I'll discuss physiological differences with the medical team later. There is one thing. I… It's a little awkward. I want to help protect your lands and… I can stop other rogues from attacking, but… I have to claim your pack. It means nothing to the way your pack runs, really. If rogues came to the pack land, they'd sense it was protected by a rogue Queen. I'd meet them at the border and call this my territory." I blushed as he looked appalled. "They'd smell my connection to the pack and would back off. A rogue Alpha rarely claims a territory they can't defend. Word would spread and we'd be treated as a rogue collective rather than a pack."

There was some heavy mental messaging in the room. I picked at my food. I wanted to offer my protection. Giving them a voice when facing larger rogue groups would be very helpful. I wouldn't do it unless they wanted it.

"What would it entail exactly?" Alpha Kieran inquired.

Honestly, it shocked me. Most Alphas would feel threatened if another Alpha tried to claim their pack and territory. That told me they'd had issues with rogues earlier. I could at least be helpful.

"When you swear me into your pack, I will ask that you're as loyal to me as I am to you. You just answer with yes, and we'll be set. Rogues don't like a lot of chatter when getting things done. This is probably the most I've talked in one sitting." I laughed.

"You won't require anything but my loyalty? What does it mean, though?" he questioned.

I sighed. Alphas weren't very trusting with outsiders in their packs. He was doing what he needed to do for his people. I just really wanted to go to sleep for a while.

"It means we talk about things, especially decisions that'll affect me or the territory I'm claiming. You won't try to get another rogue Alpha to kill me, I won't try to get another pack Alpha to kill you. If I see anything that could harm you and yours, I tell you immediately or try to protect whoever it is, you promise the same. Pretty basic," I replied.

He had a thoughtful look and mind-linked to Daniel and Tobin. They all nodded. I hoped that meant they were accepting my offer.

"You're a twelve-year-old girl! You can't protect anything! It doesn't matter that you're a rogue Queen, none of the rogues will take your claim seriously and others will think we're weak! What kind of pack could be claimed by a little girl!?" an older man growled. He shocked the ranked members and their families with his venom.

"Dad, chill out. She's just trying to help," Gamma Tobin hissed.

I pushed my chair out and stood. My energy was low, but I needed to see if I could calm him. I hoped I wouldn't pass out from the attempt. I took a deep breath, closed my eyes, and mentally scanned the room. The moth in the corner, the small crack in the windowsill where a slight breeze tried to come in, each person and their existence. The way each one breathed, the way they smelled, the way the air made space, the sound of their heartbeats.

When I opened my eyes, I focused intently on him. I could taste his age and experience. I could feel his life and its connections. He was a widower. Too old to need a second chance, so his connection was empty.

His son and grandson were right there. I could feel the connection to Tobin's mate. The boy's connection to his mate was light and wispy. She wasn't in this pack. I focused again on the older man. He was angry and embarrassed. As the previous Gamma, he probably had a lot of pride in his pack. Without a mate to spend time with, he was lost and wandering like a spirit.

I sat down again and started snacking. It was too much. I couldn't pull his fear from him. I couldn't bring him someone to soothe him.

"Then don't accept. I already explained the benefits. Like gender, age doesn't matter to rogues only skill and strength. The threat of a twelve-year-old who could take on a pack and claim them is more frightening than you'd think. I'm sorry you're lonely and feel useless, but I won't let you have a home in my head. Too many things already live there," I replied quietly, with a slightly quivering voice.

Part of me was angry because I sounded like I was upset. Most of me was too tired to care. If he wanted to win in a fight against a child, I'd let him. There were more important things for me to worry about.

"Let me think about it, Amy. You make a good point. I'm not going to discount you. You look tired. Let's have your parents take you home and get you to bed." Kieran smiled.

"Okay. I'm not feeling great anyway," I told him.

Daniel stood and picked me up. The younger boys and Olive followed. The oldest was talking quietly with his future Alpha. I wondered what they were discussing, but wouldn't question it.

When we reached my room, Olive helped me change into a nightgown. She told me we'd have dinner in the small kitchen in their living area, so I wouldn't have to change.

Once Olive tucked me into the soft bed, I fell asleep almost immediately. I couldn't help but wonder if I'd sleep without the nightmares. This was a big shift in my life, and I knew my brain would want to replay the others.

Chapter 6: Strength Test

[Bellamy]

—Five days later—

After breakfast, I threw on a tank top and workout pants. Today, I'd get to take my physical ability test and get sworn into the pack. Last night, Alpha Kieran accepted my offer to claim the pack. He said his son, Jason, convinced him of how it could help provide a safer place for the pack. They'd been having issues with rogues for years. In the time I'd been there, rogues had attacked the border guards three times.

Galen met me at my door. He was just about six feet tall, with dark brown hair and light brown eyes. He had the same thick build as his dad and was well-muscled. Galen belonged to the warrior's elite fighting class. I was determined to reach the top class in the shortest time possible.

He was excited. It was easy to bond with the people in the packhouse and my new family. We'd all grown closer in the last few days. The boys had visited with me and took me around to the garden in the back for some time in the sun. We played video games together, and they talked about their family and friends.

Bruce introduced me to Cara, Kieran's daughter, and we really hit it off. She was beautiful with strawberry blonde curls, impish blue eyes, a sweet button nose, and a self-assured smile. Of course, Cara was taller than me, even though we were the same age. But she was fun, friendly, and didn't rub it in. Everyone loved her.

Cara insisted they introduce me to Todd's two younger cousins. Their names were Drake and Dillon. They were both really fun in different ways. Drake enjoyed playing fighting games with me and Dillon would sneak snacks from the kitchen and gossip about all the things he heard while sneaking around. They were a year older than me and Cara, but we all got along really well.

"You ready to show us what you got, Amy?" Galen asked with a grin.

"I hope no one's disappointed. I haven't really been able to train in about a year," I replied.

"Just do your best. As you grow we'll move you up into the other ranks of training."

"What can I expect here?" I asked.

"First, we'll check your strength. Then, speed and coordination. After that, you'll fight Clint. He's the only one who didn't think he'd have a problem with fighting a little girl." Galen laughed.

"Thanks. I'm ready." I smiled, and we headed to the training grounds.

The sun was warm, and everything felt electric. Training soothed me when I was without a home. I remembered my father's deep patient voice encouraging me and telling me what I needed to do to be better. He was the best teacher. It made me feel safe when there wasn't any safety to be had.

We approached the field. There was a raised platform at one end and some metal bleachers on the sides. The Alpha, Beta, and Gamma were all in attendance, along with their oldest sons. It made me a little nervous. I was fine with training around other people, but having people watch me was weird.

Clint met me at the edge of the field and sent Galen to sit with his friends. I saw my other brothers sitting under the bleachers with Cara, Drake, and Dillon. They'd all been told not to come but had anyway, to 'support' me. I held back a smile as they made faces.

"I have some weights over here set up with where we think you're at. We need to find the heaviest one you can lift without strain. Got it?" Clint asked.

I nodded and went to where he pointed. The bar had two small discs on it, and I started laughing. It couldn't have been over ten pounds altogether.

"I'm just messing with you." He chuckled and added some larger weights.

It was a little over a hundred pounds now. I lifted it easily. Most wolves my age could lift more. He was probably trying to make sure I didn't overdo it so soon after healing.

We spent the next twenty minutes adding weights and lifting. He was going up by small amounts each time he added weight. Once I couldn't lift the bar without a struggle, he marked down the weight and date so we could mark my progress. I saw his gaze drift over my head. He was reporting back to the ranked members.

"Next is speed. I want you to run as fast as you can to the benches there and back," Clint instructed. "Go," he said, clicking a little stopwatch.

I ran as fast as I could, kicked off the seat of the bench to turn and ran back, stopping in front of him. Clint blinked and stopped the watch, shaking his head.

"Holy shit," he whispered. "I barely saw you move."

I blushed. "Sorry, did you need me to do it again?"

"No. You said you were an Alpha, but I didn't expect *that*." He snorted. "Let's just move to the fight. I can gauge your speed for blocking and attacking, along with your coordination there."

"Alright." I smiled.

He put down his watch and led me to the center of the field. Clint showed where he wanted me to stand and walked to his own starting spot, not too far away. I watched how he walked and moved. I'd been thinking of everything I'd seen of him since I arrived.

Clint was right-hand dominant and led with that leg. It held most of his weight when standing. At some point in the last few days, he'd taken a hard hit to the ribs and was breathing shallowly. That rib injury must have been serious if it hadn't healed yet.

I closed my eyes and took a deep breath, focusing on the area where he was standing. I could hear his heart beating, his lungs taking in breath, the rustle of his clothing. Breathing in, I could smell the scent of his shampoo and shaving cream. I could smell the scent of his wolf and his excitement. Warriors loved a good fight, and he was expecting one.

Then I smelled something else. It wasn't coming from the direction Clint was in. I opened my eyes and turned. Something moved behind a tree not far from the bleachers. I ran to the weights and grabbed a disc before taking off toward the scent.

The rogue didn't have time to react. He was staring intently at Cara and hadn't noticed me. Since he was upwind, no one watching had scented him yet. Plus, pack born wolves had worse senses of smell than rogue born wolves. But I could smell him.

An obsessed ex-pack. I knew the look and the smell. They often stole younger girls to raise as their mates. I jumped the last few feet and swung the weight upside his head as I landed.

Bringing my arm back up, I smashed his nose with the weight while repeatedly pounding my knee between his legs. He whimpered in defeat and bared his neck before my next swing. I tossed the weight aside and pressed my fingers into his windpipe.

He stared, terrified, into my eyes.

"You're in *my* territory. That's *my* female," I growled.

He coughed in answer.

"This will be your chance to gain my mercy. You tell every rogue you know that Queen Bellamy has claimed this land and this pack. If I see you, hear you, or smell you, within a mile of my territory, I'll rip out your heart and eat it while the light fades from your eyes. Do you understand?" I threatened.

The rogue nodded, and I let him up. He stumbled and ran, limping heavily, back the way he came. I watched until he disappeared into the tree line. Not the brightest bulb, trying to steal a girl with all those guys around.

"Fuck, Amy! That was awesome!" Galen shouted.

"You totally kicked his ass!" Drake cheered.

I turned to look at them. The men were already behind me, but everyone else stood further away. Clint grinned and clapped Daniel on the back.

"She fights like a demon. No mercy until he gave in. That mutt won't ever reproduce." He laughed.

"Bellamy. How did you know he was there?" Kieran asked cautiously.

"Rogues are more sensitive to the scent of other rogues. Especially ex-pack. They smell off. They're not meant to be without their people and it changes them," I replied softly.

"Do you know what he was after? Was he trying to kill the Alpha?" Daniel asked.

"He was after Cara. Those who go rogue without a mate sometimes get obsessed with finding one. They'll take unmarked girls, human, rogue, pack, it doesn't matter, and drag them around until they break and call the male 'mate'. I met a girl who was stubborn, a year and a half ago. He'd had her for seven months before she broke. I almost wasn't fast enough and he nearly marked her. She couldn't have been much older than Bruce. I returned her to her pack's territory," I answered.

"Pansy Killian," Tobin whispered.

I nodded. "That was her name."

"Pansy always said a little rogue saved her. No one believed it. Pansy was sixteen, just young looking. She found her mate at the regional gathering last April. She's in the Ice Moon pack," Tobin told me.

"I'm glad."

"Will sending that message bring anything down on us?" Kieran asked.

"The next few times rogues are spotted; I should be notified. I'll release one more to verify the ex-pack's story. All others, I'll kill," I informed him.

I didn't look at their faces. Even though we were wolves, there were some human ideals we're prone to. I knew they were shocked and disgusted. A child talking about killing so easily… no adult liked that. They would probably ask me to leave. Too much, too soon. Rogue born wolves were not meant for packs.

Two big arms scooped me up into a hug. It was Daniel. He held me tightly and rocked me back and forth.

"You did great, Amy. I'm so proud of you," he whispered as he kissed the side of my head.

I wrapped my arms around his neck and squeezed him close. "Thank you, Daddy," I whispered back.

He laughed. "She called me Daddy! Not Daniel!"

My brothers whooped, and I couldn't help but smile. They accepted me. Even though I was a killer. Even though I was a rogue. They still wanted me. I vowed to do everything I could to make sure they never regretted their decision.

Chapter 7: Welcome to the Pack

[Bellamy]

Later that evening, we gathered in the main common room of the packhouse. Nobody dressed up for my swearing in. Everyone was cheerful and grinning.

Luna Daisy had given me an enormous hug when we got home. I felt terrible about getting rogue blood on her dress, but she said it was worth it and thanked me for saving Cara. We all needed a long rest after, and Yuri only bothered me a little at lunch and dinner. It was eventually time to become one of them.

Olive looked on proudly as I stepped toward where the Alpha and Luna were waiting. There was a small golden bowl on the coffee table next to an obsidian-bladed knife. I was nervous again.

I knew an ex-pack could enter a new pack, but rogue born wolves didn't. I worried their bond wouldn't take or the moon goddess would be angry about me giving my freedom away.

In a way, being rogue born was a gift. We had different abilities. We were more physically capable because we didn't have packmates to fall back on. I hoped she wouldn't take offense at it.

I moved forward and faced Kieran. Daisy picked up the knife and handed it to him, then held the bowl in two hands, waiting. I put my hand out, and he held my wrist.

"Bellamy Carrington, do you promise to uphold all the values and traditions of the Daylight Moon pack? Following our laws, accepting our punishments, and carrying on in a way that honors our pack and its leaders."

"I do," I responded.

"Do you promise to care for its members as if they were your own family? Joining with their happiness and helping heal them in their sorrow."

"I do."

"Will you lay down your life to protect your pack and its Alpha? Using your claw and tooth to ensure the lives and wellbeing of all our people."

"I will."

He nodded.

"Kieran Moore, Alpha of the Daylight Moon pack. Will you vow to loyally join with me in the care of this territory, claiming all my enemies as yours, and fighting at my side in battle?" I asked. "Will you put the safety of your pack into my hands, trusting in my claw and fang to be your protector as I trust in your claw and fang to be mine?"

"I will," he responded.

I nodded. He sliced a minor cut in both of our wrists and took my forearm, pressing them together. Daisy held the bowl under our dripping wounds and caught the blood we shed together. We held until the cuts closed. I didn't feel any different. Wasn't I supposed to feel different?

"The bond has been forged. Welcome to our pack." Kieran smiled.

I bowed. "Thank you, Alpha Kieran."

"Bellamy? Could you hear me trying to mind-link you?" Olive asked.

"No. I can't hear anything," I whispered.

I began to panic. The goddess rejected my application. She hadn't let me join the pack. Tears began welling up in my eyes.

"Do you smell that?" Cara asked.

"It smells like the aftershave my dad uses," Daniel replied.

"No, it smells like the lotion my grandma used to use on her hands," Tobin said.

"It smells like my teddy bear that Jason threw in the lake," Cara muttered with a glare at her brother.

They all started sniffing and drew closer to me. I remembered one of the ex-pack in the collective saying that King Fuller smelled like the cookies their mom used to make. So Kieran's pack got my protection, but I got nothing. I couldn't believe it. Excluded again.

"You're not excluded, Bellamy. We can hear you. Can't you hear us?" Daisy asked.

I shook my head.

"Try focusing on one person," Galen said.

I closed my eyes and focused on Olive. She'd tried to mind-link me first. Maybe I could follow the path. After a few moments, I still heard nothing.

Bruce laughed. "Well, we can hear everything."

Could the entire pack hear me or just the people in the room? I wondered.

"We can all hear you," an omega shouted from the kitchen.

'I need Dr. Hale to come sedate me,' I thought. *'I can't sleep when everyone is attached.'*

"He's on his way. Why can't you sleep?" Olive asked.

"I have nightmares. They're really bad. I can't subject the pack to them and I can't risk trying. When I was sedated after the vampires, I didn't dream," I responded.

"Just stay calm. Close your eyes and see a ball in your mind," Daniel said.

I followed his instructions.

"Imagine lines coming from the ball and connecting to other balls. That's the link from your mind to ours."

Nodding, I could see what he was describing. I imagined switches on all the lines and started turning them off. He hadn't really told me how to block, but I was betting it was something like a wall for most people. I mentally added a bell to each line. One started ringing shortly after I added it.

'Hello?' I linked.

'Can you hear me?' Cara asked.

'YES!'

I opened my eyes and grinned. It worked. I needed to have a way to know I was being linked. It wouldn't be automatic like a pack wolf. It was more like a phone on silent. If I didn't know someone was trying to talk to me, it wouldn't get through.

"I don't think we need the doctor anymore," Cara said. "She heard me and responded. Did anyone else hear us?"

They all shook their heads.

"I'd still like to be sedated for the night. This is too new. I don't want to have an incident," I replied.

As if on cue, Dr. Hale entered. He looked a little angry and had a metal box with him.

"I was having a perfectly nice evening when I heard a child in my head. If you hadn't asked to be sedated, I would've still shown up with it. A doctor needs his sleep," he groused.

"Sorry, Dr. Hale." I blushed.

"I'm going to come every night for a week. Work on your control during the day. It'll help your control at night. Understand?"

"Yes, sir," I responded.

Olive led me and the doctor up to my room and had him wait outside while I changed. She tucked me into bed and sat next to me.

"I didn't know if it would work either. My prayer to the moon goddess was that you would become part of our pack and family. I've been asking her all week," she said softly.

"I think it's like when an ex-pack becomes a rogue. It's a shock to the system. I can adjust, it'll take time. The closest we have to a pack is a collective, and we don't have mind-links outside our link with our mates. Don't worry, Mommy. I'll be fine." I smiled.

She chuckled. "Now, *that* was the best thing I've heard all week. Thank you for joining my family. I promise to only embarrass you a little."

The door opened and Dr. Hale came in with Daniel. I was ready to let sleep come. A dreamless sleep for an entire week would be a blessing of its own. Daniel kissed my forehead and pulled Olive away so Dr. Hale could reach me.

"Thank you, doctor. I'm sorry I ruined your night," I whispered.

"Welcome to the pack, Bellamy…. Did you know you smell like vanilla? My mom used to dab vanilla extract behind her ears instead of using perfume. My dad used to say she smelled like cherry ice cream when she did that because he used to smell cherries around her." He smiled softly and injected me with the medicine.

"That sounds like a nice memory. Good night, doctor."

Everyone left my room. I knew it wouldn't be long before I slipped into sleep. My life was finally coming together. I would work to become a stronger fighter and be able to fight Kyle if he came for me.

I would work to be a good friend, sister, and daughter, and I would try to find a place in the world of pack wolves. With luck, I'd find a mate down the line and maybe even have a family of my own.

This was the first step to my new life, and I couldn't be happier.

Chapter 8: Dressed for Distress

—Six years later—

I sighed deeply as I watched Molly, Charlie, and April chattering about what accessories would go best with each of the four dresses we were trying on. They were making the process take a lot longer than it should. But it was for Cara, and I would do anything for her, even if it meant listening to torturously inane conversation while trying on bridesmaid dresses.

A few months ago, Cara went with her father and brother to renegotiate some alliances and treaties with nearby packs. She hadn't found her mate at seventeen, but didn't want to wait for the next regional singles gathering. Cara wanted to see if her mate was in one of the three nearby packs they visited.

She found him in Lune Rouge. His name was Caleb Petit, and he was the future Beta of his pack. When Cara found him, she called me and squealed and told me everything about him. I knew the exact shade of hazel his eyes were, how silky his blond hair was, how strong he was, how tall he was, how broad he was, and how amazing he looked without his shirt on. Because her description was so detailed, I could likely pick him out of a crowd.

Now, we were trying on her top four choices for bridesmaid dresses and the wedding was in a couple of months. The seamstresses in the pack volunteered to focus only on Cara's wedding party, while the ones in Lune Rouge worked only on her dress.

They were excited because no one in the ranked levels of that pack had found a mate in years. At nineteen, Caleb was the oldest of the next generation of leaders, but his mate hadn't appeared. I could imagine the worry since Cara told me the others were all seventeen or eighteen and hadn't found theirs either.

The marriage would strengthen the bond between our packs. Maybe that was what the goddess had been going for. Maybe Lune Rouge was going to be too weak on its own and needed the connection to other packs. It wasn't really my concern.

My biggest concern was getting the girls to pick a fucking dress so I could go do my ward patrol.

A couple of years ago, my vampire friend Talia had ended up in our region again, and I fed her in exchange for setting up vampire wards. She'd stayed for a while to train with me and my boys. Once the number of rogues in our area lessened, we saw fewer hunters coming along, and a rise in vampires. It kind of evened it out.

Every three days, in the evening, I had to go add a couple drops of blood to the wards to keep them running. It was like a shield that made vampires avoid the area. I wasn't totally familiar with vampire magic, but I would liken it to my rogue barrier. The one that marked the edges of my territory and kept the more violent rogues away.

"Ladies, could we please, move it along? I have places to be," I growled.

"Sorry, Amy," they chorused.

I could hear them mind-linking to each other about why I was so grouchy. Soon after I connected with the pack, I'd gotten my links under control, but I found I could hear mind-links between people if I was in the same room as both of them. It was like being able to hear people whispering all around you.

'She's probably just jealous of Cara. Amy's mate hasn't shown up in the whole year since her shift. I heard her and Cara talking about some guy named Kyle who Amy thought would come for her, but he didn't. Guess she wasn't his mate after all,' April linked the others and they tittered as they finished dressing.

I rolled my eyes. Only the ranked members of the pack knew I didn't have a fated mate. Things like this still upset me, even if they didn't know what they were talking about.

Kyle was still out there. He'd sent me offers more frequently once I turned seventeen. I got one every three months. My reputation was the only thing keeping him from coming for me.

He killed his father and took over the collective a couple years ago, but I'd taken and held one of the three largest packs in the region since I was twelve. I'd even expanded my territory to include two nearby cities. It was enough to make any male think twice about trying to pressure me into anything.

We finally had our last votes in on the dresses and ended up with the second option. A fit and flare dress with a sweetheart neckline and ended mid-shin. It went lower on me, as the shortest, but fit the other girls perfectly. When they made mine, it would fit similarly to theirs. I had my measurements taken, dressed in my jeans and t-shirt, and ran out the door.

I stopped at a guardhouse to drop off my phone and headed for the nearest post. It was a couple of miles outside my rogue border. It took a while to get to each binding area, and I didn't make it to the last one until full dark.

After I finished adding three drops of blood into the mark Talia left, I turned to go grab my phone and head home. I still had to spend some time in my office working on rogue issues and requests. First, I would stop in the kitchen. Yuri would've made sure I had something wrapped up in the fridge and I was hungry.

I hadn't even gotten two steps when I heard voices from the other side of the vampire border. They rarely got this close. The magic made them avoid our territory like the plague. I ducked behind a tree to listen.

A female laughed. "… so funny when he gets all growly. Like, I can't stop laughing when he says he's going to kill us. Doesn't he realize he's never getting free?"

"Alphas are like that. They believe they'll get the upper hand somehow, it's really fun to watch as they get weaker and finally realize it won't happen. He's nearly there. We just need a little something to keep us held over. He's powerful, but not enough for how little we're allowed to drink," a male responded.

How had they gotten an Alpha? Maybe it was an ex-pack Alpha. They were rare, but they existed. I sniffed and could tell they'd fed on someone powerful recently.

"When I was here last, around fifty years ago, I'd find teenage wolves necking nearby. There's a little grove of trees with soft grass. You know how nature makes the furballs horny." The man snickered.

"A couple teens might be nice. Something sweet and young to counter the old guy."

"He's not that old, precious. As you age, you'll understand. He's at the peak of his power. This is when they taste best. You'll see, we'll find a young one and you'll taste the difference," the male chided.

I heard them moving away. My mind was working to figure out what I should do. An Alpha, no matter his affiliations, wasn't a safe thing to let them drain. If they turned him, it would be very dangerous for all the packs in the area. I had no idea how many were in their brood. A drained Alpha wouldn't be of much use.

My vow to the pack rang in my ears. I promised to take care of them and to defend them when I joined. If Kieran heard this, he'd try to find out where they were hiding the Alpha as a point of pride. Pack wolves and their hero complexes.

'You should go. We can't defend against an Alpha turned vampire. If you kill their sire, they'll die. Remember what the little bloodsucker said,' Aurora, my wolf, told me.

'Stop calling Talia that,' I groaned internally.

'Stop being a wimp. Go save the wolf. Even if he isn't one of ours, he's one of our people. Plus, you might get rid of most of the vamps who are stalking our territory. What if one of the pups wanders out this way looking for adventure one night? What if Dilly comes out here with one of his boyfriends? Are you prepared for losing pack members because of this?'

She had a point. Dillon would often come to the woods with a guy who was on the DL and have some fun. He'd told me about the place the male vampire was talking about. It was one of his favorites. My youth elites were always daring each other to do something stupid. That gave me an idea.

Chapter 9: Master Marion

I quickly climbed the nearest tree and launched myself to the farthest one I could reach. It put me right beside them and the noise of the clumsy landing attracted their attention. Perfect.

"Who's there? Come down now!" the male vampire demanded.

I made my voice quiver. "I… I'm not going to. Leave me alone."

"Come, little girl. We were just startled and didn't mean to scare you," the female said.

"You're vampires. You'll kill me," I squeaked.

"Die in a tree or die on the ground, it's your choice," the male growled.

"Stop that, Ferdinand." The female smacked the male's arm. "Little girl, we're not mean. He just hates admitting that you scared him. You came here to see vampires, didn't you?" she purred.

"Y-Yes. But I didn't mean to actually talk to you. I just wanted to see." I sniffled.

"How old are you?" she asked.

"Thirteen," I whispered.

Ferdinand chuckled. "A marvelous age. Very sweet."

Talia told me the vintage preferences of most vampires. Puberty was a big draw because of the flood of hormones. Any age before twenty-five was good, but twelve to fifteen was the height of sweetness and vibrancy. After that, it was usually power that attracted them.

Since I only barely made it over five feet, only five feet and one-half inch, I was the same height as most thirteen- and fourteen-year-old girls in the pack. My loose t-shirt covered my curves and made me look even younger. The lack of makeup helped, too.

Faking thirteen would be a breeze. If there were more than two vampires, the Alpha would probably be naked so they could access the arteries in his legs more easily. I could easily explain any interest I showed in him on being the age where most girls really start paying attention.

"What's your name, child?" the female asked.

"Jamie," I whispered, using a name I took on when I was younger, after Talia told me never to tell my real name to a fae or a vampire I didn't know.

"I'm Louisa, this is my mate, Ferdinand. Come down and we'll take you to our home. Let us feed on you a little and we'll make sure you get back to your pack. Imagine how cool your friends will think you are."

"I'm not strong enough to fight you if you're lying. Please, just let me go home," I begged tearfully.

Suddenly, Ferdinand jumped up and grabbed me from the tree. I screamed, feigning surprise. It made them laugh.

"You're coming with us. You can either walk and live through the night, or I can carry you and we'll drain you before dawn," he growled.

"I… I'll walk. Anything. Please, don't kill me," I whimpered.

"I can't get a read on her power. That's weird," Louisa said.

"She's not a pack wolf. Here, smell." He thrusted me in her direction and she took a deep sniff.

"More wild. Is that the difference between a pack wolf and a rogue? The one we have smells like naps in the sun. She smells like stealing through the shadows," she whispered.

"You're rogue born, right?" Ferdinand said.

"Y-Yes, sir."

"Where are your parents? I don't smell any other wolves nearby."

"Dead. Killed by hunters. I've been living as a foster child in the Eaten Heart Collective," I admitted softly.

"Then, no one will miss you. Come along, Jamie. You're ours now. As long as you behave, we'll let you live," Ferdinand stated as he pulled me along behind him.

Louisa chuckled as we walked. I quickly mind-linked Kieran to let him know I'd be gone for a few days and to have Drake take over my youth elites and Clint take over the junior elites. When I was young, he'd question it. Now, he just said okay and told me he'd let my parents know.

I loved how much everyone had grown to trust me. If there was a need for backup, I would've told him. Since I didn't, he wouldn't worry. I just hoped I was strong enough and smart enough to make it back home.

We walked for two hours. They slowed their pace for me and were grumbling the whole time. I tripped a bit just to piss them off. It amused me and led to them boasting more about taking down an Alpha, just to put a little more fear in me. The adrenaline of terror would add a little extra boost to their meal.

Soon, we came to a small clearing where an old house sat next to a stream. The place looked abandoned, at least a hundred years old, and slightly crooked on its foundation. Louisa grabbed my arm roughly and Ferdinand led us up the splintered stairs to the creaky porch. He opened the door and Louisa dragged me inside.

The living room was lit by several solar-powered lamps. I bet they put them out before they tucked themselves away during the day. It was a great plan if you couldn't get electricity.

In the light, I saw there was an old plaid couch that looked like it had been there since the last occupants left… in the seventies. Sitting in an armchair nearby was another vampire. He looked up from the book he was reading and smiled.

Vampire smiles were unnerving. He quickly stood and met us by the door as Ferdinand closed it.

"What have you brought me?" he asked.

"Master Marion, we found this little orphan rogue in a tree and brought her in for dinner." Louisa chuckled.

Marion grinned. "Ah, a rare treat with how wolves care for their pups."

"She says she'll do anything if we won't kill her," Ferdinand said darkly.

My stomach dropped a little. I started praying they'd be less prone to want to use me for anything besides labor and food. The last thing I wanted was to end up a brood mother for hybrid pups. I mentally shook myself. I wouldn't be here long enough for that. They'd want to make sure I wouldn't run first.

"I haven't had a little rogue in nearly a century." Marion licked his lips.

They all looked like they were related. Pale, thin skin stretched over slightly muscular skeletons, dark hair, and black eyes. Louisa was a little meatier. She hadn't starved her body enough yet. Marion and Ferdinand were at least six feet tall, while Louisa was about five foot six. Most sires tended toward a physical preference when creating other vampires. I just needed to figure out if Marion was really the sire, or if he was the sire's mate.

"We figured she'd be good for a few meals and could clean up after our pet. We need someone to watch him during the day. Especially after the mess he made today. How is Clea?" Louisa asked.

"Angry. She didn't want to clean the mess and I had to discipline her. She's locked in the cellar. How do we know our little puppy won't run away?" Marion asked.

"I swear I won't," I squeaked. "I'm not strong and fast like other rogues. They said it was because my mom was human."

"Ah. She's honest. Do you think we're going to be more lenient because of your honesty, little wolf?" Marion laughed.

"No, sir. Lying wouldn't have helped me either. I'm used to being treated as a servant, though. The setting isn't important. I just don't want to die," I whispered.

They couldn't detect lies. That was rare with vampires. Not that it would be easy to tell if I was lying. I had a lot of practice hiding my lies.

"Someone already broke her!" He laughed even harder. "How nice of them. Let her go, Louisa."

She released my arm, and I folded my hands in front of me, keeping my eyes on the floor. I knew he'd try to test me a little. They always did when you were pretending to be broken in. I knew I was supposed to be his property and would obey as I should.

"On your knees, wolf," he commanded.

I dropped to my knees swiftly, not moving my head or hands. They all snickered.

"Stand up, wolf," he ordered.

I stood as quickly and smoothly as I could. Marion patted my head.

"What's her name?"

"Jamie," Louisa reported.

"Follow me, Jamie. I'll introduce you to our other pet," Marion said as he turned.

I followed a foot or so behind him as he grabbed a lantern and left the living room into a dark little hallway. He pointed out the bathroom and told me there was running water, just no hot water.

We stopped at a door at the end of the hall. Marion worked to unlock all the locks. A simple door like that shouldn't have been able to hold in even the weakest wolf, let alone an Alpha.

"Now, he's a little feisty at times. You need to make sure he eats three times a day. We'll bring meat every night for you to cook. There's no refrigerator, so you need to figure it out, and you'll have to use a wood-burning stove to prepare the meals. After he's finished eating, you may have whatever's left. Make sure he drinks and uses the restroom as needed. Clean him up from time-to-time. We want him to live for at least another month," Marion stated.

I nodded, and he led me into the room. There was a mattress on the floor in the corner. On the mattress was a naked male lying face down with something on his neck. It looked like the collar the witch had me in. I felt bad for him. Eight months in a silver collar was my max. It hurt like a bitch.

Above him was a boarded-up window draped with a tattered, wispy curtain that stirred slightly in the breeze. There was a bucket in the corner he'd been using to relieve himself. Someone recently washed the floor; I pieced together what probably happened.

"You'll be in charge of cleaning the rest of the house, too. I'd like to have a lot less dust and dirt on my clothing. Do you understand, Jamie?" he said.

"Yes, sir. I can do that," I replied.

"Good. We'll leave you two to get acquainted. Knock when you're ready to come out. Louisa will come back in a couple hours for her meal. She's never had rogue born before, and we dote on our little Louie. You will feed one of us every night. As you get older, you'll feed two. If you're a good girl, we might even treat you to a pup or two to care for. Wouldn't you like that?" Marion whispered into my ear as he slipped a hand between my thighs.

"Anything you want, sir. Please don't hurt me," I whimpered.

"As long as you're good, you have nothing to fear. Ferd, you keep your hands off Jamie. She's mine until I get bored. Then you can have her." He chuckled.

"I appreciate anything you're willing to give, master," Ferdinand said with a smile in his voice.

They left quickly, and I heard the locks get thrown into place. Well, Marion was definitely the sire, and they probably nested in the cellar. Now, to see what I was working with for my accomplice.

Chapter 10: The Stolen Alpha

I crossed the room carefully and knelt on the mattress. The man groaned and turned his head to me. A black eye and a split lip were visible on his face, suggesting he'd been in a fight. I rolled him over and found more bruises on his torso. There were two bite marks on his neck, right below the collar, and another over his heart. I continued examining him and found two more bites on his thighs.

He moved to cover himself as he became more conscious. I'd already seen it, but I wouldn't say anything. I checked for broken bones and found none. He was weak, though. Seeing an Alpha like this was heartbreaking. Never in his life had he experienced this sort of powerlessness.

"It's okay, sweetheart. I'm gonna help you. I'll see if they can get some food before they go down for the day and I can get you fed," I whispered.

"I don't want your help, rogue," he growled.

"I don't care what you want. If they turn you, it'll be bad for the wolves in the area. I'm not letting your pride and stubbornness keep me from protecting my family," I replied coolly.

"I'll kill them before I let them turn me, then I'll kill you, too," he snarled.

"Blah blah blah. You can call me Jamie, or keep calling me rogue. The animosity will help. Do you know where you are, sugar?" I asked.

"Leave me alone, rogue. I know exactly where I am and what I'm doing."

"Let me look at the collar. I'm going to see if I can get it off you during the day. It'll help you regain your strength faster. I'm only supposed to be gone for three days. So we need you strong enough to get out by the fourth morning at the latest," I told him as I leaned in closer to his neck.

His chest rumbled with a growl as I examined it. There was a latch that was tied with a fine silver wire. It would burn like hell, but I could get it off. I went to the door and knocked.

After a few moments, I heard the locks clicking. Marion entered and closed the door behind him.

"What do you need, Jamie?" he asked in a sweet voice.

"Can I heat up some water and clean him? The silver is keeping him from healing and he could get an infection from the cuts and bites," I murmured, looking at the ground.

"Of course you can, puppy. Has he been giving you any trouble?"

"He doesn't like me, sir. Pack wolves don't usually like rogues. And I'm working for you, so he hates me more." I shook a little as I reported.

"My poor little puppy. You're absolutely right, but he's not strong enough to hurt you. And I'll make him wish he were dead if he does," Marion cooed as he stroked my hair.

I looked at the wolf out of the corner of my eye. He was snarling and looked disgusted. It was fine. I learned a long time ago to ignore pack wolves who didn't care to listen.

Marion guided me into the hall and locked the door again. He took me to the kitchen, which was only a short distance from the room. They'd moved a couple lamps in. There was a wood-burning stove, an old electric range and oven, an old refrigerator like the ones with curvy sides and a latching handle, and a single basin sink.

"You'll have to start the fire. We don't like to be too close to flames. There's wood by the stove. In the cupboards, you'll find some food, pots, and pans. The water here is from a well, so boil any you're planning to drink," he told me.

"Is it possible to get some meat tonight? Maybe if I feed him, he'll calm down a little," I said softly.

"Ferdinand is already out hunting. We have some knives, and I'll butcher whatever he gets. We can't fully trust you yet, puppy."

"I understand." I nodded and went to start the fire.

There were some matches by the stove and old papers to help. I pulled some bark off the chopped wood and set it in the center of the wood-burning stove. Then I carefully piled logs around it and added a little paper in the gaps before lighting it.

"You're good at building fires, puppy. Don't get any ideas about burning the house down around us. The cellar has a fire door on it. There's a slab of cement and a solid stone foundation above it." He warned.

"I wouldn't do that. My parents camped a lot, they taught me how to be safe with fire. If I lit this place on fire, it would spread to the fields and the woods. I'd kill a lot of creatures for sure and probably myself," I replied quietly.

"You're a pretty smart girl for a wolf. I don't think I'll get bored with you for a while," Marion said as he approached.

I closed the door to the stove and rechecked that the flue was open. Last thing I needed was to have to spend the day healing smoke damage.

Marion stood behind me and wrapped his arms around my shoulders. I slumped a little so my breasts wouldn't show as much when the shirt clung tighter in his grip. He would know I wasn't built like a thirteen-year-old if he took off my oversized t-shirt.

"Who do you belong to, puppy?" he purred in my ear.

"I belong to you, sir," I whimpered.

"Such a smart girl," he murmured as he kissed my neck.

I stayed as still as possible. Trying to struggle would make him more eager. I moved my head slightly to the right, giving him better access to my neck. He groaned and nibbled down to where my shoulder started.

The door slammed open and Ferdinand walked into the kitchen with a small deer. I didn't move or jump. Making Marion feel more possessive wouldn't help me in my plan. He had to believe I accepted he was my owner and acting scared by a noise while in his arms wouldn't assist in that image. I had to act as if I trusted him to keep me safe.

"Got it... oh! Didn't realize you were having a little treat." Ferdinand chuckled.

"Get your water started, puppy. You're such a good girl. I'm going to take care of that meat and once he's clean you can start cooking," Marion whispered onto my skin, making me shiver.

"Thank you, sir," I replied and moved to fill a pot with water after he let me go.

Soon, I had a pot of lightly boiling water and looked around until I found another bucket. There was a bar of soap and a washcloth in the bathroom. I collected everything and headed back to the bedroom.

Once inside, I crossed to the mattress. The Alpha was glowering at the ceiling and covering himself with his hands. It was pretty weird. Most wolves were okay with nudity. I settled the bucket to the side, setting the cloth and soap on the floor and kneeling next to him again.

"I'm back, sugar. Time to get you cleaned up," I whispered.

"Why are you trying to be nice to me? I'm not falling for your shit. I'll never like you, never trust you, and never help you," he growled. "You smell like vampire, but I don't see any signs of bites. Did you let him fuck you?"

It reminded me of Ricky's little brother. Rogue she-wolves were only good for one thing, in his opinion. I'd been in the Daylight Moon Pack for so long that I'd forgotten what this felt like. Being openly hated for existing. I almost laughed.

"I'm being nice because I'm nice. I want to get you back to your pack and go home. No, I didn't let him fuck me, and I'm hoping to get out of here before he tries. I'm prepared to have to make that sacrifice if I need to if it means getting you home safe," I replied as I started soaping up the washcloth after wetting it.

I began washing his face and focused only on ensuring I didn't get soap in his eyes or mouth. Carefully, I washed and rinsed down his face, to his neck. I cleaned around the collar and down to his collarbone. I could have let him wash himself, but I was giving myself a reward for putting up with this bullshit.

Rogue born wolves enjoyed cleaning and caring for each other even in human form. Maybe he would trust me more, maybe he wouldn't, but I was going to enjoy it either way. It could help distract me from the annoyance of being pawed at by the vampire.

Weak moonlight through the boards was my only source of light. I knew he had dark eyes and hair, his nose was still straight and aristocratic, his jaw stubbornly set and covered with about three days' growth, and his lips were silky looking. If I were a weaker wolf, I'd have done something stupid. He was handsome as heck, even with the black eye.

I continued down his shoulders, chest, and stomach. The dehydration made his muscles stand out even more. I tried to wash one of his arms and he refused to move from covering himself.

"I need to get done before they finish butchering the meat. I still haven't looked through the cabinets to see what I can do with it. Now, uncover your junk, and let me clean you properly." I sighed.

He scowled. "I'm not letting some rogue kid see me naked."

"I'm eighteen. I'm just pretending to be a kid so they'd bring me here. Come on, pudding. Move your hands, it's nothing I haven't seen before." I snickered.

"You don't look eighteen."

"And thank the goddess for that, or they'd have drained me as soon as I got here. You can train a child; you can't train an adult. Now, let me get this done!" I insisted.

After a little thinking, he moved his hands, and I started cleaning his arms and the sides of his chest. I kept moving lower, and he tensed when I moved his legs so I could get at the vampire bites on his thighs. He didn't try to stop me though, and I appreciated it. I got all the way to his feet before the water got cold.

"I'll see about getting you a bath tomorrow. It'll make you more comfortable than having me wash you," I told him.

"My name's Lucien," he mumbled.

"Did you tell me that because I washed you, because you hate the endearments, or because I saw your dick?" I laughed.

"All of the above? I still don't trust you, but I'll set that aside if it gets me out of here."

"Good." I nodded. "I'll be back in a bit… sweetheart."

I stood and gathered my supplies, then headed for the door. Once I was in the hall, I locked the door and went to empty my bucket in the bathroom sink and rinse the cloth. No one bothered me. I must have done a good enough job of convincing them I didn't need to be watched.

Chapter 11: Dinner Plans

[Bellamy/Jamie]

Heading to the kitchen, I worked on a plan. I'd need to see how the daytime worked out, but I was pretty sure we could leave once the vampires retreated to their underground lair for the day. Marion told me a lot about the structure when he was telling me why I shouldn't torch the place.

I pulled out the least wobbly chair from the little dining set in the kitchen and started going through the cupboards. Deer could be gamy, very little fat was in the meat, so it could dry out while cooking. There were some noodles, flour, sugar, cans of soup, salt and pepper, rice, and canned milk.

Honestly, I was surprised to find anything decent there. Vampires didn't really eat and had poor memories of cooking necessities. Someone must have helped them.

Moving to the lower cupboards, I found some potatoes, carrots, and onions. There was a can of shortening, too. I searched for the other pans and utensils. That deer wasn't very big, but it was big enough that I didn't think we could eat it all in one sitting. I wanted to try to smoke some of it. That would help with the storage issue. But I wouldn't know what I could do until I saw how Marion would butcher it.

I worked on peeling potatoes with a little vegetable peeler I found. It wasn't the best, but it would work. Tomorrow's lunch will be bone broth, made from leftover scraps. I knew I had to convince Marion to let me have at least one knife. I didn't want to have to get creative.

Sometime later, Marion and Ferdinand brought the meat into the kitchen. His butchering impressed me. He'd taken off most of the fat and the silvery stuff that caused a lot of the gamy flavor in the meat. It was very considerate. They laid the meat out on the counter and I looked over the pieces.

"If someone watches me, could I use a knife? It's hard to cook without one," I asked softly.

"If you try anything, I'll drain you and feed your corpse to the wolf. Do you understand?" Ferdinand threatened.

"Yes, sir," I responded.

Marion gave me two knives. A fillet knife and a chef's knife. They would be acceptable. I set to chopping carrots, potatoes, and onion after putting a couple cuts of the meat into a brine of sugar and salt.

Once the veggies were done, I put the peels into a large pot with some water and salt, then started cutting some of the meat off the ribs to make the broth. I rubbed the ribs with shortening and some seasonings, then seared them before adding them to the pot on the stove. The pot was toward the back, so it would heat slowly over the next few hours.

I cut some thin strips off of the remaining carcass and pounded it with a pan to tenderize it. After mixing flour with salt and pepper, I dredged the meat and started some shortening melting in a pan for fried venison steaks. I rubbed shortening and salt onto some whole potatoes, wrapped them in foil, and stuck them in the oven.

"Would someone be willing to dig a two to three-foot hole in the yard for me? Or would I need to do that myself?" I asked politely.

"What do you need it for?" Marion asked.

"I want to smoke some of this meat to make it last a little longer," I replied.

"Ferd, go dig her a hole," he commanded.

"Yes, Master." Ferdinand sighed and left the room.

I picked up a piece of wood from the pile and inspected it. Oak. Good, it was best for smoking. Things were looking up.

"You know a lot about cooking," Marion said.

I beamed. "My foster dad was a chef and we hunted and camped a lot. I can do basic stuff with most game meat. Smoking, brining, making broth, light butchering, and I know what foods go well with them. I wish I had more ingredients, but this'll do."

Yuri taught me most of it. When I wasn't in school, training with the warriors, or training with the Luna, I was sitting in the kitchen, learning everything I could about cooking. I'd asked him about foods where I didn't need to buy anything. In case I was ever homeless again. He taught me to cook any creature I caught.

"I think this was one of the best ideas Louisa's ever had. You're pretty useful, I want to see you work hard tomorrow and get this house in order. If you do well, I'll give you a reward." He smiled.

"Yes, sir. Thank you."

I'd finished the fried venison steaks, skimmed the broth, and grated almost a half dozen carrots when Ferdinand returned. He was dirty and looked angry. Marion hid a smirk under his hand.

"Anything else, Wolfie?" he growled.

I bit my lips together. "I'm sorry. It's just… I wanted to make sure your effort in getting this meat didn't go to waste. I'll take care of the rest."

He sighed. "No. Tell me what you need."

Men were so easy, no matter the species. You just needed to show the right kind of appreciation, know when to cry, and know when to tease. He had no actual incentive to help, but it was just the right angle to get under his skin. Ferdinand wanted someone to see him and appreciate his work.

"I just need a few of these pieces of wood cut into chips, and some green branches I can use to make a grate for smoking. I have a lot of kindling stuff here. Thank you so much, Mr. Ferdinand." I smiled softly.

"You better taste as sweet as you talk, pup. Or I'm gonna be pissed," he growled and headed back outside.

I returned to grating the carrots. There were some thin wash cloths in a kitchen drawer that would be passable for making carrot juice. Lucien could use the extra vitamins. Once I had ten carrots grated, I loaded them onto the cloth and sprinkled them with some salt. I squeezed and twisted the cloth over a bowl, working to get every bit of juice out that I could.

When Ferdinand came in again, I sat at the table with them and wove the branches he collected into a grate. Then I went outside to start my kindling and load my wood chips in. I needed them to burn down to coals, then I could add the meat.

Within an hour, I had my meat smoking, my potatoes cooked, steaks ready on a plate at the back of the stove to keep them warm, and I'd made some margarine using the canned milk, shortening, and salt. It wasn't butter, and it was missing lemon juice, but it would do in a pinch. I skimmed the broth one more time before pouring the carrot juice into a cup and showing the meal to Marion.

"Impressive, puppy. He can't have a knife. You'll have to cut his meat up for him."

"I tenderized it well and the strips I made are better for using your hands. I figured you wouldn't let him have a knife if I couldn't have one," I replied.

"Go feed your charge, puppy. I'll keep an eye on everything out here," he said and waved me off.

Chapter 12: Culinary Alliance

[Bellamy/Jamie]

I gathered everything onto a tray and went to the bedroom. Lucien was sitting against the wall. Just being cleaner seemed to make him feel better. I closed the door with my foot and went to sit in front of him.

"That smells amazing," he whispered as his stomach growled.

"I didn't have butter, but I made a kind of passable margarine," I told him and set the tray on his lap.

He sniffed the juice. "Carrots?"

"It's good for you, Lucien. Just drink it. I have to work on purifying the well water before I can give you any. I plan to check the stream tomorrow to see if it's any better."

Lucien ate with gusto. He moaned with nearly every bite. I worked on flipping his mattress and finding him a blanket or some sheets.

"When we get back to my pack, you can work in my kitchens. This is fucking amazing," he moaned.

"You haven't eaten in a while. This is edible and not raw. I'm sure your kitchen staff doesn't need me." I giggled.

I found a fitted sheet in a closet outside the room and brought it in to cover the dirty mattress. Lucien had finished all the food and was lying back against the wall. He looked so tired.

"You can sleep, Lucien. Vampires usually only feed at the beginning of the night. Louisa's reward is like a dessert. I'll take that nasty bucket with me so the air will clear in here. Marion will let me take you into the bathroom throughout the day. They just couldn't let you wander before," I said.

"Thanks, Jamie. I still don't trust you entirely, but I don't think you're evil or anything," he murmured as he crawled to the mattress and laid down.

"I guess that's something."

After gathering the dishes onto the tray, I collected the bucket and put it in the bathroom. I'd clean it later. Then I took the dishes into the kitchen. I put a pot of water on to boil and skimmed the broth before I went out to check the meats. They were nearly done.

When I returned to the kitchen, Louisa was stirring the broth. I hadn't seen her since earlier. I wondered what she'd been doing.

"You almost ready to feed me, Jamie?" she asked sweetly, still paying attention only to the pot.

"As soon as the meats are done smoking and I get them wrapped, I'll be happy to feed you, Miss Louisa," I replied softly.

"No fear now, right? Master Marion put you at ease." She snickered.

"I know my role. If I'm good, my life will be okay. If I'm bad, I could die horribly. I understand my place in this house, Miss Louisa," I told her.

"Great. Let me know when you're ready. I'll be in the living room. Oh, and you can sleep in the room with the wolf. He can't get it up, so you'll be safe."

I blushed. "I… I don't know what to say."

It was a real blush. That wasn't something she should have shared. It wasn't something I wanted to know. Lucien's genitals weren't my business.

"Say thank you."

"Thank you, Miss Louisa." I bowed slightly.

She laughed and left the room. I went to the counter, there was still some raw meat. I tossed it into the frying pan and seared it a little before pulling it off and eating it while waiting for my water to be hot enough to clean with. Rogue born wolves were better equipped to eat raw meat in human form than pack wolves, but I liked the taste of it with a little heat.

When the water was ready, I poured it into the plugged sink with some dish soap and grabbed a rag. I carefully cleaned each dish before I ran out to collect the meat from the smoking pit. Once I was inside again, I wrapped it tightly in foil and set it aside on the counter.

It took some time, but I managed to get the kitchen cleaned. By looking outside, I could tell it was at least four in the morning. The sun would start rising in about an hour and my bosses would be asleep. I just had to make it through feeding Louisa.

I walked out to the living room. Ferdinand was on the couch, Louisa laid with her head in his lap, and Marion was back in the armchair, reading. I stood next to the couch and pretended to be a little worried. I'd fed Talia often when I was a kid and I wasn't really concerned. This vampire was younger, though. I hoped she was as in control as she seemed.

"I'm finished cleaning the dishes and cooking, Miss Louisa. Where would you like me to be for your feeding?" I said, quietly.

"Sit on the arm of the couch, I'll come to you," she ordered.

I climbed up on the arm of the couch and waited with my hands folded in my lap. Louisa came around and stood in front of me. She leaned in and I bared my neck to the opposite side of where Marion had kissed me. I figured he'd get angry about that being his spot, and I really just wanted them all to go to bed so I could rest and figure out my plan for the day.

She licked along my neck until she found the spot she liked. I took a deep breath as I waited for her to strike. When her fangs broke my skin, I nearly yelped. Louisa couldn't be more than a few months old. Her technique was rough, and she hadn't used her saliva properly to dull the pain. She pulled back and started sucking at the wound.

A moan from her vibrated along my neck, making me shiver. Her arms wrapped around me as she started feeding more aggressively. I looked at Marion the whole time. He seemed interested in the feeding. I remembered what Talia had told me the last time I fed her.

"Bellamy, something about your joining this pack made your blood so much better. It's like the most sinful dessert." Talia had giggled.

Marion seemed to realize Louisa was lost in the feed. He stood and pulled her off of me. I was still bleeding; she hadn't had a chance to seal the wound. Marion leaned in and licked it, helping the healing. When he pulled back, he had a dangerous look in his eyes.

"You were hiding something from us, weren't you, puppy?" he asked coldly.

"I… I don't understand. What was I hiding?" I asked in a confused way.

"You don't know? You're a rogue Queen. And at least fifteen," Marion growled.

I gasped. "My parents died when I was young. I was homeschooled. I thought I was eight, but people said I was so small I had to be six. No matter how much I tried to tell them, they insisted. I thought maybe I was wrong. But I swear I don't know what a rogue Queen is! I didn't realize how old I was! Please, don't kill me." Tears fell from my eyes.

I'd been practicing crying on cue. Sometimes my work required some acting skill. A female crying could usually defuse a situation.

"You don't smell like you're lying," Marion said slowly.

"I'm not, please believe me. I wouldn't lie, I told you before. Master, I want to live and lying will only get me killed!" I cried.

He pulled me into his arms. I continued to cry and beg him to believe me. Poised to extend my claws and strike, I would rip open his abdomen and tear out his heart if he moved aggressively. Marion pulled away from me and looked me in the eye.

"I'll believe you. You've worked hard tonight and never did anything to indicate you were scheming or lying to us. Finding out you're a rogue Queen changes a few things. I want you to take *very* good care of our pet now. And make sure you're eating and drinking as much as he does. You'll be responsible for feeding two vampires every night and he will feed two every night. You've granted him a reprieve, puppy. I bet he'll be over the moon when you tell him." Marion chuckled.

"I'll let him know when he wakes up, sir." I sniffled.

"Good. Go to bed now, I want you to clean still, but I won't expect perfection like I had been. You need to have your energy for tomorrow. I won't accept any half-assed feedings. Do you understand?" he asked gently.

"Of course, sir. I'll do my best to clean, but stay rested for you," I replied.

"Go," he ordered.

I stood and walked to the bedroom, unlocking the door and closing it behind me. I waited to hear if they would lock me in, but that didn't happen. Thank the goddess.

Chapter 13: Morning Chores

[Bellamy/Jamie]

Sleep would be helpful, but I needed to get some cleaning done, and I had to see what the security was like during the day. Most of all, I needed to get an idea of what their daytime resting place was like. It would be the best bet for getting them out of the way quickly.

"Jamie? Are you okay?" Lucien asked.

"Yeah. Just waiting for them to go to bed. I think I'll take a nap at midday. After lunch. Are you hungry? Do you need anything?"

"I need to… use the restroom," he responded in an embarrassed tone.

I walked over and helped him stand. His legs were a little wobbly. I guided him out to the bathroom and stood outside the door. I closed my eyes and focused on the beings in the house, the flow of the air through the cracks, the scratching of the insects in the wood.

I could hear the vampires below us shuffling around, preparing to die for the day. The broth needed to be skimmed again. I could hear the scum on top brushing against the sides of the pot. I heard Lucien whispering to himself.

"Do you really think we can trust her, Remus? What if she's playing both sides? … I suppose you're right. We'll have to try if it means getting back to our pack," he murmured.

Silver made talking to your wolf difficult. I felt for him, really, and I was happy he was listening to his wolf. Humans were far more suspicious than animals. Animals were just cautious.

Taking him back to the quiet room, I then went to get him a plate of food. With a satisfying thud, I added more wood to the stove, feeling the heat radiate from its surface as I put two pots of water on to boil. I'd need a lot of hot water to get the cleaning done and prepare a bath for Lucien.

Heading outside with a cup, I checked the water from the stream. Finding the water uncontaminated, I gently filled a pitcher. I wanted to get at least two pitchers full into Lucien before nightfall. I needed to make sure I was hydrated, too. Blood donation was a bitch if you didn't have enough fluids.

Pulling the chair back to the cupboard, I examined the cans of soup more carefully. In the back was a small can of mandarin orange pieces. I found a can opener and drained them, putting the slices onto a plate with some of the smoked venison. It wasn't much of a breakfast, but it would help with his iron and blood sugar a little.

I loaded the tray with his plate, the pitcher of water, a glass, and a fork. When I entered the bedroom, he was waiting by the window. I could imagine he'd probably had another conversation with his wolf.

Aurora was a true rogue. She hated chatting and got straight to the point when we talked.

"Let me take that," he said.

"You've been here for several days, beaten, bled, and starved. Sit your ass down and let me take care of you, Alpha," I chided.

His lips curved in a wry smile. Lucien sat on the floor and I took the pitcher off the tray as I set it on his lap. I poured him a glass of water and he drank it quickly, so I poured him some more.

"What do you have to do today? How can I help you?" he asked as he dug into the food.

"Today, I need to clean the house, and you. I have a bone broth that is nearly ready to be strained and it will be the base of a venison soup for lunch. I have enough smoked venison to last us until tomorrow morning. Ferdinand should be hunting again. I was thinking of asking him to look for some wild pigs. I could smoke a good chunk of a pig," I replied.

"You know; it seems like you're just going with the flow on this. Like you're actually planning to stay here. What's going on in your head? Do you have a plan?"

"How are they keeping an Alpha wolf in this broke-ass house? What's their security like? What types of skills do they have? Is it possible to kill Marion quickly enough that the others won't kill me?

"I can't just pull a rescue out of my ass, Alpha. Killing them would be the best option. One less brood of vampires to deal with. The primary goal is getting you home. You're obviously not a displaced Alpha. That means your pack is without a leader," I stated.

"My Beta's in charge. I was supposed to be gone for a week. I've been here for at least three days, maybe four. Once it hits seven and I haven't returned, they'll start to worry. What about you, though, you said you're only supposed to be gone three days. Who's missing you?" Lucien asked between bites.

"My family. My students. My team. I'm a warrior. I was adopted into a pack, even though I'm rogue born. When I heard them talking about having an Alpha, I told *my* Alpha I was taking a three-day leave. Then, I threw myself in the path of Louisa and Ferdinand." I shrugged and snagged a piece of orange from his plate.

Lucien stared at me. A flood of emotions crossed his face: shock, surprise, understanding, shame, and disappointment. I thought the disappointment was in himself. Poor guy.

It sucks to realize you were the asshole.

"I'm sorry," he said softly.

"Don't worry. I'm sure you're itching to get back to your mate and kids. It's frustrating when you can't save yourself. They have no idea what you're even going through here." I smiled sympathetically.

He winced. "I don't have a mate or kids. I lost my mate when I was young and accidentally rejected my second chance. She came along while I was still feeling sorry for myself. I didn't even realize who she was until I told her she'd never be my mate. Then I felt the pain of our connection breaking, and it was too late."

"Wow. So fucking up when you're hurt is, like, your special skill." I laughed. "Look, if you want to help, drink a lot of water and dust the cobwebs in the living room, kitchen, and hall. Working with my head tilted straight up for so long will make me dizzy."

Lucien laughed. "You just keep moving forward. Didn't even feel bad about rubbing in the mate thing. You're eighteen, haven't you found yours?"

"It doesn't work like that for rogue born wolves. I'm focused on my work anyway. My friend Drake and I are competing to be the next head warrior for our pack. I train the youth and junior elites. Plus, my mom just had twin girls last year, and I'm enjoying watching them grow up. I might try to find a mate later, but he'd have to fight me and not lose. Hard to find a male who can beat me in a serious fight. Our Alpha hasn't been able to beat me in three years. His son hasn't been able to beat me in two. And no one has beaten me since I got my wolf." I chuckled.

He finished his food and the whole pitcher of water, then moved the tray off his lap and stood. I got up, too, and gathered everything.

"You ready for a bath? The water should be boiling, and we can just add cold from the tap until it's the right temperature," I told him.

"No. We're going to clean, then we'll worry about a bath and lunch. After that, you need a nap. I want to see you drinking as much water as I do," Lucien replied.

"Oh, I forgot to tell you, you won't be feeding all four vampires tonight. I'll be feeding two. Marion said he's going to change his plan for you now. Do you know what the plan was?" I asked.

"No. They never told me what they planned. The females just keep trying to… get me hard. I don't know why. We have to kill them. I was a convenient target. If they got another Alpha, they might pick up where they left off."

"That was my assessment, too. Okay, let me get that collar off and we can get to work. There's a lot to do," I said.

Lucien bent down, and I untwined the silver wire and pulled the collar from around his neck. I carefully set it on a low shelf. He sighed in relief.

"Only have your wolf heal the injuries that aren't bites. We can tell them I stuffed you with food, which I plan to do, and it helped create enough energy that you could heal the injuries not given to you by their bite," I instructed.

"Got it." He nodded.

We headed out.

Chapter 14: Feeding Vampires

[Bellamy/Jamie]

While Lucien was working on dusting the webs and around the windows, I looked behind the other doors in the hall. In the second bedroom, I found a few totes, inspecting them thoroughly. There were blackout curtains, slipcovers for the furniture, cleaning supplies, runners for tables, and wood polish. In the corner of the room were a couple of rugs and a carpet runner that would be perfect in the hall.

I went outside and started pulling boards from the windows. Lucien came out and picked me up so I could get the tops of the windows clean. I found small, boarded up basement windows, but left them alone. We hung curtains, beat the furniture, swept and mopped, put the slipcovers on, and aired out the house completely. I boiled a lot of water for the bath before we had lunch.

I'd made a soup from one of the smoked meat packs, potatoes, onion, and carrots. The bone broth was perfect. Lucien managed another couple pitchers of water and I got one. By early afternoon, I was aching, dirty, and exhausted. I'd woken up at four yesterday morning for training after getting back from a training trip with the Elite Ten and had yet to sleep. Lucien let me take the first bath. It was heaven.

While he was bathing, I worked on making flour tortillas to go with meals. In the totes were zipper bags. I loaded a few with tortillas and partially closed the flue, letting the fire in the stove die down. Then I went around and closed the windows, drawing the curtains tight to block out the light. After that, I crawled onto the mattress next to Lucien and passed out.

It was dusk when I woke with a start. The scent of vampires got stronger when they were awake. I pulled myself from Lucien's arms and retrieved the collar from the shelf.

"Lucien, wake up, sweetheart. Time to put your jewelry back on," I whispered urgently.

He groggily sat up and I got the thing on, clasped and wrapped just moments before the sun fully sunk. They'd be in soon to feed.

"You need to act like you hate me. Got it?" I told him.

"Okay. Go over to the other corner and curl up. I wouldn't have let you sleep next to me," he said, pushing me away.

Lucien sprawled out on the mattress, and I curled up in a ball in the corner. A few moments later, the door opened. I rubbed my eyes and sat up.

"Good job on the house, puppy." Marion grinned in the lamp's light. "I didn't think you'd make it look so good."

"I worked as hard as I could, sir. I'm glad you like it," I murmured.

"And look at our pet! He's clean and pretty again. His eyes aren't all sunken in anymore. She's a miracle worker!" Louisa laughed as she held Lucien's body against hers. "Did you manage to do anything about his dick, Jamie?"

My eyes widened, and I blushed. Lucien growled and looked honestly angry. I remembered what she'd said in the kitchen. He didn't know I knew. When he explained about his rejecting his second chance, I knew exactly what was wrong with him. It was pretty good luck since their plan seemed to need that component and they couldn't get it from him.

"You and that fucking rogue have no business with my dick, you blood-sucking bitch!" he snarled.

"Is this the little pup you and Louie were going on about this evening, darling? She's so precious. With those big eyes and that innocent face. Exactly your type," a young, feminine voice chirped from the doorway.

I looked over and saw a vampire who looked like someone had turned her at thirteen or fourteen. She had the same pale skin, dark hair, and black eyes as the others. There was an innocent look about her as well. I could only imagine how long she'd had to live as a child.

"I'm Clea. I wasn't around yesterday to meet you," she purred.

"I'm Jamie, Miss Clea," I said softly.

"It's time for supper. Everyone can have double their usual amount of blood. Come, Clea, you and I will take the pup. Let Ferd and Louie have the Alpha. She likes playing with him." Marion chuckled. "Take off your pants, puppy."

I stood and pulled my jeans off.

"She takes orders just as you said. And she's a rogue Queen? I've never seen an Alpha jump to take orders from a vampire like that before." Clea laughed.

I glanced at Lucien. He looked distracted as Ferdinand was pulling him against his chest, and Louisa was prying his legs apart to get to the artery in his thigh. I hoped he hadn't heard that.

"Don't be afraid, puppy. You're a good girl and you won't fight us like he does. As long as you're very good, you won't have to be collared and forced. Understand?" Marion asked.

"Yes, sir. What would you like me to do?"

"Sit on the floor and spread your legs with your knees up and your feet flat on the ground," he commanded.

I immediately dropped to the floor as instructed. "Like this?"

"Perfect, as usual, puppy." He smiled.

Clea sat behind me. She was an inch or two taller than me, so it wasn't a big difference between us. Her arm pulled me to lean against her and she began licking my neck right where Louisa had bitten previously. Marion laid between my legs and began licking the inside of my left thigh.

It was an intimate sensation I'd never felt before. Talia had always fed from my neck or my elbow. I locked eyes with Lucien as a whimper escaped me.

I watched as Louisa and Ferdinand both struck him with their fangs. He roared with pain. It hurt to watch. They'd barely numbed the area.

"It's his punishment for being a bad boy. He had a tantrum yesterday and made a big mess. Then *I* had to clean it up, so his feedings will be with minimal preparation," Clea whispered in my ear. "Look how diligently my Marion works to ease your pain. He's going to make you feel really good. Don't be afraid to make noise. He loves that."

She went back to licking and sucking on my neck. The sensation from each of them seemed to meet in the same place, and it was like they were both licking and sucking between my legs. I felt myself heating up down there, and it was unbearably intense and painful. I started whimpering as I writhed on the floor between them.

"She's a virgin," Marion chuckled. "I can smell the innocence in her arousal."

"Hard to find in rogue society at her age, especially in this region." Clea giggled.

"Old King Fuller deflowered most of the girls in his area. He took in the orphans and trained them to be his playthings. How did you escape his notice, puppy?" Marion asked.

"I don't know who that is. I'm sorry. Did I mess up?"

"No. You're even more perfect than before, puppy. My clueless little princess. Isn't she perfect, Clea?" He grinned over my shoulder.

"Absolutely, my love. Let's have our meal and we can go enjoy the clean, fresh house our little one has provided," she purred and sunk her fangs into my neck at the same time he sunk his into my thigh.

I felt an intense energy thrum through me, followed by the most extreme pain I'd ever experienced in my life. I cried out before everything went black.

∗∗∗

[Lucien]

I heard Jamie's scream, and it shook me from my pain. The leeches sucked my blood, and I worked to focus and make sure she was okay. Marion had stopped feeding and began laughing uproariously. She was out cold and the little leech was giggling as she sucked the bite on Jamie's neck.

'What the hell happened?' Remus demanded, but I couldn't answer.

Marion laughed. "I haven't seen a woman pass out from an orgasm in years. I wasn't even doing anything. She's so perfect. And she's ours, my love."

"Mmm. Her blood is delicious. Like the most decadent dark chocolate cake and a rich full-bodied wine all wrapped into one. Bitter, sweet, tart, and heavy," Clea moaned.

Marion returned to his meal. My anger flared as I watched his fingers slide over the damp cloth between Jamie's legs. Louisa grabbed my dick and started stroking. They'd tried to get me hard before.

If it had been a different Alpha, they'd have gotten what they wanted. It wouldn't work. It hadn't for half my life. Ever since I accidentally rejected Regan. They didn't know that.

She eventually gave up on it and finished her feeding with a scowl. I was relieved when they started licking again and the wounds sealed. I saw the other two finish up with Jamie. Marion picked her up and left, the other three following close behind and locking me into the dark room.

Chapter 15: Return of Jamie

As I opened the curtains, a cool stream of moonlight poured in, brightening the room and casting long shadows. The scent of Jamie's arousal and completion was still lingering in the room. I knew what they could do.

When they'd taken me, the males strapped me to a chair, and the females used their saliva to make the bite feel amazing. If I could have come, I would have. Instead, it just hurt like a son of a bitch once it got to that point.

For a while I had them believing it was just my own force of will, but they figured it out just last night. Not why or for how long I'd been impotent, but that I wasn't what they wanted. I was certain they'd try to kill me, but they just said there would be a change of plan.

Now they had Jamie. Would she take my place in their plan? I heard them say she was an Alpha. Once I was thinking straight, I recognized that myself just from how she acted, how she held herself, how she cared for others. She was smart and commanding. She did what was best for someone, even if they didn't realize it.

I couldn't believe my arrogance in telling her she could work in my kitchen. Even if she wasn't an Alpha, offering that to a pack wolf.… She couldn't have been raised as an omega. No one could look at that girl or talk to her for more than a minute without seeing her potential.

It was a wonder she didn't have a mate. If I were a younger man, a complete man…. That wasn't important. What was important was getting home.

There wasn't anything I could do, but lie there and try to figure out how we could escape. The biggest problem I could see was that I couldn't get over five feet from the house without collapsing from searing pain shooting through my body. I'd have to tell Jamie. Maybe she would have some ideas.

A couple hours later, I heard the locks click open and Jamie walked in with a tray. I moved from the mattress. When I sat again, I saw what she was wearing.

They'd made her change into a blood-red dress with thin straps. It fit her tightly on top and flared out at her hips. It only went halfway down her thighs. She was entrancingly beautiful.

Her hips swayed slightly as she walked, and her breasts overflowed the top of the dress. Now, I could definitely believe she was eighteen. Her sinful figure was a perfect contrast to her angelic face.

She had another glass of carrot juice on the tray, along with a glass of water. Mashed potatoes, slices of smoked venison, two tortillas with her homemade margarine, and a small, weedy salad were on the tray.

"Dandelion greens," she said softly. "Sorry, I don't have the stuff to make a dressing and you need the vitamins."

"Are you okay? What happened when you woke up?" I asked.

"Eat your food and I'll tell you," Jamie ordered.

I started eating. She was fantastic at making meals with very little. I wondered what pack she was in. Whoever her adoptive family was, they did a hell of a job raising her. The questions she posed earlier regarding what she needed to know to plan a successful rescue showed a great strategic mind.

She'd infiltrated the house, gained the trust of the vampires, and actively worked to get me healed and fed. Not to mention getting me to trust her when I was being such a defensive ass.

"So, I found out what their plan was for you and what their new plan is. It's really fucked up. Louisa is under a year old. Since she's still able to breed, they wanted her to get pregnant with your child. Not so they could take over your pack, but to gain an Alpha wolf/vampire hybrid," Jamie explained.

"That wouldn't have worked." I snorted.

"Because you got 'the vengeance of the goddess' when you rejected your second chance mate. It's the only way a male wolf could become… you know." She blushed.

Knowing what I had was bad enough, knowing a pretty girl knew it, too, was brutal. I'd been better able to focus on my pack because of the vengeance of the goddess. We became stronger because of it. This was pretty much the only time I regretted having it.

"Impotent. I know. And there's no cure unless I can find another female who'd want to be my mate. Hard to do when you have to consider a pack. I couldn't just grab some random unmated female and hope she'd be a good Luna," I replied.

"And you couldn't just grab a girl who'd be a good Luna and risk making the goddess angrier by taking someone else's mate." Jamie nodded. "I understand."

"After a few years, I gave up. I've been looking at sons of other Alphas to take over my pack. There are some good options, but I want to wait until they find their mates. My reluctance for a mate was because of the Luna position. I'm not going to select a replacement whose mate isn't right. They're a partnership to care for my pack, not a couple to do as they please."

"You're a little young to be thinking of retirement." She laughed.

"I'll be thirty-seven this year. A very old man compared to you." I grinned.

"Bullshit, you don't look a day over twenty-five. Anyway. Their new plan is to breed me with Marion and Ferdinand. They wanted me to get you to mark me, to remove your curse so you could still have a child with Louisa. They were *so* gracious and told me that you could have me after each time I got pregnant with one of their babies. We could be together until it was time for one of them to knock me up again," she growled a little. "Like any wolf would be happy about that sort of arrangement."

I ate quietly and considered it. She was beautiful, intelligent, caring, and strong. Marking Jamie... having a mate... seeing her grow round with a pup... but it wouldn't be mine. She was right. I wouldn't want a mate in name.

My stomach turned at the idea of that skeletal bloodsucker having my child. Worse was the idea of Jamie being used as a broodmare for the two men. She was still young and had a chance at life. I had no doubt she'd find a mate.

"I'm going to try to get into their daytime resting place tonight. I'll offer to clean it while they're awake so they won't have to worry about me doing something while they sleep. Marion sent Louisa to the store for other things I need for food and cleaning. She's supposed to buy me some clothes, too. I hope it isn't as slutty as her and Clea's wardrobe." Groaning, Jamie gestured toward her dress. "Ferdinand is out hunting. He agreed to go for the wild pig, it could take him a while. Clea's almost as old as Marion, or I'd say we should attack them now. You still aren't back to fighting form and I'm not quite good enough to take on two vampires over three hundred on my own."

"I needed to tell you, I can't get far from the house without pain. I think they did something while I was passed out, back when they brought me here," I admitted.

Jamie bit her right index finger and made a circle, using her thumb and index finger on her left hand. Then she rubbed the blood from the finger onto the circle and looked at me through it.

"Yeah. It's a blood barrier. Probably using the blood from that bite over your heart. Once we kill the one who cast it, you'll be free," she replied and licked the blood from her hands.

Damn, the girl was a badass. I had to wonder what her friend was thinking, competing for head warrior against her. She almost reminded me of my friend Jean-Luc. He was smart, thorough, and one hell of a fighter.

Chapter 16: Demon Dust

[Lucien]

"How'd you do that? How do you know about vampire magic?" I asked.

"I lived with a vampire for five months when I was a kid. She taught me a lot about fighting. A couple years ago, we ran into each other and she came to stay with my pack for a few months. She helped me with training and taught me more about vampires. Because she and I have a blood bond from my childhood, I can see vampire magic through a circle of my own blood," Jamie explained. "I don't know everything, but I know enough."

"You were taught and trained by a vampire? And your pack let her come on their land?"

"Yeah. And she helped me with training the senior elites, most of my friends in that group always thought my 'vampire attack' game was silly. She took on anyone who wanted to fight an actual vampire. Talia is well over seven hundred years old. Marion is just about four hundred. Imagine the difference in fighting between the two. My boys found out I wasn't messing around. They all lost, but the ones who took my training seriously lasted longer than the ones who goofed off." She chuckled.

"Would you be willing to come train warriors in my pack for a few months?" I asked.

"First you want me in your kitchens, now you want me in your training field. I'm not going to tell you anything else about me or you might try saddling me with your pack." Jamie laughed.

It wasn't a bad idea. Female Alpha wolves were rare. There were females with Alpha blood, but an actual Alpha female was hard to find. I could help her with running the pack until she found a mate. He'd just have to be willing and able to take on the duties of the Luna. But would my pack accept a rogue as Alpha?

I was just about to say something when her face went neutral and the door opened suddenly. Clea crossed the room and pulled the now empty tray from my lap, then blew something in my face, causing me to inhale sharply. I saw Marion blowing something into Jamie's face and ordering her to stay where she was before they swept out of the room and locked the door.

Coughing, I went to check on Jamie. She looked a little panicked. I wanted to hold her, kiss her, mark her, and make her mine. She'd never have to be afraid again once she was mine. I'd take care of her forever.

As I advanced, she backed away, pulling herself backward with her arms. I crawled on. She'd hit the wall eventually and there'd be nowhere for her to run. She couldn't reject me, and she couldn't stop me. Jamie had promised to get me safely home and I wouldn't stop until she was mine or I was dead.

"Lucien, please. Calm down," she whispered slowly.

"I am calm, Jamie. This is exactly the answer, as mates, we'll be stronger. I should mark you. You can help me run my pack. I'll give you all the pups you want and all the freedom a beautiful rogue needs," I told her.

"That was demon dust. It makes you less inhibited, more aggressive, and a lot less rational. I can't be your mate, Lucien. Please think. I'd be a terrible Luna. I'm a warrior, not a party planner. Your pack would hate me for being a rogue. They wouldn't accept me. You'd never be happy because this isn't really you thinking, it's a passing fancy the dust magnified," Jamie pled.

Her eyes were beautiful in the moonlight. The golden glow of her honey-brown irises gave my life meaning again. Finally, I'd have more than just my pack. I'd have the mate I'd been longing for since I was seventeen. I could imagine how good it would feel to hold her every night and have her look up at me like I was the strongest man in the world.

I was over a foot taller. She'd never have to stand on chairs again. I'd run to get things for her from the high shelves. I'd dote on her endlessly.

Those curves in that dress were deliciously dangerous and I could see from the position she was crawling in that she wasn't wearing panties. I wanted to taste every inch of her. I needed her like I needed air.

"This *is* what I want. You're everything I ever wanted in a mate. If they don't like you, they can leave. Or I can leave. I'll join your pack and be the best head warrior's mate ever. I'll give everything up for you," I insisted.

Even as I said it, something in my head was screaming not to. I didn't really want to give everything up, but I would for her. For my own little Jamie. For my perfect mate.

"Stop, Lucien! You were just telling me how carefully you were picking your replacement. Giving up your pack for me would make you unhappy. Think! Listen to the part of your brain that's still trying to be sensible," Jamie begged.

"Why aren't you affected? What's it magnifying for you if not this? We were just talking about making you a part of my life. Talking about marking you."

There was a slightly pained look in her eye. She was fighting the same urge. I was sure of it. Jamie must have seen it as giving in to the vampire's plan. She was afraid. I wouldn't let her make a mistake by turning me down. We belonged together.

"I'll protect you. I'll keep you safe from everything. You never have to cook, clean, or fight again. I'm here to take care of you. For the rest of my life, I'll shield you from anything that could harm you. I promise. Be mine, Jamie. Let me save you," I murmured.

Her eyes narrowed, and her lip curled. I didn't know why she was angry. I was there to take care of everything now.

"What the *fuck* did you just say to me?" she growled. "I'm an Alpha. A rogue Queen. Not some weak bitch who needs a male to take care of her. I'm a fucking warrior. An *elite* warrior. You're telling me you want me to do nothing, but raise your pups and depend on you to solve my problems?!"

Jamie kicked me in the face. It hurt like hell and she followed it up with a kick to the chest, sending me back onto my ass. I wouldn't give up. I'd never give up, not until she wore my mark.

I lunged for her, but she rolled away and stood. It would be better this way. Once I showed her I was stronger than her, she'd back down and accept my mark. She'd be mine before the sun rose in the morning. I stood and prepared to fight the woman I loved.

No one had won a fair fight against me in ages. Those sneaky-ass vampires only got me because they set up a trap. I could beat her. Then she'd see.

She charged forward. There was no finesse, no style. Just aggression and violence. I braced myself for the attack. Suddenly, it was like she disappeared. I felt a kick to the back of my leg and a hard punch to my kidney as I fell.

Spinning on my knee, I landed a hit to her stomach that threw her at the wall, but Jamie twisted and used the force as a springboard and launched herself back at me. Her right fist hit my chest as her left went across my face. When she landed, I grabbed her hair and slammed her into the wall near us.

Jamie fell to the floor, and I grinned. Now she couldn't stop me. I knelt down next to her and leaned in. Her fist seemed to come out of nowhere and connect with my chin. I heard something crack and fell backward.

Once I was on the ground, her leg came up and crashed down, full force, on my chest. That was a broken rib, for sure. I grabbed her leg and held it. She wouldn't get another chance.

Chapter 17: Then Remus Did a Thing

We were lying there, panting, pained, and bleeding a little, when my mind cleared. I realized what I'd done… what I'd tried to do. I had never in my life thought anything like that. What the hell was wrong with me?

How could my brain have felt it was rational to beat a female I wanted to mate with into submission? It was disgusting. I was all for a good fight in fun, but I'd been trying to injure her until she couldn't stop me from marking her. I didn't know if she'd ever forgive me.

"That was fun. Next time, let's do it in a place with fewer walls." Jamie laughed.

"I'm so fucking embarrassed. It was like, I knew what I was saying and thinking wasn't right, but I couldn't stop. Marking you became the most important thing in my life. Please, forgive me," I begged.

"Demon dust is a bitch. I trained with it when I was ten. It took three months before I could control my mind, but some triggers would knock out my control. Yours made you want to treat me like a pack she-wolf. They would love to hear how you would protect them and pamper them. That's not for me. I've always been a warrior, and I'll always be a warrior." She smiled.

"So… who won?" I laughed.

"I think it's a draw, at this point, I don't think I could have gotten another attack in."

"Me, neither," I admitted.

"No one has fought me to a draw in years. We should fight again once we're out of this mess and healed. I think you might actually be able to beat me." Jamie chuckled.

We laid there for a while, recovering. Suddenly, I heard Remus in my head.

'Hey, Lucien. So I did a thing… I think you'll like it. Don't fuck it up,' he growled.

I had no idea what he was talking about. My wounds were healing slowly, but Jamie was already moving. She untwined the silver wire and helped get the collar off. I felt almost instantly better. Wearing silver hurt like a son of a bitch and dulled my senses. I probably would've won that fight if I weren't wearing it.

I took a breath to say something about not wearing silver next time, when the most amazing scent of honeysuckle and jasmine hit my nose. Nothing had ever smelled as heavenly. Jamie gasped.

"I'm so sorry," she whispered.

Her voice was angelic. I'd thought it sweet and songlike before, but now it was more than before. I tried shaking my head. It must have been more of the demon dust. I put my hand on hers to reassure her that I was in control and sparks jumped at the touch of our skin.

"Jamie, what's going on?" I asked warily.

"Aurora, she said the fight was only a draw because of the silver. She requested that the moon goddess bind us. Your wolf accepted the offer. Aurora told me they decided we were too stupid to know what was good for us." Jamie's voice quivered.

"Bind us? Like the mate bond?"

"That's how rogues find mates. We find someone with no mate bonds and request to be with them. I didn't tell her to make the request. There has to be a way to undo his acceptance. You didn't want this. I'll find a way to fix it," she murmured.

That couldn't happen. Too many opportunities had slipped through my fingers. I didn't want her to undo our bond. I didn't want to lose another mate.

"No! Don't. Please. You can be a warrior, you can teach, cook, clean, hunt, fight, anything. Just do it as my mate. Be my partner, not my princess," I pled.

My crazed thinking hadn't been entirely wrong. She would be perfect for my pack, perfect for me. I was protective, but I didn't want to have to be on guard all the time. I didn't want to worry about my mate *and* pack during an attack. Knowing she could fight well enough to be an elite warrior would mean I could be confident in her making it through and helping protect my people.

"That's a pretty quick turnaround from 'I'll kill you' to 'Marry me', Lucien. You might change your mind again."

"It was before I knew you better. I thought you were some rogue kid who didn't value loyalty to your species over your own interests. By this morning, I considered you a friend and ally. Everything you said and did made sense once I wasn't hungry, thirsty, and in pain anymore. If you walk out of here unmarked, what do you think the vampires will do? They might try something stronger than demon dust next time," I told her.

"You have no idea how much I've wanted a mate, Lucien. I just don't feel you're thinking this through. There are too many things going against us. No rogue Alpha has ever mated with a pack Alpha. We have no idea what we're really facing," she whispered.

"Then we'll be the first and make all the mistakes so everyone after us can learn. Or we could end up being the best leaders our people have ever seen. It's been years, Jamie. I'd given up. You truly are a good match for me and my pack. Even before the dust and the bond, I thought you were beautiful and strong. I've never met anyone like you. Please. Be my mate."

She nibbled her bottom lip as she thought. Her nose wrinkled at something, then she looked annoyed and irritated. Finally, Jamie sighed and smiled.

"I think you need to mark me, Lucien. When we get back to my pack, we can talk about whether or not to keep the mark and add mine. I want us to think about this when there isn't some sort of danger around us," Jamie said.

"Why your pack?" I asked.

"I know where it is, and it's only a two-hour walk at a slow pace. Plus, I'll need to re-secure the vampire barrier soon and check if there was any rogue business I missed out on. The peaceful rogues in the region come to me with issues and disputes. My territory now covers two nearby cities," she confided.

"So… as a rogue Queen, you actually have a territory?"

"Yes. If we keep the marks, I hope you'll let me claim your pack land. I have four lieutenants who cover my interests in the cities so I don't have to travel constantly or spend days at the pack border dealing with disputes. I can live pretty much anywhere in the region as long as it's my territory." Jamie smiled.

"Do I lose anything from letting you claim it?" I asked.

"You just promise to be my partner and not have me killed. A little bloodshed. And we're all good. Now, are you going to bite me or keep stalling?" She snickered.

I could breathe a lot easier now. My ribs were healed, or mostly healed. I sat up and Jamie moved closer. Putting my nose to the curve of her neck, I took in a deep breath and relished her scent. I'd been waiting to mark a mate since I was seventeen.

Her skin was soft-looking. I put my lips to her neck and felt the silken texture beneath them. Licking the spot where I'd mark her just to savor the memory. Remus got impatient and told me to either mark her or he would. I laughed softly at him, making Jamie shiver.

"Wait," she whispered suddenly.

I panicked. Was she changing her mind? I couldn't handle the idea of losing another mate. I steeled myself for what could come next. If she changed her mind, I wouldn't force it. This was my third chance, but only her first.

"What is it, Jamie?" I asked breathlessly.

"My name is Bellamy. Not Jamie. Some vampire lines can have power over you if they know your real name. Like the fae. So I used an alias. I just thought you should know the name of the person you're marking," she murmured.

I kissed her neck. "Bellamy. You know that means 'beautiful friend' in French, right?"

"Yes. I took French in high school." Bellamy giggled.

"Thank you for giving me your name," I whispered as I extended my canines and pierced her skin.

She moaned softly in my ear. I licked at the wound, encouraging it to heal, feeling my soul finally completed. My Bellamy.

"That was perfect," she purred. "Now, I'll get the last parts of my plan set up. I want to leave before the sun sets tomorrow. I don't want to spend another night in this place."

Bellamy kissed me. Her lips were as silky and soft as the rest of her. I wrapped my arms around her and nibbled at her bottom lip until she opened her mouth. My tongue found hers quickly, and I set about tasting her. Soon, I'd taste all of her, but for now, this would have to do.

I released her, and she let out a disappointed sigh. A chuckle rose from my chest. She was really mine now. How completely strange to think I had to wait until now to find her. I couldn't imagine anyone else I'd trust with my pack, though.

She stood and crossed the room, knocking on the door. A few moments later, the sound of the locks being thrown filled the room. The door flew open and someone entered with a lamp. It took a little while for my eyes to adjust. All the vampires were in the room with lamps in their hands.

Ferdinand and Clea were inspecting the damage to the room. Marion was checking Bellamy over. And Louisa came to look at me. I knew they didn't need the lamps for seeing, but it made sense if they wanted to see what was a shadow and what was a bruise. The noise from the fight had to have made it out there.

"What the hell happened?" Marion asked with a growl. "You didn't give yourself to him, did you? I told you *that* belongs to me."

"No, sir. I didn't give myself to him. Many wolves fight before marking. I'm still untouched in that way," Bellamy murmured with her head down.

"Good. How long until your heat now you're marked?"

That bastard. She was mine. I snarled and started to growl.

"Where's your silver?" Louisa asked.

"He took it off. The burning probably didn't affect him as much because he wanted to fight more than he wanted to not hurt," Bellamy replied.

"That demon dust stuff is crazy," Ferdinand muttered.

"You don't need to put it back on me. Just don't hurt my mate. I'll do whatever you want," I told them in a reluctant tone.

A grin spread across Marion's face, which was mimicked by the other vampires. Louisa's hand slid down to my dick and started massaging it. I looked at Bellamy. Her face was down, but I could almost feel the anger radiating from her as another female groped her mate. It was hot as hell to know she wanted me.

Louisa squealed with delight as I became hard in her hand. My curse was broken, but I didn't want to bury it in the boney bitch in front of me. I wanted my Bellamy. My soft, curvy little mate.

Marion grinned and grabbed Bellamy's wrist, pulling her from the room. Almost as soon as she was gone, so was my erection. I nearly laughed at the crestfallen look on Louisa's face. She tried stroking me again, but nothing was working.

"Get it back," she insisted.

"I can't. When Jamie's gone, it's gone. The curse is specific. I can only get hard with my mate," I informed her. "Only a person given the curse would know. It's never lifted, only excepted."

She shrieked and stormed off, followed by the other two. The door closed, and the locks latched. I moved to the mattress. It wasn't true, but it would work to keep her from trying to screw with me tonight.

Bellamy was just a hell of a lot more attractive than Louisa, and my arousal was going to be a little iffy for a day or two. I hadn't had an erection in about nineteen years, except the one that came with bathroom needs.

I hoped Bellamy wouldn't suffer for it. There was nothing I could do to fix it. All I could do now was wait and hope Bellamy's plan worked out.

Chapter 18: Setting the Stage

[Bellamy]

Marion dragged me back to the living room. He examined the mark on my neck. It was on the side he'd claimed as his. I'd offered that side to Lucien on purpose. No male owned me. Especially not a gross vampire like Marion.

The things he did to me when I woke up after the feeding…. I wouldn't let them live in my head with my other trauma. Instead, I would focus on where I needed to be.

I was still reeling from the shock of Aurora telling me she wanted the Alpha and was going to request him whether or not I wanted it. The story I spun made it seem better, but she wanted to let Lucien mark me as soon as Marion started talking about it. Aurora could sense his power and I had been resistant, ignoring her as she persisted.

The feelings associated with being mated were almost immediate. I'd never had a kiss like the one he gave me. It wasn't my first kiss, but it was the only one that felt so good and perfect that I didn't count the seconds until it was over. The only time I'd actually *enjoyed* being touched by someone.

My possessiveness wasn't something I'd been expecting, either. I wanted to rip Louisa's head off for touching him. I'd never felt jealous before. It was intense. I wondered how the other wolves did it.

"You've done very well, puppy. Go put away the groceries, there's no animal to cook tonight. Louisa brought other options so you could spend the evening how you wanted after going through something as harrowing as being marked against your will," he purred.

Like it had been Lucien's fault and not Marion and Clea's with that damned demon dust. I kept my emotions contained. This was not the time to let my façade slip. Just a few more hours and we could leave.

"Sir, may I clean your room tonight? I can imagine it's as bad as the rest of the house. None of you should have to sleep in a place that's dirty and dusty. I saw a lot more decoration stuff in the other bedroom. Maybe I could make things a little nicer for you and Miss Clea," I suggested.

He chuckled. "You've been offered a night to do as you wish, and you'd rather clean? I don't understand this. Explain, puppy."

"I feel like I'm not doing enough to make you comfortable. You've already told me that, once I'm old enough to mark him, I can have one pup with my mate in exchange for giving up all the others. You treat me so nicely and care for me so much. If I could have tomorrow night off and take care of you and your mate tonight, I'd feel like I've earned it more," I replied softly.

Marion looked thoughtful for a moment. He was about to speak when Louisa came shrieking down the hallway. I wondered what had happened. It seemed like Lucien was playing his part without instruction.

"He's soft again! He said he could only get hard for *her.* It's part of the curse," she whined at Marion.

My eyes widened in surprise. That wasn't how the curse worked. We broke the curse entirely when he marked me. I'd been expecting the feeling that comes with your mate cheating on you. I had honestly been waiting for the piercing feeling I'd heard about.

"Did you know about this, puppy?" Marion asked in a dark tone.

Why the fuck was he always going back and forth between loving me and hating me? It was really beginning to piss me off. Pick a damned side.

"No, sir. I only knew one Alpha who'd had the curse, and he said it was broken with his mate... oh... could that have been what he meant? It was only broken *with* his mate? I'm so sorry!" I covered my face with my hands and waited for the reaction.

Marion started laughing. I wasn't relieved. He seemed like the type to do that angry, laughing while he beat you to death thing. I was ready, though. The fight with Lucien had limbered me up.

"Oh, well. You can raise the pups she has with Ferd. Wolves were made for breeding. No need to put you through the rigors of pregnancy when we have a perfectly good broodmare. Isn't that right, puppy?" he said.

"Yes, sir. I'm happy to bear pups for your family," I murmured with a blush.

"You can go clean the cellar and decorate it tonight. First, tell me how long until your heat now that you've been marked, and then go put away the groceries," Marion insisted.

"My heat should be in five days. I'll let you know when I start to feel it coming," I replied with a bow, and headed to the kitchen to put things away.

She'd bought everything I asked for. I looked forward to making Lucien breakfast with the powdered eggs and the pre-cooked bacon… not. At least, it would help him have the energy to make it through the day of work we had ahead of us. There were cans of juice and bottles of water. She'd even picked up the fondue set I asked for and an extra pot of glycerin.

When I got to the bag of clothes, a pleasant surprise awaited me. I hadn't been looking forward to trying to walk home in the short dress with no underclothes. A lot of the items were lacy or had ruffles. All the bras and panties were white or pink cotton with little ruffles and bows. Marion was obsessed with my 'purity' and had probably decided to enjoy the reminders until he could take my virginity.

Louisa had gotten me exactly two pairs of pants. One was a pair of white yoga pants and the other a pair of light blue jeggings. There was a white, lacy baby-doll nighty I decided I'd use as a shirt because it was the only one that didn't look like a little girl picked it out or wasn't skin-tight. It was just long enough to go mid-thigh, like the dress I was in, it didn't crowd my neck like the others would, and it had tight capped sleeves instead of the poufy ones.

I took the bags of clothing to the end of the hall and set them next to the bedroom door. I'd take them when I went in later on. Heading to the other room, I thought of the items I had seen earlier in the day and how to arrange them in the best way possible. I loaded a tote with the things I needed.

The entrance to the cellar was actually in a small addition with one external door and another door that led into the house. Whoever set them up made sure they wouldn't have to wait for sunset before coming in. A battery operated push light was the only light in the windowless room.

Ferdinand carried my cleaning supplies, so I could carry a couple of lanterns, then brought me a toolbox so I could use the hammer and nails to hang things. Once I had my brand new step ladder, I got to work dusting, sweeping, mopping, and working to pry the lower windows open. I hung wide strips of cloth against the ceiling and against the walls, then changed out the bedding on the two queen-sized beds.

When I was finished, it looked like the inside of a satin jewelry box. I closed and covered the windows, then went to gather some of the heavier pieces of chopped wood from the pile outside. I wrapped the wood in the bottom of some of the cloth to keep it weighed down. There was enough loose cloth to wrap around a good bonfire's worth of wood. I grinned. One last touch.

I grabbed the fire extinguisher from the corner and headed carefully up the stairs. Just in case someone was powerful enough to wake at midday, I wanted to ensure they didn't survive.

After I was sure the coast was clear, I went out the back door. I ran as fast and far as I thought I could get away with, pulled the pin, and emptied the canister of its contents. It was a lot of work to get it to look unused again, but I managed it and ran back to the cellar.

Chapter 19: Ready… Set…

[Bellamy]

Once everything looked good, I went up to the living room to get the vampires. They followed me out to their room and the girls squealed with delight at the transformation. The men were happy with their mates' reactions. They patted my head and called me a good girl. I couldn't wait to kill them.

"You can go play with your mate now. Remember, you belong to me. He doesn't get to have you until you're pregnant with my child, puppy," Marion stated.

"Yes, sir. I'll leave now so you and your mate can enjoy the room." I bowed, picked up the tote, and climbed the stairs.

Outside the bedroom, I grabbed the bags of clothes, stacked them on the tote, and unlocked the door. I knew Marion wouldn't lock us in for the day, because he was worried we wouldn't be able to resist each other. He knew he could command and threaten all he wanted, but, in the end, vampires all believed werewolves to be closer to their canine family than their human one.

I opened the door, and Lucien smiled at me. He had almost completely recovered from our fight. It took less time for an Alpha or ranked blood wolf to heal than for a common wolf to heal, but his healing was still slower than mine because he was a pack born wolf. It would probably be a little longer for him to heal the effects of the feedings, the silver, and the lack of food and water. I closed the door behind me and set the tote down before joining him on the mattress.

"How'd it go, Bellamy?" he asked.

My heart thrilled at him using my real name. It was dangerous as hell, but I didn't want to hear him call me Jamie ever again. I could go the rest of my life without hearing that name from his mouth.

"All set for tomorrow. They got me some stuff that will make for a good enough meal and we can prepare snacks for the walk home. How are you, Lucien?" I smiled at him.

"I missed you. You should have seen Louisa's face when you left the room and my boner left, too. I almost laughed." He grinned.

"I wanted to tear her arm off and beat her with it. Never let any other female touch you there. You're mine," I growled.

He chuckled. "Didn't you say we should wait and see? I'm fine with it, but I thought you wanted to wait and talk about this."

"I do… it's the Alpha in me. We're very territorial, you know." I winked. "Let's move on. They're busy enjoying their room, so we can talk more freely. I grabbed some pants and shirts for you from the vampires' room. They're smaller than you, but I had to try. It would be better if we could make this walk in our human forms. If Marion survives, it will be easier for him to track us in our wolf form. Their scent increases when they wake up, and ours increases when we shift. We just need to make it to the vampire barrier."

Lucien nodded. I was happy he wasn't questioning my decision. I scooted closer and leaned against him. It made Aurora happy. The whole bond thing made me relax. I couldn't wait to get home and call Cara…. No, I had to talk to Lucien and make sure it was what we both really wanted. Then I could call Cara.

"We have a couple hours until sunrise. Tell me about your family. Do you have any siblings?" I asked.

Anything to distract me from my gorgeous, naked, possibly temporary mate. He was delicious, and I was starving. I needed to focus on something else and talking was a favorite pastime of all pack wolves.

"I have a sister, Liana, she lives on the other side of the country with her mate. She's Luna of her pack. My mother lives half the year with me and half the year with her. I told her to just stay with Liana because she has children, but she refused to be unfair to me. I have two nieces and a nephew. The girls, Gabrielle and Nadia, are fourteen and Julian is twelve. What about your family?" he replied.

I winced a little. He wasn't talking as much as I'd hoped. Asking that question always got the question returned. It was a much longer answer for me now than it had been six years ago.

"I have four adoptive brothers, two adoptive sisters, and two heart brothers. My heart brothers are Warrick and Tyson O'Connell. Both have mates. Warrick's mate is expecting their second child. Tyson is still waiting on their first. Galen is my oldest adoptive brother. He hasn't found his mate yet, but he's hopeful. I think she's human or ex-pack. I might take him on my next visit to my lieutenants. Maybe we'll see her.

"Then Hollis, he found his mate three years ago and moved to her pack. She was the only child of the Beta of the pack. He's taken up that position. Porter is one of my elite warrior companions. He's found his mate and they're expecting their first child. Bruce is the youngest of my older brothers. He hasn't found his mate yet. Then there are the twins, Blossom and Anise. They're just over a year old," I answered.

"That's a pretty big family. What are heart brothers?"

"Basically, we felt like we were meant to be family, but fate didn't agree," I explained.

"And your adoptive parents? Where are they living?" Lucien asked.

"The packhouse. My father is the Beta of our pack." I smiled.

He laughed wryly. "So I managed to land a Beta's daughter."

"We'll the Alpha's daughter was taken, so you get what you get."

"My first mate was a Beta's daughter. I was just amused at the coincidence," Lucien murmured.

"Sorry to remind you of her," I whispered.

He moved his arm to wrap it around my shoulders. I really enjoyed the warmth and comfort there. I sighed contentedly.

"Warrick O'Connell? The Alpha of Hunter's Moon?" he asked.

"Yes. He saved my life. His mom was the one who picked my family," I told him.

"He's a very smart young man. I've enjoyed seeing the changes he's made to his pack. Remind me to send him a thank-you gift," Lucien said softly.

We talked more about our earlier lives. I told him about my travels and my time in the rogue collective. He told me about playing in his father's office as a child and hiding frogs in various drawers all over the packhouse with his friends.

We stuck to the happier stories. The heavy stuff would come later when we weren't in the middle of a difficult situation. The room lightened as the sun rose. It was almost time.

—Three hours later—

I had Lucien dress in the only thing I'd collected that fit. Black sweatpants, which only just fit him. All the shirts were too small. It did things to me in uncomfortable and enticing ways. Whenever he was nearby, my hand seemed to slip itself along his waist, down his back, or over the curve of his delicious ass. He didn't entirely mind.

Once we finished cooking and eating breakfast, I gathered clothing from the bags and dressed. I put on the most basic of the bra and panty sets. It was white cotton with little bows, the nightie, and the jeggings. I brushed my hair out so it would cover my mark. The last thing I needed was one of the guards telling the entire pack I had a mate when I didn't even know if I could keep him.

We started drenching the area around the house. If I was going to use fire, I didn't want to risk it getting out of control. Once nothing was feeding the flames, it would die, but the flames could easily get out of the basement from a window. Better safe than sorry.

I was sitting on the couch when Lucien came out to join me. We were in the waiting stage. It was another four hours until midday. I didn't want to risk missing my chance by falling asleep. Nothing on earth was going to make me feed that disgusting vampire again. Not after I was marked.

"What are you thinking about, chouchoutte?" Lucien asked.

"I…. What did you just call me?"

"Chouchoutte. Don't you like it? Ma choupinette."

"Did… did you just call me a cabbage? Chou means cabbage!" I laughed.

"Yes, my cute little cabbage." He winked.

"I don't know how I feel about that."

"It's actually referring to a pastry. A *choux à la crème*. I'll have the kitchen make you some when we go home," Lucien said.

I bit my lips together. Home for me was Daylight Moon, not wherever he was from. We'd been talking to each other, learning more about each other, our friends, and our families. Maybe he thought that meant I was agreeing to keep the mark. We weren't out of the woods yet.

He seemed to read my mind.

"Right, we haven't talked about it. The moment you said they wanted me to mark you, I started thinking of how amazing it would be. Bellamy, I love that you're a warrior. You're strong, confident, and intelligent. You're beautiful, caring, and bold. I know you think I'll change my mind, but I won't. And, I won't give up my pack for you. I'll spend the rest of my life trying to convince you to be mine," he murmured.

"I didn't really think I'd ever have a mate. I thought you were handsome from the moment I saw you. Your fire amazed me. Even after nearly a week as vampire food, you were fighting back still. That shows a strength very few would understand. You're different from other Alphas. Are you really sure you want to be tied to a rogue forever?" I asked.

"Yes. I know I'll learn a lot from you. My pack will benefit from having you as their Luna. I want you to be my mate, chouchoutte. I want *you*, Bellamy," he replied.

The last time someone said they wanted me, it was my adoptive family. They changed my entire life path and made me into a stronger warrior and a stronger queen. Because of them, I had a life with the safety and security I'd coveted. Maybe, now, I could have the love I desired, too.

"Tell me again when we get back to my pack. We'll go from there." I smiled.

"What do we have to do still?"

"We need to make travel snacks. You're still not completely healed, I think one more day of food and rest should do it. The walk will be difficult, being able to eat will help," I said.

"Then, let's make some snacks and rest. Maybe we could leave a little early," he suggested.

"Once we get to the guardhouse, I'll grab a car to drive to the packhouse," I told him.

Chapter 20: Go!

[Bellamy]

We spent the next couple of hours going over our exact plan. He told me what he was doing in the area. Every year, he took a week-long sabbatical in his cabin. It was off his pack's land and it gave him a brief break from his duties as Alpha. Only his Beta and Gamma knew where it was. While going there, he heard a child crying and fell into the vampires' trap.

"It sounds like they knew what they were doing and where they should be, Lucien. Is it possible your Beta or Gamma set this up?" I asked.

"No, Robert and Thierry wouldn't do that. If they were unhappy about something, they would've talked to me. I'm a fairly reasonable man when I'm not a prisoner." He chuckled.

"Then it must be someone else. If this person found out where your cabin was, then they'd know Daylight Moon was the closest pack. We should hide your identity when we get there, just until I talk to Kieran, Toby, and my dad," I said.

"You're Daniel Carrington's daughter? I've met him. I thought he only had sons," Lucien replied.

"Well, he did. Until I came along six years ago, and the girls were born last year. Which pack are you from? I forgot to ask."

"Lune Rouge. Alpha Lucien Devereux." He bowed a little.

I laughed. "My best friend is marrying your future Beta. I can't believe I didn't make the connection. I actually have an appointment set with you next week to talk about security."

"B. Carrington. I remember seeing that on my books. I thought it was Bruce, Daniel's youngest son." He snorted.

I giggled. "Yeah, it's a pretty common thought. Bruce is an artist, not an elite warrior. Bet you would have been shocked to see me."

"I would have. I think I probably would've started falling in love at first sight. Instead of being an ass like I was here."

"No, you would've insisted it was some sort of joke. Then, I'd have had to fight you. Trust me, it happens a lot." I sighed.

"And I would've won, but you would've kicked my ass pretty hard on the way to my win. So I'd believe you." Lucien nodded.

"And we'd be right back here. Aurora made the offer because of how strong you were. You sealed it by nearly beating me in a fight when you were wearing silver. She would've made the offer to your wolf and he would have accepted without telling you until it was done, like this time," I whispered.

"No matter what path we took; you would've been my mate. See, Bellamy. You're mine and always would have been mine. Mark me. Keep me. I promise to never fall out of love with you. I promise to never leave you. We can protect each other forever," he insisted.

I turned to look at him. He was sitting at the kitchen table, rolling snack wraps with peanut butter and raisins as if he hadn't just said that. It was a cozy scene. I watched the play of muscles under his skin as he moved, focused on his work. Probably hoping I'd give him the answer he wanted, but trying not to apply too much pressure.

He was right. I knew it now. The connection through Cara and Caleb would've brought us together. Whether it happened now or next week, I was going to mark him.

I bit my finger and made a circle with my other hand, tracing it with my blood. Marking changed a person. Maybe the blood barrier was weaker. We wouldn't have to wait for the bodies to actually be gone… I looked through my fingers. The barrier link had dark spots. I needed a good excuse for what I was going to do next. I had to convince myself there was more than just my craving to possess him driving this.

After cleaning my hand, I walked up behind him and stilled his arms with my hands. His skin was golden and looked edible. I licked along the curve of his neck and he inhaled deeply.

He started to say something, but I covered his mouth with my hand and pulled his head to the side. Softly kissing the spot where I intended to mark him, feeling the sparks at each touch. I extended my canines and bit down. Lucien groaned against my hand and started kissing my palm as I cleaned the mark.

I released his mouth and stepped around to the front of the chair. Lucien pulled me into his lap and kissed me deeply. It was even more amazing than our first kiss had been. His mouth was soft, yet demanding. My Lucien. My mate. I never wanted it to end.

After a while, we needed to breathe. Pulling away, his lips found my neck and began their slow descent to my mark. I moaned and started kissing and sucking his mark. Under my bottom, I could feel him getting hard and gave in to the urge to rub myself against his rising erection.

"Bellamy," he breathed. "We should stop. Your first time should be in a soft bed, not on a rickety kitchen table with vampires sleeping beneath us. As soon as I get you to your pack, though, I'm going to worship every inch of your sweet little body."

I sighed in frustration. He was being considerate, but I hated it. I'd never felt an attraction to a male. Ever. Never wanted to do the things my boys told me they did with their mates and girlfriends. Nothing had ever felt this good in my entire life. I appreciated their appearance, but I wasn't physically attracted to them.

"Pack the food up. We're gonna torch these bitches and head home. I want you naked and in my bed right after I give my report to Kieran. Do you understand, mon saucisson?" I growled.

Lucien laughed. "Wow. My dirty rogue Queen. I love it, chouchoutte."

I knew he'd love me calling him my sausage. Most males liked to be a little dirty with their mates. I still got a little squicked out remembering some things I heard Dad say to Mom when they were mind-linking each other at dinner.

We got up, and he worked on packing while I grabbed my shoes, the matches, and the pots of glycerin. Once we had put everything together, we each went to one side of the house and gently opened the windows. I poured the glycerin down the wall under the window and up to the sill. After my pot was empty, I lit a match and held it to the liquid. The fire caught after a few moments and ran into the room.

I carefully closed the window and went to wait for Lucien at the front of the house. He was only a few moments behind me.

Taking my hand, he pulled me toward the woods and the path home. When we were a few feet from the house, he squeezed my hand. I looked up, and he appeared to be in a little pain.

"Are you alright, Lucien?" I asked.

"Just fine, chouchoutte. It only hurts a bit. Let's keep moving." He winced.

I pulled him forward this time, through the blood barrier, and we headed to the path into the woods. It was a nice day and I could almost pretend we weren't walking away from a vampire barbecue. We held hands as we walked. I felt like such a little kid being excited about holding his hand like that.

After walking for nearly an hour, we stopped for a snack and some water. Lucien sat on a rock and looked like a lizard sunning himself. I realized he hadn't had direct sunlight in several days. My poor mate. I almost giggled at the thought.

Mine.

"What's making you smile, chouchoutte?" Lucien asked.

"Just thinking of you. And it's so weird. I've never felt like this before."

"I'm honored to be the first," he purred.

"Eat your snack. We've still got a long way to go," I replied, trying to hide what he did to me when he talked like that.

After we'd eaten and had some water, we continued on. It was another hour before we had to stop again. The closer we got to home, the better I started feeling.

Being away from my territory for extended periods drained me a little. I missed the feeling of my places of power. I missed the people who depended on me and my community. Even those yammering bridesmaids.

Soon, we passed the vampire barrier. It was only a mile or so to reach my rogue barrier and the border of my pack lands. Lucien took my hand again, and we had a nice, safe walk through the woods. I could feel the power of my barrier reaching for me. It missed me, too.

When we finally reached the border, I stopped, and we waited after I mind-linked the patrol. Dilly was on for this section. I could feel his excitement through the pack link. I loved Dilly to death. He was always fun to fight and to play with.

"Brace yourself, mon saucisson. The warrior coming is a little… excitable," I warned as I adjusted my hair to hide my mark.

"You don't want him to know about your mark?" he asked, sounding hurt.

"Dilly is a terrible gossip. This isn't something I want going live to the entire pack before we have a chance to talk to my parents. And, Cara will kill me if she finds out from someone else." I chuckled and released his hand.

"I guess…" he pouted.

"How would your friends feel if they heard about us from someone else?" I asked.

He looked at me from the corner of his eye and sighed. "They'd be pretty pissed. I get it. That doesn't mean I have to like it."

"Trust me, I don't like it any more than you do." I sighed. "He's almost here."

Suddenly, Dilly dropped from a tree, right in front of me. I felt Lucien tense with surprise. He hadn't heard Dilly springing from tree to tree.

Dilly was six feet tall with a natural glowing tan, dark blond hair, and pale green eyes. He was my best vampire mimic. Every jump was precise, every landing near silent, no motion wasted. Talia liked him a lot when she visited and gave him extra attention.

"Bemmy!! Ooh! Did you bring me a present?" Dilly grinned, eyeing Lucien.

"No. We're heading to the packhouse. I need to grab my phone from the guard station over there. You tell no one about this meeting or our guest. I'll speak with Kieran myself. Is there a car or do I have to call for one?"

My tone was businesslike and held no humor. He knew I was serious and needed him to be serious, too. It was mostly because I was fighting the urge to scratch out his eyes for looking at my mate.

I wondered how long I'd be like this. It had to go away, right? Maybe after we fully mated.

"There's a car at the station, Captain. Keys are in the code box. I turned off your phone yesterday. The battery was nearly dead. Cara's been trying to reach you. We're on extra high alert. She told me there's a problem at Lune Rouge and no one's talking," Dilly reported.

"No reports or contact from them?" I asked.

"No, Captain. The Alpha is going to check in with them today to see if they need anything. He's trying not to let them know we know something's up."

"We'll be going now. I'll see you at dinner. Watch your landings, that one was rough and I'm not going easy on you tomorrow," I warned.

"Yes, Captain. Welcome home." He bowed and sprung up into the canopy.

Chapter 21: Home Again

"There's a problem at Lune Rouge? I need to get home," Lucien whispered, looking up at where Dilly had disappeared. He was already gone, but Lucien wouldn't be able to track him.

"Let's go to the packhouse and see what we can find out. Maybe they just realized you were gone sooner than you thought they would." I took his hand and led him to the guardhouse.

I went in and grabbed my phone and the keys to the car. I dug through the bins and found a large shirt that looked like it would fit Lucien and some sunglasses. He put them on while grumbling about needing to go home.

'Kieran, I'm home. Taking the car from guard house eight. I have a guest; we need to update you on the mission I took on the other night.'

'I'll have Daniel and Toby here in a minute. Come to my office. Something's going on at Lune Rouge and I want to find a way to get Cara and her mate here if it's not safe.'

'I'm hoping it isn't as dire as that. We'll be able to get a clear assessment soon.'

'Right. See you soon.'

We got in the car and drove quickly through town and up to the packhouse. Harrison, one of my team, came out, and I tossed him the keys as we walked past. He knew where it needed to go. We entered the house and the obstacle course started.

I paused for a moment as I heard a familiar noise. Lucien looked at me oddly when I put my arms up and Anise flew into my grasp. She giggled madly as I tossed her to Lucien and put my hands up to catch Blossom.

Werewolf children advanced faster than human children. That meant they got into trouble a lot younger than human kids. The girls were little adrenalin junkies and would do things like this often.

"What have I told you two about jumping at people coming in the door?" I scolded.

"Bemmy home!" Blossom squealed.

"Bemmy angry. You naughty babies," I growled.

"That's where they ran off to! I swear, the boys weren't nearly as crazy as these two," Mom groaned.

"We have to get a net put up there. One day, someone's not going to be fast enough." I sighed. "We need to get moving."

"Glad you're safe, baby. Have a good meeting," Mom said while kissing me on the head.

"Thanks, Mommy," I replied, handing over a wiggling Blossom and pulling Anise out of Lucien's arms before handing her off and starting toward the back stairs.

"Bebe! I was so worried! I woke up and your dinner was still in the fridge. Have you eaten? Do you need a snack?" Yuri called out as we passed the kitchen.

"Sorry, Yuri. Sudden mission. I gotta go talk to the Alpha. No snack needed, just tell me you're making my favorite dessert, please," I replied.

"Of course, Bebe! You always get a treat when you come home safe. See you at dinner!" He grinned and popped back into the kitchen.

I almost reached the back stairs' door when someone stopped me again.

"Amy, we have a request for aid when you have a moment. The lieutenants have filed their reports for the week, and there are twelve additional requests to join the collective," Drake said, holding the door to the stairs closed.

"Thanks, Drake. I'll review the aid request just put it in my office, and get the applications for new members to Galen for review. Have Todd look at the reports. I'm still working on a previous mission. I'll be with the Alpha for a while and I'm taking the rest of the day off. How did my babies do without me?" I asked.

"They're doing good. They all tell me I make training boring." He chuckled.

"Good, they need to take it a little more seriously. The next level is more work and less play. I'll make sure to get you a rundown of how the games work for the younger kids next time. I need to go, and you're in my way. You can move or I can move you." I winked.

"Of course, Captain. I'll see you at dinner." Drake bowed and moved from the door.

We entered the stairwell, and the door closed behind us. Lucien grabbed my arm and pulled me to him. He wrapped his arms around me and held me for a while.

"That was intense, chouchoutte. Is it always like that?" he asked.

"Only when I leave unexpectedly and don't come back for a couple days," I murmured as I squeezed him tightly.

"You handled everything beautifully. I didn't expect the flying babies." He laughed.

"No one expects the flying babies their first time in. Eventually, you get used to it. Can you handle the stairs or do you want to use the elevator?" I asked.

"I can manage it. We still have some snacks," he replied.

'Yuri, can you make an omelet with spinach, mushrooms, and sausage. Bring orange juice and milk with it. Our guest is healing still and needs food.'

'Got it, Bebe.'

'Thanks, Yuri!'

'Meet you in the Alpha's office.'

"Let's go. Yuri's going to bring you a better snack while we're in the office," I told Lucien.

He released me and we headed up to the second floor and down the hall to Kieran's office. I took a deep breath before I knocked, and adjusted my hair to make sure it still covered the mark. After a few moments, Kieran linked me to come in. I opened the door and stepped into the office.

Kieran's office was large with a sofa bed and three nice armchairs around a coffee table, a little dinette set, a large oak desk with three comfortable office chairs, a map of the region with his territory marked in blue and mine in green on the wall, and ceiling to floor bookshelves crammed with books on supernatural law, biology, history, and customs.

The men stood as I entered. Kieran was behind his desk, and the others had been in the chairs surrounding it. I bowed once I stepped inside.

"Alpha, Beta, Gamma, I've returned from my mission and am prepared to report," I stated.

"Captain," they chorused.

"Please, come make your report," Kieran said.

I turned to the doorway. Lucien was standing in the hall. Reaching out, I took his hand and pulled him into the room. Once the door was closed, Lucien took off the sunglasses and I turned back to the men.

"I've brought a guest."

"Alpha Lucien? What are you doing here?" Kieran asked.

"Let's sit on the couch. Yuri will be up shortly with food for the Alpha. He's healing and needs to eat. I'll give you my report and you'll know everything," I said.

I guided Lucien to the couch and sat next to him while my dad, Kieran, and Toby sat in the armchairs. Just as we got settled, Yuri knocked on the door and served the food to Lucien. My mate grinned and dug in, drinking as he ate.

Once I was sure he was comfortable, I turned to Kieran and started telling my story, starting with hearing the vampires and ending with the information Dilly gave us when we arrived. They stayed quiet through my entire report. I skipped some parts, like what Marion did to me, the plan change, and being marked by Lucien. I included the demon dust, though. They'd need to know about the fight.

"Are you sure the vampires are dead?" Kieran asked.

"I'm fairly certain. I'd like to take my team up tonight. If any of them are alive, they'll be easier to kill. I need to sleep before I can do anything," I replied.

"We can arrange it," my dad said.

"Thank you, Beta." I nodded.

"Now, we need to find out what's going on in my pack. No one should've worried about me for another couple of days. There must have been something else," Lucien said.

"I'd like to keep the fact that you're here quiet," Kieran told him. "Bellamy's right. Someone had to tip those vampires off. They couldn't have had that trap set up just on the off chance they'd snag an Alpha."

"I'll agree, but I don't think my Beta and Gamma had anything to do with it. We haven't had any conflicts in years and they talk to me when we have issues," Lucien stated.

Kieran pulled out his phone and scrolled through the directory. When he found the number he was looking for, he hit the dial button and put it on speaker. The phone rang a few times before someone answered.

"Lune Rouge, Beta Thierry speaking. How can I help you?"

"This is Alpha Kieran from Daylight Moon. I'm just checking in on how everything's going. I thought I called Alpha Lucien's phone," Kieran said.

"He's away at the moment. Everything is on track for the wedding. Cara's getting along well with everyone and is healthy. Did you want to speak with her?" Thierry asked.

He was hiding whatever was going on. I could hear the worry and nervousness in his voice when he said Lucien was away. Lucien looked concerned as well, so I knew I'd interpreted it correctly.

Chapter 22: An Accidental Announcement

I nodded to Kieran. *'Have her come in for a report.'*

'Got it, Amy.'

"I was going to call her later. You know how girls are, she'll go on about things that are important to her, but not important in general. It might be a good idea to get it out of the way, then I can relax." Kieran chuckled.

I tried not to laugh. Cara and I had gotten good at reporting to each other and our parents without seeming like we were doing anything. The way we did it made it seem like we were talking about inane things.

"I'll have her come now. How are things at Daylight Moon?"

"We had a little vampire issue, but the captain of our Elite Ten took care of it. There's a brood nest nearby. I bet the recent issues have been caused by them and their children."

'Those damned neighbors and their troublesome kids,' I linked to Lucien.

His eyes shined with humor. He was finishing his juice and had to work so he wouldn't laugh while drinking. Lucien leaned against the back of the couch and discretely started tracing shapes on my back.

There was a knocking sound over the phone. We heard Thierry call out for them to enter. He told us he was putting us on speaker.

"Your father's on the line, Cara. He wanted to know how everything's going," he said.

"Hi, Daddy!"

"Hello, princess. How's everything going?" Kieran asked.

"Well, we've still got a couple months, but I kept feeling like something was missing. The dress is perfect. I have something new, something borrowed, and something blue, but I'm missing something old. It's important. I worry because it's just *so* important," Cara said.

"I think I found your something old," I answered.

"Amy! I didn't know you were there."

"I asked to be on the call. You know how I fuss. I'll be up next week to speak with Alpha Lucien about security measures. Until then, I just have to hope you're safe," I said.

"Yeah, things are safe here. You said you have my something old. Are you sure? I need that specific one. It's got some black and gray at the top and has a really somber sort of feel to it. It's like my something new, but you know… old."

Lucien tensed up at the description he probably recognized as himself. I couldn't see his face, but I was pretty sure he sported that grumpy look he had when I'd hidden my mark from Dilly.

"Well, it is rather large and got pretty banged up. I found it in the woods. I'm working on getting it back to perfect. Do you want me to bring it to you once it's ready?" I asked.

"Yes, I can't get married without it. I'm relieved you found it. It was supposed to be here. I've just been tearing the place apart looking for it. It was supposed to be tucked away in a little box, but I guess it never made it in." She sighed.

"I've got you, honey. Sorry about not calling you after the dress selection. I got called away. Unexpected guests, you know how it is." I chuckled.

"No worries. The girls called me and told me all about it, including how rude you were. April thinks you're jealous of me." She laughed.

Lucien slipped his hand under my shirt and wrapped his fingers around my side.

'Mine,' he growled in my head.

'I was never jealous of Cara. Chill, mon saucisson.'

"April is projecting. You netted a ranked hottie and she's still waiting and hoping. By the way. I wanted to make sure you were the first to know, I found my mate," I said nervously.

My dad, Kieran, and Toby turned to me with wide eyes. I looked at Lucien and winked. He grinned broadly and pulled his hand from under my shirt, twining his fingers through mine.

Cara squealed with excitement. "Oh my goodness! It isn't Kyle, is it?"

"Who's Kyle?" Lucien growled.

"Lucien?!" Thierry shouted. "Where have you been? We sent a messenger to your cabin and they said it was empty like you never got there. We've been looking everywhere!"

"Well, I guess being sneaky didn't work out." I giggled. "You had to mention Kyle, Cara. Like I'd be excited about that prick."

"Who is Kyle, Bellamy?" Lucien asked with a scowl.

"I'll address everyone by order of information importance. Thierry, we found your Alpha and he'll call you privately to update you on what happened. Cara, Daddy, Uncle Kieran, Uncle Toby, Alpha Lucien is my mate." I smiled and moved my hair to show my mark. "Lucien, Kyle is a man who thinks he has a right to me because his father promised me to him. I've refused all his offers. He's no one to me, mon saucisson."

The tension in Lucien relaxed. He closed his eyes and took a deep breath. When he opened them again, he smiled back at me.

"Lucien, is this true? You found a mate?" Thierry asked.

"Yes. She's a perfect match for me. An Alpha female, a leader, a warrior, and a beautiful soul," Lucien replied.

I saw my dad become a little less tense. If Lucien had said anything about my body, I'm sure Dad would've gone off. I sat back and leaned against his arm. Kieran grinned at us.

"Warrick said you were meant for great things. I thought it was just being the best rogue Queen in the region. Now you can be the best Luna, too… well… after my Daisy." He chuckled.

"She is the master of her craft. Her lessons will come in handy." I winked.

"Thierry, don't tell anyone I was found. Someone set up a trap and I would have died if not for Bellamy. To my knowledge, only you and Robert know where my cabin is. Who was the messenger?" Lucien asked.

"Jean-Claude. He traveled during the day, stayed the night in your cabin, and returned the next day. We were aware of the vampire activity in the area. There's no way any of the boys would do something like that," Thierry said.

"You're right. I don't think it was him. I'll stay at Daylight Moon for a few days," Lucien told him.

"My team and I will escort you home when you're ready. We'll look over your defenses and help weed out the assassin. When I get there, I'll extend my territory's borders to include the land between our pack and Lune Rouge. Alpha Kieran, I'd like to appoint Drake as my lieutenant in Daylight Moon when I move to Lune Rouge," I stated.

"That sounds acceptable, Queen Bellamy," Kieran responded.

"We should end this call. Lucien and I have been up all night, and we walked a lot today. He's still healing and needs rest. I could use a nap before dinner."

"I'll call you later, Thierry," Lucien promised.

"Do you want me to keep this from Robert or should I let him know?" Thierry asked.

"Have him with you for the call. Make sure no one else is in the room. I'll tell him myself. I'll talk to you later."

"Expect a call sometime around six, Beta Thierry. Cara, keep this all quiet. I'll see you in a couple days. We can talk then," I said.

"Got it, Captain." She giggled.

Everyone else said their goodbyes, and the call disconnected. I bit my lips together. I could see my dad trying to piece together what he wanted to say.

"When were you planning to tell us? Or was this your plan?" he asked.

"Sorry, Daddy. I didn't really know how to say it. I really wanted Cara to know first and not hear it from anyone else, I just got a little excited. It's a girl thing. You guys know I didn't think I'd ever find someone who wouldn't lose to me in a fight." I blushed.

"That isn't the only reason you offered for him, right?"

"No. After being violently fed on for at least three days by four vampires, he still didn't break, he didn't give up. He asked me how he could help. Lucien didn't assume he needed to save me as well as himself. He'll be strong enough to deal with what I have to do to be an effective queen," I answered.

"I'll never stop Bellamy from what she needs to do to care for her people. She's smart and intuitive, not impulsive and reckless. She's as much an Alpha as I am. I promise to support that and act as a partner, not a ruler," Lucien told him.

I smiled. He really was perfect for me. I needed someone to support me and lead with me instead of protecting me and trying to take my power.

"Go get some rest. I'd prefer if you were in separate rooms, but you're marked and legally an adult. Set an alarm. We'll gather some clothes for Alpha Lucien if he'll write down his sizes. I'll get the team together and brief them on your mission and the task you'll undertake tonight," my dad said.

I stood up and hugged him, giving him a kiss on the cheek while Lucien wrote his sizes on a notepad. Toby and Kieran came over to congratulate me on finding a mate. It was a pretty big deal for them. They had placed bets. I was betting none of them had the Alpha of our nearest neighboring pack for their pick.

Chapter 23: Alphas in Love

[Bellamy]

I helped Lucien up and guided him out of the room and to the elevator. I didn't want him walking up two more flights of stairs. When the elevator doors closed, Lucien leaned down and kissed me gently.

"I don't know that I have the energy to properly worship you, chouchoutte. This has been a long day," he murmured.

"There's always tomorrow, my love. I figured the walk would probably wipe you out, so I'm not disappointed. I really didn't intend to tell your friend, though."

"I got possessive. You know how Alphas are. You never told me someone else had a claim on you, chouchoutte." He chuckled.

"Kyle's a little bitch. He's made offers but doesn't come to talk to me himself. I kicked his ass when I was eight, and I'll gladly do it again," I growled.

"And, when he's healed, I'll kick his ass, too, so he understands I'm not some weak pack wolf he can try to steal you from," he growled back.

"You're so fucking sexy when you get all violent like that," I purred and wrapped my arms around his neck, pulling his lips to mine.

Lucien's arms went around my waist, and he pulled me up, deepening the kiss. I locked my ankles behind his back. He was delicious. We kissed until the elevator shuddered to a stop. Lucien lowered me gently to the ground, and I led him to my room.

Once we were in, I pulled my phone from the little pocket in my pants and set an alarm for six before putting it on the charger. When I turned back, Lucien was taking off his shirt. I licked my lips and shimmied out of my pants.

He chuckled. "That isn't going to help me sleep, chouchoutte."

"Those sweats aren't exactly putting me in a napping mood, either." I giggled and climbed onto the bed.

Before I could turn to sit, I felt Lucien's large hands on my hips. He pulled me back to the edge of the bed and against the bulge in his pants. I moaned as I felt him rubbing against me through the cloth. Nothing had ever felt so good.

"I haven't had sex in almost nineteen years. You can't just shake this luscious little ass at me. You're going to kill me, ma choupinette," he rumbled.

"You're the one who said you didn't have the energy, mon saucisson," I groaned.

"I have the energy to fuck you silly, but you deserve better than that, bel amour."

"Then let me go, my love. Trust me, we'll get there. I'm not like Cara. There's no illusion that I can resist you until a wedding or something. You're mine and I intend to claim all of you." I sighed.

Lucien released me. I scooted nearer to the wall and slipped beneath the covers. He climbed into the bed next to me and wrapped his arms around me. I rested my head on his chest and inhaled deeply.

"Lucien, what do you smell in my scent? I smell strawberry and basil. Like my favorite ice cream."

"Honeysuckle and jasmine. Two sweet and beautiful flowers," he replied sleepily.

"I love you," I whispered.

"I love you more than you could ever know." He yawned and, in moments, he was asleep.

'Yuri, can I ask a favor?'

'Anything for my Bebe.'

'Do you know how to make choux à la crème?'

'No, but I have someone in the kitchen who's great with pastry. Would you like some?'

'If you can get some made, I'd appreciate it. And do you think the cream could be sweetened using that simple syrup you use for your springtime cupcakes?'

'I'll see what we can do.'

'Thank you! You're the best, Yuri!'

'I love you too, Bebe.'

With that taken care of, I closed my eyes and let myself drift to sleep in the arms of my mate.

***

[Lucien]

I woke up with a start, smelling vampires. Groaning, I realized I'd shifted in my sleep, expelling the scent from my sweatpants with the rush of air from my movement. I didn't think I could get to sleep again. Over the last few days, I'd trained my body not to rest after smelling vampires.

"Are you alright, Lucien? Did you have a bad dream?" Bellamy asked.

"No, just smelled vampire and it woke me. Go back to sleep if you can, chouchoutte."

She grumbled and was still for a moment. I watched her beautiful face; the way her lashes splayed over her cheekbones, how her hair wrapped itself around her like a bronze sheet, the soft pink lips that I loved kissing. Everything about her was perfection.

"I linked Melly. She'll bring up the clothes for you now and strip the bed. I want to make sure you have a restful sleep. What time is it?" she mumbled.

"You don't have a clock. I have no idea."

Bellamy sighed and started climbing over me. She straddled my waist and reached out to the nightstand for her phone. Her breasts pushed against my face and I pulled her down so she couldn't escape me. Bellamy let out a giggling moan as I rubbed my face against her soft, full breasts.

"It's five-thirty. We still have an hour before dinner. Do you want to have a shower and shave?" she suggested.

I pulled my face from her breasts. "Are you saying I'm a stinky furball?" I laughed.

"No, I'm implying it. Saying it is rude," Bellamy giggled.

"I guess I'd make a pretty poor impression if I went to dinner smelling like vampires and looking like a caveman," I said.

"Let me go and I'll grab some soaps and a toothbrush for you."

"And my breath stinks, too? I have no clue why you marked me when I'm this disgusting, chouchoutte."

"Because, even when you're disgusting, you're beautiful. I never thought I'd see a beautiful man until you," she murmured and sat back, rubbing her backside against me. "I think you'll be even more gorgeous when you're clean and shaved."

"Then go get the things I need so I can turn you into a puddle with my beauty," I joked.

"Mmm. Too fucking late, mon saucisson," she purred as she climbed off me and exited the room.

I grinned at the ceiling.

'Told you you'd like it. And you said I never make good decisions.' Remus laughed.

'Best choice ever, Remus. She's perfect. We're so lucky she wanted us, too.'

'Her wolf is great. Do you know what she said to me after I accepted?'

'What?'

'She said, 'If you fuck as good as you fight, we'll be able to forgive damn near anything.' Aurora says Bellamy is just like her in a lot of ways. She only acts like a proper good girl so she won't scare her family. She promised to be the best Beta's daughter she could and that meant saving the dirty or violent stuff for when she was with other warriors.'

'What do you mean by that?' I asked.

'She talks to them like we used to talk with our friends when we were young warriors. Down to the dirty jokes and dirtier play-by-play from bedroom sessions. She's violent, serious, and strict in leader mode, but just one of the guys otherwise. Aurora said she was taught by the Luna how to take care of a pack. So she actually is a party planner! And she'll tell you anything! If she's upset, she'll tell you why if she thinks you can help. If you don't understand something, she'll explain. She'll train and fight with you all you want.'

'A perfect match. I'd prefer a partner to a simple support. An Alpha female is rare and I couldn't think of anyone more suited to helping me navigate two generations of leadership. I can't wait to really see her in action. We've seen her as a spy, as a leader, and as an actress. I want to really see her as a warrior, as a bold woman, and as a queen,' I said.

'I want to run and hunt with her wolf. Aurora felt powerful. I bet she's gorgeous.'

If she was anything like Bellamy, she most definitely was. I couldn't wait to see her.

Chapter 24: Innocent Eyes

[Lucien]

Bellamy entered the bedroom, the door swinging inward with a soft click, a wicker basket filled with bottles in her arms. She closed the door with a soft click and crossed the room to me, her footsteps barely audible on the carpet.

"I have a shampoo and conditioner that I think would smell fantastic on you. There's a body wash, shaving cream, razors, washcloths, toothbrush, and toothpaste. I have mouthwash in the bathroom. Did I miss anything?"

"Someone to help wash my back?" I teased.

"As wonderful as that sounds, I have a mission this evening and I can't afford to be worn out or stiff. There's a sponge on a stick you can use in the shower. Now, move that ass or I'll move it for you," she growled playfully.

I sniffled. "Mother was right. You sleep with a warrior once and they stop wanting anything to do with you."

"Come on, babe. You knew what this was." She winked. "Now, get your sweet ass out of my bed."

I gave her a light kiss on her lips and took the basket before heading into the bathroom to take my shower. I loved the way she sighed each time I kissed her. She was on my mind while I showered and shaved.

I knew I was much better looking clean-shaven. There was a light sprinkle of gray starting in my beard from the strain of handling my pack while searching for a mate or someone to take over. That probably didn't help with her dad's disapproval. He'd been glaring at me pretty hard when she announced we were mates. I knew the ranked members of this pack were only five years older than me. They knew it as well.

Once I was clean and shaved, I brushed my teeth and stared at myself in the mirror. Before, I looked like I was in my thirties. Now I definitely looked closer to twenty or twenty-five, like Bellamy said last night. I opened the door to head out, but stopped when I heard her talking.

"… like you wouldn't believe. Oh, goddess, Cara, I don't even know. How am I supposed to act? … No, I don't want you to tell me what you'd do. You'd get separate rooms and sneak secret kisses thinking you're being naughty. That wouldn't work for me. I'd pull him into an abandoned office for a kiss and end up going down on him. I may be a virgin, but I'm not some innocent prude. Full offence.

"I mean how do I act so I'm not behaving like some idiot? What's going too far or out of line for a pack wolf? Where's the line? What do I do if I cross it? Fuck, Cara. I'm dying," she groaned.

I smiled. She'd lived in a pack for six years and still didn't know how she should act. It made sense when I thought of it. She became Queen of a territory right away and started training right away. Normalizing had all been a façade, so others wouldn't reject her. Now she was trying to figure out what kind of mask to wear for me.

"What if he takes back his acceptance? Rescinding acceptance is the closest thing a rogue can get to the actual pain of rejection. I'd die, Cara. Not literally, emotionally. I wouldn't be able to handle that. I've lost too many people in my life and been pushed away too many times. You're my only real female friend. I don't trust anyone but you on this…. I know you love me, I'm amazing. But that's not the point." She laughed. "I don't say that to people, Cara. You know how I feel about you. You're my best friend. Cara, you're my heart sister."

Before this morning, I'd never heard of a heart family, but I felt it. Thierry, Robert, their mates and kids, they were my heart family. She wanted love so much that she made a family. I wanted to give her everything she needed, everything she wanted.

I'd wanted a mate, someone to love me, care for me, share my life with, for so long, and she gave that to me. I wouldn't let her down. Nothing would ever make me leave her.

Bellamy sniffed and sighed. "I was all distracted. Damn it. Lucien, how long have you been listening?"

Busted.

I walked out of the bathroom with the towel around my waist and smiled. A dark, predatory look came over Bellamy's face as her eyes skimmed over my body and landed on the knot in the towel. She licked her lips.

"I have to go, Cara. I'll talk to you later," she murmured and hung up the phone.

"Sorry, Bellamy. I didn't want to interrupt your conversation, then I wanted to hear more. I like listening to you talk to your friend. Can I help you? Could you trust me with your worries? I'm your mate. Your happiness is my happiness," I told her.

She looked away. I wished I could read her mind. There was a struggle apparent in her features. More than anything, I wanted to soothe her worries and pain. Was there a way to do that without dominating her, though?

"I don't know how to act. There's a chance I'll do something to embarrass you when we get back to your pack. I'm concerned about potential backlash from your pack for mating with a rogue. Kieran had a lot of people angry when he allied with me. An alliance is different from a relationship." She shrugged.

"So you're not worried about how to act right now, just how to act when you're around my pack?" I asked.

"Of course, mon saucisson. I know how to act here and now. I need to go take a shower and get ready for work before we have dinner. When I get home, I'll debrief with the Alpha and then come up here, shower again, and suck that beautiful cock of yours before I go to sleep. I've been wanting to taste you since the first time you kissed me.

"But, when I'm at your packhouse, I'll be staying with you. I have this powerful urge to touch you all the time. I'm really jealous. The way Dilly looked at you made me want to claw his eyes out. I don't know what's appropriate outside of my territory.

"What if your Beta and Gamma don't like me? What if your pack hates me? Would you leave me? Would you take back your acceptance if they didn't want me? How should I act to make them like me enough to not encourage you to leave me? Cara says to be myself, but myself is kind of an asshole with few restraints on conversation topics," Bellamy grumbled, covered her face with her hands, and leaned back on the couch.

My mouth had gone dry and, no matter how much I tried to focus on her issues, I could only focus on the sucking my cock part. It wasn't until I felt a slight breeze that I realized I had an erection.

The feeling in my dick was off and on since the curse lifted. For nineteen years, the thing wouldn't stand at attention for anything. Now it did it from the slightest thought of any part of Bellamy's body, any touch, any breath, any little sound she made.

"Th… they can go to hell. It's my pack. I decided you were the best possible Luna. The best possible mate for me. If they have a problem, they can challenge either one of us to a fight. We'll kick their asses until they learn to respect their Alpha *and* his Queen," I growled.

Nothing was going to stop me from feeling that sweet little mouth on me tonight. If I had to fight every wolf in the region, I was going to feel her lips surround me. She'd never been shy with me and I loved it. I wanted a woman who was as bold as I was. One who said what they wanted and did what they had to in order to get it.

"Really? You won't leave me because I'm not a good Luna?" she asked, peeking between her fingers.

"You'll be a perfect Luna, Bellamy. I will never leave you. If you run away, I'll chase you and make you fall in love with me again. If I'm ever stupid enough to cheat, I'll kill myself. I'll let you kill me. I won't deserve to live."

Bellamy laughed. "A little dramatic, don't you think?"

She pulled her hands away from her face and smiled. I didn't think it was, but if it made her smile, I'd keep going. There was nothing as glorious as the twinkle of happiness in her eyes.

"Chouchoutte, nothing is dramatic when it comes to making you feel loved, accepted, and happy. I'd fight every wolf in the world. I'd collect every gem in existence. No quest would be too great. I'd hunt down every enemy you've ever had. I'd buy you anything you ever desired. I'd let toddlers ride on my back. I'd… babysit your sisters!" I told her.

Bellamy was holding her stomach and started snorting a little when she laughed. I walked over and knelt on one knee in front of her, picking up her hand and kissing it lightly before placing it on my shoulder. She stopped laughing and leaned forward as my towel dropped and the bedroom door opened.

Chapter 25: Phone Home

[Lucien]

There was a squealing shriek, and the door slammed closed, making Bellamy laugh again. She gripped my shoulders and laid her head on my chest while she tried to catch her breath. I didn't think a person could die of laughter, but she seemed to be trying. After another minute, she got ahold of herself.

"I linked Melly to apologize. She'll be back in a couple minutes. You should pick up that towel before you scare her away again. She has your clothes," Bellamy snickered.

I picked up the towel as I stood and tied it again.

"You said my cock was beautiful. How could she possibly be scared of something as gorgeous as this?" I winked.

"Because I would have ripped out her eyes and shoved them down her throat before tearing off her head if she'd done anything other than scream and run. Never show that to any female other than me. You belong to me. Your cock belongs to me. Don't ever forget that," she growled.

"And who do you belong to?"

"You. The only man who can handle me. The only man I love. But, as much as we own each other, we still own ourselves. There's only so much control that either one of us will give up. It's the nature of being Alphas." She shrugged.

"So I can say that no male is permitted to look at you or touch you. That your body belongs to me. And you won't fight me on that?" I asked.

"No. But, I do shift as a part of my work sometimes, so how about no lingering looks?" She winked.

"You permitted lingering looks before?" I snarled.

"I didn't stop them. I will from now on. A full third of my team is either related to me or gay, and it's not like the entire pack's been permitted. I'll stop giving them lingering looks too. Sound good?" Bellamy smiled.

"You fucking better." I turned away.

I knew I shouldn't be angry about things she did before I knew she existed. That wouldn't be fair. She didn't act like this over the things I did before we met. Of course, she didn't know all of them. Not that I would tell her. At least one of us had to have boundaries.

"Don't be mad, my Lucien. They're just boys. Boys try to look at girls all the time. And girls do the same, but lie about it. If it makes you feel any better, you're much hotter, much stronger, and much… bigger than any of them. And that isn't even the bond talking." I felt her arms wrap around my waist as she started kissing my back. "I definitely took a few good long looks at you over the last couple of days. Even before you marked me."

That made me smile. It was nice knowing she'd been looking at me, too. Maybe it was part of why her wolf made the offer.

The door opened again. I looked over and a girl was sticking her head in with her hand covering her eyes. Her voice was small and nervous.

"Miss Amy, I brought the clothes back. I'm sorry I ran away," she said.

I felt Bellamy's arms slide away and watched her cross to the door. For a moment, I was a little scared for the girl. But Bellamy took the bundle from her and patted her on the head.

"It's fine, Melly. You got a shock. I'm glad you didn't run too far. I want you to put together a small wardrobe for Alpha Lucien. Make sure he has something for working out in. If he'd like to join one of our warrior groups, I want him in appropriate attire. He'll need something to sleep in as well.

"I want you to strip the bed, wash everything that smells of vampire, and deodorize the mattress. If that doesn't work get it replaced before nine o'clock tonight. When you redress the bed, use blues and greens. Lucien seems to prefer them and I'd rather he was comfortable while he's here. Once we've left for dinner, you can get to work in here. Sound doable?" Bellamy asked.

"Yes, ma'am. I'll go work on the wardrobe now and have it settled in your dresser and closet before he returns from dinner. Thank you for understanding." She bowed a little and left.

Bellamy put the bundle down on the couch and ran her fingers across my waist as she went past me to the bathroom. The way she was always touching me was wonderful. The feeling of her fingers trailing over my skin was one of the best feelings I'd experienced in years. I turned to watch her leave.

She'd handled that perfectly. An ideal Luna, fair, calm, and effective.

"You can use my phone to call your Beta. That way you can have time after dinner to relax. Or be questioned by my parents… I never know exactly what's going to happen around here, but that seems like something they'd do. I'll be about twenty minutes. Lock the bedroom door," she said as she closed the door.

I locked the door and finished drying myself before looking at the clothes in the bundle. There were a pair of black boxer briefs, a white tank style undershirt, a pair of comfortable looking tan slacks, a belt, socks, shoes, and a forest green short-sleeved button-up shirt. I dressed quickly and picked up her phone from the couch cushion before sitting and dialing Thierry's number.

The line rang twice before he picked up. He told me he was putting the phone on speaker, Robert was the only other person in the room, and he'd locked the door. I gave them a quick rundown of the attack, my imprisonment, and my rescue.

"You're going to stay at Daylight Moon for a bit, then come back?" Robert asked.

"Yes. Call off the search. Tell them it was a false alarm and I was taking my sabbatical elsewhere this year. Keep things calm in the pack. I'm planning to take an extra day. I want to try out their elite training, but I won't be up to it tomorrow. If it's as intense as I've heard, I might need a day to recover." I chuckled.

"And when you come back their Elite Ten will be escorting you? How long will they be staying?" Thierry asked.

"They'll be coming with, yes. I'll have to talk to the captain, but I think they were planning to stay through the wedding. The captain will be staying indefinitely," I replied.

"Why would the captain stay indefinitely? Did you coax him into leaving?" Robert asked.

"I accepted an offer from their captain that benefits us both a great deal. The pack will be safer and stronger than ever. And I finally have my Luna." I grinned.

"Luna? Did you find a mate? What does that have to do with the captain? Is it his sister or something?" Robert asked.

Thierry started laughing. I really enjoyed being vague about things sometimes and seeing if they could pick up on what I was saying. The communication between Cara and Bellamy made me a little jealous. I'd known my friends for our entire lives, and Robert never seemed to pick up on things.

"Or something, Robert. My Luna *is* the captain of the Elite Ten. She's the one who rescued me. You're gonna love her. She's funny, smart, and hard-working. Her acting skill is amazing. I actually thought she was some rogue kid, not one of the top warriors in, possibly, the strongest pack in the region. The entire time she was working for the vampires, she was putting together a plan. She's heading back to their nest tonight to ensure they're all dead," I told them.

The bathroom door opened and Bellamy came out, wrapped in a towel. My eyes followed her path. I wanted to pull her towel off and lick every drop of water off her skin. She dug through her dresser drawers, then moved on to the closet before heading back to the bathroom. I heard a hairdryer starting up.

"Congrats, Lucien. I'm happy you found someone acceptable. Your search was a little painful to watch. Are you sure she's the one though, and you're not just enamored of a powerful female? I want to be sure you're not going to suffer," Robert said.

No. I'd thought Bellamy was beautiful from the moment I saw her. Even though I'd been angry, I thought she looked like an angel. She was kind and funny throughout our entire time with the vampires. She was strong in ways other than her physical strength. I was most tempted by the idea of marking, because I could actually see myself with her.

As if summoned by my thinking of her, Bellamy exited the bathroom. Bellamy tied her hair back in a tight bun. She was wearing a body-hugging long sleeved black top with a black zipper she'd zipped all the way up under her chin. Her pants were the same black material and went down past her ankles a bit. She had black sneakers on over them.

She went to a long, wide box on her computer desk and started pulling out pieces of wood so thin that they looked almost like paper but stiffer. Each piece curved differently. She put her leg up on the computer chair and slid a long, wide piece into a seamless pocket on her inner thigh.

I watched as each piece of wood found its home in an invisible pocket somewhere on her person. Once she was done, she pulled out fingerless gloves, which she buttoned into the wrist of her shirt. I'd been so distracted, Robert worried I was mad and started rambling.

"Sorry. I was preoccupied." I chuckled.

"Oops. I didn't realize I'd disturb you while adding my armor," Bellamy giggled. "You want to put the phone on speaker? I've been working with the boys on a plan for when we get to Lune Rouge. It will give us the best security coverage for you, let us investigate with little interference, and will explain why everyone was panicked about losing you, then no longer concerned."

I knew Robert and Thierry had heard most of that. I put the phone on speaker.

"Alright, Captain. What's your plan?" I asked.

"We're going to have my brother, Bruce, pretend to be the captain of the Elite Ten. Since our appointment was logged as B. Carrington, no one would realize it was Bellamy and not Bruce. Drake and Dillon will train your warriors for the two months we're there. Bruce will spend time with Cara, making sure she's safe. He's a warrior, but not as strong as my boys. Everyone else will be assessing and strengthening your defenses," she explained.

"Where will you be in all this?" Thierry asked as she took a breath.

An angry look came across her face. I actually felt a little frightened for him and for me. He was over a hundred miles away. I was right here, in easy hitting distance. I could beat her in a fight, but I didn't want to fight and ruin my chances of her following her plan for the night.

"Don't speak when the captain is speaking, Thierry," I ordered.

"Sorry, Alpha," he replied.

I nodded to Bellamy, who took a deep breath and smiled at me. Relief washed over me. She wasn't angry anymore.

Chapter 26: The Plan

Bellamy focused on the phone again. Her anger apparently gone, for now.

"I've talked with Kieran, Dad, and Cara. As far as anyone else seems to know, you lost your first mate and your second never appeared, well, except for my dad. His brother was *her* second chance. They keep it quiet because he doesn't like people upsetting Aunt Regan. I'm guessing your curse wasn't common knowledge, either.

"I'll be coming as Lucien's mate and future Luna. The story we've decided on was that Lucien came across the Elite Ten doing heavy field training in the woods and asked to join. He ended up camping with the team and training with them for a few days before following them to their pack lands. When he got here he found his second chance mate. We'd just returned from field training the day I found him, so the timelines match up.

"Dillon's already spreading it to the gossip mongers that Alpha Lucien came for a visit and was my mate. He's telling them we met while I was out checking the barriers and you were out for a walk. They all know about those and it's the best reason to explain why I disappeared for a couple days.

"The fact that I was unmarked the last time anyone saw me and I'm marked now will help. I have to go shopping with the bridesmaids so they can confirm it. Cara called them and asked them to try some necklaces. It's a good chance to get eyes on my neck. People will tell their friends or family in Lune Rouge. When I show up, they'll already know I exist.

"I'll act like a typical girl. People will probably say I'm an elite warrior, but we have fifty elite warriors. No one here knows I'm the captain of the Elite Ten except them and their mates. And the ranked members, of course. I can keep an eye out for whoever might be trying to kill Lucien," she finished.

It was a solid plan. No one would suspect her of being anything but an abnormally small female. She did 'frightened and clueless' really well with the vampires. I smiled.

"You realize you can't act like an Alpha wolf, right? And I'll have to act as a typical male and protect you. You can't act like you can take care of yourself further than a typical female," I reminded her.

Bellamy sat on her knees in front of me and looked up at me from under her lashes. She nibbled her lip nervously and worried at her fingernails.

"You'll make sure I'm safe from anything that can hurt me. If I get startled by a loud noise, you'll cuddle me until I stop crying. You know, thunder scares me a lot. I might not even be able to move if I hear any," she said in a soft, delicate tone. There was a slight quiver in her voice and the beginnings of tears formed in the corner of her eyes.

Remus surged, wanting to protect her. I felt it, too. I wanted to gather her in my arms, but when I leaned forward, she leaned away until she rolled backward and stood again.

"No touching. I've worked to get every scent I can off of me. We work scent-free when going after vampires. Or they can find the people we care about. We don't want to leave anything if they have friends in the area. I'll touch you plenty when I get back, mon saucisson," she purred.

"I actually thought you were starting to cry, chouchoutte," I whispered.

"I'm actually afraid of thunder. Admitting a vulnerability makes me tear up. I watch how the females here act with their mates. Don't worry, I'm good at what I do." Bellamy winked.

"When did you plan this?" I asked.

"I gathered information while you were in the shower, I talked with the boys while I was in the shower. Bruce is on board. He's hoping to have the same luck as Cara. Everything is in order on this end. There's only one thing I don't know," she said. "Why were you sending a messenger to Lucien?"

There was silence on the other end of the line. I could tell they didn't really want to tell me, even though they needed to. My mind went through everything I could think of that would make them hesitant.

"It's your mother, Lucien. She's really sick, but told us she wanted to stay in the Alpha's quarters. Your maid has been taking care of her. She had a stroke the other day, it's why we sent Jean-Claude to you. You're the only one who can supersede her orders," Thierry replied.

My mind reeled. My mother was one of the most important people in my life. More than my friends. She was the one who kept my pack together when I fell apart after losing Angelique.

Getting up, I made for the door. I needed to go home. My mother needed me.

Bellamy stepped in front of me. Where I moved, she moved.

"Please, stop, Lucien. Let's figure this out. What were her other symptoms?" Bellamy asked calmly.

"Nausea, vomiting, diarrhea, tingling in her extremities with some loss of feeling, difficulty talking at times. The doctor can't figure it out," he said.

"Get her and the maid to the pack hospital. Put them in separate quarantine rooms. Sedate the maid if she refuses. Post two guards outside the doors. No one gets in or out unless it's a doctor, nurse, or your Alpha.

"Run a thallium test on both. Order Prussian Blue for treatment. You may have to mix it with a little colloidal silver for it to take effect in the first dose. Once her body accepts it as a medicine you won't need to have the mix." Bellamy ordered coolly. "I saw this once in a witch. She thought she was being cursed, but it was her human husband poisoning her."

I froze. Someone was poisoning my mother? Who would do something like that?

The maid. That was why Bellamy wanted her held. Keeping her in the hospital instead of the cells was different. I turned to look at her.

She was biting her lips together. I could see her having a conversation in her head. Not with someone else, just the way she did when she was thinking things through.

"Once the maid is sedated, run a pregnancy test on her. She's most likely at least one week pregnant," Bellamy said.

"Why do you think she's pregnant?" Thierry asked.

"Because Lucien's curse wasn't widely known. She probably decided to get pregnant with his child. Have you ever had an extreme discomfort in your groin after a meal, Lucien?" She questioned.

I thought about the last few weeks. That had happened. I went to the doctor and had tests. Nothing in my blood. No blockages. The pain went away after a few hours.

I nodded. "Two weeks ago."

"Did you have blood tests? Did they check for toxins?" she asked.

"They checked for everything. I insisted. Nothing showed up," I told her.

"Succubus pheromone. It wouldn't show up on tests. It's used to assist supernatural men with sexual dysfunctions. The curse wouldn't let it work. The pain you felt was the pheromone trying to fight the curse. When you didn't try to find an outlet for your desire, she probably decided to use someone else and kill you to make sure no one would know you didn't impregnate her.

"It's a big risk and a multiple-level plan. I think she either had help or was being manipulated. Keeping her safe and sedated will ensure we can question her. Dilly can get information from anyone. He's one of our best, non-lethal, interrogators. Keep her alive until we get there," Bellamy said.

I stared. I'd kill her for poisoning my mother and trying to take my pack from me. After the child was born, I'd tear the maid into pieces. I was seething.

"Get it taken care of. I want visuals on her at all times. Get cameras into wherever you put her so we can be sure no one kills her before I get the chance," I growled.

"Yes, Alpha," they chorused.

"We'll head home in three days. I want Lucien to be completely healthy before bringing him back. We need to head to dinner. Keep my mother-in-law safe until she can tell me how much I don't deserve her son in person," Bellamy joked.

"Yes, Luna," they replied and hung up.

"Aww, my first 'yes, Luna'." She giggled.

"Will my mother be okay, chouchoutte?" I asked.

"Yes. Wolves are less likely to suffer long-term effects of poisons as long as they don't get a lethal dose. I promise, my love. She'll be fine. Come on. Yuri's freaking out. We're five minutes late for dinner." She smiled.

I nodded and followed her down to the dining room. Everyone sat around the table. On one side were the ranked members currently in power, Alpha Kieran at the head with his wife to his left and his son to his right. Bellamy guided me to the foot of the table.

"Allow me to make introductions," she said in the polite way I'd heard her speak to Marion. "At the head of the table, I'm sure you know Alpha Kieran to his left is Luna Daisy, then Beta Daniel Carrington and his wife, Olive, then the twins, Blossom and Anise. Next to Anise is Gamma Tobin Franks and his wife Bren. Next to her is May, the future Luna, and Gail, the future Gamma female. On the Alpha's right is Jason, future Alpha, then Galen, future Beta, and Todd, future Gamma. Next to Todd is his cousin Drake, future head warrior." There was a small gasp from everyone at the table, but no one said anything.

"Then Dillon, Freddy, Harrison, Sam, and Porter. These young men are the nine elite warriors who serve under me in the Elite Ten. Everyone, this is my mate, Alpha Lucien Devereux of Lune Rouge," she finished.

I noticed that the men to the right of the Alpha were all wearing a similar uniform to the one Bellamy was wearing. She sat next to me and placed a napkin on her lap. I nodded to them and sat as well. Everyone, except the three ranked members in power, looked shocked. They all sat quietly as dinner was served.

"Are… are you sure, Amy?" Galen asked.

"Absolutely. I don't want to risk breaking my collar or I'd prove it. Lucien?" She smiled.

I pulled my collar aside, showing her mark. Everywhere I looked, I could see people having mind-link conversations. I thought I saw Bellamy wince a few times.

'Are you okay, chouchoutte?' I asked.

'They don't actually realize I can hear them when they mind-link someone in the same room. It's not something I want people to know. I like to know what they're discussing.'

'You don't feel bad about spying?'

'Only when my mom and dad get all horny at the dinner table. Then I feel really, really bad.' She swallowed hard.

I started laughing. I couldn't help it. After the stress of finding out my mother was being poisoned, it was a relief to laugh at something. Bellamy was always making small jokes and trying to make me smile. When she left the room, after cleaning me at the vampires' house, I'd chuckled at her calling me 'sweetheart' again, even though she knew my name.

Bellamy smiled at me and ate her dinner. It was superb. I wondered if Yuri would write some of his recipes for my kitchen staff. The soup was light and sweet; the meat was seasoned well and tender, and the baked potatoes were like the ones Bellamy had made at the house. Real butter improved the soft, salty skin.

"So, you're going to run off and become Luna of Lune Rouge, then?" Dillon asked.

"Yes, Dilly. It's where I belong," she replied softly.

I wanted to hold her hand or touch her, but I assumed everyone had the same rule as she did. To avoid undermining her authority, I wouldn't give the impression that I was above the rules. I ate and watched everyone at the table.

Her parents leaned together, whispering. Luna Daisy was chatting quietly with her husband, who was nodding and listening. Drake smiled to himself as he ate. I bet he was excited to be the new head warrior.

"Alpha Lucien, how did you meet Bellamy?" Bren asked.

I looked at Bellamy. Who was supposed to hear what story? I needed a diagram.

"I found him in the woods and decided to keep him, Aunt Bren," Bellamy winked.

I snickered and everyone listening laughed a little. We continued our meal pleasantly. Mostly, people were asking about my pack and family. I felt really comfortable. Bellamy took on any tough parts of conversations. I knew she didn't really enjoy talking, but she'd been a pack wolf long enough she knew we were chatty.

When dessert was finally served, Bellamy got a bowl of pink ice cream with little dark flecks in it. She grinned broadly. I loved watching her so excited. She scooped up a spoonful of it and held it up for me to taste. The strange combination of ripe strawberries and cream sweetness with a slightly peppery, minty undertone worked.

"That's what you smell like," she whispered.

Bellamy took a big spoonful and licked it sensually while looking directly into my eyes. I swallowed hard, imagining her little pink tongue licking other things. Someone placed a plate in front of me, and the scent of honeysuckle and jasmine intensified. I looked down at my dessert.

It was a *choux à la crème*. I picked it up and inhaled. The scent was coming from the pastry. I looked at Bellamy and she nibbled her lip.

"Did you have this made for me, chouchoutte?" I asked.

"Of course, mon saucisson. You're my favorite dessert. I want to be yours, too," she murmured.

I took a bite and the flavor of the honeysuckle and jasmine cream spread over my tongue. I felt a surge in me. Remus danced inside my head. This was definitely my new favorite dessert.

"Yuri," I called out.

He turned and smiled. "Yes, Alpha Lucien?"

"Would you be willing to share this recipe with my kitchen?" I asked. "I'd love to have it more often."

"Certainly, Alpha. We'll get it written up for you to take home with you." He bowed.

"Thank you. I think I could eat it every night," I said, looking directly at Bellamy. She blushed beautifully.

Chapter 27: Best Intentions, Worst Execution

[Lucien]

When the meal was over, the Elite Ten said their goodbyes and left to their work. I wanted to go with them but knew I'd only be a hindrance to their cohesion and Bellamy's concentration. It had been a long time since I was on this side of a mission. Waiting on someone I loved to return, hoping they weren't hurt.

"Alpha, can we speak with you?" Daniel asked.

I turned and saw him with his wife. Bellamy said they might question me. It would be a distraction, at least. I nodded and followed them to the living room of their quarters.

It was a homey place with big, soft furniture, a television in the corner with a game console connected. Pictures of their kids were all over the place, on walls, on shelves, on the mantle of the fireplace.

Olive pointed to the couch and sat with her husband on the loveseat across from me. She wove her fingers through his and smiled softly at me. Bellamy looked a little like her. If I didn't know she was adopted, I would never suspect she wasn't Olive's daughter.

"We wanted to know how much you know about rogue born wolves and rogue Alphas," she said.

I thought for a moment. Most of my experience with rogues had been in fighting them when they came onto my lands. I only knew a little about actual rogue born wolves. Just the stuff my dad had in his books. And what Bellamy told me.

"They have better senses and are faster than pack wolves and ex-pack rogues. Bellamy said they make offers for their mates instead of being granted them. She's an Alpha so she's called a rogue Queen… I guess I don't know much else," I replied.

"That's what we figured. Why did you accept Bellamy?" she asked.

"My wolf accepted her without telling me about the offer. He knew I wouldn't have accepted it. I didn't think I deserved her. You know I rejected my second chance mate. I searched for someone to accept me, someone who would be good for my pack, but never found anyone who fit. She's like me, but calmer. She controls her anger better than I did at her age," I answered. "I think she's perfect. You raised her well. She's caring and thoughtful, but not afraid to be strong and commanding."

"She was like that before we got her. Bellamy's grown in many ways, but a lot of who she is had already been ingrained in her. You have to understand. For six of the most important years of her life, she had no one she could truly depend on. She's always been afraid we'd make her leave or stop wanting her. We know she loves us, but she's never said it," Olive said quietly.

Tears were forming in her eyes. Daniel put an arm around her and squeezed her to him. I hated the idea of Bellamy being a little girl with no one to protect her.

The thought of her alone, afraid to tell anyone she loved them in case she lost them.... Then I remembered, she told me she loved me. She trusted me to never leave. I wouldn't tell them, though. It felt like it was rubbing in our connection.

"When we took her in six years ago, we had no idea what we were starting. During her warrior-level test, she lifted nearly as much as Kieran could. Her speed was amazing. Before she could fight Clint for an assessment, she spotted a rogue who planned to kidnap Cara. She beat him into submission and released him to get her message out. I was so proud of her for protecting Cara. I never stopped being proud.

"Her territory is the largest rogue collective in the region. It's the third largest in this part of the country. If she expands to your lands, it could be the fourth largest in the entire country. It's considered the safest as well.

"She's started programs to bring ex-pack children back into packs and printed up little booklets for ex-pack parents having their first rogue born child. All supernaturals are welcome as long as they contribute to some part of keeping the collective safe. For some, it's financial, for others, it's work or spells.

"Bellamy has always done what needed to be done for her people. She's always been focused on her collective and this pack. As she grew closer to her seventeenth birthday, we began to worry.

"There's a rogue king called Kyle Fuller, who runs the other major rogue collective in the region and was promised Bellamy when she came of age. She told us he might come for her. She told us not to try to protect her, but we did.

"He started requesting to travel into our land. We denied every request. Drake was encouraged to deny requests to meet with her without showing them to her. If she found out, we knew she'd be angry, but we didn't trust him not to try something to make her change her mind, like threatening someone she loves. He's as ruthless as his father. We've heard stories from rogues who switched collectives. His is a nightmare," Daniel told me.

"Is she in danger?" I asked.

"He's accepted every denial without a request to challenge. I don't think he's going to try anything. She told us he'd been offering for her, but she refused. When she came home saying she was mated to you, I thought she might have made the offer to stop Kyle from coming for her," he admitted.

"Her wolf said she knew I would've won the fight if I hadn't been wearing silver," I told them.

"Aurora looks at facts and makes decisions based on those rather than on what feels right, or who could get hurt. She'll also manipulate Bellamy if she thinks it's in her best interest," Daniel said. "I think that's why she went with the vampires. They'd been drinking your blood for a few days. After spending so much time with a vampire, Bellamy knew how their scent changes based on their food source. I think she smelled you and your power on them. Aurora may have assumed you could beat her because of your power level."

She'd just wanted me because I was powerful? Or had she decided that sort of power was too dangerous for them to hold? She told me she couldn't risk them turning me.

Did that mean taking me as her mate? Did she not really want me, but offered so she could keep tabs on me? Or was it to keep the rogue king away from her? Was I a tool she was using? She gave in awfully easily when I asked her not to leave. She was a skillful actress with the vampires.

"You're saying you don't think she really wants to be my mate. It's just a means to an end? She lied?" I murmured.

'Don't listen to them, Lucien. Bellamy loves us. She told you that. Bellamy gave us a nickname. She kisses us like we're the air in her lungs. She wants to stay with us. You promised you'd never leave,' Remus growled.

'Why would they lie? What benefit could it have? She'll find someone else to manipulate. Someone else with power. Why did she really want us? Just because we beat her in a fight? This all happened too fast. The curse is broken; we can pick a mate by breeding. We'll talk to her. If she doesn't give the answers we need, I want you to take back your acceptance.'

'You want to reject another mate? How many females have to pay for your broken heart? How many will you hurt? I won't reject her. You can't make me.'

I stood and bowed to them. "Is there a guest room I can sleep in tonight?" I asked.

"You won't sleep in Bellamy's room?" Olive asked.

"No. I need to think about this," I replied.

"She'll be upset. You can stay with her and still talk things out. We just didn't want the two of you to start this relationship without understanding each other," Olive said.

"Rogues think differently than we do. This is the first time she's done something out of character. I don't know exactly what's going on in her head. She's normally more calculating than this. I just didn't want you to be surprised if she said or did things that made it seem like she was cold or cruel," Daniel told me. "She's everything she seemed when you met her. But just a little more restricted than most pack wolves are used to. She has to do things for her people that don't seem right by our standards. It doesn't mean she doesn't care for you."

'If you ask her to explain she will. Please, Lucien. Don't hurt our mate.'

"Please take me to a guest room. I'll gather my clothing," I said and turned to get my things from her room.

They settled me in the empty room across from hers. I wanted to get further away, but Alpha Kieran refused to give me a room anywhere else. I put away my things and sat on the bed.

Why was my life going like this? I didn't think I was really a bad guy. I'd been a completely normal kid. Respectful of my elders, striving to be the best Alpha possible, and trying to do my best for my people.

At every turn, someone was hurting me or attacking me. Taking away the things and people I loved. Other Alphas at least got to have someone to soothe and care for them.

I laid down, blocked Bellamy and Remus from talking to me, and let sleep take me. At least when I was sleeping, I wouldn't have to think. I wouldn't have to deal with another betrayal, another person using me, another rejection. I just hoped she'd been right when she suggested the treatment for my mother.

It was the least she could do.

Chapter 28: Alone Again

The vampires had been toasted nicely. I ordered my team to crush their remains. They didn't turn to dust like they did in movies. Their skeletons always stayed behind after their flesh was gone. I gave them a few extra good stomps. Especially the ones I knew were Marion and Louisa.

Dilly made a few comments about my aggression level while I was jumping on the rubble that had been Louisa's skull. He'd never seen me as vicious as I was while smashing all the corpses. The special attention I was paying Louisa was much more than I did Marion.

"What the hell did they do to you, Captain?" he asked.

"She touched my mate's dick. Make note of that, Dillon," I growled. "No one but me touches Lucien like that."

"Yes, Captain." He grinned. "Stomp the bitch some more. She deserves it."

When we'd ground them all into sand, we searched around for evidence of who'd sent them information but didn't have our hopes up, since I'd lit the place on fire. Soon we headed home. I felt a million times better. My mate was safe and my territory would see fewer vampire incursions.

"So, real talk, baby. Work's done. Now spill," Dilly said.

"Yeah, we tell you about our ladies, you tell us about your Alpha." Drake grinned.

"I don't want to hear this. I vote you keep it to yourself." Galen groaned.

"Seconded!" Porter shouted.

I laughed. "It's two to two. Five votes left. Guys?"

In the end, it was five for and four against. Much to the dismay of my brothers.

"I don't know what to say. We haven't done anything really. He kisses nice. His body is fucking amazing and he's packing some serious heat in his pants. To be honest, I'm a little afraid of it, but willing to face that fear." I snickered.

There were some catcalls and whistles. I could hear Porter and Galen groan and gag.

"Do you love him, though? You're different when it comes to mating," Todd said. "We fall in love immediately. Is it like that when he accepted the offer?"

"It is. I love him. I've even told him. You guys know I don't say that shit out loud. It was the first time I've said it since I was little. He says he'll support me as a queen and not try to protect me unless I need it. He doesn't question my decisions. Aurora likes him, and she barely likes anyone," I admitted.

"Dad's worried you only went with the vampires because you smelled him. He thinks you picked him to expand your territory," Galen said.

"I know. I heard him and Mom mind-linking." Only my team knew I could hear them. They'd kept it quiet, understanding the benefit.

"Well?" he asked.

"They were talking about having an Alpha. I could smell he was powerful. If they turned him, he'd be a very powerful vampire and immune to our barrier because of his wolf genes. I had to save him. I didn't have any idea of what pack he was Alpha of... until right before I marked him.

"If Dad said anything like that, Lucien *might* think I only did it for the territory. Shit. We were talking about how we would've probably met and ended up marking each other even if the vampires didn't happen. It was what pushed me to mark him instead of waiting until I got home." I froze and stooped down, hugging my knees.

It was like all my breath left me. There wasn't any way I could convince him I loved him. He'd never believe I wasn't pretending. They'd been doing it to protect him, not me. I knew they all thought Aurora and I were cold because we kept our distance and behaved differently.

"He's going to reject me," I whispered tearfully. "Oh, fuck."

"No, he won't. I saw how he looked at you when you got to the border, how he looked at you when we were at dinner. He loves you, Amy," Dilly said, patting my back.

He never used my name unless he was serious. It didn't matter how much he tried, though, I wouldn't be able to believe it until I saw Lucien again. I let him comfort me. Maybe I could lie to myself for the rest of the walk home.

"If he tries to reject you, we'll kick his ass," Galen growled.

Jason picked me up and carried me as they ran for the pack lands. I was the fastest of all of them, but I didn't want to move from where I'd planted myself. Staying away from home prevented my fear from becoming a reality. My men would never let me hide from something that scared me, though.

My apprehension grew as I got closer to the packhouse. Aurora was pacing. My assessment was correct. Lucien had blocked me from linking him. I tried to let him know I was back, and felt the message disappear into nothing against his barrier.

When we reached the packhouse, Jason set me down on the porch. Harrison, Sam, Porter, and Freddy had broken off to go to their homes. Galen, Jason, Todd, Drake, and Dilly lived in the packhouse with us. Dilly was Bren's nephew, and Drake was Tobin's. Both lost their parents in a rogue attack a year before I moved to the pack.

They went in ahead of me. I stood on the porch. It was about eleven-thirty. I still needed to give my report. Kieran was waiting in his office. I steeled myself and headed to the offices on the second floor.

The door was open, and I tapped lightly. Kieran told me to come in, and I did. My dad and Gamma Toby were there. The last time I'd been here, Lucien had been right behind me. Now, I was alone… again.

"Alpha, Beta, Gamma," I said softly.

"Captain," they responded.

"I've come with my report. The vampires are dead and their remains turned to dust by my team. The Alpha of Lune Rouge needn't worry about them coming for him. We'll start preparing for our trip after tomorrow. After the wedding, we'll return. At that time, we can discuss the path of my collective and my place in the pack. I'm going to bed," I said and turned, leaving the room and ignoring them calling for me and trying to mind-link me.

Staying in the pack would be almost impossible if Lucien left me. I'd always remember that my parents had ruined my chance at happiness. The pack would stay in my collective, but I'd move to one of the nearby towns. It was the only option.

I went to the Beta's quarters and headed down the hall to my room, ignoring my mom as she tried to talk to me. I could feel Lucien in the room across from mine. After a few minutes of staring at the door, I went to my room, locked up, got my rowan and ash planks, and then showered.

Crawling into my cold, empty bed, I curled up and huddled under the covers. This wasn't how my night was supposed to go. How could they do this to me? I thought I'd done everything right.

I talked and smiled. I played and trained. My grades in school were good, and I volunteered.

Wasn't I good enough? Didn't I deserve to be happy? To have what I saw my friends have? I'd only marked him twelve hours ago, and now he wasn't talking to me. He wanted space. I had to give it to him. He was an Alpha.

If my parent's banishment taught me anything, it was that Alphas don't think well when they're upset. As an adult, I still didn't agree with what my mother did, but their Alpha could've told them to move to another pack. Banishment was only slightly less extreme than execution.

I didn't sleep. Every time I closed my eyes, I saw Lucien leaving me. Being left by everyone. Wandering again because no one wanted me. Ending up alone again, forever. When my alarm went off, I was grateful and dressed quickly.

Leaving my room, I paused and went to the door of Lucien's room. He'd probably still be asleep. I tried the handle and it turned. My breath caught. I should leave it and go to training. Just a few moments wouldn't hurt, though. I needed to see him.

Chapter 29: Giving Him Space

[Bellamy]

I opened the door and crept into the room. I could see the bump under the blankets. He was sleeping. The rhythm of his breathing was familiar and made me feel calmer. I hadn't really realized how upset I still was.

I couldn't make myself get any closer to him. If he woke up, he'd talk. I'd fail to convince him and he'd take back his acceptance of my offer. I left and headed for the training field.

We started training with a ten-mile run. It wasn't much for us, but we had to run it at our top speed with no resting. We encouraged everyone to push and beat their previous time. When we returned to the field, we did some calisthenics stuff, muscle building exercises, repetitive motion training, and sparring.

After medics carried away my third opponent, Clint told me I was done. I just wanted to feel something other than the dread that had eclipsed everything else in my life since last night. They needed to be better fighters. I wanted them to hurt me. I wanted to hurt them.

I ran from the training field and to the western border of my territory, then I kept running. At some point I shifted, but I didn't know when. I ran for hours and was nearing the border of our closest neighbor to the west. Hunter's Moon.

It was over one hundred miles from home. I shifted back and grabbed one of the large shirts from a false rock with clothes. I eventually found some small shorts and slipped them on, too. Even if he didn't want me anymore, I was sure Lucien would be upset if I was wandering around with my bottom half naked. I settled on the rock and waited.

Soon, a border guard approached. I got off the false rock and bowed. He relaxed a little but stayed on alert in case it was a trap. I knew I looked like a kid in the outfit.

"State your name and business with our pack," he ordered.

"I'm Bellamy Carrington, daughter of Beta Daniel Carrington of the Daylight Moon Pack. I request an audience with Alpha Warrick," I said.

He mind-linked someone for a few moments. When his eyes cleared, I waited for his response.

"Alpha Warrick is in his office. He says you know the way. Welcome to the Hunter's Moon Pack, Miss Carrington." He bowed.

"Please, call me Amy. Thank you for your help." I smiled and started running toward the packhouse.

After light witches hunted down the dark witch and stripped her of her powers, Warrick's mother contacted our pack, and I visited whenever I could. I felt the strain of being away from my territory after a day or two and usually had to head home within a week.

Warrick refused my offer to claim his pack, but I didn't mind. I hoped he'd accept someday, but he had a pretty decent team of warriors. I'd helped train them myself.

His office door opened almost immediately after my knock. I threw my arms around him and he squeezed me tightly. I felt tears pricking at my eyes. One of the things I hated most was crying, but I couldn't help it.

The strain of everything crashed over me and I started bawling my eyes out. Warrick pulled me to the couch in his office and cradled me in his arms like he had when I was a child. He was practically the only person I really felt comfortable crying around.

When I was calm again, he held me for a little longer. He was my first big brother, and I felt more at ease with him than I did with my other brothers. I felt safer with him than anyone else until I'd found Lucien. It wasn't something I craved often, but a safe place, a safe person, made everything feel a little easier to handle.

I crawled out of his arms after a while and sat cross-legged on the couch, leaning against him. He took my hand and stroked the back of it. My mind was on Lucien. He'd appreciate this amount of space. I knew he probably hadn't wanted to be put in a room right across from mine.

"What's going on, Ames? Your parents called as you arrived at my border and asked if I'd seen you. They said you ran away from training. That doesn't sound like you," Ricky murmured.

"You didn't let them know I'm here, did you?" I asked.

"No, I wanted to understand what was going on. In case you needed sanctuary for some reason. Is that what happened? Did you need to be protected from your pack?"

I blushed. "No. I need time and space. Staying in my territory wasn't going to work this time. I could've stayed in one of the empty houses in town if it were possible. It's just…. I can't be there, Ricky. I feel like I'm going to die if I have to stay there another minute."

"They said you sent three men to the hospital, including one of your brothers. Your parents said you refuse to talk to them. Kieran called and told me you gave a report last night and then left without answering any questions. No one will tell me why you're being all rogue-ish. This isn't you, Ames. Tell me what happened," he pled.

I hadn't realized how badly I'd hurt them. I took a deep breath and told him everything. The vampires, what Marion had done to me, finding Lucien and falling in love with him, marking him and being marked by him, the plot against him and his family, what my family had probably done, and how Lucien didn't want to be around me and blocked me from linking him. I never kept secrets from Ricky. He was the only one who I'd told about my parents' banishment.

"That's some heavy shit, Ames. Maybe he just needs to process. I don't think he'll reject you. It sounds like he likes you as much as you like him. Are you hiding here so he can't do it?" he asked.

"No. He can do it anytime and anywhere. This feels like a punishment. I don't know what I did to deserve it, though. I've done everything I could to be a good pack wolf and a good rogue Queen. My schedule is so full I hardly have time to rest. This was supposed to be a chance to have the peace and love I see my pack mates finding every day. It's not fair, Ricky. Why does my life have to be like this?" I sniffled.

"Life isn't fair. It would be terrible if it were. This is a minor struggle, Ames. You just have to figure out how to make him see you love him," Ricky said softly. "I won't tell your parents you're here. They think they have to protect others from you and, I think, they protect you more than you know."

"Thank you, Ricky." I smiled a little.

"You can stay in the packhouse. My mom and dad moved to a cottage near the woods. If they see you, she might call your mom. I'll take you to a guest room. You don't look like you've slept much," he said, standing and helping me up.

"I didn't sleep last night. I couldn't. Bad dreams started as soon as I closed my eyes," I admitted.

"I called Dr. Blair to come sedate you. You need sleep or your brain is going to do stupid things. Come on. He's on his way." Ricky led me out of his office and up to the guest rooms.

Shortly after we reached the room, Dr. Blair knocked. He gave me a hug before I laid down and he gave me the shot. Ricky sat by my bedside until the darkness finally came for me.

Thank the goddess.

Chapter 30: Mistakes and Misunderstandings

[Lucien]

I woke up to the sun streaming in my windows. I could smell Bellamy's sweet scent and reached over to hold her, only to find the bed empty. My eyes flew open. I wasn't in the bedroom in the vampires' house or in Bellamy's room. It didn't make sense. How did I get here?

Remus snarled, *'You seriously don't remember talking with her parents and running to a guest room to sulk and feel sorry for yourself? You don't remember blocking me and our mate out? She came in this morning but left without coming near us. Aurora said she didn't sleep last night. **You** did that. **You** left her alone after you promised not to. She'll never forgive you.'*

The memory of last night flooded my mind. I doubted her, even though she told me she loved me. It felt like I was thinking clearly. It seemed like she'd lied, but everything Remus said was right. Everything she said and did told me she loved me.

Her parents didn't understand her. Alphas function differently than other wolves. So do rogues.

Throughout the entire ordeal with the vampires, she kept talking about getting me home. She wanted to figure out how to undo the offer back when it happened. She didn't even think of asking my pack's name until we were discussing where we were heading. Bellamy wasn't faking her feelings. She loved me.

'Do you think Aurora loves you?' I asked.

'I haven't had the chance to know her. It was fun to talk to her.'

'Do you think she could've been manipulating you at all?'

'Maybe. There wasn't any reason to. She seemed genuine. Are you going to talk to her? You're not still thinking of rejecting her, are you?'

'That would be the stupidest thing I could ever do. I'm going to talk to her. She needs to hear what happened from me. I need to apologize for blocking her out like a child throwing a tantrum. We'll fix this. She's our mate.'

'Good. From now on, just listen to me when it comes to her. We could've had her this morning if you'd done that in the first place,' he replied.

'Could you not with the pervy wolf stuff? When we make love to her the first time, it won't be a rollover in the morning rut.'

The alarm clock on the bedside table said it was eight in the morning. I got out of bed, showered, brushed my teeth, and dressed for the day. Once I was certain I was presentable, I headed out to the hall.

As I was about to knock on her door, I heard soft voices and Olive sniffling. My curiosity got the better of me. I moved toward the living room area and peeked around the corner. Olive and Daniel were with a man in a suit with a satchel.

"The casts can come off tomorrow. This is just to make sure he doesn't move while his wolf is healing everything. He should consume plenty of protein. Give him those shakes every couple of hours. We can take the wire from his jaw tomorrow when we take off the casts. I have to go deal with the other havoc your daughter caused," the man growled.

"Thank you, Dr. Hale. Sorry for the trouble," Olive whispered.

"You should be. After what Dillon and Drake told me when they brought the boys in…. Millie *told you* Bellamy's sensitive. She's insecure. You meddled in her relationship. You tried to take over and acted like you knew better.

"They were less than a day into their relationship and you bombed it. I'm disappointed in you. You're our Beta couple. I know you were both impulsive kids, but I'd hoped you'd grown up a little. Because of your inability to let Bellamy settle her own affairs, three boys are in full body casts." He shook his head disgustedly.

"Sorry, doctor. As soon as we find her, we'll make it up to them," Daniel said somberly.

I came out of the hall and could feel the emptiness for the first time. She wasn't here; she wasn't in the house. How had I missed it earlier? I stared at the trio as they registered my presence. Where was Bellamy?

"What happened?" I asked.

"I'll leave you to this. The border guard should be waking up soon. Maybe he can tell us more," the doctor said as he headed to the door.

"Bellamy seriously injured three members of her team. Galen first, while sparring, then Freddy and Sam when they tried to calm her. Dillon tried to get us to get you up, but we didn't realize how serious it was. We thought you two needed space and refused. Clint, our current head warrior, kicked her off the training field and she ran. No one realized, until thirty minutes ago, that she hadn't come home. We didn't realize she'd left training. She'd been gone a couple hours by then," Daniel told me.

"Which direction did she head? I'll go after her," I said.

"We've called Warrick. The guard was found on the west border. He's the most likely option," Olive replied.

I felt my anger swell. If they'd gotten me, I could've fixed this. Now my mate was running to another male for comfort instead of me. I growled at the idea of Bellamy in the arms of the young Alpha. I knew she didn't see him as anything more than a brother and he had a mate, but it should be me she wanted when she was upset.

'You cut her off. What the fuck did you expect? Of course, she went to the boy. He's probably always been there instead of only being there when his feelings aren't hurt,' Remus snarled in my head.

'Will she take back her offer? I need to find her. I need to go to Hunter's Moon.'

"Kieran is calling a meeting. We need you, Alpha Lucien," Daniel said.

I walked past him and headed to Kieran's office. He'd have to loan me a car. I wasn't healthy enough to shift and run. I told her I'd follow her if she ran and I would. No matter what, I was going to get her back.

The door to the office was open. I walked in and saw Alpha Kieran, Gamma Tobin, Jason, Todd, Drake, Dillon, and a man I didn't recognize. Daniel followed me in and we sat in the empty seats.

"This is Clint. He's the current head of our warriors. Dillon is here to act as Bellamy's advocate. He's her closest friend currently in our territory," Kieran said.

"As her mate, I should be her advocate," I growled.

"You lost that privilege when you blocked her," Jason snarled.

"How did you know about that?" I asked.

"I was carrying her home and told her to link you when we entered the border. She tried and whispered that you blocked her and hated her now. Dillon is the person here she talks to. Since her father was involved in harming her, he isn't permitted to speak for her either," he replied coolly.

Daniel nodded sadly.

"The first order of business here is repercussions for her actions. Bellamy is an Alpha and she's the captain of three of the four people she harmed. She abandoned her pack without notice. For these actions together, we'd typically be talking about banishment. None of us want that for her or for our pack. She'll be asked to leave the pack instead," Kieran said solemnly.

The air in the room was tense when he mentioned banishment. She'd have been joining my pack, anyway. This was an easy issue to resolve, but banishment shouldn't have been the first option.

"Once she returns, she'll have two hours to pack her things and say her goodbyes. I'm assuming your claim of being her mate means you're accepting her into your pack. She has to stay out of pack territory for sixty days but can come to visit after that. She'll be relieved of her post as captain of the Elite Ten and her students will be reassigned. Drake, she's previously indicated that she'd like you to become her lieutenant for the Daylight Moon arm of her collective," he stated. "As her second in command of the Elite Ten, Jason will take on the role of captain and promote a new member."

"As Bellamy's advocate, I'd like to ask that you reconsider. She's a benefit to the pack. Ending relations with her like this will only cause trouble for her and us," Dillon said.

"It's her plan and her mission, Alpha. We can't add a new member mid-mission. It's a two-month assignment. I'd like to ask that we keep her as well. A change in leadership at this point will throw the entire team off," Jason added.

"I don't want to risk her harming another member of the pack. She's too unpredictable. Anyone can see she's too dangerous to stay in our pack full-time. She's already going to leave; this won't change much. Gamma, Beta, any input?" Kieran asked.

"No, Alpha," they replied.

I stared at Daniel. He looked broken up. When they'd taken her in, they'd promised to be her family forever. They'd said they'd always take care of her and never harm her. They promised to always treat her as their child. He'd hurt her and now she'd lose everything they'd given her.

It wasn't a fair punishment for the infractions. This should be a first warning. I wondered how often she'd done something like this.

My guilt was immense, either way. She'd trusted me to be there for her, to talk to her, and to support her. I'd been selfish, and it hurt her so much she couldn't function as a member of her pack. She was afraid of losing people and I'd played a part in her losing her entire community.

"Alpha, I'd like to ask that this punishment be delayed until the Elite Ten is scheduled to leave for Lune Rouge. It would throw their timeline off otherwise. Let her leave without shame. It was partly my fault, and I understand if you refuse, but she's worked hard for this pack and had a momentary outburst," I said.

"She seriously injured four men! Three are in full-body casts! Two had to have their jaws wired! We've all had to work hard, none of us have outbursts like this. The most damage I've done is a hole in the wall and a few destroyed punching bags," he responded.

"When I entered this house with her yesterday, Bellamy had to immediately catch two small children who hurdled themselves from the second-floor, deal with rogue issues, and make a report. She had to specify she was taking the day off, but that only meant she had a short break before dinner and then went on a second leg of her mission. There was no reset period before she was expected back in training. She should have had time off.

"Three vampires fed on her! Do you have *any* idea what that's like? Those vampires violated her and took her power.

"I don't know what they did to her after she passed out and they took her from the room, but I *do* know they'd told her she'd become their broodmare for wolf/vampire hybrids. They wanted me to mark her so her heat would come sooner. If I couldn't take on four vampires, she certainly couldn't. Her report didn't say anything bad or upsetting about what happened to her.

"No matter what she did, she always focused on being strong for the people depending on her. Her wolf told mine she's afraid of being abandoned because of her rogue tendencies. After being *assaulted*, she's suffering her greatest fear. She needed to get away, so she didn't hurt anyone else. She's a Queen, she's trying to take care of her people!

"Do any of you even realize how much you depend on her? She was just a *little girl!* You let her take on the role of protector for over six *hundred* wolves! How many times has she done anything like this? How many times has she lost control and hurt her pack mates?" I asked.

"None. This is the first time," Daniel said, his face pale after my revelation about the vampires.

"If anyone else did this you wouldn't be talking about banishment or asking them to leave. You'd do what I'd do and put them on leave with counseling and a warning. If Jason did it, you'd definitely make sure he got help instead of kicking him out. Why are you so quick to get rid of her? She didn't kill anyone. She didn't hurt anyone who couldn't protect themselves. Why talk about making her leave now?" I pushed.

Kieran looked tense. I didn't think he'd really reflected on the idea much. I knew a lot of Alphas acted without thinking when they were angry. A lot of us stood by those decisions out of stubbornness.

Last night had been a mix of all the stressors and my own exhaustion clouding my ability to be rational. I wouldn't make that mistake again.

Chapter 31: Lost Luna Located

As we were waiting for his response, his phone rang. He looked thankful for the interruption. Kieran pulled his phone from his pocket and looked at the screen. He breathed a sigh of relief. I knew he was hoping this would distract us, but I fully intended to have an answer before I went to retrieve my mate.

He hit talk and put it on speaker.

"This is Kieran," he said.

"Good morning, Kieran. It's Warrick. I'm calling to let you know one of your pack members is here. She arrived safely about forty-five minutes ago and has been put in a guest room and sedated," Warrick replied. "She asked that I not call her parents, so I'm calling you instead."

"Thank you for taking care of her. Why'd you sedate her?" Kieran asked.

"She hadn't slept in a while and told me her nightmares were back. After she told me about everything going on, I knew she wouldn't get restful sleep if her mind was allowed to roam," he answered.

"Is she okay? Uninjured?" Kieran inquired.

"Physically, she's exhausted. I think she ran here at top speed the whole way. Mentally, she's not great. She's still trying to think logically, but her logic is skewed. Emotionally, she's a mess. I'm pretty fucking pissed myself. She feels like she's being punished. I know what kind of workload you've given her. I know the things she pushes herself to do.

"I don't blame you for the vampires and what they did. I do blame your Beta for hurting her relationship with Alpha Lucien. Did he seriously tell her mate she might have only wanted him for the territory expansion?! Do you even realize how much stress she had to have been put under to run from her territory after only being back less than twenty-four hours? The energy required to control her territory from a distance is massive. What the fuck were you all thinking?!" he shouted.

I had no idea what it meant for a rogue Alpha to hold a territory. We could hand it off to our Beta or Gamma and leave for an indefinite period. She'd talked about rogue barriers. Was she the battery for her territory's defenses?

"Kieran's talking about kicking her out of the pack," I said.

Kieran looked aghast. I could tell he felt betrayed, but I didn't care. This guy was the closest thing to an actual advocate Bellamy had. Dillon was still bound by his need to be respectful to his Alpha.

"First of all, don't you fucking dare kick my sister out of your pack. Secondly, who the hell is this?" Warrick growled.

"Alpha Lucien Devereux," I replied.

"If any other Alpha had done this, we'd be considering it-" Kieran started, but Warrick cut him off.

"Bullshit! That is the biggest load of shit I have *ever* heard! You're pissed because she didn't listen to you and walked away when you were talking to her! You told me yourself it was difficult to deal with having an unrelated Alpha under you. This was just your frustration coming out.

"She's always tried to act like a normal wolf and be respectful of you, but didn't play the obedient pup when you wanted her to! If you kick her out, you can tear up our contracts. I'll let her claim my territory and leave yours unprotected. Do you understand, Kieran?" he threatened.

"You can tear up mine as well. Lune Rouge will not be associated with a pack headed by someone that insecure," I added.

"If you kick her out, I will respectfully resign from this pack and go wherever she is. I'm not going to stay somewhere that would treat a powerful member of our community like this," Dillon murmured.

"I'll go, too," Drake said.

Kieran was pissed. He looked over at Jason, who had been thoughtfully listening.

"Dad, I agree. Kicking Bellamy out isn't healthy for our pack. Even in the way you were planning. It's just cold. We're her family. We have been together for six years. If she takes her protections, we go back to having rogue attacks whittling away at our pack. As the future Alpha, I can't approve of what you're suggesting," Jason stated. "I'd have to ask you to retire for the good of the pack."

Kieran looked away from us and scowled at the map on his wall. It seemed like he was considering things. I knew he'd have trouble going from being in power and being threatened with losing it.

"Ames is staying here for a while. She told me she needed to be back for the mission. You think about what's more important, your pack, or your pride," Warrick told Kieran. "Alpha Lucien, I expect to see you within the next few hours. My Luna and I will help mediate the issue with your Luna. You will be respectful of her and you will *not* block her out. If I hear about you pulling that shit again, I'm going to kick your ass."

"I'll be there as soon as I can," I replied.

"Dillon, I want you to bring him here. Ty's on the gate today and he'll recognize you. Pack for a couple days and bring clothes for her. She's wearing loaners. I have work to do," Warrick growled and hung up.

I liked Warrick more and more. He would help fix our relationship instead of telling her to leave me. He didn't shy away from talking to older Alphas. This man was definitely Bellamy's brother.

"I linked Olive. She's getting a bag packed for Bellamy. You guys can be on the road in less than thirty minutes," Daniel said.

"Kieran, I think you got mad about her ignoring you like Warrick said, and it was built on by your pride and stubbornness. Take the next couple of days to calm down. We can all write this off as a high-stress reaction. I'm going to go now. We'll be back in a few days and pretend this conversation didn't happen," I told him and left the room.

When I got up to the guest room there was a small duffle bag sitting on the bed. I quickly grabbed clothing and zipped it up. I wasn't going to waste any time. Olive was in the living room, waiting with a bag.

"I packed up some of her favorite outfits. Her wolf pendant is in the front pocket. She likes to wear it when she's dealing with things. Tell her we're sorry. We didn't mean to imply she didn't care for you. I hope you understand. We thought we were helping, but we did it wrong. We love Bellamy, we just wanted you to know how difficult it can be to get where she's coming from. I'm so sorry we didn't get you when Dillon asked us to." She wept.

I took a deep breath. "She still calls you 'mommy' and 'daddy'. That's Bellamy telling you she loves you. Even if she can't really say the words. She'll forgive you because it's what family does. Thanks for getting her stuff. I need to go."

Olive hugged me and handed me the bag. She was really good at 'mom hugs'. It made me miss my own mom a little. I left and headed to the front of the packhouse. Dillon pulled up in a light blue sedan and popped the trunk. Soon, we were headed to Hunter's Moon territory.

Yuri sent along road snacks and we ate while we drove. The silence was a little heavy. I was trying to think of what I would do or say when I saw Bellamy again. I felt pain in my chest every time I thought of how broken up she must have been.

"Why was Jason carrying her home last night?" I asked softly.

Dillon sighed. "She hunched over into a little ball on the grass and refused to move. It was like she didn't want to go home and find out you hated her. Why'd you block her out instead of talking to her? Bellamy doesn't lie unless she needs to, usually for work. She would've told you anything you wanted to know. You could've at least left her a note."

"My brain wasn't working great. I'd been held and fed on for three days. The night before, I didn't sleep. My mom was poisoned by my maid. And suddenly, the only good thing to happen to me in eighteen years was a lie. My wolf was yelling at me to ignore them and wait to talk to her, but I just wanted to feel sorry for myself," I explained.

"You have to understand. You're one of the few good things to happen to her in eighteen years, too. She watched her parents get killed and dismembered by hunters. A year and a half later, she and her friend were attacked by six vampires and she almost died.

"He took her to a rogue collective and they took care of her, but tried to betroth her to the king's son, who hit her when she refused and said he'd beat her until she accepted him. She ran away and things were okay for a while until a witch took her in and started poisoning her, then put her in silver, beat her, and started taking blood for a spell that would end in her sacrificing Bellamy.

"When Warrick found her, she was trying to kill herself. He saved her and offered to keep her, but the witch was poking around the pack lands, so they had to send her away. When we were fifteen, she told me she hoped to find a mate one day who'd accept her and support her, but she wasn't going to hold her breath. You're exactly the type of guy she likes. I thought she'd gone and convinced a witch to summon you." Dillon chuckled.

"I had no idea. She talked about her travels and pack a bit, but never said anything. I'll never let anything like that happen to her again. I can't be her protector, but I can be her partner. I promise to always have her back and never leave her behind. I'll fix this." I swore to him.

"Good. She told us she loves you last night. Don't be a dumbass. Lots of guys in school were hoping to be her mate when she turned seventeen. She's a good woman. If I were into chicks, I'd have been all over that." He looked over and winked. "I can just imagine her in leather with a whip and me at the end of her leash… She's the girl I'd go straight for, you know."

I growled. The image he painted was an interesting one. Bellamy had been his commander for a couple years at least, so I could imagine dominance fantasies being a thing for some of the men. That only made me growl more.

"Chill. No one would ever try anything with her. Until she found you, we were all pretty sure she wasn't into guys at all. I thought she was just making up her description of her dream guy when me, her, and Cara had sleepovers. You know, to stay in the closet. Wait until you see her around Cara and you'll understand better." He snorted.

Shaking my head, I went back to trying to figure out what to do. The miles passed quickly and silently. Dillon seemed to be entirely focused on driving as fast, and insanely, as possible. When we finally reached Hunter's Moon, we stopped at the border gate.

Chapter 32: Hunter's Moon

A sign with the name 'Hunter's Moon Township' in gold was placed on the high river stone wall. The idea of turning their pack into a private, gated community had intrigued me. They got fewer people wandering into their territory from the roads. We were waiting to see the five-year report before doing something like that at Lune Rouge.

A little guardhouse held a single man in a guard uniform who came out as we stopped. He was about six feet tall, with dark brown hair and a healthy tan. When he leaned down to the window, he wore a friendly grin.

"Hey, Dil. Warrick told me you were bringing Amy's mate. How was the drive? Kill anyone?" He chuckled.

"No, but the day's still young. Tyson O'Connell, this is Lucien Devereux. He's the Alpha of Lune Rouge and Amy's mate," Dillon said.

"Nice to meet you, Alpha. Don't hurt my sister again or I'll hurt you. Here's your parking pass. You know the way to the packhouse. The omegas will take care of your car." Tyson smiled and tipped his hat before heading back to the guardhouse and opening the gate.

We drove through and Dillon started laughing.

"You think that's funny?" I asked.

"Yep. Hunter's Moon has the best atmosphere. They don't care if you're an Alpha or not. Warrick made sure people are comfortable enough to tell him when they think he's being an ass. It's not as strict as a lot of places. I just loved the shocked look on your face."

"It's going to come back and bite him one day. You can't maintain authority while letting your people treat you as an equal. The Alpha isn't just a leader, he's the protector, the negotiator, and the one responsible for all wolves in a pack. His word is law and should be followed," I replied.

"Yes. All rulers are men; some men are crazy. Just look at the old Alpha of the Ivory Moon Pack. He destroyed it. There's nothing left. Smart people left and went rogue since he wouldn't approve applications to other packs. The others all died when he declared war on the Limb Torn Collective. King Fuller didn't leave anyone alive. Not women, not children. He even killed the pet fish," Dillon stated.

I remembered hearing about that. It was five years ago. We'd taken in a few of the ex-pack rogues from that incident. Alpha Mitchell had his Beta and Gamma executed for treason. They'd only suggested he find an heir from another pack when his son died young. He'd gone insane from grief when he lost the last connection he had to his mate. No one knew what was going on until it was too late.

"What's the name of Bellamy's collective? I never thought to ask."

"Eaten Heart Collective. It's her promise to anyone who tries to harm her people or take her territory. It's super effective," Dillon said.

"She actually eats hearts?" I asked.

"Yep, a few dozen. She only does it until the rogue dies, as long as none of the other rogues are watching, then she has to eat the whole thing. Once she told me if she had to eat another rogue heart, she was going vegetarian for a month." He laughed.

We pulled up in front of the packhouse. I grabbed my bag and Bellamy's from the trunk. Dillon grabbed his own before handing his keys off to an omega who was standing by. Alpha Warrick and his mate were waiting for us.

He was six foot two, at least, with dark brown hair, gray eyes, and a friendly face. He looked like one of the guys who would have been popular in high school with a trim, muscular build, and natural tan.

His mate was about five inches shorter than him. Her skin was a rich golden brown and her eyes were so dark they were nearly black. She had beautiful curves and a big, pregnant belly. I remembered Bellamy saying they were expecting their second pup.

I smiled and strode forward, extending my hand. The last time I'd seen him, he was probably ten. I wanted to make sure I approached him as an equal now. He was important to my mate.

"Alpha Lucien. A pleasure to see you again," Warrick said, taking my hand in a firm grip.

"Thank you for having me, Alpha Warrick."

"We're happy you're here. This is my mate, Janya," he told me, putting his arm around her shoulders.

"Luna, I appreciate you taking the time to meet with me and help us out." I nodded politely.

"Anything for my mate's little sister, Alpha Lucien. Greta will take your bags to the room where your Luna is resting. Dillon, if you'll follow me, I'll show you to your room," Janya replied curtly.

"Sure thing, Janie." Dillon grinned.

"I told you, do not call me Janie," she growled. There was a sparkle in her eye, though. This was something they probably did often.

"I only give nicknames to people I love," he teased as he batted his lashes at her.

"We should head to my office, Alpha Lucien. They'll be doing this for a while. He doesn't stop until she beats him with her shoe," Warrick laughed.

I handed our bags off to the omega and followed him into the house and to his office. Unlike Daylight Moon, the offices for Hunter's Moon were on the first floor. I entered and found it to be fairly standard. Desk, chairs, couch, dinette. Most of us had a setup like this since we could end up living in our offices when things got hectic.

Bellamy's scent lingered in the room. I sat in the chair across from his at the desk and let the smell of my mate calm me. I hadn't realized how anxious I'd been.

"Tomorrow, Janya and I will help you two navigate how to cope with a relationship between Alphas. Janya is an Alpha female. We have the experience you need," he told me.

I was a little amazed. Alpha females were rare and even more so in pack wolves. Alpha blood females were more common. Warrick and Janya would have some of the knowledge I needed. His being so close to Bellamy would help more with her listening.

"Thank you. I don't know if you realize how much this means to me, but I hope you do. I love her more than anything and I feel like an ass for having hurt her," I confided.

"I'm glad to hear that. It's just about lunchtime now. The sedative will keep her knocked out until about three. I suggest eating something, we'll have a snack delivered to your room around the time she should be waking. Dinner is served at seven. We have a casual table.

"Dillon is your guard. If you or Bellamy want to go to town, take him with you. She told me about the attempt on your life and your mother's. Dillon is one of the best on her team without rank or Alpha blood. I didn't want to have too many Alphas here. It makes my wolf antsy." He smiled.

"I can understand that. What should I do? Bellamy tells you everything. How mad is she? How can I get her to forgive me?" I asked.

Warrick sighed deeply. "She feels like she's at fault. Amy says she should've told you before she marked you that she didn't want you for your territory or anything like that. I suggest having lunch then lying down with her and begging her forgiveness as soon as she wakes up. Let her know you were the asshole, and she was the injured party. Make sure she understands you won't accept an apology from her, because she did nothing wrong.

"Amy wants to feel safe. She trusted when you said you wouldn't leave her. You broke that trust. It could take a while before she fully forgives you. I hope it doesn't. I love that girl as if she really were my sister. A long time ago she told me she hoped my mate accepted me when we met. I want the same for her. Even though rogue born do it different, you made that connection. I'm going to make sure you can accept her."

That was an odd sentiment, but it was a nice thing to wish for her friend. I wanted to make sure I could accept her, too. Simply accepting the offer wasn't enough.

Just like a rejection can be given at any time, so can the rescinding of an offer. I was glad she hadn't taken her offer back because I was an idiot.

"I told Kieran she probably left to protect her pack. I don't understand why she ran. Can you give me more insight into her motivations? I can only go off of what I would do. She takes on all these things in her life and handles everything with confidence. There's something vulnerable in her that makes me think she wants to be protected, but she can't ask for it. It's the way she looks sometimes. Like she's lost," I said.

"She *is* lost. She's a true rogue living as a pack wolf. It's safer, but not as free as she needs. A lot of her work is from trying to be accepted by her pack. That's why Kieran pissed me off. And you were wrong. She ran because you wanted space. This was the furthest she could go safely.

"Every day she's outside of her territory, Amy gets a little weaker. You can't stay long. She needs to go home. Just today and tomorrow, then head back and let her spend a full day in her territory. It'll recharge her," Warrick explained.

"I'm going to let her claim my territory as hers. As my Luna, my pack is hers anyway. This will make it safer for her, right?" I asked.

"Yes. Living in her territory, no matter the size, will keep her and her people healthy. We should get going. Ames told me what you went through. Food and rest are what you need. I'll take you to the dining room and show you where you'll be staying." He stood, and we left his office.

An hour later, I'd eaten and was following Warrick to the second floor. At the end of the long hall was a door. He paused outside it and turned to me.

"This is our guest Alpha suite. To the left is where Dillon is housed. Greta is the maid assigned to both rooms. Don't be late for dinner," he said and walked back down the hall.

I hadn't heard of a guest Alpha suite. I opened the door and took in the room. There were some large couches and overstuffed chairs in a corner near the door.

A king-size four-poster bed was on the other side of the room. French doors looked like they opened to a balcony. I wandered through the room.

The bathroom was immense, with a large tub and a shower with at least five heads. There was a walk-in closet that had built-in drawers. I opened some to find our clothing neatly tucked away.

Heading back into the room, I approached the bed. Bellamy was curled onto her side and looked like an angel. Tears had clumped her long lashes, and her hair curled around her like a bronze blanket. I tucked a strand behind her ear and she turned her face toward my hand.

Moving back to the door, I locked it and took off my clothes before climbing into the bed next to Bellamy and pulling her into my arms. No matter when she woke up, I'd know and be able to get her to forgive me. I drifted to sleep with the scent of sweet honeysuckle and jasmine surrounding me and my little mate in my arms at last.

Chapter 33: The Things You Learn About Yourself

[Bellamy]

The weight of the sedative lifted and I started waking up. I was so comfortable. Warm, relaxed, and unworried. I took in a deep breath and the smell of strawberries and sweet basil filled my nostrils. I tried to sit up.

Something was holding me down. I panicked a little and my eyes flew open. A tanned, muscular chest was all I could see. I recognized it and looked up.

Lucien was just opening his eyes. He held me tighter to him and I stiffened. What was he doing here? I pushed at him, but he kept his grip on me.

"I'm sorry, chouchoutte. I was childish. Blocking you was a mistake; I should have spoken to you. Please don't leave me again," he whispered.

My mind reeled. I left because he was mad and needed space. I couldn't handle the idea of seeing him angry with me, and I wanted to give him what he needed. Why was he apologizing?

"You don't have to apologize. I should've made sure you didn't have any reason to doubt me. I won't leave you. Lucien, I love you. I don't want to lose you," I replied.

"Tell me you forgive me, chouchoutte."

"Of course I do, my love. I forgive you. Will you forgive me for not making sure you were secure in our relationship?" I asked.

"You didn't do anything wrong, chouchoutte. I was exhausted and my brain wasn't working. When I woke up and remembered the night before, I knew you loved me and I was in the wrong. I went to your room to apologize when I heard what happened. As soon as I knew where you were, I came after you. Just like I promised you I would," he murmured, rubbing his face in my hair.

"Please, say you forgive me. Even if you don't think I did anything wrong. My brain doesn't like to let things go. If you don't forgive me, it'll make me think you're holding it against me any time we disagree in the future," I told him.

"You did nothing wrong. I forgive whatever you think you did, though. But if you want to be sure you gained my forgiveness, there were promises made about your mouth and my cock…" he chuckled.

I laughed and ran a hand down his chest and under the blanket. He felt much thicker and longer than he'd looked. I grasped him at his base and stroked. Lucien groaned under my attentions. I started kissing down his chest and he relaxed his arms as I wiggled down the bed.

"I was joking, chouchoutte," he said breathily.

"I wasn't," I purred as I slipped my tongue over his tip.

I'd never licked a man before. The way he groaned was exciting. I ran my tongue over him again while stroking him. His breath quickened. Taking a moment, I remembered Dilly talking about how to do this right. I wasn't going to mess it up.

Gently, I pressed my lips to his tip and kissed him. I stuck out my tongue and ran it from the base of the underside of his cock to the tip. When I got back to the end, I slid him into my mouth and focused on suction and moving my tongue firmly over and around him while I stroked the rest of him with my hands.

Lucien moaned and panted as I worked him. It was empowering. I controlled his pleasure, and he was certainly appreciative of it. One of his large hands stroked my hair, and I felt him twitch a little in my grasp.

Pushing myself a little more, I decided to see where my limit was and took him further into my mouth and a little down my throat before I had to submit to my gag reflex. I tried it a few more times, just to see if it got any better.

"Bellamy, oh, goddess, I don't know how much more I can handle. It's been so long, chouchoutte. I'm so close," he groaned.

I liked how that sounded. Moving one of my hands from his shaft, I stroked his balls and massaged them in my hand. I could feel them pulse a little before they drew up against his body.

The hand Lucien had been using to stroke my hair was now holding my head in place while he pushed himself into my mouth and throat. I nearly gagged when he started pouring hot, thick cum into me. With no other options, I started swallowing.

When he finished, he sighed. I didn't know how I felt about what had just happened. I knew what happened with oral sex, but hearing about it differed from experiencing it.

Lucien reached down and pulled me up into his arms. This was definitely something I liked. Being in his arms made me feel good, why was I so nervous?

"That was amazing, chouchoutte. That was the first time in years…. Thank you," Lucien murmured.

Now I couldn't even be entirely mad. I was still a little upset, but I'd forgotten about his situation while thinking of my own. I *had* told him I would do that. He'd been looking forward to it. Somehow, he'd managed not to touch himself since his curse broke. It wasn't like I told him not to hold my head like that.

"Are you okay, Bellamy? You're very quiet and look like you're having a fight in your head. Did I hurt you?" Lucien asked.

'That was my first time… I just feel really nervous now, I guess.' I told him in the mind-link.

"So nervous you can't talk?"

'Yeah. Sorry.'

"Let's get you out of those clothes and I'll help you find your voice again," he purred.

My stomach clenched. I realized I wasn't nearly as ready for this as I thought I was. Apparently, I talked a big game but had no follow-through. When there was a knock at the door, I was so relieved I almost cried.

"Warrick sent a snack. I'll go get it. You relax here. You're probably still exhausted from your run," Lucien said, kissing me on the head and getting out of bed.

I watched him walk into the closet and come back with some shorts on before answering the door. An omega brought in a tray with food and fruit juice.

'Dilly, I need a distraction.' I linked.

'What's up, Amy?'

'I'm not ready! Help, please.'

Silence answered me. I panicked slightly. I couldn't do this yet. My stomach twisted at the idea of being alone with Lucien again. He looked over and smiled softly. I nearly melted, but my nerves kept me in one piece.

"Come on, chouchoutte. I want you to eat something. You haven't had food since dinner last night," Lucien insisted.

I walked over to the sitting area in the room and curled up in one of the overstuffed chairs. Lucien brought me a little bowl of fruit and a sandwich on a plate. He set a glass of juice on the side table and went to sit on the couch.

After I took a few bites of the sandwich, there was another knock on the door. Lucien got up to answer it, too. I heard Dilly tell him he needed to give me a report, now that I was awake. Thank the goddess.

Dilly entered the room and saw me on the chair with my food. His eyes widened a little.

'Bems, you look like a scared kid. Did he hurt you? Do you need to leave?'

'No, I just need to get him distracted. I need time. I rushed into things a little and didn't realize my mouth was writing checks my body couldn't cash,' I replied.

'You never ask for help, Captain. I've got you. The good news is there's something you need to know about that will definitely distract you.'

'Have a seat and make your report.'

He sat on the couch across from me and crossed one leg over the other. Lucien sat in the chair next to mine. He seemed annoyed. I could deal with annoyed Lucien. It was horny Lucien I was worried about.

"Captain. I've received a report from Daylight Moon. The guard they believed was attacked by you woke up. He reported that he saw you go past an hour before he was attacked. Before the attack, he smelled someone familiar. A member of the pack, but the scent was nearly like his brother's. His brother died three years ago," Dillon reported.

I set my sandwich down. "Are you sure? He was certain it was nearly like his brother. Only very slightly off?"

"Yes, Captain. His brother was cremated like everyone else, so this couldn't be a resurrected corpse. They've gotten a couple witches out, but they haven't seen any death magic or life magic traces," he replied.

"They wouldn't. It's a potion. Someone infiltrated my territory," I growled.

"You know what this is?" Lucien asked.

"I can't remember the name of it… something like… 'Pack Scent'. Witches use it to gather ingredients in pack lands without permission. It makes them smell like trusted members of the pack. There are only a couple issues. One, our guard experienced, the wolf who scents you may not trust anyone living. Two, if you run into a couple wolves who aren't members of the same pack, the spell is broken," I explained.

Dillon nodded. "What should we do, Captain?"

"Do you have your phone?" I asked.

He pulled out his cell and handed it to me. I unlocked it and dialed Kieran. He picked up after a few rings and we did the pleasantries thing.

"There's someone on our land. I need to talk to the guard who was attacked," I told him.

"I have the guard here. I figured you would be up soon and want to talk to him," Kieran replied. "I put the phone on speaker. The guard is Vernon Dyers."

"Vernon, I want you to close your eyes and focus on the scent you smelled before you were attacked."

"Okay," he answered.

"The first thing you smelled was pack, then your brother, under the scent of your brother, was something else. It didn't make sense. It didn't fit, so your brain ignored it and just registered as slightly not your brother. I need you to focus on that scent. What was it most similar to?" I asked.

There was silence from the other end of the line while we waited for Vernon to dissect the scent and catalog the sensory information. I quietly kicked myself for having had a meltdown that led to them writing off this incursion as part of my tantrum. Who knows what reason this person was in my territory? They'd had hours to do whatever they intended.

"Bear. It was a bear," he breathed. "Holy fuck. I could've died!"

"We need to go home. If the bear didn't kill Vernon, it means he was after something that a murder would've hindered. If he's still in the territory, it could be an issue. How many wolves do we have who have experience with bears? How many can track minor scents? They would be tracking the wisps of bear. We need rogue born noses. I'm the only one in the pack," I said, getting out of the chair and crossing to the closet.

I could smell which drawers had my stuff. They smelled like me and my mom. Digging around, I pulled out my favorite jeans and t-shirt. It was an extra-extra-large lavender shirt with 'pop culture reference' written on it. I found underclothes and socks while I was looking.

"Queen Bellamy, I've called in rogue born members of the collective who are registered as trackers. They've been on site for an hour. The intruder went to the packhouse and guard station eight. Then left the territory in the east," Drake said.

"It was tracking me or Lucien. It didn't go to the training field?" I asked.

"No. It appears it may have been after the Alpha," he told me.

Shit. There went my hope of heading home this evening and hunting bear instead of sleeping with my mate. I wasn't planning to never sleep with him… I just needed time to feel ready.

"So it could come back to the pack lands… Conscript the rogue born in my name and have them walk patrols on my border. We'll be back tomorrow afternoon instead of the morning after," I ordered.

"Yes, Queen Bellamy," Drake responded.

"Kieran, I wanted to apologize for this morning and last night. I was a little overcome with everything and acted out of line. When I get home, I would be happy to answer questions you have about the mission last night," I said softly.

"Jason already answered them for me. I appreciate you apologizing, Bellamy. I'm sorry, too. My anger almost led me to make a terrible mistake. Your mate and Alpha Warrick helped me see where my emotion was clouding my judgment." Kieran stated.

"I don't know what you almost did. I don't want to know. Okay? I forgive you. Thanks for taking responsibility. I'm going to let you go. I need a shower and some more food. See you tomorrow," I told him and we hung up.

Turning back to the room, I saw Dillon and Lucien sitting deep in conversation. I ignored it and went to take a shower. Lucien wouldn't try anything once I was clean and dressed, right?

I locked the bathroom door behind me, peeled off the loaner clothes, turned on the water, and stepped into the spray of the shower. Time to think.

Chapter 34: Acting Like an Alpha

Bellamy took her call into the walk-in closet and started digging through the drawers. There was no way I'd be able to get her back in bed while she was worried about her pack. Damn it. Dillon had some shitty timing. I glared at him and he motioned me to come over.

I got up and sat near him on the couch. He leaned in and briefly glanced at Bellamy as she was talking and pulling out clothes.

"I don't know what you were doing, but you freaked her out. She knows things and says things, but she's a *total* virgin. Slow your roll," he whispered.

A blush spread across my face. I remembered what I did. I lost control at the end and came in her mouth. Only vaguely registering her pushing against me while I held her in place. Pinching the bridge of my nose, I closed my eyes. It had been so long; my body just took over.

"She told you that?" I asked.

"Bellamy doesn't ask for help, but she did today. I was already waiting for her to get up for this report. It would've happened either way. If you keep doing whatever it was, she might push you away. None of us want that. How can I help *you*?" Dillon asked sincerely.

"You want to help me? I'd think you would want to get her away from me. What can I do here? I lost control a little, and then she got quiet and nervous. I thought it was regular nerves…" I replied.

Bellamy walked past us into the bathroom and locked the door. She didn't lock the door when she showered with me in her bedroom yesterday. I turned to Dillon. I'd broken her trust twice now.

"You have to be straightforward about everything. Bellamy doesn't like it when people beat around the bush or hint at things. Let her know how you feel. Let her know you noticed the change in her. Listen to what she says.

"She doesn't play games. There's never a hidden meaning. Watch her body language if she's not saying much. Rogues don't like talking, but she forces herself to a lot of the time. Cara and I get a lot of her silent talk, but not as much as the rogues," he explained.

I nodded. All of this was important. I didn't want her to run away from me because I pushed her too far, too fast. I cursed myself for not seeing. She couldn't talk. That's some pretty intense anxiety.

"I can't stop trying to be with her, though. She might think I'm going to leave if I do. I feel like I might die if I can't touch her. It wasn't like I was just using her, Dillon. I need her. Bellamy is everything." I sighed.

"Look, just tell her you want to slow it down until she's comfortable. Bellamy doesn't realize what she does to men. I can help more as you go. I'm kind of the expert on her, but I can't lead you to the key. Sometimes she's cautious, sometimes she's all in. If you can get her really into it and feeling powerful, you could have her by morning. If not, you might not get any until Cara's mate does." He snickered. "I'm gonna head out. She'll probably be nervous when she gets out of the shower. If I'm here, she'll make it about work. Don't talk to Warrick about this. He's her sounding board, but he's still her brother and will *not* be helpful at all."

Dillon patted me on the shoulder and left. I had to make her feel powerful and confident. Then she'd go back to how she was. This nervous Bellamy was too innocent and wide-eyed. I felt like a dirty old man when I saw her in the bed after the omega left. I wanted the girl who teased and rubbed herself on me. The girl who touched me whenever she went past. I wanted *my* Bellamy.

Lost in thought, I startled when she emerged from the bathroom. Her hair was damp and pulled back in a braid. She looked like a younger teen again. Baggy shirt over jeans and no makeup. She nibbled her lip.

"Sit down and finish your snack. Dillon had to go. I wanted to talk to you," I told her.

She sat cross-legged in the chair and picked up her sandwich, nodding to me. I wanted to hear her voice again.

"I realized I lost control when you were… anyway, I want you to know I didn't mean to do that. You were amazing, and I forgot myself. Please forgive me," I said.

'No problem. I figured it was something like that.'

"Are you really not going to talk to me?" I asked.

'I'm eating.'

I raised an eyebrow. Bellamy winked as she took another bite of her sandwich. It made me laugh.

'I realized that I may not be as ready as I thought I was for this step. I didn't mean to lead you on with… how I am,' she told me.

"I want you to be comfortable. We can go at your pace. I only have one request." I smiled.

'What?'

"Tonight, let me taste you. I promise, my cock will not be involved in the process. You made me feel wonderful, chouchoutte. I want to do the same for you. If you get uncomfortable, I'll stop," I promised.

Bellamy turned red as she stared at me. I could see her thinking and a couple of winces threw me off.

'Aurora says I should do it. She doesn't like me like this. What would you be doing? The guys never talked about exactly what that involves. I know how it works on guys because Dilly tells me everything. No one ever said more than a simple 'I went down on her' or 'I ate her'. None of which helps me understand.'

It was my turn to blush and stare. She wanted me to tell her what I planned to do to her and it wasn't in the sexy 'then what' sort of thing. She honestly wanted me to give her a rundown of what I would do. I wished I could mind-link Dillon for advice.

No. I had to stop acting like a nervous kid. I'm a fucking Alpha. She was too, and we needed to get back to who we really were. The thing with the vampires, the marking, the fight, it all changed us into something we weren't for a while.

"Come sit in my lap and I'll tell you," I purred.

She blushed, but came to sit on me. I wrapped my arms around her waist and leaned my head into the curve of her neck. Her heart was hammering.

"Calm down, chouchoutte. I won't do anything right now. I'm just talking," I whispered, making her shiver.

'I'm trying to calm down! I don't like this any more than you do.'

"You're an Alpha. Act like it," I hissed in her ear.

Bellamy stiffened and took a deep breath in. Her heartbeat slowed and the light scent of fear went away. I knew she'd pulled herself out of this to talk with her pack about their intruder. She needed to keep her head.

"Better?" I asked.

"Much. Thank you," she replied and relaxed in my arms. "I got lost for a while."

"Is it because of how much time you've spent outside your territory?"

"Maybe. I become more nervous once I've been away for two or three days. If I compound it with the whole mate thing…. That could be exactly it. Thank the goddess. I thought I'd turned into Cara for a minute there." Bellamy laughed.

I laughed, too. She wiggled in my lap, reminding me of my mission.

"Do you still need me to explain what I'm going to do to you tonight?" I asked.

Bellamy swallowed. "Only if you do it slowly and thoroughly," she whispered.

I chuckled into her skin and kissed her neck. There was my mate.

"First, I'm going to have you take off these clothes. Then, I'll need to touch all this beautiful skin. When I'm done, I'll lay you out on that bed and begin tasting your sweet, sassy mouth." I ran my fingers over her lips and started trailing them over her as I spoke.

"I'll move to your jaw and cute little chin, then down your neck and over your collarbone. Once I've reached these gorgeous breasts, I'll take my time worshipping every inch of them. I'll continue over your stomach, lower and lower. Then, you'll spread these legs for me." I tugged at her knee a little and she opened to me. "Every inch of them from your knees up will be covered in my kisses, licks, and nibbles. Then, I'll kiss these lips."

Bellamy moaned as my fingers caressed her between her legs. I could smell her arousal as her breath quickened. She was perfect.

"I'm going to kiss, suck, and lick you until you lose control like I did, chouchoutte. You'll come over and over, grabbing my hair and riding my face in ecstasy. Then I'll hold you until we fall asleep. No matter how much you beg, I won't enter you with anything but my tongue or my fingers. Your sweet cream will be my reward. The taste of you will rest on my tongue, bringing me the most pleasurable dreams of you, my little queen, accepting me in every way possible," I murmured.

She was close. I knew just a little more, and she'd reach her peak. When I moved my hand away, she groaned in frustration.

"Don't stop, Lucien. Please," Bellamy whined.

"I'm done with my description, chouchoutte. I should get dressed. If we're only staying one night, we need to tell Warrick. He and Janya will be talking to us about how to navigate a relationship between two Alpha wolves. Now, your mother put your favorite necklace in the front pocket of your bag. Why don't you go get it on?" I smirked.

"You are a terrible man and I will never forgive you for this." She huffed and bounced off my lap, storming over to her bag.

I grinned and followed, pulling out jeans and a T-shirt of my own. Bellamy slipped her wolf pendant on and trailed her fingers along my back as she returned to the sitting area to finish her snack.

She forgave me.

Chapter 35: Marriage Counseling

We left our room and headed for Warrick's office. He answered after a couple of knocks and waved us in, sitting behind his desk.

"What's up?" he asked.

"We need to leave sooner than we thought," Bellamy answered. "Lucien said you and Janie had some stuff to talk to us about."

"When are you leaving?"

"We need to leave tomorrow after lunch. I want to have at least one full day at home before heading to Lune Rouge," she replied.

"Janya's on her way. Dinner's at seven, which gives us about two and a half hours to talk. In the morning, the two of you can join us for training. Bellamy needs to train every day or she gets antsy. Remember that. She'll be easier to handle that way." He winked.

"I'll handle you. You're my first sparring partner tomorrow," she growled.

Warrick laughed and nodded. "Just don't break my jaw. Janya will be very upset if you do."

Bellamy blushed. Making him laugh even harder. She looked like she was going to say something when the door opened. Janya entered and looked irked.

"Care to tell me why I'm rearranging my schedule again, Amy?"

"My pack needs me home earlier than planned. We're hunting," she said seriously.

"Not vampires or rogues... humans?" Janya asked.

"Bear," Bellamy smiled.

"Tough hunt."

"More fun."

They both chuckled, and Janya sat on Warrick's lap. She grabbed his chin and made him look at her.

"You owe me, Alpha."

"Of course, Luna," he replied.

I was a little lost and must have looked it. Bellamy tapped my hand.

"He owes her because she's pregnant and not allowed to come hunt and fight with us. Janie isn't a rogue, but her pack was fairly roguish and she's a warrior, like me. We connect on that level," she explained.

"I see. Am I going to owe you for things like that, too?" I asked.

"Only if it's a really fun one. The safety of our pups will always come first," Bellamy promised.

"We should get started," Warrick said.

"Where do we start, though? I mean, obviously, two Alphas would have a difficult relationship, but we just have to remember ourselves. Right?" Bellamy asked.

"Kind of. An Alpha likes to be in charge, they like to win, and they hold themselves up to a higher standard. Whereas humans with Alpha tendencies can be narcissistic, Alpha wolves don't quite reach those heights. Don't get me wrong, we love ourselves, but we love our pack more. Our pack is part of us, like your collective is part of you. Your past made you a little different," Warrick told her.

He continued. "Because of the ill-treatment, abandonment, witnessing your parents' murder, and the fear you have of the Alpha who banished them, you're not as confident or assured. Most Alphas naturally pull away from their parents. You were torn from them before you were ready. There was no one to give you the safety to grow on your own and come into yourself as an Alpha."

She nodded. It certainly explained why she shut down. The lost, afraid girl was still in her. I needed to help her get over that. My mate was a strong, independent queen.

"Why are you afraid of the Alpha who banished them?" I asked.

"Because, if he finds me, he'll probably want to kill me. I'm less afraid now. As the head of a large collective and an elite warrior, I know I have a good chance of beating him if he comes around," Bellamy told me.

"What's his name, or his pack name? I'll make sure we cut off any ties we have with him and ban him from our lands," I promised.

"I don't know. My parents never told me. I only knew them as Mama and Papa. I don't even know my real last name. Only that it started with a 'P'. I remember seeing it on a file. Bellamy P," she said sadly.

"You're hoping making her feel safe will help. We looked into murders nearby and none had a survivor. We didn't want to risk looking further and having things traced back to our packs. It was a decision Ames, Kieran, and my dad came to. I agree with it. Whoever it is, he hasn't found her yet and might not even know where to start," Warrick stated.

"If he comes, I'll end him, chouchoutte," I said, taking her hand in mine.

She smiled. "Thank you, mon saucisson. I'm glad I have you."

"Being a rogue means Ames needs less restriction than a pack wolf. Everything's heightened by her senses, abilities, and emotions. Remember that as we go forward," Warrick warned. "Since you're both Alphas you need to figure out which domains belong entirely to one or the other. There is little to no sharing with Alphas unless you define everything. If you can work to support each other instead of trying to best each other, it would be helpful. We can easily define two roles for each of you."

"Alpha and Rogue Queen," I said.

"And their partners, yes." Janya nodded. "As Alpha you're in charge of your pack. Amy's your Luna, a support and a confidant. You work together, but she lets you have the lead. For me, since I'm not a rogue Queen, I take on responsibility for the children, the elderly, and the omegas in the pack. They're mine. Warrick takes care of the pack as a whole but has to consult with me if he wants to do anything with those three groups and has to back off if I tell him to. Amy will have her own people to focus on."

"Ames is the Queen of all the rogues in her territory, which will include yours. She is the Alpha and you are like a Chief Lieutenant. When she's in 'queen mode' she is Queen Bellamy, not 'chouchoutte'. You need to be her support like she'll be yours. Both of you will work to protect your people. Pack and collective.

"With your children, you'll need to make decisions before they come. Not taking the lead in your own home is hard. Compromise is difficult for Alphas, but you can learn. We created a way to make decisions without conflict. You need to make your own system. One you both agree on," Warrick added.

"The most important thing is really knowing about each other. Once you truly know your mate, you can understand and remember their motivations. We know Amy and her values. We don't know yours very well, Alpha Lucien.

"The fact that you were willing to apologize and follow her, means you're already open to admitting faults. Amy will do that if she feels it's appropriate, which is more often than you'd think. You two need to talk about where you fall on other things. More than in other relationships, you need to honestly communicate. Really listening can be hard. *Never* assume, always question your reactions," Janya lectured.

I felt like I should take notes or something. Bellamy looked like she was calmly absorbing everything. Maybe she could help me when I forget.

"So, make a method of compromise, communicate, know your place and role, compare values, and let me be free. Awesome. Anything else?" Bellamy sighed.

"Are you getting bored, Belly?" Janya asked, annoyed.

"Your face isn't pregnant, Janie," she growled.

"They like each other, but they can't be in a small space with each other for too long," Warrick explained when he saw my concerned expression. "They get feisty. How about a break you ladies can take a walk and get some air on opposite sides of the house?"

"Let's go to the garden, chouchoutte. Fifteen minutes sound okay, Alpha Warrick?" I asked.

"Just call me Warrick. You're my brother now. Fifteen should be fine. We'll go over your fight and anything else you want to talk about. We can even help you two talk through some of your past. Go on. We'll see you soon." He waved us off.

I tightened my grip on Bellamy's hand and pulled her out of the room. They'd started properly growling. I'd never had that happen with another Alpha. We headed to the back and out to the gardens.

Bellamy calmed down after a while. She pulled her hand away and looped her arm around mine, leaning against me as we walked.

"Alpha females are more territorial," she said unexpectedly. "Janie and I love each other, and I can visit, but we normally have to hang out in larger rooms than that office if we're going to be together for more than a half hour. Because our mates were with us, it was worse. If we're in a small room and Ricky is there, Janie always has to sit on his lap. It's annoying, but we figured it out."

"Have you two ever fought?" I asked.

"Yeah. She's really good. I'm better. That's part of our problem. When she's not pregnant, we fight within a couple hours of me getting here. It makes our wolves calm down. We're not great when we can't hit each other for a while," Bellamy laughed.

"Would it be easier on you two if you sat on my lap like she does his?"

We walked on the path in the garden while she thought. She was probably consulting with her wolf. Aurora would know what would make this easier better than Bellamy. She was the one who was elevating the tension.

'Did you notice the young Alpha looks a little like us?'

'This isn't the time, Remus,' I told my wolf.

'I'm just saying, if his hair were black and he was a little thicker, he could easily pass for you when you were young.'

'What's your point?'

'Maybe that's what the Luna was picking up on. Didn't Dillon say you were her exact type? That means he is, too,' he suggested.

'Her brother, Galen, looks almost exactly like me at his age, except for his eye and hair color. You didn't feel the need to point that out.'

'Maybe she has a crush on him, too.'

I felt a growl low in my chest. Remus did this a lot. His brain got distracted, and he pointed out things that drew his attention. Even inane things like this.

He could be as possessive as I was. It boiled under my skin. He knew I had problems with jealousy, but here he was, making it worse.

"Are you okay, Lucien?" Bellamy asked.

"Yes, chouchoutte. It's just Remus causing problems." I smiled tightly.

"I would like to sit in your lap when we go back. If it can make my relationship with Janie easier, I'd love to try it." She grinned up at me.

"Good, we'll do that when we get back."

We continued walking, and Bellamy leaned on my arm. The smell of the different flowers mingled with her scent. She hummed a little as we walked and I found myself relaxing.

"We should head back soon," Bellamy murmured.

"Yeah. Just tell me one thing so I can make Remus shut up," I said.

"What, my love?"

"Tell me honestly if you were ever attracted to Warrick or Galen." I insisted.

Bellamy stopped walking. I paused and looked down at her. She was biting her lips together and her eyes were sparkling. Soon, she started laughing.

It annoyed me. She shouldn't laugh at this. It was serious. She was mine and should only want me. I growled.

"Oh, Lucien. You're so cute. They're my brothers. That's super gross." She giggled.

"They're not your actual brothers. You didn't answer the question," I replied.

"And I don't need to. *You* are my mate. The only male who I've marked and I've permitted to mark me. Nothing from before should matter. Are you planning to tell me about every woman you felt attracted to, but never did anything with? I already know you slept with my Aunt Regan. How many others did you sleep with before you got punished?

"Did your maid have a *reason* to believe she could have your child? Were you secretly panting after her, wishing for your curse to break so you could bend her over something and dominate her? Did you imagine whipping it out while she was on her knees cleaning the baseboards? Did she smell your interest in her and decide to make you hers? You don't get to own my past, Lucien. Only my present and my future." She pushed me and walked back down the path.

'So… that's a yes.' Remus snarled. *'She needs to stay away from that Alpha. She's ours.'*

'He has a mate. She wouldn't do anything with a mated male. She's right. We have no room to try to claim her past. Remember how we fantasized about all those females over the years? All the women we did sleep with? The things we imagined doing with Angelique?'

'We're male, it's different for us,' he reasoned.

'No. It's not. Now stop. You're going to fuck it up for us. Don't encourage me to hurt our mate. You're supposed to be on her side, remember?'

I blocked him. I needed to remember to be more thoughtful and not fall into these traps. My jealousy was going to cause problems if I didn't get it under control.

Running, I caught up with her as she walked into the packhouse. I followed her to Warrick's office. He and his Luna were already there. I sat in my seat and Bellamy crawled into my lap, wrapping my arm around her waist. She slid her fingers between mine and leaned against my chest.

'Are you done being an ass, Lucien?' she asked.

'If I buy you a maid outfit, do you think I could get you to clean my office? I'll pick you up to reach the high places.'

'Pervert.'

Chapter 36: A Matter of Breeding

I looked at Warrick. He didn't look happy. I put my other hand on Bellamy's knee and smiled politely.

"What's going on, here?" he asked.

"I thought by sitting on Lucien like Janie sits on you, I could stay calm. She sits on you to deal with the possessiveness. Right now, we want to stay in the room together long enough to learn. Taking fifteen-minute breaks all the time will cut into what you have to say. So, we're claiming our territory and hoping it will keep our wolves calm," Bellamy explained.

"That sounds perfectly acceptable, Amy. He's just doing the big brother thing. Let's see what happens." Janya said.

"The fight. We need to talk about why Ames ran." Warrick sighed.

"It wasn't really a fight," Bellamy said.

"That's true. Her parents decided to talk to me and let me know she thinks and acts differently than a pack wolf. They ended up implying she only wanted me, only followed the vampires, because I was powerful. Powerful enough to keep her safe from Kyle," I growled.

I didn't know who Kyle was, but he'd already become a hassle in my relationship with my mate.

Bellamy snorted. "At dinner, they were saying they thought I only wanted you to expand my territory. I thought that was why you were upset. It was because you thought I was using you as a shield? I never need you to protect me from Kyle. I was worried when I was twelve.

"When I was seventeen, I had spies go into his territory and report to me. He never trains, he relies on his added power from being an Alpha wolf and on the size of his collective. When he took over his collective, he killed King Fuller as he slept. I whipped his ass at eight, I can easily do it again at eighteen."

"I never worried about you wanting to expand your territory. As my Luna, my pack is your pack. Co-ruling isn't enough to make me give up on a mate as perfect as you," I told her.

"Why did you leave me then?" she asked.

"I didn't like the idea of being used and I wanted to pout for a while. Honestly, I wasn't really thinking straight. Once I woke up, I realized I was wrong," I said.

"I left to give you the space you wanted. I figured you'd cool off and we could talk. That in the meantime I could figure out how to show you that I didn't want you for your territory. I wasn't mad. It hurt that you wouldn't talk to me and the pain was too much to bear. Being close, seeing you angry at me, it was too hard. I hate stuff like that. I want to fix things as soon as I can," Bellamy whispered as she kissed my jaw.

"From now on, I'll talk to you instead of pouting like a child. If I walk away, I'll be back as soon as I'm not stupid anymore. I promise. I'm not leaving forever, just until I can be the mate you deserve," I vowed.

"Well, that was anticlimactic. Let's move on," Janya said.

Over the next hour, we talked about our beliefs and values, our people and needs as their rulers, our families and what we want for them, and our goals for our territories. I felt like I had a much better idea of who she was and how she thought.

We really were the same in a lot of ways. Neither one of us was afraid to fight alongside our people, to kill for their safety, to sacrifice if we needed to. We wanted to make a safe place and home for them. We wanted that for ourselves, too.

"So, now we've covered all the boring stuff, how many nieces and nephews can Rick and I expect?" Janya grinned.

Bellamy blushed. We actually had to have sex for that. I knew it wouldn't be much longer. Her heat would come soon. It would be harder for her to resist me then. Until then, I'd make sure she got over her fear of being with me.

"Rogue born wolves only have heat twice a year. Not monthly like pack wolves. It's a lot more intense than yours and lasts the same amount of time. Most rogue born wolves can only get pregnant during their heat. We rarely breed outside that time.

"Since I'm an Alpha female, I usually leave to an outer corner of my territory when it happens. There can be a mini baby boom if I have my heat in the pack lands. Kind of similar to the Alpha female in a natural wolf pack. My pregnancies will only last four months instead of five. And my heat starts three days after marking," Bellamy said softly.

"It's five for pack wolves. That's pretty crazy. When were you marked?" Janya asked.

"Two nights ago," she squeaked.

I'd been expecting five. I didn't realize it was less. That meant she'd start her heat tomorrow night. I could have a pup before Christmas. A smile tugged at my lips.

"I see this is news to you, Lucien," Warrick chuckled.

"If Bellamy wants to wait, I'll find a way. If not... I certainly wouldn't mind a pup or two for my birthday." I winked.

"Your birthday is in October?" Bellamy asked.

"Yeah. October sixteenth. What's yours?"

"Well... I thought it was September. But Aurora showed up around June sixth last year." She smiled. "Kids aren't great with calendars."

Everyone laughed. I could imagine trying to guess your birthday when you didn't really have a good grasp of the months. I wondered how she decided on September, but something struck me as more important.

"How were you planning to do your mission while in heat?" I asked. "We'd be driving up, so the space would be small. If we rode with the guys, they'd be affected too."

"The first couple days of heat don't have the scent or pheromone associated with it. Generally, it's just me flirting a lot more than normal. Day three is when it gets irritating. Then it's four days of... well... heat. I don't know how to explain it. I just know I couldn't be at home.

"The one time my heat came early, I ended up with two little sisters because we were camping when it started," she groaned. "It kicked mom's heat in early and hard. Not an experience I recommend. No one should ever have to camp with their parents when their mother is in heat." Bellamy shuddered.

"So you were planning on getting established and then disappearing for almost a week?" I asked.

"I'd just be in our quarters, Lucien. No males would be allowed on that floor. The Alpha's quarters are always their own floor. At home, we shared the floor with the Gamma family. None of my family is actually related to me. No one in that house is immune to it. I couldn't stay there at all," she explained.

I could understand what she was saying. My home's setup differed from most packhouses, and we had a completely separate living space. It was a good plan. No one would intrude on my home and she would've been safe.

"Sorry to interrupt this… interesting… conversation, dinner is about to be served," Warrick stated. "We need to go. You two seem like you have this under control. I suggest just getting to know each other more. You should tell each other everything, no secrets. The more you know the fewer surprises can mess you up."

We nodded, and Bellamy crawled off my lap. We walked to the dining room, hand-in-hand. I thought about the chance we could have a pup by the end of the year. I was telling the truth. If she wanted to wait, I'd sleep in one of the guest rooms. I really hoped she didn't want to wait, though.

Dinner was fantastic, a warm and satisfying meal that left everyone feeling content. Dillon shared the story of Bellamy's exhibition fight with Talia when she was visiting. She didn't win, but the fight sounded like it was pretty amazing.

When it was over, we went for another walk. Bellamy rubbed against me as we meandered through the garden in the fading light. She gripped my arm and hummed the same song she was humming earlier.

I hoped it would always be like this for us. She seemed so happy. Closing my eyes for a moment, I thanked the moon goddess for bringing us together.

"Do you want to go to our room, Lucien?" she asked softly.

"Of course, ma chouchoutte. I always want to be alone with you," I purred.

She giggled, and we made our way to the suite. I couldn't wait to worship my little queen. I'd make sure she wouldn't be afraid of me again.

Chapter 37: Finding Her Voice

[Lucien]

I locked the door after I closed it and turned to see Bellamy taking off her necklace and pulling her clothes off. Her clothing fell away piece-by-piece, leaving her standing in nothing but her underclothes. She turned to look at me, making eye contact while she reached behind her and unclasped her bra, pulling it off, then sliding her panties off her hips and down her legs.

My lungs burned, and I realized I'd been holding my breath from the moment she bent her arms behind her. I let my breath out and licked my lips. Bellamy swayed her hips a little as she slowly made her way over to me, stopping within arm's reach. She clasped her hands behind her and looked up at me through her eyelashes.

Reaching out, I ran my fingers along her collarbone and down to her chest. My thumbs brushed over her nipples, making her whimper a little. I moved my hands lower, to the soft skin of her stomach, and around to her waist. Picking her up, I moved to the bed, laying her down gently.

Stepping back, I removed my own clothes. I wouldn't have sex with her tonight, but I wouldn't make myself sleep uncomfortably, either. Looking at my bare mate as I stood nude in front of her made me incredibly hard. She gazed at me with a hungry look in her eyes.

"You ready to be tasted, chouchoutte?" I asked.

"I've been ready for hours, mon saucisson," she murmured.

I smiled and climbed on the bed, straddling her legs. Bellamy looked down at my engorged cock and licked her lips. It made me chuckle.

"None of that tonight. But I will have to lay it against you for most of my tasting," I told her.

She nodded, and I pressed myself along the line of her body. Her skin was soft and warm against me. I had to fight the urge to rub myself against her.

Gently, I nibbled and sucked on her lips. Once I'd gained entry to her mouth, I let my tongue dance with hers, tasting every inch. She moaned and writhed a little while I diligently traced my tongue over every part of her mouth.

Moving to her jaw and chin as promised when I'd finished and down the line of her throat to my mark. I licked and nibbled while she rubbed my cock with her body. Thank the goddess I'd already had a release, or I would have embarrassed myself all over her beautiful stomach.

Every part of her was silky and sweet. My tongue wanted more, and my hands craved the touch of her skin. When I reached her breasts, I permitted them. Groping, fondling, pinching the gorgeous globes that had eluded me for the last couple of days. I sucked and licked her nipples, giving each one languorous attention while she moaned and panted, calling my name like a mantra.

I moved down to the plain of her stomach, feeling her deliciously toned muscles underneath. She squealed and arched as I continued my tasting, getting ever closer to my prize. I kissed and nipped at her hips as I slid to the side, freeing her legs.

"Open for me, chouchoutte," I purred.

Bellamy bit her bottom lip as she spread her legs. She gasped when I moved to lie between them. I kissed her knee and up her thigh to the sweet center of my love. She was dripping with need and the scent of it caused me to feel my own surge. I kissed her lightly, making her cry out before I went to her other knee and repeated my journey.

"Please," she whispered. "Lucien, I need you. Please."

I had heard nothing so beautiful in years. Starting with a kiss on her mound, I then followed the path of her center line down her body before gently using my fingers to spread her sweet lips. I explored her with my tongue and fingers, taking her clit into my mouth and alternating swirling my tongue around it and sucking. Her legs danced on either side of me, shaking with the pleasure I was giving her.

Sliding down, I finally gave in to my urge to lap and suck every ounce of her juices up. For all that I called her chouchoutte, she was just as sweet and creamy as my new favorite dessert. I rubbed and teased her clit with my fingers while slowly fucking her with my tongue, curling it, tasting every bit of her sweet center, as she bucked and cried.

Her muscles grasped at my tongue as I stroked in and out of her. Suddenly, her legs wrapped around my head, pressing me into her and riding my face. I growled with satisfaction as she screamed and arched, her sweet nectar filling my senses until I was desperate with desire.

When she released me, I crawled up and kissed her deeply, sharing her essence between us. Bellamy purred with pleasure as her hands clutched my back and shoulders, and her hips moved.

It took every bit of my willpower to pull away and lay down next to her. My entire body ached with the need to delve into her and plant my seed deep inside. I only had to wait until tomorrow night. Then she'd be entirely mine.

I closed my eyes and tried to get my erection to go away. I needed to sleep and this would only be a hindrance. There was some movement in the bed. Bellamy was probably trying to sleep. I smiled, thinking of how beautiful she was when she'd been sleeping earlier.

There was a light growl from next to me and I suddenly felt something on my waist. I opened my eyes and Bellamy was standing over me, one foot on either side of my hips, hands on my waist, looking down at me. She winked and lowered herself onto my hardened length.

Once the tip was in, I stared in disbelief as she pushed herself down with one stroke. She didn't stop until she was resting in my lap. The pain on her face was agonizing to me. I never wanted to see her suffering because of me.

"Holy shit, that hurt!" She cringed.

"I thought we weren't going to do this until tomorrow. Chouchoutte, you have to go slow. It always hurts the first time, but going slower can give you time to adjust," I explained.

"I'm not a fan of prolonging pain, even if it lessens it. How long before it stops? I need sleep so I can be rested for training in the morning, but I needed this dick more," Bellamy grinned.

"It can go away as you move, it can take a few minutes if you don't want to. Or that's what I've heard," I answered.

She pushed herself up, then came back down tentatively. The hiss of her breath was soft as she worked herself up and down my shaft. Soon, it turned to light moans and panting.

"That's much better," Bellamy groaned. "Oh, Goddess, Lucien, that feels so much better. I love how you feel in me, mon saucisson."

I moved my hands to her waist and stabilized her motions, moving her body more steadily, rotating her hips to change how it felt, driving my body up to meet hers.

Nothing in the world could ever be like my little love. The feeling of our bodies combining was like the creation of the universe, amazing and immeasurably powerful. I never wanted to do anything but live in this moment.

Sitting up, I wrapped my arms around her and stopped her motion. Bellamy looked up at me and I kissed her deeply. She moaned against my lips and tried to move.

Pulling away from her sweet lips, I held her tight and rolled until she was under me. Taking the lead, I pushed into her until I felt the stop that made her squeal.

"What was that?!" she gasped.

"Your cervix, chouchoutte. I'm pressed against the door to where our pups will grow inside you. Do you want me to put a pup there, chouchoutte? Do you want me to come in you, ma belle?" I asked.

"I want pups, Lucien, but are you sure you're okay with me finishing my work while pregnant? I need to make sure our family will be safe," Bellamy whispered.

"Let me help. Lean on your team more. Manage, delegate, and only fight if you need to. We'll take care of whatever you need. I want to have a pup with you, chouchoutte. I want it more than I've ever wanted anything, but I'll wait if you want," I assured her.

I made sure not to move while we were talking. This was a conversation I'd been planning to have before we got to this point, and I didn't want her influenced by an orgasm.

When I'd started getting close to my end, I had to stop her. No child of mine would be an accident. No child of mine would have regret as part of their life story.

"Will you listen to everything I say? Even if what I tell you isn't the same as what you know? Pack born and rogue born wolves are the same species, but some differences go deeper than what you can see or smell," she stated.

"I will. You might have to remind me and sometimes give in to the overprotective urges I have. Can you do that? Can you let me take the lead while you focus on creation?" I asked.

"It'll be difficult, but I think I can. Will you talk to me if you get upset? I can't stand the idea of having to worry about relationship stuff and you running off when I'm in my final weeks."

"I won't run any further than the next room. I will talk to you, but I might need to calm down first. Will you stay near me while giving me space instead of running off to your brothers?" I smiled.

"I will. Okay, let's do this. There's a good chance I won't get pregnant since I'm not in heat, but at least we got that hammered out before we forgot." She chuckled, tightening the muscles surrounding me.

I groaned and started moving again. The edge I'd felt earlier had dulled, and I was ready to take my time with my beautiful little mate, stroking in and out of her firmly and slowly. Her soft sighs and moans filled the room.

There was nothing more beautiful than her face full of ecstasy as we made love. She moved with me. Sliding her fingers up and down my body, occasionally digging in when her body would spasm around me. I'd never felt a woman like her before, and was thankful for everything that brought us together.

Eventually, I felt my end coming again. There was nothing I could do to stop it, as my Bellamy reached the heights of her own. She milked my body as wave after wave was hitting her and her moans turned to exclamations. I let myself go, holding deep inside her, feeling her body tense and relax over and over while I pulsed in her, coating her walls with my seed.

When we finished, I rolled again so she could rest on my chest. She released a shuddering sigh and kissed right over my heart. I smiled as I trailed my fingers over her back. We were finally complete and bonded. I'd never felt so fulfilled.

"What are you thinking, Lucien?" she murmured against my skin.

"That you're perfect, chouchoutte. That I love you more than I've ever loved anyone else. I can't wait to take you home and make love to you in our bed. And you, mon petit amour? What are you thinking?" I asked, kissing the top of her head.

"I'm thinking I was an idiot for being afraid of this. And I'm lucky to have found a mate who's so perfect for me. I can't wait to go home with you and really start our lives together. Did you want a wedding, or should we just go get married in a nearby courthouse? I think my family would be upset if we didn't have a wedding, but the headache of one like Cara and Caleb's doesn't appeal to me," Bellamy giggled.

I hadn't even thought of a wedding. Thinking about it now, I loved the idea of seeing her in a wedding dress, her father giving her away, my mother and sister watching as I vowed to keep her forever.

"We don't need to do anything like what they're doing, chouchoutte. Cara wants a grande fête. We only need our family and friends. I think you'd be gorgeous in a wedding dress, Bellamy. You're certainly gorgeous out of one." I chuckled.

"If we're trying for a baby, then we should do it in the next month. Rogue born are more prone to multiple births to begin with and I remember my parents saying twins run in both of their families. By the end of my second month, I'll start getting big. I'll be a whale by the time of the birth," she said thoughtfully.

"The cutest whale on the planet," I whispered.

"Certainly the deadliest one if I ever hear you call me that again," she growled.

We laughed and Bellamy slid off of me, pulling the blankets over us and curling into the curve of my body. I closed my eyes and drifted to sleep. Dreaming of the day when we would be joined in the eyes of human law as well.

Chapter 38: Training

[Bellamy]

The alarm clock went off entirely too early in the morning. I was used to only getting a few hours of sleep, but sleeping alone had never been as comfortable as sleeping in Lucien's arms. I crawled over him to reach the clock and turn it off. Thirty minutes to training.

Getting out of bed, I dug through the drawers until I found my spare training outfit. My normal one had probably shredded when I shifted yesterday morning. I went to the bathroom, then changed, tying my hair back in a high ponytail again, before I left. Lucien walked groggily past me as I went to find my socks and sneakers.

Warrick's warriors didn't train as hard as mine. I knew this would only be a light workout before the sparring started. He probably already had a couple of people asking to fight me. His brother, Rhys, would be among them. I thoroughly enjoyed handing that boy his ass every time we fought.

Lucien sat on the couch to put on his shoes. "How are you feeling this morning?" he asked.

"A little sore, but excited for training." I grinned.

He looked a little disappointed.

"What's that look for? Should I be feeling something else?"

"I don't like the idea of you training while you're in pain," he replied.

I laughed. "I said sore, not hurt. Moving helps healing. It's not like I plan to take a lot of hits to my girly parts."

"I still don't like it," he grumbled.

Standing, I moved between his legs, taking his face in my hands. He really was beautiful. I got a little lost in his silver eyes before I remembered what I was doing.

"You don't have to like what I do, but you have to accept it. I won't change something like this because you don't like it. It's just training, Lucien. I'm not going to war… yet. Come on, if we're late we have to do doubles and I'd rather have breakfast," I told him and reached for his hands to help move him along.

We ran out to the training field and made it just before the whistle blew, indicating the start of the session. It was pretty good. Six-mile run, sit-ups, squats, planks, push-ups, and a dozen other fun exercises to make our muscles burn and our bodies sweat.

Then came my favorite. Sparring. I loved a good fight.

We would have a team of four and all four would face off against each other in individual fights. The fights went to five hits, usually, but people could tap out whenever they wanted, and some went further than five. Out of the corner of my eye, I saw Rhys smirking as he made his way over.

He must have been training hard since the last time I kicked his ass because he looked very confident. Warrick was already standing with me. And we were looking for a fourth.

Most people were wary of fighting Warrick. Only Rhys was stupid enough to be eager to fight me. I looked for Dilly, but he had his own group already put together with Tyson.

"You mind if I join your group, Warrick?" I heard Lucien behind me.

"Only if you don't go easy on your mate, Lucien," Ricky warned jokingly.

"I wouldn't dream of it. This could be my last chance to fight her for a while," Lucien chuckled.

I turned to them. My face felt like it was on fire. I didn't want Ricky thinking of me like that. It really was gross. Lucien was the first guy I ever wanted. I didn't even know I could feel that way before him. When he asked if I'd ever thought of Ricky and Galen that way, I nearly gagged.

It was offensive that he thought I liked men I considered brothers, but worse, that he felt entitled to ask. I didn't question him about women he felt attracted to or the ones he slept with. I didn't even ask the name of his original mate. Our individual pasts and past interests were our own business unless we felt like sharing.

"Hey, Rogue, ready to have your ass kicked?" Rhys asked, his smirk still in place.

"Ready to watch you cry again, Pack Bitch." I sneered.

Lucien growled, and Ricky put a hand on his shoulder. He shook his head at my mate, letting him know this wasn't the time. Rhys and I would always be like this. It was nice to hit someone I disliked. It was a shame he looked so much like my friends.

"First match is me and the bitch. You two Alphas can fight each other. I'll watch after he's on the ground. Shouldn't take more than a minute," I announced and went to an empty patch of grass, followed by Rhys.

I watched his movement as we circled. He was more fluid than before. That earned an appreciative nod from me. Unfortunately, he still telegraphed and was really stuck on the idea of a certain fighting combination being the best. It didn't take long before he was on the ground.

"Use different moves, Rhys. I'm getting bored," I groaned as he limped to the side.

His next couple of fights wouldn't go well. He wouldn't quit until I hurt him. Poor boy.

I sat on the grass and watched Ricky and Lucien fight. They were both very good. Fluid, instinctual movements, solid observation, quick thinking, and acting. I could tell they'd landed a few punches on each other, but neither was down. It had only taken me a little less than two minutes to take Rhys down.

Glancing over, I could see Rhys was watching them and probably regretting his choice of group. He was basically an Alpha-blood wolf fighting three true Alphas. He just wasn't a match for us at all.

I turned back to the fight to see Lucien take a hard hit to the stomach and hunch over. Ricky approached haughtily. I knew this move. When I'd hit Lucien, I'd been closer. He was feigning injury to get Ricky in range.

Once Ricky was close enough, Lucien sprung up and gave him a powerful uppercut. If there wasn't a wall handy, I guess that would do. Ricky sprawled on the ground and I saw him weakly tap. A feeling of pride washed over me. That was my mate, the strongest Alpha male. It turned me on.

He helped Ricky up and let him lean on him for support until he could sit him on the grass near me. Rhys crawled over and sat next to his brother. Lucien held his hand out to me.

"We should let them rest, would you like to fight me, chouchoutte?" he asked.

"Most definitely," I purred.

"Oh, Goddess, it's foreplay. Gross," Ricky groaned.

We laughed and headed to the spot where Ricky and Lucien had fought. I bit my lip and stood with my knees together and my hands behind my back. The innocent girl pose was one of my favorite ways to start. Lucien's eyes took me in with a lustful sheen.

I noted he was favoring his left leg. Ricky enjoyed attacking the dominant leg to weaken his opponent. Lucien was watching me, but I gave nothing away. I just waited.

He tired of waiting for me to attack and took the initiative. Lucien struck, throwing a punch meant to knock me out. He had to bend down to reach, but ended up over-extending, as some people did when fighting someone much shorter than them. I bent backward until my hands could reach the ground, twisted my legs around his neck, and rolled.

His body landed with a thud as I held his head locked between my legs. Lucien reached up to work on pulling me off. I fought off his hands as best I could, but he finally knocked me down. It turned into a grappling match for a while until I slipped from his grasp and kicked him in the chest.

Lucien got up and winced. A rib must have cracked. Breathing would be hard for a while. I might actually win this.

The idea of me being pregnant obviously distracted him. Even if he didn't mean to, he was going easy on me. It made part of me bristle, but I kind of liked that he was so protective of our imaginary baby.

We fought a little longer. Lucien landed a few good hits and kicks, none anywhere near my stomach. We were both bloody and bruised, but neither one would give up. Both of us wanted to see who would really win. In the end, we had to call it a draw.

"Another stalemate, chouchoutte," he chuckled as we lay on the grass.

"Seems to be our destiny. Maybe we should try it when you don't think I'm pregnant." I giggled.

"That's ridiculous. I don't think you're pregnant," he scoffed as his face turned red.

"Mm-hmm." I snorted. "Of course not. That's absolutely not why none of your hits landed in my stomach, or why you didn't throw me once."

He was quiet for a while. It wouldn't take long before we were mobile again. I wondered what was going through his head. He was probably cursing his inability to fight me without some sort of hindrance to his ability. Alphas love to win, and a tie isn't a win.

Chapter 39: A Sexy Shower

[Bellamy]

Ricky made his way over to where we were and then stood directly above us. "So, I think we should call that good for today. Rhys is a little scared of fighting Lucien now, and I don't want to fight Ames if she might be pregnant."

"I'm not pregnant, Ricky," I growled.

He laughed and sat next to us while we waited to heal enough to get up.

"There were three openings where I could've killed you, Lucien. Don't go easy on an opponent because they aren't male. If they're smaller, like I am, you need to focus on kicking, then punch when they're down. You hyper-extended and I could have broken your neck when I grabbed you," I said.

"I'll work on that. I'm not used to fighting people over a foot shorter than me," he replied. "You weren't moving as smoothly as you normally do. Just because this is practice, is no reason to let your form fall. Halfway through it was like you stopped trying. I wouldn't have gotten nearly as many hits in if you were going as fast as I know you can."

"Got it. It was probably because it looked like I could win with little effort, so I stopped putting the effort in." I sighed. "I need to work on that."

Rising to a sitting position, a smile spread across both our faces as our eyes met. With someone equally matched in fighting ability, my training would improve significantly, pushing me to my limits. I found his insights helpful.

We stood up with Ricky's help and returned to the packhouse. It was a decent workout, but nothing compared to what I do at home. But the sparring was so good, it made up for everything.

Lucien locked the door when we got to our room. I turned and sprung onto him, wrapping my arms around his neck and my legs around his waist. He grinned at me and pressed me against the nearby wall. He captured my lips in a searing kiss, his body grinding against mine, the heat of his skin igniting a fire within me. It was heavenly. I wanted him ever since I saw him beat up Ricky.

"We need to get to breakfast, chouchoutte. Let's take a shower and get dressed. We have plenty of time to indulge in each other before we leave. And I fully intend to," he purred.

"A sexy shower?" I asked hopefully.

Lucien groaned and kissed my neck. "It would save time… good thinking."

I squealed as he bit down on my mark, pleasure ripping through me like electricity. He chuckled as he carried me into the bathroom, setting me down while he turned on the shower. I pulled off my clothing as quickly as I could and was completely nude by the time he turned back.

Lucien licked his lips as he took in the sight of me. I loved the look in his eyes. It made me feel like I was the most beautiful woman in existence.

"Well… strip, Lucien. We don't have all day," I said as I walked past him, trailing my fingers over his muscular waist as I passed.

I'd only just stepped into the spray of water when his hands slipped under my arms and encircled my breasts. I leaned back against him as he massaged and manipulated them with his strong, thick fingers. He turned me around and caressed my face before reaching down and lifting me, settling himself inside me and pressing me to the cold tile wall.

I yelped and arched away from the icy tiles. He didn't seem bothered as he started pushing into me harder with each stroke. He was hitting all the sensitive spots inside me, creating wave after wave of delicious shocks that built into an overwhelming wave of ecstasy. My muscles clenched around him as he pushed into me faster and harder.

It was different from last night, but just as wonderful. I squeaked as I felt him hitting deep inside me. Even that felt different. There was still some pain, but it was like the pain my body had after a good fight. I craved the feeling of him demanding entrance to my deepest parts.

When he came, it was powerful. More than either of the other two times. It felt never-ending as he pulsed and jerked inside me. Even Lucien seemed surprised.

"If you weren't pregnant before, you are now, chouchoutte," he gasped.

I laughed as he slowly let me down from my perch. Quickly, I rinsed my hair, washing it too often, made it static-y, and I'd just washed yesterday. Grabbing a washcloth, I added soap and started washing myself. I needed breakfast after all the activity of the last twelve hours.

Lucien diligently cleaned himself as well. He was probably just as hungry as I was. I helped him wash his back, and he helped with mine. He probably didn't realize how important helping clean each other was to rogue born wolves.

It was one thing I'd noticed while living in the Limb Torn Collective. A lot of couples would clean and brush each other. I knew one guy who would give his mate manicures and pedicures.

Now I knew why everyone looked so blissful when they did it. When I'd washed him before we marked each other, it was good, but this was a whole new level of pleasure.

It was amazing to be cared for and to know I was caring for my mate. Did pack wolves feel the same, I wondered? I never saw my parents brush each other. I'd see them groom each other in their wolf forms, but never human.

We got out of the shower, dried off, and dressed for the day. I picked a dark pink tank top and wore a thin white t-shirt with a stylized pale pink rose on it, and a dark green handkerchief skirt that stopped mid-thigh. Normally, I wore bicycle shorts with it, but I didn't want to this time. I could sit like a girl for one day.

Lucien was wearing comfortable looking tan slacks with a royal blue polo. I loved how the color made his skin look even more delectable. He held out his hand, and we headed to the dining room.

Chapter 40: Traveling and Tiaras

We spent much of our day preparing for the mission at Lune Rouge. I was eager to make sure Lucien and Dilly knew their roles. Especially Lucien.

As the target, he was at more risk than any of us. Though, I might have drawn a little bit of a target on my back by becoming Luna of his pack. At least I was going into it knowing what I was getting into.

After lunch, we said our goodbyes. Janie promised to send pictures when the baby was born. Ricky told me they'd be at our wedding. I just had to give them a date once we'd figured it out. Ty was going to come with his mate, too. I was excited to know I'd have my whole family there.

Since I didn't think I'd ever find a suitable partner, I hadn't given much thought to weddings. Unlike Cara, I wouldn't go to extremes. I don't need to be a princess. I'm already a queen.

Dilly drove and Lucien sat in the front passenger seat while we headed home. He needed a lot more legroom than the backseat could afford. I sat behind Dilly and Lucien reached his hand back to clasp mine as we drove.

I called Cara on the way home to let her know, so she wouldn't hear it from anyone else. She was thrilled until I told her it would take place before hers. Then she yelled at me about not taking my wedding seriously. Her rant lasted nearly an hour. Lucien and Dilly looked pretty awestruck at some of her reasoning.

"How can you take your marriage vows seriously if you aren't dressed like the royalty you are? Will you even have a tiara? How can you get married without a tiara, Bellamy?!" she lectured over the phone.

I hadn't realized a tiara was required.

Eventually, she calmed down with a pouty 'do what you want, you always do' and told me we'd talk more about it when I got to Lune Rouge. I wasn't looking forward to that conversation.

We reached home in record time. Dilly was on fire, wanting to get back as soon as he could so he could tell everyone Lucien and I planned to get married. I told him he couldn't tell my parents, but everyone else was free to know.

When we pulled up to the packhouse, my parents were waiting along with my team. Seeing Galen, Sam, and Freddy out of their casts was such a relief. I'm sure Freddy's mate was pretty pissed off at me. I would have an apology gift sent before we left.

My parents looked concerned. I knew they were probably still worried I was mad, but I really wasn't. Not entirely. I was mad the issue with Lucien made me act out of character enough that people thought I would hurt a border guard. It opened us up to the infiltration. But I wasn't mad about them talking to him. They tried to do the right thing, it just backfired.

"Hi, Mommy. Hi, Daddy. We're back." I smiled.

They looked relieved and came over to hug me.

"I'm so sorry, Amy. We really weren't trying to mess things up," my mom cried.

"Please forgive us, Amy. We'll make it up to you," my dad promised.

"Of course. You didn't mean to upset Lucien, it just happened. I'm sorry I hurt Galen and scared you. I'm sorry I was rude when I came home from my mission," I said.

"We forgive you, sweetheart. You had a hard experience. The way you cover up your pain makes us think you're alright when you're not. We should know better. We failed," Dad said, softly.

"You did your best. That's all you can do. I need to go talk to my boys." I smiled and headed over to my team.

Dilly had joined them after handing off our bags and keys to the omegas standing by. They all looked very serious. I was hopeful they would accept my apology. I didn't want to lose their trust.

I bowed deeply. "I'm very sorry. As your leader, I shouldn't have let my own problems affect my treatment of you. Please accept my apology."

I stayed like that for a while, waiting. They knew I wouldn't stand until they said something one way or the other.

"Captain, you've always looked out for us. We all have each other's backs. Sometimes we fail, and sometimes life gets in our way. Your mate explained that you left so you wouldn't harm anyone else. No one here feared you, but we were worried you would do something you couldn't take back to someone too weak to defend themselves. That would hurt you deeply. We need our captain strong if we're going to be hunting bears and saving Alphas," Jason stated.

I stood up and grinned at my men. They were really the best in every way. I was glad Lucien thought of that story. It made me seem less weak and selfish. I would definitely not be correcting anyone.

Alpha Kieran met us in the entryway with Toby, Daisy, and Bren.

"The girls are waiting for you at the jewelry shop. We contacted them when you got to the border. You still have necklaces to try on. My daughter called and said something about you needing a tiara…." He quirked his eyebrow.

I looked at Lucien. Of course, Cara called her father. If we didn't say something now, someone would before we got the chance.

"I've asked Bellamy to marry me," Lucien smiled and took my hand. "I'll go with you to the jewelry store, chouchoutte. We can pick out a ring while you and your friends are trying on necklaces."

"Oh, Goddess! My baby's getting married!" my mom squealed.

Daisy and Bren ran to hug her, and they bounced. They were so cute sometimes. I couldn't help but laugh. I closed my eyes.

'Mama, Papa, I'm getting married. I found a mate who loves me. Please watch over us,' I silently prayed.

My stomach twisted a little. This was all too much. Too noisy, too many people. I backed out of the house, pulling Lucien with me.

Once we were outside, I took a deep breath. No matter how much time I spent with pack wolves, I couldn't deal with the way they celebrated things with group hugs and screaming. Large groups weren't really my thing, either.

"Are you okay, chouchoutte?" Lucien asked.

"Yes, mon saucisson. It just got too loud, too fast. Let's walk to the store. It's only a ten-minute walk from here. They can wait. I've waited for them enough." I smiled and led him toward town.

As we walked, I leaned against him. Another natural wolf trait rogue born wolves tended toward. We leaned against our mates when we were together. It made us feel happier. Like a hug, but not as constricting.

I hummed the song my mama used to sing to me when I was little. The tune always made me feel calmer. When I did have a pup, I planned to sing it to them, like she did to me. It was one way my pup would be close to my mother.

"Are you sure you want to do this, chouchoutte? We only just got back, and I'm pretty sure we nearly died a few times on the road," Lucien whispered.

"This'll be okay. It's an hour to look at shiny things and listen to the girls squeal over them. Then we can walk back. This helps. Being with you, leaning on you, touching you. And you'll be with me," I murmured as we approached the shop.

He opened the shop door. I walked in to see April, Molly, and Charlie hunched over cases. They didn't even look up. I heard their linked conversation, though.

'Amy better have a damned good excuse for making us wait,' April linked them.

'She never does. It's always 'warrior business' or 'rogue stuff'. It's like she doesn't even care about Cara's wedding,' Charlie replied.

'Because she's never going to have one of her own. It was too bad that Kyle guy wasn't hers, then we wouldn't have to deal with her anymore,' April responded.

'This must be pretty painful for her. She and Cara do everything together. Maybe that's why she seems like she doesn't care. I couldn't stand not being with my mate.'

'Stop rubbing it in that you found your mate, Molly. We don't need to hear it.' April snipped.

'I wasn't rubbing anything in. I was just saying-' Molly was cut off by an exasperated Charlie.

'Quit fighting. If she's not here in five minutes, then we'll pick the jewelry and she'll have to deal with it.' Charlie fumed.

I wanted to turn around and leave. April was in a mood, and it always made me grumpy when she was a bitch. Molly didn't have a mate when I last saw her, though. I wanted to know everything.

Chapter 41: Engagements

"Sir, may I see your engagement rings," Lucien said, stepping around me.

His voice drew the attention of the bridesmaids. I wiggled my fingers at them and walked over to where they were standing. Molly grinned and took my hands in hers when I got there.

"I found my mate! He's an ex-pack child in the collective! Alpha Kieran says he can join our pack once you release him. Can you release him, Amy? Please!" she begged.

"Of course. Is he on pack lands today? Can he be here before we're done?" I asked.

"I'll call him now! Thank you so so so much!" Molly squealed and pulled out her phone to call.

I was happy an ex-pack child found a pack to call home. I always felt bad for them, having to be banished with their parents even if they did nothing wrong, or losing their entire pack and having no family in other packs willing to take them in. It was a tough existence and the primary reason for my re-inclusion program.

"Finally, Amy. Where have you been? Alpha Kieran called us almost an hour ago," April growled.

"It was like thirty minutes, maximum. I was out of town. I had to address some 'warrior business' before I could come. Now, let me take care of this 'rogue stuff' and we can get started. Why don't you ladies ask the clerk to pull the options Cara picked and any of the ones you thought were nice. If we like something enough, I can talk Cara into pretty much anything." I smiled.

April rolled her eyes and Charlie bit her lips together. I knew they wanted to say something, but were afraid to say it to my face. They went to talk to the other clerk while I waited for Molly.

She finally returned with a grin. "He can be here in forty-five minutes! I hope we won't be done before then."

"When have Charlie and April ever made a decision in less than an hour?" I snickered. "I can wait if we, miraculously, do."

"Thank you. I'm so happy. I love him so much. He's perfect in every way. Oops! I'm sorry, Amy!" Molly covered her mouth with her hand in horror.

I could hear April and Charlie snickering. They certainly got over the fact that they also didn't have mates pretty quickly. I guess they didn't hear Dilly's rumor, or see the mark on my neck.

"Chouchoutte, I have a few options. Can you come look?" Lucien called.

"Coming, mon saucisson," I replied. "Go help the girls. I'll be back soon."

I walked over to the counter where Lucien was standing. He had four rings in front of him. I looked at them. They were all beautiful, but right away, I saw two that wouldn't work.

"The big diamond is a no-go, love. I don't do big stones. The smaller one won't work either. I'd hate to lose the ring because I have to take it off for work and diamonds catch light easily, so I couldn't really wear it on a chain. Hmm." I inspected my options.

'What the hell is she doing? Who is that guy?' April asked in their link.

'I don't know, but he's hot. Damn,' Charlie responded.

'Maybe he's a rogue, too,' Molly said.

*'She **would** bring a rogue into town. Probably wanting to show him off. Pathetic.'* April scoffed.

One ring caught my eye. It was a matte white gold band with two inset holes for tear cut stones to make a heart. I picked it up and looked closer. Nothing big and flashy about it, no fancy designs, just a ring with a heart. I smiled and looked up at Lucien.

"Can we get this one with a pink and a green topaz in the settings?" he asked.

"Let me see if I have any stones that match the cut and size, if not I can get them cut and set then send them to your pack, Alpha Lucien," the clerk said.

"Thank you." Lucien smiled. He turned to me. "I think that will look perfect on you, chouchoutte. Can I put it on you?"

I nodded and handed him the ring. He took my hand and kissed the spot where the ring would rest before slipping it on my finger. It fit perfectly. I only hoped they had the stones he asked for.

"Why topaz?" I asked. It wasn't either of our birthstones.

"It was once believed that wearing topaz increased body heat." He winked.

I laughed. "Using human superstitions to get me pregnant, now? I guess you lost faith in your… abilities."

"I have tons of faith in my abilities, but every little bit helps," Lucien grinned.

"I should probably pick one for you," I said.

"Chouchoutte, I don't need one right now."

"If you collar me, I collar you, Alpha," I whispered.

His eyes turned dark with lust. "I can see you in a collar, ma belle."

I took a deep, shuddering breath. "I can see you in one, too, mon cœur. Maybe we should stop at the pet store on the way home."

He bent down and pulled me to him, pressing his lips to mine. I wrapped my arms around his neck and held him tight while he lifted me and put my legs around his waist. The whole world fell away as he delved into my mouth with his super-talented tongue and reminded me of all the things he made me feel last night. I moaned into his mouth. I needed him in the worst way.

After a few minutes, a man cleared his throat. "Umm… Alpha Lucien? Sorry to interrupt. We have the stones you wanted. I just need the ring back from your Luna so I can set them."

Lucien placed another soft kiss on my lips before lowering me to the ground. I took off the ring and handed it to the clerk. He smiled tightly.

"Thank you. I'll be right back."

"Amy, the necklaces are ready. Come decide with us," Molly called.

"Have him pull all men's rings in your size. I'll come look when I'm done with the girls," I told Lucien.

"Of course, chouchoutte. Have fun."

I went back to where the girls were set up with the necklaces. They were all very pretty. There were three that I felt would really look nice with the neckline of the dress we were wearing.

"Who's that guy you were making out with?" Molly asked.

"My mate. Alpha Lucien Deveraux. We found each other just a couple hours after I last saw you all. He's perfect," I said softly.

"Bull. You're stealing him from a pack wolf who deserves him," April replied snottily.

"I know you don't get it, but that's not my problem. Our wolves chose each other. He is mine and I am his," I said and looked more closely at the necklaces.

"A rogue can't be a Luna. There are better options. Options who are proper, well-bred pack wolves," she said in a snippy tone. "Not some rogue born trash. Alpha Kieran shouldn't have let you in our pack. Cara's too simple to see what you are. A power-hungry, rogue slut."

Lucien growled from behind me. "You do *not* talk to my Luna like that!"

April yipped and cowered away from him. Pissing off an Alpha was a terrible idea. I had no clue what she was even thinking, saying that stuff out loud instead of keeping it to herself and linking it to others like she normally did.

I turned and put my hand on his chest. "Lucien, please. I'm used to April's hate. Don't get upset, my love. She's not worth it."

"No one should talk to you like that, Bellamy. I'll speak with Kieran about this," he stated.

"Don't, Lucien. I don't need to go running to the Alpha because some girl doesn't like me. She just got over-excited and said the things she's only ever linked others before," I murmured.

"They can pick the necklace themselves. Come choose my ring, chouchoutte. I don't want you around such a hideous girl," Lucien insisted.

"This is for Cara. I won't let someone's hate ruin the celebration of my best friend's love. Go wait for me. I promise I'll be done as soon as I can," I said softly.

He growled at April again, but turned to leave after giving me a kiss on top of my head.

I turned back to the counter and started talking to Molly about her thoughts, completely ignoring April. Molly agreed with me about three of the options working better. Charlie liked a festoon style necklace with white and pale pink stones. It wasn't one of the options Cara picked, but it looked absolutely perfect when I pictured the pink of the dresses.

"I think we can talk her into this one, Charlie. It'll look fantastic on you and goes really well with the dress style and color. What do you think, Molly?" I asked.

"I like it. I could totally wear it on other occasions, too. April?" She turned to the, now quiet, final member of our party.

"I don't like it. We should go with the pink and pearl choker. It's sexier. I'd be able to wear it other times," April answered coolly.

I looked at the choker. The dresses had a sweetheart neckline. I felt it would look nice to have something that hung a little, but I could see her point.

"Why don't we do both? If the choker is worn a little high, then the festoon necklace won't be crowded. Let me show you," I said and put on both necklaces.

When I turned around, Molly, Charlie, and April examined the look. They smiled and nodded. I was glad they liked it. April could really dig in on things she wanted. She was a little spoiled.

I took off the necklaces, and we placed the order. Charlie and April left, but Molly stayed behind to wait for her mate. She came over and stood next to me as I joined Lucien at the counter.

"Amy, I'm glad you found a mate. You did a lot for our pack. You deserve to be happy," Molly said softly.

"Thanks, Molly. Lucien, this is my friend Molly. I need to release her mate from the collective so he can join the pack. We're gonna stick around until he gets here." I smiled.

"Nice to meet you, Molly. Don't spend too much time with that ugly girl. Her kind of ugly rubs off on a person," Lucien replied.

I shook my head and looked over my options. There were about fifteen rings in the store that would fit his finger. Matte was better than polished because it cut down on reflections in the dark. There was a beautiful dark tungsten band with a strip of moonstone encircling it.

Moonstone was my birthstone. According to those crystal healing sites, it was supposed to soothe emotions and relieve stress. Exactly what my mate needed.

Picking up the ring, I held it up for Lucien to see. He took it from me and looked at it with a smile.

"It's beautiful, chouchoutte."

"That's moonstone, my love. It's supposed to help with providing calmness," I told him.

"Precisely what I need." He winked. "Especially with an Alpha for a mate."

I laughed. "I thought the exact same thing. Shall we get it?"

"Of course," Lucien smiled and turned to the clerk. "We'll take both, and send the statement to Lune Rouge. We'll pay as soon as it is received."

"Yes, Alpha. Would you like them in boxes or will you wear them out?" the clerk asked.

"We'll wear them out. Thank you," Lucien replied.

He picked up my ring from the counter and slipped it on my ring finger. Lucien handed me the ring we picked for him and I slid it onto his finger. We didn't need the ceremony. We were already married in our hearts. The wedding was just for everyone else. He bent down and kissed me softly.

Chapter 42: Releasing Declan

[Bellamy]

'Queen Bellamy, there's a rogue at the border requesting entry. Did you want me to contact Drake or should I send this man through?'

"Molly, what's your mate's name?" I asked.

"Declan Moss."

"Seriously? Molly Moss?" I snickered.

"Don't tease. I can't help the fact that the Moon Goddess didn't consult my parents when she picked my mate," she pouted.

'Is his name Declan Moss?'

'Yes, Queen Bellamy.'

'Send him through. I'm expecting him.'

'He's heading your way.'

'Thank you!'

A few minutes later, a man entered the shop, and Molly's face lit up. He was fairly tall, as most werewolves were, and thickly built. He had dirty blond hair and green eyes with dimples that showed as he smiled at Molly.

"Sorry, I'm late. They weren't going to let me through. I was arguing for ten minutes with the guards." He apologized and bowed. "I'm Declan Moss. I've been a member of your collective for four years."

"You don't have to bow, Declan. Let's head up to the packhouse. We can get you released and accepted after I've looked over your file," I said.

"Thank you, Queen Bellamy." Declan smiled.

He went to Molly and held her tightly. It made me smile, too. I always loved seeing members of my pack find their mates. They were always so blissful. Until I found Lucien, I didn't think I'd ever have that.

We left the shop and headed back to the house. I linked Kieran to let him know what was going on and he said he'd meet us in the entry.

Leaning against Lucien, I walked and hummed. I wanted my mama to see me as happy as she'd been with my papa. I felt her around me when I hummed the song.

When we arrived, Kieran took Molly and Declan to his office to get to know the new member of his pack and figure out a place for him. Lucien followed me to my office. I punched in the code to unlock the door, turned on the light, and went to my file cabinet to pull Declan's file.

"How many rogues are in your collective?" Lucien asked, sitting in one of the chairs on the other side of my desk.

"Two hundred and fifty, give or take," I answered and sat at my desk to look over the file.

That was never a question I enjoyed answering with an honest number. It made the pack wolves nervous. I had nearly three hundred. It wasn't the amount of people that mattered; it was the amount of actual territory that mattered in a collective. If you have five hundred wolves, but they live in a pack-like town, and your neighboring collective has one hundred, but spans the size of a western state county, you have the smaller collective. Too many wolves, and not enough resources.

"That's a lot of rogues," he breathed.

"Yep. Largest in the region," I replied distractedly.

They exiled Declan, his mother, father, and two sisters. The Beta accused Declan's father of having an affair with his wife. He and his own wife swore he hadn't, but the Beta insisted on banishing them. They weren't from the region and had come to my collective because of the rumors that it was a safe place.

In the four years they'd been in my collective, Declan excelled in the private school I'd created for rogues; he was valedictorian of his class. He did very well in the rogue warrior training. There were no reports of fighting or improper use of his wolf. No issues with the pack. Or any of its members. All in all, a good boy.

"Queen Bellamy?" Lucien said quietly.

"Yes, Alpha Lucien?"

"You look really sexy right now," he purred.

I looked up at him. He was staring at me with that dark, lustful gaze again. My heart beat wildly. I wanted him so badly it hurt.

"That is inappropriate, Alpha Lucien. What would you do if I interrupted your work to say something like that and give you bedroom eyes?" I scoffed.

"I'd bend you over my desk and take you roughly from behind until you were crying from the amount of pure pleasure I was unleashing upon your naughty little body," Lucien growled.

I swallowed hard. That sounded amazing. I closed the folder and stood, picking it up and walking around the desk. I paused in front of the chair and looked down at him.

"I suppose that's the difference between an Alpha and a Queen. I have to go deliver this file and assist in the release and acceptance of my rogue. You can stay here," I said in a cool voice.

Lucien seemed a little upset. I leaned in close.

"You better be in that seat, naked from the waist down when I get back, Alpha," I commanded.

A slow smile crossed his face. "Yes, Queen Bellamy."

With that, I left and headed down the hall to Kieran's office. I handed him the file and went to stand between Declan and Molly. They were sitting in the guest chairs in front of his desk.

"Alpha Kieran, if your interview went well, I see no reason this wolf cannot be released from my collective to join your pack. He's skilled and intelligent. I think he would make an ideal candidate for the upcoming opening with the Elite Ten," I stated.

Kieran nodded. We'd done this before. He trusted me to assess the wolves who wanted to transfer into his pack, and I took it seriously.

"I'll accept him. While they're on their mission, he'll train with the other elite warriors. When they return, the captain will evaluate him," Kieran said.

Molly looked excited and reached out to grasp her mate. Being an elite warrior meant he wouldn't have to get another job. The Alpha paid the elites well for their work for the pack. It was an ideal post.

"Declan, please stand. Molly, I need you nearby so he doesn't get lost. This is harder on ex-pack rogues than on those of us born rogues," I told them.

Declan stood and Molly stood nearby. I took a deep breath and focused on him. I could hear Kieran readying his supplies. Pack born wolves needed to be brought in quickly. Especially unmarked ones.

"Declan Moss, you are no longer welcome as a member of the Eaten Heart Collective. Your links and connections have been severed. Goddess watch over you," I said as I removed his tie to my wolf.

It was incredibly painful to release wolves. I wished it were as easy as it was for pack Alphas. Banishment only needed a few words, and it just happened. Alphas didn't have the same connection to their people that I did.

Declan's eyes went wide, and he started hyperventilating. Molly stepped forward and held his hand. She whispered soothingly to him.

'Molly, ask him if he wants to join your pack and be with you. Turn him to Alpha Kieran when he accepts and say "Alpha, this wolf would like to join our pack, will you accept him?" The ceremony will begin from there.'

'Got it.'

Molly did as I said. She was great at following direction. It was no wonder April liked having her in her little group. Kieran said his ritual and mixed their blood as he had when I joined the pack. I held the bowl to collect it, since Molly was hanging on to Declan, keeping him calm.

Kieran smiled. "Welcome to the Daylight Moon Pack, Declan Moss."

"Thank you, Alpha." Declan bowed and then hugged Molly.

"Thank you, Amy. I hope you and your mate have a wonderful life together." She smiled at me.

"Same to you." I nodded. "I need to get back to my office, an important matter needs my attention there. See you at dinner, Alpha Kieran."

"See you then, Queen Bellamy." He waved and sat in his seat, directing the others to sit.

Kieran would outline the next steps and introduce Declan to Clint and Drake. I left the room and headed back down the hall to my office. As I was about to reach for the knob, my father stepped out of his office.

"Amy, can I talk to you for a moment?" he asked.

"Sure thing, Daddy," I replied.

'Sorry, Lucien. My dad needs to talk to me. You might want to lock the door if you're planning to stay in there. I'll be done as soon as I can.'

'When we get to Lune Rouge, my strategic meetings with the rogue Queen will all be locked door. No interruptions allowed.'

'That sounds very conducive to successful and… satisfying meetings.'

Chapter 43: Curses

I followed my father to his office. It was about halfway between mine and Kieran's. Unlike my office, he had a window. His was also more spacious and very similar to Kieran's office in a lot of ways. We sat in the armchairs and he got that look like he was trying to put words together.

"Your mother wants to know more about the wedding." He smiled.

"I'll talk about it at dinner. That way I don't have to repeat myself too much," I replied.

"Good. Good. Now, there's some stuff I wanted to talk to you about. It's about marking and… things that come after." Dad looked nervous.

Oh, Goddess. He wasn't trying to give me 'the talk', was he? I would nope on out of there if he did. I didn't want to talk to my dad about that stuff.

"As you know, you're going to start your heat soon. You need to be prepared for what can happen." He cringed.

"Please, stop. Shouldn't Mom be talking to me about this?" I winced.

"She doesn't understand."

"So this isn't a sex talk then? Because I was on the camping trip where the girls were conceived. She understands sex." I snickered.

Dad blushed.

"This is about males, not females. Have you talked to Lucien about any of your past relationships, people you were attracted to, or men you may have flirted with in past heats?" Dad asked.

"He asked me if I was ever attracted to Ricky or Galen. I told him it wasn't any of his business. I didn't ask about his, he has no right to ask about mine," I replied.

"That might not be good. In the first heat of a mating, the male often becomes violently jealous. Since Lucien is as strong as you, I needed to see if anyone was in danger of an attack. Galen should wait until your heat is done to head to Lune Rouge. If you look at him in a way that makes Lucien jealous, he could get hurt," he said.

"This is so stupid. I have *never* been attracted to *any* male. *Ever.* I was just mad and made it seem like I might have. Galen is my brother. That's super gross." I stuck out my tongue.

"You're… not pretending… that was an honest answer. You're eighteen and you've *never* been attracted to a male at all?" he asked, leaning in.

"No. Is that not right? I didn't give it much thought. My life was already too complicated, and a boyfriend would have only made things worse. I appreciated how they looked, but I didn't want to do anything with them," I answered.

Dad looked thoughtful. "During your first heat, the thing with Bruce…"

"When he came into my room and I kicked his ass?" I asked.

"You were in the height of it. You shouldn't have been defensive… I never thought of it. When you have your heat, during the active times, what does it feel like?" he pressed.

This was going somewhere, and I was pretty curious. One thing Dad and I really connected on was our desire for knowledge. If he was asking questions, that meant something was there to investigate.

"It felt like stabbing, burning pain. I didn't want to eat, I had to force myself to drink, I couldn't really move."

He shook his head. "I asked Olive once what it was like, so I could have a better idea. She said it was like she was always aroused and aching for completion."

"It's nothing like that for me. Maybe it's a rogue thing? No, if it were none of them would have the amount of children they do. I know young rogue born wolves are interested in dating and mating," I said, trying to think.

"Have you ever had a crush on anyone? Mild puppy love? Anything?" Dad asked.

"When I was seven I had a crush on Stanton. He was ten years older than me, but cared about me a lot. I asked if he'd marry me when I was older. He refused. Said I was like a sister and he wasn't attracted to werewolves," I whispered.

"But no interest in males after. Pain during heat. Before you were marked, did anyone touch you?"

"In what way? I don't get what you're asking," I replied.

He sighed. "I don't like asking this… In a… you know… sexual way." Dad winced.

I bit my lips together. "The vampires. Marion rubbed between my legs when he talked about giving me pups to care for. He kissed me. His family line creates pleasure with their saliva. Inducing orgasm with their bites if the victim is properly prepared. When he bit me, I passed out. It wasn't from pleasure, it was power and pain. When I woke up, I was stripped and tied to the coffee table. I didn't know what was going on."

He covered his mouth. There was a pained look in his eyes. I'd only told Ricky what happened. My dad was onto something, so he had to know. I wanted to make sure I wasn't unhealthy. If there was anything to stop me from having pups with Lucien, I needed to know.

I continued. "Marion said he tasted something and needed confirmation. He… he put his finger in me and it hurt. It hurt worse than my first time with Lucien. He rubbed something that was extremely painful. I begged him to stop hurting me and he moved it out to touch me outside.

"It was uncomfortable, but not as painful. When he licked my skin anywhere, it felt good, then started hurting. That was when he asked me if I knew anything about Lucien's condition and said he would hurt me again if I didn't tell him."

I could remember the look in his eye. He realized I'd been pretending to enjoy his kisses and touches. It was dangerous not to tell him.

"I told him about the vengeance of the goddess and how I heard it was cured. He untied me and had Clea get me some clothes. She picked out the tiniest, tightest dress. He told me to cook for Lucien, then dress and talk to him about marking me while he ate. Marion said I would be punished if I didn't come out of the room marked, but I knew I couldn't. I'd never fought Lucien. But Aurora wanted him from the moment Marion told me to get him to mark me."

"Then the demon dust and the fight, which led to the marking," Dad said.

I nodded. He sighed and stood, crossing to his bookshelves and looking them over until he found the one he was looking for and came back to sit. After a few moments of flipping pages, he read for a bit.

'Lucien, I'm not making it back anytime soon. You should probably head to the room or something.'

'I'm outside his office, chouchoutte. I heard everything,' he replied.

'Why were you listening to a private conversation, Lucien?!'

'Because I love you and your parents are bad at private conversations. Can I come in? I want to hear what he's thinking.'

'I'm worried. What if there's something wrong with me? What if someone poisoned me? What if I can't have pups at all?' I asked him in our link.

'Don't worry. We can adopt. I just want you, Bellamy. Anything else is icing.'

'Come in. I'd rather have you here than have you out there.'

I told my dad Lucien was coming, since this seemed serious and could involve him. He nodded and continued reading. This was completely stressing me out.

Lucien walked into the room and stood by my chair. He pulled me out of it and then sat with me on his lap. I curled up and rested my head under his chin. Lucien stroked my back while we waited for my dad to finish what he was reading.

"I don't know why they would have done it, though…" Dad whispered.

"Done what?" I asked.

"You have all the signs of a female with the vengeance of the goddess, but you were too young and not a pack wolf. There was no way for you to have gotten it. The only other option is a chastity curse. It mimics the vengeance of the goddess, but in any species and without the normal cause. It's cured the same way, too. I just don't know why." He shook his head and muttered.

"I was a taste tester for King Fuller. He decided he would pick a child to test food for him, figuring no one would poison a child just to get to him. King Fuller liked to have women without their consent. He would make it part of joining his collective.

"He would have prospective female members, mated or not, become his concubines for a year before they would officially join. Their mates and families would be permitted in while they were… working. You heard Marion, Lucien. King Fuller deflowered every female orphan he found. He liked them around thirteen or fourteen, just like Marion," I told them.

"Someone could have decided to curse him and you were collateral damage. Well, that's the bad news, I suppose." Dad smiled.

"What's the good news? Will it cause me any problems since it happened before puberty? Can I have babies, Daddy?" I asked.

"The good news is, one, you were cured without knowing it was a thing. Two, you could focus on building your territory and solidifying your collective because of it. Three, you've been in heat since Lucien marked you. That's why he suddenly asked if you were attracted to Warrick and Galen.

"It's probably also why he got so upset when we talked to him. The exhaustion makes sense, but males can get pretty emotional if they think their female doesn't really want them during this time. He's probably been having jealous thoughts, too," my dad explained.

My stomach twisted. I've been in heat since I was marked. There wasn't any pain. Just the constant desire for Lucien. I *could* have been pregnant this morning. Holy shit!

"Thank you, Daddy. I was beginning to worry. I know it wasn't supposed to happen until tonight, but I still was expecting something. That means my active heat will start tomorrow, not in two days! This messes up my timeline."

"No, it doesn't. Your active heat will be more like your mother's and Cara's. If you leave first thing in the morning, you should have all day before the scent starts. Since the vampires were up, that means you were marked after dark. Tomorrow night will be when it starts. Unless you're already pregnant," he told me.

Lucien tensed, and his hand moved from my hip to my stomach. I knew he was hopeful for a baby. I was, too. There was so much going on so fast, but I knew I could handle pretty much anything, especially to protect my family.

"Right, because pregnancy ends the progression of heat. I guess we'll find out in a couple days," I said, slipping back into Alpha mode. "I need to talk to the rogue patrols and get a defense plan put together for when I'm gone."

I pulled Lucien's arms off me and stood up. He looked confused. I smiled and caressed his cheek.

"Sorry, I forgot. I want to be sure we have everything in order. There's a lot to do to get my territory ready. You guys should hang out. Or you can go talk to Jason about what he needs to know about your pack," I said softly.

I sent a call out to the border patrol, asking them to bring the rogues to the lecture hall. They would help me a lot. I needed a plan of action and I wouldn't be able to relax until I had one.

"Will you be at dinner?" Dad asked.

"Yes. Please don't tell anyone about the curse. No one needs to know," I requested.

"I won't. We'll see you in a couple hours. I'll find someone to keep Lucien distracted so he won't interrupt you." Dad grinned.

"Thanks, Daddy. Lucien, be good. I'll see you at dinner. You can come sit in my office after or go to bed. I have a lot of work to do and I don't think I can get it all done in the two hours before dinner. Okay?" I smiled.

"Don't overdo it. I don't want to risk the baby if you are pregnant," he warned.

"Daddy, can you see if Dr. Hale or Dr. Cleary can come educate Lucien on rogue pregnancies? He doesn't get that I'm not as fragile as a pack wolf or a human." I asked.

"Sure thing, sweetheart. Go to your meeting, I've got this covered." Dad nodded.

I headed out the door to the end of the hall. Blocking the lecture hall door open and heading down to the front where a tall seat was. I didn't want to risk flashing the room, so I needed to climb up before anyone got there.

Chapter 44: Rogue Stuff

[Bellamy]

When I got seated, I straightened my skirt and prepared. Two young males entered the room. They were the same height, one with black hair, the other with brown. Both were relatively good looking. I didn't know their names, but I would remedy that before the meeting started. They stopped and slowly scanned over me. They were unmated, so it was to be expected.

With rogues, looking at an unmated female told her you found her attractive. It was like a compliment. But I wasn't unmated. They just weren't aware of it. I needed to send out an announcement before I left, so my collective would know.

"If you want to keep your eyes, take them off me," I growled.

They stiffened and bowed deeply.

"Apologies, Queen Bellamy," the black-haired one said.

They took seats in the front as the rest of the group filed in. The last one secured the door. In all, there were ten rogue born trackers, four females and six males. I had them go around the room and tell me their names. With nearly three hundred rogues, I couldn't remember them all.

"Thank you all for coming to work with the pack. We will make sure you are compensated. Has there been any sign of the bear since it left our territory?" I asked.

A young woman stood. Her name was… Jenny.

"I've been on the border it left from. No signs or scents," she reported.

The other wolves reported the same. It was good and bad. It meant we didn't know where the bear went after.

I got reports on the status of the borders and the barriers. Kieran would feed the vampire barrier and would continue until we had confirmation there would be no more incursions. I hoped all the vampires in the area had come from Marion's line. Any who were under three hundred needed their sire to live. They would've died when he did.

"Any other news?" I asked.

"Some of my cousins have requested to join. They'll be a big help. They come from the collectives in Alaska. Useful for hunting bear," a man called Ross offered.

"There's some paper and pencils at the back of the room. Before you leave, give me their names. I'll pull their applications and, if I approve them, I can swear them in before I leave. Anything else?" I looked around the room.

They shook their heads.

"I have just a little more for you before I let you go. First, an announcement. This announcement will go out to the whole collective via e-mail. I've made a mate offer and it was accepted. My mate and I have marked each other. Lucien Deveraux is my consort. He is my claw and my fang. His voice is mine," I stated.

They cheered. I smiled. People in my collective were loyal to me. Everything I did fueled our growth. Having a mate, as a rogue Alpha, was going to give us a stronger base. It would keep me from losing control and keep me stable.

"The second is a question. Could you all confirm for me, if I'm pregnant?" I asked.

Rogue born wolves could smell slight changes. If it had been long enough, there would be the slightest scent of hormone changes.

Because of the rapid nature of our pregnancies, they were detectible by normal means within a week of impregnation. Rogue noses caught it before a test would. Our sensitive senses of smell made for a great detector of a good many things.

"We can't tell. If you are, it's too soon. Your body isn't giving a clear signal. So… maybe?" Jenny shrugged.

The others nodded. It was too much to hope. They'd probably be able to tell in the morning.

"Would someone be willing to come see me in the morning and either give me a nod, shrug, or head shake? I need to know as soon as possible. If I'm going into a dangerous situation, I don't want to risk the child," I told them.

"I can," Troy announced. "I meet my patrolman here and we walk the running paths the warriors take."

"Thank you. That's it for me. Go and be awesome." I smiled.

They got up and started coming up to congratulate me on my mating before leaving. Ross went to the back to write the names of his cousins before returning with the paper and congratulating me as well.

Once they were gone, I climbed off the stool and headed to my office. I linked Galen to bring the files Drake had given him. He said he'd meet me in my office.

I went and sat at my desk. Pulling a map of the area out, I found Lune Rouge and plotted the most likely course to expand my territory. It covered a major city in the area and three smaller towns. I'd know better once we did the blood oath.

Galen knocked and peeked his head in the door. "No funny business going on in here, right?" he asked.

I laughed. "So you've walked in on them, too?"

"It was bad enough when I walked in on Alpha Kieran and Luna Daisy. Once I walked in on Mom and Dad. Both times, they'd forgotten they called me down. It was terrible. I wasn't about to walk in on my little sister getting nailed on her desk," he snorted.

"Gross. Never say anything like that again, Galen. That's an order from your captain." I winced.

"Trust me, I regretted it as soon as I said it." He shuddered and came in, closing the door. "Here are the files, you want any help getting through them?"

"Okay, I'm looking for these names in particular." I handed him the paper. "I'll need to call their ex-king to be sure they are what they say. We just don't have time for the traditional digging."

Galen nodded and split the stack in half. I looked through and pulled out three files. He pulled another two out of his half. We began reading.

It looked like they wanted to move to my collective for the security. That was often the case. Four were brothers, the fifth was the mate of one of the men. All were rogue born. I got the number for Jonas Harper from their file and called.

He was one of the High Kings of the Werewolf Association. The Alaskan territory he owned was the largest in the country. I was familiar with the High Kings, though I had never met them.

"Harper," he stated firmly when he picked up the phone.

"Hello, King Harper. This is Queen Bellamy Carrington of the Eaten Heart. I hope you're well."

"Queen Carrington, how can the Icy Death help you?" he asked.

"I have five prospective members looking to join me. They're from your collective. I'm trying to get applications sorted before I go visit a new territory I'm taking over," I told him and gave him the names.

Galen sat back in his chair and watched. My family and most of my boys had never seen me interact with another rogue Alpha. Rogues don't function the same way pack wolves do.

"Another expansion in less than two years. Congratulations. Soon you'll own the entire lower forty-eight." He chuckled.

"I intend to own the entire continent. Or, at least, have it be at peace," I replied coolly.

"I would like it to be at peace as well. Accept my offer of friendship, as the largest collective in the US, I want us to share our home."

"Of course, I accept. I will put our friendship in my books and keep it in my heart."

"I have the information."

"Did they leave peacefully and without crime or misbehavior?"

"Yes. Joy is pregnant. We have bear and pack problems. The whole family decided to move down," he answered.

"Great. Thank you. Anything else?"

"They were five of my best trackers. The boys are all third-generation rogues, Joy is first. Parents are dead on both sides."

"I will ensure they live to see their children grown," I promise.

"That's all I want for any of my collective. Safe days and journeys," he said, signaling the end of the conversation.

"Same to you. Don't die," I replied.

"Same to you." He hung up.

I replaced the phone on the cradle and signed off on accepting them. There was a number to the motel they were staying in. Before I called to have them come up to the packhouse, I called my lieutenant to come in with housing options. The collective would pay them directly for their skills and abilities. We would give them a home and they would only have to pay for utilities.

Galen sat quietly. He looked curious at times, but didn't question anything. The family was thrilled and would come after dinner to be sworn in. That was when my lieutenant, Henry, would guide them to their new home.

Henry was mated to Katie, the woman who brought me to Daylight Moon. They were both lieutenants for the town at the base of the forest mountain we lived on. She covered the work for the ex-packs there. He covered rogue born. They met through me and hit it off. I was happy she found a love match.

"All done. And it's nearly six-thirty." I grinned.

"That was cool, Amy. I've never seen you actually be a queen before. I hope my mate is as good at her job as you are." Galen chuckled.

"You'll find her, Galen. If nothing else, Charlie still has a crush on you." I winked.

He scoffed. "I'd rather not. The last thing I need is April thinking she's big shit because her friend is the Beta female. And you just know she would."

"Yeah. April's like that. Let's go get dinner. I hate rubbing it in, but I miss my mate," I told him.

"Never apologize for your happiness. I'll find mine. I believe you." Galen stood and left my office.

I straightened up my files and went to the dining room. Lucien was standing by the chairs we'd sat in the last time we had dinner at the packhouse. It would be fine. They were for visiting leaders and their mates. I wouldn't be sitting with my family anymore.

He held his hands out to me and I grasped them like they were the last solid things on earth. It had only been a couple hours, but it felt like days since I last touched him. I smiled up at him and he kissed me lightly on my lips.

"I missed you, chouchoutte. Did everything go well?" Lucien asked.

"Yes. I have five new members coming into the collective tonight. After dinner, I'll add them and get them sent off to their new home. Do you want to come see?" I offered.

"More than anything, ma choupinette."

I giggled, and we took our seats. Yuri made spaghetti with a salad and his amazing garlic bread sticks. It was one of my favorite dinners. We chatted with the ranked members of Daylight Moon about the wedding.

Galen told everyone about the calls I made and how I handled things. Kieran already knew how I was in 'queen mode', but he pretended to be impressed. I nearly laughed because of the fake surprised look on his face. It was a great meal and helped me feel a lot better after the revelations of the day.

Chapter 45: Bringing in the Berkers

[Bellamy]

When we were done, I led Lucien to my office to wait for my new wolves and Henry. I let him know what to expect while we waited. It didn't take long, just as he suggested some very enticing ways to pass the time there was a knock at my door. I laughed at the crestfallen look on his face as I went to open it.

My office and Kieran's office were soundproofed, so we either had to answer the door ourselves, or mind-link the person. Since rogues didn't have links outside mating, that meant I had to answer it. Henry was grinning on the other side of the door.

"A little bird told me our queen found her mate." He chuckled.

"Noisy little birds. I'm sending it in an e-mail to everyone." I sighed. "Come meet my consort, Henry."

I led him into the room; the Berker family followed him. The men were all over six feet tall, and Joy was about 5'9". They looked amused at the fact that I was so small, but they got less so when Lucien stood up. They actually got a little hostile.

"What's a pack wolf doing here? This is rogue business," the man next to Joy said, pulling her behind him. "It's fine if you choose to live in the pack lands you hold, but they shouldn't be included in these things."

"What is your name?" I asked calmly.

"Derek Berker," he responded.

"And you are the mate of this female?" I asked.

"Yes."

"Then neither you nor she are welcome in my collective. Good night," I stated and turned back to my desk, pulling Lucien with me and having him stand by my chair as I sat.

'Let them stew. He has no right to question how I run my collective. He wants us, not the other way around.' I told him.

'I would've had him explain himself or yelled at him.'

'That's what they expect. Even rogues. I don't have time for this.'

"If our brother and his mate aren't welcome, then we aren't either," one of the other males stated with a growl.

"Then your temporary permits will be revoked. You have twelve hours to leave my territory or a bounty will be put on your whole family," I said, opening another file and focusing on it.

"Please. My mate was just thrown off by the presence of a pack wolf. We don't have friendly relations with the packs back home. My parents were ex-pack and had to fight to be accepted into the Icy Death. Literally, they had to fight anyone who opposed their entry. The price of admission to most collectives is terrible. We really want to be here. Let us have another chance," Joy begged.

I glanced up at her, then raised an eyebrow at her mate.

He sighed deeply and went to his knee, bowing his head. "I offer my apologies, Queen Bellamy. I shouldn't question your choice of company."

His brothers followed suit. I hid my smile. They were all bluster anyway. Pregnant rogue born wolves became the leaders of any family group they were in. If a king's mate was pregnant, she would become the leader of the collective until the pups were delivered. It was a hormonal imperative. They *had* to make her happy.

"You may sit on the couch. Henry, come sit up here. I'll address the Berkers in a moment," I said.

Henry sat on the chair across from me. His eyes were wary. The only pack wolves he'd ever seen with me were Drake, Dillon, Cara, and Kieran. He didn't like change.

"Henry Musgrove, this is my mate, Alpha Lucien Deveraux of Lune Rouge. We'll expand our territory to include his and all land in between," I told him.

A look of admiration and pleasure swept over Henry's features. I looked past him and astonishment was clear on the faces of the Berker family. The larger our territory, the safer we were. It meant more wolves to fight for us, more space for those who had issues in groups, and more resources, which meant less fighting each other.

"A very impressive pairing, Queen Bellamy. Congratulations. Welcome to our collective, Prince Lucien." Henry bowed his head.

"Thank you," Lucien said. There was a smile in his voice.

'Prince?' Lucien asked in our link.

'You're not my king. You're my consort. Non-rogue mates and non-Alpha mates become a prince-consort or princess-consort. King and Queen are reserved only for the Alpha.'

'I see. Tonight, I want to hear you scream 'Prince Lucien' when I take you.'

'Then you need to call me 'Queen Bellamy' and follow my every command.'

'We never got those collars....'

'Mmm. Remind me later. I have work to do,' I replied.

'As you command, Queen Bellamy.'

I managed not to blush. That was advantageous. The last thing I wanted was my queenly air to be destroyed by my mate talking dirty in my head.

"That announcement will go out around midnight. Now, on to our prospective members. We work with the packs I hold. They are members of this collective just as the rogues are. Do not forget that," I warned.

"Is it the best idea to join a collective whose Queen is a Luna?" one of the men whispered to his brother.

"She may try to run it like a pack. That would be safer, but also stupid. Rogues aren't pack wolves," another hissed.

"You *do* know I can hear you? We're all werewolves here," I said in a bored tone. "I run this collective. If you want to join, you accept that. I am the absolute authority here."

"You're expanding through a mating. You have the same name as the Beta in this pack. It doesn't seem like you're really all that strong. You just bat your eyes at a male the right way and they give you what you want," the hissy one scoffed.

"It's true I was adopted into this pack and mated with the leader of another. I have also bested many warriors and Alphas in this region. My mate is one of the strongest Alphas in the state. But, I have never lost a fight with a rogue and have held this territory for six years.

"*You* are petitioning *me*. Not the other way around. You should speak with your matriarch before trying to say I use my looks to get what I want. She can tell you, few people will literally give you the heart from their chest because you're cute." I laughed.

"We could always test his theory," Joy growled.

The man ducked back and whimpered a little. I was tiring of this. There was still a lot of work to be done, and I hoped Dilly would have my intel on Lune Rouge soon. I needed to be sure I knew everything about the pack before we left.

"Joy Berker, are you here to join this collective?" I asked.

She nodded. "Yes, Queen Bellamy."

"Come here." I waved her over.

When she was standing in front of my desk, I grabbed a dagger from my drawer and went to stand with her. She put out her hand, palm up, and calmly waited. I took her hand and looked directly into her eyes.

"Submit," I growled, filling the words with my dominance.

She struggled as her wolf tried to push against my power. It took a few moments before she was on her knees, baring her neck. I laid my teeth gently on her neck and applied small pressure before pulling back.

With the point of the dagger, I pierced the tip of her finger and took the blood into my mouth, then I pierced my own and she took my blood. The wounds healed quickly, and I felt her being tied to Aurora, who was thrilled. Gaining a new wolf more than making up for the pain of losing one. Especially since this one was bringing me two pups.

"Twins," I said.

"We hadn't seen a doctor yet. Thank you." She beamed. "And congratulations on yours."

My eyes widened. "My what?"

"Your babies," Joy answered cautiously.

"I wasn't aware I had any. Thank you, Joy. Please have a seat and rest." I smiled.

Plural. Babies. I could taste that she was creating two. The other rogues said it was too early to smell, but sharing blood wasn't something I'd considered. She could taste what I could. I chose not to look at Lucien. He'd heard. I knew he had. A burst of excitement and pride came through our connection.

"Derek Berker. Are you here to join this collective?" I continued.

It took nearly half an hour to finish swearing the Berkers into my collective. Henry and I went over information about the collective's preschool, the clinic, and their new home. The other men could move out when they wanted, but family groups stayed together for a while after joining.

I talked with them about creating an elite tracker group we could hire out to packs to help with training so incursions like the one my pack had wouldn't happen. Derek would be the captain. He liked the idea and I set a meeting for him with Clint to go over the sort of training pack wolves had with tracking and with Larry, our head tracker.

When it was all said and done, I was happy with the result. It was a good night for the collective. They left, heading to the motel they were staying in, and then to their new home. I went online and ordered two cribs to be sent to their home as a welcome gift. I also ordered the really expensive chocolates Wendy liked to apologize for breaking her mate.

It didn't take long to plan the e-mail which announced my marking of Lucien and the expansion of our territory. My pregnancy would come later. The e-mail also announced the coming elite tracker group and the appointment of Drake as lieutenant for the Daylight Moon Pack. I scheduled it to send at midnight, started organizing my new files, and linked Dilly, still avoiding Lucien's eye.

'Do you have everything I need yet?' I asked.

'I was just printing off the photos. Do you want me to bring them to your office?'

'No. I'm turning in early. Get them to me before you leave for training. We're pushing off the trip for one more day.' I replied.

'I thought you wanted to go before your heat came.'

'Lucien isn't at a hundred percent yet. I still need more time in my territory, too. It's just one day.'

'Alright. Good night, Captain. Give eye candy a kiss for me,' Dilly teased.

'You didn't call him that to his face, did you?'

'Of course I did. He loved it.'

'Good night, Dilly.' I nearly laughed.

I finished putting the files away and turned to Lucien. He was sitting in the chair, looking thoughtful. I went to stand next to him and tapped his shoulder when he didn't notice.

"I'm tired. You ready to call it a night, mon saucisson?" I asked.

"Babies?" he breathed.

"Yes. More than one." I chuckled.

"How many?"

"We'll actually have to wait until I'm further along to know that, Lucien." I smiled. "Odds of twins are high. Like I said, they run in my family."

"Twins." He grinned. "It must've been that time in the shower. That would've definitely made more than one."

I laughed. It was probably the first time, but I didn't need to correct him. He was so happy. So was I. For my entire life, I wanted a family. A real family, not people who claimed me and who I claimed. People I actually belonged to and with. This didn't mean I was going to cut off my adoptive family, just that I was more connected to my babies.

Lucien placed his hand gently on my stomach. He had a starry-eyed look. He probably didn't think this would happen on his little vacation. I certainly didn't think it would be how I'd be spending this week.

He stood and picked me up. "I know you can walk, but I'm celebrating and I get to carry you to bed tonight," Lucien whispered as he kissed my cheek and jaw.

"Fine, but I get to carry you tomorrow night." I joked.

He laughed and took me out of my office, giving me just enough time to lock the door before he headed to the stairs. Kieran was leaving his office as we went past. He chuckled, shaking his head. Lucien looked like he was going to say something.

'Hush. Let's keep our secret for a little longer. This is just for you and me, my love.'

'I want to tell the whole world,' Lucien argued.

'My family got to hear about so much first, let's save this for yours. Your mom will be the first to know. Sound good?'

'That sounds fantastic. She's going to be so happy, chouchoutte!'

We made our way up to my room. I linked the team and ranked members to tell them I needed one more day in my territory before I could safely travel. They all understood. It was as good a lie as any, and it gave us one more day before things got too crazy.

Chapter 46: Learning for Love

[Lucien]

— Four in the afternoon —

Bellamy left the office, and I felt like she was mad at me, but that couldn't be right. She'd just had an upsetting revelation. My curse was deserved, but another person was entirely to blame for hers. Sometimes there were disgusting men in power. This one had caused my mate pain.

"Lucien, Dr. Cleary is on her way to talk to you about rogue pregnancies," Daniel said.

"Thank you. Do you think Bellamy will be okay? That news was quite a shock," I replied.

"She'll be fine. It really was a good thing. She was more focused on building her collective because of it. It explains a lot about her behaviors. We see young wolves getting into relationships and having crushes, but she was entirely focused on building better lives for her rogues. And it meant she never engaged in any activities that worried me as a father… aside from her work as Queen." He chuckled.

"She said she'd never been attracted to men until she met me. That she was attracted to me before I marked her. I wonder why."

"The curse. The moon goddess wants us all to be happy. Since most wolves with no mates will mate by breeding, part of her vengeance is that you won't be attracted to most other wolves, but more attracted to others with the curse. It's meant to bring together two wolves who have been punished and became better from it. She blesses these unions.

"That's why Bellamy's heat started right away. Because you were cursed, too. Otherwise, it would have been the usual time after marking. It really is intriguing." He smiled. "I guess you two were destined in a way."

I smiled at the idea. A third mate from the goddess, just not in the traditional sense. I wondered if she could be pregnant. More than anything, I wanted a baby with her. A little pup with her strength and intelligence. With a mix of both of us everywhere else. I imagined the happiness she and I would share watching our pup grow.

There was a knock at the door, and Daniel called out for them to enter. A young woman with dark red hair and blue eyes peeked her head in. She smiled warmly.

"Just making sure I had the right place. I don't get called up here very often." She chuckled.

"Come in, Dr. Cleary." He waved her in.

She sat on the couch across from me and folded her hands in her lap. Daniel poured some water for her and she thanked him.

"So, you need to know about rogue pregnancies. Is Amy knocked up?" Dr. Cleary giggled.

"I'm her mate. In case it happens, I need to know more. I'll also need you to send all the information you have on rogue born wolves to Lune Rouge's pack hospital so we can care for her properly," I stated.

"Oh! I'd heard she found a mate, but you never really believe the gossip around here. Especially when it's about Amy. Some people make up the worst things about her. She's the one who brought me into the pack with her re-inclusion program.

"I was a pack doctor in a pack that was destroyed by hunters. No one would take me in because I was a rogue. I applied to her collective because I'd heard good things. She took me on a week after I applied and started working on getting me sane again. I'd lost it a little without a pack.

"Once I was back to normal, she had me do a year in the clinic and train rogue borns to work there. Then she had me brought into this pack. I love her so much. I found my mate because of her and I get to do what I love," Dr. Cleary rambled.

Daniel snorted. "Bea. Get on with it."

"Sorry. I talk a lot sometimes. That's why Dr. Hale loves to have me around. I take care of all the explaining because he doesn't like people that much. But he loves Amy. He just won't say it out loud." She giggled again.

This was possibly the most cheerful, talkative, and bouncy person I had ever seen. I regretted my decision a little, but I needed to do this for my mate. She wanted me to know what differences there were.

"Okay. So, to start, she will only be pregnant for sixteen to seventeen weeks. We usually have twenty to twenty-one. The odds of having multiples beyond twins are exponentially higher. Singletons are actually rarer among rogue born pregnancies. She won't start showing until the end of the second month. At that point, she can't shift for the safety of the babies. Any time before that is fine. She'll crave rare and raw meat more and will become more territorial and possessive," Dr. Cleary explained.

"More territorial and possessive? I can see territorial. She's really protective of her collective and pack. I don't think she's really the type for possessive," Daniel said.

"She said she wanted to scratch Dillon's eyes out for looking at me. According to him, Bellamy personally ground Louisa, the vampire they wanted me to impregnate, into dust and said no one but she was permitted to touch me. She told me she would've torn Melly's eyes out and shoved them down her throat, then ripped off her head if she'd done anything but run away when she accidentally saw me nude," I told him.

"Never mind. That's terrifying. You'll need to keep her calm, or you're going to have a lot of unhappy, injured people in your pack." He laughed.

"Anyway," Dr. Cleary continued. "It's almost impossible for a rogue born to miscarry. It would take her getting run through right in the uterus for that to happen, or if mom dies. They're the least fragile pregnancies ever. I saw one mom who got hit by a truck. Most of the bones in her body were broken. Barely alive. The baby was absolutely fine. It was so cool. And by cool I mean medically, not actually." She winced.

"Also, her sense of smell will get stronger and the hormones will really knock *you* out. I once had a rogue born male brought in with a fractured pelvis. His mate was pregnant with quads and in her last three weeks. He didn't seem to be too upset, just in pain. It was so cute, she sat next to him, combing his hair and dabbing the tears from his face while telling him how much she loved him."

Quads… broken pelvis…? In the last three weeks of my sister's first pregnancy, her mate said she refused to let him sleep in the bed because he was too hot and she didn't want him to touch her. In Celesta's last three weeks with Salomé, she growled every time Thierry got within a foot of her.

"Has she groomed you yet? It's so adorable how rogue born wolves do that. It's just like natural wolves. They get super blissed out. All stylists in the collective are pack born or other species. Amy's orders. Grooming is too intimate with rogue borns. It causes jealousy issues," she snickered.

"I… I don't think so… Is it bad if she hasn't?" I asked.

"No. It might mean she's being cautious since you're pack born. She's been with this pack since she was twelve, she has to have seen that pack wolves don't do it in human form. But she leans against you when you're walking together. I saw that earlier when I was on my break. That's one of the other things they do that we only do in wolf form." Dr. Cleary smiled fondly.

Maybe I should ask her to brush me or something. It seemed weird. I loved the serene look she had when we were walking together. If it made her feel closer to me, I was more than happy to indulge in the weirdness.

"Why would she include that information in a medical briefing?" Daniel asked.

"She didn't. I was a rogue for three years before I joined her collective and a year in the collective before I was admitted into the pack. These are things I know from that. I just think it's a cute habit they do."

"Katie never talked about this stuff," he muttered.

"Even though she's pack born, the lieutenant keeps things close. Like all rogues. I've always been too talkative." Dr. Cleary laughed.

"What's the deal with all the territory talk in her newsletters?" he asked, leaning in. "It seems they're all about that. She always gets a flood of responses when she announces a territory expansion. When she holds her lieutenant meetings, they focus on it a lot."

"Rogue collectives are judged by territory, not population, unlike packs. We're excited about gaining people via birth or transfer, they're excited by the addition of land. It means more wolves to help protect them, more space, and more resources. That's why she doesn't have a problem with sending ex-packs to rejoin the pack wolves, even though it hurts her physically to do it," she explained.

"How? I don't like her being hurt," I said.

"They're all connected to her. Everyone in the collective is bound to her. Alpha Kieran is bound to her and through him, everyone in this pack."

"Is that why she gets nervous if she's away too long?" I asked.

"Yes. It's like leaving your kids at home and the babysitter is new. You worry about everything. And a lot of her additional strength is from the dedication and loyalty of her people."

"Is there anything else I need to know about pregnancy or rogues in general that will help me take better care of my mate?" I pressed, we were getting off topic.

"Hmm. Well, I guess, just that their emotions are heightened. Even though she acts like she's cold, Bellamy feels things more. Things that would upset us a little, hurt her deeply. Fear is more intense, sadness is deeper, happiness is like euphoria, and love is absolute bliss. It's why she always looks happy when she is around her family. The contentment and love she feels here is rapturous. There's no other way to describe it," she said softly.

When I hurt her, I wounded her deeply. I'd never do that again. There wasn't much I could protect her from, but I could protect her from the pain I could cause.

"Thank you, Doctor. I appreciate your time," I told her.

"No problem. We'll send everything medically relevant to Lune Rouge. I better get back. Good luck." Dr. Cleary smiled and left.

"Well. That was informative." Daniel chuckled. "I never thought to ask Bea. She's a little annoying sometimes. I could've understood my daughter so much more if I'd set that aside and asked more questions."

I nodded. At least I knew that now. She hid things so she wouldn't upset people because these things upset her even worse. It was why she didn't tell me or anyone else what the vampires did to her.

Marion hurt her terribly. If the pain she felt when he touched her was anything like the pain I felt when my maid fed me succubus pheromone, then it was excruciating.

My poor little chouchoutte. She wasn't just afraid of losing everyone; she was terrified of it. Dillon said she saw her parents murdered and dismembered. I couldn't imagine the fear and pain she'd had to live through.

Chapter 47: The Bored Alpha

Lost in thought, I left Daniel's office, trying to make sense of what I'd heard. I saw Galen stick his head into Bellamy's office with a stack of file folders.

"No funny business going on in here, right?" he asked.

She laughed. "So you've walked in on them, too?"

As I inched closer to the door, I listened to their conversation. She really didn't seem to feel more than sibling affection for him. And it seemed like he felt the same about her. At least, the way he talked was familial and loving. I wanted to find out what they were doing with those files.

After the door closed, I went to stand by close by, but couldn't hear anything. That was strange. I should've been able to hear through a simple wooden door.

"It's soundproofed."

The voice, close and hushed, startled me, making me jump slightly. I turned and saw Dillon there. Busted, again. How did he sneak up on me? I was an Alpha!

"I was just curious what they were working on," I explained.

"Rogue business. Not ours. You have to learn where that line is. Come on. I was just heading to my office. You can be my eye candy for a while," he laughed.

He walked past me. I didn't really have anything else to do, so I followed. It was hard not being busy all the time. I'd been planning on spending the day with Bellamy, but I didn't have that option. At least he might give me more insight into her.

Three doors down, he stopped and punched in a code on the door lock. It was rare for offices to be locked in my pack unless there was a meeting on the other side. He opened the door and turned on the light.

Like Bellamy's office, there was no window. Unlike her office, it was full of computer equipment. She only had a desktop, and I knew there was a laptop in her room, but he had things with blinking lights and four monitors sat behind his desk. Wires came through the wall from the room next door that had an entrance to his office, but not in the hall. That door was thick, metal, and had a panel next to it.

On one monitor, there were security camera feeds from different areas in the forest surrounding the packlands. Another had some sort of spreadsheet. A third was moving text so fast that I had no idea what was on it, and the fourth had a video game paused. There was a fifth monitor coming out of the top of his desk and facing away from the chairs in front of it.

"Welcome to my lair," he said in a fake villainous voice as he sat behind his desk.

"What's all this for?" I asked.

"Oh, well, I watch the vampire wards to make sure that no one sends a human servant to erase a section. It happened once. I'm running deep background on a top-secret project. I do some accounting for Bellamy's witches. And I have to beat the high score in one of my games because Bellamy broke in and filled all the top scores with 'sukit', again." He sighed heavily.

I laughed. Tyson said the exact same thing happened the last time she visited. Apparently, she also made people cry when she played online shooting games. He told me she was cruel to the boys who told her to make them sandwiches. I wanted to see that Bellamy, too. Being much younger than me, I knew she'd connect well with my future Beta and Gamma. It would help me a lot.

"Is the top secret project for the pack or the collective?" I asked.

"It's top secret. That's what that means. If anyone wants you to know, they'll tell me to let you know." He winked. "So, why were you spying? Bored?"

"Mostly. When I'm on my breaks from being Alpha I run and hunt and sleep. Sometimes I take a book to read. There's no one else to make me think I'm slacking off. It's the nature of being alone, if you do anything, it's something. I feel a little useless here. I was hoping to hang out with Bellamy, but she's busy with rogue stuff," I replied as I sat in the chair across from him and leaned back.

"Poor you. So, I heard Warrick talking about her being pregnant. You managed to do the thing then?" Dillon grinned.

"Yes."

"Come on. Spill. I want to see if your story matches up with hers." He laughed.

"No," I replied.

"Boo. You suck." Dillon stuck out his tongue.

His face went serious as he worked on whatever was on the fifth monitor. After a while, he sighed deeply. It seemed like he was thinking of something, like he wanted to say something, but was having a little internal battle with it.

"What's on your mind, Dillon?" I asked.

"Can I join your pack? Cara's there and Bellamy's there. I don't really want to be alone. I feel alone without them. They're my girls," he murmured.

"What about the Elite Ten?"

"Those are my boys. The top four, aside from Bellamy, all have titles. Everyone else connects on some other level. Drake and Todd are my cousins, but we're not that close. I'm part of the group, but not as much as everyone else." Dillon looked downhearted as he said that.

"What would you bring to my pack if I let you join?" I asked.

"I'm the tech guru here. I'll upgrade your security and set up a municipal ISP for your pack. I can run background on anyone you want and I'm pretty good at hacking. No one mimics vampires better than me, except Bellamy. I'm the best elite warrior who doesn't have any ranked blood. Bren married into it, our family doesn't have it," he stated.

It was a solid offer. He brought a lot to the pack. Trying to upgrade was difficult and having someone in the pack who could oversee it would be great.

"I'm good with that. I know Bellamy would love to have you there. Just put in the transfer after your mission is over. I'll approve it on my end." I smiled.

"Really!? Yes!!" he cheered. "I have to write up the options for pack members to take over my position here. Before I leave, I have to locate my red folder and reinforce my security. I need a plan of action…. There's so much to do! Okay, get out. I need to focus and you're too pretty." He pointed at the door.

I laughed and headed out. He gave me a lot of help with Bellamy. It was worth it to accept him. I wandered the hall for a while, but nothing else happened. I went by Kieran's office and his door was open. He was working on something, but I decided to bother him for a while and knocked on the door.

"Come in, Alpha Lucien," Kieran said, looking up.

"Am I interrupting much?" I asked.

"Just new member paperwork. It's tedious. I could use the break. What are you up to? No, I know that look. You're bored," he chuckled.

"Yeah. It gets like that. How are you doing? Feeling better than yesterday?"

Kieran sighed. "I think I'm getting too old for this. We can't promote the boys until they've either all found mates or all turned twenty-five. That's another two and a half years, unless Galen finds his mate. I can't believe I let my territorial mind get in the way of what was best for my pack.

"I had a hard time when Bellamy first made the offer to claim my pack. After the first year, I couldn't believe I worried. We went from losing a few people a month to a few people in that entire year. She fought every rogue that came along. She never demanded anything, never fought my authority, never tried to take over my pack.

"I let her take on too much because I didn't think it was a problem for her. Rogues are different, she was different. You reminded me that I made a little girl into a soldier for my people. I was an idiot."

I nodded. "It's hard to think of her as a little girl when you see her as a warrior. And the other way around. I still have trouble seeing her as a warrior and I've fought her. It doesn't stop me from wanting to wrap her up and keep her safe from everything."

He laughed dryly. "I got over that after the first time I saw her kill three rogues in one fight. She was thirteen and fought so violently, so viciously, that I couldn't see her as anything but a killer. She was every villainous rogue we ever heard stories about, but she was under five feet tall with those big innocent eyes and little sweet voice. It was like it caused an overload in my brain."

Remembering the dark smile on her face while she talked about burning the vampires, the cool tone when she scolded me about my jealousy, the anger in her eyes when she talked about the vampires' plan, I understood. Those were and weren't my Bellamy.

She was also the scared girl whose anxiety overwhelmed her, the girl who ran away because she was afraid of being abandoned, the girl who leaned against me and hummed while we walked in the garden.

"I guess she's a lot of things we just don't understand. Any update on the bear situation? Any idea what he was after?" I asked.

"We have one of our trackers out and he followed the bear to the vampires' house. He started walking up the stream, into the woods. There were traces of chemicals from a fire extinguisher and our tracker lost the scent," Kieran said.

"He's probably heading for the place I was attacked. It sounds like he's backtracking my path. Depending on how fast he's going, he might end up at my pack before we get there. I'll call Thierry to get the patrols stepped up. I wish we had better relations with the rogue borns in my area so I could have a patrol like you have," I chuckled.

"You will soon. Give her a couple months. Bellamy will have the rogues in your area in line. The bad ones will be weeded out and she'll start bringing useful ones into your pack. Your entire life is going to change and you'll find yourself doing things you never thought you would before," he warned. "But your pack will grow stronger and larger, like mine did."

"I'm going to go call home and get some stuff taken care of. Is there an office I can use?" I asked.

"Yeah. Let me take you." Kieran stood and guided me down the hall to an office and opened the door.

I nodded, and he left. There was a phone on the desk and a legal pad with a pen. The office itself was fairly basic and had a window that overlooked the back garden. I closed the door and sat at the desk.

I'd learned a lot more about my little mate and it made me happy. The more I learned about rogues, the better mate I could be to my Bellamy. Knowing she can be frightening to seasoned Alphas would prepare me for seeing it myself.

Chapter 48: Alpha Calling

[Lucien]

Taking a deep breath, I picked up the handset and dialed Thierry's number. I doodled a little on the notepad as the phone rang. There wasn't an answer, so I tried Robert's number. He picked up after a couple of rings.

"Robert Dubois, what can I do for you?" he answered.

"It's Lucien," I replied.

"Ah, back from Hunter's Moon? We tried to call you last night. Kieran said there was a last-minute meeting with the Alpha over there. Did everything go well?" Robert asked.

"We had to cut the visit short. A bear was using a potion to infiltrate Daylight Moon. It looks like he's tracking me. I tried Thierry first. We need to increase patrols and have them doubled up. I want men paired up. If they smell someone from the pack but slightly off, they need to be on high alert and report it as if it were a rogue attack. I know it could cause issues, but a bear is serious business," I told him.

"I let Thierry know. He's on it. He left his cell in the dining room and was retrieving it when you called. How is our Luna doing?"

"She's busy. It's a lot of work getting the collective prepared for her to move her home base. Everything is going pretty well otherwise. Why were you trying to call last night?" I asked.

"Well, it was something like that actually. We realized some things you said pointed to our Luna being a rogue. Alpha Kieran said she was a 'rogue Queen' when you were first calling Thierry, you said you thought she was a rogue kid. Cara confirmed that she's a rogue born wolf. Is that the best idea for the pack?"

"Of course it is. She's an Alpha, as strong as I am, and as dedicated to her people as I am. She'll be that dedicated to our pack. Bellamy risked her life to save me even though she didn't know me. The goddess blessed our union. If anyone has a problem with it, they can leave.

"We'll be safer from rogues by having her as our Luna. Our warriors will be stronger from her training. And I'll be happier than I've been in years, which will make things run better for everyone. I love her, Robert. In the short time I've known her, she's become everything to me," I said.

Robert sighed. "I won't oppose it. Thierry won't either. We know how hard it's been for you, and how depressed you've started getting. Frankly, we thought you'd done something to yourself when we couldn't find you. With your mom getting sick and you disappearing, we were out of our minds with worry. You have no idea."

"I'm sorry you were worried. You know I would never abandon my pack like that. It was just... I couldn't sit there and listen to more wedding talk. Not when I thought I was destined to be alone," I said softly.

"There's Thierry. I'll put this on speaker," Robert replied, avoiding the vulnerable answer I gave.

"Hello, Lucien. Did you two talk about Bellamy?" Thierry asked.

"Yes. She's a rogue. Can we get past that?" I groaned.

Thierry chuckled. "Is what they say about rogue she-wolves true?"

"What do they say?" I growled.

"You can growl all you want. I'm not scared of you, Lucy. I heard they're freer in bed. They do all sorts of fun things you can't get pack she-wolves to do. They get really into it and like it rough. You have a hot young rogue; you have to share the stories. Let us live through you."

"I walked in on you and your wife in your office not two days before I left behaving like you were performing in an adult film. Bellamy's a good girl. If you talk about my mate like that again, I'll kick your ass," I warned.

"We told you about our mates. Come on. We're buddies. This is what guys do," Thierry pressed.

"She's beautiful. Her body is perfection. And she loves me. We're getting married and she wants a baby as much as I do. I'm not saying anything more. You don't need to know," I replied.

"Just one more thing." Thierry snickered.

"What?" I sighed.

"She calls you her saucisson?" He laughed.

Robert laughed, too. I grinned.

"Yeah. Is that all?" I smiled.

"You got a dirty little rogue mate. People in Daylight Moon may not know what that means…" Thierry snorted.

There was a knock on the door.

"Come in!" I called out.

Dillon opened the door. "Kieran said you were here. Dinner's almost ready. Come on, eye candy. Your queen misses you."

Thierry and Robert started laughing. I sighed. They wouldn't let me live that down. People didn't talk to me like that in my pack. I chuckled. At least one would now.

"I have to go. I'll talk to you guys later," I told them.

"Bye, eye candy. Better get your sweet ass out there for your queen." Thierry guffawed.

Robert just breathlessly squeaked a painful laugh. I hung up the phone and glared at Dillon. He was trying to hide a smile.

"You're lucky I want to get out to dinner more than I want to kick your ass," I growled.

"Sure thing, eye candy. Let's go," he laughed, and we headed to the dining room.

I was a little disappointed Bellamy wasn't there when I arrived, but I felt it more than made up for it to see her light up after she scanned the room and finally saw me when she arrived. With a happy squeal, she bounced over to me, her small hands instantly closing around mine. I felt like she was a wisp I had to hold on to or she would fade away again.

Leaning down, I kissed her gently. I had to feel her lips and know she was really there, not a figment of my imagination. It felt like it had been years since I saw her beautiful, angelic face.

"I missed you, chouchoutte. Did everything go well?" I asked.

"Yes. I have five new members coming into the collective tonight. After dinner, I'll add them and get them sent off to their new home. Want to come see?" she offered.

I nearly bounced with excitement myself. More than anything, I wanted to see my mate in her role as queen of her people. No amount of talking to people would give me that experience.

"More than anything, ma choupinette," I purred.

We sat, and Yuri started serving. The way Bellamy's face lit up, I was certain she liked spaghetti. She ate with vigor. I hadn't seen her attack food like that in the entire time we'd been together. It was adorable.

I picked up a napkin and wiped some sauce that had gotten on her nose. She leaned closer when I did. It made her look happy, and I realized something as simple as that was grooming to a rogue. I could definitely take care of her like this.

"You guys should've seen Amy talking to the rogue King in Alaska! She was so cool. Super straight to the point. No chitchat beyond warning him that she intends to take over the whole continent." Galen grinned.

"I was actually securing an alliance. He's got the biggest collective in the country. It was prudent," she mumbled into her food.

"The last thing she said to him was 'don't die'. And they hung up. No 'goddess bless you' or anything like that. I've never seen her talk to another rogue Alpha," he went on.

Bellamy kept glancing at Kieran and looking like she was going to laugh. I followed her gaze and saw him, very obviously, pretending to be surprised. He was not a good actor.

"Have you thought of a date for the wedding?" Daisy asked.

"Yeah. Three weeks from today, I think should do it. Sound good, mon saucisson?" Bellamy smiled.

"Sounds perfect," I responded.

"That's way too soon! We can't get everything together by then!" Bren cried.

Bellamy scoffed. "We have three Beta females, three Gamma females, and three Lunas. If we can't throw together a basic wedding in three weeks, we aren't very good at our jobs. The reception will be the most important part. Lucien and I are already married by werewolf law. The human part is just because of legal stuff. I don't need the frilly shiny stuff Cara does. I'm cool with a store-bought dress. Just like my ring and my mate, the goddess will give me the perfect one as an option and I will find it."

She didn't even know about the goddess' blessing and she already trusted her to help. Bellamy had seen things no one else had. She saw me under the dirt and hair. She saw how much love I had to give. Bellamy saw the truth about my mother's illness. She was more in tune with hidden things than anyone I'd ever met.

"I'll make the cake. I know what my Bebe likes. Their kitchen can make the food, but they better not mess up my Bebe's wedding," Yuri announced.

It was nice to see how much people liked her. Several members of the kitchen staff started chattering about the wedding food and the suggestions they would make to my kitchens. Dillon talked about setting up a video feed so everyone in Daylight Moon and the collective could see the wedding.

Everyone worked on planning while we ate. It seemed the future Luna and Gamma female were excited. This would be their first collaboration, true collaboration, with another pack. After dinner, Bellamy took me to her office.

I sat in one of the guest chairs on the other side of Bellamy's desk, watching as she tidied up a few things. There was tension in her shoulders.

"Is this because I'm here?" I asked.

"Kieran, my dad, and Toby watched the first batch I ever swore in, but I haven't had anyone watch since. And I want you to understand, I'm going to seem really mean. You can't be nice to unaffiliated rogues. Especially when you look like me," she giggled.

"Well, if you're nervous, I can help you relax." I reached out and took her hand, kissing her palm. "I could set you down on this desk and have my favorite dessert. Maybe add some of my own cream. I could kiss every inch of this tiny, perfect body. You could take off your panties and settle yourself on my—" A knock at the door cut me off.

Fuck. I wasn't catching a break today. Bellamy looked like she was going to laugh as she made her way to the door and opened it.

Chapter 49: A Little Roguish Business

[Lucien]

"A little bird told me our queen found her mate," the man at the door chuckled.

"Noisy little birds. I'm sending it in an e-mail to everyone." She sighed. "Come meet my consort, Henry."

Consort? I thought it was 'Chief Lieutenant'. Was being a lieutenant only for the Alphas in her collective that were her partners? I liked it. I'd rather be a consort than a lieutenant.

A group of large men and one woman followed Henry as he entered. The tension in the air thickened. A heavy silence fell as one man spotted me. His eyes narrowed before he yanked the woman behind him, his body stiffening into a defensive stance.

"What's a pack wolf doing here? This is rogue business."

Bellamy's demeanor didn't shift. She remained completely composed.

"What is your name?" she asked calmly.

"Derek Berker."

"And you are the mate of this female?"

"Yes."

"Then neither you nor she are welcome in my collective. Good night."

I let out a low breath as she turned, pulling me to stand behind her as she settled into her chair, projecting absolute authority. The man bristled at her dismissal, but before he could speak, one of the others did.

"If our brother and his mate aren't welcome, then we aren't either."

Bellamy's expression remained impassive. "Then your temporary permits will be revoked. You have twelve hours to leave my territory or a bounty will be put on your whole family."

My mate was unlike I had seen her before. I was discovering new facets of her every day. She was amazing, a true queen.

The woman in the group quickly stepped forward, pleading their case. She explained their troubled history with packs and the difficulty of joining other collectives. Bellamy finally looked up, her gaze sharp. I watched as Derek and his brothers hesitated, then dropped to one knee in submission.

Pride filled me. My mate wasn't just strong, she commanded respect effortlessly.

When the Berkers moved to the couch, Bellamy turned her attention to Henry, beckoning him closer. The man looked cautious of me. I knew most rogues didn't trust pack wolves and pack wolves felt the same way. We stared each other down a little before Bellamy spoke again.

"Henry Musgrove, this is my mate, Alpha Lucien Deveraux of Lune Rouge. We'll expand our territory to include his and all land in between."

Henry's eyes widened slightly, and then he smiled. "A very impressive pairing, Queen Bellamy. Congratulations. Welcome to our collective, Prince Lucien."

Prince Lucien. That was new. I liked it more than I should have. My mom always called me her prince. Of course, I'd found a way to become one in reality.

Bellamy explained it in our link. Everything I was learning about rogue tradition, hierarchies, and habits, the better I felt about my place by her side.

'Tonight, I want to hear you scream 'Prince Lucien' when I take you,' I teased through our bond.

'Then you need to call me 'Queen Bellamy' and follow my every command.'

I smirked but didn't respond. My mind was already drifting to the night ahead. I was going to take her to her room and make her scream and beg for me for hours.

The sweet torment I would unleash on my perfect little mate would be the ideal end to this day. I was so focused on my thoughts that I almost missed the shift in the conversation.

Bellamy had moved on to the formal initiation of the rogues. I watched as she tested Joy Berker's submission, her dominance rolling off her in waves. It was different from anything I had ever seen in a pack.

This wasn't just obedience; it was a fundamental power shift. Not a promise of submission, but proof of Bellamy's dominance over the woman.

'Our mate is powerful,' Remus said.

'Yes,' I confirmed.

'Our pups will be powerful.'

'Yes.' I answered.

'We can't beat her. Can we?' he asked.

'No. She's as strong as we are. I didn't pull any punches this morning. Only avoided things that would hurt a pup. She's stronger than we realized. The demon dust made her more impulsive. She couldn't plan her moves or she would've won,' I told him.

'Thank the goddess for that.'

Joy yielded, and the blood exchange sealed her acceptance into the collective. Then came the moment that made my entire world tilt.

"Twins," Bellamy murmured.

"We hadn't seen a doctor yet. Thank you," Joy responded, smiling.

I realized she was pregnant and Bellamy could taste exactly how pregnant in the woman's blood. It was impressive.

Then she said to Bellamy, "And congratulations on yours."

Everything in me froze. Did Joy taste the same thing Bellamy could taste? Was this real?

Bellamy stiffened. "My what?"

"Your babies." Joy's voice was careful now.

Bellamy was pregnant. Not just pregnant. Plural. Babies. More than one. The fractured pelvis then popped into my head. I'd have to be careful as my little mate grew. I fell into thoughts of pups and our lives together. She was everything and was giving me everything I'd ever wanted.

A rush of emotion slammed into me; joy, disbelief, and fierce protectiveness. My entire world rearranged itself in an instant. I wanted to jump, to shout, to pull Bellamy into my arms. Instead, I clenched my hands into fists and forced myself to stay still.

We needed to get this issue with the bear and whoever was behind the attack on me taken care of. I wouldn't let my pups be born into an unsafe life. Bellamy wouldn't raise them without me. We were going to destroy whoever wanted me gone.

After the initiations wrapped up and everyone else left, Bellamy focused on her work, but I was barely aware of anything else. I sat in the chair, my mind racing.

This changed everything. My mate was already everything to me. But now… now she carried our pups. My future. My family.

I concentrated on who my enemies were, and who would want me dead. If there was someone in my pack, I was aware of, who had a problem with me that I may have been overlooking. It couldn't be Thierry or Robert. That was absolutely impossible.

They stayed with me even through the worst things. They never held back when we discussed issues. They were my brothers.

The thought of how excited they'd be when we told them about the pups nearly made me start grinning. I thought of how excited my sister and mother would be. Everyone at the packhouse, everyone in the pack, would be thrilled. Having a mate was one thing, but I was already bordering on the age when most Alphas retired and had no heir.

She tapped my shoulder, pulling me from my thoughts.

"I'm tired. You ready to call it a night, mon saucisson?" she asked.

"Babies?" I breathed.

"Yes. More than one," she chuckled.

"How many?"

"We'll actually have to wait until I'm further along to know that, Lucien. Joy was around two weeks, so I could tell how many," Bellamy smiled. "Odds of twins are high. Like I said, they run in my family."

"Twins." I grinned. "It must have been that time in the shower. That would have definitely made more than one."

I placed my hand gently on her stomach. I couldn't feel anything yet, but knowing they were there… nothing had ever made me this happy. Nothing except for Bellamy marking me and sealing our bond to each other.

I stood and picked her up. I didn't care if she was a rogue Queen and elite warrior right then. She was mine, my mate, mother of my children, my Luna, and my entire heart.

"I know you can walk, but I'm celebrating, and I get to carry you to bed tonight."

She laughed. "Fine, but I get to carry you tomorrow night."

As I carried her toward the stairs, we passed Kieran, who chuckled, shaking his head. I wanted to tell him. Hell, I wanted to tell everyone. I wanted to tell the spiders in their webs.

'Hush. Let's keep our secret for a little longer. This is just for you and me, my love,' Bellamy murmured through our bond.

'I want to tell the whole world.'

'My family got to hear about so much first. Let's save this for yours. Your mom will be the first to know. Sound good?'

My throat tightened. She was thinking of my family, making this moment special for me.

'That sounds fantastic. She's going to be so happy, chouchoutte.'

And so was I.

***

When we got to the room, I carried her through the doorway and closed the door behind us. Finally, she was all mine. No distractions. No responsibilities… at least for a little while.

"I'm pushing our departure one day, Lucien. I still need some time in my territory. Is that okay?" Bellamy asked.

"You're the captain. We should call Thierry and Robert so they know not to expect us," I replied, though the extra time here wasn't what I wanted. We'd barely had any time alone, and it wouldn't be much better once we were at Lune Rouge. Remus was restless for more than stolen moments between meetings.

She stretched her arms over her head, sighing. "You call them while I have a bath? My back aches from the deskwork, and I have even more tomorrow."

Remus huffed in my head, mirroring my disappointment. She needed rest. She needed us.

"More work? But… I want to spend time with you. You're pregnant. Take a day off. Please." I knew I sounded desperate, but I didn't care.

She laughed, shaking her head. "That was how I got this way. Sorry, saucisson. I can probably be done by three in the afternoon, but I'm on light training, so I have to train at eleven, which throws my whole day off. You, on the other hand, will be getting up at four-thirty for elite warrior training."

"I've been wanting to try it out. After Warrick's training, I think I'm ready."

The training at Hunter's Moon was about as hard as the training we had for our elites. It couldn't be worse than that.

Her eyes glittered with amusement. "Yeah. It was a good warm-up to get you into it. Training is two hours long. Breakfast is at seven-thirty. I'll meet you there in the morning. No workout clothes at the table. So you have to make sure you shower and change before coming. Yuri won't serve anyone who isn't properly dressed," she warned.

I raised a brow. Warm-up? That training had nearly broken me. I wasn't about to admit it, though. Instead, I set her down and she went to take her bath. I grabbed her phone, dialing Thierry.

"Lucien?" Thierry answered.

"We won't be back until the day after tomorrow. Bellamy needs more time in her territory before she can travel," I informed him. "How's my mom?"

"She's doing well. Keeps trying to convince us to let her out of the hospital, but your orders supersede hers. We didn't tell her about the poisoning; just said it was a rare virus. We also didn't mention you being captured. She thinks you're just taking longer than expected."

Good. The last thing I needed was my mother worrying herself sick over me.

"Make sure the omegas are prepared to unload a truck with Bellamy's things and unpack them into my room. Get an extra dresser added, replace the mattress, and have it made up in green. She likes green. So do I. The whole house should be cleaned," I told him.

"Yes, Alpha."

"And I want all the ranked families outside to meet her when we arrive. No waiting until dinner or lunch. I want everyone introduced immediately."

"Yes, Alpha. It will all be done before you arrive. Have a good night."

"You, too. Goddess watch over you," I said.

"And you, Lucien."

Hanging up, I made my way into the bathroom. Bellamy was lying in the tub, eyes closed, looking exhausted but peaceful. The tiny bathtub barely fit her comfortably. The one at home would be better.

I grabbed a washcloth and sat beside the tub. Bellamy's eyes fluttered open, a lazy smile stretching across her lips.

"Hey there, eye candy," she snickered.

I groaned. "I'm going to kill Dillon."

"What are you up to?"

I lifted the body wash from the side of the tub. "I'm going to help you relax. Let me take care of you for a bit."

Bellamy sighed, letting her eyes close again. I washed her carefully, enjoying every second of feeling her skin under my hands. When I was done, I leaned forward and whispered, "All done."

"That was amazing," she purred. "I feel a million percent better."

I helped her out of the tub and dried her off before leading her to bed. As we settled under the blankets, she murmured, "Did you know rogue-born couples do things like this? Washing each other, brushing each other's hair... some even paint their mate's nails."

"Dr. Cleary mentioned it," I admitted. "She asked if you'd groomed me yet. I let her know we hadn't done that yet. But she saw you lean against me while we walked earlier."

Bellamy frowned slightly. "What do you mean? I washed you the first time we met. I picked out everything you needed to clean yourself when I couldn't do it for you. We showered together at Hunter's Moon. You didn't think that counted?"

Guilt pricked at me. I hadn't considered that. "You did it so naturally; I didn't realize... Was that what you were doing? Being a naughty girl and getting your kicks from grooming a strange man?" I teased, nibbling her ear.

"I was hoping you'd trust me more if I took care of you," she admitted.

"You did more than that." I pulled her closer. "I wish I could bring Marion back just so I could kill him slowly. That bloodsucking bastard was lucky I didn't know what he did."

"I love that you're angry about this, mon saucisson, but neither of us was in any condition to take on Marion and the others. He can't hurt me again. I have you to protect me from any other vampires."

"You mean that? That I can protect you?"

"From vampires."

I huffed. "What about tonight? Those rogues insulted you. I wanted to beat them."

"I'm glad you didn't. If I hadn't put them in their place myself, they would've seen me as weak. Lots of people are trying to find my weaknesses, trying to find a way to dominate me, trying to find a way to put me into whatever place they think I belong. I need to maintain control, and you standing by my side, letting me handle it, meant more than you know."

I tightened my arms around her. "Get some sleep, chouchoutte. We have a big day tomorrow."

"I'll get up when you do and start working," she murmured sleepily. "Maybe I can be done before training, and we can have the entire afternoon together."

"That would be perfect."

She didn't respond. Her breathing had already evened out. I listened to the steady rhythm of her heart as I drifted off, holding my mate close. My future, our future, was finally taking shape.

Chapter 50: Impossible Image

[Bellamy]

My alarm woke me in the morning. I pushed Lucien and he groaned at me. Pushing again made him grab me tightly and shush me.

"Lucien, you have training. If you're late you have to do doubles. You really, really don't want that, mon saucisson," I whispered.

"No training. I'm the Alpha. I want sleep, and my mate," he growled.

"You train or you're not getting either," I threatened.

"Fine, but you have to give me extra kisses when I'm back."

"Done. Now, move," I ordered.

He climbed out of bed and headed for the bathroom. I stretched and got out of bed to dress for the day. I pulled out my underclothes, jeans, and a dark green tank top. After getting dressed, I headed to the bathroom and brushed my teeth. When I was done, I found Lucien dressed for training and we headed downstairs.

Drake and Dillon were waiting for him at the entryway. I smiled at them.

'Don't let him die, boys,' I warned.

'Yes, Captain,' they replied.

"Dilly, where's that file you had for me? I'm going to try to get some work done."

"I put it in your office," he said.

"Thanks." I turned to Lucien. "Have a good time, mon saucisson," I purred.

He bent down and gave me a light kiss.

"I'll try," Lucien groaned.

They left, and I headed back to the second floor to start my research on Lune Rouge. Yuri came up with a cup of coffee. I wasn't a big coffee drinker, but I enjoyed one in the morning after training. Everyone else took a nap after breakfast, but I didn't really have that option.

The file was thick and sat right in the middle of my desk. I grabbed Yuri's arm as he started heading back down.

"Could I get some orange juice, too? I'll be here for a while and it would be nice to have a second drink." I smiled at him.

"Of course, Bebe. I'll bring it right up." He grinned.

I was trying to make sure he didn't know I was pregnant. I wouldn't be drinking that coffee, but I wanted to have something. He left, and I settled in with my file.

I barely registered the additional drink being dropped off as I read through the information on Lucien, his mother, his sister and her family, and his Beta and Gamma and their families. I knew everything from the last ten years. The files included medical, legal, social, and some personal information.

My alarm went off. It was ten minutes before breakfast. I hadn't even noticed that the time had gone by so quickly. I took the cold coffee and dumped it in the sink of the little bathroom in my office before grabbing the empty juice cup and taking them down to the kitchen.

After heading to the dining room. I saw the boys, who were all dressed properly and grinning. They'd had fun. I was betting Lucien was exhausted.

"Did you keep him alive a little?" I asked.

"We carried him to your room. He'll take the elevator down." Galen snickered.

"Ouch. That sounds bad." I laughed. "I warned him."

"He said you made him go," Dilly said.

"I wasn't gonna let him back out just because he thought we trained as lightly as Warrick's pack. He had no idea what our training was like. Now he knows."

There was a groan from the doorway. I turned to see Lucien leaning against it. The entire room burst into laughter. He looked miserable. I went to him and helped him to a chair. He grunted as he lowered himself to the seat.

"Are you okay, mon cœur?" I asked softly.

"You're all insane," he groaned.

"Wasn't it a light day guys? It should have just been a short run, light exercising, and sparring. Did you change up the schedule?" I questioned them.

"Well, we went for a medium workout. We had to do light yesterday because we had a couple injured people. No one wanted three days of light training. We didn't want to go heavy with your mate being there for the first time. You said you didn't want him to die." Drake shrugged.

A medium workout was usually a run, a game, and a group spar. It was harsher than Warrick's training, which had more running and one-on-one fights. He was probably used to fighting only one person at a time in sparring. We trained for actual fights, which meant several people attacking at once.

"How many?" I asked with a wince.

"Just three and three. We babied him for you, Cap," Todd scoffed.

"Let's get seated. I want to get him fed and then I want you boys to help him back to my room for sleep," I ordered.

"Yes, Captain," they chorused.

We sat down for breakfast. To give him proper energy without too much quick-burning stuff, I made sure he had plenty of protein and limited carbs. It would ensure that he woke up feeling better.

My dad, Kieran, and Toby tried not to laugh at him. They'd moved back to standard warrior training a few months after I took over. They couldn't keep up with us. As long as the elite squads were prepared, they wouldn't have to worry.

Once the meal was over, I kissed Lucien on the head and sent him off with Jason and Galen. They'd get him settled for me. If he stuck with it, he'd be much stronger than me in short order, and the workout wouldn't be as bad.

Most of my guys took a thirty-minute nap after breakfast. He'd probably need more for a while. I figured I'd wake him up after I got done with my training.

I headed back to my office. There wasn't a lot left to read. There was a general history of the pack. I needed to go over the heads of different areas of the pack still and complaints filed against Lune Rouge. There hadn't been anything really big and bad.

The pack lost many people in a few large raids. Those raids were sometimes rogue and sometimes hunter, but always seemed to hit when the pack finally started prospering. It felt orchestrated, but it all started after they moved from France, ruling out a connection.

I wouldn't discount the idea. I just wasn't going to bank on it. There had to be something more recent for someone to try to kill directly instead of whittling down the pack.

When I reached the end of the print files, I looked at the time. It was ten-thirty. I decided I would go for a run later in the evening instead of training with the old people. I wanted to get this done so I could spend time with Lucien. He could relax in the larger tub in the room across from mine, and I'd give him a massage. It would help him feel better.

There was a knock at my door just as I was about to move on to the photos. I liked knowing the faces of the people I was dealing with. It made me feel more confident when meeting new people.

I opened the door, and Troy was standing there. I'd completely forgotten about him.

"Sorry, my schedule got thrown off, Troy. Is it yes or no?" I asked.

Joy told me yesterday, but a second opinion wasn't exactly a bad thing. He grinned and nodded. I bowed briefly.

"Thank you. Please, keep quiet. I'll make an announcement when it's prudent," I said.

"Anytime, Queen Bellamy. Congrats on everything. I better go." He bowed back and turned to leave.

I closed the door behind him and went back to my desk. Secondary confirmation. I was definitely pregnant. With a smile, I stroked the spot where my pups were resting and growing. My family.

Shaking my head, I returned to my files. If I finished by lunch, I could have the entire afternoon with Lucien. We could talk about baby names and plans for the future. I wanted to make love to him to celebrate our babies. In a couple of weeks, we'd see them clearly. In a couple of days, we'd be able to hear their hearts. I hoped it was only two. I didn't want a whole litter my first time.

I started looking at the pictures. Lucien and his family. He got his size from his dad, but his mom was where he got those gorgeous silver eyes. His sister had them, too, but she also had their mother's reddish-brown hair. Lucien had his father's black hair.

Moving on, I looked at Thierry Petit's family. I saw Caleb, and he was exactly as Cara described him. Thierry had the same hazel eyes as Caleb. His hair was a golden blond with a slight red tint. He stood about six feet tall, like most male wolves, and had a thick build. Not like Lucien, but decent.

His wife was dainty and blonde as well. They had a daughter who looked like an angel. She had that kind and sweet look on her face. Her eyes were green like her mother's and the same reddish golden blonde hair as her father's.

I flipped the page to the Gamma family and my stomach dropped. My head shook as I stared, speechless, at the impossible sight. This wasn't right. It couldn't be right.

Robert Dubois. I read the name again and examined the picture.

He had glossy auburn hair, a little long on top, with a slight wave that gave it a carefree look. His skin had a healthy, golden glow, like sun-kissed wheat. His physique was well-toned, however, he was not as muscular as I expect. A slightly impish half smile curved his mouth.

My focus went to his eyes. His eyes like mine. The eyes that had stared blankly at me while I hid in the wicker vase twelve years ago. Eyes that gazed at nothing when his head rolled from his body. I couldn't breathe.

Darkness clouded my vision, and I sank under my desk, curling into a ball in the safety of the deep foot well. No one could find me. My door was locked. I was hidden. There were no windows. I was safe.

No one would get me.

Chapter 51: Lost & Found

I woke up with a general soreness and a feeling of panic. It wasn't my panic, though. Jumping out of bed, I ran out to the living room of the Beta's quarters and nearly into Olive. She grabbed me frantically.

"We can't find Bellamy! Everyone hears her. Everyone in the pack hears her crying. Lucien, do you know where she could be? We need to find her. She's terrified. I keep seeing things. Horrible things, Lucien. Please, find her," she cried.

"Did you look in her office? That's where she was supposed to be until training at eleven," I said. I had the feeling that she was close by, though not in the Beta's quarters.

Looking at the clock, it was eleven-thirty. She never made it to the training. They wouldn't panic if she were there. Galen ran through the door.

"We checked the perimeter, no one's seen her. A rogue called Troy said he stopped by her office around ten-thirty and she was fine," he told us.

"Her office was thoroughly searched?" I asked as they clutched their heads and fell to the ground.

"No. Not again," Olive sobbed.

Galen wrapped his arms around his mom and held her tightly. I would have to do this on my own. I ran downstairs. Every pack wolf in the house was on their knees, gripping their heads, the people next to them, or sobbing on the floor. I found the odd man out, though. Well, men.

Kieran, Tobin, and Daniel stood in front of Kieran's office. They looked relieved when they saw me. I hurried to them.

"Galen's with Olive. What happened exactly?" I asked.

"Just before eleven, I started feeling fear, panic, intense sadness, and nausea. I put up my mental shields, none of it felt like my own feelings," Kieran said.

"We did the same, we were in a meeting. No one seemed to know where it was coming from, but we got reports from all over the pack. The boys said they could block it, too, but wanted to keep it live to see if it was an attack of some sort," Tobin added.

"The first flash happened ten minutes after the feeling started. Jason reported seeing a man and a woman being slaughtered. He said it was like he was frozen inside something. There were bars, it was made of wood. Dillon rushed in and said it was Bellamy after the first flash. He and Cara were the only ones in the pack she talked to about her parents' deaths. He recognized it from the story." Daniel drew a stuttering breath.

"Has this ever happened before?" I asked.

"No. She was sedated at night for her first week connected to the pack because something like this was possible. We checked her office, and there was a file on her desk. Her scent was almost completely gone. We have no idea how long ago she left," he said.

"Can you get me into her office? Let me see what I can find. I'm not a rogue, but I'm her mate. I should be able to find her," I told them.

Daniel took me to the office and unlocked the door. I stepped in and closed the door behind me, leaving him in the hall. I took a deep breath.

Her scent was faint. It was more faint than it had been yesterday when she left to deal with the rogue release. There were some rogues who could cover up their scent and slow their hearts down to a barely conscious state.

I walked over to her desk. The file was open, and there was a picture of Robert in it. She was researching my Gamma? I picked up the file. It was on my pack, everyone of importance, and their families. The file she asked Dillon about. This must have been the top-secret thing.

A faint beat sounded. She was in the office. I started searching. I looked in the bathroom and the closet. There was a little cupboard, but she wasn't in it. I got on my hands and knees and looked under her desk.

There was a small shaking lump under the desk. I couldn't reach her. The desk was short and the foot well was deep.

Remus was frantic. He was too big to get in there, too. I didn't want to move it and frighten her if she was having flashbacks of her parents' murders.

"Chouchoutte. Bellamy. My love. Please come here. Let me hold you. I know something scared you. Please, let me help," I said softly.

She shook more intensely. The sight of her distress caused a sharp pang in my chest. I didn't know what to do.

"You lied to me, Lucien," she whispered.

"When did I lie? What did I lie about?" I asked.

"You said you lost your first mate." A whimper followed her words and wrenched my heart.

"Sorry, chouchoutte. I didn't want you to know. I didn't want anyone to know. She rejected me. I was heartbroken and angry. I banished her and the man she left me for. My best friend."

"Your Gamma's twin brother," she sniffled.

"Yes. I regretted it," I replied and leaned against the desk. "I tried to find them. For years, I searched everywhere to apologize and help them find a pack to take them in. I wanted to apologize more than anything in the whole world. A messenger came seven years later and told me they died. He said they left some things behind and asked if we wanted them. We just wanted to move on."

It had been terrible. A few months after my rejection, I rejected Regan. The pain I felt made me realize Angelique hadn't had it easy, either. She'd felt the same pain when she rejected me. It hurt for hours when it happened to me. Angelique hadn't been an Alpha, so it hurt her longer.

She'd packed a bag and left within only one hour of rejecting me. The entire time, she had to have been in searing pain. I could barely move after I rejected Regan, but Angelique fought through it. I made her leave, even though she was hurt, simply because she wasn't in love with me, because she loved Jean-Luc instead of me.

"She was wrong," Bellamy murmured.

"She loved someone else. That wasn't wrong. It was strong enough to go against the will of a deity. That kind of love should've been protected. Not thrown away," I replied.

"The goddess didn't make a mistake," she stated in a breathy voice.

That was the opposite of what Angelique said. She told me the goddess made a mistake, and I was definitely *not* meant for her. I remembered the feeling of my heart ripping in two when she told me that. It was a similar sensation when I found out I would never see her or Jean-Luc again. Losing all hope of reconciliation.

"If the goddess hadn't paired you up. If she'd given her the man she wanted instead. Their daughter would've had a destined mate, who wasn't you."

What daughter?

I turned and pulled the file down, searched through it. There was no trace of Jean-Luc or Angelique; no sign they had ever existed. Every piece of information was from the past decade, none older than ten years. All the pictures were from when we were older except for my family picture. It didn't say anywhere Robert had a twin.

Bellamy knew Angelique dumped me for Robert's twin. My rejection wasn't in the file. My mother, sister, Robert, and Thierry were the only ones who knew.

Their daughter....

"Did you get scared because Robert looks like your father, chouchoutte?" I asked softly.

"Do you want to hurt me because they made me?" she answered.

"Warrick said you were afraid of the Alpha who banished them.... You were afraid of me."

My heart broke again. It really was too good to be true.

No matter what, Bellamy would've found out my pack was where her parents came from. If she'd come for the security meeting, she would've met Robert in person and Goddess only knows what that would've done to her.

Would she have reacted with fear, or with aggression and violence? We wouldn't have mated. The moment she learned my identity, any chance of a relationship would have vanished, her feelings for me never growing.

I couldn't imagine that possibility. I adored her completely; my heart, soul, and mind were hers. She had my whole heart.

The weight of not apologizing for kicking them out still burdened me. Their apology for hurting me never reached me. I refused to hear them. They would've kept trying until I heard them. I grew up with them. Neither was cruel enough to think they were entirely in the right.

"Forgive me, Bellamy. Forgive me for banishing them. They made you from love. I could never hate something so pure," I begged, praying to the goddess that she would forgive me. "I never would've hurt you."

"They forgave you. You were a child, a heartbroken child. I don't need to forgive you. You didn't do anything to me. They hoped you found your second chance mate and were happy, and that you forgave them once you found love."

"Once I got over my pain… once I felt the pain of hurting someone I was supposed to love… I forgave them. I understand if you want to take back your offer, Bellamy. We'll do whatever you want about the pups. You don't have to be tied to a person like me," I told her.

"Only one person, aside from my parents, knew where they came from. The messenger was from Limb Torn. I was something they left behind. You didn't want something to remind you of them. You wanted to move on. I can't force you to stay in a bond with me, not when I'm all those things. No matter how much I love you, I can't make you love me," Bellamy wept.

"Please, come out here. Let me see you. I want to make sure you're okay. I can't focus on anything until I know you're not injured," I pled.

There was some shuffling behind me. Soon, she crawled out from under the desk and sat on the other side of the opening. I glanced over.

Tears had dried, leaving red, irritated eyes and nose, and visible trails on her tear-stained cheeks. A hollow look, devoid of light and life, haunted her eyes. She looked away when she saw me looking at her.

"I loved your parents, Bellamy. I was young and stupid. Like most Alphas, I dug my heels in and stuck with a bad idea. Fixing that flaw has been a primary focus in my life. The person I am today isn't the angry, emotional boy I used to be.

"You were right. You can't make me love you. I adore you completely, and I don't believe it's possible for me to love you more. You don't have to stay with me, though. Stay only if you're sure you want to. I'll never stop loving you, *l'amour de ma vie*." I set my hand down on the ground between us.

"You don't hate me? You still want me?" she asked.

"Yes. Forever, chouchoutte. I always want to be yours," I insisted. "Do you still want me?"

Her hand found mine, and I closed my eyes. My tiny little mate. My best friend's daughter. The true love of my life.

"Forever, mon saucisson," she whispered.

I grabbed her hand, pulled her into my lap, and hugged her tight. She pressed herself against me, her body shaking with sobs, and cried silently. Gently rocking her, I hummed the tune she'd hummed on our stroll. I had a pretty good ear for tunes. Now I knew why the song was familiar. Angelique used to sing it to her baby dolls when we were little.

"Lucien?" Bellamy said softly.

"Yes, chouchoutte?" I asked.

"What were my parents' names?"

I remembered she said she didn't know their names when we were at Hunter's Moon. They were only Mama and Papa to her. It broke my heart that she'd spent the last twelve years not knowing something so simple about them. I'd make sure she never had to wonder again.

"Angelique Petit and Jean-Luc Dubois. Thierry and Robert are their older brothers. We'll answer any questions you have about them. I'm never going to hide anything from you. I promise."

I kissed the top of her head.

"I wonder why the file had 'P' as my last initial… maybe they decided to take Mama's name…."

"We'll figure it out, chouchoutte," I promised. "As soon as we get everything settled."

She was quiet for a while. I knew she was still reeling from everything. I certainly was. Robert and Thierry would be happy to know some part of their little sister and brother existed. I would make her as happy as possible and give her everything she desired for the rest of my life.

"There's so much ringing. Everyone's trying to talk to me," Bellamy mumbled into my chest.

"Your emotions were too strong, chouchoutte. Everyone felt them. They all saw what happened to your parents."

"Only the adults. I have a hard lock on children. It would have bled through to the ranked members first. If they blocked it, it would have started finding other places to go. It would have started with people close to me and warriors, then spread from there. I hurt them all. They'll never forgive me," she sniffled.

"Open the links up. You'll be surprised," I told her gently.

After a moment, she gasped. "They want to know if I'm okay. April apologized for being mean to me. So many people are saying sorry. So many are worried about me. Why? I did this to them."

"Because you're a member of their pack. You hid your pain for so long, and so well, they didn't know. None of them really knew what you suffered. You don't have to hide it from me, though. It's why I'm here. I'm your mate. Your other half. Give me some of your pain. Let me help you heal, chouchoutte. You don't have to be strong for me. Not until you're better," I murmured.

Her small body relaxed against mine, her breathing becoming shallow as I held and rocked her until she peacefully slept in my arms. I struggled a bit, but I managed to get up and walk to the office door. To avoid disturbing her, I gently knocked on the door with my foot and stepped back. A few moments later, Daniel opened it and let us out.

Chapter 52: Revelation of Loss

The hall was completely full, overflowing with so many people that it was difficult to move around. With a breathless gasp, Olive rushed over. Concern filled every face present.

"What happened, Lucien? Why did this happen to her?" she asked.

No one knew anything about the reason for her parents' banishment. But most people knew she was afraid of the man who'd banished them. I couldn't lie. I knew there were too many noses. Someone would scent it.

"Bellamy found out what pack her parents came from. Her father was a twin. When she saw a picture of his brother, she started having flashbacks to their murder," I replied.

It didn't take long before I could see it registering in the ranked members and some of the warriors. Their expressions changed from concerned to cold anger.

"Did you banish her parents, Lucien?" Kieran asked.

"Why do you think I'm so good at knowing how anger and pride cause issues with the judgment of Alphas? I was eighteen and I made a mistake because of that anger and pride. In fact, I made several big mistakes because of it. I worked to make sure I never would again," I told him.

The air in the hallway grew tense at my revelation. The entire Elite Ten was there, the ranked members and their wives, the kitchen staff, Dr. Hale, Bruce, several rogue born trackers, and a bunch of warriors. If I wasn't holding her, I was pretty sure someone might have attacked me.

They had just seen the result of me banishing her parents. They felt her fear and pain. And, of course, they knew the death of her parents wouldn't have happened if they were safely in a pack.

"Give me my daughter," Daniel demanded.

"I can't do that. I'm her mate. She only calmed down because of me," I said.

"She's spent her entire life *afraid* of you. She was exhausted from hiding once she figured out who you were. Bellamy probably fainted. When did you figure it out, Lucien? Was it before you marked my daughter or after? Did you decide you'd get your revenge on them by taking their child? What could they have done that was serious enough to cut them off from their families?" Daniel growled.

The hall buzzed with low growls, almost everyone echoing his tone. I almost laughed at how hard this whole relationship was. We couldn't catch a break. Nothing worth having was easy, though. I knew we'd be happy once this was all over.

I closed my eyes and breathed deeply. There had to be some way out of this. She needed rest and comfort. That wouldn't happen without me.

"Lucien, I don't feel good," Bellamy whimpered in my arms.

"When's the last time you ate, chouchoutte? How much have you had to drink?" I asked, my attention now fully on my mate. Everyone else could wait.

"I had juice before and during breakfast. I ate at breakfast, too. It's only lunchtime," she whispered and curled into me.

"Sounds like you might be dehydrated. Let's go get you a glass of water," I said softly and started walking forward, but we weren't getting far.

"I'm glad I found you, mon saucisson. No one else gets me like you do. They would've rushed me off to Dr. Hale. I just need water and you." She sighed.

"Amy, sweetheart, do you understand what's going on?" Olive asked.

"My mate is taking me to get water and have a nap. Then we have to figure out how to tell my uncles about me," Bellamy giggled.

"They'll be thrilled to know who you are, chouchoutte," I told her.

"I apologize for hurting everyone. Please forgive me. I had a big shock," Bellamy said.

"Here's some water," Yuri announced, holding up a glass.

The crowd split for him and he brought it to her. Bellamy took the glass and drained it quickly. She handed it back to him.

'They're mad at you. Why?' she asked.

'I told them why you were upset. They think I knew who you were. They think I'm planning to hurt you,' I replied.

'They don't know why you banished my parents. Only that I was afraid. I'm sorry, Lucien. I can try to fix it.'

'I don't have any idea how. They'll only think you're being tricked.'

'I can try. The first thing is easy. I can get rid of the rogues. Help me sit up more. It's hard to look queenly when you're being cradled like a baby.'

I helped her to sit in my arms. Bellamy straightened her back and glared around her. I stood still and kept myself planted. This wasn't something I could really fix. None of them would listen to me.

"Rogues, return to your patrols. You aren't needed here," she commanded.

"The pack wolves think you're in danger from that Alpha, Queen Bellamy," one answered.

"He is my consort. He would never harm me. Go on. The bear is more of a concern than a little family squabble," Bellamy stated.

They bowed briefly and left the hall. The warriors assigned to them had to leave, too. It cut our crowd down a lot.

"Dr. Hale, I don't need your help. Thank you for coming," she said coolly and looked away from the older man, effectively dismissing him.

He raised an eyebrow at Kieran and left. I was impressed. She was going to clear out a lot of people.

"Has lunch been served, Yuri? I'm very hungry. If you all are up here, then that means it must be over." She made a little pouty face.

"No. We didn't even start it yet. We were looking for you, Bebe. I'll go make you a good lunch. As long as you promise you're safe with the Alpha," he said.

"Lucien won't hurt me. I'll make sure you know everything later. I really am hungry." Her voice softened as she spoke to him.

I could tell Bellamy really cared for him as a friend. She told me during our trip from the vampires' house to Daylight Moon that he'd taught her how to cook and was like a grandma and big brother rolled into one. He always wanted to feed her.

"Okay, Bebe. I trust you. Come on, kitchen folk. Back to your ovens. We have to feed our pack," he ordered, and another ten people left the hall.

We were just left with the Elite Ten, Bruce, the ranked members, and their wives. Much easier to get around. Bellamy seemed to have come out of her funk altogether.

"Put me down, Lucien," Bellamy said.

I didn't question it; I just set her down. It was her home and pack, not mine. When we got to Lune Rouge, it would be a different story.

"Daddy, do not *ever* speak to Lucien like that again. You have no idea what my parents did to warrant getting banished. I told you I didn't want my life as a pack wolf to be connected with what they did. Lucien and I had a long conversation. We love each other too much to let what happened before I was even born affect it. I will *not* have you deciding what he does and does not intend to do with me," she lectured.

"When did he figure it out, Bellamy? How long do you think he's known?" Daniel asked.

"Lucien figured it out when I told him. No wolf is good enough at lying to make me honestly believe them. He was genuinely shocked when he found out I was their daughter. I picked him. My wolf made the offer. Not the other way around.

"After all the other stuff. With our history of miscommunication, your and Mommy's intervention, and our constant problems, please… can't you just let us do this our way? I'm a rogue Queen, an elite warrior, a straight 'A' student, and *your* daughter. I couldn't possibly be as stupid and gullible as you're making me out to be," Bellamy sighed.

"If he hadn't banished them, you wouldn't have had to watch them die," Galen said.

"If he hadn't banished them, I would've been a pack wolf. The rogues would've kept attacking your pack. None of the rogues in my collective would've been safe. An unknown number of girls would've been abducted, including Cara. Blossom and Anise wouldn't exist.

"How many people lived because I was rogue born? Many things in my life may have sucked, but how many lives were made better because of it?

"I didn't *have* to travel; you know? There's a reason behind my decision. I trained for a reason. Even before I had the issue with King Fuller and his son, I was training for my primary goal.

"I killed the hunters who killed my parents. I drugged them with a paralyzing potion I learned from some witches when I was nine. Then I cut them to pieces while they screamed inside their heads. I was the monster people wanted to imagine I was, then I lost purpose and drifted. It was just three months before I met the witch who tried to sacrifice me.

"Lucien was never part of my vengeance. I've already avenged myself, and my parents. Bad choices were made. Those who were actively evil paid for their involvement. I just want to be happy now. Can you let me be happy? Can't I just be a girl who found her mate? Why can't I have what I've had to watch everyone else have for all these years?" There were tears in her voice.

None of this was her burden. I wished I had been there to help her avenge them. Even if I couldn't be there for her back then, I was here for her now.

"I don't want to hurt Bellamy. I forgave her parents and tried to find them to bring them home or get them into a different pack. My hope was that they'd forgive me for my anger and we could be friends again. A messenger came after they'd died but was vague. If I'd known the messenger was talking about Bellamy when he said they left some things behind, I would've accepted her and brought her home.

"I don't know how our lives would've turned out, but I do know I would've done everything I could to make it up to her. And I still will. I'll give her the life she deserves. She's not just my mate, she's the daughter of two people I loved dearly. I would never let her come to harm," I promised.

They were considering it. Bellamy turned to me and put her arms up. I grinned and picked her up, cradling her. She wrapped her arms around my neck and kissed me on the cheek.

'I love you, Lucien.'

'I love you, too, Bellamy.'

Dillon approached us and placed a hand on my arm. I looked over at him. He fixed a sad gaze on Bellamy. Not pity, something different. He loved her. Perhaps he resigned himself to supporting her despite disagreeing with her decisions.

"I'll take you to your room, Alpha," he said softly.

"Thank you, Dillon." I nodded and followed him as he led us up to our room. No one tried to stop us.

When we arrived, Dillon opened the door and I carried her in. Bellamy rested her head on my shoulder, relaxing more when we were inside her space.

"Grab some clothes for tomorrow and something to sleep or relax in. Tonight, you're staying in the guest room across the hall. Melly and another omega will get your lunch and dinner. A few other omegas will be packing Bellamy's belongings. You guys were in the office for a while, but you might still have things to work out. Maybe you two should have some alone time to sort out everything else. I'll guard your door so no one comes to bug you," Dillon told me.

"Thank you for believing in me, Dillon," I said as I set Bellamy down.

"I've had to stand by and watch everyone find their mates, too. If my best friend can find a way to be happy, if she can find her mate in even the most unlikely place, then I have hope. I just want to know, and I won't tell anyone else, why did you banish her parents?" he asked.

"Lucien was my mother's fated mate. My mother rejected him because she was in love with my father," Bellamy whispered.

"I was young and heartbroken. My anger overwhelmed me and banished them. I regretted it after I realized how much pain her mother had been in just trying to have the love she wanted. If I'd known… I wouldn't have banished them. I would've relocated them. They would've been safe." I sighed.

"Their death wasn't your fault. Please, stop. It was the fault of the hunters and the King of Limb Torn, not you, not them. They could've been safe if King Fuller hadn't had that rule. Mama refused to be his plaything. She refused to be with any man other than my papa. That's why my only requirement is service. I won't leave any family out if I can help it," Bellamy stated as she turned and wrapped her arms around my waist.

I stroked her hair. She was right, but it was hard to accept. I knew my part in their deaths. If not for me, they'd be alive. She wouldn't have had to grow up without them.

"Sorry, chouchoutte. Let's get our things," I said.

"Good. You do it again and I'm going to punch you," she growled and went to gather her clothes.

Chapter 53: Regret Not Permitted

[Lucien]

After we'd gotten everything together, we went across the hall and set them in the dresser there. Dillon followed us. He'd been quiet since Bellamy told him what I'd done. I didn't know if he'd change his mind about guarding us. I hoped he wouldn't and that he wouldn't change his mind about joining my pack.

"I'll be right outside the door. I let Yuri know to send the food up. He says it's nearly done." Dillon smiled and headed to the door.

"Wait," I called out. "Aren't you going to say anything? Does this change your mind about our discussion yesterday?" I asked.

"No. I've had my heart broken before. It wasn't even to the level of having a mate reject you, but, if I could, I would've made sure I never saw them again. I get it. See you soon." He waved and left the room.

I stared at the door. I never actually thought anyone else would understand. Robert and Thierry had because they felt betrayed, too. Like me, they regretted their actions. Maybe this was Angelique and Jean-Luc giving us a chance to heal and give their daughter the life she deserved. I wasn't sure I could ever fix things, but I'd try my best forever.

"I told you to stop, Lucien Deveraux," Bellamy scolded from behind me. "Look at me."

Turning, I looked down at her.

How did I miss all the ways she looked like her parents? Her glare, the way she crossed her arms, and the air of disappointment, were all like Jean-Luc when he was scolding us for being stupid.

"I can't. I keep trying. Can you forgive me for—"

"No. Because you did nothing to me. I will tell you that every day forever. Stop." Bellamy pulled her tank top over her head and started unbuttoning her pants.

Goddess, her body was a sight to behold; I had completely forgotten how stunning she was. She came up to me and started undoing my pants.

"Take off your shirt, Lucien," she ordered.

"Bellamy, I don't know if this is a great idea right now," I whispered.

She rolled her eyes up to meet mine. Never before had I felt so threatened with just a look. She grabbed my shirt, her eyes blazing, and tore it in half.

"When I say strip, you strip," she growled as she ripped my pants down the front.

"What the hell, Bellamy!?" I shouted.

A growl rose in my throat as I swiftly picked her up, keeping her away from my underwear. I was determined to have a conversation, and we were going to fucking have it. She needed to calm the hell down.

"Let me go, Lucien!" she demanded, trying to wrench my arm off of her.

"No. We're going to talk. You are going to listen. I'm not going to have sex with you until we do," I snarled.

"I don't want to! You'll just sit around feeling sorry for yourself about things you can't change. All you're going to do is whine about what you did wrong and what you should've done instead. You're a fucking Alpha! Act like it!" Bellamy commanded.

She bit my mark, sending a jolt through my body. I'd act like a fucking Alpha if she insisted.

Pulling her off, I threw her on the bed and jumped, trapping her body under mine. Bellamy pushed at me and I grabbed her arms, holding them above her head.

"You are mine. You'll do what I say," I told her.

"I do what I want, and I want to do you. Give me what you've been promising for the last twenty-four hours. If you want to own me, you have to let me own you."

She strained, pressing her body up as much as she could. I pulled back and flipped her over, ripping off her panties and pulling her body up to meet mine.

My cock strained to make contact through the cloth of my underwear, but I would have what I wanted before I gave her what she wanted. Grinding into her, I knew exactly what I wanted to say, what she had to know.

"Say you forgive me and I'll give you the pounding you crave, little mate. I'll make you scream and cry and come until you can't move anymore. Say it if you want your Alpha to fuck you into madness," I ordered.

Bellamy moaned and rubbed herself along my length. I reached with one hand and wrapped it in her hair, pulling her head back. With my other hand, I rubbed her clit, drawing more of her sexy little moans and groans out.

"Forgive me, Bellamy. Give me what I need and I'll give you what you need."

"No, I'll never forgive you, Lucien," she replied breathily. "I will never forgive you for regretting me. I will never forgive you for regretting us."

I stopped moving. "You think I regret you?"

"If you hadn't banished them, I wouldn't exist as a rogue. I wouldn't be your mate. Every time you ask me to forgive you, you're asking me to forgive my existence and our connection. You're saying you regret this, me, our pups.

"I never wanted to live under the shadow of what my parents did. Put a wall around it. Leave it alone. Let it be dead, too. Stop making me talk about this. Show me you don't regret me," Bellamy insisted.

Letting her go, I got off the bed. Bellamy laid on her stomach and covered her face with her hands. I took off the boxer briefs and rolled her over, spreading her legs and laying between them.

Softly, I kissed her damp mound and slid my tongue over her clit. Her back arched and her hands moved to grasp the blanket she was lying on. Slipping my fingers inside her, I rubbed her g-spot as I suckled at the tiny bundle of nerves that made her sigh and writhe until she cried out and grasped my hair. I would show her I didn't regret her.

Moving my fingers out of her, I crawled up, replacing them with my cock, and pressing further into her until I filled her completely. I kissed her sweet mouth and moved slowly but firmly, letting her feel every inch of my desire for her. Her muscles tensed over and over, squeezing me as I eased myself in and out of her tiny body.

I hadn't ever considered that I was saying I regretted her. She was perfect. She was everything. My Bellamy, my mate, my heart.

I trailed kisses down her neck and nibbled her mark. It was only a few days ago that Bellamy changed my entire life. She gave me what I was craving, the love and family I wanted and thought I would never have. Bellamy never pushed against it, never tried to rein it in. She embraced her love for me and moved forward.

Bellamy murmured my name over and over, telling me how much she loved me, as I made love to her, reveling in the heat and tightness of her body. Nothing was ever like her. I felt my end nearing amid a cascade of her small sweet squeezes. I wanted to feel her clamp down around me and hold me tight.

Picking up the pace, I moved my hips in a circular motion while I pumped into her. Holding back with everything I could while her fingernails dug into my flesh and I worked her into a state of bliss. She tightened around me more, milking my cock. I finally released, pouring into her.

"I never regret you, chouchoutte. I'm just an idiot," I whispered as I kissed her.

"I'll forgive you for being an idiot," she giggled breathlessly.

"Get used to it. I can be an idiot a lot." I chuckled and got up.

"No cuddling? That's cold, mon saucisson."

"Our lunch is probably going to be here any second. Unless they screamed and ran away and we were too distracted to notice."

"I forgot about lunch!" Bellamy laughed. "I just checked with Dilly. He says he has our food and will bring it in when we're decent."

I grinned and grabbed the little silky shorts and tank top she'd picked out. After putting on some basketball shorts, I took her clothes to her.

"No panties?" she asked.

"No. Never," I growled playfully.

She laughed again and went to the bathroom to clean up and dress. I vowed I would never hurt her, then I basically told her I regretted her. I'd never do that again.

Once she was out of the bathroom, I opened the door and helped Dillon with the trays. There were little finger sandwiches, glasses of water, and fruit.

"Yuri sent this up after I told him it would be a while before you two would be ready to eat. He's making pizza tonight. Just let him know what you want on it. Alpha Kieran came by, but I told him you two weren't up for company. He seemed to understand, but Bemmy may want to link him, in case it was important," he said as he set his tray down on the dresser.

"Thanks, Dilly. I appreciate you so much," Bellamy smiled and gave him a hug.

"Sure thing, Cap. I'm just glad you're feeling better. You two need to stop having stuff happen. Life as a werewolf is tough enough, quit finding more drama." Dillon chuckled as he headed to the door.

He closed it behind him and I realized what a good idea it was to bring him into my pack. Bellamy needed the support of familiar people. Having Cara and Dillon would help her acclimate to our pack more easily.

We sat on the bed and ate quietly. There would be time to talk about everything later. I needed to process more, or I'd keep saying things that hurt her. Right now, we needed to just exist without complication or interruption.

"What do you want to do with all our free time?" Bellamy asked.

"Hmm. Make love to you again. Then have dinner, and spend the night finding every spot on your body that makes you melt," I suggested with a wink.

She giggled. "Our entire relationship can't be sex, or we'll just keep having issues… and babies."

"I like the idea of having a lot of babies, but not issues. You didn't want to talk earlier." I reminded her.

"I didn't want to talk about my parents. I still don't. We'll have time for that later. I'd rather do it in a place where I don't have to deal with my other family getting overprotective and interrupting. There are other things. We already worked out a lot of our personalities and ruling styles with Ricky and Janie."

"Why does she let you call her Janie, but not Dillon?" I asked.

"Because I give nicknames out of love. And I had that one first. I don't share." She smirked. "Plus, they like fighting about it."

"So no one else is allowed to call me 'saucisson'?"

"They better fucking not," she growled.

We laughed and finished our meal. I took the trays out to Dillon and returned to cuddle with Bellamy. Having her in my arms made me feel calmer than I had in years.

"What about baby names?" she asked.

"I'd like to wait until we know what they are before we decide," I said.

"So you want to know before they're born?"

"If you're okay with it. I want to be prepared in every way we can be."

"It's fine," Bellamy sighed and snuggled deeper into my side. "I should link Kieran and find out what he wants. I wouldn't be surprised if he uses this to make me leave the pack permanently."

"I can kick his ass if you want," I offered.

"No. I've outgrown the pack anyway. I was surprised he didn't do it when I ran… unless that was the mistake he almost made," she said softly.

"It was. He saw it wasn't a great idea. There was a lot of opposition. In both cases, it was the first time anything like that happened. He should really have taken our counseling suggestion," I told her.

"I've been in counseling. Millie is my therapist. We've mostly worked on my issues as a rogue in a pack. She's the reason I'm so zen about the hate. We talked about some of the stuff, but I didn't really get into my parents' death. There were a lot of other things that needed attention," she explained.

I nodded. She'd lived a long and difficult life in only a few short years. I'd make sure she could see a therapist in my pack, too.

"Do you want me to let Thierry and Robert know who you are before we leave, or wait until we get there?" I asked.

"I don't know. What do you think will be best?"

"We should tell them. It will give them time to process, and get over the fact that they were pressuring me for details about our sex life yesterday." I chuckled.

Bellamy started laughing so hard she could barely breathe. I thought it was funny, but not that funny.

"Sorry," she squeaked. "I can only imagine how red they'll turn. It might make it worth it to wait so we can see firsthand."

"That sounds perfect." I laughed.

She laid quietly in my arms while I stroked her back. This was the kind of peaceful afternoon I'd wanted. Just connecting in the quiet calm before we left.

"I have to go," Bellamy sighed. "Kieran has Elite Ten business with me. I'll be back right after it's done."

"After we get married, I'm taking you away from everything for a week. No rogue business, no warrior business, no pack business. Just you and me and room service," I vowed.

"That sounds amazing, mon saucisson," she purred.

Bellamy crawled out of bed and changed into the clothes she'd been wearing earlier. She came back and gave me a kiss before leaving. I hoped this wouldn't take her away again. There were so many things I still had planned for the evening.

Chapter 54: Unbearable Interactions

Leaving Lucien was getting harder and harder. Maybe things would get easier once we made it to Lune Rouge. It would be a while before I knew. It could just be because of the pups or the emotional situation earlier.

When I was young, I truly feared the Alpha who'd banished my parents would find me. Like Lucien said, Alphas were stubborn and never changed their minds. I never thought there'd be an Alpha who wasn't like the rest. But he was. Lucien learned from his mistakes and was a better leader for it.

I loved him so much. Honestly, I feared someone at Lune Rouge might think he only wanted me because he couldn't have my mom. I'm glad I confided in only Ricky about why my parents were exiled; otherwise, things might have turned out differently.

The idea of having chosen the mate my mother gave up was super weird. It wasn't like he was my father or would have been my father. Everyone always said how much I looked like my papa when I was little. Mama said I was a little copy of him in a million different ways.

I couldn't imagine my mother with Lucien, though. She was too flighty for him. She might have been a better match for him back then. It didn't matter now; he was mine.

I knocked on Kieran's office door, and he linked me to enter. Once inside, he swooped in, arms wrapping around me in a tight, warm embrace. It was really fucking awkward. Kieran and I weren't big on hugging.

"Kieran? Could you not? My mate will be upset if I come back smelling like another man," I whispered.

"I'm going to hug you for a bit longer. He can fight me if he has a problem. Once we sent Lucien into the office, I took down my mental shield. I saw what happened. I'm truly and deeply sorry. It was wrong of me to let you become a warrior. I should've let you have a childhood," he said as he held me tightly.

"What are you talking about? I *did* have a childhood. I wanted to work as a warrior. You aren't making sense. I went to school, played with my friends, did extracurriculars, volunteered, babysat, had sleepovers…. I don't understand what else I needed for this to be a childhood."

"Safety. Not having to fight or defend. I should have treated you like a kid, not like a tool."

"You called me down for Elite Ten stuff, not this mushy shit. Get the hell off me and start talking, Alpha," I growled.

He pulled back sharply and moved to the other side of his desk. I grabbed a chair in front of the desk and waited for him to talk.

"I didn't know how to get you to come out of your room. I was lucky when I got a call from Lune Rouge. They caught the bear. He's being held in their cells," Kieran told me.

"That could've waited until tomorrow." I scoffed.

"He's not talking. They've had interrogators in with him for an hour," he stated.

"Call Thierry. He won't talk for anyone other than an Alpha. All wandering bears are Alphas. They see any creature lower than that level of power as weak and worthless unless it's another bear. He won't tell them anything. None of them are powerful enough," I explained.

He dialed Thierry and let him know what I'd said. I heard him say he was pulling the interrogators until Lucien and I arrived. After he hung up, I smiled.

"Anything else?" I asked.

"No, Dillon told us you wouldn't be down for dinner. I just wanted to know if you're really alright with Lucien and what he did. Daniel said he heard you two fighting, but Dillon wouldn't let him in," Kieran said.

"We had an argument. It happens. I've seen you argue with Daisy and my dad argue with my mom. Neither of you needed referees, we didn't either. Stop worrying. I told you, we decided it wasn't worth it to focus on the past," I assured him.

"You can come back home anytime. If you need space again, our house is always open to you," he promised.

"I appreciate that, Kieran, but I really want to go back now. I'm getting antsy," I said and got up to leave.

"The bus and truck will be ready after breakfast tomorrow. We figured you wouldn't want to be on the road too long. Early morning will have less traffic."

"Thanks. See you later." I waved and left the office.

As I was heading to the stairs, I remembered the request for aid I had set aside. I really wanted to get back to the room.

'Drake, there's a request for aid in the tray on my desk. Can you look it over, make a decision, and contact the appropriate lieutenant?' I asked in our link.

'Yes, Queen Bellamy. Are you doing okay?'

'I'm fine, Drake. See you tomorrow.'

'Sure thing.'

When I reached the Beta's quarters, my parents were waiting. I almost rolled my eyes and groaned. Obviously, nobody was going to let me get back to my mate easily.

Lucien really was the only one who got me. They all worked on their own assumptions of my motivations instead of accepting what I said or actually paying attention. They were better than when I was a kid, but somethings never changed. Sometimes he messed up, but he tried. I knew he would change because I could see how dedicated he was to taking care of me.

Our earlier encounter may have finally helped him realize why his apologies were upsetting me. I could understand the first time, but after I told him to stop, it felt like he didn't want actual forgiveness. It felt like he wanted me to be angry and hate him. I couldn't hate him.

"Amy, do you have a minute?" Mom asked.

"Are you going to try to convince me to leave my mate or bug me about him banishing my birth parents?" I sighed. "Are we going to have to rehash what happened in the hall?"

"No. We just want to see if you're okay. You went through a lot of heavy emotional stuff today. Did you want to talk to Millie? She says she'll come over if you need her. She saw what happened to your parents and felt what you felt, just like we all did."

"I'm fine, Mommy. I just need to go be with Lucien. We're talking about a lot of big things and Kieran interrupted. I can't work through it all if people keep getting in my way," I replied.

"So, you're talking to him about what happened then?" she asked.

"Lucien will help me deal with stuff. He's dealing with things, too. We'll work together like we're supposed to. Please, trust that I know what I'm doing," I pled.

"Can we hug you before you head back?"

I nodded. They came over and wrapped their arms around me. While I'm not a hugger, they were the type who loved to hug. I got used to them needing lots of hugs. It wasn't about me being a rogue.

Rogues were physically close to the people they cared about, too. It was probably because of the curse. It would've made me dislike being touched and just became my normal.

They released me, and I finally reached the hall. There were boxes being stacked outside my bedroom. Leaning against the wall, Dillon wore an angry expression.

"Trying to look deadly and dangerous?" I asked as I approached.

"Do you think it works? No one has really tried to talk to me," he chuckled.

"I think you're pretty when you're angry," I teased.

Dillon smirked and tossed his hair. He assumed his 'sexy' pose and winked.

"If you and the Alpha ever want to try for a devil's three-way… no, girls are still gross." He stuck out his tongue, making a 'yucky' face.

We laughed. He joked about being willing to go straight for me pretty often. I think, on some level, Toby and Bren hoped he would. Dilly was my closest friend in the pack.

He and I were even closer than me and Cara. Both a little outcast for things that were out of our control, but tolerated for what we brought to the pack. I figured I'd ask him about moving to Lune Rouge after we'd gotten there. I could handle just about anything if I had Dilly and Cara by my side.

Chapter 55: Feeling the Bond

I went into the room and closed the door. Lucien wasn't there. I knocked on the bathroom door, but there wasn't an answer. Peeking inside, I saw him asleep in the tub. It was so cute.

Entering the room, I watched for any signs he was awake. No movement and steady breathing indicated that he wasn't. The water was still warm, and the tub was bigger than the one in my room, but not big enough to submerge his huge frame. I grabbed a washcloth and decided I would wash him like he had washed me last night.

After taking off my clothes so they wouldn't get wet, I grabbed the soap and dampened the cloth. I completed one arm and half of his chest before he stirred. My focus was almost entirely on his chest, the dark swirls of hair that covered his muscles, and the feel of the soapy cloth rubbing over his skin.

"What are you doing, chouchoutte?" he groaned.

"You fell asleep, so I was helping you clean up," I stated.

"Hmm. Without any clothing on?"

"What if I slipped and fell in the water? Then I'd have wet clothes. No one wants wet clothes," I giggled and washed lower on his stomach.

"Now I'm worried about you slipping. Let me get you seated somewhere safer," he purred and slipped his hands around my waist, pulling me onto him until I was straddling his body.

"You are a dirty old man," I growled.

"Then I guess this bath will take even longer than expected." He chuckled and pushed himself into me.

"Lucien," I sighed.

"You always feel amazing, my little mate," he moaned.

The water splashed around us as we moved together, the cloth long forgotten as my hands slipped over his soapy chest and shoulders. Having him in me was fulfilling. I never felt as good as I did when I was connected to him. His thick length stretched me, demanding further entry deep inside me.

I leaned back, tensing my muscles while he pumped into me. Waves of pleasure ripped through me. I couldn't breathe for all the orgasms that crashed over me. I had no idea how he did it. He seemed to rub in all the right spots, no matter how he had me.

My fingernails dug into the swell of his chest as I reached the peak that stole my control, making my whole body tense and spasm as I screamed his name. He always lasted until that point and finished with me, but, this time, he was still going, drawing it out. It wasn't until another hit several minutes later that I finally felt the pulse of him completing as his fingers gripped my hips tightly.

The water ended up washing away the soap on him at some point. I was grateful for that because I couldn't hold myself up and laid my head on his chest. Lucien stroked my hair, and I relaxed more. This was perfect.

"Let's get out of the bath, chouchoutte. It's not nearly big enough for both of us, and the water is either cold or on the floor," Lucien murmured as he kissed the top of my head.

"You should have to suffer for what you've done," I stated seriously.

"For what am I suffering?"

"For not letting me finish washing you. It was terribly rude," I pouted.

"I'm sorry, my little rogue Queen. You were just too beautiful, I had to have you."

"Fine. I'll accept your apology. I expect you to make it up to me, though."

"How will I do that, chouchoutte?" he asked.

"Come out and run with me before dinner. Let's let Remus and Aurora play for a while. I really want to stretch my legs," I requested.

Lucien winced a little. I knew he had the same issue I had. As soon as I said it, Aurora started shouting and celebrating. She knew I was being cautious because of the bear. Now we could be with our mate properly.

"Remus loves the idea," Lucien laughed.

"So does Aurora. We have to take Dilly along. Griffin doesn't like to play as much. He's a warrior and says he'll only relax once he's found his mate. Until then, he will be my claw and tooth. He vowed loyalty to Aurora the first time the Elite Ten ran together in our wolf forms," I told him.

"Is that why Dillon is such a powerful warrior?"

"No. He fights so no one tries to hurt him. Not everyone in the pack is cool with an openly gay male. I really hate leaving him," I said as I climbed off him and carefully out of the tub.

"I told him I would accept him into my pack once his mission was over. We're a lot more accepting. Your cousin, Jean-Claude, is openly gay and the head of our warriors. Not because he wanted or needed to protect himself from the pack, but because it was tradition. The second twin is always a strong fighter in your father's family. That's why Jean-Luc was our head warrior before he and Angelique left," Lucien responded.

My heart leapt. I hated leaving my friend behind, especially since Cara was at Lune Rouge. And he wouldn't have to fight to be himself. It would be wonderful to have them both there while I was dealing with the pushback that always happened when I expanded.

"Thank you, my love. I really want my friends to be happy. Let's go run." I smiled.

"Anything for that smile, mon amour." He winked.

We dressed, and I linked Yuri about the pizzas. It turned out that Lucien and I did *not* have the same taste in pizza toppings. He liked peppers, onions, pineapple, bacon, and pepperoni. I was an 'all the meats' kind of girl, maybe some mushrooms… if I really had to. Yuri was happy to make two for us.

Dilly loved the idea of going for a run. He made sure the patrols were aware we'd be out as we made our way to the changing rooms. The rooms had large doggie doors in the walls, so we could keep our clothes there while we went for a run. Kieran's dad created it because he didn't want people seeing his mate naked.

I went into the women's side, took off my clothes, and put them in a basket that had my name on it. Then I let Aurora take over. She was itching to get out so badly that I changed almost as soon as the clothes fell from my hand. Aurora wanted to see her mate for real. She wanted to bond with him like I had with Lucien.

She bounded out of the flap door and looked around. Griffin was waiting, seated a few feet away, but Remus was nowhere to be seen. She huffed and went to sit by Griffin.

'Lucien, where are you? Remus isn't having performance anxiety, is he?' I asked.

'He's worried she won't like him. I've never seen him like this.'

'Is she the first female for him? He didn't go and rut like a wild animal even though you did?'

'Wow. Not even a week in and she's bringing up my past. No. He never even looked at another female wolf after we were rejected.'

'That's so cute. Aurora has been waiting patiently for him. She's not a patient wolf. If you guys don't get out here, we're coming in,' I warned.

A minute later, the flap moved and a large, chocolate colored wolf came out. He was shiny and sleek. His eyes were like Lucien's, impossibly silver and beautiful.

Aurora walked around him as he stood stone still. She rubbed up along his flank and licked his muzzle. When he didn't move, she stood in front of him and lowered her front end to the ground, wagging her tail in the air. It was a play position. He didn't respond, so she lunged a little and nipped near him before jumping back.

'What's going on? Why won't he move?' she asked me.

'You're his first mate. I think he's nervous.'

'He shouldn't be nervous. I love him.'

'Don't hold back. He probably needs some encouragement, if you know what I mean.'

'Oh, I know exactly what you mean. Dirty little rogue girl.'

'Get him bitch! Claim your mate before he turns into a statue forever,' I laughed.

She straightened up and sneezed at him. His eyes jumped to her, and she sauntered close, rubbing against him until she saw her goal. She lowered her head and licked him between his legs. Then, head-butted him in the haunches, making him stumble before she ran off into the woods.

Chapter 56: When Remus Met Aurora

[Lucien]

I was in the changing room, trying to get Remus to move his furry ass. He'd been eager for this, but now he was dawdling. My pervy wolf's attempt to hide in the changing room while his mate waited outside shocked me. This wasn't like him at all. Remus was always confident, and he was the one who accepted Aurora's offer to be mated.

'What the hell are you doing?' I asked him.

'I can't. Lucien, I can't go. I'm too old. I can't play like she'll want to.'

'You aren't too old! We aren't too old! If you can fight, you can play.'

'Her human half's MEDIUM level training kicked your ass! She'll be disappointed.'

'For fucks' sake! Get out there! Bellamy just linked me. They're waiting. She says if we don't come out, they're coming in.'

'Fine! Damned females,' he grumbled.

We left the changing room finally. Once we were out, Remus looked up. A silver and white male was sitting a few feet off. From behind him came a female. It had to be Aurora.

Her fur was golden yellow over her stomach and legs leading up to her back and head, which were the same bronze color as her hair with a strip of dark auburn down her spine. Aurora had Bellamy's honey-brown eyes and was as big as Remus, not nearly as tiny as her human form.

She rubbed against us and licked Remus' muzzle. We froze. He was panicking as she bounced into a play pose.

'She's beautiful. I don't know what to do!'

'It's been years since you thought you'd be in this situation. Come on, Remus. She wants to be with you. You told me you liked talking to her. If you can't play, she'll think of something you can do together. At least try.'

Aurora lunged and nipped before jumping back into the play position. I knew she would have as much patience as Bellamy, which was not much. When she straightened up and sneezed, I knew she was tired of this. I hadn't expected her to just walk up and start licking our junk before knocking us over and running off into the woods.

That seemed to be all it took to get Remus over his nerves, though. He took up the chase, and we ended up running, rolling around, and wrestling with her. After playing for a while, we rested in a meadow. Aurora and Remus groomed each other before curling up together. He put his head on top of hers.

'Glad he got over that, mon saucisson,' Bellamy giggled in our link.

'She's just as bold as you. I'm glad, too, though. He's usually the one to push me to act.'

'We know what we want. Once everything is calm again, we'll be able to go out hunting. Finding prey while rogues are on patrol is hard.'

'I'll look forward to it.'

We spent another hour letting our wolves play and explore together. I could feel them bonding even more. It would help our relationship in the long run if they had this connection.

Aurora was perfect for Remus. By the end of the afternoon, he was feeling more like a pup himself, even if he was a little worn. Playing for Alpha wolves was more physically trying than playing for other ranks of wolves. And they were just as frisky as Bellamy and I were.

As soon as the romantic tension started to build between Aurora and Remus, Griffin would immediately and discreetly remove himself from the situation. He went hunting with the wolves, but didn't take part in any of the games, exactly as Bellamy said. Despite being smaller than Aurora and Remus, Griffin was unusually strong and self-assured.

Dillon and his wolf would definitely be a positive addition to my pack. After seeing him in training this morning, I was already feeling more confident about inviting him to my pack. I knew our warriors would benefit a lot from having him and Bellamy helping Jean-Claude with training regimens.

Once we were back at the house and changed, we headed to the room. With Bellamy's belongings packed, the omegas were carefully loading them into the truck Kieran provided for our move. Entering our room, she gave my hand a gentle squeeze.

"This time tomorrow, we'll be in the Alpha's quarters in Lune Rouge. I bet you're excited to get home, mon saucisson," she purred.

"Of course, I am. I want you to meet my mother and some of my closest friends. I want to make love to you in our bed and start planning the nursery for the babies. Most of all, I want to have your Luna ceremony and have you join my pack," I told her as I pulled her to me and swayed her gently.

"Do you think they'll like me, Lucien? I'm worried they'll hate me and try to make me leave. Especially when they find out who my parents were," Bellamy gripped me and pressed her face into my chest.

"I think they will love you. You are so perfect, Bellamy. Jean-Luc would be proud of the woman you grew into and Angelique would, too. No one at Lune Rouge hates your parents. We all made our peace with what happened a long time ago. Even my mother and sister forgave them after a few years. You're not to blame. No one will blame you for what they did. If they do, I'll kick their asses. I promise, chouchoutte."

"I trust you, Lucien. You didn't try to hurt me and only tried to leave when you thought it was what I wanted. What about the ones who think I'm too young for you?" she asked.

"They're just the jealous ones. It's more likely they'll say I'm too old for you." I chuckled.

"You know I don't care about your age though, right?"

"Remus was afraid we were too old to run with a pup like you. I kept telling him you wouldn't push us too hard."

"Once you get used to training with me, you'll do much better." She giggled.

"I'll probably die," I groaned, remembering how difficult the training had been just on medium.

"Then I'll be the Alpha of your pack until the children are grown. So, you can't do that," Bellamy said jokingly.

"I think I need a drink from the fountain of youth. Come, chouchoutte, I'm going to make you scream," I growled.

"How is that going to make you live longer?" Bellamy asked as I pulled her to the bed.

"When I'm in you, I feel twenty years younger. All I experience is your pleasure and it makes me happy. Happiness creates long lives, you know," I told her.

"I see. Then I just have to make you happy all the time and you'll live forever?"

"That is exactly how it works." I nodded, kissing her and peeling off her clothing.

We made love and spent the rest of the evening cuddling, kissing, talking, and eating. Yuri made some amazing pizza. I stole a little of Bellamy's and it led to a wrestling match, which I won. She could make anything fun, even just dinner.

Right before sleep, I stroked her stomach, thinking of our babies. No other pack wolf would have a better start than they would. With a full understanding of wolf culture, our first child would be the greatest Alpha in history. No matter the circumstance, I would always be there for them; they were my most precious treasure, a jewel second only to my mate.

Chapter 57: Leaving Daylight Moon

Lucien and I pulled ourselves apart and out of bed with only twenty minutes before breakfast. We'd worn ourselves, and each other, out the night before. I was so happy to have my life moving forward. Stagnation made me nervous.

We went down to breakfast and only just made it. Yuri clucked his tongue at us and shook his head. I was going to miss him so much. Breakfast was all of my favorites. It made it a little better. He was obviously trying to make my last memory of home a good one.

When we were done, the boys met us out front. I hugged my parents and the girls. This was the sort of occasion where it was called for. I also had to hug Daisy, Kieran, Bren, and Toby.

When I hugged Clint, he spun me around. He was always supportive and never got weird about any of my rogue work. Honestly, he was the first adult I had ever connected with in the pack.

I turned and saw my men giving last goodbyes to their parents and mates. I would make sure they could come home from time-to-time, but it was still a long while in between seeing their mates and families.

"Alright men!" I shouted as I walked back.

They straightened, and their families move to the sides. I looked them over as I got closer. They were ready. I could see their excitement. A long-term mission was rare. This one would help an allied pack and would cement them as a powerful force in the world of pack wolves.

"The trip to Lune Rouge isn't long. I want you to spend this time getting Bruce up to date on everything. Make sure he understands how to act if he's going to pretend to be me.

"When we arrive, Lucien and I will disembark first, you will follow on my signal. The first day will be spent getting your rooms set and exploring your assigned areas. I want you fluent in the geography of Lune Rouge by twenty-two hundred hours. Understood?" I ordered.

"Yes, Captain!" they responded.

"I want information on guard rotations, training, warrior status, and pack squabbles. I need to know any connections that may be risky for the Alpha and his family. Drake, Dillon, and Galen, I want the status of any rogues in the area and any rogue settlements. If you have time on the first day, you can start on the second day's work. I expect all of this by tomorrow night at twenty-two hundred hours. Understood?"

"Yes, Captain!"

"Say any last goodbyes and get on the bus. We leave in fifteen minutes," I directed.

"Yes, Captain!" they chorused.

I went to Lucien and took his hands. "Are you ready to go home, my love?"

"Yes, Captain." He winked.

I giggled as he lowered his lips to mine. This was so different from the missions we'd had before. Normally, I would watch everyone else say goodbye and look after the final preparations. I suddenly realized this was the last mission I'd have with my boys.

"Are you crying, chouchoutte?" Lucien whispered.

"I think, a little. Can I have a team when we get to Lune Rouge? I don't like the idea of never having fun like this again." I asked.

"Anything you want. I know you'll be the best option for running a team like this, as long as you don't do it while pregnant. I want our family to be safe."

"Of course, mon saucisson. I promised you already, our pups will come first. Always." I smiled.

"Let's get on the bus. I can't wait to introduce you to my mother. She's going to love you," he murmured as he turned and guided me to the steps, helping me to a seat.

Soon, we were on the road. I cuddled close to Lucien and listened to the guys try to instruct Bruce on how to pretend to be their captain. They got silly after some time and Lucien couldn't hold in his laughter.

"You have to scowl and wrinkle your nose when Dillon gets weird." Galen laughed.

"No, more scowling, you look like you smelled something bad. You have to look really disgusted by him," Freddy instructed.

Dilly snorted. "And you need to look a little tired of it. Like 'this again' sort of thing in the eyes."

I turned in my seat and scowled at them.

"Like that! See! Bellamy's perfect." Jason laughed.

"Stop instructing him on my facial expressions and tell him how to make it seem like he has any sort of control over you. Then tell me the same, because you're all really fucking insubordinate," I growled.

"Go back to your mate, Luna! We're doing warrior work," Porter called out.

I turned back and huffed as I plopped back into my seat. Lucien kissed the top of my head.

"You need to remember to let go of control, chouchoutte. You are only a basic female warrior. I'm the protector and leader here."

I sighed. He was right. I needed to get into my role as well. Aside from everyone on the bus, only Cara, Thierry, and Robert knew I was the captain of the Elite Ten.

I smelled enough like a pack wolf to confuse the noses of common wolves and omegas. The ones with ranked genes would know. They had a more sensitive sense of smell. Lucien would link them before we got off the bus, so they said nothing. Any rogues hiding in the pack would know, just as I would know what they were.

The rest of the ride was mostly listening to the boys and trying to hold myself like a ranked she-wolf. They weren't as rigid as I could be, but still kept themselves a little closer. I tended to take up space. Which was impressive with how small I was. I also needed to not be as bold. That would take work.

Nearly an hour later, we passed the border marker, two trees that had been manipulated to grow with a slight spiral. Not enough to draw a ton of attention, but enough to show any entering that it was a purposeful shaping. I was excited to see the place my love, and my parents, had grown up.

"Are you ready, chouchoutte? The guards have waved us past and we'll be entering the village soon," Lucien murmured as we left the forest and entered the cleared pack lands.

I looked out the window. The town was very cute. We drove on the main road. Most people were walking or riding bikes and scooters. A lot of the roads were too small for most motor vehicles to drive down. There weren't many cars on the bigger roads either.

A cobblestone square with a large fountain was in the center of things. All the buildings were fairly close together. Clothing hung from windows above shops. There were cute little apartments over them!

Children stopped in the street to look at the sleek bus we arrived in and followed us as we went past. There were older people sitting outside of buildings on porches or on balconies, chatting with people across the street like they were right next to them. Young women pushed baby carriages, not the running type I saw around my old pack, but bulky ones, that they rocked as they meandered down the streets.

"Holy shit," Dilly whispered. "This place is fucking adorable!"

That made everyone laugh. It really was, though. I couldn't imagine what living here would actually be like. I loved the idea of my kids being able to run and play in the streets without worrying about too many cars.

We pulled up to the packhouse. It was as much a mansion as every other packhouse I'd seen. I was curious about how… short… it was. There only seemed to be two floors. Most of the packhouses were three or more. I looked at Lucien.

"You see the slightly taller area over there?" He pointed to the west side of the house.

I nodded.

"That entire building is the Alpha's quarters. There are two similar ones in a semi-circle behind the main building. They all have halls leading into the main house. That's where our guest rooms and offices are. We each keep our own homes rather than apartments like at Daylight Moon," Lucien told me.

"How many meals are served in the main dining hall?" I asked.

"We serve three meals. Omegas, guests, and anyone who doesn't want to eat their own cooking will eat there. The slightly larger area to the east is where unmated omegas are welcome to live. They have small apartments. The offices are on the second floor. Guest quarters are to the south. The first floor is public and common areas including the kitchen and ballroom." He grinned.

"Ballroom?"

"Yes. For welcoming guests, celebrations, and wedding receptions. We have some pack members who get married in the gardens and have their reception here at the packhouse. The ones who want something a little fancier." Lucien winked.

"I bet Cara loves it." I chuckled.

"She does. She says it's like a castle," he replied.

The bus stopped in the cobblestone courtyard. Lots of cobblestones in this place. I saw a group of people working on getting a receiving line set up, faces peered out of the windows of the packhouse, and the children who had been chasing the bus went to sit on the ground nearby.

Chapter 58: Luna of Lune Rouge

[Bellamy]

Lucien got up and left the bus. I stood and straightened my dress. It was a nice, light summer dress that went down past my knees and had wispy pieces of cloth on the shoulder that could almost be called sleeves. It was carnation pink, and I paired it with some white strappy sandals.

When he stepped onto the cobblestones, people cheered. Kieran had never gotten that kind of reaction to coming home. I looked at the guys, who were just as shocked as I was and turned back to the steps.

"I'm so happy to be home!" Lucien announced loudly, getting more applause. "I've brought with me some guests and my mate! Allow me to introduce, Bellamy Carrington. Your new Luna!"

I got to the bottom step before Lucien reached into the bus and pulled me out, setting me down beside him. It hadn't just been the kids following. It looked like most of the pack was now surrounding the courtyard. I pressed myself to Lucien's side. My nerves were going crazy. It was too many people.

"Wave, chouchoutte. They've been waiting a long time to meet you," he whispered.

I waved a little, and people cheered. It made me jump, and they chuckled. At least I was amusing the pack.

"I didn't think this would be so loud. I wasn't prepared for anything like this," I whispered back.

Bemmy! My mate! I see him! He's so hot! Dilly linked me.

Where, Dilly? I asked.

Standing in the line, next to a not-as-hot guy who looks like him.

I looked down the line. Next to my uncle Robert stood his mate and then his sons and daughters. Two sets of twins. The boys were tall, the first one more thinly built and the other thicker. That must be Jean-Claude. He had the same light auburn hair as our fathers did and looked very serious.

'The one with muscles and light brownish-red hair?' I asked.

'Yes! You got it. Who is he?'

'The future head of the warriors if I'm thinking correctly. His name is Jean-Claude.'

'Goddess, a sexy name for a sexy man.'

'Chill. You'll get to meet him soon,' I replied.

"Chouchoutte? What was that?" Lucien asked quietly.

"Jean-Claude is Dilly's mate," I answered.

"That's great news. I can't wait until they meet." He laughed.

'Bellamy,' Galen linked.

I paused and looked back at the bus. *'Yes?'*

'Dillon says his mate is the guy over there and you knew his name.'

'Yes.'

'Who's the girl next to Cara?'

I looked next to Cara. It was Thierry's daughter. The one who looked like an angel. What was her name? I read it just yesterday.

'Salomé. Why?'

'I'm pretty sure she's my mate, but I can't be certain. I don't think she has her wolf yet. She's glaring at you a lot.'

'I noticed. She's sixteen, so you're right about the lack of a wolf part. I bet she'll like you.'

I linked the rest of the group. *'Anyone else see their mate in the crowd? I'd really like to get on with this.'*

'No, Captain,' they responded.

"Something else or can we go? I want to get to the hospital soon," Lucien chuckled.

"Galen and Thierry's daughter," I replied as we started toward the receiving line.

"Maybe it'll distract her from her crush." He smiled.

"On you, right? It's a good thing he looks like you. I think it'll be an easier sell," I giggled.

"So you *noticed* he looked like me, but you were never attracted to him."

"You stop being so insecure. My brother has a mate; he couldn't possibly interest me. Now, introduce me to my family. Let's keep it quiet until there isn't a crowd," I whispered as I leaned against him.

We finally arrived at the head of the line. Thierry smiled broadly and stuck out his hand to Lucien.

"Congratulations, Alpha." They shook hands. "It's nice to finally meet you, Luna."

He bowed and took my hand, kissing the back of it. I guess it was better than a hug.

"Thank you, Beta. It's nice to meet you as well."

His wife, Celesta, curtsied. I was a queen, but no one had ever treated me like this. Caleb mimicked his father, which made Cara purse her lips. When I got to her, I smiled.

"I better get a hug, Luna," she growled.

I hugged her tightly. I missed her so much and was absolutely thrilled that she would be with me here.

"Jean-Claude is Dilly's mate," I whispered into her ear.

"Dillon's coming to live with us!? Yay!" she squealed and jumped, drawing attention.

"You are really bad at secrets lately." I laughed.

"It won't be a secret for long. Everyone has been watching Richard and Jean-Claude to see who's next."

"What?" Caleb asked.

"Shut your mouth, Cara," I sighed.

"Yes, Luna," she pouted.

"You'll see, Caleb. Just wait." I winked and moved on to his sister.

She looked like she wanted to hit me or cry… or both. Instead, she curtsied and introduced herself.

"Please forgive me for taking him from you," I whispered to her.

"So you knew? Did he tell you?" Salomé sniffed.

"No. I could see it in your eyes. Your mate is waiting for you, as soon as you turn seventeen, you'll have him and never regret it," I told her.

"I was going to reject him and ask Lucien," she murmured softly.

"Now you don't have to. Lucien is mine. I'll give you my brother instead."

"Like I'd want him," she sneered.

I shrugged and moved on to my uncle Robert. He really *did* look like a slighter version of my papa. I wanted to hug him, but I hadn't hugged Thierry and it would be suspicious if I did. I wanted them to be really shocked like Lucien and I were. He kissed my hand and patted Lucien on the back.

Robert's wife was Simone. She had bright blue eyes and dark red hair. I hadn't gotten around to seeing her picture in my file because of the shock of Robert's. She was regal, but in that sort of way that made her seem like a kind queen. She curtsied, and I felt like I should, too. But I didn't because I hadn't with anyone else.

Next was Richard, the future Gamma. His eyes were like mine and his smile was like his father's, like my father's. He was polite and gracious. I felt he was very much like Robert. Jean-Claude didn't try to kiss my hand. He bowed stiffly. I liked it.

I bet his wolf loved to play. It would loosen Griffin up a bit. I shifted a little, stepping nearer to Lucien.

Suddenly, Jean-Claude took a step back and eyed me. He looked at Lucien and I could see he was mind-linking. After a bit, he looked back and bowed again.

'I told them when we arrived that you were a rogue. He was surprised that you were a warrior.'

'He's observant. Papa taught me how to see if a person could fight without them getting aggressive. It seems my cousin is adept at it as well.'

"Don't worry. It surprises a lot of people," I whispered as I walked past to his first sister.

"I won't underestimate you, Luna," he responded.

I nodded and stopped in front of his sister. The first of the twin girls was Isabelle, and the other was Felicia. They were both ten and almost as tall as me. They had their mother's dark red hair and their father's light brown eyes. Both had big, bright smiles.

After the introductions were done, the group moved closer to the bus behind Lucien and me. I linked Bruce, letting him know it was time to introduce the men and we moved next to Thierry. I wanted to see Salomé's face when she saw Galen.

Bruce stepped out of the bus and stood rigidly next to the door.

"Bruce Carrington, Captain of the Elite Ten," he announced.

Jason stepped out and announced his name, followed by Galen. I looked over at my cousin and her mouth dropped open. I knew she couldn't sense he was her mate, but she had a type and he fit it. Galen winked at her and I thought she would swoon.

'Smooth, big brother.'

'I aim to please.'

Drake was next, and I saw Cara bouncing a little as Dilly stepped out. Lucien, Cara, and I looked at Jean-Claude. Caleb followed our gaze. Jean-Claude gasped a little and took a step forward before seeming to remember himself and moving back, clutching his brother's hand.

Even without a pack connection, I could almost hear what they were saying. Richard grinned. I was glad he was so happy for his brother.

After Bruce introduced the last of my boys, he dismissed them to unload their things. Dilly looked at me, then leapt to land right in front of Jean-Claude. The crowd gasped.

It was exactly the motion and movement of a vampire, showing off his skill and also giving a warning to any opposition. Dilly was talented and I could see the effect it had on my warrior cousin. He caressed Jean-Claude's face.

"Hello, gorgeous. I've been looking for you," he purred.

Cara and I couldn't keep our smiles contained.

"Our new Luna brings many blessings," Jean-Claude breathed.

"She really does. I'll talk to you later. First, I have to get settled." Dilly winked and rushed back to the bus to grab his bag.

Robert hugged his son. "I knew he was out there."

"He's a warrior. He's an elite warrior. Thank the goddess." Jean-Claude grinned.

"Should we talk to them before we see your mother?" I whispered to Lucien.

"No. I want to see her. She would've been here if not for the illness. The hospital isn't far; do you want to walk?" he asked.

"Yes. I love walking with you." I smiled.

"We're heading to the hospital. Have the omegas take my Luna's things to our room and unpack them. I'll meet you and Robert in my office later," Lucien told Thierry.

"Yes, Alpha," he replied with a bow.

Lucien looped my arm through his, and we started walking out of the courtyard. People greeted us as we walked along the narrow road. Some of the older people on balconies and in front of buildings asked who I was and shouted their congratulations when he told them I was his mate. I heard older men talking about how lucky he was to have a young and pretty girl as his mate.

Chapter 59: Meeting Maman

[Bellamy]

By the time we reached the hospital, I was sure we'd seen every elder in the village. Lucien chuckled as I leaned more heavily against him.

"Is it overwhelming, chouchoutte?" he asked.

"A little. I'm trying to remember how to move and act at the same time as I'm meeting these people." I sighed.

"They all keep saying what a sweet and timid girl you are. A couple asked if I kidnapped you from your pack and you just went with it because you're so docile." He laughed.

"Then I've been successful," I replied jokingly.

We entered the hospital, and the staff greeted us. A doctor updated Lucien on his mother's condition, and then led us to her suite. The maid was in the one next door. There were guards on both doors and I saw them check credentials of the doctor who led us. That made me feel better.

We opened the door and went in. Lucien's mother was sitting in her bed, looking angry. Her expression changed to pure joy when she saw her son.

She was beautiful. Her silver-streaked, reddish-brown hair was braided to the side and she was wearing a nightgown instead of a hospital gown. She looked like a queen even in this situation.

"Lucien! Mon prince! I missed you! Where have you been? Tell them to let me go home," she commanded.

"Not yet, Maman. You still have a couple days of treatment. Now, calm yourself before you get hurt. I want to introduce you to someone." He grinned.

"Who could you want to introduce me to while I'm in the hospital? I'm not even properly dressed, Lucien," she scolded.

"Genevieve Deveraux, this is Bellamy Carrington. My mate. Bellamy, this is my mother," Lucien smiled.

I almost bowed, then remembered that females curtsied here. No one laughed, so I must not have looked too ridiculous. Her silver eyes grew large.

"A mate? Did you find someone? Oh! And she's so beautiful! Like a little angel!" She smiled.

"Thank you, very much," I replied.

"She sounds like a little angel, too! He didn't force you to accept him, right? He's big and scary, but actually a sweet boy," Genevieve cooed.

I could feel Lucien laughing. I almost laughed, too. He was pretty big… in so many ways.

"Wait… you're a rogue? I can smell it. Lucien, you mated with a rogue? Why do you smell like a pack wolf and a rogue at the same time? What's going on?"

"Doctor, we need some privacy," I said.

"Yes, Luna. I'll be in my office when you're ready for the update on your maid, Alpha," he said with a bow and left, closing the door behind him.

"Bellamy was born a rogue, but adopted by the Beta of Daylight Moon, Maman. She's a rogue born pack wolf, so she smells like both," Lucien explained.

"You couldn't have found a pack born girl? A rogue can't be Luna. She won't know how to take care of the pack," she said sadly.

"I was taught by Luna Daisy Moore. She taught Cara and me everything about how to care for a pack. I promise, I know what I'm doing," I assured her.

"You're so pretty. Why did you have to be a rogue?" Genevieve sighed.

"Maman, you're being rude. Bellamy is perfect the way she is. She saved my life. I was captured by vampires and they planned to kill me. Bellamy risked her life for me. She loves me and I love her. Please, get to know her and don't judge her on how she was born. That wasn't something she could control," Lucien pled.

"You saved him? Why?"

"Because it was the right thing to do. Because his people needed him and… because I fell in love with him." I smiled softly.

Lucien put his arm around me and I cuddled into his side. It never hurt when other people didn't trust me, but I really wanted her to like me. I understood. Most pack wolves didn't trust rogues. My stomach turned, and I felt a headache starting.

"And he was conveniently an Alpha with no mate so you could take over the pack as his Luna?" she questioned harshly.

"One more insult like that, Maman, and you can go live with Liana full-time. I thought you were better than this. If not for Bellamy, you would be dead, too. She recognized the symptoms of your illness and told us how to treat it.

"She lost everything, lived a rough and dangerous life, and nearly died countless times before she was even a teen. None of that made her cruel, cold, or evil. She is a good person and I won't have her insulted. You can stay here, alone, for the next couple of days. I hope you have a better attitude when you're released," he lectured.

"I'm a rogue Queen, Madam Deveraux. It means I'm an Alpha myself. My people were worried when they learned I'd taken a pack Alpha as my mate. I understand your concern. I'll do as I always have and you will either accept me or not.

"A long time ago, I came to terms with who and what I am. I'll never harm this pack. I'll keep it safe as a partner to my collective. Just like Daylight Moon. I hoped Lucien was correct when he said you'd love me, but I was prepared for the opposite. Even if you choose to continue hating me, I hope you'll love our children as you do your other grandchildren," I declared.

"Grandchildren?" she asked.

"Bellamy's pregnant, Maman. She wanted you to be the first to know. She felt it was your right to have this news before anyone because you're my mother. I thought you'd be happy for me, for us. I guess some prejudices are hard to get past. Come on, chouchoutte. We have some work to get done," Lucien said, turning to me.

"I need to rest for a while, I don't feel well," I murmured.

"You've only been out of your territory for around an hour. You shouldn't be feeling bad. Let's find the doctor. I want to check on you and the babies," he replied and pulled me from the room.

It didn't matter how much I objected. He was worried and it was only a small ask. I ended up giving in. The staff quickly had me in another suite across the hall. I was pretty sure not all the rooms in the hospital were so nicely decorated with such large beds and fancy bedding, but I was happy to have this one. A different doctor came in.

"Hello, Luna. I'm Dr. Mellette, you can call me Trina if you like. We received the information Daylight Moon sent regarding rogue physiology and I've read over it. I'll be your doctor until we have more people trained on it. Can you tell me what's wrong?" she asked.

"I'm pregnant. I feel nauseous and headachy. Lucien overreacted," I sighed.

"It could be something serious. I want to be sure you're okay," Lucien pouted.

"I'll take a look. Any idea how far along you are?"

"About two days. I'm not worried, but he needs some reassurance," I told her.

She nodded and started examining me. Lucien danced back and forth next to the bed. He was making me nervous.

Dr. Mellette pulled out her stethoscope and listened to my stomach. She picked up a tablet at the foot of the bed and started putting information in.

"Everything looks fine, Luna. I couldn't hear anything, but that's to be expected. If you come back tomorrow, we can check again. I would say the headache is stress and the nausea is your body changing for the pup." She smiled.

"Pups," Lucien corrected. "A rogue tasted her blood and said it was more than one."

"I didn't realize that was possible. Be that as it may, until I can confirm it, I need to work under the assumption of it being a single pup. We should know more tomorrow. Did you want to come back in the morning, Luna?" Dr. Mellette asked.

I nodded. "Yes. I'd like to stay on top of anything developing with the pregnancy."

"Great. I'm scheduling you for ten in the morning. Just check in at the front desk and you'll be taken to an exam room," she replied.

"Thanks, doctor. Can I go? I have a lot to get done still."

"Just take it easy. This is your first pregnancy, we want our future Alpha to be healthy and safe." She smiled again and took her leave.

"See. It was nothing to worry about, mon saucisson. Can we go talk to Robert and Thierry now? I think you could use a laugh and their faces will be hilarious." I winked.

"Get dressed, chouchoutte. I'm going to sit for a moment. That scared the hell out of me." He chuckled as he sat in the armchair next to the bed.

"I can't imagine how scared you're going to be in a couple weeks then."

"What's going to happen in a couple weeks?" Lucien asked.

"Everything stretches faster than a pack wolf or human. It will cause cramping. I want to have you safe before random pains start making me less useful," I replied, getting my underclothes and dress on.

He blanched a little. "How can you be calm knowing that's going to happen?"

"Because, my love, it will happen so I can make room for our pups. Pain is inevitable, and it won't be nearly as bad as what I went through during my heats. You're just sensitive to me getting hurt." I walked over and caressed his face. "I love the hell out of that."

"You like that I don't want to see you hurting?"

"Yes. It makes me feel cared for. I don't want to see you hurting either. But I don't know how to save you from the pain you feel when you can't protect me." I sighed.

Lucien wrapped his arms around me and held me close.

"I suppose we'll just have to suffer for the next few months, chouchoutte," he murmured.

"Yes, we will. Are you ready to go talk with my uncles then?" I grinned.

"More than anything," Lucien laughed and stood, picking me up as he went.

He shifted me until he was carrying me like a princess. I wrapped my arms around his neck and let him walk with me like that. Lucien needed to feel strong and capable. I loved being in his arms. It worked for both of our needs.

"Pardon me, Alpha. Your mother is asking to speak with you, alone, sir," an orderly said, stopping us in the hall.

"I should make her wait until tomorrow. She needs to think about what's important and not act rashly," he sighed.

"But you've never let your mother stew and it makes you nervous." I giggled.

"I know I'm a grown man, but I'm pretty sure she'll take me over her knee, chouchoutte. And she'll do it where everyone can see," Lucien chuckled.

"Can't have that. I'll go check out the maternity ward. You go talk to your mom. Okay?" I offered.

"I'll do that." He smiled and set me down.

I turned to the orderly and asked him to show me to the maternity ward. I wanted to see what the situation was for birthing rooms and stuff. Plus, it would give me an idea of what the general fertility was like in the pack. It was important to pack wolves, and I wanted to understand more.

Chapter 60: Rogue Attack

[Lucien]

When I entered my mother's room, it looked like she'd been crying. I hated seeing any of the women in my life cry. I really hated causing their tears in any way.

"Maman, why are you crying?" I whispered as I approached her bed.

I pulled some tissue from the box on the wall and sat in the chair next to her, handing the tissue to her. She worked to pull herself together. My mother hated looking weak or unkempt. I thought she was always beautiful, though.

"I thought you left with your mate. How is the baby?" she asked, sniffling.

"Babies. There doesn't seem to be an issue. Bellamy was just stressed and her body reacted, and I overreacted. Don't tell her I admitted that," I chuckled.

"Babies? How wonderful, Lucien! I acted horribly. I've been in a mood and… I didn't mean to attack your mate, mon prince, but I was thrown off by her being a rogue. She really must be a queen. She was imperious and aristocratic. What will our people think, though?" Maman pressed.

"They will think they are lucky to have the protection of a rogue Queen, or they will think of what other pack they want to live in. She is my mate, whether they like it or not," I responded.

"A perfect answer. Do you think she'll forgive me? I want a chance to know her. She said you told her I would love her. You don't say that lightly. I don't like many people. I loved her as soon as I saw how she looked at you, but I was scared when I realized she was a rogue. You wanted a mate so badly. I just don't want to see you hurt. She won't hurt you, right? She loves you like she seems to, right, mon prince?" Maman worried.

"Bellamy is very smart and thoughtful. She said she understood, and she did. I know she wants you to love her. She truly loves me. Bellamy trusts that I'll never hurt her, and I trust that she'll never hurt me," I assured her.

"Will she come in and see me too, or was this visit just so you could check if I'd found my manners?" She chuckled.

"You called me, Maman. An orderly came and said you wanted to talk to me alone," I told her.

"No, I didn't, Lucien. I was married to an Alpha and I know you need space when you're upset. I figured I'd wait until tomorrow." Her eyes widened.

'Bellamy! Where are you? Are you with the orderly?'

'Yes. Jason and Galen are on their way to take him to the cells,' she responded in our link.

'Are you alright?'

'I'm fine, mon saucisson. Would you link the doctor and tell him we'll meet with him about the maid tomorrow? I almost forgot, because I wanted to get out of here.'

'I can do that. Are you really okay? Should we have the doctor meet with you again, just to be sure?'

'Lucien. I'm an elite warrior. He wasn't even a trained assassin. He didn't land a hit on me. As soon as we were in the elevator, I could smell the silver on him. I love you. I'll see you after I get him handed off to my boys. Stay with your mom in case someone tries to use the confusion to come after her. Have the guard on alert outside the maid's room.'

I linked the doctor and guards, then sat back in the chair. This was nerve-wracking and seriously pissing me off. I just brought my mate home and someone was already targeting her.

"Bellamy's alright. She has the orderly in custody. Thank the goddess." I sighed.

"Someone tried to kill her? Why?" Maman asked tearfully. "She just arrived in Lune Rouge."

"I have no clue, but I'll find out once we question the man. It was lucky my mate is an elite warrior. Any other woman may not have done well."

"You picked a good one then. I look forward to getting to know her. If you can overcome your dislike of rogues, I can try for the sake of my family. This isn't the time to have infighting," she replied softly.

"Thank you, Maman." I smiled.

We talked about the things that had happened over the last few days. I filled her in on everything I'd experienced with the vampires and the entire story of how Bellamy and I met. She laughed at some parts, especially when Bellamy called me by endearments, which Maman knew I disliked from people I don't know, and when she scolded me about letting her take care of me.

"Do you truly love her, Lucien?"

"More than anything ever, Maman. She's perfect in so many ways. I almost forgot she was a warrior because she was acting so sweet and docile." I chuckled.

The door opened and Bellamy sauntered in. Her dress was a little ripped and there was some blood on the skirt. She grinned and leapt onto my lap as smoothly as Dillon had jumped across the courtyard earlier.

"Did you miss me?" Bellamy asked, kissing me on the cheek.

"I always miss you, chouchoutte," I replied, wrapping my arms around her tiny frame.

"That was so much fun! He even said one of those stupid lines. I almost got hit, I was laughing so hard." She giggled.

"Did anyone see you?"

"No. It was in the elevator. I stopped it between floors, took care of the dude, linked Jason and Galen, and restarted it once they were in position. Then I flung myself out of the elevator, into Galen's arms, crying that he was trying to kill me. Jason rushed in, made it sound like there was a struggle, and cuffed him.

"I had Galen bring me here, he's going to come in and guard your mother until after the meeting tonight, Sam will come to take over until morning and will be relieved by Freddy. Twelve-hour shifts until she's out of the hospital," Bellamy explained.

"That's impressive," Maman said. "It's good for Lucien to have a mate he doesn't have to worry about. He already has enough to worry about as an Alpha."

"Oh, that never stops him. He likes to worry," Bellamy laughed.

Galen walked in at that moment. He bowed.

"The orderly has been properly disarmed and detained," he told us.

"Thank you, Galen. Please keep an eye on my mother," I requested.

"Of course, Alpha. You should take your Luna home so she can change and rest. She needs to expand her territory soon. We don't want her getting sick." Galen smiled.

"Right." I nodded and stood, sweeping Bellamy into my arms again. "We're heading out. We'll come see you after her appointment tomorrow, Maman. Get some rest."

"Alright, mon prince. Have a good day and take care of that girl."

I carried Bellamy out of the room and she snuggled closer to me, looking like she was upset still. I could hear people whispering about the attack already. Most of them were worried. They all loved seeing me carrying her out of the hospital.

'Lucien! I just heard about the attack, is everything okay?' Thierry linked me.

'Everything is fine, Thierry. Can you have someone grab another dress from Bellamy's things and take it to my office. Hers is ripped and a little bloody.'

'Yes, Alpha.'

'We'll meet you and Robert in there in about ten or fifteen minutes.'

Bellamy looked distracted. I'd learned that was the look she got while mind-linking people. She was probably informing her team and getting things settled. After a few minutes, she closed her eyes and sighed deeply.

"Is something wrong, chouchoutte?" I asked.

"I'm still puzzling out the orderly and what the general plan is for the assassin. He said some things… I'll have it soon. I feel like there's something right at the back of my brain. I need an office. Can you show me the Luna's office when we're done with Thierry and Robert?"

"Of course. Have you thought of how we should tell them?"

"I went over a few options. I think it would just be best if we sat them on the couch and told them. Once everything is settled, we can let others in the pack know, but they were siblings to my parents. I would feel terrible if they didn't know. Especially with how much Robert reminds me of my father. I have to fight the urge to give myself away. If he were in on it, I might do better," she chuckled.

"Then we will be sensitive and to the point, but remind them that they shouldn't try to get details of our sex lives anymore. Just to see the embarrassment. Though I'll enjoy seeing their reaction to finding you just as much, I think." I smiled.

"Yeah. That'll be good, too," she whispered, snuggling closer to me.

We walked through the streets of the village and it became apparent that news of the attempt on Bellamy's life spread quickly. People were hanging out of windows and lining the street. They called out well wishes to her. She was getting more comfortable with how my pack treated us. She was thanking people and waving.

Though she may have actually been a queen, Bellamy hadn't experienced this. My pack was truly grateful for how we cared for them and protected them. We didn't stay separate, like some pack leadership, but actually spent a lot of our time in the community.

It was one thing Bellamy and I had in common. She would have events for her collective so they would feel closer to her. She was a big part of their lives and their protections. They all knew she was there for them.

Chapter 61: Reconnecting

[Lucien]

When we arrived at my office, I put Bellamy down and we walked in together. Robert and Thierry were already in the chairs in front of my desk. I picked up the folded dress from the corner of the coffee table and showed Bellamy to the restroom so she could change.

"Let's move to the couch and chairs. I want Bellamy to rest," I said.

"You carried her through town. Everyone saw it. We've had a lot of people asking about her because of it. How much more rest should she have?" Thierry asked.

"I don't like your tone, Beta," I replied coolly.

"She was attacked less than *two hours* after arriving. I'm pissed. He was a member of our pack. If it had been someone like Cara, she would've died. Bellamy is stronger than that. She's the captain of the Elite Ten. She should've gone with him to the cells but had to play broken doll.

"How many other spies and assassins are in our pack, Lucien? The maid was a member since birth. How unsafe is this pack for our families? Should we send the girls and our wives to Daylight Moon?" Thierry probed.

"No," Bellamy sighed as she came out of the restroom. "It would look odd if they left and I didn't. None of the attacks, so far, have been on anyone other than the Alpha's family. The man wasn't even really trying to kill me. If I died, he wouldn't have cared much, but I wasn't the target."

"What do you mean, Bellamy?" Thierry asked.

"He was trying to kill the future Alpha," she answered angrily, with her hand over her stomach.

I stood and crossed the room, putting my hand over hers. They were trying to kill my pups. I was going to tear him to pieces. He wouldn't see the light of day again.

"Let's sit. I need to rest. The stress isn't good for the pups. Now that I don't have to stay calm and smile, I want to castrate him. Slowly. With a dull, rusty butter knife," Bellamy growled.

We sat in one of the chairs. I held her in my lap with my hands protectively over her stomach. I had to send her back to Daylight Moon. This wasn't safe for her or the pups. I couldn't have her here, risking her life.

"Pups?" Robert asked.

"Bellamy's pregnant. We'll have the official test tomorrow. Did he say why he wanted to kill the pups, chouchoutte?" I whispered.

"Their plan involves wiping out your entire family line, Lucien. He was in it for the money. He said he was accepted into your pack, but couldn't get a decent job and couldn't make friends because of how most of your pack members feel about rogues. So, he accepted the offer when someone wanted him to kill your mother. But, he couldn't get in to see her. He decided to target me instead. When he contacted the person who hired him, they offered a bonus if I didn't die, just to make you suffer more," she reported.

My blood ran cold. If it had been any other woman. He might have made her miscarry just from the stress of having to fight him off, and she *would* have blamed me. He made sure of it when he told her it was to cause my suffering.

That meant the person who wanted to harm me and my family also knew my mate was pregnant. They knew where to attack to hurt me the most.

"You and the other women should go to Daylight Moon. It's the seat of your collective. You'll all be safer there," I said softly.

"Bullshit," she growled and grabbed my arm. "You aren't the boss of me, Lucien. You are not my ruler," Bellamy bit my hand, then her own, and held the wounds together. "I'm sorry I have to do it this way. I don't think you'd be rational right now."

"What are you doing?"

"Alpha Lucien Deveraux, will you protect me and let me protect you? Is all you own mine and all I own yours, until the day we die?" Bellamy asked.

"Yes," I replied, a little shocked.

It was like a super simplified wedding vow. Maybe a rogue union of some sort…. She used her other hand to pull my face to hers and kissed me deeply. Our wounds healed, and she pulled away.

"Sorry, I couldn't dress it up for you like I did for Kieran. Your pack is now part of my collective. Welcome to the Eaten Heart," Bellamy murmured, pressing her forehead to mine.

The smell of honeysuckle and jasmine intensified. I felt myself calm. My mate was a capable woman. I needed to trust her more than I had. I could feel the power in our connection increase like she was sharing her strength.

"I smell my grandmother's cassoulet," Thierry gasped. "I haven't smelled that since I was fifteen."

"I smell Jean-Luc. The scent of my brother." Robert whispered. "Like he's right here."

"What do you smell, Lucien?" Bellamy asked.

I sniffed. All I could smell was her. My honeysuckle and jasmine queen.

"You, chouchoutte, but stronger." I smiled.

Bellamy's eyes widened. "Really?"

"Yes. Why?" I asked.

"When under the protection of a rogue Alpha, wolves smell the scent of something comforting. Often foods made by people they loved or perfumes and colognes worn by loved ones. No one has ever smelled me." Tears formed in her eyes.

"You're my greatest comfort, Bellamy. Ever since the first night I met you," I told her.

"Please don't worry, mon cœur. This expansion is a little earlier than I wanted, but I wanted to lock down the borders. Any rogues in your pack will feel the urge to come to me. The ones in the territory in between the packs, that's mine now, will send a representative for each family if they want to join the collective or give me an estimate on how long before they can safely leave. Others might come to try to fight me. Whoever's trying to hurt our family will know you've been claimed by the Eaten Heart. We'll stand together against our enemy," Bellamy vowed.

"Thank you, Queen Bellamy, for doing that. I understand the sacrifice. You like sticking to your plans. This will make me feel like the lives of our pups are safer. Let's get everything else figured out, then I'll take you home to have lunch and rest," I said.

"Robert, Thierry, we need to address the bear issue, then the issue of my family," Bellamy stated, turning in my lap to face them.

"Go ahead." Thierry nodded.

"As Kieran told you, the bear won't see anyone but an Alpha as worth speaking to. I don't want Lucien to be alone with him. He may have a plan that hinges on the next person he speaks with being Lucien. If he was hired to kill him, it would all be going to plan. I'll interrogate him," Bellamy replied.

"What if he decides to kill you instead? What if he doesn't see a female Alpha as being worth speaking to?" Robert asked.

"Bears function like rogues. They don't see age or gender when deciding worth. The reason the orderly failed, was because he grew up in a collective that treated females as property. It's a sick collective. If he'd come from a different collective, he may have had a chance. The bear will see me as an Alpha. He may try to hurt me, but I trained with a vampire and a bear in the past. I know how to fight them," she explained.

"We'll have warriors on standby in case he tries anything," I added.

"I'll have a couple of my boys go with me. Don't worry."

"And what about your family?" Thierry asked.

"Yes, what does this have to do with the Carringtons?" Robert questioned.

"Nothing. It has to do with my birth parents," Bellamy replied.

She pulled my arms a little tighter around her. I knew she was worried. For all that we'd laughed about embarrassing them, I knew she was concerned about them not wanting or liking her. Even if they didn't, I knew Salomé and Jean-Claude would be on her side. She brought them their mates, after all.

"What about them?" Thierry leaned in.

"I… My… Well…." She squirmed uncomfortably.

"Her parents were Angelique and Jean-Luc," I told them.

'Thank you, Lucien. My nerves got me.'

'I understand, chouchoutte. I'll help in any way I can. You know that.'

'I love you, Lucien.'

'I love you, too, Bellamy.'

I was learning. Overwhelmed by nervousness, Bellamy stopped speaking. She would become that scared girl again. Neither one of us liked it, and I decided to make it my mission to keep her from falling.

I held her as we watched Thierry and Robert process the information.

Chapter 62: Family Squabbles

They were silent and frozen in place. My Beta and Gamma just stared. It seemed like their brains overloaded. They were barely breathing. It was quite a shock, but I couldn't think of any other way to tell them.

Robert gasped. "They had a daughter? Why didn't the messenger say something?"

"He was probably under orders to be as vague as possible. Alpha females are rare. King Fuller wanted one for himself, for his son," she murmured.

"What does that mean?" I growled, already having some idea.

"He was going to have me trained like one of the other orphaned female rogues. Use me until my wolf came, then let his son mark me. In the year it took them to get ahold of me, I grew. I wasn't a lost child anymore. I was already learning to be a queen and a killer. Plus, I was a lot smarter than he thought a female, or a child, would be. I figured a lot of things out and set myself to learn everything I could. I was planning to leave before I was ten, anyway. That was when they started grooming the girls." Bellamy shuddered.

I wanted to kill him. Even though he was dead, I wanted him brought back to life so I could kill him a second time. I pulled her to me more tightly.

Thierry put his head in his hands. "Oh, fuck."

Bellamy looked up at him.

"I can't believe… Oh, goddess. I can't believe… Why didn't you say something the other day, Lucien? You let me go on about rogue she-wolves. I was talking about my own niece!" he growled.

Robert's eyes widened, and he turned red, then a little green. "The things we talked about after we hung up…. I think I'm going to be sick. We were identical twins. She's practically my daughter! How could you? Goddess, forgive me."

"In his defense, I didn't know my parents' names or what pack they came from until I saw your picture yesterday. Lucien found out an hour after I did. He's the one who told me their names," Bellamy offered.

Her shoulders were shaking a little. She was silently laughing. I pressed my lips together to hold back my smile and hid my face in her hair.

"You think this is funny?! It's not funny, you two!" Thierry shouted.

That, apparently, was all Bellamy needed to push her over the edge into peals of laughter. I held her so she wouldn't fall off my lap as she laughed at her uncles' discomfort. I was glad for something to make her happy and take her mind off of the clusterfuck she walked into by becoming my mate.

"I'm so sorry, Uncle Thierry," she wheezed. "Your face!"

"Lucien, you got my niece pregnant…." Robert glared. "You marked her and… and… did things to her… and… got her pregnant."

"Well, it would have been weird if I got him pregnant, Uncle Robert. My wolf offered the match to his wolf. None of us knew about the connection. I love Lucien. You don't get to be mad at us, or at him, for falling in love," Bellamy scolded.

"Now I see it." Thierry laughed dryly. "She sounds just like her mother."

I remembered Angelique said something similar when they'd been yelling at her about rejecting me for Jean-Luc. She said she loved him, and we couldn't be mad at him for it. She said no one should ever be mad at someone for falling in love.

"What are you saying? I'm rogue born. Unlike you, I wasn't born with a promised mate. I'm allowed to find love *and* my mate. No one did the work for me. I didn't have the *luxury* of leaving it to the goddess," Bellamy growled.

"I'm wondering just how much of you is rogue and how much of you is my sister. Maybe you did fall in love. Maybe it happened before you officially met him. Did you fall in love with the sad Alpha in whatever story she told you? Were you chasing your fairy tale prince?

"Lucien is the only Alpha in the region without a mate. Everyone knows that. I bet you knew who he was. Cara could've confirmed it for you. She's an excellent spy. You said you knew vampires and bears, now we have issues with vampires and bears…. Seems pretty peculiar, don't you think?" Thierry countered.

"When I was little, I wanted to help him find his second chance mate so he could be happy. Then, I was afraid he'd still be mad about what they did and would want to hurt me. I wasn't interested in Lune Rouge. It had no bearing on me or my collective until Cara ended up with Caleb. She only ever talked about Caleb or the wedding when she called. I told her to let me know if there were any big issues here that we should worry about or could cause her harm," she answered softly. "I only know one vampire. Talia. She wasn't associated with those ones. I have no clue who the bear you have in the cells is. He couldn't be Stanton. Stanton was a mercenary, but not an assassin. He specialized in retrieval."

"You will always be a rogue, Bellamy. Just because you're my sister's child, doesn't mean I'll forget that you're my enemy." He glowered.

"You're exactly as my mom said. An ass who thinks he knows everything without having learned anything. You chased her away with your opinions about her romantic attitude. Now, you're trying to do the same to me. This is where my mother and I differ. She was raised around your bullshit. She respected and loved you. I don't. You can go suck a dick," Bellamy scoffed.

"You're like Jean-Luc. I see it in the way you move and your facial expressions. Like him, you won't put up with Thierry's attitude. It's good. Our Luna shouldn't be cowed by our Beta. Welcome home, Bellamy." Robert smiled. "I'm still not exactly happy about my friend being your mate, but he makes you happy and I know he loves you."

"Thank you, Robert," I replied. "I'll take care of her for the rest of my life, you know that. Bellamy is my heart."

"I think we can call this meeting over. Please don't tell anyone else about me. You can speak to your mates if it stays between just the four of you. Later, we'll address it with the rest of the pack. Right now, I think it would be best if people got to know me outside of my connections with my parents," she said.

"Yes, Luna," Robert responded.

"I'll stay quiet, but only because Lucien needs to have less going on. There will be pushback from having a rogue as Luna. I don't want others to assume this is some sort of revenge for your parents' banishment," Thierry stated.

"Thank you. Please leave. I need time to talk with Lucien about the next moves and what joining my collective entails," Bellamy dismissed them and climbed off my lap.

Robert came over and hugged her. She held on to him tightly. He was right about one thing, she was, essentially, his daughter and she felt it, too.

They left shortly after. Bellamy sighed.

"That wasn't great, but one of them likes me, at least," she chuckled. "Thierry will get over it as he gets to know me. He's just mad about being embarrassed. Mama always said her brother was sensitive about that."

"You aren't upset, chouchoutte?" I asked.

"No. I usually expect pack wolves not to trust me. Their faces were pretty funny, though."

"Yeah. They were. Now, what do we need to go over?" I stood and crossed the room to my desk.

Bellamy followed me and straddled me once I was sitting in my chair. She traced along my jawline and gazed into my eyes.

"I didn't get the bear or vampires to hunt you. I was unaware of an unmated Alpha in the area. The idea of rescuing my damaged prince appealed to me, but not the boy who had banished my parents. I was in love with the idea of having found you and getting to keep you before I knew who you really were.

"The things I said before I marked you weren't because of the mark you gave me. I wanted to keep you from the moment you begged me to stay. You wanted me and it made me want you more. I love you, Lucien. More than anything or anyone else," she murmured.

I wrapped my arms around her.

"I love you, ma choupinette. I know you didn't hire those people. You hated the vampires and you were pissed about the bear in your territory. I loved the idea of keeping the girl who saved me. You saved me in so many ways, Bellamy. I realized I wasn't really living before you," I told her.

She kissed me softly, and I felt her relax in my arms. My need for her was overwhelming. I hadn't expected so much opposition from the people who loved me. I thought they would be happy enough for me, that they wouldn't treat her like an enemy.

I slid my hands down her back and under the hem of her dress. It had bunched behind her delicious bottom and made it easier for me to reach my goal. I pulled it over her head and pressed my face into her full breasts, kissing them and teasing her nipples through the cloth of her bra.

Bellamy moaned lightly, twining her fingers in my hair. I trailed my hand up to the catches at the back of her bra and unhooked them, sliding it from her and attacking the bare flesh in front of me. She arched her back and sighed as I tickled down her spine, grabbing her and moving her onto my desk.

I slipped my fingers around the waistband of her panties and pulled them off. Now she was bare and sitting on my desk with lusty, half-closed eyes. I quickly dropped my pants and positioned myself at her entrance.

"You're mine, and only mine, forever. Nothing will make me give you up," I whispered. "No one can take you from me. I've waited too long to find you. I'll never let you go."

"I'll never let you go, either. I'll hunt down and kill anyone who tries to take you from me. They shouldn't have tried to hurt our pups. I'm going to destroy the person who ordered their death. I need you, Lucien. Please, before I have to go deal with that bear," she pled.

With a stroke, we became one. Bellamy cried out as I moved in her, reveling in the feeling of my sweet little mate. No one could take her from me. No one could take our pups from me. I'd protect them until the day I died, and I wasn't planning for that to happen anytime soon.

It was a desperate union for both of us. We needed each other deeply. I wanted to feel her loving me, feel the way she held me, feel her body accepting mine. We wouldn't always be like this, but right now I couldn't imagine us ever being any other way.

Bellamy chanted my name like a breathy mantra as I stroked in and out of her, kissing her face and neck, nibbling on the mark I'd given her. I felt her muscles grasp at me as she wrapped her legs around me. When her climax hit, it was electric. I could feel her milking me and the way she moaned my name sent me over the edge.

Chapter 63: Luna's Office

After we'd finished, cleaned up, and dressed again, I took her down the hall to the Luna's office. It was as big as mine, with a balcony and big windows. The desk was a little smaller and the couch a little larger, but it was like mine in every other way. She glared at the windows.

"Can I redecorate when I'm officially the Luna?" Bellamy asked.

"Of course, chouchoutte. What are you thinking?" I sat in the chair across from her desk as she took her seat behind it.

"I want the windows coated in a reflective film, so no one can see in here. My office didn't have windows for a reason. Rogue business is no one else's business and I don't feel safe being visible to whoever might try to look in. Otherwise, a bigger desk, some new tech, replace or reupholster the furniture, new curtains, new rugs, and getting rid of the artwork. I get distracted sometimes and pictures don't help. I need the room soundproofed, too," she replied with a smile.

"As soon as we have time, we'll get you everything you need. We never went over the things you were saying. Next steps, what it means to be claimed by you, like you said," I reminded her.

"Oh. So my rogue barrier has expanded. I'll need to check the perimeter to have an absolute idea of my territory. It might be easier for me to run it. Like I said, rogues will feel the urge to join me or leave. Some might try to fight, but that's only if they're dominant enough not to be deterred by my power. It means your pack will be treated as a rogue collective when dealing with rogues. I'll help integrate any useful ex-pack families or children and start working on finding lieutenants to get my social programs up and running in nearby towns," Bellamy explained.

"Would you like me to run with you?" I asked.

"Sure, if you want. It's a long run. It could take the whole day," she said.

There was a tap at the door. We looked at each other and Bellamy called out for them to enter. The door opened and Celesta came in, followed by Simone.

"Robert and Thierry just told us you're Angelique's daughter," Celesta said after they closed the door.

"I am." Bellamy nodded.

"Can I hug you?" Celesta asked. "She was my best friend."

Bellamy stood and walked around the desk. Celesta rushed over and hugged her tightly. I knew she wouldn't be like Thierry. She'd never been happy about the banishment and tried to get me to change my mind before Angelique and Jean-Luc left. She was precisely the aunt Bellamy needed.

"Thierry's just mad about being embarrassed. He'll get over it and everything will be fine. He doesn't actually see you as an enemy. Thierry was upset with himself over his reaction once he got home. Just give him time. I won't let anyone hurt you like they hurt your mother," Celesta crooned as she rocked Bellamy.

'I think she's going to strangle me!' Bellamy linked me.

"Let her go, Celesta. I don't think she can breathe," I chuckled.

"Oh! I'm so sorry, Bellamy!" she squealed and let go.

"Don't worry. I'm glad my mother had a friend still," Bellamy smiled. "Please, call me Amy. I prefer it."

"Of course, Amy. I'm so glad you're here!"

"I'm glad, too. Robert missed his brother terribly after his anger subsided. I always wished they would come home," Simone stated softly.

"I hope no one is too disappointed. I'm not a typical pack wolf. Just let me know if you have any concerns. I'll be happy to address them."

"We should go have lunch, chouchoutte. You need lots of vitamins and protein for growing our pups." I smiled.

"I am feeling a little hungry," she replied and moved to wrap her arms around me. "Though, I suppose a meal first might be a good idea."

I traced a finger over her lips. "I truly do have a dirty little rogue Queen."

"I know you wouldn't want it any other way, mon saucisson," Bellamy purred.

Celesta giggled and grabbed Simone. "Let's go make sure my husband can behave himself. Come have lunch in the Alpha's dining room. Everyone wants to get to know you better. We'll see you in a little bit."

I thought to wave goodbye, but the loving look in Bellamy's eyes entirely consumed me. The door closed as I gazed down at her. We'd get everything resolved, get everything in order, and then we could be happy.

"Do you want to have lunch with everyone else, or should we go to our home and eat there?" I asked.

"We should eat with everyone else or I won't be able to pull myself away from you long enough to go see the bear today. I liked Celesta. Was she really my mama's best friend, Lucien?"

"Yes. They were very close Celesta's mother was the main housekeeper for most of our lives. Common wolf, not omega. She was always around and the girls were thick as thieves. My sister used to follow them around and they would always look after her. She was a couple years younger," I explained.

Bellamy nodded. "That makes me happy. Shall we go eat then? I want to see Cara again and I'm sure Jean-Claude has questions."

"Of course, chouchoutte." I smiled and wrapped her arm around mine before leading her out of the office.

***

[Bellamy]

The parent revelation hadn't exactly gone to plan. My mama told me what an unbearable ass her brother was when he felt insulted. She'd told me the things he said to her after she rejected Lucien. I was prepared for something worse than what he said to me.

I leaned against Lucien as we walked to the first floor. Right next to the main dining room was a set of double doors. We went inside and found a long table with a bunch of seats. People were sitting and standing in the room. My uncles weren't there yet.

"When we normally have meals, we eat with everyone. If we want to eat privately, we eat in our own homes. When we have important guests or matters to discuss, we eat here in the Alpha's dining room," Lucien explained.

Cara was standing near the table with Caleb and Jean-Claude. She was talking excitedly until she heard Lucien speak. Turning to me, she grinned widely and raced over, enveloping me in a deep hug.

I wrapped my arms around her waist and laid my head on her chest. Cara had grown to be 5'7", so my head came up just under her chin. She stroked my hair and held me tighter.

"I missed you so much," she whispered.

"I missed you, too," I responded, feeling the comfort of her embrace for the first time in months.

We stayed like that for a while. She was the one of three people I felt comfortable holding on to until I met Lucien. When I claimed her as my female to the rogue who tried to kidnap her, it created a strong bond between us.

She saw me as her primary protector in the pack, and I cared for her as if she truly belonged to me. I knew part of it was because of my bond with Kieran and my promise to protect what was his. It would last until her mate and marked her and she was no longer a child who was dependent on her father.

Now I understand what Dillon was talking about when he said I would see when you two were together,' Lucien said in our link.

'I don't know what you're talking about,' I replied.

'You look like two reunited lovers, chouchoutte. I'm both jealous and turned on.'

I pulled away from Cara and turned to look at him. *'Pervert.'*

'Maybe I should've been asking if there were any females you were attracted to....'

"Stop it, Lucien," I growled.

He laughed and walked toward the head of the table. Cara took my hand and led me to where Caleb and Jean-Claude were waiting. Caleb looked a little annoyed and jealous. Maybe it wasn't just my mate being a perv….

"Jean-Claude and I have been talking ever since you left for the hospital. He wants to know everything about Dillon. I thought you might be better at answering, you two were always a bit closer," Cara said.

"I'll answer what I can, but a lot of stuff is better answered by Dilly. He'll be off work after ten-thirty," I answered.

"He seems like he's a skilled warrior, but he was the sixth introduced. Are all the other warriors as good?" Jean-Claude asked.

"Sounds more like a head warrior question than a mate question. I can answer. Dilly is actually the third-best fighter in the Elite Ten, but tradition requires that ranked members be higher in the pecking order. It's the captain, Jason, Dillon, Drake, Galen, Todd, and so on. Since Drake has ranked blood and is the future head warrior for Daylight Moon, he's ranked higher in the team," I explained.

"Sit down, chouchoutte. We can't be served until everyone is seated," Lucien called.

I looked around. It was just the four of us standing. Thierry sat next to Celesta and Robert was next to Simone. Their unmated children at the end except the two younger girls. I'd seen them in the main dining room eating with some other little girls when we went past.

We took our seats, and they served the food. It was pretty basic, chicken, salad, wild rice, and pan seared broccoli. A light midday meal. We ate and talked about general things. It was like being at home. Celesta kept grinning at me… so not quite like being home.

"I was wondering… and it might make me sound a little stupid, but, why didn't Dilly recognize Jean-Claude as his mate while he was putting together the file for me?" I asked Lucien.

"You can't feel the mate bond through a photo or video. It has to be in person," he replied.

I nodded. I guess it made sense. Dilly only ever glanced briefly at things he got for me. He probably didn't even look at the information that had names. There were still a lot of things I didn't know about pack wolves.

"There is one more thing I needed to tell you about some rules here, Bellamy," Lucien went on. "Because of a… particular incident, when you find your mate, even if they haven't gotten their wolf, you let them know. It gives time for attachments and relationships to be resolved."

'She was already in love with him. She just gave him up to his mate, though she refused to give herself up in the same way. Trust me, Lucien, there was nothing that could have changed it.'

'I know. And I don't want it to change now, but we made these rules because of that.'

"Galen is watching over your mother. I can't call him away and leave her unguarded for something like this. She'll just have to wait," I murmured.

"You could tell her."

"No. Galen is a bit of a romantic. He has big ideas about wooing his mate. I won't take that from him. I will help, though," I whispered with a smile.

'Galen.'

'Yes, Captain?' my brother replied.

'There's a rule here that says you have to confess to your mate, even if they aren't of age. As soon as you see they're your mate you're supposed to tell them. I talked to Lucien and we've been granted a little more time because we were unaware, but you need to tell Salomé tonight.'

'It's really okay?' he asked.

'Yes. You just can't do anything about it until she's seventeen. According to my file, that will be five weeks from now.'

'Can you get her to meet me at eleven by the rose fountain in the garden?'

'Sure. You want me to keep which brother she's meeting a secret?'

'Yeah. I know she likes me. I want to surprise her.'

'Got it. I'll let you know.'

I smiled at Lucien. He was eating and talking to Thierry, so he didn't see me. I loved watching him with his friends.

"Salomé, my brother would like you to meet him at eleven tonight by the rose fountain in the garden," I said, silencing the table.

Thierry stared at me. Celesta bounced.

"Which brother?" Salomé asked, pretending to be nonchalant about it.

"My older brother."

Cara laughed. "All three of them are older than you."

"The warrior…" I smiled.

"All three of them are warriors," Robert chuckled.

"The unmated one."

"Well, that means it's not Porter," Cara snorted. "Why are you being vague?"

"He asked me not to tell her which one he was." I winked.

'Is it Galen? It seems like his style. He loves water features. Bruce would've asked her to meet on top of the packhouse.' Cara inquired.

'Yes. Please keep this secret. I know it's hard for you, but you know how Galen is, plus, I'm planning on sneaking us nearby so we can watch.'

'I'll be good! I want to see!'

I worked on finishing my food. Everyone tried to figure out which of my brothers it was, but I wasn't telling. Lucien just shook his head when he was asked, and Cara focused on her meal. Probably the quietest that girl had been since she was born.

After we'd finished, I linked the boys to find out who was closest to the cells. Freddy and Sam said they could meet me there. I told Lucien I had my guards for the questioning, and Thierry offered to walk me there. I was a little wary, but happy to let him if he wanted.

I kissed Lucien and told him to be good before I left. Cara squealed. She was such a sucker for lovey stuff. I was pretty sure Celesta did too, though. They were a perfect match as mother and daughter-in-law. Daisy would feel very comfortable when they were all together. She was the same way.

Chapter 64: Bears and Babies

[Bellamy]

Leaving the packhouse, Thierry and I walked together quietly for a short while. I was on the lookout for anything that might harm us. No one was going to get another chance at my pups.

"I'm sorry for how I acted," Thierry murmured.

"No worries. My mama told me how you are." I shrugged.

"Do you think she would've forgiven me?" he asked.

"I asked her when I was five if she'd ever forgive you all. She told me she did forgive you, all of you. My dad taught me when to fight and when to run, but my mom taught me when to forgive and when to dig in," I told him.

"And you forgive me for chasing her away?"

"It wasn't me that you chased away. It wasn't me who you cursed and disparaged. I have nothing to forgive. Don't ask me again," I stated coolly.

"You really are a lot like your father," Thierry chuckled.

"I'd rather be a lot like me."

We continued on until we reached a bland, square building. It was nothing like the rest of the village. Freddy and Sam stood near a nondescript door silently. They nodded as we approached. Thierry hit a buzzer and waited for the door to open.

Entering the building, I saw there was a small reception area with doors that led to the back. He guided us to the door on the right and down a dark hall. There were small rooms with silver bars. I felt my connection with my collective weaken a little.

"There's silver in the paint on the walls, ceiling, and floor. The bars are coated with silver, too," Thierry said.

"I can't stay here too long. It'll cause an immense strain on my body and bonds," I whispered.

'Understood, Captain,' Freddy answered.

Thierry reached another door with a code box. He punched in the code and the door unlocked. We went in and faced a large barred cell. I moved next to Thierry and could see the bear stretched out on the bed.

The bear glanced over and raised an eyebrow. He had a thick build, about as thick as Lucien, but stood taller, around 6'7". Dark eyes and sandy brown hair complemented his broad face and features. I'd seen other bears, they all had a similar broad sort of facial structure and thick build.

"She's a little small for my taste, but I guess she'll do," he said.

"Thank you, Thierry. I've got this from here." I smiled.

Freddy and Sam stood near the door. I'd trained my men to treat me as an Alpha. They didn't get defensive over insults and only got involved if things were dangerous. Thierry had snarled a little at the bear's implication that I was there for his pleasure. It wouldn't be helpful.

"I should stay in case you need me," he insisted.

"No. You should leave. You can wait outside, but I don't want you in here," I said firmly.

He huffed, but left the room. I was grateful. Protective males weren't very useful.

"You want to come over and lift that skirt, baby?" the bear said, leering at me.

"Not especially. I want to ask you some questions," I responded.

He laughed. "What makes you think I'll answer them?"

"I don't think you'll answer anything you don't want to. Don't get your hopes up about Alpha Lucien coming here. I'm the only Alpha you'll see."

"I don't care if I see him. I'm not a killer and, even if I was, I haven't been paid for that kind of work." He winked.

"Would you tell me your name, so I know what to call you?" I asked.

"Randy Bruinwald," he answered.

That surprised the hell out of me. It wasn't a common name. I'd only ever heard it once before. Thank goodness Lucien trusted me, or this wouldn't look good.

"Bruinwald? Any relation to Stanton Bruinwald?"

Randy laughed. "That's my cousin. He asked me to take this job since I was in the area."

"What job?" I asked.

"Track the Alpha, find the wolf who was hired to kill him, and report back to the client. The job is paid in advance since we don't trust the client." He shrugged.

"Who is the client? Did you find the hired wolf?" I pressed.

"The wolf's dead. I guess she let some vampire turn her a few weeks ago, according to my sources. Found her in the basement of a burned-out house… well, found the dust that used to be her. The client's anonymous. That's why we don't trust them," he answered.

"What would you do if we released you?" I inquired.

"Report back to the client. Contact Stan to let him know what happened. Head off to whatever's next. Still, a few years before I settle down if you want to try a little bear in your bed," he replied with a flirty tone.

"Has that line ever worked? You just implied that you're little." I laughed. "I prefer my big bad wolf. Thank you for the offer."

I turned to the boys. "Get me his personal items."

Sam bowed and left the room.

"You gonna let me go, little wolf?" Randy asked.

"My name is Bellamy. Queen Bellamy of the Eaten Heart Collective. You trespassed on my territory and work for someone who is trying to kill my mate. Do you think I'm really going to let you go?" I chuckled.

Randy finally started looking worried. "Oh, fuck. I didn't know. Look. I have no problem with rogue wolves. I don't like getting involved with shit like this. Stan asked me to do this job because it was low risk and just an info grab."

"Why is Stanton involved in this? He's a retrieval specialist, not a killer," I replied.

"He'll kill when he has to. How do you know Stan?"

"I worked with him for a while."

Sam returned with a bag. I dug through it and found a cellphone. There was no lock on it. He must have figured no one could get it from him. I looked at his texts and call logs. Nothing that would indicate contact from a client. I opened his e-mail and found the correspondence.

Reading through, I could see where the client asked if Randy could kill Lucien. Randy refused. I liked that. He wouldn't bend to any offers or threats and told the client he'd hunt him down if he tried to make good on the threats.

I opened one attachment to see a picture of Louisa, pre-vampire, staring back at me. The e-mail said she was the assassin, and the client was sending something with her scent. She wouldn't have had much memory of her life before, so I didn't know how she had the information on Lucien unless she gave it to the vampires before they turned her.

"I killed the assassin. Then I ground up her bones," I told him.

"She's one of the best. How did you manage that?"

"Memory loss from vampirism. It would've been another thirty or so years before she would have remembered her previous life. I started the fire that killed them. We're going to call Stanton now. He can come retrieve you under the condition that you never trespass on my territory again, and you never contact this client again. Do you understand?" I asked.

"Got it. I don't know exactly what's going on, but this isn't business for bears to be involved in." Randy shook his head.

I looked up 'Stan' in the contacts list and dialed. He picked up after the first ring.

"Randy. Where are you? You missed your check-in call," Stanton growled.

His voice was deeper than I remembered, but I was happy to hear it. I could almost hear the boy he'd been when I'd last seen him. It brought back a lot of memories.

"Stanton, Randy's in the cells at Lune Rouge. If you want him released, you have to come and get him," I said.

"Who is this?"

"Queen Bellamy of the Eaten Heart Collective, Luna of Lune Rouge. It's good to hear your voice again, Stanny-bear." I smiled at the phone. Randy snickered.

"Baby Belle?" Stanton gasped. "I thought you died. They told me you didn't survive the vampire attack."

"King Fuller didn't want to give me up. He told me that you left me in his care because you felt guilty about me getting hurt. I left the collective at eight and started my own at twelve. Your cousin trespassed in my territory," I explained.

"I can be there in three days. Thanks for not killing him. I know it's in your rights as a Queen," Stanton said.

"If he was trying to kill Alpha Lucien, I would've killed him," I stated.

"Lucien is the Alpha who banished your parents. The one you were afraid of… but if you're Luna…" he trailed off.

"Lucien is my mate, yes. I'm not afraid of him. He's not using me or hurting me. I just need to get your bear out of our territory so I can focus on whoever is trying to kill my family. They targeted my babies, Stanny. I need them dead," I growled.

Freddy and Sam gasped and looked at each other. I knew that information was going out to the whole of the Elite Ten. I had to question that orderly before the boys decided to kill him.

"I'll be there as soon as I can. I have no idea who the guy is, but I want in on this hunt. If you're happy with Lucien, I won't oppose it. No one has any right to kill babies. Especially not my Baby Belle's babies.

"Your cubs will be safe until we destroy your enemies. I promise. Gotta go. I need to get my travel arrangements put together. Call me at this number if you need me. Keep Randy's phone with you so I can reach you," Stanton told me.

"Thank you, Stanny. I'll let my mate know you're coming. Randy will stay in the cells for now."

"As long as he's healthy, it should be fine. I'll see you soon," he said and hung up.

I looked up at Randy. "He's on his way."

"Good. I'll help. I didn't realize you were the little wolf he used to run with. He always said you died."

"I got better. I'm heading out. You'll get more to eat and drink while you're our guest, but I'll keep your phone. I need to go deal with another prisoner now. Get some rest." I waved and left the room, followed by Sam and Freddy.

We walked out to the main reception. Someone pounded on the door as I reached Thierry. He looked startled.

"The Elite Ten just found out I'm pregnant and that the orderly was targeting the babies. If they get in, they'll kill him. I need to question him, now," I told him.

"I'll have to be with you. Lucien would kill me if anything happened to you," he responded, and we headed through the other door.

It was another corridor with cells lining it, but there were more people there. I realized the door on the left was the prison for pack members. The one on the right was for rogues and non-wolves. It was a decent setup.

We came to a cell where Thierry stopped. The orderly lay on his cot, bruised and beaten. He looked over and sighed.

"Come to see what you did? Rub in that I was beaten by a *female?* What the hell do you want? Isn't my blood enough?" he snarled.

"I want to know who you were working for. You deserved everything you got. You tried to kill my pups. They did nothing but exist," I growled.

"I'm not telling you shit. I don't answer to anyone in this pack. Not the Alpha, not the Beta, and most certainly not the fucking Luna."

"Because you don't identify as a pack wolf even though they accepted you?" I asked.

"They didn't accept me. They let me live here. A ranked bitch like you wouldn't understand what it's like living as a rogue. The humiliation, the violence, the fear. All of that's lost on you," he scoffed. "When I finally got a pack to take me, I was treated like garbage. Less than human. Not allowed to be even a common warrior, but servant work like a fucking omega."

"Omegas aren't servants. They work hard for their pack because they aren't strong enough to protect it like everyone else. You aren't much more powerful than an omega, so they put you somewhere accordingly. You told me you came from a collective, which one?" I demanded, channeling my dominance into my voice.

"Flayed Pelt," he strained, unable to resist.

"That makes sense! It isn't even a collective! Just a bunch of low-level ex-packs who think they're big shit. You're in my territory now. You've threatened the core of the Eaten Heart and you will die for it." I glared. "Tell me who hired you."

"I… I don't know. A burner phone was delivered to me and I got e-mails on it. I never heard a voice, saw a name, or was given any information about why." He struggled against my commands.

"Get me his phone. I'm done with this. Let the boys have him if they want." I turned and walked away.

I was exhausted. It was already a long ass day, and it was still hours until it was over. We walked back to the reception area. The pounding was even louder. They were practically beating the door down.

'Stop right now!' I commanded in our link.

The pounding stopped, and I nodded to Sam to open the door. Everyone except Harrison crowded into the little room. I glared.

"What do you think you're doing, Galen? I gave you a job. Why are you here?" I growled.

"That man tried to kill your pups, Amy. I'm not going to let everyone else kill him without me," he responded heatedly.

"Lucien wants to be the one to kill him. It's his right, they're his pups, too. You can beat the guy, but leave him alive," I said. "When you're done, get back to Madam Deveraux. I want my rotation stuck to. Everyone else, remember your jobs for today."

I walked out of the building. Normally, I'd be right there with them, but I couldn't handle being around so much silver. It was making me have to push harder to keep my connections to my collective. The strain could hurt the pups and I wouldn't risk them for a little fun.

"Are you alright?" Thierry asked.

"It was too much silver. I'll be fine. Now that this is my territory, it's like a battery to me. I just need to rest and recharge," I explained.

"I'm having a car meet us. I don't want to risk the pups. Those are my little sister's grandbabies. I'm not letting anything happen to them." He smiled.

A few moments later, a black car pulled up and Thierry opened the back door, entering after me. I hadn't realized exactly how tired I was and in the few minutes I was in the car I fell asleep.

Chapter 65: Finding Equilibrium

[Lucien]

I'd been working on some of the things that were on hold while I was away, trying not to worry about Bellamy while she was with the bear. It was hard to let her take on things, even though I knew she could take care of herself and she was with two other elite warriors.

'Lucien, Bellamy fell asleep in the car. Do you want me to take her to your quarters?' Thierry asked in our link.

'No. I'll come get her. I have a lot of work to do and I don't want her to be alone.'

'We're pulling up now.'

I left my office and rushed out to the courtyard to meet them. Pulling open the back door of the car, I saw Bellamy leaning against Thierry. She looked peaceful. I reached in and gathered her in my arms.

Thierry got out of the car and opened the front door, leading us to my office. Once inside, I laid her on the couch and covered her with the blanket that hung on the back of it. She snuggled down and sighed softly as I tucked a strand of hair behind her ear.

I went back and sat behind my desk. Thierry sat in the chair in front of it.

"I apologized to her. She said not to worry because Angelique told her how I was. Bellamy told me Jean-Luc taught her when to run and when to fight, and Angelique taught her when to forgive and when to dig in. They really were well-matched," he said softly.

"They were. It's too bad we didn't see it sooner. Though, Bellamy says I'm not allowed to apologize for banishing them. She told me it makes her feel like I regret being with her. I wish I'd found them before they died. Then we could have them and her at the same time," I sighed.

"Do you honestly think Jean-Luc would've let you mark his daughter?" Thierry chuckled.

"If Bellamy wanted me, I don't think anyone could have stopped her. My little queen does what she wants. She's a leader, a fighter, and a ruler in all things."

"I don't think I've ever seen you like this, Lucien. You used to be so cold. Even before everything happened, you weren't like this. Is it just being mated, or is it Bellamy?" he asked.

"I think it's her. She's not just strong. She needs to be taken care of in just the right way and it's making me stop to think about what I'm doing. I have to be more honest and straightforward in my interactions. She's unlike any woman I've known. Bellamy makes me think differently about everything and I love fighting and training with her. You should've seen her at Hunter's Moon. She's a warrior queen."

"Maybe this was all for the best then. Robert is thrilled to have her here. He's been bugging me all afternoon about how she's doing and if she needs anything." Thierry shook his head. "You should've seen her with the orderly. I don't think I would have been that calm questioning the man who tried to kill my pups."

"What do you mean? She was just supposed to question the bear," I growled.

"The Elite Ten found out she's pregnant and the babies were the target. She said she had to question him before they got there. Before she left, she told them they could beat him, but to leave him alive for you. Three of them are her brothers. I don't think she felt they'd be able to stop themselves," he answered.

I hoped they left a piece of the bastard for me. If not, I knew they'd at least make sure he suffered before he died. Looking over at her, I got a little lost. Seeing my pregnant mate resting, growing my pups, safe in my sight, made me feel calmer.

Thierry grabbed a stack of papers and started helping me get through the pile of things that had built up. There were some things that needed me to sign off on them and had to wait while I was away. He sorted out the things he could take care of and we worked quietly for a while.

There was a knock at the door. I looked at the clock on my desk. It had been a couple of hours. Thierry got up to answer the door.

Robert walked in with a tray of food. On the plates and in the bowls, Robert piled fruit, nuts, cheese, and sliced meat. There was a pitcher of orange juice in the middle and a single glass next to it. He'd gotten three people's worth of food for Bellamy to eat. I managed to hold in my laughter.

He set the food on the table next to her and joined Thierry and me at the desk. He smiled tightly and took the papers Thierry handed him. No one said anything. No one needed to. We were content to work silently so she could rest.

A short time later, I heard movement from the couch and looked up. Bellamy was staring at the tray of food, pressing her lips together. Her eyes sparkled with amusement. She looked up at me, and I nodded over to Robert.

Bellamy started eating her snack. Robert glanced behind him briefly and turned back with a cheerful smile. Thierry shook his head and kept working.

She picked up one of the three cell phones Thierry had brought in with her and looked through it while she ate. I returned to my work and focused on getting as much completed as possible. I wanted to spend the evening with Bellamy before she had her meeting with the Elite Ten.

"Oh, Lucien, Stanton will be here in a few days to help us," she said as she looked at the device in her hand.

I vaguely remembered her mentioning him. The boy she'd had a crush on when she was young. It made me growl a little. I didn't like the idea of a man she was interested in around her.

"Calm down. He's coming because he wants to help get whoever is trying to hurt you. He's only a friend. Remember, he doesn't find werewolves attractive," Bellamy snorted.

"What is he?"

"A bear. The one I was traveling with the first time I was attacked by vampires. Apparently, King Fuller told him I didn't survive. Randy, the bear we caught, was only gathering information, not trying to kill you. He's Stanton's cousin. I told him he could have him back," she calmly stated.

It could be useful to have some bears on our side. She was a good tactician and had to have realized a benefit. Even if I couldn't see it.

"As long as you're safe, I don't mind. We'll have guest rooms made up for them," I told her.

"Randy will stay in the cells until Stanton gets here. I want him to have more food and water while he's there. He needs to be healed in time for us to work out our plan."

"Got it." I nodded and returned to my work.

It was nearly time for dinner when we finished. I'd never made it through that much work in such a short time. I felt more focused than ever before. Maybe it was seeing how focused Bellamy was.

She'd had an omega retrieve her laptop and was working on something with the cell phones. Nothing seemed to distract her for long. I knew she was also consulting with someone through her mind-link. Her dedication was amazing.

"Are you hungry enough for dinner, chouchoutte? I know Robert brought you a fairly large snack," I chuckled.

She'd eaten all of it while working. I couldn't imagine her still needing more. She was so tiny; I didn't even know where she put it all.

Robert turned red as Thierry snorted. He'd been the same during both of Simone's pregnancies. Robert doted on pregnant women, no matter who they were. I saw him make an omega sit down while he mopped the floor. She was less than a month pregnant.

Thierry was pretty sure Celesta was going to leave him for Robert when he found him giving her a foot rub after having delivered a tray of junk food while she was pregnant with Caleb. Thierry had been making her eat very healthy, and she complained all the time. It was the first pregnancy of our group and Robert was excited.

"I'm fairly hungry still. I'm usually hungry, though. My barriers and connections to my collective take up a lot of energy. You can pretty much always assume I'm up for more food," she giggled.

I got up and helped her put her things into my safe. She was very security conscious and wanted to make sure sensitive items were locked away. Robert and Thierry listened to her ideas for securing the Luna's office while we walked to the Alpha's dining room. They were beginning to see what I did. Soon, I wouldn't have to tell people how amazing she was. They would just know.

Chapter 66: A New Home

Dinner was an amusing event. Most of the ranked members and their families were still trying to get me to tell them which brother was meeting Salomé in the garden. Thierry tried the 'I'm her father' argument. Nothing would work. Cara played dumb and told them I wouldn't tell her either.

Spending the last couple of months with this pack had gotten her into some bad habits. I knew she'd straighten up now that I was there. After all, Cara was the captain of the Dark Angels, Daylight Moon's elite spy group. She'd started letting herself go.

It was probably partly because she only really had to do the minimum while she was there and just tell me when there was trouble. She only had to be sneaky when gathering additional information, and her emotions were making keeping secrets harder for her.

Dillon came in to give his report to Lucien on the 'unfortunate accident' the orderly had. He was still alive, though, not for long. Looking at Lucien told me that.

After feeling powerless for nearly a week, I knew he'd relish killing the bastard who tried to kill our pups. The dark look on his face was such a turn-on.

I asked Dilly to join us for dinner. It was his break time, and I knew he was itching to see Jean-Claude. It was probably why he volunteered to make the report and didn't do so until dinner time. If it were more time sensitive, I would've been upset. As it stood, I felt for my friend. He'd been like me, thinking he'd never find a mate either.

Dilly sat in the chair next to Caleb, across from Jean-Claude. My poor younger cousin looked like he might cry. I could practically feel Dilly's excitement about affecting his mate like that, even though he seemed calm on the surface.

"Sorry, gorgeous, I can't sit next to you or I might forget to go back to work. Being able to gaze at your beautiful face will have to do until I sign off for the night," Dilly said, winking.

Jean-Claude blushed. This was apparently not something he did often, because a lot of teasing started up. Especially from Richard. I loved watching my family talking and being playful. I still didn't feel a big connection to them, but I knew I would over time.

"What time do the elites train?" I asked nonchalantly.

"Oh, yes! When do I get to see your warriors, gorgeous?" Dilly pressed.

"Our elite warriors train at six in the morning in the north training ground. Our general warriors train at eight," Jean-Claude replied.

"Can I come and see?" I requested.

"Sure, Luna. We're always happy to have observers. Did you want to join our training?" Jean-Claude answered.

"I think I'll just watch this time." I chuckled.

Training in the south field at four in the morning, everyone. We're done by six and then we'll go watch the elites here train. That way we don't slack off too much. We're doing five-and-fives, twelve-mile run, and hide-and-go-seek. Anyone on mother-in-law duty is allowed to train with the Lune Rouge warriors at eight,' I announced.

Lucien looked at me like he was going to cry. Maybe he thought being here would let him off the hook. That wasn't going to happen.

"Please tell me you didn't mean to link me on that," he whispered.

"You can do it. It's only a heavy day. Not a brutal one," I snickered quietly.

"What do you mean 'not a brutal one'?! There's harder than heavy?!" Lucien sounded panicked and drew attention from everyone.

"I'd rather not…" Cara said softly. "I hate getting up that early."

"You're getting soft, Cara." I shook my head.

"What's going on?" Thierry asked.

"The Elite Ten is planning on training at four tomorrow morning in the south field. They invited Lucien, Cara, and me to join," I explained. "We'd be done by the time your elite warriors started, that's why I wanted to see when they trained. Lucien was just thrown off by it being a heavy day."

"I barely survived a medium day, chouchoutte. I'd like to live to see my pups born," he scoffed.

"Pups? Amy? Are you pregnant?!" Cara squealed.

"Yes. Tomorrow we'll have the official test, but it's already been confirmed by two rogues." I smiled. "Lucien and I are very excited."

"I'm still not going to training in the morning," he grumbled.

"Yes, you are. Otherwise, you're saying your little, pregnant mate is stronger than you. No one will respect you after that."

"That's true, Lucien. We will lose all respect for you if you don't go." Thierry nodded.

A wicked look came across Lucien's face. Thierry had fallen right into my trap and Lucien picked up on what I was doing.

'Good job, chouchoutte. Now we can make him suffer.'

'I may have forgiven his outburst, but I'll never forget it and I'll make sure he pays for being an ass.' I replied.

"Great! Then we'll see you there at four as well! I'm so excited." I grinned.

"No…. I wasn't going to train, I just thought…."

"You just thought only Lucien should go? Oh, no. All of the ranked males get to come. You, Gamma Robert, and your sons. Cara, don't you want to play with Caleb?" I smiled.

"Hide-and-seek is fun…." She bit her lip.

Jean-Claude scoffed. "You're playing hide-and-seek during training?"

"Yeah! Will you be there? Dilly is one of the best hiders." I winked.

"Sure. I've been wanting to see what they do that makes Daylight Moon so strong." He smirked.

Dilly chuckled. Rogue hide-and-seek was one of our favorite games. Me, Dilly, and Cara absolutely dominated. We'd often get the Angels to come train with us on hide-and-seek days because their team was fourteen people and we could make teams of either three or eight. Adding Lucien, Robert, Thierry, Richard, Jean-Claude, Bruce, Caleb, and Cara, we could do teams of three or six.

We finished our meal while Dilly and I worked on getting to know everyone a little better. When we were done, Dilly headed out to finish his work. Lucien took me to the ballroom to meet the household staff.

It was a very different experience from any I'd had before. They all wore name badges, which was good because there were over fifty of them and I would never remember all their names. Lucien introduced me and there was applause, like honest applause and not the forced type. The kind I only ever got after announcing an expansion.

He led me through the packhouse and to our quarters. They were at the end of a long hall and there were locks on the front door, which I appreciated. After unlocking and opening the door, Lucien picked me up and carried me in. I laughed the whole time.

"Chouchoutte, I'm going to show you around, then you can rest until it's time for your meeting. Have your men come to our quarters. It's more private and no one will overhear anything. We haven't gotten a new maid assigned yet. You and my mother will be in charge of that," Lucien said, setting me down.

I sent out the message to my boys and followed him around as Lucien led me into the living room, dining room, kitchen, and study. He showed me where a small elevator was in a closet on the main floor.

"This is mostly used to get injured Alphas upstairs. My mother used it when she was pregnant. My grandfather had it put in because of how often he was coming home injured from fighting rogues. Did you ever hear about the 'red rogue wave' of the sixties?" he asked.

"Yes. Everyone knows about that. The wave of over a hundred ex-pack rogues led by a displaced Alpha. They destroyed almost every pack they came across and even attacked human towns. They took women, children, valuables, and anything else they wanted. The death toll was horrendous." I shivered.

"They killed my grandmother and several of my aunts and uncles. My grandfather joined the party of pack wolves that went after them."

"Every rogue collective in the country sent their best warriors to help fight them. They gave our people a bad name. We don't stand for that. It's why a lot of collectives will kill undesirable applicants," I explained.

"Good. You'll have to teach me more about how rogues work and the role of collectives. I realize, I'm not the most well educated on your people," Lucien smiled.

"I appreciate that you're willing to learn, mon saucisson. Show me the rest of our home. We can have lessons some other time. I want to cuddle with you for a while. It's been a very long day," I sighed.

Lucien took my hand and guided me around our home, up to the third floor. The entire floor was the master suite. It had an enormous closet, bathroom, and a balcony. A small, unused nursery was tucked away to one side. I planned to clean it up and decorate it for the pups. It would be perfect for our family.

Chapter 67: Meeting with the Boys

[Bellamy]

Lucien and I were lying in bed. He had his head in the middle of my abdomen and was talking to the pups while he rubbed lower on my stomach. I stroked his hair and listened to his soothing voice while he spoke in French. He was telling them a story.

I remembered the story from when I was little. My papa used to tell it to me. Of course, I heard it in English when I was a pup. My parents rarely spoke French. Now that I knew most of this pack was bilingual, speaking French and English, I felt like it was one of the ways they were trying to put their past behind them.

It was about a warrior who became Luna of her pack. Unfortunately, her mate died prematurely, leaving their son too young to inherit his father's position or duties. Driven by grief and a fierce loyalty, she avenged his death and spent ten years caring for her late mate's pack, demonstrating remarkable strength and commitment. Just two years before her son came of age, she found her second chance mate.

He was a displaced Alpha. A greedy and desperate Beta ran his Alpha from their pack. The Luna mated with the Alpha and accepted him into the pack, giving her son the time he needed to find his mate and prepare to take over. The Alpha helped to teach the Luna's son how to run his pack and supported him after he took over. I loved the story.

My papa always said it was a story of how the moon goddess trusts and loves us. How she provides what we need when we need it. How she would make sure I was safe, because the goddess loves all children. That was why she gave the Luna an Alpha who wasn't selfish and power hungry. He was a perfect father for her children. Like my Lucien.

"I love you, my Alpha," I whispered.

"*Je t'aime plus ma reine*," he murmured. *'I love you more, my queen,'* he linked me at the same time.

I giggled. He was so precious to me. My own lost Alpha, trying to find safety in the world. Just like me in so many ways; in all the ways that mattered.

"Why do you laugh, chouchoutte?" Lucien asked.

"Because you're cute when you speak French and I just couldn't help myself. You make me feel giddy, like a schoolgirl crush sort of thing." I smiled.

"Then I should speak French to you more often. I love your little giggles, mon bel amour," he purred.

"Now you're just trying to entice me," I laughed.

"I'm succeeding. I can smell your desire, chouchoutte."

'Captain, we're right outside the door. No one answered when we knocked. Pull yourself off that hunky Alpha and get this meeting over with. I want to find a good hiding place for Galen's confession,' Dilly linked me.

"Sorry, my love. The boys are here."

He sighed and groaned in frustration before getting up. I climbed out of bed and grabbed some dark blue yoga pants and a dark blue T-shirt. We had to get settled before Galen got there or he'd figure us out. I planned to leave from the meeting because I had to help Cara find a good place, too.

When we got down to the living room, I sat in a chair while Lucien opened the front door. The men filed into the room. Ranked members of the Elite Ten sat on the couch. Almost everyone else found a place on the floor.

Dilly pulled the ottoman next to the chair I was in and sat there. He was practically my right hand, so it made sense that he would be right next to me. Lucien sat in the chair across from me after locking up.

"Alright. Let's have the report," I said.

Jason stood and delivered the information they'd collected. The border patrols were solid, well-timed, and with few gaps. The general mood in the pack was one of happiness.

"There were very few squabbles reported, Captain. Almost everyone loves Alpha Lucien, most of them were happy to hear about you. Even more people were totally smitten by Lucien carrying you through town after the attack. They felt it was a sign you trusted him to protect you.

"Some commented about you leaning against him while you walked through town earlier. They thought it was cute. The general sentiment at this moment is that the pack is extremely happy to have a Luna who obviously loves their Alpha very deeply," he reported.

When Jason sat, Drake stood. I'd trained him, Galen, and Dilly, to scent rogues, even if they were using something to hide their scent. Part of their mission was looking for rogues. They were in every pack no matter how secure they thought their borders were.

When I joined Daylight Moon, there were ten rogues living in their border. They'd found their mates there but were afraid to petition to join. I helped to get them into the pack and they were all living happy and productive lives.

"I found five rogues living in the pack secretly. All mated, as usual. I'm having them meet us at the training field in the morning. I made sure they knew they weren't in danger. Most of them are females. One is rogue born," Drake said before sitting.

Dilly stood. "I found two. Both male ex-pack. I told them the same thing."

He sat again, and I mentally assessed the information. It could be a lot harder to find out what our enemy was planning next. I told the boys I wanted Dillon, Galen, and Drake to head to the nearby city to gather information on the rogues there.

"I'm preparing to run my borders after Stanton arrives. It'll take all day, and possibly a good portion of the night," I announced.

"I can help. If we designate a starting point, we can each take half," Dilly offered.

"Hmm. It could be dangerous… You might want to see if Jean-Claude wants to run it with you. He'd know the area well enough, having grown up here," I suggested.

Dilly blushed, making everyone laugh. I figured it would give their wolves time to know each other. It occurred to me that I hadn't told the boys we were keeping my relations quiet.

"Just one more thing, then we can head out. Because the attacks are on Lucien's family, I want to keep my relationship with the Beta and Gamma families quiet. It's easier to protect a small group than to protect the whole of the leadership. Lucien, don't forget to contact your sister. I want to make sure she's safe," I said.

"I called her while you were questioning the prisoners, Bellamy. Her mate is stepping up their patrols and monitoring everything. Their pack is small, only a couple hundred, so they're all very close. No attacks so far," he told me.

"The person pulling the strings may have decided to wait until she came for funerals. It's hard to orchestrate this sort of thing for how little he was offering Randy and the orderly. Okay, we're good, everyone has their assignments for tomorrow, and we only have twenty minutes before the show. Let's get a move on." I grinned.

We headed out to the gardens. They really were lovely. The rose fountain was right in the center of a ring of rose bushes. Three jets of water shot from the center of the fountain, which was shaped like a cabbage rose. Cara, Caleb, Richard, and Jean-Claude met us there.

"Okay, the wind is coming from the south and a little west. Let's look for places that won't carry our scent to them. Galen will know we're here, but that's because he's trained to find people who are hiding," I said.

"Right, let's go. It's ten forty-five. My sister will be here soon," Caleb said urgently.

We quickly found spots. Most of my team were in trees. The ones that couldn't find one were hiding under rose bushes. I tossed Cara up to a tree with very high branches. Caleb looked sad and hid in the bushes at the base of the tree. I didn't want him trying to get romantic and giving us away.

Lucien helped me up to a tree that had a little deck built around the trunk. He climbed up, too. I raised my eyebrows at him.

'Lucien, you better not try anything. I want to see this and I don't want you messing it up.'

'I promise; I'll be on my very best behavior… until they leave.'

'I am not having sex in an old tree fort.'

'We'll see.'

I controlled my laughter. He always found ways to make me smile. I sometimes wondered if he really loved me as much as I loved him, or if it was just the connection between our wolves and his desperation. As he put his hands on either side of the railing around me, I found I didn't actually care.

For so much of my life, I had to give up things I wanted. I had to work harder than anyone else and had no one to talk to about it. No matter how much my friends tried, they couldn't understand me. It felt a lot like Lucien understood, though. He got me in a way no one else did.

Chapter 68: Proclamations of Love

[Bellamy]

Salomé's entrance near the fountain disturbed my reverie. She was in a different outfit than earlier. She piled her hair atop her head and wore a white dress with a ruffled top that flared to her knees. White sandals with little heels gave her an extra couple inches, lifting her 5'6" frame up to 5'8". Galen was only just six feet tall, so the height difference worked.

She kept glancing at her phone, looking anxious. I could tell when it turned to eleven because she looked all around rather frantically. Her face fell when he didn't show up, but I knew exactly where he was.

Galen stood under a darkened archway off to the side, watching her. I hoped he gathered himself before she left. I wondered what was going on in his mind.

'I know you're here, Bellamy,' he linked me.

'You need support. I can tell you're nervous.'

'I waited so long for her. What if Bran's wrong? What if he just got desperate?'

'Do you want me to double-check?' I asked. *'It would mean I have to come out of hiding.'*

'I know you don't like to do it, but I'd really appreciate it.'

'It's not some party trick, but I'll do it for you because you're my brother. You have to go out there and start the conversation. Use that flower thing you told me about a couple years ago. If she's like her mom and Cara, you'll have her swooning for you. I'll come along with Lucien once you've talked to her.'

'Thanks, Amy. You're the best.'

'I know. Now, MOVE!'

Galen reached out and snagged a rose off one of the bushes as he headed toward Salomé. She looked down a path, away from him. When she turned back, he was standing less than a foot away, holding the flower.

"Thank the goddess, it's the cute one," she whispered.

Lucien covered his mouth, and I bit my lips together. Bruce was ranting in our link with the team about not being 'the cute one', and I was sending it along to Lucien. Lucky for us, Galen and Salomé had gotten caught up staring at each other. It took me a couple of minutes to calm Bruce down.

"I… I… Umm… I didn't mean to say that out loud," she murmured, turning bright red.

"I'm sorry I was late, I was trying to find the most beautiful flower in the garden, but none of them compare to you," Galen said softly.

She squeaked a little and took the flower from him. It was so cute. Salomé traced along the petals and collected herself.

"So…. What did you want to talk to me about?" she asked.

"Well, my sister told me there was a rule here. As the future Beta of the Daylight Moon Pack, I don't want to break any rules, you know. So I have to tell you, I think, you might be my mate. I know you don't have your wolf yet, but I was hoping to ask if you would spend time with me. I'd like to get to know you more," he requested.

Salomé nodded vigorously. "Yes. Absolutely!"

"You have no idea how happy you've made me." He grinned.

'We need to head down there, Lucien.'

'Why?'

'Galen asked me to verify if she was his mate. It's not something I like doing, but he's been looking for his mate for seven years. I just need to tweak his connection to his mate. If it's her, even if she's not old enough, she'll feel something,' I told him.

'That's cool. How are you able to do it?'

'A witch taught me. It's part of a soothing spell. It can bring a comforting presence to the person I focus on. The talent works easiest with mates. I can see the connections to any relative nearby. The strength of the connection depends on how close they are to the person I'm working on.'

'Will it be safe for you and the pups?' he asked.

'I don't see why it wouldn't be. Are you ready?'

'Ready for what?'

I turned and swept him in my arms like he was a princess. It was awkward because of how much bigger he was, but he wrapped his arms around my neck and held on as I jumped up to the railing and down onto the ground.

The landing was fairly quiet. I impressed myself. I'd never jumped while carrying someone over a foot taller and at least a hundred pounds heavier.

Setting him down, I smiled to myself. That was a lot of fun. I wanted to do things like that more. Looking at Lucien, he didn't seem as amused.

"Don't ever do that again, Bellamy," he growled quietly.

"Why not?" I asked.

"I don't like it," Lucien said sternly.

I cocked my head to the side. "Why not?"

"I just don't. It's weird."

"Fine. That's one. You get three more unreasonable rules. If you can pick me up, then I should be allowed to pick you up," I told him.

"It's not unreasonable. You could have been hurt. The pups could have been hurt. I could have been hurt," he insisted.

"Fine! I said fine, Lucien. Can we go now?" I groaned.

He huffed and took my hand. I wrapped my other arm around his forearm and leaned against him. He was cute when he was mad. I understood his protective feelings, so I let it go. We walked toward the fountain.

Lucien was still grumbling a little. I chuckled as we caught sight of Galen and Salomé. She was looking up at him like he was a god and he was stroking her hand while gazing into her eyes.

"Hey, guys." I smiled, startling them a little.

"Oh, hey, Amy. Out for a walk?" Galen asked.

"No. We came to see how you two were getting on. I told Salomé I was giving you to her back when we met. What do you think, Salomé? He's a good one, right?"

She nodded and blushed. "I didn't know you could have such handsome brothers."

"Yeah, they're all pretty boys. Let me get a hug from you two." I grinned.

I really wasn't fond of hugging, but it was a great way to give their bond a tweak. I could already sense their connection to each other. Now, I just had to prove it.

First, I hugged her, and she thanked me as quietly as she could. I was happy that my cousin and my brother found their mate. If nothing else, it ensured that Anise and Blossom would stop jumping off the second and third floor railing. I bet Mom and Dad would get a single level after the last couple months of flying babies.

After I let her go, I hugged Galen and focused on the invisible bond to his mate. I could almost see it, like a tread that linked their hearts. Taking a deep breath, I prepared myself and gave the thread a tug.

"Mine!" Salomé growled and pushed me away from Galen.

Lucien caught me as I stumbled. He growled at Salomé and she looked really embarrassed. I could imagine she had no idea what just happened, but Galen was grinning broadly as he held her to him. We totally confirmed she was his mate.

"I'm not going to steal your mate. He's my brother, that's gross," I snickered. "Come on, mon saucisson, let's get to bed and leave these two to get better acquainted."

"Next time, remember that Bellamy is your Luna and future sister-in-law. This is your warning to never harm my mate again, Salomé," he said sternly.

"Yes, Alpha. Sorry, Luna. I have no idea what came over me," she whimpered.

"Don't worry. I'm not hurt or offended, I'm just tired." I smiled and pulled Lucien from the garden.

'Galen, get moving soon. I don't want everyone to be tired and you know they're all watching.'

'I know, Captain. We all watched Jason and Todd when they found their mates. It's practically a rite of passage.'

'Good night, big brother.'

'Good night, little sister. I love you.'

'Of course you do. I'm amazing.'

With that settled, I took my mate home and went straight to bed. I needed so much more rest and Lucien was more than happy to cuddle me all night. I looked forward to the coming days, seeing the pups, seeing Stanton again, getting my new territory settled, and all the Luna/pack wolf things. Most of all, I looked forward to finding the person who was trying to hurt my family and killing the bastard.

Chapter 69: Elites in the Lune

[Bellamy]

Training the next day was a lot of fun. Jean-Claude surprised me with his adaptability. He almost made me lose in our five-and-fives. I picked him for the head of my hide-and-seek rival team. He didn't have as many people to choose from, but it gave me a great idea of how strong they were and how good at hunting rogues they were.

We required teams to be made of people from the same pack so they could communicate. Jason tried to argue when Cara, Dillon, and I joined up. Until he found out our mates were going to be our opposition.

If we'd been against anyone else, he would have insisted we change. It was important for all six of us to understand the capabilities of our mates. We won, of course. Dilly and Cara were fast and stealthy. I was in charge of the distraction so they could make it to the designated pack land.

Once training was over, the rogues and their mates arrived. I was happy my cousins had all cleared out to get to the north field in time for their training. Lucien and I talked with the ex-packs and got their stories. Pretty much all of them were children from fallen packs. One of the men was the brother of the rogue born woman.

Their parents were from a southern pack that fell. No one in their region would take them in, so they headed north, hoping some pack would accept them. Hunters attacked and killed both parents two years ago. When the kids ran away, they bumped into the guy's mate and her older brother.

The older brother had lost his mate in an attack and didn't seem to have a second chance. I could feel that he'd only had one. The rogue born offered for him and he accepted. She was relieved because she didn't want to lose the only family she had left. The pack wolves snuck the rogues over the borders and they'd been living together on their family farm.

"Lucien, I'd like to try an experiment," I said.

"What would that be, Bellamy?"

"I want to accept the rogue born into my collective and have her accepted into your pack after her bond is secured and I've been named Luna. I think the reason I could be accepted was that I created the alliance with Kieran and, as a queen, I am always connected to the rogue side of the moon," I explained.

"You think she might be able to be a pack rogue?" he asked.

"Yes."

"This would be an amazing chance. I approve of the suggestion and will accept her," Lucien smiled.

I turned to the rogue and her mate. He was holding her and stroking her hair. I liked seeing other rogue born finding mates. It was hard out there for us.

"Maple, would you and your mate come here, please?" I asked.

She pulled away from her mate and dragged him along with her.

"I'm here, Queen Bellamy," she whispered.

"I want to do an experiment with you." I smiled.

A look of terror came over her. I knew that look, they'd had experience with a rogue collective. Some of the rogue Alphas were terrible people. Though, that could be said of pack Alphas as well.

"I'd like to accept you into my collective for one week, then have you attempt to join Lune Rouge. Are you willing to try that?" I asked.

Her eyes widened. "I didn't think we could join packs."

"I managed it. I think you can, too. Your mate is a member of this pack, and I will be too once the Luna ceremony is complete."

She grinned. "I'd like that. I want to stay with my mate and my brother. They need a pack, even if I don't."

"Perfect. Lucien, what time did you want to accept these rogues into your pack?"

"After lunch. All of you come to my office at one o'clock this afternoon."

"A member of the Elite Ten will come to escort you. Once you leave, you shouldn't have issues with the guards. Maple, you'll join my collective at that time. Your scent will be like mine and it will be hard to determine if you are a rogue or a pack wolf. This should save you some hassle until we can try bringing you into the pack," I told her.

"Thank you, Queen Bellamy!" She bounced.

"Call me Luna. I am not the Queen of the Eaten Heart here yet. I am simply the mate of the Alpha," I warned her and made sure to meet the eyes of everyone remaining in the group.

"Yes, Luna," her mate said with a bow. Others followed suit. This would work out perfectly.

We dismissed them and headed to watch the elite training for Lune Rouge. I nearly laughed when I saw it. It wasn't nearly as intense as even a light day for us.

My cousins were all trying to keep up, but they weren't in any condition. The hunt of hide-and-seek was more exhausting than it seemed. The fights when you're found or when you found someone were intense.

I looked over at Dillon and Cara, who looked just as worried as I was. They didn't have the stamina for this, even though it really wasn't difficult. I wouldn't stop them though. They were trying to prove themselves. Lucien, Thierry, and Robert sat near us.

'Will you guys need help carrying them back?' I linked Lucien.

'Have Dillon carry Jean-Claude. We can get the others,' he responded.

'They're going to be useless for most of the day.'

'But they want to show their mates and Luna that they're strong. It's the folly of young men. They'll have to learn from it.' Lucien chuckled, followed shortly after by my uncles chuckling too.

When training ended, Jean-Claude dismissed the warriors and almost immediately after the last one left the field; the boys collapsed. I sent my team off to clean up and have breakfast. Freddy would take over for Sam so he could train, and then Porter would take the overnight shift. Depending on what the doctor said, Madam could be back as soon as tomorrow.

We approached the groaning young men. Caleb seemed embarrassed and tried to look away. Cara stroked his hair and called him an idiot. It was very cute. Thierry picked up his son and carried him home while Cara followed behind. Robert picked up Richard and went in the same direction.

Dillon laid on the grass next to Jean-Claude. I could see my cousin turning red. No warrior wanted their mate to see them like that, especially not a head warrior or future head warrior. I know I wouldn't want Lucien to see me so weak.

"So… did that make you feel powerful, gorgeous?" Dilly chuckled.

"I just wanted to rest for a bit before breakfast and enjoy the early morning sky," Jean-Claude scoffed.

Lucien hid a smile. I sat quietly and watched. I loved seeing my friends happy. Dilly was glowing. He always told me how adorable he found stubborn boys.

"Then you're not out of energy! Great. I was thinking of a quick four-mile run before breakfast. I got a lot of energy back while I watched you train. We can run together for a while!" Dilly grinned.

Jean-Claude whimpered. He looked like he might cry. Poor boy.

"Stop teasing your mate, Dilly!" I called out.

"He's just so cute when he pretends he's not exhausted," Dilly purred.

I winked at Lucien. "Dilly, he can't protect himself right now. What if someone attacked? I think you need to help him to his room and get him cleaned up."

Both of them turned red at that suggestion. I'd never seen Dilly get flustered over a boy. The way his eyes raked over Jean-Claude's prone form showed he was definitely thinking of how he could help him.

Dilly stood and scooped Jean-Claude up in his arms. "Come on, sexy. I'm gonna protect you until I can deliver you to your parents," he said, nuzzling my cousin's neck.

Before I could see Jean-Claude's reaction, Dilly took off running toward the packhouse. Lucien helped me stand, and I leaned against him as we walked and followed everyone. It was a perfect start to the day.

Chapter 70: Vampires and Pups

The boys ate in their homes. Celesta told me Cara said she'd be taking care of Caleb all day. He was thrilled. She usually spent a lot of time out in the pack trying to get to know everyone or working on the wedding. Thierry told me a month ago that Caleb was worried he wouldn't remember what she looked like by the time they were married.

Robert missed breakfast to help his mate with their boys. After feeding and cleaning them, both exhausted boys immediately passed out. Simone told me Dillon cooked for the family while she and Robert took care of the boys. She was already in love with her new son-in-law.

I almost laughed when she told me the man who called me 'eye candy' and asked if I was a present for him was a sweet and respectful boy. The way she went on about him was endearing. Bellamy told me he had difficulties in his pack because of his orientation, but he would be embraced at Lune Rouge like he never had been before.

After a shower and some breakfast, Bellamy and I went to my office to work for an hour before her appointment. I tried to focus, but was too excited about seeing our pups. It wasn't that I didn't know they'd be little shapeless dots. I knew that. It was entirely about knowing they were there and healthy.

Bellamy worked on her laptop for most of the time. She seemed deep in thought. I turned back to my work and tried to focus again. The ringing of a cell phone drew my attention.

"Hello? Hey, Stanny-bear…. Yes…. I wondered who told her that…. No. Stanton. You can't! Because Lucien isn't ready yet! I don't care. No. No. Shit. Fucking, fine. Just make sure she knows to behave. Right. I'll see you tomorrow." She sighed and hung up, pressing her fingers to her forehead.

"Is something wrong, chouchoutte?" I asked.

"I'm sorry, Lucien. Stanton is bringing Talia. She was in his territory. He had her come over so he could tell her I was alive. I guess he was the one who told her I was dead. I know you hate vampires, especially after what they did to you, but there's really no arguing with him. He had a point. Having a powerful vampire on our side will help," Bellamy explained.

"Talia is the vampire who trained you. You talked about her when we were still playing captive…. Will she try to hurt me or any member of my pack?"

"No. I can feed her. She only fights to protect herself and others. It's just… when I told you about her…. I fudged the truth just a little." She blushed.

I closed the file folder I'd been working on and went to sit in the armchair across from her. This wouldn't be something small if she was worried like this. Bellamy didn't give emphasis to unimportant things.

"Tell me," I stated, firmly.

"I told you she was over seven hundred… but not how far over seven hundred. I was trying to hide the fact that I was extra weak from only having twelve hours in my territory and just four hours of sleep before I threw myself into your rescue. If I'd been fully rested and been in my territory just a day longer, I would've been able to kill them easily. Talia trained me. I can't beat *her*…. But I *can* beat four vampires under five hundred." Bellamy nibbled her lip and looked away.

"When you were young and attacked by vampires. Dillon said it was six…" I questioned.

"Yes. Three vampires over six hundred and three vampires ranging from one hundred to four hundred. I killed the three younger ones, but one of the older ones attacked me from behind. The two other older ones had been focusing on Stanton, but their attention was drawn to me and they jumped in. Stanton had to pull them off of me."

"Tell me about Talia."

"How much do you know about vampires?" she asked.

"The Werewolf Association is loosely based on their High Council. Instead of having the oldest, like they do, we have the most powerful. Three rogue Alphas and three pack Alphas. They have the four oldest living vampires. All vampires have the eye color of their master sire. Each vampire has a certain talent or talents from that line," I answered.

"Yes. Talia told me all vampires are descended from the first two. The council is made up of the oldest four. Two from each of the originals. They passed on a long time ago along with some of their oldest children. The council goes by nicknames. The Prince, The Angel, The Traveler, and Death. Talia is over ten thousand years old, mon saucisson. She's 'The Traveler,'" Bellamy said quietly.

"And she's coming to help kill whoever wants to harm our family. I can rein myself in, chouchoutte. I promised you a home for her, remember? I want this threat taken care of and I would call in any creature in the world to make it happen," I vowed.

She smiled. "I'm glad you're okay with it, Lucien. I was worried you'd have trouble because of Marion and his group."

"What color are her eyes?" I asked.

"Violet."

"Then she wasn't his sire and I have no problem with her." I nodded.

Bellamy got up and climbed into my lap. She snuggled close to me and inhaled deeply. I wrapped my arms around her. This morning she told me no sex before the appointment. I wished I'd known that last night. It would be a long day for me.

We arrived at the hospital ten minutes before ten o'clock. I led Bellamy to the offices for the doctor we'd be seeing. After a few minutes in the waiting room, a nurse took us back to a room.

In the room, she gave Bellamy a gown and a cup after taking some of her blood. She sent Bellamy to the adjoining bathroom. When she returned, she was dressed in the gown and set her clothing on one of the extra chairs. The nurse asked some question, took some vitals, and left us.

"I've never done this before." I chuckled.

"You've never been to a doctor before…. That's pretty unlikely," Bellamy snorted.

"Right. Neither have you. Are you nervous, too?" I asked, moving to stand in front of her and holding her hands.

"No. I have nothing to be nervous about, Lucien. Today we'll get confirmation of the pregnancy and maybe hear their hearts. If we're lucky, we might be able to see them. You have no idea how much I've wanted a big family, Lucien. It feels like a dream. I had one request though…." She smiled shyly.

"What can I do for you, ma choupinette?"

"I know you wanted to wait to pick names… but, I wanted to make a couple suggestions."

"If it makes you happy." I caressed her cheek.

"When my mama was killed, she was pregnant, Lucien. She and my papa had already picked names," Bellamy whispered.

My heart sank. She was pregnant. Angelique fought to save all of her children but only managed to save one. I remembered how she'd volunteered at the child care center, how she sang to and cared for her baby dolls, and how hard she worked to care for Liana when she was little. Angelique loved children and always said she wanted a large family when she grew up.

"What names did they pick?"

"Étienne for a boy and Lunette for a girl. We don't have to… but I wanted to, maybe, let another part of my family live," she murmured.

"I love you, Bellamy. I would love to have our children named in honor of your parents and your lost sister or brother. If they're boys, our first son will be Étienne and if they're girls, our first daughter will be Lunette. But I get to pick the names for the other pup." I winked.

Bellamy giggled and wrapped her arms around my waist, pressing her ear against my chest. I stroked her back and held her.

"I love you, too, Lucien. Thank you," she sighed.

"You never have to thank me for honoring my friends and making you happy. Those are the sorts of things I live for," I told her, kissing the top of her head.

The door opened and Dr. Mellette came in. She smiled at us as we pulled away from each other.

"It's always nice to see happy couples. Now, we have the results from your blood test and urine sample. It is absolutely confirmed, you are pregnant." The doctor smiled.

I grinned. I never doubted that Bellamy was pregnant. Having medical confirmation was thrilling. It made it all more real.

"I need to do an exam and we can hear the heartbeats. At this stage, I could use an internal ultrasound and we may be able to see them. Three days would be similar to a human at six to eight weeks. It's a hard equivalent to properly say. If you were a pack wolf, I'd say you wouldn't be likely to see them. So, it's up to you," she said.

"I'd like to check. It couldn't hurt just to see," Bellamy replied.

Dr. Mellette nodded. "That's what I figured you'd say, Luna. Let's get started."

I sat in the corner of the room for the exam. Remus wanted to go look at what the doctor was doing, but I convinced him it wasn't going to make Bellamy happy. He wanted to keep her happy as much as I did.

Once the exam was over, the doctor pulled a machine out of the wall that had a screen and a wand attached to it. I watched as she put gel on it and put it in my mate. Bellamy squeezed my hand when I growled a little. I didn't mean to, it just slipped out.

After some maneuvering, the doctor turned on the sound.

"There's one little heart," she said before moving the wand a bit. "And there's another. It looks like twins."

Dr. Mellette turned the screen to us and showed us the two little dots that were our pups. Bellamy had her print out four copies. One for my mother, one for Robert, one for Celesta, and one for us. She said she'd scan it and send it to her parents, too.

When she'd dressed again, and we had the prescription for her vitamins plus all the papers, books, and forms, we headed out to visit my mother. I knew Maman would be as excited as I was. Our pups were the most perfect little dots in the world.

Chapter 71: Curses…. Again….

I couldn't resist looking at Lucien as he practically floated down the hallway next to me. Through our bond, I could feel his happiness and pride. When he said we could use the names my parents were planning to use for my little sister or brother, I was so happy. It would be a great way to keep my family with me, without doing something like naming our children after my parents. I didn't like that idea.

We walked to his mother's room and the guards let us through. Freddy was sitting with her, talking while they crocheted little squares I knew would become blankets. Most of my guys knitted or crocheted for the dexterity and focus aspects. Most presents from them were blankets or scarves because of it.

Lucien strode over to his mother and gave her a hug. I relieved Freddy and told him I'd let him know when to come back. He gladly put aside his work and headed out.

"Look, Maman. See our pups!" Lucien was grinning as he pushed the ultrasound photo at her.

He reminded me of a little kid showing off something he made in school. His mother had the same smile I did. She looked at the ultrasound and squinted.

"They're beautiful, Lucien." She smiled softly.

There was no other answer he'd want to hear. No amount of telling him they were barely visible would get through. They were his pups, and he wanted everyone to tell him how perfect they were. I was going to have to deal with a lot of the rule-making and punishments if they had him like this already. We'd have to talk about it later.

I sat in the chair next to Lucien's while he told his mother about Galen's meeting with Salomé last night and about Jean-Claude and Dillon. I was relieved to see she was happy for them. We chatted for a little longer. I could see how much he missed talking to her. I bet he talked to her every day, even when she was staying with his sister.

"I'm going to go talk with the doctor about my mother's release and the status of our maid. Do you want to call Freddy back?" Lucien asked.

"No. I can watch your mother. We need to get started on plans for the Luna ceremony and the wedding. Freddy's probably calling his mate. Let him have some time. This is a long mission for the boys and only a couple have their mates here. Go on, Lucien," I urged.

"Okay. Link me if there's an issue," he said, standing and giving me a gentle kiss before he left.

The door closed, and I was suddenly nervous about being alone with his mother. I wasn't necessarily afraid of her. I could beat her in a fight easily. What I was more afraid of was that she wouldn't be as friendly now that he wasn't there.

"Your brother told me all about you yesterday. He was trying to make sure I understood what kind of person you were," she said softly.

The memory of how my parents messed up a similar conversation with Lucien flashed in my head. I was going to kick Galen's ass if he messed up my relationship with Lucien's mother. It's hard to win over the only person who might love your mate more than you do. It was even harder when you're starting from a negative value.

"Please tell me it wasn't all terrible," I groaned with my head in my hands.

Madam laughed. "It was grand, and terrible, and glowing, and dark. Your brother seems to idolize you even though he's older. He cherishes you in a way you rarely see with siblings. You are his sister and more. I think that is a precious thing. What do you think of your brothers?"

"I love them. My brothers made my life so much better. They played with me and fought with me. They weren't scared of me and always stood by my side. I never knew I could have such caring people in my life. I think they gave me the ability to be who I am now as much as any training or life experience ever did," I admitted. "But don't tell them that. They'll never let me hear the end of it."

She laughed again. "I had seven brothers and sisters. Only two still live. You should definitely tell them before anything happens to them. My brothers used to tease me about things like that. So I understand."

"Are you actually okay with me? I hold no ill will. Accepting rogues is hard for most pack wolves."

Madam sighed. "You're something I never thought I'd see. More than a mate for my little prince. You're the one who will break our curse."

That got my attention. It couldn't have been the Vengeance of the goddess. Not with the weary way she spoke. There was something else.

"What curse?" I asked.

"About four hundred years ago, we lived in France. Our pack was large, powerful, prosperous, and a little arrogant. One day, the Alpha was out for a run and came across a rogue she-wolf just inside the border," she told me.

I knew this story. My parents told me a lot of stories as a child. I knew they were all based on things that had actually happened.

"He killed her and dumped her body on the other side of the border as a warning to others. But she hadn't been there to harm anyone. She was lost after leading enemies away from her pups," I continued her story.

"You've heard this? I know Lucien didn't tell you. He never listened to this story very carefully. He always said he didn't believe in curses."

I chuckled. "He certainly does now. My parents told me this story when I was little. They could never remember what the requirements were to break the curse. Only that the pack would never prosper again as long as someone from that bloodline was Alpha. The pack moved from their homeland, hoping the curse wouldn't follow, but it did."

She nodded. "Yes. To break the curse, an enemy must become a friend and our Alpha must learn to love that which he hates. Lucien hates rogues because of what the wave did to our pack and what the random attacks have done over the years. But he came home mated to a rogue. I think you're what we need to break it."

Thinking about it, the solution seemed obvious. The past Alpha had brutally murdered an innocent rogue, then showed no remorse when he found out about her situation. He said all rogues deserved to die. It would mean becoming friends with and understanding rogues and their culture.

Lucien did that with our relationship. With luck, our pups wouldn't have to worry about a curse taking away the people they love. I needed to look at old documentation, if they had any, and speak with some of the oldest members of the pack. The ones who told them the story would have been closer to the original telling.

"Galen also told me your parents were banished by Lucien. In the time he has been Alpha, there have only been three occasions where he banished someone. One male who took his mate and pups, one single male, and one unmated couple. I just have to look at your eyes to see the answer. Would you like to tell me?" Madam smiled softly.

"I forgot to tell the team not to reveal that before we got here. I don't want to endanger my mother and father's families. Please don't tell anyone else. Your assumption is right. I am Angelique and Jean-Luc's daughter," I admitted.

"You aren't planning to hurt my son for what he did, right?"

"No. I love Lucien. My parents forgave him, and he forgave them. None of that has anything to do with me. He said he doesn't hate me for being their daughter. Don't make me out to be guilty of their crimes, too.

"My mother said she felt nothing for him. Not even the pull of the mate bond. The first moment I saw him, I wanted to be with him. I'd never thought about a man the way I thought about him. My wolf doesn't really like anyone, and she liked him. I saved him for your pack, not for myself," I explained.

She nodded. "You're sincere. When you have your pups, you'll understand a mother's concern. No matter how old he is, Lucien is my baby. My little prince. I don't ever want to see him hurting like he did back then."

"I will never do anything to make him hurt like that. I can't imagine any reason I would ever think it was okay to let my mate suffer the way he did. Is there anything else you want to ambush me with, or shall we start planning this ceremony? I want to have it settled so I can focus on my other work and the wedding," I said.

"Of course. I have nothing else right now. Let's start planning." Madam smiled.

We spent the next half hour going over things. She valued my understated approach. I appreciated her taking charge with my ideas in mind. Every available minute needed to go to settling my territory and finding the killer.

She also offered to take the lead with my mother and plan the wedding and reception. I gave her my mom's phone number and asked her to keep the pregnancy quiet for a day or so. I quickly linked the same to everyone from Daylight Moon.

When Lucien came back, he told us she would be able to be released the next morning. Her vitals and levels were doing great. I called Freddy back, and we left after he returned.

Lucien picked me up and carried me home. He said he intended to do that every time we had an appointment. It made me laugh.

"That's two unreasonable rules," I giggled.

"This one is worth it. From now on, our pack will know you're pregnant when I start carrying you from the hospital. It will become a tradition." He winked.

"You're terrible! That's embarrassing, Lucien!" I blushed.

"No, it's sweet and adorable and everyone will love it."

On the way back, several people asked if I was okay. Lucien told them, 'more than okay' with a wink. I could hear them whispering their guesses about whether or not I was pregnant. They all seemed excited.

Chapter 72: New Wolves

When we reached the packhouse, Lucien set me down, and we had lunch with everyone. I was excited about the beginning of my pack rogue experiment. Having rogue born wolves in the pack would strengthen it. My team could be mostly rogue born and I wouldn't have to worry about toning things down for the difference in pack and rogue abilities.

After lunch, the boys started bringing our rogues in. Lucien accepted all of his into his pack, as promised. He announced it to the pack through the link. Bringing in six new, mated wolves was tremendous news, especially with the losses suffered at the last attack.

My uncles came in to witness me bringing Maple into my collective. She was fairly submissive, so it didn't take long for her to submit to my wolf. When she left with her mate, Thierry and Robert were still staring at me.

"What?" I asked.

"You're much more powerful than you seem. It's a little surprising," Robert whispered.

"You have to be one of the most powerful Alphas I've ever met. And to think, you chose our little Lucy to be your mate," Thierry chuckled.

"Lucy?" I giggled.

"I'm going to have to kill you now, you know this," Lucien growled.

"I'm more afraid of her than of you now, Lucy." Thierry laughed and dodged behind me when Lucien grabbed for him.

"Enough roughhousing. I have a lot of work to do. If you boys have all this energy, you should go for a run. You're all out of shape," I scolded.

"Only compared to you, chouchoutte. We're some of the strongest warriors in our pack," Lucien grinned.

"That isn't praise for you, mon cœur. That's a condemnation of your warriors," I chided, as I picked up my laptop and sat on the couch.

They scoffed and turned to their own work. I loved working in the same room as them. It gave me a sense of peace.

Using my phone, I scanned the ultrasound and prepared an email for my collective with information about the recent expansion to Lune Rouge, the pups, and the wedding. I set it to send at midnight, giving myself time to contact my parents.

After a couple more hours, I was mind-linked by Drake.

'Queen Bellamy, there's an issue in your new territory.'

'What is it, Drake?' I asked.

'It seems the larger city is fully aware of werewolves. The mayor is rogue born. One of the major problems is a gang run by an ex-pack Alpha. I was hassled by them a little.'

'Did you kill them or just beat them?'

'Killed one, beat three. Their Alpha definitely knows about us now. The mayor is trying to figure out where the pull is taking him. He announced in the local news this morning that the territory has been claimed by a rogue Alpha and he plans to make sure it will not harm his residents,' Drake said.

'Amazing. Contact the mayor and have him meet me this evening. I'll come to town with Lucien. This portion of the territory needs to be well meshed with the pack.'

'Got it. I'll have him name a time and a place.'

'Public. I will not go to someone's home if I don't know them,' I replied.

'Yes, Queen Bellamy. I'll let you know.'

I returned to my work. There was no point in upsetting Lucien yet. I wondered if he knew humans were aware of wolves nearby.

Mostly, humans were aware of supernaturals. Their brains had a hard time processing it, though. They would generally forget we existed. Unless faced with a shapeshifter, fae, or vampire in person, they were more likely to believe it was all myths and legends.

Three types of humans came from this: hunters, who wanted to eradicate us; allies, who wanted to live peacefully alongside us; and fanatics, who were obsessed with us. The fanatics were good for the vampire community, not for wolves. They treated us like some sort of frightening amusement.

Having an entire city know about werewolves meant the rogues involved had caused enough problems that the human mind couldn't just write it off. I'd have to deal with him for the safety of our people. I dug into the news from the city over the last ten years.

Starting eight years ago, a slow shift combined gang violence stories with those of werewolves. Editorials from humans and supernaturals showed the conflict in the population. Soon, a consensus grew. Not all supernaturals were bad, but the ex-pack gang most definitely was.

This was the mayor's second term. He ran on a platform of being a rogue born wolf who wanted peace in the region. I found articles about his supernatural police force and the building of a jail to house supernatural beings. I liked him. We seemed to be like-minded.

Drake linked me again. *I contacted him. He wants to meet in a rogue-owned restaurant. When he found out who the Alpha was who claimed the territory, he was relieved. It was a good thing I approved his request for assistance the other day.'*

'What do you mean?' I asked.

'The request that was on your desk. It was outside your territory when we got it, but, by the time I read it, I knew you were mated to the Alpha here. So I approved it because you would never let this stand.'

'Good. I'll give him a little more trust because he needed help badly enough to contact a collective. The Association is known to be a little slower to assist rogue communities. I'll fix this.'

Drake gave me the details, and I wrote them into a document. I didn't want to miss anything. Now I had to let Lucien know, and I was concerned. He had no idea about what was going outside of his borders. It wasn't healthy for his pack.

"Lucien? We need to go to the city this evening," I said.

"What for, chouchoutte?" he asked.

"The mayor wants to meet with me," I replied.

"What? What do you mean?"

"The mayor is a rogue born. He ran on the platform of being a werewolf. A gang of rogues has been terrorizing the city. This city is aware of us because of that. The mayor previously asked for help, now that this is my territory, I'm inclined to assist," I explained.

"We seldom go to the city. I know I've seen the marker for wolf-friendly businesses, but I didn't think…. Okay. We'll go." He shrugged.

"We need a nice car to take us. Humans know and they expect some sort of show."

"Right." He nodded and stared off to the side for a moment. "Got it."

We worked on our business for a little longer and I called my parents to let them know about the pups. Mom was thrilled and said she was coming down to help on-site with the Luna ceremony and wedding. She wanted to be there for the next ultrasound.

At five, I locked up the extra phone and the laptop, then took Lucien's hand and we went to our quarters to change. This was an important meeting. Neither one of us was going to put on a poor display.

An hour later, we were ready to go. An omega helped me with styling my hair. She piled it on top of my head in a way that didn't look like I was sporting a weird creature up there.

I was wearing a formfitting black dress that tied around my neck and reached an inch above my knees. Dark gray silk stockings, four inch spiked heels, my wolf pendant, and my engagement ring finished it.

Lucien was in a black suit with a light blue button-up shirt and no tie. It was a fairly relaxed look, but also a little serious. The way the suit fit his body showed it was custom made, not off the rack. He styled his hair in a way that made it both business-like and terribly sexy…. However, that could just be the hormones talking.

"You look beautiful, chouchoutte," he purred when he saw me in the living room.

I'd dressed in a guest room on the second floor of our quarters because I knew how itchy Lucien's hands were. I felt the same pull. We had to be responsible leaders. That meant not throwing him down on the nearest flat surface and screwing his brains out whenever I felt him looking at me.

"You're practically edible, mon saucisson. We shouldn't attend any other business tonight. It's been over twenty-four hours since the last time we were intimate. I need my Alpha." I sighed with longing, straightening his collar when he bent down for a kiss.

"I wish we didn't have to meet this man. I'd carry you upstairs and spend the rest of the night making you squeak and squeal," he said heavily as he pulled me to him.

"Ew. Stop! We have to go. I don't want to hear or see anymore!" Galen insisted.

He was driving us, since I wanted our team to take point on everything involving rogues. I hadn't realized he was there. It made me feel guilty. We'd just been talking about walking in on the ranked couples a few days ago.

"Sorry, big brother. I didn't see you there." I blushed.

"I just walked in. Luckily, it was just in time to avoid whatever was going to come after that comment." He chuckled.

"Are our people in place around the restaurant?" I asked as we headed out the door.

"Yes. Jason and Freddy are seated near the window to look out for trouble from the front. Todd and Sam are seated at the kitchen door to watch that entrance. Dillon is with his mate still, Harrison is with Madam, and Drake is with the mayor. Porter is outside the restaurant on top of a building in the back, watching the alley. I'll watch the street from next to the car," Galen told me.

"I wish we had Dilly with us, but his mate is still having trouble. Cara said she was seeing the same issue with Caleb and Robert reported that with Richard. They pushed themselves far too hard today. I hope they learned their lesson," I sighed.

Galen nodded and led us to a black SUV. He opened the door and helped me in. Lucien got in behind me. We buckled our seatbelts and headed to the city. I was very interested in what could happen next.

Chapter 73: Meeting the Mayor

[Lucien]

Riding into the city next to my beautiful mate in a skin-tight dress was one of the hardest things I'd experienced. I longed to slowly remove her dress and savor every bit of skin that was uncovered.

I probably would have taken the risk had our driver not been her brother, a fact that gave me significant pause. He shot me warning glances through the rear-view mirror, his expression hardening with each look. My face must have betrayed my thoughts.

We pulled up to a charming restaurant nestled amongst other buildings downtown. People filled the wide sidewalk, many carrying cameras and microphones, eager to capture the event. I didn't realize exactly *how* aware of us the humans in this city were.

"Holy shit," Bellamy whispered.

"They have security and a roped-off walkway as if we're some sort of human celebrities." I chuckled.

"Look at the fanatics with their little wolf ears. It's so cute," she giggled.

"I'll step out first, chouchoutte. I don't want them rushing you and making you more nervous," I told her.

"Thank you, Lucien. The rules for this are Alpha and Queen. We are both representing our people. I will call you Alpha Lucien, you will call me Queen Bellamy. Sound good, my love?" She smiled.

"Sounds perfect," I responded.

Carefully, I moved to the other side of her. Galen opened the door for me and I stepped onto the curb. A sudden roar from the crowd shattered the peaceful quiet of the night, punctuated by the blinding flashes of cameras. I didn't like it at all.

Some of the fanatical humans in the back of the crowd howled. How fucking embarrassing. I refrained from sneering.

I reached into the car to help Bellamy out. She grasped my hand, and I helped get her on the ground without flashing the cameras. I offered my arm, and she took it, holding on lightly instead of clinging to me like usual.

"Are you the Rogue King? What's your name? What are your plans for the territory?" people shouted.

'If we ignore them, it might lead to issues with the press later,' I told Bellamy.

'True, but if we answer them, it would be without preparation,' she worried.

'Just a little. We can prepare something else. We can at least clarify who we are and our titles.'

'True, mon saucisson,' she responded with a small smile.

"Is she your mate or just your date?" someone called out.

"My name is Lucien Deveraux. I am the Alpha of the Lune Rouge Pack. This is my mate," I announced.

"I'm Bellamy Carrington. Queen of the Eaten Heart Collective and this territory. We will be happy to answer questions after the territory is fully settled," Bellamy stated.

"Seriously? *You're* the Alpha of the territory?! Is this a joke? You're not even tall enough to see over the steering wheel! How old are you? You can't possibly be the sort of threat we'd been expecting." One man surged forward. "How are you going to scare anyone away?"

I sniffed, human. Pack wolf structure was a little patriarchal, but we could tell when we were in the presence of someone powerful. Once I wasn't starving and dehydrated I could easily see Bellamy was strong. A human wasn't a wolf; he didn't pick up on the danger. At least I could say something, do something, about this disrespect.

When I stepped toward the man, Bellamy tugged on my arm. I stopped and turned to her. Her eyes were gentle, and she wore a small smile.

"No, Alpha Lucien. We have an appointment. I've proven myself to the people who matter. Threatening someone a child could beat isn't going to make this better," she said softly.

"I don't like people disrespecting you. He's not a wolf," I growled.

"And he's not someone I need protection from. Come, the pups are hungry. I need my Alpha with me," Bellamy purred.

I sighed and moved back to her side. If I hurt a human in front of these cameras, it would be bad. I almost messed up. She looked up at me with a tender expression. I could feel her contentment and pride.

My Luna, my queen. I wouldn't let her down.

"Wow, looks like he's a tamed wolf! He's not that much of a threat either!" the guy jeered.

Suddenly Bellamy disappeared from my side. There was a shout, and she reappeared. The man was nowhere to be seen.

"Humans may not be aware, but the name of a collective is our promise. My promise. I will defend my people, my territory, and myself. I eat the hearts of my enemies, take care not to become one," she warned the crowd coolly, before guiding me to the door.

'Where's the human?' I asked.

'On the roof with Porter. He's teaching him a quick lesson about taunting my mate.'

'You can defend me, but I can't defend you?'

'Sorry, Lucien. This is my territory, not yours. Right now, every rogue is watching. They saw me rein in my protective mate, and then take care of the issue. All other creatures saw what they were dealing with. You are not my muscle, Lucien. You are my heart. I protect my heart and don't let it act for me,' she replied.

We stepped into the warmly lit restaurant and were guided to a table set with crisp linens in the heart of the dining area. Aside from Bellamy's men, there were some men who were watching out for the mayor and a few people who looked like reporters.

"Are you planning to share this meeting with the humans, even though they may not understand what's happening?" I questioned the man who stood at our table next to Drake.

"No. These are supernatural reporters. They're familiar with tradition and our culture," the mayor huffed. "Information will be altered so humans will understand."

"My apologies for my mate's rudeness. You hadn't warned us about media coverage. I dislike having my privacy invaded without notice." Bellamy glowered.

The mayor looked nervous. He bowed and apologized. It had a rocky start, but I still hoped for an outcome Bellamy would be happy with.

"Allow me to make introductions." Drake smiled. "Mayor Byron, this is Queen Bellamy Carrington of the Eaten Heart Collective and her mate Alpha Lucien Deveraux of the Lune Rouge Pack. Alphas, this is Dale Byron, leader of this land."

"Thank you for meeting me, Queen Bellamy. I've heard much about your collective and we were eager once we knew who'd claimed our land," the mayor stated with a bow.

"Let's sit. I fully intend to treat this area as any other location in my collective. It is the central-most hub to many of the smaller towns that were included in the expansion," Bellamy said as she took a seat in a chair I'd pulled out for her.

I sat next to my mate. We glanced over the menus and placed our order. I ordered some wine to go with my meal. Bellamy ordered orange juice.

The mayor smiled. "An odd choice."

According to Bellamy, he should've known she was pregnant based on her scent. I knew pack wolves could drink in small amounts during pregnancy, but most didn't. We tended to process alcohol quickly, so it wasn't worth the risk.

"Not at all. It has many required vitamins and I'm not old enough to drink alcohol by human law. Not that I would while dealing with territory issues." She smirked as she looked pointedly at him.

Somehow, I'd forgotten that she wasn't twenty-one yet. Bellamy was so calm and commanding. She seemed like she knew what she was doing. I hadn't seen the frightened girl peek out for a while. This was exactly what I knew my mate could be.

Dale looked nervously at the wine being poured in front of him. I sipped mine while I watched him debate what to do. Bellamy chuckled.

"Please, drink. It's not like a glass or two of wine is going to cause your city to collapse, especially since we're not really affected by alcohol. Alpha Lucien is drinking. I just live by different rules."

"Thank you, Queen Bellamy." He sighed and took a drink.

"Let's begin. Tell me about this ex-pack that's causing trouble in my territory," she requested, leaning in.

He told the story of an Alpha from another region moving into the area with a dozen ex-packs. The rogues in the area had lived peacefully until he arrived. He tried to name himself 'rogue king' and demanded compensation for keeping his men in line.

The rogues not associated with this Alpha worked to protect human and other supernatural businesses, but it was difficult. Once the humans realized what they all were, it became easier. Not hiding themselves gave them more chances to help others. To fight an Alpha without another Alpha was difficult. I was impressed they were able to keep themselves free for so long.

They should've made a request of my pack. This was close enough to my pack lands for us to get involved. Though we didn't have the best reputation with rogues. I could see why they worked so long on their own. It disturbed me. My prejudice prevented me from being a more positive influence on the region around my pack.

"I understand. I'll take care of him. If you don't have too much on your plate as mayor, I need a rogue born and an ex-pack lieutenant for the area. Do you have any suggestions?" Bellamy asked.

"I am rather busy, actually, but I have a good idea of who would work for your needs. There is a pastor who leads services in praise of the goddess. He's beloved in the community and a rogue born. His mate is an ex-pack and she's just as cherished. I think they would make excellent lieutenants," he suggested.

"You would answer to them as well. You understand they are my voice and hand."

"Yes, Queen Bellamy. It would be good if I could just focus on helping our community combine safely. If they could take care of rogue issues, it would actually clear up some time for me."

"Get their number to Drake. I haven't brought my phone with me. I need a place set up so I can take the rogues in town into my collective. Drake will give you a web address, I need all rogues in the area to answer the questions, then we can look at scheduling for a massive intake," she stated as our food was being delivered.

"I can do that." Dale smiled.

Bellamy put her hand on mine as I reached for my fork. I looked at her and she shook her head.

"Don't eat that, Lucien. It's poisoned," Bellamy told me.

I smelled nothing. I glared at the mayor. He'd already taken a bite of his food. Since the mayor was rogue born, if his food was poisoned, he would have smelled it. Bellamy sniffed her food.

"Someone tried to poison my mate, but not me or you. An interesting move. What did you think would happen, Dale?" Bellamy gave a deadly smile.

"I didn't do that!" he insisted. "Why would I? He's the mate of one of the most dangerous rogue Alphas in the region."

"Someone did this. Someone ordered it. I want the staff out here. Now," she growled.

He swallowed hard. "Of course."

A quick hand motion sent his guards spreading through the restaurant. Someone brought fifteen people out. The reporters were watching with great interest. I was certainly interested.

Chapter 74: A Poisoned Plate

[Lucien]

The staff lined up before Bellamy. She surveyed them with a stern gaze and considered them carefully. She was radiating anger because one of them had insulted her by attempting to poison me.

"My mate's food has been poisoned using extract of wolf's bane. It's mostly scentless, but a rogue born Alpha has a stronger sense of smell than an average rogue. That means I can smell if you've had contact with it. My guard has blocked all exits. Now is the time to come forward," Bellamy stated coldly.

There was some shuffling among the line. A few of the people in chef's coats looked over at our server. He blanched. That was the man who tried to kill me.

"You." She walked over to him and glared. "Why did you attempt to murder my consort?"

"I…. I didn't," he started, but realized it wouldn't work when she started growling. "You're a Rogue Queen! Not a Luna! You shouldn't have a pack wolf for a mate! You should stick to your own kind! He doesn't care about wolves unless they're pack wolves. Even now, he doesn't really care about you, only your power! You should be with a rogue. Someone who cares about our people! We don't need a pack Alpha looking down on us!"

I felt a growl deep in my chest. "This time, I get to say something."

"I will gladly wait for you to correct him before taking my turn," she chuckled darkly.

"Queen Bellamy is my mate and I have dedicated my pack to her collective. I want a mate for the same reason as any wolf. Not for power, but for balance. She's *mine* and I'll kill *anyone* who tries to take her from me," I growled as I leaned over the man.

"You're guilty of an attempt on my mate's life. Your life is forfeit. I will give you a two-hour head start before I hunt you down and eat your heart. Run, little man. I hope your friends weren't part of your decision, or they'll suffer too," Bellamy said in a deadly tone.

The look on the man's face was unlike any I'd seen before. First amusement, then confusion, then fear. He realized how badly he'd messed up. This wasn't a simple misunderstanding. He'd tried to murder the mate of his queen, and she wasn't a forgiving queen.

He ran out the front door, not waiting for a car, but dashing down the road. Bellamy picked up the plate and headed to the kitchen staff. She handed the plate to the first person in a chef's coat.

"Remake this, without the poison or I kill everyone in here," she demanded.

"Yes, Queen Bellamy," responded the chef, before running into the kitchen.

Bellamy returned to the table and looked at one of the guards. "Make sure they follow my instructions."

The guard bowed. "Yes, Queen Bellamy."

I sat next to her and sipped my drink. She scooted her chair closer, began cutting her steak, and alternated between feeding me and herself. I kept a napkin in hand to ensure she didn't have anything on her face or any smudged lipstick. Her deadly, regal air was such a turn-on. I wanted to take her back home as soon as possible.

"Your eyes are telling your secrets, my Alpha," Bellamy purred.

"Your scent is telling yours, my Queen," I whispered back.

The mayor cleared his throat, and we looked up at him. He seemed even more nervous than before. I could imagine he was upset about this happening while he was trying to negotiate a peaceful takeover.

"I am so very sorry, Queen Bellamy. I had no idea. Truly, I have no problem with your mate being a pack Alpha," the mayor swore.

"I'm inclined to believe you. You aren't responsible for the actions of all the wolves in your care. I want you to report to me directly until the lieutenants are in place. Your work with the other beings in this territory has been invaluable." She nodded and continued feeding me until my plate returned.

***

[Bellamy]

My anger was still intense and unrelenting because someone had the audacity to attempt to murder my mate. More than anything, I was looking forward to that hunt. Judging from the information the mayor gave me, the waiter headed straight for the ex-pack Alpha. He ran toward the highest incidences of trouble, according to Porter.

We finished hashing everything out and had a delicious meal. The mayor was in contact with wolves in the smaller towns as well. His estimate was that there were about two hundred rogues and three hundred other supernaturals in my territory.

Turning to the reporters, who had watched everything silently. I smiled. This was our best chance to take the region peacefully. I could make sure that the humans and other supernatural beings felt comfortable. Others often underestimated me because of my size. I'm small and when I get angry, it is a very intense feeling, but I also wanted to avoid being perceived as overly temperamental. I'm not a chihuahua.

"Do any of you have questions I can answer? I'll have a prepared statement of intent within a week. But I can answer little things," I said.

"What do you intend to do with the self-proclaimed 'Rogue King'?" a woman with black hair that looked like it was actually a really dark purple asked.

"I plan to eliminate the threat to the population," I answered.

"So, you're going to kill him?"

"If that is what is called for, yes." I nodded.

"How did you and Alpha Lucien meet?" another female reporter asked.

"He was visiting the Daylight Moon Pack. I've been living there for six years. We liked each other immediately. There were some… misunderstandings, but we worked through them and fell in love," I responded.

"Alpha, your dislike for rogues is well known even outside your pack. What compelled you to mate with a rogue Alpha?" She smiled, changing her focus.

I slid my hand in his and laced our fingers together. I didn't like this woman, but this was something people would be curious about if she was right and his dislike of rogues was widely known. It was understandable that she would ask.

"Bellamy is my destined mate. I didn't realize it at the time, but I do now. Since before she was born, we were meant to be," Lucien said in a dreamy tone.

He shook his head and looked shocked that he said that. Now I understood. She was good.

"Seriously? Wow. I wasn't expecting you to answer like that," she laughed.

"A Heart's Truth spell. Now I know why I didn't like you," I chuckled.

"Sorry. Gossip mag. We need the juicy stuff. How'd you know about that spell?"

"I've trained with pretty much every supernatural species that lives in the region, including witches. You must be pretty good to pull that one off without drawing attention."

"Normally, I am." She winked. "You didn't seem to be affected, though. You lied right to my face."

"Never underestimate a rogue Queen. We're stronger than we seem in many ways," I answered in a chilly tone.

Giving a warning was important. Establishing myself in the region meant establishing my threat. Tonight, I would do it in speech and in action.

"Can we come with you for the hunt?" a man asked.

"No. You all smell very strongly. Sorry." I shrugged.

"When's the pup due?" a rogue male asked.

"October," I responded.

Lucien smiled softly at me. I smiled back, knowing he was happy about the announcement and the timing. One heck of a birthday present.

"Will Alpha Lucien be taking over your territory after the birth?" the first man questioned.

"No. I can run a territory while caring for a pup. Anything else? I'd like to go home and change for the evening's activities." I smirked.

"Is there a message you'd like to pass on to the citizens of the city, no matter the species?" the first woman asked.

"What Mayor Byron said earlier is true. I am one of the most dangerous rogue Alphas in the region. That's a boon for anyone I claim. I'll make the collective's web address available to you. Cloak it with viewing magic so only supernatural beings can see it. Any who wish to join my collective are welcome to apply. In one week, I'll start swearing in new members. Any werewolves who don't wish to join will have seven days, starting tomorrow, to leave my territory. All other species are free to do as they will, joining would benefit them more, though," I replied.

Lucien stood up, and I wrapped my arm around his. Sam and Todd went to the door. They led us to the SUV, trailed by Jason and Freddy. The reporters out front had mostly gone, a few were still hanging around. Lots of flashbulbs went off.

"Wait!" a girl shouted from behind the crowd.

We paused and turned as the crowd parted. It was one of the fanatics. She had short red hair, a chubby frame, and a baby face with big blue eyes. The wolf ears she wore looked a little like Aurora's. I fought a smile.

"Can we help you?" I asked.

"I want to be a wolf. Will you make me one? Please?" she pled.

"What's your name?"

"Becky Thornton. Rebecca," she replied as she blushed.

"I'm sorry, Becky. That's a myth. You're either born a wolf or you're not." I smiled softly.

"Oh." Becky looked down sadly. "I guess you're laughing at me a bit for not knowing."

"Never. We keep a lot of secrets and that's one thing we never corrected. We love all of our human neighbors. Please, come closer."

As she came near, I could see she was about the same height as me. She was very pretty, and I desperately wanted a pair of those ears. I hoped to earn some good will, so she'd tell me where she bought them.

Becky stopped a little over a foot away from me and bowed a little.

"If we could make others into wolves, I would consider your petition. Unfortunately, only vampires can change people into their species. I am very sorry. I must say, though, I love these little ears you have. They look quite well made. Proper proportions and everything. Can I see them?" I asked.

She nodded and took them off, handing them over. The fur used was nice, soft to the touch, and the stitching was barely visible. I showed them to Lucien, who looked amused.

'You have ears of your own, chouchoutte. Why are you teasing this human?'

'I'm not, Lucien! I'd love to have these. They're cute. Imagine how nice they'd look with the right lingerie and a pretty collar.'

'I agree; we need these…. You should have a dozen of them.'

I giggled. That was a little much. I knew he just needed some incentive to see their value. But, my plan for them was a little bigger.

'There are a lot of other uses. My junior elites, the young teens, all knew they were wolves, but nothing showed it. Some little ears could make them happy. Especially the ones who are new to the pack link. It could be part of a welcome to being a wolf package. Since twelve is when they start experiencing more of what it is to be a wolf.'

'That's silly, chouchoutte. I love it. It would encourage them to work harder as members of the pack. Like we're acknowledging them as proper wolves.'

"Exactly what I was thinking, Alpha." I smiled.

"Where did you purchase these?" Lucien asked Becky.

She blushed harder. "I… I make them."

"Would you make some for our pack? Let me know the prices. Umm… Galen! Get my cellphone number for Becky." I bounced.

"Really? Oh my goodness! Thank you!" Becky grinned.

Galen handed her a little card with my number and email address on it. She looked at it with glittering eyes and flung herself onto me. I hugged her back.

"I'm so excited!" she said as she pulled back.

"You'd never guess it," Lucien snorted.

"Lucien, stop. Head home and be safe, Becky," I told her.

"I will. Don't die." Becky smiled as she stepped back from me.

"Same to you." I bowed slightly.

She knew rogue goodbyes. Her knowledge impressed me. People rarely realized we weren't being snarky when we said that. With luck, this would cement some goodwill with the humans. I suddenly realized I still had her headband.

"Becky! Your ears!" I called out to her retreating form, waving them.

"Keep them! I have a ton more!" she called back.

I grinned broadly up at my mate. He was looking at me in a soft and lovey sort of way. It made me blush a bit.

"You made a friend, my Queen," he whispered as he helped me into the SUV.

"I've never had a human friend before." I smiled back.

Lucien sat next to me and wrapped an arm around my shoulder. I cuddled into his chest. It was a nice, relaxing drive before I had to head out to deal with my rogue business. I found I thought more clearly when I was with Lucien. So I worked on formulating my plan while he held me.

Chapter 75: The 'Rogue King'

[Bellamy]

Lucien wasn't thrilled about me leaving again after we returned home. He grasped that I needed to find the man who'd tried to kill him, but didn't want me to go it alone. I offered to take Dillon and Drake with me, and then I had an idea.

"I'll take Randy, the bear, too," I told him.

"You trust him enough?" he asked.

"He's Stanton's cousin. He won't run away and he won't try to hurt me. Dilly and Drake are two of my best fighters. I'm the best warrior in Daylight Moon. Adding a bear to the mix will make us even more formidable," I offered.

He seemed to think about it. I could smell his discomfort. It was hard for an Alpha to let their mate go into a dangerous situation, and even harder if that mate was pregnant. I know I didn't want him in a situation where he could get hurt.

"Let me come, too. He tried to kill me. I should have some involvement," Lucien stated.

"I don't want a war right now. If he is with the Alpha in town, adding you might spark something. Please, Lucien. I want to kill this man and come back home. I still have to see what this Alpha has to say for himself and do more investigating than a simple news archive. If there's a way to settle him peacefully, I would rather take that course," I explained.

"When we talked before, you told me you'd try to accept some of my possessiveness and overprotectiveness. This isn't one of those things I can just set aside, chouchoutte. You said the ex-pack Alpha has a gang. I can't just sit here and hope you and the pups return. It's not that I doubt you. You're an amazing warrior. I just…. I can't imagine not being by your side in a dangerous situation like this," he strained as he looked away.

I moved closer and reached up to his face. There was a tear threatening to tumble from his long lashes. I hadn't thought like a mate, but like a queen, like a warrior. I hurt him. His fear was filling our bond.

"Lucien, don't be afraid. I'll do everything I can to make this end safely," I promised.

"Just, let me come with. I'll stay out of sight unless you call me. Please. I love you. I can't lose you," Lucien whispered, taking my hand and kissing it.

"Fine. Don't act before thinking. Don't come until called. Trust that I'm good at what I do, please." I smiled.

"I trust you. Thank you. I'll go change. Are we running?" he asked.

"No. We'll take a car into town and track from there We'll need to dispose of the body. It'll make it easier to bring him back," I answered.

Lucien nodded, and we went to change and gather our men. I didn't really want to take Dilly from Jean-Claude, but he was one of my top fighters and I needed to make sure that we'd have an advantage. No one would expect the strength of our small numbers.

An hour later, we were ready to go. Randy was happy to get out of the cells for the hunt. Dilly felt thrilled to hunt down the person who tried to hurt Lucien. Drake was mostly along to act as my lieutenant until I could get one set up in town.

When we reached the city, I had Drake slow and stuck my head out of the window. Two hours was the maximum for a strong trail scent and we were just outside that marker. Once I caught the scent of the rogue, we started following it.

The scent got stronger as we neared a city park. It mingled with the scent of at least a dozen other wolves. I directed Drake to a parking area, and we got out of the car. In the distance, there was a covered picnic area. I could see shadows there. That had to be them.

"There are too many," I sighed. "Lucien, you'll have to come with us. I don't smell more, but that doesn't mean they aren't there."

"I'll follow your orders to the best of my ability. My first priority is protecting you and the pups, though," he replied.

"Got it. We'll do a basic formation. 'V'-shaped. I'll take point, Dillon and Drake next, then Randy and Lucien. Keep your ears, eyes, and noses open. I don't want a sneak attack."

The men nodded and took up their positions. We made our way toward the gathering under the metal roof. As we neared it, I could smell the rogue and his blood. They better not have killed him before I got the chance.

When we were about fifteen feet away, a man emerged from the picnic area. He was as tall as Lucien, about 6'2", with light-colored hair. It was difficult to tell in the dark if it was brown or blond. He had a 'jock next door' thing going on. His face looked friendly and there was a confidence in his movement that told me he could fight, and it would be a rough one if we did. We stopped our approach.

The man smirked as he paused about ten feet from me. "Can I help you?"

"I'm Queen Bellamy Carrington, of the Eaten Heart Collective. Are you the one who calls himself the Rogue King?" I asked, mirroring his condescending smile.

"I called myself that once as a joke. Rogue borns can never take a joke," he scoffed. "My name is Thomas Lorrie."

"You're not an ex-pack Alpha," I murmured as his scent hit me.

"I'm an Alpha who has no pack. What else would you call it?"

"A displaced Alpha. That clears a few things up at least. You lost your pack by no fault of your own. You weren't ejected with reason by the rest of your pack. I'd like to schedule a meeting with you in a more… well-lit location. I need information before I decide what to do in this region of my territory," I replied.

"Seriously? You send a messenger to tell me you're coming after me and my people, then try to pretend like you didn't. I thought a Queen would be better than that."

"I've sent no messengers. I'm only here hunting an attempted murderer. Alpha Thomas, I mean no harm to you and yours. I just want that man's heart." I smiled.

"You don't smell like you're lying. Who did he try to kill that the Queen is hunting him?"

"My mate," I answered in a cold tone.

"Bring him out," Thomas called back to his men. "That's a fairly serious crime among pack wolves."

"It's a pretty serious crime among rogues as well. The mates of our leaders are important for keeping them calm and sane," I told him.

Two large men dragged a bleeding, battered, and bound rogue between them. They stood him up once they were next to their leader. The rogue looked frightened. He'd made a very poor decision. I'd been looking forward to this and now it wouldn't be as fun.

"What do I get for giving him to you?" Thomas grinned.

I could hear a low growl from Lucien. He didn't like how this was going, but I saw a possibility in it. I remembered something from the map I'd been studying previously.

"Do you have a map of the county?" I responded.

He turned and ordered someone to go get him a map of the county. Thomas looked interested. I thought it was perfect. A third pack added to my collective.

It took a little bit while someone ran to a corner store for the map. We took our conversation to a picnic table under a tree. Dillon held a flashlight while Drake grabbed a pen for me. I examined the map and drew out my assumed territory borders. It was exactly where I thought it was.

"Listen, Alpha Thomas, you aren't a rogue. You're a displaced Alpha. That's why you don't really have a scent that says one or the other. If we can find a territory for you to claim, you can reestablish a pack. On this edge of my territory," I pointed to the map, "we have the old pack lands of the Silver Moon pack. They were wiped out in the red rogue wave in the sixties. A couple packs have tried to move in but didn't have the resources. The pack land is half in my territory and half unclaimed. I can give you the land in my territory to start your pack. There are some buildings, I have contractors and builders who can come assist in getting everything livable again. My collective can help with other resources."

"For the life of one man?" he asked.

"That and for you joining your pack with my collective. I think the conflict with the mayor and this city can be resolved by removing you to a more acceptable habitat. You would have all the resources of a pack in my collective and you would be safer from rogue attacks.

"Since the last pack to try fixing it up has been gone for about five years, hunters won't even show up for a few. You could get safely established. I'd ask that you take on some of my ex-pack children while growing your pack as well. We could have you fully peopled inside of a year and prospering inside of two," I offered.

"You would do this for us? No killing or fighting involved?" Thomas asked, shocked.

"Alpha Thomas, I want my territory to be at peace. I opt for non-violent resolution when I can. I do still intend to kill that man and eat his heart." I chuckled.

I felt Lucien's hand on my shoulder and fought the urge to rub my cheek on it. Alpha Thomas looked up. He glared over my head at Lucien.

"You're a pack Alpha," he said.

"Yes," Lucien answered.

"Why are you here?"

"He's here to watch me kill the man who tried to kill him. Alpha Thomas Lorrie, this is my mate, Alpha Lucien Deveraux," I said, straightening myself between them.

"Is that the reason this man tried to kill him?"

"That's what he said. I was hoping to question him a little, but it looks like that won't be possible," I sighed as I looked at the man.

The men turned to the rogue. He was dead. The two warriors holding him looked shocked. I walked over and examined the body. I found a small dart embedded in his back.

I pulled out the dart and sniffed it. Concentrated wolf's bane extract. He died as I introduced the Alphas. Whoever did it was stealthy. I didn't hear or smell them. It's hard to sneak up on me. I looked around, but couldn't see any movement giving away where the killer would've gone.

"That body needs to be burned," I stated, standing up.

"We'll take care of it, Queen Bellamy. Here's my phone number, if you're still interested in making this offer," Thomas said. "But you have to know. My people have been blamed for things we didn't do. We aren't the ones extorting and bullying people."

"I want everyone in my territory to be comfortable. This would make it infinitely easier to get ex-pack children into packs. I'll call you later. We can talk about the accusations and our plans then. I want to go home and rest. I have a long day tomorrow."

"Thank you for giving us a chance. I didn't expect anything like this."

"Don't misunderstand, Thomas. I'm doing this for my collective. It's because I don't want to lose people in a fight, not because I feel sympathy. Have a good night." I waved and walked away.

Chapter 76: Home Again

When we got back in the car, Bellamy sat on my lap. She wouldn't answer any questions. She didn't kiss or cuddle me. I wrapped my arms around her and held her. It seemed like she was processing. Maybe thinking of who could've killed that rogue. They could've killed all of us.

Throughout the entire drive, Bellamy didn't move. She barely blinked. Her scent started fading, and I heard her heartbeat slow. Dillon sat on my left, and Drake drove with Randy in the passenger's seat.

"Don't worry. She's planning. Bellamy uses this as a deep meditation sometimes. She'll be fine. Just, don't try slapping her. She dislocated every joint in Hollis' arm when he did that." Dillon chuckled.

"How long will she be like this?" I asked.

"Dunno. No one does. Sometimes it's an hour, sometimes a couple days. She'll eat if you put food in her mouth and she'll drink if you use a straw. It's like having a baby doll. She doesn't need much food or water, though," he replied.

I nodded. Another aspect of my little mate I had to figure out. I was more grateful than ever that Dillon was there.

When we arrived at Lune Rouge, I had an omega take Randy to a guest room and another get his things from the cells. He'd been an excellent resource to have tonight, and I wanted him to be rested for when his cousin arrived. He was important to Bellamy and her plans.

I carried Bellamy to our quarters and up to our room. She didn't move. She barely breathed. I laid her on the bed while I ran a warm bath.

Bellamy preferred being clean when she went to sleep, so she usually bathed or showered before bed. I ensured she followed her tradition. I felt certain I'd be rewarded after her meditation.

I was pretty sad about not getting to make love to her like we planned. Most Alphas wouldn't be cool with this. They'd try something, but I wasn't going to risk her breaking or dislocating something sensitive on me. Plus, I would never disrespect her when she was working on something important.

Once the bath was ready, I stripped her and carried her in to be cleaned. She still didn't move. I elected not to try washing her hair. I didn't want her to think I was drowning her. Her unconscious mind might not fully realize what was happening.

Diligently, I worked to clean every inch of her before wrapping her in a towel and setting her on the bed. I put a pillow on the ground and settled her there so I could brush her hair. It was in a bun and I hadn't taken it out, so it was mostly dry.

She sighed while I brushed her out, but didn't say or do anything to show she was back. I returned Bellamy to the bed and finished drying her before putting her under the blankets and taking my shower.

When I returned, she was still staring blankly at the ceiling. I sighed and tucked myself in next to her. I hoped she would be healthy and rested when she woke up.

I awoke to the familiar feel of Bellamy's small hands on my body; it was still dark. A small groan escaped my lips. I was exhausted and wanted to sleep. I had training in the morning.

Once she reached her goal, I suddenly didn't care. Her hands wrapped around my shaft and she began stroking. She started kissing my chest as she worked my cock.

"Chouchoutte, what are you doing? It's late." I sighed.

"Actually, it's early, mon saucisson. You took care of me last night. I got you up an hour early to say thank you. Just lay back, my love. Let your Luna take care of you," she purred.

I smiled and did as she said. Her lips trailed over my chest and abdomen. She nipped at the bulges of my abs while keeping a slow but firm motion going with her hands. The path of her nibbles and kisses went down.

Licking my lips, I waited to feel her mouth surround me. All I got was a firm lick over my tip as she went lower and nipped at my balls. Her tongue danced over them and she took one into her mouth, sucking on it gently.

One of her hands left my cock and started trailing lower. Tickling under my balls to the sensitive skin beneath. Bellamy stroked that area in time to her sucking and other stroking. I'd never felt anything as intense. Then her finger slipped lower, and I yelped.

"Are you okay, mon saucisson?" she asked innocently as her finger swirled around my backdoor.

"What are you planning, chouchoutte?" I strained.

"I'm just learning more about how to please your body, Lucien. Where all the fun spots are. Where you like to be touched, but would never tell. No one will know, my love. This is for me and you," Bellamy murmured and applied some pressure with her finger.

I cursed myself as I moaned. Her other hand never stopped stroking and her lips were right against my skin as she talked. All the sensations flowed together, and I felt myself drawing closer to my end.

"What do you think, saucisson? Do you want me to keep going, or should I stop?" She offered as she kissed and licked the skin in front of her.

"I'm not ready for that, Bellamy. Not yet. I really like how that feels, though. I'm so close," I grunted.

She buried her face in my balls, licking and sucking them as the tempo of her hand around my cock increased and she fingered my asshole. I couldn't hold back anymore and roared my completion.

My whole body shuddered as I came. It was one of the most intense orgasms I'd ever had. After I finished, she went to the bathroom and returned with a warm, wet washcloth. She cleaned everywhere I'd reached when I came, then went to rinse the cloth.

When she came back, Bellamy covered us with a blanket and snuggled in close to me. Her fingers trailed up and down the centerline of my body. It wasn't exactly what I'd been hoping for, but every time with her was amazing.

It was the difference between just having sex and having sex with my mate. I'd never been so connected with a partner. We shared so much more because of our bond.

"Would you like me to taste you again, chouchoutte? We have time," I suggested.

"No, Lucien. I needed to feel powerful and in control of something. Thank you for going along. Last night just left me a mess. I didn't kill the man who tried to kill you. I wasn't the one to end his miserable existence. Someone stole that from me and I want to know why. They couldn't have been part of it. If they were, then they would've tried to kill you, too. I don't understand," she sighed.

"We'll figure it out. We have the resources, the intelligence, and the strength to overcome anything, ma choupinette," I murmured, kissing the top of her head.

"I don't want anyone to take you from me and I feel like we're treading water in a shark tank. I'm scared. What if I fail and I lose you, too?" Bellamy asked quietly.

"*We* won't fail. The goddess brought us together. We just have to focus and use what we have. There's an answer. It may not fall in our lap, but it exists. Have faith in her, have faith in you, have faith in me. I refuse to die now that I've found you. You are my reason for living, Bellamy. You and those pups," I told her, holding her tight.

"Thank you. You always make me better, Lucien. I'm not acting like much of an Alpha right now, am I?" she chuckled.

"You are acting precisely as an Alpha. If we didn't worry, we wouldn't be nearly as effective. It's okay to be scared of losing something you love. That's what makes us get up in the morning. We need to protect the things and people we love. Our pack, our collective, our mate."

"It was a great idea to mate with such a wise old man," Bellamy giggled.

"You little brat," I growled and tickled her.

She squealed and squirmed, but I had her held tight. After a bit, she started tickling back, and we didn't stop until the alarm went off. Alphas shouldn't have tickle fights. We never concede.

Chapter 77: Mothers and Monsters

[Bellamy]

Training went better than it had the day before. We had a light day and all of my teenage cousins were there. Salomé joined us, making Galen act like an idiot. It was a great laugh and exactly what I needed to lighten my mood.

He was so attentive to her that he ended up falling behind, tripping over things, and missing blocks. During our repetitive motion training, he let his form fall. Bruce scolded him about watching his form and not pretty girls. Coming from a standard warrior, it was definitely grounds to tease Galen mercilessly… and we would.

We joined the Lune Rouge Elites for their training as well. Except for Lucien, Thierry, and Robert. They watched us. I could feel Lucien's pride when I sparred against Jean-Claude and Caleb. I put them down fairly quickly, and the rest of the warriors started looking at me with a lot more respect.

After breakfast, I got a call from my mom letting me know she was heading out from Daylight Moon at nine and was bringing Gail, May, and the twins. I let Todd and Jason know their mates were coming to help with things. They were thrilled.

Lucien ordered one of the second-floor rooms in our quarters to be made up for my mom and the one across the hall from it made up for the girls. There were eight rooms on the second floor. Perfect for a large family, like we were planning.

His mother's room was on the same floor. We had it cleaned and prepared for bringing her home. It was a busy morning, but it felt great to get things in order.

At ten, we went to retrieve Madam from the hospital. Until she told me to call her anything else, I decided that would be best. I always tried to be respectful of my elders. Especially the ones who were in charge of my big life events.

We got back to the packhouse right as my mom pulled in. I linked Todd, Jason, and my brothers. Lucien linked my uncles and their wives. Everyone met in the courtyard.

My mom rushed over to hug me and gush over me. She said I was glowing, asked about my health, and fawned over me. It was a little suffocating. Luckily, I had an out. Galen arrived in the courtyard a little late, holding Salomé's hand and chatting quietly.

"Mom, did Galen call and tell you he found his mate?" I asked.

She pulled back and looked at me with wide eyes. "No, he did not! Where is she? Where is he? I'm going to whup that boy."

"Over there." I pointed to my now fearful older brother.

Mom turned and launched herself at him, telling him he was a rotten, ungrateful child. All the while fawning over my younger cousin. Salomé went back and forth between trying to protect Galen and thanking my mom for the praise. Celesta and Thierry went to introduce themselves to her. Learning Galen's mate was Caleb's sister thrilled Mom. It essentially made her and Daisy sisters.

Jason and Todd embraced their mates and helped them with their luggage while Bruce and Porter got our sleepy little sisters out of the van. I was happy there wasn't much for them to jump off of here. We'd made sure their bedroom window had a baby lock on it.

My mom returned to me and smiled softly. "You've always given us so much, Bellamy. Now, we have a daughter-in-law, more grandbabies, and even more reasons to celebrate. My sweet daughter, I always knew you'd grow up to be amazing."

I blushed. "Mom, not in front of everyone."

"Olive, this is my mother, Genevieve Deveraux. Maman, this is Olive Carrington, Bellamy's mother," Lucien said with a little chuckle.

"Genevieve it's so nice to meet you. Lucien is a wonderful man and makes our Bellamy so happy. I thought there would be problems because his first mate was her birth mother, but neither one seems to mind it. I'm so glad everyone here has accepted her."

"Mom! We aren't telling people that yet!" I whisper-yelled.

Thierry and Robert sighed. Genevieve looked like she was going to laugh. Celesta and Simone covered their mouths with their hands. None of the omegas were near enough to hear. The only person who didn't know was Salomé. Her eyes widened.

"Your birth mother was…. You're my cousin?" she murmured.

"Don't tell anyone, please. Someone is trying to hurt Lucien's family. If they find out your parents are my aunt and uncle, they might try to hurt you and your family," I told her. "We're waiting until we were sure it wouldn't harm any of you."

"Did you know, Galen?" Salomé asked.

"Yes. I kept the secret to protect you," he replied.

"Dad?"

"Yes. We knew. They told us on the first day here. Bellamy's right. We need to protect all of you from these people. They tried to kill Luna Genevieve, Lucien, and our future Alpha. We didn't want to risk your lives. You can't tell anyone about this, Salomé," Thierry said.

"I don't know what to say. I… you should've told us. We can keep secrets. Did you tell grandma and grandpa?" She scowled.

"No. Only we know. They'll be told when the time is right," Celesta answered.

"Let's get off this topic. We need to get everyone settled. I have a lot of work to do. Mom, don't tell anyone else. May, Gail, I need you two quiet on this as well," I stated.

They nodded. My mom looked embarrassed. But it was my fault for not saying anything. I reassured her that I wasn't upset and it wasn't her fault.

Once everyone settled, I went to Lucien's office with him, Thierry, and Robert. We went over the plans for the next few days. Tomorrow, we would run the borders. We would start in the east. Lucien and I would take the north, and Dillon and Jean-Claude would take the south. When we reached the old border line, we would head back.

Our estimates were that we'd need to leave around dawn and should return no later than three in the afternoon. It was generous, but running had different things to take into consideration than driving. Dillon and I had specially designed bags that would carry our tools. We would have maps we would mark with the curves and turns. Borders were seldom straight lines.

We had lunch in the Alpha's dining room with everyone else. No one could know I was involved in the investigation. The story was that I was getting accustomed to the workings of the pack. Most people didn't expect to see me much until after the Luna ceremony. I was still working with the heads of every section of the household via text to get things running more smoothly.

Madam, Mom, Gail, and May recruited Salomé, Celesta, Cara, and Simone to work on the Luna ceremony and start work on the wedding. We would go dress shopping later in the week. They were all excited to go with me. It was a relief to have them all working on that stuff for me. It made focusing on the killers easier.

After lunch, we returned to the office and started a board with everything we knew about the attacks and plans. Randy came to help and Dilly went to interview the maid. He would have his report by three. He was fantastic at making people comfortable enough to talk.

We had a decent timeline that started when the maid gave Lucien the pheromone and went to the poisoning last night. It could've been a coincidence, but I wouldn't take it off my list just because we couldn't properly connect it. That incident had a question mark next to it, but stayed up there. The mayor was having his supernatural police digging into the waiter, his friends, family, and other affiliations.

Randy and I were on the couch, going through emails sent to him and the orderly. He used some of Stanton's people to trace them. They were from a web-based mail server, so they had to pull out the big guns and it would take a while. They made the payments through cryptocurrency and numbered accounts. It was basically untraceable.

Dilly came in and we all set aside our work. The information he gathered would, hopefully, help pull things together. We were getting ready to hear his report when Lucien put up his hand.

"Stanton's here. They just let him through on the main road. Let's have everyone here for the report, if that's okay, Dillon," Lucien said.

"Works for me. I can't wait to see Bemmy's bear." Dilly grinned.

Randy snorted. "He's gonna love this."

In the courtyard, we met up with the remaining Elite Ten. I held on to Lucien's hand and linked my mom and Cara that Talia had arrived. They loved her when she stayed with our pack a few years ago. With them came all the other women. We had a decent sized crowd by the time the SUV pulled in.

They parked and Stanton got out of the driver's side. He was a lot taller and thicker than he'd been before. When I knew him, he was just over six feet, but bears could grow in height until they were in their mid-to-late-twenties. Now he was the same height as Randy 6'7".

He wore his chocolate brown hair long, framing his face and flowing down his back over his shoulders. He had wide-set, nearly black eyes, naturally dark skin from his mother's Native American heritage, a hawk-like nose, and a small cleft in his chin.

He was just as handsome as I remembered, but his muscles were much bigger. All of him was much bigger. A small smile tugged at the corners of his mouth. I grinned and pulled Lucien forward.

"Hey there, Baby Belle. You grew up… ish," Stanton chuckled.

"Not all of us can be giants." I laughed. "This is my mate, Lucien Deveraux. Lucien, this is Stanton Bruinwald, my childhood friend."

Lucien released my hand and reached out to shake Stanton's. After looking at the offered hand for a moment, Stanton accepted it and they gripped each other's hands tightly. I rolled my eyes. Alphas.

The passenger side door opened, and I walked around them. Talia climbed out. She was smiling like she almost always was. I loved her to pieces, but vampire smiles creeped me out. Her skin was pale, but she wasn't bony like Marion and his crew were.

She indulged in blood-mixed foods. Soups, shakes, drinks, and soft foods were mixed with blood so their bodies would digest it. The people in her bloodline didn't get that sickly frailty I saw in Marion's line.

Talia was only a couple of inches shorter than me. Average height for a woman back when she died was around 4'8", so she would've been on the tall side. She had copper colored hair and violet eyes. Her mouth was a little cat-like. Talia always looked like she had an amusing secret.

"Bellamy, you look radiant," she purred and rushed forward to envelop me in a hug. "Congratulations on finding a mate, pheata."

Pheata meant 'pet'. She taught me a little Irish when I was young, along with a few other languages. It was where I got my nickname tradition from. She said she only called me that.

"Welcome to my new home, Talia. How much direct sunlight have you had today?" I asked.

"Always taking care of others. I still have an hour before I start to get uncomfortable," she replied.

We turned back to the group. Lucien and Stanton had stopped their dominance game and Lucien was staring at Talia. I worried about him. He looked absolutely stricken. I wondered what was wrong.

Chapter 78: Dillon's Report; Making Plans

[Lucien]

I was shaking the bear's hand when the smell of vampire hit me. I thought they'd have her in a box or a bag or something, but there she was, in direct sunlight, hugging Bellamy. The idea of being safe during the daytime had been one thing keeping me calm about having a vampire in my home.

'Lucien, are you alright?' Bellamy linked me.

'She's out in the sun, how?'

'Don't be afraid, mon cœur. Talia will only feed on me or the boys while she's here. She's well over ten thousand years old. The older they are, the more powerful they are. At her age, they can handle a couple hours of direct sunlight,' she explained.

Bellamy smiled. "Lucien, this is Talia. Talia the Traveler, this is my mate, Lucien Deveraux. He's the Alpha of this pack."

Talia put her hand out to me. I regained my composure. As Alpha, I wouldn't let a small vampire stop me from representing my people well. I bowed, taking her hand and kissing the back of it, as was tradition in our pack.

"It's a pleasure to meet you, Talia. I've heard much about you from Bellamy."

"I can smell your fear, Alpha. Don't worry. I mean no harm to you and yours," she said so quietly I could barely hear her.

She was ensuring no one else would, either. I appreciated it. Talia didn't look like the other vampires, it made it easier to trust her.

"Let's head in. We still need Dilly's report and Talia shouldn't be in the sun much longer," Bellamy said softly.

She wrapped her arms around one of mine and led us into the house. Once inside, Talia finished greeting everyone she knew, and then she introduced the bear. Bellamy looked very happy. I was glad to have more allies and the resources of a member of the High Council would come in handy.

We headed back to my office for Dillon's report and to read Talia and Stanton into the investigation. Bellamy leaned against me and Talia would sneak looks from time-to-time. She really seemed to dote on my mate. It was a little strange to see.

Though vampires, wolves, and bears rarely got along, Bellamy managed to befriend creatures who would normally have nothing to do with her. She was amazing.

Once we were in the office, and the door secured, we took seats around the coffee table. Randy, Stanton, and Talia were on the couch. Robert, Thierry, and I were in the armchairs. Bellamy sat in my lap and Dillon pulled one of the desk chairs over.

I knew Robert and Thierry were uncomfortable with Bellamy sitting on me. I didn't realize how uncomfortable it would make the bears. Stanton was glaring at me. I didn't know what his problem was, but I didn't like how he looked at Bellamy.

She told me he didn't find wolves attractive, but the look in his eye when he saw her earlier and the posturing made me think he wasn't entirely honest. Maybe I wasn't used to the type of protectiveness a bear had over younger siblings. It just seemed suspicious to me.

"Lucien, you're growling," Bellamy whispered, rubbing my chest.

I smiled. "I didn't realize, chouchoutte."

"I know. Everything will be okay," she replied with her hand over my heart.

"Stanton said you were captured by vampires. Would you mind telling me about it and giving me their names? There is no master for the region so I need to make sure their final deaths are recorded with the Council," Talia requested.

I nodded and told my story. They were quiet, and Talia listened intently. I revealed my curse in the telling so they would understand the pain I was in. Bellamy told what she knew about Marion's bloodline and his eye color. It would make it easier to track down his sire.

Talia snorted. "Marion and Clea. I've heard of them. Marion Bane. He's obsessed with Death. That's why he picked a name so similar to my broodmate's. I'm glad they're dead. Marius will be as well. He hated hearing tales of that boy's misdeeds being attributed to him because of the name similarity."

"Marius is Marius Aconitum. Wolf's Bane," Bellamy added. "A plant poisonous to more than just us. Death is Death to all."

"He wanted me to let you know you can call on him if you need. He's bored." Talia chuckled.

Bellamy wrinkled her nose. "No. Marius isn't allowed to come. He's an ass."

My tiny mate called Death an ass. She's not even bothered. His offer to come annoyed her. Goddess, that was hot.

"Let's get on with the meeting. We want to get the report while it's fresh in Dillon's mind." Robert smiled at his future son-in-law.

We turned to Dillon, and he began.

"Miss Corbisier said she's pregnant with the child of a rogue. He wanted her to pass it off as yours once you were dead. An assassin was hired to kill you, then kill your sister and her family while they traveled to the funerals. The maid was supposed to kill your mother, but accidentally broke the vial of concentrated wolf's bane extract. She talked to some people and someone told her about thallium. All it took was an order of rat poison from China. It came just in time for your trip.

"She had to give a much higher dose than the guy told her because Madam is a wolf. That's why she got sick for a couple days before the stroke. The day the guards took them in, was the day she resolved to load it into everything she could. Madam was still insisting on some solid foods, pudding, mashed potatoes, and soft bread with butter. If they hadn't come, Madam wouldn't have survived that dose with her already weakened state," Dillon reported.

I was shaking with a mix of fear and rage. If not for Bellamy, my mother really wouldn't be alive. If that woman wasn't pregnant, I would tear her apart.

"Why the pregnancy?" Bellamy asked.

"Spite. Putting a rogue child in power over the pack would be a slap in the face to pack wolves."

"That would only be possible if she disavowed the pack and if the rogue was an Alpha. It narrows down the suspects. There are four rogue born Alpha males in the region. Kyle Fuller of Limb Torn, Percival Hanks of Flayed Skin, Calvin Bourne of Blood Drained, and Ashley Oakes of Bough Broken," Bellamy listed.

"I've never heard of most of these men," I said.

"This is why the Association requires 'Rogue Studies' in high school now. Most packs only know about collectives that are threats. Everyone in the area has heard something about Limb Torn because of how aggressive Kyle's father was, especially in the later years. I'm allied with Ashley and Percival. Calvin doesn't like other Alphas and I don't speak to Kyle," she replied.

"Sorry. Bough Broken? Like the nursery rhyme?" Thierry scoffed.

"Our name is our promise. Ashley breaks limbs off of trees and… violates his enemies with them. No one with half a brain is enemies with Ash. Your spirit is broken long before your body succumbs to death." Bellamy winced.

"Ash is half bear and half wolf," Dillon said. "He's about as tall and built as Stanton and his wolf is twice as big as Lucien's."

"With half breeds, you either get a gigantic wolf or a small bear. It's rare for a bear to breed with a wolf. We're generally not attracted to them," Randy said.

"There are some exceptions. Bears who come from a brown bear or polar bear line are more likely to breed with wolves. Black bear lines are peaceful and don't like the more aggressive side of apex predators," Stanton added.

"What kind of bear are you and your cousin?" I asked.

"Ursus arctos horribilis. Grizzly bears." He smiled. "Despite the name, we're not nearly as bad as our northern cousins."

"Ash is half polar bear," Bellamy said, looking him in the eye.

"Shit. I hope that's not the guy you're after." Randy chuckled nervously.

"I doubt it. Ash likes to stay in his territory. He's grown it all he wants to and found a wolf mate. His focus is on his collective and pups. I don't see Percival doing this either. He's first generation, like me. We're not as aggressive toward pack and ex-pack. He also has a mate. So it's really down to Kyle and Calvin," she speculated.

"Do you think it's more likely to be Kyle?" I asked.

"I think it's a toss-up, Lucien. Kyle and Calvin are both so many generations that they don't even count them anymore. Neither is particularly fond of pack wolves. But neither one has a reason to kill you and your family. Their territories aren't even that close to here." Bellamy sighed.

"Did she give a reason for wanting to kill my family? For herself or the man she worked with?" I asked.

"She said you killed her mate. He was an ex-pack who was waiting in the woods right outside the border about a year ago. They were going to run away together. She was just getting her pay and packing her things. You found him and killed him," Dillon replied softly.

I looked at Bellamy. She bit her lips together and looked sad. I didn't know how to fix this. I might have changed a lot about myself, but I hated rogues back then and this sounded like something I would've done. Me not remembering it was in line with my attitude at the time.

"And the other?" she asked.

"She told me he wanted to finish what an ancestor started and it happened to benefit him in two ways. Nothing else," Dillon answered.

"This is fantastic." Bellamy grinned. "This takes our suspect pool from vast to just two. I don't think it would be a rogue Alpha outside of the region. I can make some calls and see if any of the ones in nearby regions are likely to have tried. If not, we just need to investigate Kyle and Calvin."

She laid her head against my shoulder. I could feel her relief. I was glad we got some movement on the investigation. Our family was important to me and I didn't want anyone trying to harm Bellamy or the pups again.

"Let's get everyone settled. I had the omegas prepare the room next to Randy for Stanton. We have a guest room we rarely give out because of the lack of windows. So, I thought that would be best for Talia," I said. "We serve dinner around seven. I'll have someone retrieve you for it."

"The kitchen is making a special meal for you, Talia. I'll make sure there's some blood tea to go with it," Bellamy said.

"Thank you, pheata. I love your blood tea. What's my meal? Did you make my favorites?" Talia asked.

Bellamy smiled. "Yes. Salmon mousse, blended vegetable soup, and white wine."

"You eat actual food?" I asked.

"It needs to be mixed with a certain amount of blood, but I can eat many soft foods."

"I thought it would be more comfortable for you if she were on a solid diet while here. I know you dislike the idea of me being bitten. The Elite Ten has offered to donate for the next few days," Bellamy replied.

"Thank you both for that," I said.

"Well, let's go. I'd like to relax for a while," Stanton said gruffly.

They stood, and Talia slipped over to where Thierry and Dillon were.

"You can walk me to my room, handsome," she purred to my Beta.

Thierry turned red, and Bellamy giggled. Dillon looked playfully offended.

"I can't believe you, Tally. After all, we meant to each other," he sniffed.

"Darling, I have two arms." She winked and reached over to link her other arm through his.

"Goddess, Talia. Could you not?" Stanton growled.

"He's just jealous, ignore him. Let's go boys."

Everyone left, closing the door behind them. Bellamy sighed and kissed my neck. I wrapped my arms around her and held her closer.

"I love you. I'm so happy we've figured this much out. It doesn't seem as hopeless now," she whispered.

"I love you, too. Did you want a little nap or did you want to work some more?" I asked.

"What I want and what I have to do, are two very different things, mon saucisson," Bellamy sighed.

"Work it is, then." I smiled.

We separated and started on our tasks. She worked on preparing a statement for the new territory. I tried to work ahead so I wouldn't have too much piled up after we ran the borders the next day. Maybe I could set up another workstation in my office so we could work together most days. I loved having her near me.

Chapter 79: Dinner with the Family

As it neared seven o'clock, I headed down to the kitchen and started giving instructions. The staff was happy to see me, and quickly retrieved what I was asking for, then started a kettle boiling. Once I had Talia's meal, a glass measuring cup, a clean towel, a measuring spoon, and a knife all setup, I started preparing her food.

I sliced my finger and bled into the cup until the cut healed. After wiping it up, I added three drops of blood to the wine and stirred it gently. Three tablespoons of blood went into the mousse and two went into the soup. There was just enough blood left for the tea.

When the water started barely boiling, I poured it into a cup with a tea ball full of the leaves I brought from home. They needed to steep for an exact amount of time and temperature, or the flavor would be too intense. Talia taught me the technique when I was young and it was like riding a bike. I never really forgot.

Once I pulled the ball and added the blood, the scent was exactly as I remembered. The kitchen staff watched in slightly horrified silence. I arranged everything on the tray. An omega stepped up.

"I'll carry that, Luna."

"Thank you. We'll be eating in the Alpha's dining room since we have guests," I replied.

"Of course, Luna."

I left her to it and headed to the dining room myself. It was a lot louder than the previous meals. Dillon, Bruce, Galen, Porter, Jason, and Todd joined us for the meal. They made the table much longer so everyone could fit.

My mom insisted on the boys sitting next to their mates. She fawned over how precious they all were and took pictures to send back to Bren and Daisy. I sat next to Lucien and took his hand.

After everyone sat down, the staff served the meal. Talia smiled at her plate and began eating. We all talked about the Luna ceremony and the wedding.

It turned out that having all those ranked females together turned a daunting job into an afternoon's chat. They had practically everything figured out. They set the Luna ceremony for the end of the week. The date confirmed for the wedding. And they planned a trip to the dress stores for the day after we ran the borders.

"Can I go, too?" Dilly bounced.

"Sure. I wouldn't want to exclude one of my best friends." I smiled.

"If you can wait until an hour or two before dusk to leave, I'd love to go as well," Talia requested.

"We planned it for that time so you could, Talia. Don't worry." My mom winked.

"Does that mean I get to go, too?" Stanton grinned.

"No," Lucien growled.

They stared each other down for a while. It made everyone uncomfortable. I didn't know what was wrong with them. Competition between Alphas was generally only for Alphas of the same species. Even Jason wasn't getting involved in this.

"Stanton, stop teasing him," Talia scolded.

"I just want to make sure he values my Baby Belle as much as he should. I love that kid. A part of me died when they said she died." Stanton looked sadly at his plate.

"Stanny, don't tease Lucien. We've had enough stress in our relationship." I sighed.

"Sorry, Baby Belle. I just got a little angry and sad. Lucien, I have no interest in your mate as anything but an old friend. If I go outside my species, it's strictly cats. I love me a little tigress or lioness."

I laughed. That hadn't changed, at least. He always said he wanted to marry a bear or a lioness and wouldn't settle. Stanton didn't intend it. He was always unapologetically honest. He felt it was better for relationships.

"I'll take pretty much anything, as long as she's mine," Richard said quietly to no one.

Bruce nodded heavily. "Same."

"Stop pouting, you two. You'll find your mates. I know you will." I grinned. "Even if I have to send you traveling with Talia."

"Mmm. I'll be happy to help two handsome young wolves see the world," she purred.

Richard blushed, but Bruce was used to Talia. She flirted a lot and was fond of making people uncomfortable. Bruce gave her a wink and focused on his food.

"Tally, have you met my mate yet?" Dilly asked, distracting her.

"No. I assume he's this gorgeous warrior next to you." Talia smiled.

"Jean-Claude DuBois," my cousin said, bowing slightly.

"Stanton should train him. He's not elegant enough for me," she sighed.

"Wow. Fucking rude, Tal. You want to learn to fight like a bear, kid?" Stanton asked my cousin.

"Yes. Please." Jean-Claude lit up.

Stanton snorted. "He looks like Belle did when I offered to train her."

"It's an amazing offer that not many receive. He's the future head warrior for the pack. This will benefit us greatly." I nodded.

"Talia, you were the first to find and train Bellamy. How did you meet?" Lucien asked.

"I was in a larger city on the other side of the state looking for a place to spend the day. It was about an hour after sunrise when I found an abandoned building on the outskirts. I went in and only smelled rats, feral cats, and a dog.

"Once I was about halfway into the building, I realized it was a wolf I was smelling, not a dog. I went hunting for it so I could secure the building for myself. I found her bundled up in some old tarps and blankets behind a wall of pallets." Talia chuckled before she continued.

"She was just this tiny little pup, deeply asleep. I pulled back the blanket covering her face. Bellamy woke up, looked directly into my eyes, and said 'I'm not ready, you'll have to wait.' Then she went back to sleep."

Everyone laughed a little. I blushed. Talia talked about me with the tenderness and pride of a mother recounting fond memories of her child.

"So, that's what I did. I took my rest right next to her. I only need to sleep for three hours a day. When I woke, she was staring at me. She said, 'You were dead, then sleeping, how did you do that?' I told her I was a vampire and she got excited. She told me her papa talked about what amazing fighters vampires are.

"Then she put out her hand and introduced herself. It was the most adorable thing I'd ever seen. She wasn't afraid of me and was very polite. She told me she wanted to learn to fight like a vampire and offered to feed me in exchange. It's against our law to feed on children and I told her that. She said it wasn't me feeding on her, it was her paying for her training." Talia sighed. "I couldn't say no after she told me why she wanted to learn to fight like me."

"Why'd she only train for six months?" Dilly asked.

"I was called away to the High Council. One of my children had abandoned his territory and was hunting one of *his* children. I was needed to officially name one of his *other* children as the new master of his territory. We managed to reach him and confirm he was still hunting. He willingly turned over his territory. The boy he's hunting is tricky. I don't know that Victor will ever find him. It's been nearly fifteen years now." She shook her head. "I wasn't the only vampire she trained with. Just the first."

"That's how Marius knows me. He was in the area when I was nine. I was out training one night and bumped into him. He's an ass, but he trained me for another six months," I told them.

"So you were trained by the Traveler and Death?" Lucien asked.

I looked over at him and saw the hunger in his eyes. He always got turned on by things like that. No other man was as perfect for me as him. I nibbled my bottom lip and nodded.

"Stop flirting. Some of us are trying to eat," Galen groaned.

"I have no idea what you mean," I stated and worked on eating my dinner.

For the rest of the meal, we all talked and joked about things. It was a really comfortable feeling. Like I was truly home. When we finished our dinner, Lucien and I turned in early. We had a long day ahead of us. I wanted some time alone with my mate before we slept.

Chapter 80: A Marked Issue

There was no training in the morning for those of us running the borders. Lucien and I told everyone to give us an extra hour or two out there. We were heading to the area where Silver Moon had been. I wanted to get an assessment of how much it would take to get the pack set up.

We met the boys on the easternmost border of my territory, which was two miles east of Lucien's. Once Dillon and Jean-Claude arrived, I noticed something a little different. I tapped Lucien's arm and nodded to them.

'Looks like someone didn't want to wait,' I linked him.

Lucien laughed. *'I thought Dillon would be the one to mark first.'*

Neither one of them was wearing a shirt and Dilly had a mark on the curve of his neck, but Jean-Claude didn't. Actually, Dilly looked pretty grumpy. He was walking ahead of Jean-Claude, who looked upset, too. Not what I was expecting.

'Dilly? Are you okay?' I asked.

'Your cousin is a jealous asshole. You know Randy, Stanton, and I sparred last night after dinner. I was so tired I forgot to take a shower. He smelled them on me and threw a fit! He pretended to calm down, but it was a trick to get close and mark me. I don't want to run with him. I'm so pissed.'

I walked over and punched Jean-Claude in the stomach, then the face. He fell to the ground and didn't even try to fight back. It was seriously not cool to mark someone without consent. I grabbed Dilly's hand and pulled him over to where Lucien and I were.

"Call Richard or Caleb out to run with Dillon. I don't want Jean-Claude to be alone with him," I growled.

"I… I said I was sorry," Jean-Claude groaned.

"Sorry doesn't fix this, Jean-Claude DuBois! Go home! You aren't welcome here!" I shouted.

"What happened?" Lucien asked.

"He marked Dillon without consent," I replied.

"Jean-Claude, you know better," Lucien sighed. "I'm notifying your parents. Richard's on his way, but I can have Caleb come instead if that makes you uncomfortable, Dillon."

"It'll be fine. I don't have a problem with his brother," Dilly answered, looking away.

Jean-Claude winced and held his head. Seemed like one of his parents got involved and was yelling at him. He was lucky I was still reigning myself in.

Richard came through the trees a short time later. He helped Jean-Claude stand before slapping him hard enough to knock him down again. Jean-Claude held his cheek and looked up at his brother tearfully.

"You found your mate first and pulled this bullshit? I can't believe you! What happened to caring for and cherishing your mate and their opinions?! You know he can still reject you, right? You really risked *everything* because he smelled like bears?" Richard growled, standing over his brother.

"I didn't want to lose him. They're better looking than me and better fighters than me. I… I didn't want it to be like Pavel all over again," Jean-Claude sniffled.

"Who's Pavel?" Dilly growled.

"Pavel Montclair was Jean-Claude's boyfriend for a year. Neither had their wolf yet. Everyone was sure they would be mates. One day, about a month ago, Pavel dumped Jean-Claude out of nowhere," Lucien explained.

"No. Pavel dumped Jean-Claude after getting him into bed. The new transfer that came in the day after was gay, so Pavel decided he didn't need to pretend to love my brother anymore.

"He told him it was because he was too wrapped up in being head warrior, too bulky to be attractive and made Pavel uglier by association, and something to pass the time until someone better came along or Pavel found his mate," Richard replied with anger, stopping as if to calm himself.

His voice shook slightly as he started again. "That doesn't mean your mate is going to do that to you, Claude. He loves you. I watched him take care of you. I talked to him. Dillon is nothing like Pavel."

My heart ached for my cousin. Pavel was a fucking asshole. Dillon was gripping my hand tightly. I could see the rage on his downcast face. He was definitely angry about both Pavel's actions and Jean-Claude's lack of trust.

"Go home, Jean-Claude. Take some time to think about what you want your relationship with Dillon to be. He needs space after this. It was a total violation. He would never do what that boy did to you," I said.

"Bruce told me how much Dillon got around at Daylight Moon. I had *one* boyfriend my whole life. If I couldn't keep the man I had a yearlong monogamous relationship with, how could I keep one who had a new lover every week? I just didn't want to lose him."

"You can't fault Dillon for his past! You're his present and his future, but his past isn't who he is anymore," I said and went to kneel by my fallen cousin. "He was excited to find you. Just as excited as you were. Dillon's a couple years older than you. Most gay wolves *never* find their mates. A lot of them pick an opposite-gender chosen mate and live unhappily. You *know* this. Yes, he had lovers, but he never had a *real* boyfriend. You have no idea how much he was looking forward to finding you and having a relationship like he saw everyone else having. You took that from him when you marked him without his permission."

"You don't understand. None of you do," Jean-Claude whispered.

"I do," Lucien said. "Did you forget?"

Jean-Claude shook his head.

"I chose to wait for my first mate to come of age. She fell in love with someone else and rejected me. I thought that was the worst pain I'd ever felt, until a few months later. I was negotiating a contract, went to a party, got drunk, and slept with my second chance mate.

"When she asked about marking each other, I told her she wasn't my mate and never would be. She ran out of the room and I felt the goddess' vengeance sear into my soul," Lucien sighed. "I took my pain and forced it on someone else without thinking of them or what it meant for them."

Lucien told me before that only his immediate family, his Beta, and his Gamma knew about Regan. I wondered if he felt it was worth it to reveal it now to help Jean-Claude understand.

"That sounds a bit like what happened here," I told Jean-Claude. "You couldn't see him through the pain of your past, so you hurt him while thinking of yourself and your betrayal."

"I didn't realize I was doing that. Why can't this be easier?" Jean-Claude asked.

"Because it wouldn't be worth it if it were easy. Lucien and I haven't had it easy either," I said.

"You're both happy. Aside from the attack, there hasn't been anything that would cause a problem," Jean-Claude pressed.

"My adoptive aunt was his second chance mate. He hates rogues and I was born one. I have some mental and emotional issues because of my past. He gets really jealous because of what his first mate did. All of that has nothing to do with the attack. All of it colors the nature of our bond. It's easier for some couples because things fall together perfectly. The relationships where they don't are more precious," I replied.

"Will he ever forgive me?" he whispered.

"If you give him space and show him you're trying to be better. If you put in the work and communicate, then I can guarantee he will. He's been hoping to find you. Now you have to show him how much you value him. You lost a lot of trust," I sighed.

Robert came through the trees. He looked around and saw the situation. Walking over to his sons, he put a hand out for Jean-Claude and pulled him off the ground.

"I'll take him home. Have a safe run. Dillon, I'm sorry," he stated, shaking his head. "I thought we taught him better."

"I just want to get my work done. Can we get on with this? Griff needs to run," Dillon said softly.

"Go on, Robert. We'll be back this afternoon." I smiled at my uncle.

He led Jean-Claude away and Richard walked over to join us. I pointed out the assumed borderlines. We made a plan for how the run would go. Dillon shifted, and I showed Richard and Lucien how to put the bags on and take them off of us. The boys headed out.

"Lucien," I said, once they were out of sight.

"Yes, Bellamy?"

"Where is Pavel?" I asked.

"He's the manager of the village theater. His parents built it. His house is only a few blocks from there."

"Was the new guy his mate?"

"No. He hasn't found his mate," Lucien replied. "Why?"

"No reason. Just wanted to see if this was a concern." I smiled.

Drake,' I linked him.

'Yes, Captain?'

The manager of the local theater is called Pavel Montclair. I want him detained until I return.'

'Can I ask why?' he asked.

'I need to speak with him and I don't want him to run away,' I replied.

'Is this about the murder plot or is it about your anger?'

'Why do you ask?'

'Because Dillon just asked me to find a wolf called Pavel and lock him up, but wouldn't say why,' Drake responded.

'It seems like you should be doing that, then. I'll see you this afternoon.'

'Yes, Captain.'

Lucien and I shifted and headed along the path of our border.

Chapter 81: Silver Moon

Whenever there was a turn or curve in the border, Aurora would stop us and we'd have to shift back to mark the edges on the map. It was pure torture seeing Bellamy naked and not being able to touch her. Aurora was all business, and Remus couldn't get her to play at all. She growled when he tried.

It was after ten when we reached the old borders of the Silver Moon Pack. Aurora was sniffing carefully. Remus did the same.

We could smell all sorts of animal scents crossing the border. There were some supernatural scents as well, but they weren't fresh. A natural wolf had marked a nearby tree. Aurora marked over it.

'Keep your nose up. There's no telling what could have settled here. Not everything is as it seems,' she warned.

'What do you mean by that?'

'Some of these scents are artificially aged. We want to smell them before they smell us.'

'Got it.'

We stalked into the old border as quietly as we could, sticking low to the ground, and moving slowly. Aurora didn't walk straight into the pack lands, instead, she kept to the edges. She was still tracing the borders of her territory.

'As long as we don't run into anyone, I want to focus on this. We'll come back to investigate once our work is complete.'

'We were wondering about that,' I replied.

As we went, we would do our shifting and logging of territory boundaries. She kept going, leading us out of the Silver Moon lands until we reached the area where she said we should turn back. At that point, we hunted a deer and had lunch.

When we returned to the border of Silver Moon, we started heading toward where the settlement would have been. On the edge of the forested area, we saw two little boys playing in a field. Aurora sniffed the air.

'Ex-pack pups? I don't smell any others, though.'

'What do you want to do?' I asked.

'Help me out of the bag, then shift back to a wolf. I'll go human and dress. I'm not as intimidating as you in human form. Let's see what we can learn.'

'Sounds good.'

I shifted and took the bag off her. Bellamy shifted and dug through until she found a light summer dress and some sandals. She dressed while I changed back, and then she slung the bag over her shoulder. We exited the forest, and I stayed near her side, sniffing and looking around to ensure no one snuck up on us.

The children spotted her. The taller boy pulled the small one behind him and took a defensive stance. We stopped a few feet from them.

"Hello, my name is Amy. Are your parents with you?" she asked.

"Go away. We have an army of warriors and they'll kill you if they hear us scream. This is our territory," the older boy warned.

"This is my territory, actually. I'm not here to harm you. I just want to know if someone has settled this old pack land." Bellamy smiled.

"No! We were here first! This is our territory!" the boy shouted.

"That's not how this works." She chuckled.

"Go away!" he screamed, grabbed the smaller one, and ran.

Bellamy stood next to me, running her fingers through my fur as she watched the children disappear in the distance. I turned my head. Her eyes were watering while she was trying not to laugh.

"Let's see their army," she sighed.

We followed the path the boys ran down. The settlement came into view. Cracks and weeds covered the streets.

Fire had burned out several buildings, while others were half-collapsed or in various states of disrepair. The buildings showed signs of attempted repair, but the work was incomplete, with tools scattered and paint cans rusting. Piles of tarp covered materials dotted the sidewalks and filled alleyways.

Bellamy stopped to look under a few tarps. Most of the materials appeared to be in good condition, with only a few minor imperfections. If they didn't have rot when properly examined, that could lower the cost of rebuilding.

The only people I could smell in the settlement were the two children we saw. That was unsettling. I wondered what happened to their parents as we trekked after their scent.

Soon, we were standing in front of the old packhouse. Broken windows marred the packhouse, vines climbed the siding, and the roof appeared a patchwork of mesh and boards. Bellamy tugged at my fur.

"This isn't good. I need you in human form."

I shifted quickly. "What's wrong?"

"Close your eyes and smell," she instructed.

Following her instruction, I took a deep breath in through my nose. Decay. Bodies in different states of decomposition, and something else, something bitter. Bellamy handed me shorts, and I put them on before we entered the house.

A wave of stench nearly knocked me over. My eyes watered from the smell. There were little giggles and the sound of running feet. That wasn't creepy or anything….

Bellamy reached into her bag and pulled out two chains with nails on them.

'I only gave them my nickname. I'm safe, but I'm going to call you Luke. You only call me Amy. Understand?'

'Fae?'

'Possibly. I think goblins. It's best to be safe if I'm wrong. Remember what I told you about fighting smaller opponents.'

'Got it.'

"We told you we had an army of warriors," a small, venomous voice echoed off of everything.

I couldn't figure out where it was coming from. I slipped the necklace over my head. Nothing changed, but I trusted Bellamy's judgment. She had more experience with other supernaturals.

"Ah. I can smell them now. I thought you were saying it was an army of wolves. Not goblins. Are you really wolf children, or is that just a glamour?" she asked.

Dozens of laughing voices echoed the tittering voice. This wasn't a good situation. It wasn't safe for Bellamy and the pups. I started growling.

"Stay calm, Luke. Demon dust," she whispered.

"Demon dust?"

"It's made using a powdered gland from goblins. They exude a mist called goblin haze before they attack to weaken or distract their opponents. We need to think, not act," Bellamy explained.

"The big bad Alpha takes orders from a tiny female? I never thought I'd see an Alpha male who was so weak," the voice taunted with a snicker.

It was right. Bellamy shouldn't be giving me orders. I wasn't a rogue; I was her mate. She was smaller, weaker, and younger than me. She should respect me and stay behind me. Bellamy was endangering our pups by following that decoy here, and now we would die.

I looked down at Bellamy, and she took my hand in her little grasp. Her hand was chilly. She gazed into my eyes with love and confidence.

"I love you. You are the strongest Alpha male in the region. Probably in the entire state. They think strength is in dominating others. You know strength is in knowing when to lead and when to follow. I always feel safe with you and I know you'll protect me when I need it," she murmured.

Her scent got stronger. My mind cleared. I forgot how powerful the thoughts demon dust created were. I had to focus. The goblins were the issue, not my mate.

The voice deepened. "Aw. You're no fun. This is our territory. Leave."

"I told you, that's not how this works. This is our territory. We will not leave. We will fight if we need to. You are not welcome here," Bellamy insisted.

"Then fight. It'll make the taste of your flesh even sweeter," the voice growled.

A shrill battle cry sounded.

"Stay in human form, but grow out claws. Our wolves are too emotional. Watch my back. Protect the pups," Bellamy warned.

About thirty goblins soon swarmed us. Some had weapons, pikes, and spears, others had broken boards, and a few had knives. They began attacking a few at a time.

I kept track of Bellamy to make sure none of them attacked from behind as I kicked at them. They were fighting as hard as we were. I got a pike from one and started stabbing at others while kicking the bastards away.

The goblins were only about three to three-and-a-half feet tall, so I wasn't in a great position. Their strikes and weapons were getting dangerously close to my sensitive parts. I turned to check on Bellamy as she grabbed a goblin by the throat, used it to block the spear of another, and tossed it into a small bunch of them.

She fought them with a cool determination that made it seem almost effortless. I felt a sudden pain as I looked at her. Glancing down, I saw a small dagger sticking out of my chest. It wasn't deep and the goblin who put it there had obviously thrown it and gotten lucky. I pulled it out and threw it at one who seemed to be celebrating, piercing through its throat.

When I kicked the last goblin through the broken wall, I turned to help Bellamy. She tore the throat out of a goblin who launched himself at her. I grabbed the one sneaking up on her and snapped his neck. We looked around. There didn't seem to be anymore.

"Are you still here? I didn't find anyone powerful enough to have tricked my eyes and nose," Bellamy called out.

"What are you? We've had two Alphas at once. We've had mates. We've had rogues and pack wolves. You killed our *whole* clan."

She shrugged. "They were trying to kill me. Turnabout is fair play."

"We're tired of this game. Come fight or leave our territory," I ordered.

"We are not stupid. You would kill us. We watched you fight. She moves like a vampire but smells like a wolf. You fight like a teammate, not like a soulmate. She said she loves you, but you didn't fight like either one of you actually feels love. Neither one of you tried to protect the other! When you were stabbed, she didn't even flinch!" the voice shouted, sounding more annoyed.

"She's a powerful Alpha female. I'm a powerful Alpha male. We don't mix emotion into our work. Right now, we're working." I grinned.

"When we get home, we'll lick each other's wounds, kiss, cuddle, and be sweet. Right now, we have a vermin problem in our territory. Leave and don't return." Bellamy smirked.

There were some whispers and skittering noises before we heard the backdoor slam. I closed my eyes and focused. I could hear my heart and breathing, Bellamy's heart and breathing, and nothing else.

I picked up the bag from where it had dropped and went to her. She hadn't moved since the last goblin attack.

"Are you okay, chouchoutte?" I asked.

"Tired. Can't move or I'll faint."

"How?"

"Fighting off the goblin haze. It made me want to run away to protect the pups. It made me want to leave you behind. I had to force myself to stand and fight," she whispered, her voice quivering.

"That speech about feeling safe with me wasn't just for me was it?" I inquired gently.

"I was s-so scared," she whimpered.

I scooped her into my arms and held her tight. Her skin was cold and slick from goblin blood. My strong, beautiful queen. My delicate little mate. I'd keep her safe for the rest of my life.

Chapter 82: Clean Getaway

[Lucien]

When we got outside, I told Bellamy I wanted her to ride Remus home. My wolf was almost as tall as she was and thickly muscled. He could easily carry our tiny mate.

I shifted, and she strapped the bag on me before climbing on. She hugged it and gripped my fur underneath. Not needing to stick to the border exactly, I sped up by taking a few shortcuts.

It was about five when we arrived at the border of my pack lands. I slowed down to a trot and the border guards let us through. We went through the wooded areas and the gardens to get to the packhouse. I didn't want anyone to see Bellamy covered in blood.

'Thierry, we're in the garden. We're trying to get to my quarters without anyone seeing us.'

'Got it. Sending Cara and Caleb for a distraction.'

'Thanks.'

After a few minutes, people started rushing past the spot we were hiding in. I got to the back door of our home and scratch at it. Olive opened the door and sighed.

She pulled Bellamy off of me and carried her inside. After settling her on the couch, Olive came back and removed the bag, allowing me to shift.

Bellamy had fallen asleep. I changed back and picked her up. The bitter smell of goblin blood tainted her normally sweet scent. It was an assault on my senses.

"We'll meet everyone in the Alpha's dining room. She needs some time," I said.

"What happened?" Olive asked.

"Goblins. We took care of it." I smiled and headed up to our room.

Halfway up the stairs, Bellamy woke up and snuggled into my chest. She sighed happily. I held her tightly against me as I opened our door.

"Let's have a shower, then you can rest," I said softly.

"Will you help me get clean, Lucien?"

"Of course, ma belle. I want to get the smell of those things off you."

I carried her into the bathroom and settled her on the bench before starting the water. When I returned, I pulled her dress off and threw it into the tub, adding water so I could get the bulk of the blood off.

"Are you able to walk or stand?" I asked.

"Not really. I fell asleep halfway home. If not for Aurora, I might have fallen off." She giggled.

"So… what you're saying, is that you're entirely at my mercy." I smiled evilly.

Her eyes widened. "Oh, dear, Mr. Alpha. You wouldn't torment a weak little girl like me, would you?"

"No one can save you from my grasp little wolf," I murmured as I picked her up. "You're all mine."

"Whatever shall I do?" Bellamy purred as I stepped into the shower.

"Never let me go," I whispered.

"I never will," she replied.

Once I washed the bulk of the blood down the drain, I began kissing her neck and nibbling her mark. I pressed her against the wall and slid into her eager body. Watching her fight today aroused me. I loved seeing my warrior queen destroying our enemies.

"You feel amazing, chouchoutte," I groaned as I slipped my arms under her knees and braced against the wall.

She moaned as the change in position spread her further and altered the tightness inside her. Her muscles grasped at me while I slid in and out of her sweet little body. I captured her lips with my own, tugging at them and sucking them.

Her arms wrapped around my neck, and she deepened the kiss. Our tongues danced together while our hips met and parted. My mouth against hers muffled the sound of her desire.

I kissed along her jaw and back down to her mark. When I felt her nearing her climax, I bit down on it. Bellamy arched and screamed my name. I loved that sound. Pressing through her orgasm, I went on sucking and biting her mark. Her legs shook against my arms and her fingernails dug into my shoulders.

My movements increased in speed and strength. The feeling of her body gripping mine, needing mine, was overpowering. I struck one final time, stiffening as I filled her. I moved my hands to support her and went to the bench in the shower.

Sitting down, I kissed her softly and languorously. Taking my time to enjoy the taste and texture of her mouth. My hands roamed all over her body, along her spine, over her breasts, up and down her legs. I licked and nipped every inch of her neck down to her collarbone, my tongue exploring every curve and groove.

Bellamy hummed as her head lolled back, baring her neck to me. She trusted me completely. I never thought I would experience that level of trust from someone. I nibbled along the artery in her neck up to her ear.

"We should finish cleaning up. I'll carry you to dinner. You were amazing, even completely exhausted. I love you so much, chouchoutte," I murmured.

"Only because you are amazing, saucisson." She sighed. "I love you, Lucien."

I grabbed her shampoo and washed her hair, then washed the rest of her with her favorite soap. Once she was clean, I washed myself while she relaxed on the bench in the shower. When all the blood was completely gone, I took her out to dry off, and we laid in our bed.

"Mm. This day wasn't too bad. We definitely needed the alone time," Bellamy smiled.

I caressed her stomach. "I love watching you work. You were so strong and focused. You protected our pups so well."

"We did that together. Now we just need to clean up that pack land and we can move Thomas out there with his pack."

"You called this our territory. Is it really ours?"

"Yes. And no. It's not yours when you're acting as the sole leader of your people. It is when you're acting as my mate. Today, it was because those goblins were a danger to our people. Both pack and rogue," Bellamy smiled.

"What are you planning to do with Pavel?" I asked.

"I have no idea what you mean."

"His parents linked me that he was taken by a member of the Elite Ten and locked in the cells. They wanted to know what crime he committed. I didn't think being a terrible ex-boyfriend to the Luna's cousin was an appropriate answer. So?" I inquired.

"Tell them I wanted to speak with him, but given the attack on me the other day, I didn't want him waiting in my office. I also didn't want him wandering off. So he was taken somewhere safe to wait," she stated simply.

"What is your plan, Bellamy? He's a member of my pack."

"I want to talk to him about moving to Silver Moon to help them get settled… and not coming back."

"You want me to kick him out of the pack for being an asshole?" I asked.

She huffed. "You've kicked people out for that before…."

"Low blow, chouchoutte." I winced.

"Sorry. He pisses me off. I'm not talking about banishment. I'm offering him an important role as a lieutenant. He'd be in charge of ex-pack intake requests. His experience as a theater manager would give him the ability to suss out viable applicants," Bellamy reasoned.

I had to admit; it wasn't a terrible bit of figuring. It would get him away from Dillon and Jean-Claude while they worked on their relationship and kept him away from her. Bellamy wasn't one to anger, and he'd run the risk of making her angry enough to injure him if he did anything to Jean-Claude or Dillon.

"I'll allow it. Good thinking. I'm proud of you for not giving in to your urge to hurt him." I kissed her gently.

"I never harm anyone who doesn't deserve it. We should head to dinner soon. I'm starving. Do you think they'll serve us a little early?"

"Of course they will. Then we just need to work on the maps and we can come back to bed," I replied.

"That sounds wonderful," Bellamy sighed.

Chapter 83: Boundaries Confirmed

Dinner was a fairly uncomfortable meal, punctuated by awkward silences and strained looks. Dillon sat between Bellamy and Cara. Jean-Claude was at the end of the table with Stanton and Randy, who didn't look too happy with him, either.

I felt bad for him. I understood the effects of a nasty breakup and how it could mess with your head. It was no excuse for marking Dillon without consent, but it was difficult for me to be angry with him. In the end, I probably would have done it too… if I had known Regan was my second chance.

Once we finished the meal, we headed to my office with Talia, Richard, Dillon, and Drake. I settled Bellamy on the couch and sat next to her. We pulled out the two maps and started filling in the border lines on each of them. One would stay in my office and the other would go to Bellamy's. I understood the map I saw in Kieran's office better now; it was a combination of his territory and hers.

"It's a lot bigger than I originally thought," Bellamy sighed. "Is it possible to extend the vampire wards, Talia?"

"No. You're too big. The positive about that is your size and power will deter many," Talia replied.

"Can someone explain exactly what we were doing? I have no idea what this was about. Those aren't the boundaries of Lune Rouge," Richard stated.

"I'm a rogue Queen, Richard. Like an Alpha with a pack, I am the head of a collective. I expanded my territory when Lucien and I mated. We needed to find out the borders in case of any territory disputes. Was there anything else to report from your run, Dillon?" she asked.

"We found a few stray families and gave them the website and phone number for the collective. A couple knew of you and were excited to join. Mostly roaming ex-packs, but there were a few rogue born," Dillon reported.

"The old Silver Moon pack land was taken over by goblins. Lucien and I ran them off. We'll want to take a force with us for the settlement of the new Silver Moon Pack. I'm not going to risk the lives of our new pack or allies out of hubris," Bellamy said.

"Goblins?" Richard gasped.

"That's why Bellamy is so tired. It was a fairly draining fight and she's pregnant. Everything took a little more energy than it normally would," I answered.

Bellamy smiled. *'You make me sound less weak. I appreciate that, mon cœur.'*

'You're the strongest person I know, ma choupinette.'

"I have an update on the resources we've secured for the investigation," Talia said.

"We're ready for a break from the territory stuff. What've you got?" Bellamy grinned.

"Stanton contacted a sleuth Alpha on the other side of the region, nearer to the two collectives we're looking into. They'll work to gather information on the Kings you singled out. One of my broodlings is here. A grandchilde, if you will. She will take on more of the stealthy, night work and report back. There is no master vampire in the region. The territory is lawless and wild. Probably what drew Marion in." She scoffed.

I had no clue. As far as I knew, vampires wandered until they found the place they wanted to terrorize. Of course, that could just mean there hadn't been one for a long time.

"Was there ever one?" I asked.

"I contacted the council and confirmed there was one around a hundred years ago. He met the sun sometime after settling the land. His last missive to the council was that the territory was cursed."

Bellamy laughed. "Everything I get involved in seems to be cursed."

"What do you mean?" Talia asked.

"Well, it turns out someone tried to curse King Fuller with a chastity curse back when I was his taste tester, so I was cursed. Lucien had the vengeance of the goddess. This pack was cursed by a rogue King four hundred years ago. I wouldn't be surprised to find at least a dozen more curses as we go," Bellamy chuckled wryly.

I didn't know what she was talking about for a moment. The story my mother used to tell me popped into my head. *That* was the rogue King's curse she was talking about? I'd forgotten it.

"Do you know anything about the curse? Was there anything in the letter?" I asked.

"Nothing. Just that the land was cursed and it was centered in the vampiric territory seat. We're trying to find a master to take on the territory and investigate. No one wants to manage a cursed land." Talia shrugged.

"Will you take it?"

"No. I don't like dealing with all that. It's why I'm 'The Traveler.' I am hosted, but never host. I need no permission to enter any vampire's home or territory because of my talents and place in the high council. The ones who do not fear me, do not live long enough to realize their mistake." She chuckled.

I didn't like the sound of that. Until now, she didn't seem like much of a threat. Something deadly flashed in her eyes and the scent of vampire increased. My stomach twisted like it used to when the vampires at the house woke up. I could feel my panic rise.

Bellamy slid herself into my lap and wrapped her arms around my neck, pressing her chest into mine. She breathed slowly and evenly, and I calmed in her embrace. I pressed my nose into the curve of her neck and took in her sweet honeysuckle and jasmine scent.

"Talia, I know you want to ensure others understand your threat, but please consider what Lucien has been through before you do that again," Bellamy murmured.

"My apologies. Someone patted me on the head today. It makes me angry." Talia scoffed. "I will not harm the family of my pheata. You're all safe."

I nodded and held Bellamy closer. She said I could protect her from vampires, but she was protecting me. I was honestly beginning to doubt myself.

My entire life, I'd been the strongest and bravest. After three days with vampires and nearly a week with a rogue Queen, suddenly, I needed a security blanket. I was a disgrace of an Alpha.

'Trauma needs time to heal. Remus told Aurora you're worried you've become weak. I couldn't have taken on those goblins by myself. If I'd had anyone else with me, they might not have fought as well as you. You put just as much effort in as I did, and you still had the energy to move after. In case you haven't noticed, my love, I'm much weaker than you.'

'You're creating life. It takes a lot more energy. I felt your power. You're stronger than me in so many ways. Maybe I should just give you my pack and take over as Luna.' I sighed.

'I knew it! I knew you were just trying to saddle me with your pack! Think you can just fake being weaker than me and make me do all the work while you play with the pups? Nice try, Alpha. You're stuck with it until out oldest pup is old enough to take over.'

I laughed and squeezed her, making her squeak. She pulled me out of my funk. I wouldn't be one of those pouting, brooding Alphas. Bellamy wouldn't let me.

"Only happy thoughts. Enough difficult things have homes in our lives. Let's not let them have homes in our heads," Bellamy whispered.

"Of course, my Queen," I replied.

"Can you two stop for a while? I love that you found each other, but I don't need to see it right now," Dillon hissed.

"You're just jealous because you want to sit in my lap, but there's no room." I winked.

Dillon and Richard looked shocked. Drake snickered and Talia start laughing. Bellamy tried not to giggle, but could never seem to help herself when someone else was laughing. Dillon snorted.

"You got me." He laughed. "Thanks, eye candy."

"We need to get out of our negative thinking habits right now. It's not going to help us in the long run," I said.

"Let's adjourn for the evening. I'm still tired and need to rest if I'm going to be anything but a rag doll tomorrow. I still have to go deal with my guest in the cells," Bellamy smiled.

"What guest?" Richard asked.

"Pavel. She had Pavel put into the cells with no explanation. He's been in there since we left," I answered.

I linked the guards at the cells to bring Pavel to my office. I didn't want Bellamy around so much silver. Not after what Thierry told me it did to her last time.

"Why would you do that? Just because he was an asshole to my brother?"

"What he did wasn't just 'being an asshole'! Sleeping with your partner, taking that special 'first time' from them, then telling them they're worth nothing isn't a personality quirk! It's a deficiency of compassion, class, and conscience! It's immoral, unethical, and fucking evil! A pack, a collective, functions on a set of rules of behavior and conduct. You do *not* harm a packmate if you can avoid it. Not physically, not mentally, and not emotionally! I want him gone," Bellamy snarled.

I stroked her arm and rocked her a little. I had no idea she felt that strongly about this. She seemed so cool earlier. In every sort of interaction with other wolves, she was calm, even bordering on cold at times. This was one place she seemed to draw the line.

"I understand, but this isn't something you can banish him for," Richard said calmly.

"I don't intend to. I plan to offer him a job as a lieutenant in the new Silver Moon Pack. He would be in charge of reviewing ex-pack applications to join. Almost a hundred miles away."

"What makes you think he'll accept the position?" he pressed.

"I know you all aren't familiar with me. I am as much an Alpha as Lucien. My anger is the same in strength, violence, and length. Every time I see Pavel, I will become angrier. One day, I won't be able to hold back. Selfish people like that know when to run. He'll accept." Bellamy glowered at him.

"Richard, stop pushing it. I've already approved this decision. Had his actions been brought to my attention, I would've had Jean-Claude in counseling and given a warning to Pavel about his behavior. This marking was the result of a lack of communication. If you are to be my Gamma, Richard, then I expect you to bring things like this to me immediately. It affects the health of our pack," I told him.

He looked at the ground in shame. Our future head warrior was suffering. His mate was suffering, because no one told me what was going on. This wasn't helping. I needed my pack to trust in me to give this sort of information.

"Sorry, Alpha. I'll do better," Richard mumbled.

"Good. You can leave. I'm having Pavel brought here. The cells are too dangerous for my Luna right now. Talia, you can leave if you'd like. You don't have to stay," I offered.

"I want to see what happens. If nothing else, the threat of a vampire's anger might help him make the right choice. Dillon is my sweet puppy. Hurting him is hurting me," she replied coldly.

Richard left the room. Drake and Talia worked to help Dillon calm down in preparation for meeting the man who'd caused so much pain for him and his mate. I hoped Pavel wasn't stupid enough to cause a problem.

Chapter 84: The Problem with Pavel

[Bellamy]

Dilly settled in on the couch after I moved off of Lucien's lap. I wanted him near me. Dealing with Jean-Claude's ex wouldn't be pleasant. I knew Dillon's anger stemmed from someone hurting my cousin. He was angrier about that than he was about the mark.

There was a knock at the door and everyone prepared themselves for the devil himself to come through. When it opened, a young man with black hair and nearly black eyes came in, following the warriors.

Pavel was about six feet tall and lanky. He looked down quickly, but I could see the harsh lines etched around his eyes and the down-turned corners of his mouth showed his scowl.

He was like a photo negative of Dilly. They were the same height. Pavel was wispy looking, but Dilly was a wiry sort of muscled that didn't look it until you see him without clothes. Dilly had golden blond hair and pale green eyes. Where Pavel was pale-skinned, Dilly had a luscious tan that glowed.

Both were very attractive in their own ways. The robust, gregarious way Dilly acted and carried himself was much more appealing to me than the elegant, chilled vibes Pavel was putting out. Dilly might be my best vampire mimic, but Pavel exuded the vampire aura.

'Ew,' I linked Dilly and Drake.

They snorted. Pavel's eyes, blazing with fury, met mine, and he glared as if he'd heard the comment.

"You better lower those eyes if you want to keep them," I growled.

"My apologies, Luna. I have no idea why I've been detained all day. I was hoping to see what amused them," he replied in a smooth voice.

"Have a seat," I ordered.

He took the empty chair between Talia and Drake. Pavel looked around the room. I could feel him assessing the atmosphere. He was trying to make a plan to get out of any trouble.

"We recently found out that you treated a fellow packmate in a heartless manner. We understand break-ups happen, but what you did was shameful and could harm the function of our pack," I explained.

He scoffed, "I was thrown in jail because I broke up with Jean-Claude? Seriously?"

"I wanted to see you because you used him and were cruel without reason. We decided to hold you in the cells to keep you safe," I clarified.

Pavel snorted. "Safe from what? He wouldn't hurt me. He's still half in love with me."

Dilly started growling. I placed a hand on his. He needed to stay calm. Losing his temper now wouldn't help.

"I doubt that." I smirked. "You have three options, Pavel. The first is to stay here and risk your health and safety every day. The second is to apply to join another pack. I don't recommend Daylight Moon or Hunter's Moon. The third is to take on the position of rogue/pack liaison for the new Silver Moon Pack. I'll give you twenty-four hours to make your decision."

"You can't do that. What's this threat that could harm me? I'm a warrior, too, you know."

"The threat is Jean-Claude's mate and his mate's two best friends. None of them want you here and all of them are more important and useful to the pack than you. They are all elite warriors and no one will ever be able to prove any of them did anything when you disappear." I smiled.

"That's bullshit! You'd let them attack me?! I've been a member of this pack since birth. My family was one of the original families to follow the pack instead of leaving when it moved to America. All I did was break up with someone who didn't fit and wasn't my mate!" Pavel shouted.

"You did far worse and you know it. Go home. Think about your options. We'll expect your answer by tomorrow evening," I replied.

He looked to Lucien but saw he'd get no help there. Pavel stood up and straightened his clothes. Turning to the door, he sneered a little.

"I don't know what he was so upset about anyway. It's not like he didn't have a good time," Pavel said smugly.

That was the wrong thing to say. I couldn't even stop Dilly from springing across the room, knocking the younger wolf down, and punching him repeatedly. Not that I wanted to. Drake pulled Dilly away before he did something he couldn't take back. Talia was right behind him, dragging Pavel to face her.

She bared her fangs and hissed at him. The bloodied wolf started whimpering. He was a basic pack warrior, a common wolf with combat training. Only the elites of a pack would have experience with vampires.

"If you ever talk to, think of, or fucking *breathe near* my mate again, I'll rip your balls off and shove them down your throat!" Dilly growled.

"I suggest you run away, mutt. No one here will save you if you shoot your mouth like that again," Talia snarled.

Pavel dashed out of the room. Talia wrapped her arms around Dilly and hugged him. She only came up to his lower chest, so it looked like a little girl trying to comfort her big brother. I wished I could help.

"Dillon, take as much time as you need before heading to bed. Make sure to get some rest tonight. Will you go to training in the morning?" Lucien asked.

"Of course, I will. I need to blow off steam. How about a ball-breaker, Captain?" Dilly responded.

"Are you sure, Dilly?" I asked.

"Yeah. I need it," he seethed.

"No one from Lune Rouge can join our training tomorrow, Lucien. Most of my team will be unavailable until the day after," I said softly.

"Why? What's a ball-breaker?"

"It's a training we only do a couple times a year. None of you are well-trained enough to survive it. I'm sorry." I offered a smile.

"I don't like the sound of that. Will you and the pups be okay?"

"Yeah. We should be fine; we are just not available until after four. I want everyone to stay away from the south field and the eight acres of forest right next to it until someone gives the all-clear," I told him.

"Stanton and Randy might be useful. I was there for one of those days. I won't join this one, but they should contribute," Talia said.

I nodded. "That could be good. What do you think Dilly?"

"They can come. We could definitely use the extra muscle." Dilly chuckled mirthlessly.

"Head to bed, then. Talia, let the bears know where to go. I expect them on the field no later than three-forty-five," I said.

They nodded at me and left the room. I curled into Lucien's side. Ball-breakers were awesome, but I didn't want to go after everything I had to deal with today. I needed a vacation.

"Are you going to tell me what a ball-breaker is, chouchoutte?" Lucien murmured.

"We're going to try to kill each other. The fights aren't done until only one person is left standing. No rules, no tapping out, no breaks, no mercy. It usually takes about twelve hours. It's everyone against everyone else. We call it a ball-breaker because of the time one of the boys actually got hit hard enough to rupture a testicle. Wolves can heal that, but it's a very long process," I explained.

"That doesn't sound safe," he growled softly.

"It's not. We'll be fine. There are no weapons. Don't worry."

"I don't like it. I know I don't have to. You'll let me know when you're done so I can come carry you home, right?" Lucien asked.

"Yes, whoever is left standing arranges for the others to get home safe. I'd love to have you carry me home... and a bath. I'll be pretty sore," I sighed.

"Alright. I'll trust you. Let's go to bed. You need rest if you're going to beat the Elite Ten." He got up and lifted me into his arms.

Lucien carried me to our quarters and to our room. I reveled in the warmth of his arms. I needed rest. Tomorrow just got even longer.

Chapter 85: Warrior Wounds

[Lucien]

Bellamy left so early in the morning that I nearly slept right through it. No matter how much I asked, she refused to let me join and said any attempts would cause a shift in the plan. She promised I would eventually have enough training to participate. I didn't like the idea of them fighting each other with actual harmful intent.

Bruce would stay in my quarters while the training was going on. Bellamy said he lacked adequate training, too. Not even Cara could go. Bellamy linked me that Stanton and Randy confirmed they'd go. That worried me even more.

I didn't have much work to do, so I went out to visit with my pack members for the day. After helping a few people out, I had lunch at the high school. Some of the staff had been my classmates and two of my favorite teachers still hadn't retired.

In the summer, our school had options for students to take intensive classes to graduate early. There wasn't any class after noon, so we had time to hang out. Everyone wanted to know more about Bellamy and why she wasn't with me. They accepted when I told them she was busy with Luna and wedding stuff.

I told them everything I could about her without saying she was a rogue. Maurice, the history teacher who used to be on the football team with me, asked if she was ill since there had been rumors about me carrying her around yesterday and my carrying her home from the hospital both times we'd gone.

I grinned. "I'm not supposed to say anything."

Reaching in my pocket, I pulled out my wallet with the ultrasound and showed him. Maurice laughed and showed it around. He linked his mate, Teresa, and told her.

Bellamy was going to be a little miffed, but I'd watched every one of my friends have and raise their pups. I waited so long to be the one showing off my pictures. It was one of the best feelings in the world.

"Twins! What he lacks in timing he makes up for in strength!" Maurice laughed. "I'm proud of you, Alpha. You got over all the bullshit and found a pretty little mate to give you pups. Not bad for an old man."

"I'm not that old. I have more than enough energy for my young Luna." I winked.

He smiled. "My cousin says she was impressed by how quickly our Luna adapted to running the house, even without the pack link."

"What do you mean?"

"She's been texting with the section heads to change how some things are run. Claire says everything's more efficient now and they're able to enjoy more of their day. Her number is available to anyone who needs it and she always answers messages by the end of the day," Maurice explained.

"Don't take this the wrong way; some kids in my summer English section texted her a couple days ago as a joke," Carole said with a grimace. "They can't get enough of her."

"What did they text?" I asked.

"The first time, they asked her how you are in bed. After that, there were a few more joking texts, but they started asking her more serious stuff. She doesn't sugarcoat things, or tell them they'll understand when they get older. She's only a year or so older than them and they really connect with that," she went on. "They all love her."

"It's pretty much all any of the kids are talking about." Maurice grinned. "Will she be coming to school before the pups are born?"

"Why would she?"

"Because she hasn't finished her senior year yet. Didn't you know? One of the girls in my history class saying she hoped the Luna would have classes with her. Is she just planning on not finishing high school?"

Where did the girl hear that? I thought she was done with school. I was confused.

'*Lucien.*' Bellamy linked me.

'*Are you done, chouchoutte?*'

'*Yeah. I need some people to carry the boys home. I'm in the south field, but they're in the woods.*'

'*I'll come get you. I'm at the high school. Did you want me to get you a map of the building while I'm here?*'

'*Why would I need that? I'm only one class shy of graduation and I'm taking it online from my old school. I hate math,*' she growled in the link.

I chuckled. "I have to go. My Luna needs me. She will not be attending school in the Fall. The only class she needs is available online. I'll see you all later."

"Have a good day, Alpha. We're excited to meet her after the Luna ceremony." Carole smiled.

I nodded and took off toward the south field.

When I got there, it looked like a battle really *had* been fought. Chunks of dirt and strips of grass lay pulled up on the ground. There was blood on the grass and I thought I saw a couple of teeth as I walked toward the woods.

Looking around carefully, I tried to find Bellamy. I didn't see her on the bleachers or on the grass. I worried a little.

'*Under the bush to your right, saucisson.*'

I looked under the bush and saw my mate curled up on her side. She had several nasty-looking cuts and bruises, and blood covered her. I crouched down and swept her into my arms. She squeaked in pain.

"I dislocated my arm a little. Well… Jason did," she chuckled.

"My warriors have found everyone and are taking them back to their rooms. It's an hour sooner than you thought you'd need," I whispered as I turned toward the packhouse.

"Good. I need a lot of protein and I should be all healed for the dress shopping. My mom can put my arm back in when we get to the house. We need to make sure Dilly gets a meal with a lot of protein and iron. He needs to go with." Bellamy carefully cuddled closer.

"You look worse than yesterday. Are you going to be up for dress shopping today?"

She giggled. "I wasn't fighting a goblin haze this time. I'll heal up and be ready in time. They want to go at seven. That gives me five hours to heal and rest."

"I don't know if I'll get used to this, chouchoutte." I sighed.

"You will. Eventually, you'll be one of the guys I leave bleeding in the woods." She laughed and groaned in pain.

I chuckled and carried her home. Olive had Porter and Galen moved to two of the other rooms in our quarters and was already applying first aid to them when we came in. My mother looked worried when she saw Bellamy.

"What happened? Did she get attacked by someone again?" Maman started checking her over.

"Bellamy Carrington! I cannot believe you broke your brothers' arms! Galen can't even open his eyes!" Olive shouted from the stairs.

"I didn't break their arms! I *did* punch Galen pretty hard in the nose. Honestly, I'm really surprised it didn't break. Look at my knuckles, Mommy! I cut them on Drake's teeth. Jason pulled my arm out of its socket. I think Porter broke one of my ribs," Bellamy pouted.

Olive tsked in disapproval. "Is the rib break on the same side as the dislocated arm?"

"No." She looked down dejectedly.

"I'm going to need help then. Lucien. Can you hold her? It's going to hurt and I can't use any sort of traction on it because of the rib," Olive sighed.

My mother looked horrified. I nodded, and we took Bellamy to our room. After some more scolding, Olive got her bandaged up, pulled in place, and settled with food.

I helped her eat until she could move her arm again. She ate seven plates of food before she started getting sleepy. I tucked her in and went to check on her brothers. They were healing a little more slowly but were coming along.

The omegas were reporting in on the progress of the men without mates. I assigned a few omegas to ensure the men without mates ate and received wound treatment. The omegas were concerned there had been an attack. I assured them they were safe, and no one was too seriously hurt. I told them it was a type of training for elite warriors at Daylight Moon.

Stopping in the living room, I found Salomé sitting with Olive and my mother. She was upset and Olive was doing her best to help her calm down. When she saw me, Salomé jumped up and scurried over.

"Is Galen alright? What happened? Please tell me, Alpha," she pled with tears in her eyes.

"Intensive training. Everyone got hurt and they're all healing. They should be fine soon," I replied. "I'm going to check on everyone else."

"We'll keep an eye on Bellamy." Olive smiled.

"Thanks."

I found everyone resting with the omegas or their mates watching over them. When I got to Dillon's room, Jean-Claude was standing outside the door. He looked like he was guarding it.

"Have you been in to see him yet?" I asked.

"He doesn't want me there. I understand. What happened? I didn't think anything could hurt the Elite Ten that badly. Randy and Stan are bears for Goddess' sake!" He growled a little.

"They did this to each other. It's one of the ways they train and why they didn't want us in the south field today. We aren't trained enough."

There was a scoff behind me. I turned and Cara was standing there. She had a sardonic smile on her face and her arms crossed.

"That's bullshit. They didn't want you two there because they didn't want either of you distracting them. I watched a ball-breaker once. I was never really afraid of them until that day. They fight coldly and ruthlessly. Their goal today was to be the last one standing. There's no doubt Dillon and Bellamy were going to end up facing off at the end. My brother tries his hardest, but he's just not as good as the two of them in an actual fight." She smirked.

My eyes widened in shock. Cara's voice was sharp, a stark contrast to her usual sweet and gentle tone. Bellamy predicted Cara would act more like herself once Bellamy had been at Lune Rouge for a while.

"I thought they were your friends. How can you be afraid of your friends?" I asked.

"They're my *best* friends. That doesn't mean I'm blind to what they are. The last time we had a massive attack on Daylight Moon, those two killed the most hunters. They'll never let you two see them like that," Cara said sadly. "You don't understand. They thought they'd be alone forever. No matter how badass you are, they'll worry about you seeing that side and leaving. Whatever you think you need to hide from them, isn't nearly as bad as what they'll be hiding from you."

I looked at Jean-Claude. He was young. Only seventeen. I had far more to hide than he did. I never would, though. Bellamy needed honesty, or she'd feel less secure, and I wouldn't give her up for some worthless secrets.

"Eventually, they'll feel like they can tell us and show us who they are," I replied. "I learned my lesson about keeping secrets. I'm never keeping anything from her again."

"I'm going to tell Dillon everything. I want him to tell me everything. That's never going to be me again. I learned, too. I'm never keeping another secret from him."

"Good. Dillon says you can go in, Jean-Claude. He's ready to talk and work this out. Lucien, Olive, and your mother want us back at your place. We're going over the last few things for the Luna ceremony and we wanted to have your opinions on what Bellamy's dress should look like. C'mon." Cara smiled, turning instantly back to her chirpy self.

With a chuckle, I followed her as Jean-Claude went into Dillon's room. I hoped they'd resolve it quickly. I didn't like my house being in such an uproar.

Chapter 86: Wedding Stress

[Bellamy]

After dinner, we loaded up in a couple of SUVs to head to town. Cara told me April, Charlie, and Molly would meet us there. April wanted to show me she was attempting to change. I grumbled a little, a lot less than Lucien, but allowed it.

On the way to the shop, I texted the number Alpha Thomas gave me. Meeting while doing this would be good. I had two powerful warriors and a vampire with me, not even counting April, Charlie, and Molly, who were all well-trained. Being among so many females would relax the Alpha. I told him to meet there and he could bring one trusted wolf with him.

My research came back showing there was a group of ex-packs who were using the name 'The Rogue Kings' and causing general mayhem. The men who attacked Drake belonged to that group, not to Thomas. He was just trying to care for his people and offered his protection to others.

The hostility between pack wolves and rogue wolves led to a misinterpretation of his offer. This would be the perfect solution. I would put a bounty on the ex-packs if they didn't submit to me.

After getting the confirmation, I chatted with Cara for a while. My phone buzzed, and I checked the messages. It was Becky wanting to know how I liked the ears. She was probably waiting on pins and needles for a time to message that wouldn't seem desperate. I invited her, too.

The store would be officially closed after we got there. It was owned and operated by ex-pack rogues. Cara told me they were excited to have me and the shoe store next door, which was also run by rogues, would bring options in my size.

I was excited to get it done without a huge hassle and multiple shopping trips. I had absolute faith that the goddess was watching out for me.

We pulled up to the shop. It was a cute boutique-style place. As we were getting out of the SUVs, Becky pulled up in a beaten-up little car. She bounced over and bowed deeply.

"Queen Bellamy! Thank you for letting me come along." Becky grinned as she straightened up.

"Please, don't bow. Call me Amy. You need to calm down."

"Sorry, I'm just so excited. I thought you were just being nice the other night and weren't serious. I didn't expect this." She blushed.

"Don't worry about it. I'm fairly straightforward and I was serious, I love those little ears. I hope you can give us some information on how much it will cost for the materials and your time. Let's head in. Talia can't be in the sun too long." I smiled.

"Why not?" she asked.

"Because I'm a vampire, little human. No… not entirely human," Talia sniffed. "This is an excellent learning opportunity, pheata. Get close and smell her deeply."

I did as Talia instructed. Becky seemed nervous.

"I promise you won't be hurt. Just relax," I told her softly.

Focusing, I got really close and inhaled. I could smell human, but there was something under it. I dug deep into my mind and concentrated on the underlying scent. It was slightly metallic and a little sweet. If I hadn't been told to look for something, I would've missed it.

"What is that?" I asked Talia.

"She's a low-level dhampyr. One of her ancestors was a vampire." Talia explained. "It's rare to find low-level dhampyrs since most children created by vampires are collected by them."

"What does it mean for me?" Becky asked.

"It means you're a little healthier and stronger than humans. You heal quickly and won't scar from injuries made by supernaturals. Other than that, there's little difference between you and a human. You may have a slightly longer lifespan, but no more than a werewolf," Talia replied. "And possible fangs. At your level that may or may not be possible."

"Let's head in and you can tell us some more," I said.

Inside, introductions were made; we met the manager and her sales associate. They would gather dresses after figuring out my size. While we waited, Talia told us more about dhampyrs.

The higher level ones were first generation and usually taken from their mothers and sold. Masters often turned males into warriors, and sold females as breeders. It was sick, and Talia swore they stopped doing it a hundred years ago. There was a black market that dealt in things like that, though. It's much harder to stop those.

Breeding with a vampire was difficult. If the person they were with was human, it was nearly impossible. Fae couldn't breed with the undead at all. Shapeshifters had an easier time, but not as easy as a dhampyr.

The vampire blood never diluted to less than one quarter. They had to be first generation for the very best results, though. Worse, people considered them property from birth. They never got a chance to do anything or have any normal relationships. I felt so sorry for them.

"I'm glad I'm only a quarter then," Becky breathed.

"You're officially a supernatural, Becky. Would you like to join my collective?" I asked.

She squealed and nodded. "Yes! Please!"

"You can't tell anyone what you are. There's no master for this territory, so it wouldn't be safe," Talia warned. "Even at only a quarter, you are a better breeding option than a human. We don't want someone trying to use you."

"Right. I'll keep it quiet."

"We'll get you an invite to the intake gathering. It looks like they've got the options ready for us. Come on." I smiled.

They moved our group to the back of the shop, where chairs and couches were lined up. There were only five options in my size. I was looking at each carefully when Alpha Thomas arrived.

"Alpha, thank you for meeting me here," I said graciously.

"Happy to do it. This is Julio, he's an ex-pack Beta. He'll be my Beta in the new pack. I still need a Gamma and I was hoping to find one with ranked blood. I have a head warrior and about fifty families who are ready to go when we have a place," Thomas said with a smile.

Julio was a little short for a werewolf at only 5'10". Of course, he was much taller than me. He had blue-black hair and dark chocolate-brown eyes. His naturally brown skin glowed even in the artificial light. He was quite handsome. Not as handsome as my Lucien, though.

"Fantastic." I grinned and introduced him to everyone.

As predicted, he and his Beta felt very comfortable with the group. They sat and talked while Dilly went over the information Lucien and I had, along with his own research on the land and buildings. I returned to the dresses.

Immediately, I wrote off the two princess-style dresses. They would encumber my movement too much. Those big skirts were hard as heck to move in. I needed to be able to move if something happened and even ripping the skirt on those wouldn't give me the range I needed.

I also said no to the sheath dress. Lucien had envisioned a more breathtaking and dramatic gown for me to wear as his bride on our wedding day. A sheath dress just didn't work.

The remaining two dresses hung before me. One dress was a mermaid style and the other an A-line. They were both perfect in so many ways and could easily give me the chance to free my legs to fight or run. Of course, this decision wouldn't be easy. I needed to try them on.

Just as I was about to take the mermaid cut dress to the back, the manager guided Molly, April, and Charlie to us. I went to greet them. Charlie started sniffing the air.

"Mate?" she whispered.

Only two unmated men were in the store. I stepped out of the way so Thomas and Julio could be clearly seen. Both men had their eyes fixated on our new additions.

Rising to his feet, Julio walked past Charlie. He grabbed April around the waist and pulled her to him. She was only a couple of inches shorter and easily wrapped her arms around his neck. They kissed deeply and passionately as if they were already a couple and hadn't seen each other in a while.

Cara giggled. "April and July."

I smiled a little, but was more focused on Charlie and Thomas staring at each other. They looked like they were afraid to blink. I knew Charlie's mate died before her wolf came. When a mate dies, even if they haven't met, the other mate goes through a depression at the breaking of the bond.

Second chances were pretty rare. They mostly happened in the cases of ranked blood wolves losing their mates like Thomas had. He was about ten years older than her and probably thought he would never find his second chance.

"Alpha Thomas Lorrie, this is Charlaine Benson," I said softly.

He stood and approached her. Charlie looked like she might faint. Molly was bouncing behind her, looking back and forth at her friends.

Thomas stopped in front of Charlie. "Please, don't reject me. I'm not a rogue. I'm building a new pack. Charlaine, be my Luna. Help me make a safe place for my pack."

"I would never reject you, even if you *were* a rogue. I've been praying to the goddess for almost three years to grant me a new mate. I'd love to help build a pack." Tears welled in her eyes. "My Alpha."

Thomas grinned and wrapped her in an embrace. He buried his nose in the curve of her neck and the look on Charlie's face was one of pure bliss. I loved these moments. The times when two souls connected and found each other.

This was a perfect time to make a decision. So many things were falling into place. I grabbed the dress and headed to the changing rooms.

The mermaid dress had no straps and would have to be worn with a strapless bra. It had ruffles that started just above my knee. It clung to my curves tightly, but I could still move and didn't worry much about ripping it if I needed to. Lucien loved me in form-fitting clothes. It was a nice mix of sexy and dramatic. My mom and Madam hated it.

Next, I tried the A-line. It was free enough that I'd be able to run and climb if needed. It had a fitted bodice and straps that were thick enough that I could wear one of my cute bras. There was a lacy applique that trailed down to the top of the skirt and a v-cut neck which was just low enough to show me off, but not enough to make Lucien jealous.

It was perfect. Everyone approved. Shoes were delivered; we then picked out a veil and matching accessories. Just like I said, the goddess made sure the perfect dress would be there. She always looked after her children.

Chapter 87: Loving Lunas

It took a while to leave the shop, even after we found and purchased all the accessories to go with the dress. I worked with Alpha Thomas to get his ideas for what to do with the pack lands. Charlie was awesome. She had some wonderful suggestions and I could tell she'd make the best Luna for the pack.

They would level the old packhouse and plant a garden there in memory of the people lost on the land. They would rename it the Rose Moon pack.

A nod to Lune Rouge and our work in clearing the place and settling the pack. Charlie even picked the perfect place for their new packhouse.

Thomas watched her in awe and looked very proud. Julio and April were still eating each other's faces. I guess she got to have a rank after all. Since the girls were Cara's second and third in command, I knew they'd whip that roguish pack into shape.

Dilly took notes while we talked and planned. He'd get them sent off to our construction guys for quotes. We warned them to stay off the land until we confirmed the goblins cleared out. In a couple of weeks, we were deploying some of my rogue warriors to clear out the premises.

We said our goodbyes after reminding Charlie and April that they had to take Molly home. Neither one wanted to leave their mates, and we stuck around for longer to make sure they left. I understood the pull of having found your mate.

Molly couldn't wait to get home and tell Declan about the girls finding their mates. I couldn't wait to get home and climb my mate like a tree. Who knew wedding dress shopping was such an aphrodisiac?

When we reached Lune Rouge, I became more eager to get out of the car. My mom laughed at me. I couldn't help it. Lucien and I were apart for most of the day. I just wanted to curl up in the curve of his arm and feel the heat of his body seep into me.

"I never thought I'd see you like this. I always figured you'd be as cool and aloof as you normally were once you got a mate." She chuckled.

"Once the bond is accepted, a rogue is just like a pack wolf who found their mate. I feel everything like you do. We've only been mated for a little over a week now. It's hard to spend so long without him. I know it'll get better, but I just want to see him," I replied.

The SUV stopped and before I could even reach for the handle, the door flew open. Lucien's scent hit me like a brick wall. I was stunned after going so long without him. I'd felt that way when he came to get me from the field earlier, but was too tired to do anything about it.

Lucien pulled me from the backseat and wrapped me in a hug. He buried his nose in the curve of my neck, making me giggle at the feeling of his breath. I was finally home in every sense of the word.

"Let's go to bed, chouchoutte," he purred against my neck.

"Did you hear from Pavel?" I asked.

"He'll go to the new pack as soon as they're ready," he said.

"Then I'm ready. I found the perfect dress today. I can't wait to show you."

"I'll see it at the wedding. We have enough curses and bad luck; we don't need to tempt the fates," Lucien whispered as he carried me to our quarters.

I quickly linked my mother to put my wedding outfit somewhere safe and hidden. Lucien consumed my entire mind. More than anything, I wanted to get to our room and be alone with him.

The next day was the day of the Luna ceremony. We'd hold it at dusk. My mother and Madam were insistent I not be involved in it further than being there and planning my introduction.

Lucien and I decided it was time to let the pack know about my rogue status. I agreed it was a good idea so the pack would understand as more of my work started coming to the pack lands.

Over the next two days, I'd be doing mass intakes for my collective. It would take a lot out of me, but I wanted to secure my territory. This would ensure that our people were loyal.

After training and breakfast, Lucien and I headed to his office. I put together an email for my collective, letting them know about the intake and plans for the new territory. I also let them know about the rogue pack that was being created and our need for warriors to help secure the pack's land. Then, I turned my attention to organizing my social programs and getting schools set up.

One of my collective members was a rogue born who had a small chain of grocery stores. We arranged to have one built just outside Rose Moon's pack land. It would serve the pack and the rogues in the area, providing food and employment, no matter the status.

The mayor sent me the contact info for a realty company run by rogues. I sent them my requirements for the buildings we'd need in town and the two smaller cities nearby.

Once that was complete, I addressed the need for lieutenants in the area. I'd already received an email from the pastor and his mate about taking on the city. They had suggestions for the surrounding area.

The lack of pushback from the rogues pleasantly surprised me. They all seemed excited about being in a collective that would care for them and didn't have horrifying requirements. Not a tremendous surprise, but there were a fair amount of rogues who didn't want life in a collective. They liked the more dangerous aspect of being a rogue.

I hadn't even noticed how quickly time was going past until Lucien cleared his throat and told me we needed to head out to lunch. I would've preferred eating in the office, but I needed to be there. Spending time around the pack would be beneficial.

We ate in the main dining room. A lot of omegas came to talk with me. They were all very nice and had happy reviews of the new workflow initiatives I'd put forward.

It would go a long way toward getting the pack to accept me. I knew Lucien wouldn't tell me to leave if they didn't want me, but it could make my life at Lune Rouge very difficult if they didn't. It was a bit of a relief.

Unlike the Alpha's dining room, the main dining room had a head table on a slightly raised platform. I sat to Lucien's left and Thierry sat to his right. It was tempting to lean against him. He made it even more difficult by pulling my chair close to his and setting his arm behind me.

"Would you like to go for a run after lunch, chouchoutte?" he whispered softly.

"I have so much work to do right now, saucisson. Preparations for tomorrow's intake have been set aside for far too long." I sighed.

"Will it always be like this? I know a lot of Lunas have to deal with their mates being busy, but I wasn't really prepared to be on the other side of that experience," Lucien chuckled.

"Expansions take a lot of work and I've been busy with the investigation and pack matters. We should see things calming down a lot more once the territory is settled and we've dealt with the person who's trying to kill you," I assured him.

"Then I'll be patient, chouchoutte, but not for long."

"You're being awfully possessive today, my love. Are you alright?" I asked.

"Just frustrated with how hard everything is and worried about my pack's reaction to you. With how everyone treated you on the first day…. I don't want to have to kick out most of my pack, but I will if they won't accept you," he growled softly.

Thierry was suddenly paying more attention to our conversation. I could see the concern on his face. This wasn't a worry only Lucien had.

"Don't worry, I have faith that we'll be fine." I smiled.

I didn't want to tell him I'd already been working on the issue with some teens in the pack. They'd gotten me a list of pack members who were the most anti-rogue and I'd focused on them with some of my changes. In the brief times I'd been out in the community, I'd talked with a few. A majority of them were elite warriors and they had really warmed up to me in the few times I'd trained with them.

My main focus was making sure people had positive opinions of me. The packhouse staff spread information about how Lucien and I behaved with each other and how I interacted with everyone there. Galen reported the general opinion of me was that I was a positive influence on Lucien and was a good Luna so far.

"Just a little run. A small break. Only an hour," Lucien replied, kissing right below my ear after each sentence.

"Fine. You win." I giggled. "One hour. No more."

"I love winning." He grinned and returned to his meal.

"Of course you do, Alpha."

Chapter 88: The Messenger

After lunch, Bellamy and I headed to the forest at the end of the garden. Remus was excited to run with our mate again. I just wanted to spend more time with her. Though I was happy she was working in my office, I also wanted her attention. It was hard trying not to disrupt her when her mere presence drove me to distraction.

We stripped and shifted. I led our run into the woods. Remus wanted to show Aurora our favorite place. I wanted to make love to Bellamy there. I could imagine her hair and body surrounded by wildflowers. Her scent added to their perfume.

I guided her to the meadow, which was surrounded by thick bushes and trees. The long grass tickled along the underside of our wolves as we ran and played. Aurora liked to wrestle, and she was fantastic.

Remus tried not to get competitive, but no Alpha enjoyed losing. He wanted to enjoy her while he could. In a little under two months, Bellamy wouldn't be able to shift without hurting the pups. None of us wanted that.

We played tag and rolled in the grass. For a little while, we didn't have the responsibilities that strained us and kept us apart. We could have a little of our earlier freedom back.

Once our wolves were ready to rest, I shifted back and sat next to Aurora. I stroked her fur and scratched firmly behind her ears.

'Not that we don't love this, Lucien, but it's a little silly,' Bellamy linked me.

"When you can't change and run with us anymore, then you can pet Remus. It's about bonding, chouchoutte. Aurora and I haven't bonded much. Soon she won't be coming out anymore. This is important," I replied.

'If I could, I'd be blushing right now. That's so sweet, Lucien,' she replied.

"We love both of you very much. You are our world. You've given us everything we ever wanted. We hope to do the same for you," I murmured into her fur.

'You have. More than anything, we wanted a family and a mate to make us feel whole. I can't imagine someone being as perfect for us as you,' Bellamy answered.

I laid next to her and continued rubbing and scratching as we soaked in the heat of the summer sun. It was perfect. Well, almost perfect.

"Change back, chouchoutte," I purred.

Aurora rolled onto her back and shifted back into Bellamy. She smiled and nibbled her bottom lip. I took her hand and pulled her to me. Our lips met. It started as a gentle kiss but soon became a need-filled entanglement.

I maneuvered her until she was on her stomach and started nipping and kissing her back and shoulders. Her skin was soft and fragrant. My hand slipped between her legs and I teased at her opening, rubbing my fingers around the edges and then up to her clit.

When Bellamy tried to turn, I held her in place. She was mine, and I wanted to own her completely. I continued my tender assault on her body as she whimpered and moaned. I moved my hand from between her legs and grasped her hips, raising her beautiful bottom into the air.

Positioning myself behind her, I rubbed against her. She tried forcing herself onto me, and I delivered a slap to her ass. Bellamy yelped.

"I decide when you get that, chouchoutte. Be good," I growled.

"Please, Lucien," she begged.

"Hush. Raise up on your elbows, ma belle," I ordered.

She did as I said without arguing. I slid my hands up from her hips to her ribs and around to tease her beautiful breasts. My fingers tickled the soft flesh until they found her taut nipples proudly standing at attention.

I rolled them between my fingers, occasionally running my thumbnail over them while she hissed and groaned. My hips still working and rubbing her from behind.

I could feel her wetness dripping onto me as I stroked near her sweet center. I pulled back and slid into her. Bellamy moaned as I filled her. I moved my hands back to her hips and gripped them roughly, pounding into her firmly and eliciting the most beautiful little squeal from her.

"Who do you belong to, chouchoutte?" I demanded.

"Y… you, Alpha. I belong to you," she panted.

"Damned right," I replied, sliding in and out of her as I felt her muscles grip around me.

Remus loved dominating our mate. Neither one of us could believe she wasn't fighting for control. I pushed it a little further and reached under her, pulling her against my chest and slipping my hand up to grasp her throat. I moved one of my legs up, so I was on one knee and used my other hand to pull her leg over mine.

She wasn't touching the ground anymore and the tension in her body as it tried to use her legs to keep from falling increased the pressure inside of her. My roaming hand found its way between her legs and I manipulated her firm little nub while forcing myself into her tight body.

Bellamy leaned her head back against my chest and cried out. Her moans and whimpers fed my desire for her. She was perfection in every way. Her sweet submission to my control made me feel even more powerful. I could feel her end coming. I wasn't far behind.

Moving my head down, I bit her mark and Bellamy's body tried arching away from me as she came with a scream. It put me over the edge and I emptied myself into her. For a few moments after, I held her to me, softening my grip on her throat and supporting more of her weight with my other hand.

"You *were* feeling more possessive, mon saucisson," Bellamy purred roughly.

"Did I hurt you, Bellamy?" I asked.

"Mm. No. Rogues are a lot tougher than pack she-wolves." She chuckled and pulled away, getting to her feet.

Bellamy turned, and a dark smile came over her face. She closed the short distance quickly and gripped my hair, pulling my head back. Her lips came down on mine and she fed at me hungrily, biting and sucking my lips and tongue. When she pulled back, her cheeks were red, as if she had been running a marathon, and her lips swollen.

"My turn, my prince," she growled. Her dominance flooded over me.

"Whatever you desire, my queen," I groaned.

Bellamy lowered her mouth to my throat and started nibbling toward my mark. I bared my neck, submitting to her. Two Alphas can struggle for dominance, but I would be more than willing to give a little up from time-to-time to have her like I just did.

'Alpha, there is a messenger here from the Werewolf Association,' I heard through my link and growled a little before telling the guard to take the messenger to the packhouse.

My mate pulled back and looked at me quizzically. I sighed. Our time was over.

"There's a messenger here. We have to head back," I told her.

"We'll just continue this tonight. I have a lot of work to do anyway. Plus, it'll give you time to prepare for me to claim that sexy ass, saucisson," she murmured into my ear, sending chills through me.

What did that mean? No… I knew. Oh, goddess, why did it make me so excited?

We shifted and ran back to where we left our clothes, just inside the tree line. Aurora nipped at Remus as we ran, making him yip and run faster. It ended in a tied race. Much to everyone's disappointment. Once dressed, I took Bellamy's hand and led her into the house.

When we reached the main entry, two of my pack guards stood on either side of the messenger. He was a rogue. I could sense the nervousness of some of the household staff.

Messengers from the Association were always rogue born wolves. They took their jobs very seriously. Before I met Bellamy, they were the only ones I tolerated in my territory. Being sent a message from the Association was either a blessing or a curse, and refusing one was a dangerous prospect.

It was deadly to kill one of the messengers. The Association would destroy anyone who did so. Only a few Alphas very early on were that stupid.

The messenger was about my height, with dark orange hair and pale blue eyes. He had a youthful face with an easy smile that got larger when he saw us approach. Most rogue born wolves seemed to be happier when they saw Bellamy.

"Good to see you again, Queen Bellamy." He grinned.

She sighed. "Braden, damn it."

The guards were stone-faced, but one of the older ones raised his eyebrows at me. They'd all know by tonight, anyway. I just didn't want them telling more people.

"Neither one of you say anything. It will be announced at the Luna ceremony. Do you understand?" I commanded.

"Yes, Alpha," they said as they bowed.

"Sorry, I didn't realize it was a secret. She's the most recognizable Queen in the country. Tiny, deadly, Queen Bellamy." Braden chuckled.

"Who is your message for, Braden? I'm busy," Bellamy growled.

"For you, Queen Bellamy." His smile turned a little nervous.

Bellamy released my hand and folded her arms. She looked at him expectantly as he fidgeted. I didn't understand what was happening. Normally, the messenger handed the letter off and left.

"Well?" she asked angrily.

Braden reached for the messenger bag he wore slung over his shoulder. He opened it and dug around, finally fishing out a thick envelope. An apprehensive look came over him as he held it out.

"What did you do to piss them off, Braden?" She laughed.

"I was flirting with the daughter of one of the Chief Alphas. If you don't take it, I'll get punished." He blushed.

"You're a fucking idiot. He's just going to keep giving you shitty jobs until you mess up and he can punish you without retribution. Give me the letter," Bellamy groaned and held out her hand.

"Thanks, Bells. You're my favorite Alpha," Braden replied, pressing the letter into her hand.

"Let's get him a room for the night. We should have some free. You can leave after breakfast," I offered.

"Thank you, Alpha Lucien. I appreciate your hospitality," he said with a bow.

Some of the household staff was called to take him to a room. I dismissed the guard and followed Bellamy out of the room. She didn't seem to want to even look at the message.

I wondered what it could be.

Chapter 89: Jury Duty

[Bellamy]

When we got to Lucien's office, I tossed the envelope onto the coffee table and went to collect my electronics from the safe. I had a great idea for the next expansion of my collective. I just had to look at the map of the area I kept on my computer.

There was a small pack and another collective nearby. If I could get my stuff set up ahead of time, then the expansion wouldn't take as long. I was pretty sure I knew what was in the envelope, there was no point in holding back on expansions now.

I was happily setting up my things when I noticed Lucien standing by the table, looking down at the envelope. He looked confused. It was really adorable. I pulled out my phone and took a picture. The sound of the camera drew him out of whatever was going on in his head.

"Aren't you going to open that, chouchoutte?" he asked.

"Nope. It's from a Chief Alpha. Rogues only answer to the High Kings. The Association is to make sure we don't suffer from something like the rogue wave again. Our respective representatives handle the minor regulatory stuff. You answer to the Chief Alphas, I do not," I explained as I settled on the couch.

"What if it's important?"

"Then I'll get a text or brief call from one of the High Kings." I pointed to my phone. "Nothing yet. It's not hugely important. We have work to do."

"Can I open it?" Lucien requested.

"No. Go to work, Alpha. That's not your business yet. I'll let you know when it is," I growled.

"You're so cute when you get growly like that." He chuckled before heading to his desk.

I smiled and returned to my work. Several emails came in covering the information I needed for the intake and the buildings to be purchased. I forwarded the building information to the accountancy firm that handled our business.

I'm bad with math, so I was thrilled when we had a couple rogues and other supernaturals who wanted to start an accounting firm up. Eaten Heart was one of their biggest clients. I wondered if they would open a branch in my area since I moved.

After a while, my phone chimed and I picked it up.

Damn. The envelope was exactly what I thought it was. Braden's reluctance to pull it out of his bag had already made me wary. Rogue Alphas didn't like thick missives from the Association. It was always bad.

High King Dolph messaged me two words: 'Open it'.

"Alright, Lucien. It looks like I'm opening the envelope," I groaned.

He jumped up from behind his desk and rushed over to sit next to me, picking up the envelope on the way over and setting it in my lap. He looked like a little kid, eyes wide with anticipation, waiting for someone to read his birthday card. It made the situation less annoying.

A small piece of string, looped around two tiny pegs, kept the envelope closed. I unwrapped them carefully. Lucien's eyes shone with barely contained excitement, his body practically vibrating.

"Why are you so excited about this?" I asked.

"I've never gotten an envelope that thick. If they were disapproving of our mating, I don't think it would be that big. It could be anything. I'd rather think positively. I know you believe worrying is my hobby, but, I assure you, it isn't."

"You have a point. I wouldn't care if they were disapproving of our mating. It's not their decision. If it were a problem, the goddess wouldn't have allowed it," I told him.

"Just, open it," he sighed.

I opened the flap and pulled out the stack of papers. On the top was a single sheet with a short message on it. I read it and groaned. Lucien pulled it from my hands and read it aloud.

"Congratulations on your latest expansion. After receiving the map of your borders and calculating the size of your collective, we are pleased to inform you that you have the third-largest collective in North America. We'll see you at the next meeting in September, High Queen Bellamy…. You're a member of the Association, chouchoutte! Why aren't you happier? This is a huge honor," Lucien looked at me with shocked eyes.

I snorted. "Only for pack wolves. For rogues, it's the equivalent of jury duty to humans. We don't want it."

"Why wouldn't you want it?"

"It's a hassle, Lucien. Two days every quarter we have to spend in conference with the other heads. The meeting is outside of anyone's territory because no pack or collective gets along well enough to share. It's not comfortable. Plus, travel and dealing with so many humans. Then there's being on call for anything that might come up. It sucks." I stuck out my tongue.

"You know an awful lot about it."

"Yeah. I figured this would happen with the expansion. I already had one of the largest collectives, now it's the third largest. I was warned about what could happen if I kept expanding. It didn't stop me. I won't give up the protections I gave to Daylight Moon and I won't give you up.

"I wanted the country to be at peace. So it either has to become mine, or I have to make a ton of alliances. Once I saw the size of the envelope, I started planning for more expansions. There was nothing for it and this 'honor' isn't optional. I have to accept." I grimaced.

My phone chimed and I looked at the message. It was from King Dolph, the now previous third most powerful rogue Alpha in the Association. Rubbing it in, the bastard.

'Congratulations, High Queen. As the fourth largest collective in the country, I wanted to inform you of my decision to stop expanding. Have fun.'

"Asshole." I scoffed.

Two more texts came in. One from King Jonas Harper and the other from King Quinn Sharpclaw, both welcoming me to the Association. I saved their contact information and replied with my thanks. They'd be important to have on hand in the future. At least I knew one thing, I had a whole new powerbase to pull from.

I leaned against Lucien and he wrapped an arm around me. We looked over the welcome documents together. He was very proud of me. I could feel it in our bond. It made me feel incredible. Even though this wasn't an ideal post to me, he thought I was wonderful for having it.

"I love you more than I think you could ever understand," I whispered.

"Of course you do, I'm amazing," he chuckled.

I laughed. That was the exact sort of thing I used to say to people when they said they loved me. I'd be stopping that. Now that I had Lucien, I felt more like I deserved the love others tried to give me and that they wouldn't disappear if I loved them.

"You are forever my queen, my Luna, and my love. I do understand. I wasn't broken in the same way as you, but I was just as broken. You're fixing me, one kiss, one smile, one cuddle at a time. I hope I'm fixing you, too," he murmured and held me tighter.

"We're just too in awe of each other still. I think it'll take a few months before we're entirely comfortable and not acting like this all the time." I giggled softly.

"No. We're going to act like this forever. I'm certain I will never get over my excitement about you loving me," he purred.

"Let's get back to work. I want to take you straight to bed once we're done with the ceremony," I replied.

"I finished my work. Would you like me to go through these papers, summarize them, and pull out the important parts?" he asked.

I widened my eyes and moved to straddle his lap. Holding his face between my hands, I gazed into his silvery eyes. He really was amazing.

"Are you offering to do the boring stuff for me, saucisson?"

"I'm really good at the boring stuff." Lucien winked.

I moaned and kissed him passionately on the mouth. Lucien's arms wrapped around me and he held me to him while I fed at his lips. I rubbed myself against his, now bulging, lap as I continued kissing him. His hands slipped down to my hips and he forced me down more firmly making me cry out from the pleasure of the increased friction.

Lucien steadied me and I pulled away from our kiss.

"You shouldn't get me all excited like that or we'll never finish our work, chouchoutte," he teased.

"It's so hot that you want to do the stuff I hate, saucisson." I smiled.

"Alright. You've expressed your gratitude. Off. I have work to do and so do you. Maman will be here in a few hours to steal you away for the ceremony," Lucien reminded me.

"Okay. Head back to your desk or I may not be able to control myself, Lucien." I kissed him again lightly and climbed off his lap.

Lucien picked up the envelope and sat behind his desk. I began sorting through the emails that came in while I was busy with my mate. Soon, our territory would be the envy of the supernatural world. Peaceful, safe, and secure, a perfect blending of pack and rogue wolf. I couldn't wait.

It was about six when Madam came to get me. There was a banquet at eight and the ceremony would take place afterward. That gave me two hours to get ready. I didn't really need that long, but everyone was insisting I do more than just wash my face and put on a dress.

I understood. It had been about forty years since the last Luna ceremony and everyone was looking forward to this. The entire pack was on pins and needles for the formal presentation of Lucien's long-awaited mate. Their cheerful mood permeated the entire pack lands.

In my room, my mother, Cara, Simone, Celesta, Daisy, and May were all waiting. I was a little apprehensive as Madam pushed me along. They looked evilly gleeful at the prospect of whatever they were about to do to me.

'If I don't make it out of this alive, just remember, it's all your fault. Stupid Alpha,' I linked to Lucien.

'Suck it up, Queen Bellamy. It's just a little makeup,' he replied.

I sighed and steeled myself. Dressing up for a night out was way different from what they were planning. Leave it to a male to call it 'a little makeup'.

Chapter 90: Preparations

I chuckled as I went back to examining the documents Bellamy received from the Association. I couldn't believe she didn't see the appointment to the Association as an honor. My name was far down the list of Alphas in line for the coveted title; I had little hope of receiving it. The prestige it would have brought my pack was immense, a glorious weight of respect and power. Bellamy's seat would do the same, at least among pack wolves.

Thierry and Robert knocked on the heavy oak door, then cautiously poked their heads inside. I waved them over, and they sat in their chairs. I'd called them to give them the news and see what concerns they'd found for the Luna ceremony.

"So? How are our people?" I asked as I separated the papers.

"They all seem excited. No one is saying anything against her and everyone is talking about how much happier you seem," Thierry reported.

"The warriors are behind her since seeing her in training over the past few days. Jean-Claude told them how hard he had to fight in their match and how pleased he is that our Luna can defend herself," Robert said.

Thierry nodded. I knew he was eager to get to something. He had been growing more and more proud of his niece since Bellamy came to live with us. It seemed their conflict early on left him more open to how she differed from her parents, and how she was like them. I knew Robert loved her more and more each day, but seeing Thierry soften so quickly was amazing.

"The guests have started arriving. Alpha Kieran is in his room and Luna Daisy went to help with Bellamy. Beta Hollis and his mate arrived soon after. Alpha Warrick and Luna Janya are getting settled. Both of his brothers are here.

"Tyson's mate is a little intense. She went straight to work on the efficiency of the people organizing the grounds for the ceremony. Bellamy told everyone to let her. Apparently, she needs to do something or she gets upset.

"Bren Franks is with her daughter-in-law and Porter Carrington's mate helping the staff with the banquet. Randy and Stan are out walking the borders. And Talia is in her room resting." Thierry smiled. "Our Bellamy has some powerful alliances."

"Hunter's Moon, Daylight Moon, and Silent Moon are all strong packs." I nodded. "Having a connection to the Vampire High Council will be useful as well."

"There was one other addition that just arrived and we needed to warn you. It seems she invited her other uncle and his mate… Regan." Robert winced.

"Shit…. I should see them before dinner. I don't want anything to mess this up. If they object…." I sighed. "Let me finish sorting these papers and we can call them down."

"What are the papers?" Robert asked, leaning forward.

"You heard about the messenger from the Association?" I inquired.

"Yes," they said in unison.

I grinned. "Bellamy has been appointed as the third rogue Alpha. She's now *High Queen Bellamy.*"

"That's incredible! I'm so proud of her. Is she excited?" Robert asked with a broad grin of his own.

"No. She says it's like jury duty for humans. No one wants the job, but refusal isn't an option." I snorted.

They chuckled and shook their heads. It was confusing, but very much what we'd learned to expect from Bellamy. They helped me sort through the rest of the papers quickly. I didn't look forward to dealing with Regan and Michael, but it needed to be done. For my mate's peace of mind, and my own.

***

I stood to prepare for my guests. My dealings with Thunder Moon a few years back were challenging, and Alpha Michael was unpleasant and unhelpful during that time. Regan hadn't even come out to greet me.

To not greet an honored guest was extremely improper for a Luna, but I understood. My rejection and words to her were truly awful. If it were me, I'd have a hard time forgiving someone for causing that level of pain. Now I regretted not trying harder to mend my relationship with them earlier, but I never had a reason to until I had Bellamy.

There was a knock at the door, and Robert opened it. With a gracious bow, he gestured for our guests to enter, a warm smile on his face. Michael, with a small scowl etched onto his features, was the first to enter the room. With her head lowered, Regan trailed behind Michael, her hand gently grasping his arm.

His build mirrored that of Daniel, his older brother; they shared the same height, dark hair, broad shoulders, and naturally tanned skin. Michael always wore a more serious look than Daniel, at least every time I saw him. I was sure Michael could be softer and kinder, but he had no reason to show that side of himself to me.

Regan was 5'9" with long black hair and brilliant blue eyes. Even though she was over thirty-five, she had a youthful face that made her seem ten years younger. She was truly an elegant beauty. It was one of the many things I regretted once I realized I'd lost her. She was an amazing Luna to her pack. Michael was lucky to be her second chance.

"Alpha, Luna, please have a seat. Thank you for coming to see me." I smiled.

"We're here for our niece. Don't expect this to change our relationship," Michael growled.

"Please, Lucien. Tell me you didn't pick her because she's our niece," Regan begged softly. "If you did, just end it now. Don't hurt her. She's had so much pain in her life already."

I looked over at Thierry and Robert, who had suddenly found something interesting on the floor to stare at. She sounded like they did when we first met up alone after we told them who Bellamy was to them. None of them even considered we were meant to be.

It didn't bother me anymore. A wave of irritation washed over me, but I understood their hearts. Something about her made people want to protect Bellamy, even though she was strong and capable. Once they saw us together, I knew they'd realize we loved each other.

"Let's sit," I replied, gesturing towards the plush, velvet couch as I settled into the worn leather armchair, "and I'll tell you everything."

Thierry and Robert took a seat after Robert closed the door. Michael and Regan seemed apprehensive, but sat. I took a deep breath. I needed to fix this a little. Nineteen years is a long time for negative feelings to fester.

"I understand your suspicions and concerns. We need to resolve our issues. Bellamy is my mate and that makes us family now. I'm going to make you privy to some information that will be revealed to everyone else later, but we need you to keep quiet about it," I told them.

"Why would you tell us this?" Michael asked.

"It's important, so you understand how this all happened," I said. "I need you to know why all of this happened, from before I ever met Regan. Please, listen until the end and I'll answer any questions you have."

With that settled, I revealed everything from Angelique's rejection of me and my subsequent rejection of Regan, followed by what Bellamy had told me about her parents. I disclosed the murder plot we were investigating, my abduction, our earlier encounter with the vampires, along with our fight, and how we marked each other. Their expressions shifted from polite interest to utter astonishment as I spoke.

"So, Bellamy is the daughter of the woman who rejected you, but you didn't choose her or even know about the connection? Nothing has anything to do with Angelique or Regan, it was just an odd twist of fate?" Michael asked.

"Exactly." I nodded.

"What do you expect from us?" Regan asked.

"I want you to know; that I am truly sorry for the pain I put you through. I didn't recognize you as my mate because I was too depressed. If I had, I would've accepted you.

"As it stands, I honestly feel like Michael was a better fit for you. Bellamy believes we were fated to be together. Everything had to work out as it did," I said. "I'd really like for this to be a step toward healing our relationship. If for no other reason than Bellamy's happiness."

They looked at each other for a while. I could tell they were discussing how to proceed. If it encouraged them to agree, I'd wait any amount of time. It was excruciating, but I'd do anything to keep Bellamy happy. She was the most important thing in my life.

"We can do that. Amy was a blessing to Olive and Daniel. She's done so much for Daylight Moon. She's a good girl. If you ever hurt her, Lucien, I'll personally castrate you," Regan said with a glint in her eye.

I smiled. "I'd deserve it, Luna. Thank you."

We shook hands, and they left to get ready for the banquet. I breathed a sigh of relief. It would make the Luna ceremony and the wedding less tense. I was grateful for their agreement. Now, to get my pack to accept us as well.

Chapter 91: Dinner Announcement

They decorated the field nearest the packhouse with fairy lights, tables in nice tablecloths, decorations hanging from the surrounding trees, and centerpieces that glowed with the pack's colors. I was pretty surprised when I arrived. It was a totally different place than I'd seen before. A feeling of pride filled me. They'd all done so well.

Madam guided me to a platform. We stood toward the back, away from the table. Several tables in front of the dais where my guests, future ranked members, and past ranked members of the pack were seated.

Warrick and Janya gave me a huge smile. I knew he was proud of me for many more reasons than just mating with an Alpha. He was always my biggest support. Janya was looking particularly round. I settled my hand over my stomach. I couldn't wait to be there, too.

Lucien came up from the other side of the platform. Another flawlessly tailored suit clung to and draped his frame. The suit was black, his shirt was brilliant white, and his tie was forest green with a gold wolf tiepin. He styled his hair perfectly, and a gentle smile made my heart swell.

I hoped he liked my dress. It was bright rose red. Those pale reds clashed with my complexion, making me look sickly and drawn; I much preferred deeper shades. A lot more makeup had to be applied for me to look anything less than sickly.

The dress fit tightly with a square neckline over my top and flared out low on my waist. A white and gold belt rested on my hips; my shoes were simple white flats. I rarely liked heels, and heels on grass wasn't going to happen.

He crossed to me and caressed my cheek softly. I looked up into his beautiful silver eyes. This was a very special day for both of us, and I wanted to cherish every memory we made. One day, I'd be telling my daughter-in-law all about my Luna ceremony while helping her get ready for her own.

"You look beautiful, chouchoutte," Lucien murmured.

"So do you, saucisson," I replied quietly.

"Are you ready for this? We'll announce before the meal so they can get used to the idea of you being a rogue Queen, and then we'll have the ceremony, tomorrow morning I'll process the transfers for anyone who wants to leave," he told me.

"I hope they don't decide to leave. I intend to claim every pack in the region. They'll have to deal with me eventually."

"I never realized you were this ambitious, Bellamy. It's exciting as hell. Almost like you're a pack Alpha." He chuckled.

"Slurs. Slurs against me and my nature. How shameful, Lucien. I never thought you would be so cruel as to call me something as horrid as 'pack Alpha'." I wrinkled my nose and shook my head.

"I am, in fact, an evil horrid man. Alas, the innocent rogue has fallen in love with me and cannot escape. Whatever shall she do?" Lucien laughed.

"She doesn't have to do anything. Your mother is about to slap you for being so silly," Madam said in a dry tone, making Lucien blanch and me laugh. "Make your announcement. Everyone's hungry."

Lucien pulled me to the area of the stage right behind our seats. Everyone sat down. The servers had finished placing plates on the tables before taking their own seats. I scanned the area. A few tables had younger pack members who waved at me. Some warriors nodded when they saw me looking at them.

"Pack! Your attention!" Thierry called out and everyone quieted.

"Thank you all for coming to celebrate our new Luna as she joins our pack. As is tradition, we welcome the family of our Luna and her allies to this event. Not all could make it on short notice, but we are pleased to those who are here," Lucien announced.

He stepped back a little, giving me a nod. Daisy and Madam explained this part. All Lunas announced the benefits and alliances they brought with them. If they brought none, they would talk about their future plans for the pack and their love of the Alpha. I think I would have preferred that.

"Thank you for coming tonight. As your Luna, I bring with me stronger ties to the Daylight Moon Pack, Hunter's Moon Pack, Thunder Moon Pack, and Silent Moon Pack. I bring a connection to the newly forming Rose Moon Pack. I bring links to future bear sleuths via my guests Randall and Stanton Bruinwald. Also, I bring connections to the Vampire High Council via my guest Mistress Talia the Traveler," I stated.

Whispers swept the area. Most of the pack seemed appreciative. The added strength of the connections would create a safer territory.

Now was the part I was most worried about. When I'd first registered my collective with the Werewolf Association, I recommended rogue and pack classes to be taught to young wolves. The lack of knowledge I'd seen when I joined Daylight Moon fed into their distrust of collectives and rogue born wolves.

We weren't as bad as wandering ex-packs or ex-pack communities. Their behavior became more violent and aggressive. Nationwide, we distributed a new curriculum filled with engaging lessons and diverse perspectives to foster greater understanding among younger generations of wolves. I worried about the older ones who didn't get the same education.

"Through my connections, as a rogue born Alpha, I bring even more alliances and benefits. As Queen of the Eaten Heart Collective, I grant safety to this pack against rogues. The threat of my collective is immense and frightening to many. My alliances include the Icy Death Collective, the Bough Broken Collective, the Flayed Skin Collective, and the Entrails Strangled Collective. I also bring a voice in the Werewolf Association as the recently appointed holder of the third rogue representative seat and first High Queen," I declared.

Scattered cheers and applause came from the teens and some warriors. A few people gave me the side-eye, their expressions clearly suspicious. Pack wolves rarely trusted rogue wolves. I figured there'd be a lot of resistance.

"Any who don't see the benefits of our new Luna are free to apply to other packs. I'll take care of any transfers tomorrow. Queen Bellamy carries our future Alpha. She's my mate, and I will not give up all she offers to me and our pack over outdated beliefs about rogues," Lucien announced sternly.

"Does the Luna promise we won't lose our status as a pack? This won't cause the Association to dissolve our claim?" a man near the front asked.

I looked at him. He was older, in his late fifties or early sixties, about Madam's age, and had dark blond hair with silver streaks along the sides. From the position of the table, he was a previously ranked member of the pack. It was likely that he was one of my grandfathers.

"I reported our mating to the Association, but they don't decide whether or not a pack is a pack. Only the goddess does. If this pack were turning rogue, I would've smelled it. You're all still pack wolves. I've been a member of a pack for six years. It didn't change the fact that I am a rogue. My collective is strong. I believe the goddess blessed this union. She wants her children to be happy and safe. That can only happen if we grow together and support each other," I replied.

'Beautifully said, chouchoutte. That's your mother's father, Gerard Petit.'

'I assumed something like that. Thank you.'

"How do we know you'll represent our pack properly and not start making it more like a collective?" a woman sitting next to him said.

She looked like an older version of my mama. My eyes ate up the sight of what my mama could have grown into if she'd lived. I gripped Lucien's hand, and he rubbed my arm comfortingly.

"A rogue collective is only different from a pack in a few ways. I was trained by Luna Daisy Moore and my adoptive mother Olive Carrington in the ways and traditions of packs. When acting as Luna, I will represent this pack properly because of their teachings," I said.

"If there are no more questions, let's have our meal and get the ceremony completed. It would be nice to finally retire," Madam said loudly and cheerfully, making the pack chuckle.

We took a seat to enjoy our meal. Much to my relief, the expected walkout, the cacophony of boos, and the threat of rioting never came. Everyone seemed to be processing. It was much more than I'd hoped for when the day started.

Chapter 92: Luna Ceremony

[Lucien]

After dinner, the servers cleared away the plates and everyone in the pack turned to look at us. Some of my friends from around the pack had linked me to make sure I wasn't being threatened or forced to be her mate. A Beta's daughter isn't much of a threat, but Bellamy was a rogue Queen, and my little mate's powerful connections were quite terrifying.

My mother brought out the ceremonial dagger and bowl. They'd come with our pack from France when we emigrated. The blood of every new pack member for centuries had graced the bowl. The blood of every sworn Alpha, Luna, Beta, and Gamma had dripped and swirled there.

Maman took Bellamy's hand. "You are officially becoming Luna. You are my son's mate and the mother of my grandchildren. Call me Genevieve or Maman from now on."

"Thank you, Genevieve. I appreciate that more than you know." Bellamy smiled.

They turned their attention to me, and I smiled a little, too. I was glad my mother permitted Bellamy to call her by her name. It meant she liked her, just as I thought she would.

"Bellamy Carrington, do you promise to protect and represent this pack as its Luna?" I asked.

"I do," she responded.

Suddenly, a cloud passed over the moon and thunder sounded. There wasn't another cloud in the sky.

The goddess objected.

Bellamy ducked into my arms and shook. I forgot she was afraid of thunder and stroked her hair, trying to soothe her. The goddess could have picked something that didn't terrify my mate as a warning.

Murmurs spread through the crowd. That had never happened before. My pack was obviously growing concerned about the obvious divine interference with the ceremony.

The goddess hadn't objected to Aurora offering to be our mate. An Alpha's mate had to be the Luna of his pack. Why did she object to this?

"Lucien, Aurora says the goddess requires my full name to be used," Bellamy whispered. "She tried to argue that my family would be in danger, but… the goddess insists."

"We'll make sure they're under guard and aware of the danger. Alright? Plus, who would mess with the family of a High Queen of the Association?" I replied.

I raised my hand, calling for quiet. The pack quieted and watched expectantly. I knew we couldn't just change gears without addressing it.

"My apologies to the goddess. We will do this right," I said loudly enough for everyone to hear.

Bellamy took a deep breath, then nodded. She carefully repositioned herself for the ceremony. We restarted the process, picking up where we had left off.

"Bellamy Petit Dubois Carrington, do you promise to protect and represent this pack as its Luna?" I asked again.

"I do," she stated loudly.

For a moment, we waited, a hush falling over the gathering, to see if another objection would surface. The goddess remained silent. The pack was confused. We'd explain it after she told her grandparents what we meant with the name change. I could already see a couple of them working it out.

"Do you vow to give your life in service to this pack?"

"I do."

"Will you assist and guide your Alpha to the right decisions regarding this pack and support his resolutions as law?"

"I will."

"With these vows and promises, you are granted membership to Lune Rouge as its Luna. All of the duties and responsibilities of this title are now yours to uphold," I announced, cutting into her forearm, then my own, and entwining our fingers so the blood would drip from our elbows into the bowl my mother held.

When the wounds healed, the ceremony was complete. Bellamy closed her eyes for a few moments. I remembered being told she had to put up mental blocks when she joined Daylight Moon. She must have been setting them up.

Her eyes fluttered open, a soft smile gracing her lips as she looked at me. Bending low, I brushed her hair from her face before kissing. The kiss was chaste. A light brush of lips, barely more than a whisper, just enough to show my love without bending her over a table.

"Feel free to enjoy the desserts on the back table and relax. Our Luna will come around to meet everyone," Thierry announced.

"Great job. You two handled that perfectly," Robert said.

"I was surprised the goddess would object over a name," I chuckled.

"These ceremonies are more than tradition, Lucien. The magics that created us etch our names in her scrolls. Once my name was known to me, I became Bellamy Petit Dubois Carrington in them. I couldn't be anything else until I take your name," Bellamy said with a blush.

"Bellamy Deveraux. I love it, chouchoutte." I grinned.

"As do I," she purred.

Taking her hand, I guided her from table to table, introducing her and helping her answer questions. Most of the pack was friendly, especially the younger ones. They all wanted to talk to her about how cool it was and if they could go talk to her vampire friend. A few of the oldest members were curt. Bellamy didn't seem upset by this. None of them were rude.

I finally took her to where Gerard, Annette, René, and Margot were sitting. My mother and her friends were deep in conversation, the red wine swirling in their glasses as they waited patiently for our arrival. We stood next to my mother, waiting for a break in the conversation.

'Did you tell them why we called her that?' I asked.

'Non. Of course not! I knew you and Bellamy would want to tell them. They were just complaining that none of their children or grandchildren were saying anything,' Maman replied.

That was good. Everyone who knew was letting Bellamy have the chance to tell them herself. I knew Bellamy would want that. She valued family and would want to have that memory with them.

"So, would you like to explain what that was?" Gerard asked.

He was my father's Beta and like a father to me. He looked a little angry and upset; his fists were clenched, and his shoulders were tense. If I were a younger wolf, I might have worried.

As I was older, I knew there was nothing he could do to me. Not that he would've if I were younger. He was stern, but also a little soft.

"I'm sorry. We didn't want to announce it like that, but it's unwise to anger a deity," Bellamy said softly. "I am the daughter of Angelique and Jean-Luc."

Annette gasped, her eyes widening as she covered her mouth with trembling hands. A brief, almost imperceptible nod was Gerard's only response. Tears welled in their eyes as Margot and Annette grasped each other's hands, the weight of the news settling upon them.

"Is there proof of that?" René asked.

Even though he was a Gamma, he was very prudent. They handled the broken mate bonds in the pack, helping people through the hardest times of their lives. He was there to help support me after his son stole my mate. But I never blamed him for it, just like I never blamed Robert.

"The goddess made it clear that swearing in as Luna without using their names was not an option. What proof do we have? Other than that she has the Dubois eyes? Besides using many of the same facial expressions as both of them, and all the other ways she's exactly like them? No, we're just hoping our hunch is right," I scoffed.

Bellamy snickered and leaned against me. She was getting tired. I knew the pups were taking it out of her and she was having to talk a lot more than she liked to. I knew René was just worried about my guilt over banishing Jean-Luc and Angelique making me believe anything to absolve myself, but I was getting tired of people doubting us.

"René, stop being an ass. She has almost exactly the same coloring as your mother," Maman growled.

"Angelique had a daughter." Annette smiled and pulled her hand from Margot's so she could hug Gerard. "We have another granddaughter."

Annette suffered the most from Angelique and Jean-Luc's relationship. She blamed herself and there were some times when I knew my mother and Margot struggled with similar feelings. They got over them with some therapy and time to talk things out. I knew she needed this relationship with Bellamy more than any of the others.

"You're going to take good care of our granddaughter, right, Lucien?" Gerard asked.

"Of course I am." I smiled.

"You promise to do no harm to our Alpha?" René asked.

"I would never harm him. My parents told me what they did. I don't want him to ever hurt again. He's mine and I'll keep him safe and healthy for the rest of our life together," Bellamy replied.

"We need to go visit with Bellamy's guests. I'm sure there will be times in the future for all of you to catch up," I told them.

Annette and Margot sprang up and pulled Bellamy away from me, wrapping her in a hug. Gerard looked on with a soft smile. He loved his mate, and I knew losing Angelique hurt them. This was almost like a second chance for them, as much as for me.

René watched. He really wasn't as bad as he seemed. Jean-Luc was his son, and he missed him. Like Robert with Richard and Jean-Claude, René was very close to his sons.

He retired once I'd gotten out of the worst part of the rejection, after the banishment. It affected our relationship worse than my relationship with any of the other parents. He never trusted me not to lose my temper and do something terrible again. It didn't mean he stopped caring, but we were never as close as we were before.

Bellamy pulled herself out of the arms of her grandmothers and wrapped herself around my arm again. Her eyes looked heavy. I smiled and picked her up.

"Just one more table and I can take you home, chouchoutte," I said.

"I'm not used to being so tired, Lucien. I feel useless," she pouted.

"Dillon told me how little sleep you used to get. You need to sleep a normal amount now that you're pregnant," I told her as I made my way to her guest table.

"I should've been fine for the first couple of weeks. This sucks," Bellamy groaned.

"I understand. We can push off sex until tomorrow night."

She laughed. "No, I'll find the energy. Tonight, your ass is mine, Alpha. You're not going to distract me or make me forget."

I sighed. It was worth a shot. She was intent on it.

When we arrived at the guest table, Talia stood on her chair and looked me in the eye. She looked a little crabby. I wondered what was making her upset.

"Put my pheata down. I need to hug her and you're too tall," she demanded.

Chuckling, I put Bellamy down, and Talia jumped off the chair, hugging her. Warrick ambled over, his face a mask of slight irritation, a grumpy look etched on his features. I turned toward him, bracing myself for the familiar sting of doubt, the same skepticism everyone else had thrown at me.

"I'm glad you killed the Alpha who banished her parents. You're probably a lot better for the pack than that guy was." He grinned and winked. He'd been faking being upset. I was relieved after so much doubt from others.

"I believe I am. Plus, I have one of the best Lunas in the region to help keep me from resurrecting him." I smiled.

"You gave her back her family. I always wanted Ames to have people who loved and cared for her as much as I did. Now she has her real family."

I saw Olive and Daniel look disheartened at his words. They didn't deserve that. He probably didn't even realize what he'd said or implied. Before I could say anything, Bellamy cut me off.

"You're all my real family, Ricky," Bellamy said. "Some were given to me by blood, others by fate and the goddess. That doesn't make any of you less than the others. Without my family, I wouldn't be here today. I wouldn't have found my mate and I wouldn't have my pups. I love all of you."

"Sorry, Ames. I didn't mean to say any member of your family wasn't real." He blushed and gave an apologetic look to the Carringtons.

Bellamy hugged him and went around the table, thanking everyone for coming and giving them hugs as well. Regan and Michael were a doting aunt and uncle. I was always amazed by how easily Bellamy attracted people to her; it was as if she had some sort of magical charm that drew them in. It was definitely something she got from her mother.

She returned to me and wrapped her arms around my waist. I put my arms over her shoulders and held her close to me. My very own Luna. My beautiful mate.

I stiffened as her hands drifted down to my butt, and she squeezed it. Laughs, catcalls, and whistles rang out behind me. The pack loved seeing their Alpha groped, apparently.

I pulled her off of me, picked her up over my shoulder, and headed back to the house. Might as well turn into the spin.

Chapter 93: Pain in the….

When we reached our bedroom, I set Bellamy down. She smiled and tugged me toward the center of the room. I was a little apprehensive, but I wanted her to be more open to letting me take over. That meant I had to let her take the lead sometimes.

"Get undressed and lay on the bed with your arms over your head, Lucien," she said as she headed into the closet.

I started stripping, setting my clothing in the hamper to be taken care of by the house staff later. My heart was in my throat. I didn't know what she was going to do once she came back. Remus was growling and pacing in my head.

'You should march into that closet and take her against the wall. Let her know you're the Alpha.'

'There are worse things in the world than giving into whatever she plans on doing. If we make her mad, she might withhold sex. I'm not going to risk that because you're a coward,' I replied to my wolf.

'You know a finger is a gateway probe. You let her do this and soon enough she's going to be pegging you with a giant strap-on.'

'Shut up, Remus.'

'Don't say I didn't tell you so when you've got your knees up by your ears and you're begging her to be gentle this time.'

'I wish I could kick your ass,' I growled.

'Blah, blah, blah. I'm going to sleep.'

I didn't mind him sleeping. I didn't want to hear any more of his wild theories. There was no way it would end up like that… I hoped.

Once I was undressed, I laid on the bed with my hands resting against the headboard. I was on my back. If nothing else, she might just think I misunderstood. My nerves were going crazy.

Bellamy walked out of the closet. She was wearing a violet bra and panty set that barely covered anything. Her skin glowed next to the dark material. As my eyes trailed up, I saw she was holding a scarf in one hand and wearing the wolf ear headband. The color was just like Aurora's ears. It made me smile.

"Are you ready, saucisson?" Bellamy purred.

"Absolutely not. Let's do this."

She giggled and glided toward me. When she reached the bed, she climbed up near my chest and started tying my wrists, looping the scarf through the thick bar at the bottom of the headboard. There was just enough slack I could move.

I had the urge to try to escape. My heart was beating wildly. It might be too soon for something like this. Bellamy saw my face and looked worried.

"I won't harm you, my love. This is just to keep you from taking over. I know my big, strong Alpha will want to turn this into a fight for dominance. I want to own you as much as you want to own me, Lucien. Neither one of us is used to giving up control. I did earlier, but it was a struggle. Just relax, like I did. Let me possess you," she whispered as she stroked up and down my chest and kissed me lightly.

"I trust you. It's just really close to the last time I was tied up and… I guess some part of me just freaked out," I confided.

Bellamy smiled. "Just breathe and let me take over. If you start to panic again, tell me to stop and I will. We'll talk about safe words when we get to needing them. For now, I just want you to learn that you're safe when I have you like this. There will be very little pain tonight."

"Very little pain?" I asked.

"We're both dominant wolves. I know you like some pain as much as I do," she whispered and nipped at my mark.

She was right; I did. I nodded, and Bellamy slid her hands down my chest. She teased at my nipples before pinching them and twisting them a little. I moaned at the feeling. It wasn't violent or rough, just strong enough to hurt, but gentle enough not to kick in my fight-or-flight response.

Her lips passed delicately down my chest, and she released my nipples as her tongue came in to soothe away the remaining pain. She drew her fingernails down my chest to my stomach. I looked down to see a couple of small, bloody lines. Bellamy looked into my eyes as she licked the blood from my cuts. It felt like her tongue was everywhere.

I gasped as she slid lower, not seating herself on my erection, but pressing it down between my legs with her body. She moved to the side and reached under my knee. I closed my eyes in nervous anticipation of where her hand was going.

When she gripped my erect cock instead of putting a finger in me, I opened my eyes. Bellamy nudged me to roll over while securing my sensitive parts so they wouldn't get hurt. I could turn easily because the scarf was loosely tied.

Once I was on my stomach, Bellamy moved the pillows from the head of the bed and directed me to turn my head to the left. Gently, she lifted my head and adjusted my arms to support a small, decorative pillow on them before resting my cheek on it. Bellamy kissed me lightly.

After she had me in position, she got off the bed and then moved the nightstand. She pulled the wide, full-length mirror from the closet. Bellamy climbed over me, sitting on the opposite side so I could see her in the mirror. She ran her fingers down my back to my ass.

"Look at that gorgeous man," she murmured. "Every curve and bulge perfectly sculpted into an artwork of sensuality and strength. All of it belongs to me. My own precious Alpha."

I watched the reflection of her adoring my form. I was as vain as any Alpha, as any man. This praise of my body filled me with pride.

Her ownership of me wasn't as rough as mine of her. It highlighted another difference between us. She didn't dominate with her strength, but with her heart.

Bellamy moved to sit between my legs. She ran her hands over the curve of my ass and gripped it tightly. I tensed and squeezed my eyes closed.

"Open your eyes," she commanded and delivered a firm slap.

My eyes flew open. Bellamy was looking in the mirror with a stern expression on her face. I squirmed a little. She was hot as hell when she looked like that.

"You will watch me when I touch you, Lucien. You belong to me and will do what I tell you," she growled.

I nodded. "Yes, Queen Bellamy"

She smiled and returned to what she was doing. Her hands slid down my thighs, and she drew them back up with her nails dragging over my skin.

"This is how I first saw you. Dim light. Bare, beautiful, body. Flawless skin just begging to be touched by warm hands. All I could think when I cleaned you was how I would've done something stupid if I were a weaker wolf. Even when I didn't think of males sexually, your beauty called to me," Bellamy purred. "Did you ever imagine this, that you tried to hide from me, would one day belong to me? The dirty rogue would possess the Alpha prince?"

Her hand moved down to grip my hard cock, while the other massaged my balls. She was just rough enough to send pleasurable waves throughout my body. I tried to answer her, but words escaped me when her little hands were on me.

"Mmm. Speechless. Just how I like a man." She chuckled seductively.

Bellamy released me and slid her hands back up to my ass cheeks. I watched as she gazed at me with lust in her eyes. Her tongue glided over her lips before she leaned forward, laying a soft kiss on my left butt cheek before she bit it.

I felt her teeth sharpen as my flesh was in her mouth. They pierced my skin, and I shouted a little. It hurt, but it felt so good. She cleaned the wound, and I realized what she'd done.

"You marked me again," I whispered.

"Now everyone will know who this ass belongs to, mon saucisson. You're mine," she growled.

I smiled. Bellamy rolled me over again and straddled my waist, rubbing her own beautiful ass against my rock-hard erection. She wanted me so much that she marked me twice. I pulled against the binding on my wrists.

I needed to have her. I needed to mark my Luna again like she had me. Nothing was as important as showing her she meant as much to me as I meant to her.

"Stop struggling. I'm not done with you yet."

Bellamy reached up and turned my head toward the mirror. I watched the reflection as she got off of me and removed her panties, then slid me inside of her. She was hot and wet, making me groan with pleasure.

She started riding me. At first, she was gentle, but eventually, she built up to a furious pounding. Her fingernails dug into my waist.

I felt my end coming as her body spasmed over mine. Suddenly, she reached behind her and flicked my balls. The unexpected, sharp pain made my orgasm stop. I whimpered my frustration.

The next few times I nearly finished, she did the same thing. She forced me to watch her repeatedly reach orgasm while she continually stopped me. The pressure was immense. I needed completion so badly.

Anytime I started thrusting, she smacked my thigh and told me 'no'. Bellamy used me as she wanted. I was nearly crying with need.

"Please, let me come, chouchoutte," I pled.

"Who do you belong to, Lucien?" she asked.

"You. Only you. Always you, my Queen," I answered.

She smiled. "Damned right."

Bellamy rode me harder and faster. When I'd nearly finished, I winced, expecting her to stop me again, but she didn't flick me this time. My end was explosive. The pleasure and the pain rocketed through my body, unlike anything I had ever felt before. I arched with the power of it.

When it was over, Bellamy kissed me deeply and untied my arms. The muscles had locked up a little. She rubbed my arms, shoulders, and wrists to relieve the pain. Afterward, she took off the headband and tossed it on the nightstand. Bellamy curled up next to me with her head on my chest, and I gently wrapped my arm around her.

"You were perfect, saucisson. Thank you," she murmured.

"I thought I was young enough to keep up with you, chouchoutte. I think I was wrong," I chuckled.

She didn't respond. I looked down and saw she'd fallen asleep. I was too tired to clean us up, so I just pulled the blankets over us and went to sleep with my mate in my arms.

Chapter 94: Next Expansion

The alarm on my phone went off at the usual time for training. It interrupted the nicest dream I'd ever had. I wanted nothing more than to turn it off and go back to sleep. I felt like I hadn't slept in a month.

It stopped ringing, and I sighed. I'd get up when the snooze alarm went off. Training was important. I couldn't slack off when the lives of my family hung in the balance.

"Bellamy. Are you alright?" Lucien asked gently.

"Tired," I groaned.

"Take today off from training. You've kept going this whole time. You need to rest or you're going to get sick."

"Werewolves don't get sick, Lucien. What am I going to do? Come down with the awoo-flu?" I snickered.

Lucien laughed. I loved making him laugh. He had the richest, warmest laugh I'd ever heard. This must be why my parents were always happy. Seeing your mate happy was so fulfilling.

"You had two big, hard battles. You've been doing Luna work and Queen work whenever you're not fighting. The closest thing you've had to a break was when we ran your borders and our small jaunt yesterday. I'll tell everyone the pregnancy is wearing you out. They'll understand," he offered.

"Okay. I'm not going to argue. If I'm exhausted, I won't be helpful in a fight," I replied.

"I'm going to head out to the field. You sleep," he whispered and kissed the top of my head before climbing out of bed.

It didn't take long for me to drift off again. I felt like such a lazy wolf, sleeping away my morning, but I knew I needed it. If not for me, then for the health of our pups.

***

When Lucien returned to wake me, I felt a lot more rested. The intake would start just before noon. I had to wrap up my final preparations and get to the convention hall by eleven.

Wearily, I crawled out of bed and joined Lucien in the shower. While washing his back, I let my fingers trail over the new mark I'd left on him. There was no reason to mark him twice, but I wasn't as big and intimidating as him.

Some females last night had been checking him out. During the last week in the pack, I'd heard women talking about how they'd been flirting or trying to entice him for years. Every one of them talked about how hot his ass was. It took everything in me not to attack them like some jealous harpy.

"Chouchoutte, please stop. We aren't able to spend the day in bed and that does the exact same things to me as if you were stroking the other mark," Lucien whispered, turning to me.

The evidence of his claim stood proudly between us. I laughed.

"Sorry, saucisson. I was just admiring it. I think it makes your ass even more gorgeous than before."

"When do I get to mark you a second time? I didn't even realize it was an option." He chuckled as he pulled me to the bench in the shower.

I moaned softly as he seated me on his erection. He filled me up perfectly, rubbing every sensitive spot inside of me. The feeling of his muscles under my hands was glorious. His skin sent sparks along mine as he kissed my lips and held me close.

Putting my face in the curve of his neck, I nibbled at the mark there while I rode him. Lucien's large hands stroked down my back and gripped my hips. He guided my motion as we rose to our climax.

"I swear to the goddess, if you flick my balls, I'm going to tie you to the bed and torment you mercilessly for a whole day," he growled.

I chuckled against his skin and wrapped my arms around his wide shoulders.

"Don't threaten me with a good time, saucisson," I purred.

Pulling him closer, I reveled in the feeling of his body connecting with me inside and out. I murmured his name and my love for him in his ear. Lucien's breath quickened, and he finished with me.

"You can decide when you want to mark me a second time. Don't feel pressured to do it, though. I don't mind waiting," I whispered softly as he held me.

"I just have to decide where else on this beautiful body I should claim," he growled heatedly.

"Mmm. Let's finish getting ready for the day. Are you coming to the intake?" I asked, sliding off of his lap and returning to the spray of hot water.

Lucien soaped up a cloth and moved my hair aside to wash my back. I loved how he had gotten into the habit of grooming me. The feeling of contentment that went through me was wonderful.

"I'd love to, chouchoutte. Will it be okay? Your rogues won't be upset?"

"They can deal with it. You're my consort. It means you have a role in their lives now. I want this to be a community, with no hierarchy between rogue and pack. All our people should be able to work together. We can guide them to a new era of acceptance," I replied.

"That's a fantastic idea, chouchoutte. Our people will be happier and healthier if they know they can depend on both of us," Lucien said.

"It will make your next expansion much easier." I smiled and turned to wrap my arms around his waist.

"*My* next expansion? What are you talking about?" he asked.

"There's a small pack near an equally small collective. The pack is dying. Most of the wolves there are older, the younger wolves apply to other packs after high school. We could offer a merger. The Alpha there has no heir since the last attack and is searching for someone to take over.

"No one wants a dying pack. If you offer the merger, we can gain another two hundred wolves. I'll take over the other collective, their king isn't a fighter. The expansion for us would be a tremendous boost to our strength. I think we could have it all put together within the next three months, if not sooner," I explained.

"With another two hundred wolves, I would have the largest pack in the region," Lucien grinned.

"Yes. And we could set up those pack lands to house accepted rogues until they can be filtered into this pack," I purred.

"We need to get out of the shower. When you talk like this it makes me want to take you back to bed," he growled provocatively.

"Everything I do makes you want to take me back to bed." I giggled.

He winked and finished rinsing off. After we left the shower, we went to dress for the day.

I picked some black jeans, a black tank top, and an off-the-shoulder shirt Dilly had made for me. It was black and had a heart shape with a bite taken out of it and a little crown on top. I loved it.

Rogues had a sense of humor. Most of my collective liked it back home. Searching the shelves of my shoes, I finally found the ones I wanted. Black leather ankle boots with a small, wide heel.

Back in the bathroom, I pulled my hair into a French braid, tying it at the bottom with a black band. After putting on a little eye shadow and lip gloss, I was ready.

Lucien stood in front of his side of the closet, wearing only boxer briefs, as I came out of the bathroom. He looked like he was having a hard time deciding what to wear. I watched him internally debating things.

"Need help?" I asked with a grin.

"If this were a pack thing, I'd wear a suit or something else formal. It looks like you're planning to go out to a club. I don't think I have much to compare with your outfit." He chuckled.

I walked around his side of the closet, pulling things out and looking at them. I handed him some black jeans, a blood-red t-shirt, and a black blazer. Some black oxfords completed the outfit perfectly. It would show some uniformity in our appearance. Black and blood red were the colors of my collective.

"Perfect." I smiled.

"Are you sure? This seems a little… on the nose for supernatural stuff," Lucien said, with an eyebrow raised.

I sighed. "My collective's colors are black and blood red. The colors of heart blood. This will just make it easier to point us out and signify what we represent. Now, let's go eat. I'm starving and it's making me nauseous."

Lucien dressed, then took my hand and kissed it before looping it over his arm and guiding me toward the door. We got a few strange looks as we made our way to the dining room, but I didn't mind them. Our clothing was just different from what they were used to seeing us in.

***

The quiet hum of conversation filled the dining room as all my guests settled into their seats. Even Talia was there. From his seat at a corner table, Braden gave a small, friendly wave in my direction.

We sat in our seats, and the servers brought our plates. Mine had a lot more protein than normal. I looked up at the server who set my food down. She was the same girl who delivered the food I made for Talia on their first day at Lune Rouge.

"We were informed that rogue pregnancies require more protein and rare meats. The kitchen has made alterations to their recipes and meal plans to take care of you and our future Alpha, Luna." She bowed.

"Thank you. I really appreciate that." I smiled.

"Anything for our Luna. The Alpha is much nicer since you came and everything runs more smoothly. Everyone who works in the house is happy to have you here."

I looked at the name badge she was wearing. Geraldine. That was an unfortunate name.

"Do you have a name you go by?" I asked.

"Like a nickname? No. Sometimes my brothers call me Gerry, but I hate it." Her nose wrinkled.

I understood that feeling. I hated being called 'Bella'. Everyone at Limb Torn called me Bella. No matter how much I asked them to call me Amy, they never did. I'd help her find a better name.

"Can I call you Allie?" I inquired.

Her eyes widened. "Yes, please."

"You can call me Amy unless something official is going on," I replied with a smile.

"I… I don't think I can. Sorry, Luna." She blushed.

I sighed. "No problem. It was worth a shot."

She bowed again and trotted off. Warrick snickered. He knew how much I hated the hierarchy in packs. I understood they were serving the pack in whatever way they could, but I didn't like people feeling like they had to use honorifics with me outside of my rogue business.

I began eating. I needed to get back on track for the day. There was a lot to get done. I still needed to collect the tablets Drake and Dillon programmed for anyone who didn't have internet access to fill out the intake forms. Then I needed to sign the papers the Association sent and fax them in. I had to check my emails and get things rolling on the plan for properly clearing Rose Moon.

"Missed you in training, Ames," Warrick smiled.

"I was tired. I'm allowed to take a day off, Warrick," I growled.

Janya laughed. "Oof. Not 'Ricky'? What did he do?"

"Sorry. Busy," I muttered while I powered through my breakfast.

Explaining things so often was getting boring, and I had talked way too much in the last week. I just wanted to get things done. It was one thing I hated about pack wolves. Too much talking.

Braden wandered up to the table. I glanced at him and he nodded.

"Don't die," I said, nodding back.

"Same to you." He winked and headed out the door.

I finished shortly after and Allie took my plate to the kitchen before I headed to my unfortunate office. Once Lucien finished, I knew he'd be right behind.

Waiting wasn't an option for me. The sheer volume of this intake, coupled with its inherent complexities, suggested it would be a challenging undertaking. I prayed to the goddess that it wouldn't.

Chapter 95: Unconventional

A few hours later, we had an SUV packed up with just under a hundred tablets and a lunch the kitchen staff made for us. Randy and Becky were going to be there for the first half of the intake. Stanton and Talia would come for the second half. They were in charge of non-wolf intakes.

Lucien and I sat in the back, while Randy drove us to the smaller convention center in the city. Randy was pretty chill now that I'd gotten to know him a little. I was glad to have another powerful ally.

"Is there anything I should remember or any rules I need to know about, Bellamy?" Lucien asked.

"The ex-packs will want to call you 'Alpha'. I think we should let them. Before we go in, I want you to release your Alpha aura. We need to show the rogues we're stronger and more dominant than they are. It'll lower the chances of a challenge," I told him.

"I can do that. I haven't had to let it out in a while. Going the whole day like that might make me a little unbearable." He chuckled.

"You think you're tougher than me, Alpha?" I inquired, raising my eyebrow.

"I don't know. Remus and I know you're strong, but we've never let our full power out when not fighting strong enemies. Maybe you'll be surprised."

I was excited to see exactly how powerful he was. Just from what I felt when I first sensed him, I knew he was strong. The dominance in our fights hadn't been full force. Even when fighting the goblins, he held back so he wouldn't lose himself in the emotion of the fight.

We arrived at the convention center twenty minutes later. Randy parked and turned to us.

"Let me get out so my bear doesn't freak at being in a small space with two other Alphas. Then you can do your thing," he said, reaching for the door.

"Thanks, Randy. And thank you for helping with the non-wolf intake." I smiled.

"Anything for Stan's little wolf. See you soon," Randy replied, leaving the car.

"Okay, saucisson. Show me what you've got."

Lucien smirked and suddenly the SUV filled with power. It washed over me in burning waves. I almost couldn't breathe. He was the most powerful Alpha I'd ever met.

'Our mate is powerful,' Aurora purred.

'More powerful than us, I think,' I replied.

'Our pups will be powerful.'

'They'll dominate all other Alphas. Our territory will be safe.'

'Wish we didn't have this intake. I want to take him back to bed,' she pouted.

'Same. And mark him a few more times. Goddess, he's amazing.'

A small moan escaped my lips. His power was intoxicating. My own power struggled to break free.

"Are you alright, chouchoutte?" Lucien rumbled in a sexy tone.

"I think we should have done this much sooner." I breathed.

He chuckled. "Finally seeing how outmatched you are?"

I bit my lip and allowed my power to come out. Lucien gasped. I hadn't let it out fully during my intakes previously and held back during the fights. He only felt a portion of it before.

"We should definitely have done this earlier," he growled.

Our powers pushed against each other. With no clear victor, they mingled, a vibrant fusion of sensations washed over us. Our combined power became much more robust. In terms of dominance, we were evenly matched. Together, we were even stronger than before.

"Amazing," he whispered and leaned in to kiss me.

It wasn't a hungry, passionate kiss, but a gentle, caring kiss. Normally, I would push it further, but this was perfection. We didn't need to fight to see who was more powerful. We knew we were equal.

"Let's get this over with, saucisson. I want my territory settled. Then we'll kill whoever's after you and spend time exploring our combined strength," I murmured.

He nodded and exited the car, holding his hand out to assist me. Randy was standing a few feet away and seemed shocked. I tilted my head at him.

"You're stronger than me. My bear keeps telling me to look away." He chuckled.

"Sorry. That must be difficult." I offered a small smile.

"I already knew *you* were stronger, Amy. You kicked my ass at that ball-breaker. But him, I didn't realize pack wolves could be that strong. You two are as powerful as Stan," Randy snorted.

"Good. He's meant to have a large sleuth. We'll be able to hold an even larger territory." I grinned.

"You're going to make my pack large enough to gain a seat on the Association. Aren't you, chouchoutte?" Lucien asked.

I turned to Lucien and wrapped my arms around his waist. He looked down into my eyes. My pride in him grew. He was a perfect Alpha, a perfect male, and a perfect mate.

"Imagine the power we'd have as the heads of the Association, Lucien. The seat of the Association would move to our territory. No one would dare harm our people," I replied.

"I thought this was jury duty."

"Joining your pack made me think more like the head of a pack. I didn't realize how intoxicating it could be to desire power and prestige. Don't worry. It won't change me. You want a seat in the Association like I have, and I want you to have everything you desire," I purred.

"I already have all I desire, Bellamy. You gave me that when you accepted me when you didn't give up because of our past, and when we made those pups you're carrying."

A blush rose to my cheeks. I knew he'd given me the same. Stepping back, I put my hand over my stomach and he covered it with his hand. I felt the sparks of our connection and gazed into his eyes.

"Same. Come on, Lucien. We have a lot to do." I moved my hand to hold his, and we went into the building.

***

Randy followed us as we headed through the lobby area. When I opened the door to the main convention area, a guttural growl, like a wild animal, echoed from the room. Not how we needed to start this intake. Lucien and I threw the doors open and stepped in.

Our combined energy filled the room, a palpable wave that silenced the chatter and drew attention to us immediately. The wolves fell to their knees and averted their gaze. I tried to figure out what happened.

Becky was cowering in a corner. Two well-dressed older wolves were kneeling in front of her like they were guarding her before we entered. Two female wolves were keeping a couple of male wolves at bay in the middle of the room. A man and a woman lay knocked out on the floor. Three other guys were lying near the wall, unconscious.

"What the HELL do you think you're doing?!!" I roared.

One of the men looked at me. It was Thomas. The other embarrassedly looked up. Dale, the mayor. It was pretty simple to see what happened.

"Sorry, Queen Bellamy. This mutt tried to send Julio and me away. He threatened to kill us. I told him if he had a problem, he should fight me and not threaten my people," Thomas explained.

"He's a menace. He shouldn't be here," Dale growled.

I sighed. Of course, this wouldn't be easy. I let go of Lucien's hand and strode purposefully toward the men, my boots thudding heavily on the wooden floor. The closer I got, the more they shrunk back, their fear practically tangible in the tense silence of the room.

Maintaining a one-step distance, Lucien's measured steps followed mine. The combined force of our power overwhelmed everyone present. The wolves all sank closer to the floor, even Thomas.

"Alpha Thomas is our ally. He stays to vow his loyalty to me. I already told you what I found," I answered, glaring at him.

"They wouldn't have gotten the idea if not for him."

"They would've still formed a gang and would've still fucked with people. We're going to take care of it. Pull this bullshit again, and you'll be banished from the collective," I stated coldly.

"Yes, Queen Bellamy," he whispered.

I went to the corner Becky was standing in. Terror filled her large eyes. The couple in front of her didn't move aside.

"Please, she's just a little human. Don't hurt her," the woman pled gently.

"She's my friend. I want to make sure she's okay. Thank you for protecting her," I told the woman.

Becky's face lit up, a wide smile spreading across it, as I called her my friend. I knew it would get her out of her fear response. I smiled at her.

"Really? I'm really your friend?" She bounced.

"Of course you are."

I carefully examined her, checking for any visible injuries or wounds. A wave of relief washed over me as I saw she was okay. I should've had her wait outside for us.

Reaching out, I gently took her hand and led her to where Randy was waiting. Glancing over, he immediately began staring at her with his eyes wide open in surprise or shock. I saw his pupils dilate, his breath hitching in his chest as he inhaled deeply.

"Randy, this is Becky. She's a dhampyr. Can you take care of her while I tend to the wolves?" I asked.

"Becky…" he whispered.

She blushed. From what I'd learned about her, Becky was eighteen and lost her father when she was eight. She lived with her mother.

Aside from her activities as a fan of wolves, she mostly focused on school and caring for the house, so her mother didn't have to worry. She never dated. Becky squeaked and pulled me aside.

"Amy, help."

"What's wrong, Becky?" I asked.

"I want to bite him. I've never felt like this before," she whimpered. "My teeth hurt."

"Open your mouth," I ordered.

Becky opened her mouth, and I looked at her teeth. Behind her canines, fangs started emerging. The fangs baffled me. Turning, I looked at Randy. Randy balled his hands into fists, his knuckles white.

"I need to call Talia. Can you resist the urge to bite him?" I asked Becky.

With a hesitant shake of her head, Becky squeezed her eyes closed. I waved Lucien over. He was concerned.

"Watch over Becky. I'll take Randy out with me. I need to talk to Talia about this," I murmured.

"Got it."

I looked at the other wolves, who were staring at us. We needed to get things in order. All of this was putting us off schedule, and that wasn't how I wanted the first day of intake to start.

"Look after the injured, clean this mess, and do *not* fight again," I commanded.

Grabbing Randy's arm, I pulled him out of the room. He fought it a little, but went along. When we got out of the room and closed the doors, I looked at him. He seemed nervous.

"Randy, is she your mate?" I asked.

"Yes. I'm not old enough to settle down yet. Why isn't she a bear? It doesn't make sense. What's a dhampyr?" he strained.

"She's part vampire, but mostly human. What are you going to do?"

"I don't know." He sighed. "I always thought my mate would be bear. She's really fucking cute. Goddess, I love chubby girls."

"So it wasn't my height when you said I was a little small." I chuckled.

Randy covered his face and sunk down into a crouch. Poor guy. I hoped he would accept her. Just because they were different didn't mean they couldn't be together.

If the goddess put them together, they would complement each other. I pulled out my cell phone and dialed Talia. I needed to confirm this was a dhampyr's reaction to finding their mate.

Chapter 96: Solus Amor

The phone rang a while before Talia answered. I organized my thoughts during the wait. She would have the answers.

"Hello?" she said when she picked up.

"Talia. I have a question about dhampyrs. What does it mean when they grow fangs, and have the urge to bite someone?"

"Becky?" she asked.

"Yeah," I replied.

"That has never happened to any dhampyr I have ever heard of, pheata. But it is possible. It's what happens to a vampire when they meet their solus amor, the vampire they will spend their existence bound to. They share blood with each other. It's one of the only times a vampire bites another vampire. Has she seen another dhampyr?" Talia inquired.

"No. A bear." I snickered.

"Randy?" she laughed.

A scuffle sounded on the other end of the line, punctuated by her even louder laughter. There was a sound of a phone dropping, followed by the sound of it being picked up.

"What about Randy?" Stanton demanded.

He must've only heard the last part where Talia said his cousin's name. Vampires could find some weird things amusing, and he was clearly not getting answers from our friend.

"He's found his mate," I answered. "Becky, a dhampyr who's joining my collective."

"A dhampyr? He always was a weird kid." He sighed, probably more from relief than anything else.

"I can hear you, Stan," Randy growled.

"Bears only get one mate. If he rejects her, his bear will pine for her forever and he'll never love anyone again," Stanton explained. "At least, not how he would've loved his mate. Some can find something like love, but it will never be the same sort of connection."

"It will be the same for her. If a vampire is lucky enough to have a solus amor, they only have one. If he rejects her or the other way around, she will never love anyone else," Talia added. "Or, at least, no vampire who has ever been rejected has loved again."

"I'm not going to reject her. It's just…. I'm only twenty-four. I wasn't ready to settle down yet," Randy groaned.

"Maybe she isn't either. Becky's only eighteen. She's never had a boyfriend or a date. There's still a lot for her to experience before settling down," I said.

"*You're* only eighteen!" Randy replied, standing up and crossing his arms.

"And I've traveled, learned, experienced, and tried more in that time than *you* have in twenty-four years. Unlike you, I'm ready to settle down. I'm ready for a family and responsibilities." I smirked. "You can't use me as an example."

"Let Becky bite you. Staking her claim will make the itching stop. It will help so she isn't in pain from it. Unlike you furry folk, we do not have to spend every minute of our lives with our solus amors. My solus amor, Zen, lives in Spain. She's quite happy there and doesn't like traveling. She runs her territory and lives as she pleases. I see her every fifty to one hundred years," Talia said.

"I didn't realize you had a mate, Tal," Stanton said quietly. "You sleep with a ton of people."

"Our solus amor is the one we always go back to. With lives like ours, you can't be alone or you go insane. My Zen has her affairs as well and we always come together again. Vampires who haven't found their solus amor will often arrange marriages so they have someone to keep them sane."

"What do you think, Randy? Let her bite you and go on with your life until you're ready, settle down early, or live without a mate for the rest of your life?" I asked.

Randy turned and pulled the doors open, marching into the main room. I followed, putting the phone on speaker. Quietly, I gave Stanton and Talia a play-by-play.

He walked over to Lucien and Becky and knelt down in front of Becky. With a helpless expression, she pressed her lips together and stared at me. Randy gently took her hand, refocusing her attention.

"My name is Randall Bruinwald. I'm a werebear and your solus amor. Your mate. I'm an Alpha, we're called Ursos. We usually don't look for our mates until we're around thirty. Would you wait for me, Becky?" he asked.

The entire room was still. Wolves and bears rarely interacted outside of fighting. None of them were familiar with bear mating habits. I know I wasn't. I wondered if this was normal or if he was acting like this because he was thinking of what Becky needed.

"I was accepted into a college I really want to go to. I'm fine with waiting. We can get to know each other until I leave. But…. Promise you'll wait for me, too," she said softly.

"Absolutely. You're beautiful and I want to make you mine. For now, though, I want you to bite me. Talia said it would be painful for you if you didn't. I never want you to hurt, my little tulip," Randy murmured.

"I've always liked bears more than wolves anyway." She giggled.

"Ouch, Becks. That's mean," I said in a falsely injured tone.

"Not sorry, Amy. My dad used to call my mom his solus amor. His only love. I looked up what it meant. I really have always liked bears more. But, I never saw a werebear, so I didn't know if they existed." Becky smiled.

"Well, that's taken care of. Let's get started. We have a long day and this delay hasn't helped," Lucien stated in a commanding tone.

"We'll see you two at the switchover," I told Talia and Stanton as I hung up. "You heard my mate! Let's go."

Randy and Becky found some place private to mark him while I got to know the wolves I hadn't met yet. I briefed them on the routine for intake. We distributed twenty tablets per table for any who hadn't signed up ahead of time.

The older couple were Lance and Rita Blood, the pastor and his ex-pack mate. Lyric and Melody Knight, rogue-born twin sisters who owned supernatural-friendly cafes in smaller towns, were the ones restraining Dale and Thomas. Jasper Sorenson and Petra Katz, ex-pack wolves running wolf-friendly businesses in their respective towns, had been knocked out earlier.

My lieutenants and Alpha Thomas would join my collective traditionally. I would also do the mayor and the guards he brought traditionally. It would take too much blood to do everyone and with vampires being among the people joining, there was a risk of losing more.

A mass intake differed from a one-on-one. There was no bloodshed. Just them submitting to me. I would greet each person, touch them to make that connection before sending them to find a place to wait. Once we had enough, I would command them to submit to me.

After they had, I would welcome them into the collective, and they could leave. The greeting part took the longest. I hated it, but it was the beginning of our bond.

Julio wouldn't join my collective, nor would any wolf who was going to become a member of the Rose Moon Pack. There was no reason to deal with the pain of releasing them.

Not all ex-packs wanted another pack. Not all of them would want to help set one up, but they would get the option to join instead of joining my collective. Thomas needed at least one hundred to have a solid start. We'd get the numbers he needed over the weekend easily. I could feel it.

My collective was strange in that it included species other than wolves. When I was thirteen, a witch coven approached me, asking to join my collective. No one had ever told me I couldn't accept non-wolves, so I did the submission ritual with them and it worked.

It wasn't until my expansion at fifteen that the Association told me collectives didn't accept other species. They hadn't expected that I had already had the chance to accept several other species as the slow growth of my borders spread further from the Daylight Moon pack lands.

No other King or Queen could get other beings to trust them like I could. My knowledge of other species, their habits, and traditions helped in that a lot. It made me a unique and valuable ally.

An hour later, we were officially ready to start the intake. People started filtering in. Wolves born outside packs registered at their table, ex-pack wolves at theirs, while Becky and Randy registered non-wolves.

Thomas had a room set up next to the main convention room for ex-packs who wanted to join his pack. They would have to register with the collective, and then have the file transferred. He would decide who to accept there.

Soon, people started filtering in. I'd directed all fae to show up in the intakes before dusk, so they wouldn't come across vampires. Their blood was powerful, and few vampires could resist it, at least in the species I'd met. I wouldn't risk any fae with my intake.

There were no issues. I was grateful at least one part of the process was going smoothly. The ex-packs were all gracious, and I saw quite a few head off to Thomas' room. Those who stayed with the collective were respectful to Lucien. None of the rogue born seemed to have any issues, either. They'd all seen coverage and read articles about us.

***

As the day ended, I was exhausted. Lucien helped pack everything up while I rested. We would take the tablets with us and return with them the next day. He drove us home since Randy left with Becky. Stanton messaged Randy to make sure he could get a ride back to the packhouse.

In all, it was a wonderful day. I had hope that the next day would be just as good. It would be even longer since we'd be starting at nine.

"You were amazing today, chouchoutte. I love seeing you like that," Lucien said softly.

"Thank you. I think it went more smoothly because you were there, saucisson. Two powerful Alphas run this territory. They'll fall into line or suffer the consequences." I giggled.

"I'll be there tomorrow to lend my support as well. I've been reading through the Rogue Studies information from the high school. Soon, I'll be more helpful." He smiled.

"I'm proud of you, Lucien. You're getting over your prejudice and becoming a better leader, and a better person, for it," I replied.

"You make me want to be better, Bellamy. I love you."

"I love you, too." I sighed and leaned against the seat with a yawn.

I ended up falling asleep on the way home. When Lucien picked me up to carry me into the house, I woke briefly. Mass intakes were hell on energy levels.

Thankfully, I wouldn't have to do them after my next expansion. Once a collective reached a certain size, the Alpha's power shifted, forcing any rogue within their border to submit or flee as the border solidified. I looked forward to that day.

Chapter 97: Kings and Queen

The second day of intake was going nice and smooth. Lucien was perfect. He stood by my side and didn't posture when people were disrespectful. We got that more from the non-wolves than the wolves.

Charlie came with Thomas for the second day. Many people commented on how excited they were to join the new pack, knowing their Luna was smart and capable. I had no idea what was going on in that room, but it was making the pack building go more smoothly than it had the day before.

Talia and Stanton arrived just before dusk. Randy was having dinner with Becky and her mom. I loved watching them throughout the day. He was attentive and she couldn't take her eyes off him. I don't know how things were for her with humans, but now she would be with her people, and I knew Randy would keep her safe.

As it reached nine in the evening, we were seeing smaller crowds in the intake groups. It looked like we were right on schedule. Lucien and I were standing at the front of the convention hall.

He smiled down at me and tucked some of my hair behind my ear. I leaned into his touch. Today, we were wearing black and red again. I had a flowy, blood-red shirt on over black leggings and Lucien was wearing black jeans and a tight black t-shirt.

Without a jacket, I could see the bulge of every muscle he had. I made him wear a jacket, though. I wouldn't be fighting females who looked at my mate or tried to flirt with him, and they would.

"When we get home, I'll run you a bath and massage your feet. You've been standing too long," he murmured.

"I'm not that pregnant yet, Lucien. I can stand all day and be fine," I giggled.

"No, I get to pamper you. I've behaved, even when men were ogling you. I want to spoil you so you don't get any ideas about running away with them," Lucien chuckled.

"I would never. You are the only man for me, my love." I smiled.

"Good."

A commotion erupted near the doors. I peered around Lucien to see what was happening. Fifteen young men, their faces hard and eyes narrowed, stormed through the doors, scanning the room with hostile glares. The one at the front focused entirely on me, his intense gaze unwavering.

"What's going on?" I asked in a commanding tone.

I started walking, heading directly toward the group. Lucien was trailing close behind me. He was radiating a menacing aura, the one Alphas used when protecting their land. Mine matched. This man was definitely here to challenge me.

When I got to the tables, I stood and crossed my arms. Stanton's left hand was behind his back, going for his gun. Talia wore a slightly aggressive look on her face. They'd assessed it like we had.

"We're here to tell you we aren't joining your bullshit collective and we aren't leaving. This was our territory first. If you don't want trouble, you pay us to keep the peace," the man at the front said.

"What's your name?" I asked in a bored tone.

He smirked. "I'm Eddie. Head of the *Rogue Kings*."

"I'm Bellamy. Queen of the Eaten Heart Collective. This is my territory. You will submit to me or you will die," I informed him matter-of-factly.

The men chuckled. They were young and cocky. I understood the stupidity of youth, especially young men who had power over a city the way they had before I arrived.

"There are fifteen of us and what… ten of you? This isn't even my entire crew. Most of the people here are women. We're not above putting down a few bitches to get our point across," he said with a dark grin.

None of these boys moved like they had more than basic warrior training. Lucien wasn't elite level, but he was close. Thomas was probably about the same. That left me, Talia, and Stanton to be the powerhouses. I didn't want Charlie fighting, but she was elite as well and could benefit us.

"Stanton, we're going with CP95, short stack. Green?" I instructed.

"Lit," he responded and reached into his pocket for his phone.

What was that?' Lucien asked.

'I told him to record me and Talia making an example of these boys. Stay back. My evaluation says they'll back off when six of them are down,' I explained.

'Why is he recording?'

'We'll take the video to their hideout and give them a couple options. Don't worry. I've got this.'

'Let me know if you need help.' he replied.

Talia moved closer to me as I walked through the gap in the tables. We would be the primaries in the fight, so no one could say we wouldn't be as strong without the males around. Getting your ass handed to you by two small females didn't help with a gang's image. This was meant to teach them a lesson and embarrass them too much to try this bullshit again.

"Everyone, behind the tables. Leave this to Talia and me," I ordered calmly.

They moved back. Some of the boys started looking uncomfortable. They should. Rogues rarely backed away from a fight. Rogue Alphas never let others defend us. We were often better fighters than everyone else. Our wolves didn't like letting others take over.

"You're making a mistake little girl. You should've just given up," Eddie chuckled.

I smirked and glanced at Talia. She was ready to fight. The men stepped up and formed a horseshoe around us. I watched for signs of the first attack.

A surprise attack began with a fist aimed at my face from the side, a clear signal for the rest of the group to launch their attack. I quickly grabbed the fist, twisted it, and applied sharp pressure to the elbow of the man who attacked. There was a satisfying crack to the sound of the joint breaking. It got Aurora excited.

Talia and I moved fluidly. We hadn't fought together in many years, but I was still familiar with the feeling of her presence. My observation skills and memory of her fighting style helped me know when to duck, when to assist, and when to move further away.

She was very fast, but had to slow down enough for the camera to catch her. I did, too. It was annoying.

Throughout the fight, I barely registered switching opponents. Aurora partially took over. This type of fight was the only way to satisfy her bloodlust.

The air filled with screams, groans, grunts, and the sound of shattering bones. It was exhilarating. I ripped open my opponent's chest with my claws and pulled out his heart. As his body hit the ground with a thud, silence fell, and I realized the attack was over.

A fog lifted. The werewolves hadn't retreated after six went down, like I thought they would. At least nine lay on the ground, their bodies still, while several more limped out the door, leaving a trail of blood.

Eddie paused at the door and stared at me. I caught his eye. A look of fear and disgust came over him as I took a big bite of the heart I held in my hand.

After I swallowed it, I smirked. "You're next. Now, run. I love a good hunt."

He didn't have to be told twice. Eddie turned and fled. I sighed and finished eating the heart. There were too many rogues around for me to do anything else.

I walked around, checking the bodies. Only three were dead. It was pretty good. I wanted to leave as many alive as possible. Witnesses were great for adding to a threat, but people who had experienced it made for more expert testimony.

Stanton was already in Thomas' office, calling Drake. They would pool their information to get us close to where the gang was hiding. Lyric called the supernatural police force, and they were on their way to pick up the injured wolves.

"Bellamy," Lucien said from behind me.

I knew I shouldn't be nervous. He'd seen me fight and kill before, but there was something about killing other wolves. Especially since they used to be pack wolves. He might not be happy with me. I turned to him.

Lucien used a tissue to clean some blood from my chin. He smiled softly as he took care of me. I felt tears in my eyes and he started to look worried.

His grip on my hand was firm as he pulled me from the brightly lit lobby into a dim hallway, and we made our way to the office with our temporary access key. The door clicked shut; the lock engaging with a firm thud before he turned back to me.

"Are you alright, chouchoutte? Dillon said you didn't want to eat another heart, but I don't think you should go vegetarian while pregnant," he said with a gentle smile on his face.

I snorted a little at the idea of actually trying to not eat meat with my cravings. "You aren't mad or disgusted by me?"

"Why would I be? Everyone knows you eat the hearts of your enemies. You fought amazingly, my little queen," Lucien purred.

A blush spread over my cheeks. How could I have ever thought he wouldn't love me? My mate never shied away from my darker, more violent side.

He loved me after the vampires. Lucien wanted to go with me when I was tracking the rogue who tried to kill him. He made love to me after we fought the goblins.

My Lucien was practically a rogue King himself in his attitudes. It was hard for me to reconcile after years of living with Kieran and the wolves at Daylight Moon.

Only Dilly, the boys, Clint, and Daniel ever accepted me entirely. It might seem like a lot, but our pack was large, and I had to hide so much of myself from everyone there.

Lucien pulled me toward a chair in the office and settled me in his lap. He wrapped his arms around me and just held me. I leaned against his chest and relaxed as his scent washed over me.

"I don't know why I was worried. You've always accepted me," I sighed.

"And I always will. Your violent side isn't a deal breaker for me, chouchoutte. Just like mine isn't one for you. We're Alphas. It means we have to be stronger, tougher, and more ready to kill to protect our people."

"Kieran always had a problem with it," I replied softly.

"Kieran saw you as a monster hiding in the form of a little girl. I see a vibrant, powerful, protective woman," he whispered as he nuzzled my neck.

"I love you, Lucien."

"And I love you, Bellamy. No matter what," Lucien answered. "Now, tell me about your plan."

Chapter 98: An Ultimatum

[Bellamy]

Just over an hour later, Stanton, Talia, and I were on our way to the suspected hideout of the 'Rogue Kings'. The city gradually transitioned into suburbs, which in turn gave way to a semi-rural landscape.

Because I could smell the ex-packs' scent growing stronger as we headed toward their suspected hideout, there was little need for a hunt. Rather than escape, they retreated to their not-so-secret hideaway. They didn't expect me to pursue them. I have to admit; it was a bit insulting.

Our plan was fairly simple. We'd go into whatever shelter they had, play the fight on a projector, and let the gang know they could join me or die. There was no option for fleeing the territory now. When Eddie challenged me, he ensured that fate for all of his people.

We pulled up in front of a wide, low building, its weathered wood painted a faded green. A small, weathered porch attached to the house was probably the only remarkable feature. A gentle breeze blew as we unloaded. Stanton slipped me a small handgun.

Most supernaturals wouldn't use human weapons, but Stanton showed me long ago how useful they could be. No one expected you to pull a gun in a fight between supernaturals. Knives were possible, but never firearms. We'd caught a few people off guard when we used to run together. As little as they expected firearms, they expected them even less from a child.

Stanton pulled out the portable projector, and Talia smiled darkly. She was excited about being able to kill the leader and anyone who sided with him. I was too. Securing my territory was one of the guilty pleasures of my life. I shouldn't like the violence, but I *was* a rogue born, after all.

I led the march to the front door. There would be no friendly knocking or posturing at a bottleneck. This was my territory, and they were trespassing. I kicked in the door and walked into the large main room.

Some injured wolves were still being treated in the sparsely furnished room. He hadn't lied that the fifteen wolves in his initial contact weren't the entirety of his crew. At least five more men and three women were present. I wasn't worried about any of them.

They all looked startled. Eddie pushed forward menacingly. I smirked as he stopped a few feet away. He started to speak, but I held up a hand to silence him.

"Talia, please come in," I called behind me.

"Thank you, Queen Bellamy," she replied and entered the room.

Talia didn't need to be invited, but no one needed to know that. Stanton wasn't farther behind her. He spotted a good wall to set up the projection. The wolves were too stunned to do anything. They watched it all silently, only turning back to me when Stanton nodded that he was ready.

"Ladies and gentlemen, I am Queen Bellamy Carrington of the Eaten Heart Collective. I am here to give you two options. There's no negotiation. There's no third option. There's no fighting back," I announced. "Please begin, Stanton."

He hit play on the phone, and the video of our fight played against the wall. The ones who weren't part of the initial attack gasped. I could smell their fear as they watched Talia and me tear through the wolves, who were probably their best fighters.

It wasn't a long fight. They watched as their leader ordered the retreat. They watched me eat the heart of the last wolf I fought. At the end, the video restarted. The video would continue looping until I was done.

"Now you've seen what a warning looks like, you have to make a decision. I'm going to order you to submit to me. If you want to live, you will. You will be tried and punished for your crimes against the community. When you are finished with whatever the humans decide to do with you, you will be given a job in my collective. Any infractions afterward will result in your death," I stated coolly. "If you want to die, don't submit. Talia and I will permit our bear friend to join us in the slaughter. You know how much bears like pack wolves. Eddie will not be spared. He left his people behind and never even tried to fight."

I pointed to the video, and everyone looked at it. They could clearly see Eddie backing off as the fighting began. He watched his men go down, offered no help, and waited longer than he should have to call them off.

Stanton and Talia stepped outside for the next part. We were all feeling hostile. My Alpha aura could incite them, and we didn't want to risk it. Once they were gone, I released my dominance.

"Submit," I commanded with a growl.

Out of the fourteen wolves, eight submitted. Eddie looked like he wanted to, but didn't. Two of the males who had fought at the convention center and three of the males who hadn't were glaring at me. They chose poorly.

"Those who submitted, grab what you can carry and wait outside for me to finish this," I ordered.

They scurried away. After a few moments, one female came out of the back and tried to get past two of the males who were staying. One of them grabbed her arm roughly and held her. She tried pulling away and begged him to let her go.

I pulled the little gun from under my shirt and shot him in the shoulder of the arm that held her. He shouted and released. The female ran past everyone else.

"You try to harm members of my collective or stop them from following my orders and you will be punished."

"Human weapons are cheating," Eddie growled.

"Cheating? Says who?" I laughed. "*Pack wolves?* I am the High Queen of the Association. I am a rogue. *And* I don't follow *pack* rules."

"If you hate pack wolves so much, why are you mated to one?"

"I don't hate them. I hate the way they follow idiotic traditions and all the rules they make that aren't needed. Now, let my people leave and I won't have to shoot any more of yours," I sneered.

Talia and Stanton came back into the room. He grabbed the video set up and put it outside before blocking the door shut. The remaining wolves prepared themselves as much as they could, but they had no idea about what was about to happen.

There's an aura of determination that came over people when they faced a situation of kill or be killed. The struggle to survive fundamentally alters who people are. Such a dramatic change that their families wouldn't recognize them. It can be chilling.

I would never want Lucien to see me like that. It was one reason I told him to stay behind and take care of everyone. When we first dealt with Eddie, it was just a fight to him and his people. Now it was more. Now they knew this was a fight to the death. They would fight harder, and so would we.

I let Aurora take over.

This was the thing hunters were afraid of, the monsters we could become in these instances. A slow smile spread over my face, embracing my beast.

Time to be the queen.

Chapter 99: An Unlikely Lead

Yesterday morning, while Bellamy got some extra sleep, Talia pulled me from training. She said she wanted me to stop smelling fearful around vampires. It was like a seasoning to some of them and I wouldn't be a great support to Bellamy if I had that scent.

"We are going to spend the entirety of this time getting you more comfortable with my kind. You don't have to like them, or even be friends with more than just me, but you have to be confident and fearless. You're an Alpha, you can't like how this feels," she stated.

I nodded. "That would be helpful. I can't be the best leader of my people if I am afraid of a certain threat."

"Good. We'll start with a fight, then a feeding. You've spent the last few days with me, I've made sure to talk to you and try to make you at ease. Except for the issue the other day. I don't like people patting my head. Once you are comfortable, we can talk about a binding. I am blood-bound with Bellamy. It gives her some of my ability with vampire magic and she can scent the age and power of any vampire she meets. It makes her less susceptible to mind control from my kind," Talia replied.

It made me nervous, but I needed to get over this. It was like Bellamy's shutdown. If I couldn't act and react, I would just be a hindrance to her in the long run. I wasn't acting like much of an Alpha.

Talia didn't seem to put much effort into the fight. It was more like she was assessing me. The longer it went on, the angrier I got about not being effective. Soon, I was on the ground and Talia had me in a painful hold.

"You fight well. Bellamy will have you in top form before the babies come. If you train with my precious puppy, he will whip you into shape while she is recovering. I think Stanton's training might be a better fit for you style-wise, but you would benefit from training in every style much more than just one."

"Can you let me go, Talia?" I groaned.

"Oh! Sorry!" she laughed, releasing me and sitting on the ground next to me. "Now that you know how long you can fight with me; it should give you more confidence."

"How so?" I asked, sitting up.

"Because…. Right. Sorry. I didn't explain. I was assessing and raising my fighting level as we went. You lasted ten minutes. You can fight off a single vampire of up to one thousand years old. I bet you did some serious damage to the ones who caught you." Talia grinned.

"Not serious enough," I muttered.

"Shush, mon loup. You did well."

"I'm not your wolf, Talia."

"You are my wolf as much as Bellamy is my pet. It's an endearment, loup. Get over it, I won't stop." She chuckled. "Let me give you a hug, then we'll work on other things."

I sighed and opened my arms. Talia grinned and stepped in for a hug. Bellamy and Dillon both told me it was impossible to get Talia to change anything. She always did what she wanted, when she wanted.

When Talia let me go, I stood. She had a smug look on her face. I could imagine it was from me giving in so easily.

Talia probably thought I was weak. I didn't really care. I needed help, and she was one of the oldest vampires in the world. If anyone could get me over the residual fear, she could.

"And that was a properly done feeding," she stated.

I opened my eyes wide and put my hand to my neck. There was no blood or wound. I didn't feel any pain. There was no overwhelming need or sting when it happened.

"You were fearful when they did it. That amplifies the discomfort of the bite. When relaxed, one can barely feel it. They wanted you scared because they liked it. No one of my bloodline does. I never turned anyone who would do what Marion did," Talia told me.

The realization came over me. I fought a vampire, a powerful one. She fed on me after I lost, and I didn't feel anything bad or terrifying. It was a relief.

"I've healed your fear. If you wish, we can form a blood bond later and you can be even stronger. For now, the fear and terror of the time you spent with the vampires is being bled off. You will have no emotional reaction to memories of that time. I've assisted your brain in processing."

"Why? How?"

"Bellamy's territory will include some vampires. You cannot be afraid of them, or they will walk all over you. One ability in my bloodline is to instill our allies with confidence and heal some emotional wounds. The feeding marked you as my ally. Now, I want to talk to you about something I tasted in your blood," she said.

"What? It's not something bad, right?" I asked.

"No… you just taste, a little… roguish. I've never tasted a pack wolf who was mated to a born rogue. You smell like pack but taste wilder than that. Maybe you're becoming more rogue than pack. Bellamy changed after joining Daylight Moon, as did the flavor of her blood. This might be something to look into." Talia giggled.

It had been on my mind ever since then. The way my power mingled with Bellamy's was amazing, shocking… and worrisome. She told Gerard she would smell it if we started turning rogue. Would she say anything, though?

Remus and I debated it. We discussed it whenever we had a spare moment. When Bellamy said she was thinking more like a pack Alpha, she didn't seem worried. Maybe it wasn't something to be concerned about.

What was most important to me was Bellamy's safety. If becoming more rogue-like meant I could keep her and the pups safer, I wouldn't mind it. Especially if it would protect my pack, as well.

***

After the police took away the unconscious men at the convention center, I worked with Bellamy's lieutenants and Thomas to clean everything up. We were setting up for the final intake of the night. People would just have to understand that Bellamy was away on business for now. She said she wanted to do one more group before heading home. I hoped she was alright.

As I was manning the non-wolf desk, I noticed a man staring at me. He was a wolf, rogue born by his scent. Nearly two days surrounded by rogues and ex-packs had honed my nose. I could smell the difference between types of rogues, the wrongness of the ex-packs and wildness of the rogue borns.

He was shorter, stockier, than most wolves. There was a dangerous air about him, even though he looked like the friendly good-ole-boy type with dark blond hair, clear blue eyes, and a warm smile. I wondered more about what he was carrying.

In his hands, he had a box. It didn't seem like it was anything hazardous. I couldn't smell it well because of all the different scents in the room, but it smelled a little like leather and ink.

I stood up and walked over to him. He didn't look nervous about catching my attention. I suspected he had planned it.

"Can I help you with that?" I asked politely.

"Actually, it's for you and your Queen. An early wedding present." He chuckled. "I'll take it to the table over there. I know you wouldn't like to have your hands full if something happened."

"I appreciate that." I nodded and led him to the table.

He set the box down and took the lid off. It was full of older books. I pulled one of the thick, leather-bound books out. Opening the unmarked cover, I read the first page and stared back at the man.

"A History of Rogues?" I asked.

"One of the last four copies. All of our handwritten histories were combined to create a dozen sets of books. We never thought to make more than the first set. Every hundred years since the 15th century, we collect histories and create a new book for that century.

"This is my family's collection along with some books on rogue physiology written in the 60s. There are some rare books and journals there, too. Stuff my family wrote, but never shared with anyone," he stated.

"Why are you giving me this?" I asked. "Aren't you joining the collective?"

"Nah. I'm retiring. Heading to Alaska to join Icy Death. Rogues don't become house pets like pack wolves when we get old. We go off to hunt until we die. Don't worry about Bella, though, she's an Alpha. She'll rule her collective until she has an heir or until she dies," he assured me.

"Don't you want your kids to have these?"

"I don't have any. Anyway, I gotta run. I need to get out of the region as soon as possible. Tell Bella, Kyle's gone crazy. He's obsessed. Kingston refused to give up his collective, that's why Kyle killed him. Kingston was bad, Kyle's worse. I'm not sticking around," he told me urgently.

"Can I tell Bellamy who this gift is from?"

"She may not be too happy with it. You can tell her it was Silas Greene. Let her know I was the one that took out the rogue the other night. We didn't know Bella was your mate. He got himself hired at the restaurant when one of our contacts in your house told us you were going out to dinner. I took care of that guy, too. No other spies are in your pack."

"Kyle is the one trying to kill me?" I pressed.

"Yeah. Something about an old family curse and killing your family would bring him good luck. I don't know, like I said, the kid's nuts. I better go. Goddess watch over you… that's what you pack wolves say, right?" Silas chuckled.

"Yeah. Don't die," I replied.

"Bella's gonna make a rogue of you yet." He shook his head and walked out the doors.

I looked through the box of books while I waited for Bellamy to return and worked to check-in shapeshifters and vampires. It all felt a little hollow. I knew who was trying to kill me now. I wanted to go hunt him down and kill him, but he was an Alpha.

I would have to declare my intentions to the Association. It could cause a war between my pack and his collective. Would Bellamy's collective join? She might decide to keep her people out of it.

Was it seriously because of an old quarrel? How would that improve his luck? I needed much more information than I had. I needed Bellamy.

Chapter 100: Return of the Queen

Bellamy, Stanton, and Talia returned almost an hour later. They were bloody, and none of it seemed to be their blood. Some of the pack born wolves gasped, as did a few of the non-wolves. The rogues seemed quite happy, though.

She smiled brightly when she saw me. I chuckled. She looked so proud of herself. No pack Alpha would meet with their people while covered in blood and… a few chunks now that I was looking closer.

"Let's get this last intake done. I need a shower," she announced laughingly.

The rogues and vampires tittered. My mate knew her audience. I went to her and took her hand, guiding her to the front of the room.

All the attendees came to the front to meet her. Some vampires asked for a taste of the blood she wore, and Bellamy allowed it. Even after Talia helped me, I don't think I could have handled strange vampires licking me.

The intake went just as the others had, and soon we were done. Bellamy went to talk to Thomas while I directed the packing of our items and got the SUV loaded. I would wait until we were home to talk to her about Silas. The way he said she wouldn't like it made me worry.

I wondered what their connection was. A few people in the pack tried calling her Bella, and she told them to call her Amy instead. I knew she had certain names for certain people and the other way around, but I could feel her discomfort whenever someone called her Bella.

On the road home, Bellamy chattered about what happened with the 'Rogue Kings'. She laughed about the one she shot. I agreed with them. Guns were cheating, but it got her home to me safely.

After a while, she grew quiet. She was probably tired from the fight. I tried to talk to her a little, but she didn't talk much. It was such an odd change. I figured I'd take her straight to our room to avoid more interactions with people.

When we finally arrived at the packhouse, I went to help unload the SUV. I had Thierry come to take the books to my office and lock the door. They needed to be kept safe until we could look at them and decide where the best place for them was. Bellamy might want them in her office.

I took Bellamy upstairs for a shower. I helped her wash her hair and scrub off all the remains of the men who opposed her. She was quiet and introspective. I wondered what was going on in her head.

We settled in our room, and I brushed her hair. Bellamy still said little, but a couple of quiet thanks. It was worrisome. There was no reason for the shift in behavior.

"Lucien, who did you talk to while I was gone?" she asked softly.

"A man came and gave me a box of books about rogues. He said it was a wedding present."

"Did he tell you his name?" Her voice was breathy.

"Silas Greene. He said he was retiring to Alaska and he was the one who killed the rogue the other night," I answered.

She started shaking and turned around, kneeling between my legs and looking up at me. There was fear in her eyes. Her arms slipped around my waist and she held me as tightly as she could.

"Who is he, chouchoutte?"

"One of King Fuller's men. They were called 'The Shades'. Mr. Greene, Mr. Scarlet, and Mr. Brown. Each had a specific job. Mr. Greene was assassination. Mr. Scarlet was torture. And Mr. Brown…. He trained the girls. That wasn't Mr. Greene. Halfway home, I could smell him. It was Mr. Brown. I could never forget the scent of him.

"Greene had brown eyes and a shaved head. Scarlet also shaved his head but was lazy about it. He had dark blue eyes and black hair. Mr. Brown looked like a very nice man. He had blond hair and lighter blue eyes. The girls, who didn't know him, trusted him," she explained, looking sick.

"You left before he got you, chouchoutte. Why does this scare you instead of making you angry?" I asked.

Bellamy buried her face into my chest. I could feel the hot wetness of her tears. Gently, I pulled her arms from around me and picked her up in my lap, holding her while she shook.

"He cornered me in the library once. I wasn't strong enough. He touched me and told me he was looking forward to me joining the collective. I stuffed it down so deep, I didn't even think of it when my dad asked about me being touched. It was before I was cursed.

"Before King Fuller started giving me work for my safe passage until I made a decision. Brown was the reason I knew what Fuller did to girls. He told me how training would start, what he would make me feel before he started teaching me to pleasure men."

My rage exploded. I gripped her tighter. That bastard was right in front of me and I let him go. I still didn't know enough about her past to know when to kick someone's ass and when to leave them alone.

If he lied to me about his name, what else could he have been lying about? He knew he would be long gone before she got back. Maybe he thought she'd told me. That made sense. If I had any clue about him, I would have ripped his head off.

"I'm so sorry, Bellamy. I shouldn't have let him go. I should have made him wait for you, then I could have killed him," I murmured as I rubbed my face in her hair. "He'll never get you. I promise. Now I doubt the other things he told me, though."

"What other things, Lucien?" Bellamy asked, pulling away.

"He said Kyle's gone crazy. King Fuller was killed because he wouldn't give up the collective. Kyle's even worse than his father. Kyle's the one trying to kill my family. Something about a family curse and getting good luck from wiping us all out. When Brown saw you were my mate, he decided not to kill me. He killed the last spy here and decided to retire," I explained.

Bellamy looked like she was processing. She climbed off my lap and started pacing. Sometimes she would shake her head or nod. Maybe she was consulting with Aurora. Suddenly, she turned back to me and smiled.

"He wouldn't have any reason to stay in Limb Torn. According to my spies a couple years ago, Kyle was saving himself for his mate. No need to train concubines. Are you planning to challenge him?"

"He's an Alpha who tried to kill my family. And I do intend to challenge him. I don't know what the procedure is between pack and rogue, though," I admitted.

"I'll call Jonas in the morning. We may need to investigate. Brown could've just been trying to start shit before leaving." She sighed.

"I thought that might be possible after you told me who he was."

"This will help us in the investigation, though. If Kyle isn't the one trying to kill you, then it can't be Calvin either. He told me once that he would kill Brown if he ever saw him. Several females who came to his collective from Limb Torn were really messed up. That means he's working for a king from out of the region. We can look at it later. For now, I need to rest. I'm exhausted. This is a wonderful lead, Lucien. I just wish it hadn't been from him." Bellamy smiled slightly.

"I know, ma belle. Let's sleep. You had a long day and those pups didn't make it any easier," I said, holding my hands out to her.

Bellamy crossed the room, slipped between my arms, and pushed me onto the bed. I pulled her tightly against me and kissed her. She'd shaken off the fear and was back to normal. It made me feel better about everything. She had an idea. We had a direction, and we could move forward with confidence.

Chapter 101: A Long Awaited Meeting

It had been a week since Lucien met Mr. Brown. Jonas said he'd take care of Brown if he showed up at Icy Death, and we'd have to call an emergency meeting of the Association about Kyle. It would be a conference call and Lucien would have to attend. No one was free until almost a week after the incident and it made me angry to have to wait. I wanted to just say fuck it and look into it myself, but Lucien said it would be better if we had the Association on our side.

Usually, issues between rogue and pack Alphas were settled in fights between packs and collectives. None of them were personal like this one. Usually, it was about territory issues or resource disputes.

They would need the full panel to discuss it, especially since it affected the collective of one of the High Rogue Alphas. The question of my collective joining the fight was a given. Lucien's pack was part of my collective. Daylight Moon and the rest of the Eaten Heart would fight if it came to war.

The best thing that came out of the week of waiting was the experiment! Maple and her mate came for the joining ceremony just a couple of days before the meeting with the Association, and it was a resounding success. I showed her how to close the links and set up notifications for when someone in the pack linked her. Her mate was thrilled.

Lucien said it felt different to accept her than it did to accept any other wolf. He told me I was much more powerful than any other wolf he'd accepted, but there was a unique quality to accepting Maple. A more untamed component. I was excited to see where it would lead in the future.

***

We were sitting in Lucien's office, waiting for the call to come in. It was tedious, but I had something to entertain me a little. I was leafing through one of the books Mr. Brown brought. The smell of him had only fully dissipated the day before.

Most of the books were books King Fuller had forbidden me to touch. The ones that were handwritten especially intrigued me. Sometimes they were hard to read, but I found some stuff I had never heard of before. Things that rogue Alphas used to be able to do, including mind-linking their people.

I wondered why we weren't able to anymore. Of course, no one I knew of ever tried. It would make running the territory much easier. It seemed there was no limit to the distance. The book stated that a rogue King once linked the writer from two towns over. Most likely, it was because rogues rarely lived as closely as pack wolves.

More than anything, I wanted to try it out. We found I was still connected to Daylight Moon, even though I was a member of Lune Rouge. I'd accidentally linked Dilly out of habit. We hadn't even realized it for most of the conversation.

The uproar was huge once we realized I shouldn't be able to do that. Lucien could link members of Daylight Moon who were in his territory now as well. It would make looking out for him much easier. I wanted to have every advantage.

We knew all wolves gain the strengths of their mates, but no one had imagined that meant Lucien would share my connections to the pack. It hadn't happened before the Luna ceremony. We'd never really know if it was that, the second marking, or our combining our power that did it.

***

Finally, the phone rang. I sat up quickly and tossed the book onto the coffee table before heading to sit in Lucien's lap. He answered and put the phone on speaker.

"Lune Rouge, this is Alpha Lucien."

"Greetings, Alpha Lucien. This is Chief Alpha Brett Daily. I have Stuart Malik and Vance Pappas, the other Chief Alphas, on the line. High Kings Jonas Harper and Quinn Sharpclaw are here as well. Is your mate ready?" he asked in a laughing tone.

That fucker just relegated me to 'Alpha's mate' in a meeting of the Association! I seethed. If I were to hold this seat and title, I *would* be treated with the respect that came with it.

Lucien squeezed me and I pulled myself out of my mini-rage. He was right. I needed to control myself more. This wasn't the time for a tantrum.

"I'm sure you meant to ask if High Queen Bellamy is with me. Otherwise, it would be as disrespectful as me referring to you as Luna Opal's mate," Lucien chuckled. "I can only say the High Queen is here. It is up to her if she is ready."

"Thank you, Alpha Lucien. I am ready. If we could start instead of focusing on how insecure some males are at the thought of a female being ranked among them, I would appreciate it," I replied.

Jonas and Quinn started laughing. I could've sworn I heard at least one additional snicker from the line. I was here to deal with the issue at hand, not make friends.

"I'll take over from here, Brett. You take a breath and try to find your balls." Jonas snorted.

"The issue at hand is what the results would be if Alpha Lucien challenged King Kyle Fuller. Since a personal challenge often results in the loser's people being taken on by the winning Alpha. Is it even okay for the challenge to be issued?" one of the men asked.

"Of course, it's okay for the challenge to be issued, Stuart!" Quinn growled. "The man tried to kill Queen Bellamy's pups! She should be challenging him for that alone! Lucien has precedence since he tried to kill four members of his family. If Lucien fails to kill Kyle, Bellamy can end him. Either way, since Lucien's pack is part of her collective, he would gain the ex-packs and she would gain the rest of Limb Torn."

"We don't even know that it's actually Kyle and not some sort of subterfuge from Jared Brown," I interjected. "Neither of us can challenge Kyle until it's cleared up. We need a proper investigation. Someone has to question Kyle."

"All of our investigation teams are busy right now. We've had some issues in the south and up near the Canadian border," Jonas replied.

"It would probably help if you had more than two…." I sighed.

"If WE had more than two, Queen Bellamy," he stated.

"Right…. Well, I can go talk to him. He'll answer my questions. Kyle thinks I might actually change my mind even after years of refusing his offers," I said.

"Offers?" Jonas asked. "How many?"

I gave them a rundown of my time in the Limb Torn Collective, Kyle's father promising me to him, and Kyle offering for me every three months since he turned seventeen.

The Chief Alphas were livid. The High Kings were only slightly less so. They didn't like the idea of someone giving a female away. It wasn't our way.

"So, I think it will work. I'll contact him and set up a meeting in neutral territory," I told them.

"The hell you will," Lucien growled.

I stiffened and turned to stare at him. He looked seriously pissed. If I weren't an Alpha myself, I would have been a little afraid. As it was, I was getting angry.

"What, exactly, do you mean by *that*, Alpha Lucien?" I inquired sternly.

"You are my mate; those are my pups. You will *not* endanger yourself and them by going. We will wait for an investigative team to be free and step up our security in the meantime."

I jumped off his lap and turned to him. Getting close to his face, I snarled.

"I am High Queen. I am an elite warrior. AND I am the *mother* of these pups, Alpha. The only risk is in waiting. The longer we hold off, the more likely it is that he'll try something else. What if Brown was lying? What if someone poisons me instead of trying to stab me?"

"You can smell poisons. I couldn't even smell the last one, but you did! This is not up for discussion, Bellamy! I said no!" he shouted.

"I don't care what you said. This isn't your decision!" I replied.

"Maybe we should let you two talk about this. Just give us a call with what you decide," Brett said slowly.

"There's no need for that. Send an investigative team as soon as one is available. She's not going," Lucien responded and hung up.

"You can't do that! You don't speak for me in these matters, Lucien! I'm going!"

"You are not," he stated firmly.

"What are you going to do, lock me up?" I asked.

"Don't push me on this, Bellamy. You're my mate. You will not go see him."

"Are you jealous again? Or do you just doubt my ability to take care of myself?" I seethed.

"Neither. You will not see him. This is the end of the discussion. Get out of my office," Lucien growled in a low tone.

"Fine. I'll get out. You sit here and feel proud of yourself for whatever you think you fucking accomplished with your little power trip," I sneered and slammed out of the room.

He had some fucking nerve thinking he could tell me not to go! I wasn't some idiot who would go alone. I wasn't a child with low impulse control.

Lucien had no right to forbid me from talking to Kyle. This was my family, too. I wouldn't wait just to appease his stupid whims. I needed an ally.

Chapter 102: Time and Space

After Bellamy left the room, I started to get a handle on my anger. It was like she didn't see how dangerous the whole situation was. Those High Kings encouraging it didn't help. Once the investigation was done, I would challenge Kyle and Bellamy would understand.

She was *my* mate, and she needed to do what *I* said. I was fine with her taking care of her collective however she wanted, but this was unacceptable. She was endangering our family, not saving it. If something happened to her and the pups….

My stomach twisted at the idea of losing her. I trusted she could fight. I knew she was strong. There was something in me that said I would lose her if she went after Kyle.

I learned long ago to trust my gut. Bellamy couldn't go or I would never see her again. Losing her would kill me. Not a part of me. It would destroy me and I would die.

Why didn't she see that? How could she be so cavalier about a potentially dangerous confrontation? She was acting like an impulsive child, not like an Alpha, not like a mother, and not like a mate.

I worked on my transfer papers. Only about twenty people didn't like the idea of a rogue as their Luna. They applied to other packs, none of the ones allied with Bellamy. On Monday, I reached out to the Alphas in those packs to see if they could accommodate new wolves and their families. Now, it was a matter of finalizing everything.

It was sad to lose some of my people, but the amount who stayed was terrific. I knew many people talked to Cara, Olive, and the Elite Ten about their experience with Bellamy. The stories of her fighting rogues and hunters, caring for injured wolves, and taking care of children in the pack were beneficial.

The entire packhouse staff loved her. They talked about her with glowing praise to anyone who would listen. The teens were educating their parents and Maurice was talking about getting rogue education classes together for adults.

My pack, generally, didn't like change, but they were working hard to change and grow for Bellamy. Several of the much older ones said they didn't have a problem simply because they didn't think I'd ever find a mate and it was distressing my mother to take care of Luna's work when she should be retired.

Taking care of the pack from across the country for half the year was tiring for her. We found that leaving things until later didn't help. Celesta and Simone handled the smaller tasks, but Maman addressed the larger issues from Liana's pack during weekly video calls.

In the last week, Bellamy proved herself to be a tougher warrior than the persona she adopted while playing the softer woman. We had a schedule for sparring because so many males wanted to prove themselves against her. It was how she was winning the warriors over. After she beat them, she gave them tips on how to fight better and would work with them in training.

Several of our elite warriors were getting up early to join us in the Elite Ten's training. Stanton, Randy, and Talia picked over the warriors and selected a few for personal attention in their respective fighting styles. The excitement in our ranks was palpable.

Bellamy brought so much anticipation for the future with her. She wasn't just important to me. She was important to the pack.

***

It was about dinner time when I finally finished the processing. I contacted the wolves who were planning to move and gave them the details for connecting with the Gammas of their new packs.

They were apologetic about wanting to leave. I told them they were always welcome to come visit, and I hoped they would come back once they saw this was really for the best. None of them seemed to believe it would be.

I debated having dinner at home. If Bellamy wanted to continue fighting, it would be best to do it away from everyone else. In the end, I went to the main dining room.

Being seen would make my people feel more at ease. Being around them would calm me. My pack was my comfort for most of my life.

Entering the room, I scanned the people there. I didn't see Bellamy. She was sometimes late, though.

Things would come up and she would deal with them, or she would get caught up talking with pack members. It didn't concern me until the meal was finished and she hadn't shown up.

I tried linking her, but she blocked me. Panic flooded me. Did she go off on her own to deal with Kyle? Did she run away again?

Rushing to our quarters, I searched and found she had cooked something and packed some clothes. I linked all the Elite Ten, her whole family, and anyone I could think of, asking if they'd seen her.

'Remus, can you reach Aurora?' I asked.

'She told me to go fuck myself, but she didn't want us to worry too much. She said they need time and space. They are not going after Kyle… yet,' he answered.

I growled as I walked toward the guest rooms. Maybe Stanton or Talia knew where she was. Aurora confirmed they were still planning to go see him, even though I expressly forbade it.

***

Stanton was cleaning his guns when I entered his room. He raised an eyebrow at me but continued his work. I took a calming breath. The last thing I needed was a fight with a bear who would shoot me if he felt it was helpful to him.

"What's up, Alpha?" he asked with a half-smile, his eyes focused entirely on the weapon in his hands.

"Have you seen Bellamy? She didn't come to dinner and no one has seen her since early this afternoon." I inquired.

"Yeah. She came by around two. You really pissed her off," Stanton laughed. "You're lucky she likes you, she was fit to tear your head off."

"Where is she?"

"Staying somewhere safe and away from you until she gets her anger under control. You know how it is for Alphas. We get pissed, we do something stupid, someone suffers. Let her alone," he said.

I sighed. "She's planning on going to talk to Kyle by herself. I told her not to. Aurora said something that makes me worried she's going to go still. I just want to know where she is so I know she's safe."

"Baby Belle told me all about the fight. Unlike other people, she never tries to paint herself in a more sympathetic light. I agreed with you. That didn't make her happy. I told her she needed to talk to you again with a clear head. She is on the pack lands and said she wouldn't leave unless she had business with her collective. Don't look for her. She's not ready to forgive you for commanding her," he explained.

"You're sure she won't try to leave?"

"Yes. I made her promise me. Belle keeps her promises. I made her promise she wouldn't leave until she talked to you with a calmer head. You need to chill out, too. You want to go shooting? Maybe spar with me? It looks like you need to blow off steam in a big bad way." Stanton chuckled.

I hadn't really spent time with the bears. Only training and a few meals. It would be a good chance to make alliances of my own.

"That sounds good. I've never used a gun before. Can you teach me?" I asked.

He grinned. "Not every day you get an Alpha who's willing to use a gun. Let's go. We set up a firing range shortly after we got here."

Stanton packed up a couple of guns and some ammunition, then led me out to the range he'd set up. He was right. It helped clear my head. It got a little competitive when I saw how good he was. I wouldn't stop until I was hitting the center of the target repeatedly.

When we were done, Stanton sparred with me. He didn't hold back at all. It was an amazing fight. I could fight full out, without something holding me back for the first time in months.

It was a hard fight. Bears were bulkier and more muscular than wolves. His hits were powerful.

I loved every minute of the fight. Every bruise, every cut, every injury was therapeutic. I did a fair bit of damage to him as well.

In the end, we headed back to our respective rooms worn out and well beaten. Maybe it would help me sleep without my tiny mate in my arms. It would be the first night we'd been apart since the misunderstanding at Daylight Moon.

After I took a shower, I climbed into bed and held Bellamy's pillow in my arms. With luck, she'd realize she was wrong soon enough. From there, we could work on other preparations.

Raising our security was important. Dillon was already bringing our technical security up to his standards. Jean-Claude was learning everything he could from Dillon.

I decided to make Dillon the technical equivalent of Jean-Claude, training people to care for and work our new security systems. We needed to bring our pack into current times.

I fell asleep with the future of my pack looking bright, but some trepidation about my relationship. Bellamy was strong. She just had to learn when to let others take over. I was relieved that she didn't leave me.

The idea of losing her, no matter how, gave me a stabbing feeling in my chest, but I wouldn't back down.

Chapter 103: Lost in a Dream

As if my day wasn't difficult enough, soon after closing my eyes, I found myself having one of my least favorite dreams. I hadn't had the dream since I met Bellamy and hoped I would never have it again. It wasn't the worst dream I would have, but it wasn't one I'd ever enjoyed.

I had no control over my body. As a passenger in my own memory, I observed my eighteen-year-old self, getting ready to enter the main dining room on Angelique's birthday. I would watch from behind my younger self's eyes as his heart was ripped out. I'd feel the agony of the severed bond. Worst of all, I couldn't stop him from exiling them.

Entering the dining room, I mentally groaned at the old wood paneling that used to hang on the walls. I'd practically been desensitized to the dream, except for that horrible paneling. It was one of the first renovations I headed. I never liked it, but it reminded me of that day even more after the rejection.

The room was full, as it had been back then. I saw people I knew would die or move away over the following nineteen years. My pack mates were eating and talking like I wasn't about to be destroyed.

Angelique stood near the table where we usually sat with our friends. Jean-Luc, Robert, Thierry, and Celesta were already there. Angelique was wearing one of her favorite light pink dresses. Her golden blonde hair fell down her back in waves.

Since my seventeenth birthday, I'd known she was my mate. We used to wait until our mate was of age if they were younger. For a year, I pined for my mate. All my thoughts were about our future together.

Halfway into the dining room, I stopped and she turned toward me. A look of distress was plain in her clear and sparkling hazel eyes. Back then, I mistakenly believed her worry was about being the Alpha's mate. But I knew she could do it and wanted to show I believed in her. I smiled at her.

"

Even though I watched her a lot, I somehow missed that she was in love with Jean-Luc. If I'd told my friends, I'm sure it would've turned out differently. I kept the secret to surprise her. It was one of my biggest regrets in the past.

Angelique walked over to me and stopped a couple of feet away. She nibbled her bottom lip a little. Bellamy did that sometimes. They had the same soft, pink lips.

"Can I speak to you in your office, Lucien?" she asked.

"Of course." I grinned.

My younger self attempted to take her hand, but she recoiled, folding her hands defensively. He didn't realize anything was wrong. He thought, I thought, she was shy about holding hands in public. Goddess, I was an idiot.

We walked up to my office, and I closed the door before crossing to where Angelique was pacing. It reminded me of Bellamy's pacing when she was working things out. How could I have missed all the ways they were the same?

I tried to embrace her, and she pushed herself away from me, dashing behind one of the armchairs. She put her arms out to ward me off. Now I could see the pain on her face.

Angelique didn't want to hurt me, but there was no other way to have what she truly desired. I ached for her as much as for my younger self. Knowing everything Bellamy told me about her parents made it even worse.

"Lucien, there's been a mistake," she started.

I chuckled nervously. "What do you mean, Angie?"

"The moon goddess made a mistake, Lucien. *You* are not my mate. You *weren't* meant for me. I don't love you. Not even the mate bond could *ever* make me love you as more than a friend. The thought of being with you makes me sick," Angelique said with tears in her eyes. "I, Angelique Petit, reject you, Lucien Deveraux, as my mate."

The stabbing pain shot through me like it did every time I had this dream. It felt like my heart was literally being ripped out, but I knew it wasn't nearly as much of a searing pain as she was going through. Somehow, she stood there only looking a little upset.

"Why, Angie? Why don't you want me?" I asked.

"I love someone else, Lucien. We'll leave. We'll transfer packs so you never have to see us again. You can find your second chance. Alphas usually have one. Find her and be happy. You wouldn't have been happy with me," Angelique murmured in a strained voice.

Rage filled me. How dare she love someone else? The burning anger in my stomach was at war with the agonizing pain in my chest. I lunged forward and grabbed her arm, yanking her close as she screamed and tried to pull away.

"You want to leave? Fine, I'll grant your wish as the last thing I ever do for you," I growled. "I accept your rejection. Angelique Petit, you are hereby banished from Lune Rouge. You have one hour to pack your things and leave my territory before you are considered a trespassing rogue. If you aren't gone by then, I'll kill you and whoever it is you decided you loved more than the mate selected for you by our goddess."

I flung her away, toward the door, and she tripped, landing hard against it. For a moment, I felt some remorse, but my anger fueled me. As she crawled away, the door opened and Jean-Luc entered. He looked from her to me and growled.

That was when understanding filled my younger self. All the extra fighting practice, all their time spent with their heads together when we hung out. I felt the sting of the betrayal as if it were fresh.

"Get your woman and leave my pack. Never return, or I'll kill you both!" I roared.

He gathered her up and pulled her from the room. I picked up the nearest chair and threw it against the wall. The fire of my anger wasn't sated, so I threw another. Then the coffee table. I went on a rampage that left most of my office in shambles, then sat heavily on the couch and put my face in my hands.

I never wanted to love anyone again. Never wanted to have another mate. Never wanted to open myself up to that kind of pain again.

My emotions consumed me when I heard the quiet opening of the door. The soft click of the lock couldn't draw me out of it. It was probably Celesta and my mind had shortened the time between them leaving and her coming in to scold me. I hated how she yelled at me every time. How it made me hurt even more.

Two small hands gently touched my shoulders. I felt myself being pulled into an embrace. The smell of honeysuckle and jasmine filled my senses as Bellamy held me against her. I wrapped my arms around her waist and laid my ear against her chest, listening to her heartbeat.

"Hush now, my love. I'm here. Everything is alright," she murmured as she stroked my hair and back.

"Why didn't she love me? What did I do wrong?" I asked in a quivering voice.

"It wasn't meant to be. There was nothing you could've done to make her love you. I'm sorry you had to go through that again," Bellamy whispered.

"Again?"

"Lucien, I know you're in there. Come back to me, my love. Don't let this memory hold you. You don't deserve it."

I pushed forward harder than I ever had before. If the younger me got upset again, he might hurt her. I wouldn't risk that. Even if it was a dream, I didn't want to see her harmed.

He was fighting me for control. I would win, though. I never saw how much stronger I'd grown from back then. Having Bellamy in my arms, calling to me, connected me to my power.

"I thought you were mad at me, chouchoutte," I strained.

"I am mad at you, stupid Alpha, but you needed me. Our connection let me come to you when your pain became too strong for you to handle. You were sinking into your past. Don't run back to your pain. Stay with me," she purred.

Another hard push let me finally grab control. I squeezed her tighter and rubbed my face into her breasts. Bellamy giggled.

"In dreams, you aren't allowed to be mad at me," I replied.

"You can't tell me what to do whether you're awake or asleep, Lucien," Bellamy chuckled. "Just enjoy this time."

"Why can't you just see this from my point of view, Bellamy?" I growled. "You can't go see Kyle."

"I'm not having this fight in your subconscious, Lucien. If you want to fight with me, you have to do it in real life. This is not the time or place," she groaned.

"This is the perfect place. No one can interfere and you can't run off," I said.

Bellamy applied pressure on two pressure points in my shoulders and the pain made me release her. She moved toward the door quickly.

"No. I came to soothe you and pull you out of that dream. Now you're feeling more yourself, I'll be leaving," she stated and left the room.

I refused to be discouraged. This was the best place. I could show her what my gut was telling me. Then she would understand. I jumped up and followed her.

Opening the door, I found the hall was empty and dark as if it were the middle of the night. It was the packhouse, but not. The whole thing was a twisted, shadowy version of my home.

Lightning flashed and thunder shook the walls. I heard Bellamy scream and ran toward the sound. She was lost in my mind. I had to save her.

Chapter 104: Regret Permitted

I frantically searched, my heart pounding, but Bellamy was nowhere to be found. I attempted to shift into my wolf, willing myself to become Remus, but my body remained stubbornly my own. With a roar, I slammed my fist into the nearby wall; the sound muffled by the thick plaster.

"REMUS! GET YOUR ASS OUT HERE!" I yelled with everything in me, dropping to my knees.

This was my fault. She gave me time and space to work out my shit back when we had problems, and I didn't give her the same consideration. My selfishness, and my desire to keep fighting instead of accepting her help, caused Bellamy to be lost somewhere in my mind.

"I'm here, Lucien. What's wrong?" I heard a voice like my own behind me.

Turning, I was face to face with my wolf. My actual wolf. Of course, it was a dream world. We didn't have to share a form.

"Bellamy. She's lost here. I heard her screaming, and…." More screams cut me off.

Something had her. Her screams, raw with terror and agony, pierced me to the core. Remus was suddenly on guard, every muscle tense as his head swiveled, searching for the source of the screams.

"Our mate," he growled and sniffed the air.

With a sudden burst of speed, he bounded down the hall, making me jump and instantly chase after him. His senses would be keener than mine. We were going to find her.

As we ran down the endless hallway, a door opened, and I crashed into Talia. Her eyes glowed with an eerie light, and her fangs bared in a menacing snarl as I hit the ground, but she remained standing. What the hell was my mind doing?

"Where is she, mon loup? Where is my pheata?" Talia snarled, pulling me up by my collar.

"I don't know! We're looking for her. She was screaming, but we can't hear anything now. Are… are you really here?" I asked.

"Yes. I heard my pheata begging for help. When I closed my eyes to focus I was dragged here. Bellamy doesn't beg. She doesn't ask for help unless she's desperate. Where are we?"

"My head. She came when I had a nightmare and we argued. I'd give anything to take it back. Something has her. I know it's only a dream, but something in me says this is very real," I explained.

"We don't have time for this fucking chatter!" Remus shouted.

She pulled me up, and we were off again, following Remus and Talia's noses. After a while, Talia stopped suddenly and turned to a wall with a false door. She sniffed around the door.

"Here. She's in here. We need to get through this door," she insisted and started pounding on it.

My fists connected with the wood, a dull thud accompanying each strike. It shook like a human was hitting it. With a fierce intensity, Talia pounded on the door, the sound echoing in the otherwise still hallway. We lacked the necessary strength. It was my dream, my mind. I had to have some power there.

Stepping back, I started mind-linking Robert, Thierry, Jean-Luc, Jean-Claude, Richard, and Caleb. I knew all of them for the better part of their lives. Even though they were dreams, they were still werewolves. They were still my pack.

They arrived in a matter of moments. I was a little more relieved than I should have been. Although they seemed a little puzzled, they waited to take my order.

"We need to break down this door and get into this room. My mate is in danger," I told them.

"Bellamy!" Robert shouted and started desperately punching at the door.

"Bellamy? Lucien, what's going on?" Jean-Luc asked.

"Just help with the door, Jean-Luc. We have to save her," I pled.

"You better explain this later," he growled and joined his brother.

It didn't take too long before we were through the door. Talia and I burst in, followed by Remus and everyone else. The room had stone walls with wooden shelves and a stone floor. The room contained candles and a display of strange knives. I'd never seen a room like this before. This place wasn't part of my nightmares.

Three charred, skeletal creatures stood between me and the center of the room. Muffled sobs came from behind them. Rage swept through me as I recognized Bellamy's cries and the familiar scent of vampires.

"You're too late, Alpha. I have my prize," Marion's voice rang out.

The bodies parted and revealed Bellamy strapped with silver bonds to a thick wooden table. Someone had gagged her, and she was crying; her stomach distended. I looked past her and saw Marion holding two squirming, bloody infants.

Remus attacked one of the charred things and started tearing it to pieces. Jean-Claude joined the fray and soon all of my wolves were fighting them. Talia and I closed in on Marion. He stepped further from the table.

"Killing babies isn't nearly as hard as killing anything else. Stay back," he warned.

I looked at Talia. A snarl stretched her lips, revealing gleaming white fangs as she bared her teeth.

"What are you doing with them?" I asked.

"I'm taking what you stole from me. Call off your wolves. Leave my children alone or I end yours," Marion growled.

Three figures formed behind him, seemingly out of nowhere. More vampires. This was going to be even harder. I could feel a sense of sorrow but set it aside so I could focus on saving my children, even if they were just dreams.

Two of the vampires reached around quickly and grabbed the babies before Marion could react, while the third vampire's hand erupted through Marion's chest, followed by the other, and proceeded to tear him in half.

The vampires with my children rushed them over to me and Talia. One vampire was a male with dark blond hair and golden eyes. The other female with short dark brown hair and ruby-colored eyes. They looked regal, almost ethereal.

When Marion's body hit the ground, I saw the third vampire. He was the shortest male in the room, around 5'10", but well-muscled. He had black hair and deep green eyes. All of their eyes were glowing.

"Here are your pups. We mean you no harm," the female said.

"Who are you? What's going on?" I asked as they loaded the babies into my arms.

"We had a very odd occurrence. All of our human servants were suddenly begging for help from the Traveler, someone called Lucien, and your Moon Goddess," the blond man said.

"*This* is Lucien," Talia told them. "Lucien, this is Felix, the Angel, Phoebe, the Prince, and Marius, Death. They're my cohort from the High Council."

"Thank you for coming to help." I bowed as deeply as I could while keeping my pups in my arms.

"That thing was bonded to you. I severed the bond." Marius scowled at the body on the ground.

"L-Lucien," Bellamy's quivering voice called out.

I turned and went to the table. There were pieces of burned vampire everywhere. Talia and the other members of the High Council started undoing the silver bindings on my mate's limbs. When Bellamy was free, Talia and Marius helped her sit up.

"He said I would miscarry the pups if they were born here," she sobbed. "I couldn't fight back. I tried so hard, but I was weak."

Robert pulled her into a hug. Thierry stroked her back. I moved closer with the pups, bringing them closer to her.

Our pups would be gone when we woke up? The family I'd waited decades for wouldn't exist in the real world anymore? And for what? For my pride and inability to communicate, I destroyed my family.

Bellamy pushed her uncles away. She held her arms up for the babies and I handed them over. She snuggled them close, and I stood there dumbly. This was my fault. If I hadn't caused the fight, if she hadn't come to my dream because of my pain, our pups would still be alive.

"Look, Lucien. They have your eyes," she murmured. "I thought the Dubois eyes were dominant."

Bellamy's own eyes were full of tears as she spoke. She was trying to have this time that we'd never get to have in real life. I wouldn't take it away from her.

"They have your cute little chin, though, chouchoutte," I whispered.

"There's never been a mixed-gender set of twins in our family," Robert said.

"Can someone explain this, please?" Jean-Luc asked.

Bellamy stiffened. I glanced up at him and ended up staring. Earlier, I had been in a rush to save Bellamy. Now, I saw what I'd missed.

That wasn't Jean-Luc the way I remembered him. His eyes held a different light; this man carried himself with a new confidence the one I'd sent away never possessed. He was older than he'd been the last time I saw him, but still a young man. The age he was when he died.

"It seems, you may have pulled people from their sleep in more ways than one, Lucien. Much like Bellamy called on the Vampire High Council, this shouldn't have been possible," Talia said.

"There was something about eight thousand years ago. Remember, Talia? That one wolf couple. In…. I can't even remember. It was ages ago and boundaries and names changed so much over the centuries. You know the ones," Marius replied.

"Oh, yes. I remember. We thought wolves were evolving briefly, then their collective was wiped out a generation after they passed." She nodded.

"That doesn't explain how my daughter is, *apparently*, having children with my childhood friend," Jean-Luc growled.

"Let's focus on returning the children where they belong. Then you can have your little family meeting," Felix stated, looking mildly annoyed.

"Just relax, little one. Your wolf is protecting them in the real world," Phoebe told Bellamy in a gentle voice. "Felix will heal you."

I could see why they called her 'The Prince'. Her voice was soothing and deep for a woman. Her slightly masculine air, strong jawline, and sharp cheekbones gave her the androgynous look of a pretty young man. The way she acted around Bellamy was cordial and friendly in a respectful sort of way.

Phoebe made a circle in the air with her hand and inside the circle, I could see Aurora curled up on a bed. Aurora seemed distressed, but I didn't see any signs of a miscarriage. I breathed a sigh of relief.

"Lucien, take the little girl. It will be easier for Felix if we start with the rogue," Talia instructed.

Bellamy gently placed Lunette in my arms; I felt the warmth of her small body as I cuddled her close, breathing in her faint, sweet scent. Her tiny hands, soft as velvet, grabbed at my face as I lifted her close to smell her sweet baby scent. She would be with us in a few months, but I would hold this memory until then.

"Alright, that's one down. Give me the girl, let's get her settled in with her brother," Felix said.

I handed my daughter to the vampire, and she went from being a baby girl to being a ball of light. He pushed her against Bellamy's stomach until the light disappeared. Bellamy's hands moved to her stomach, and she caressed it.

"The task is complete. We must return to our bodies. Talia, get a report on what you find. Keep us informed. The wolves have just started becoming interesting again," Marius commanded.

"I don't do reports. These wolves aren't your business. Shove it up your ass, Marius. I'll let you know what you need to know when you need to know it." Talia laughed.

He sighed and rolled his eyes. It looked like this was a common thing for them. I focused on Bellamy. She was going to hate me even more for this.

"Get me out of this place. I've never liked this room," Bellamy whispered, shaking.

Jean-Luc stopped me with his glare as he stepped forward and scooped her into his arms. He marched out of the room as the vampires, aside from Talia, disappeared. We all followed him.

Chapter 105: Ghosts of the Past

It didn't take us long to get to Lucien's office. The hallway went back to normal, now that Marion was gone. I was relieved. It was familiar.

The room had righted itself and looked more like the office I knew. When I was there earlier, it looked like a tornado had gone through a secondhand store.

My father set me in the armchair Lucien usually sat in and pulled Lucien's office chair over next to me before sitting in it. Power positions. He wasn't playing. Lucien sat on the couch closest to me, and extra chairs were brought in for everyone else.

Remus sat next to me and laid his head gently on my knee. I ran my fingers through his fur and looked up at Lucien. He was still his eighteen-year-old self. I hated it.

Sure, he was cute, but he wasn't my mate. He looked unsure of himself and wouldn't make eye contact with me. That wasn't the man I loved. It was a shadow, an echo of who he'd been once.

"Lucien change back," I ordered.

He blushed. "I don't know how. This is the first time I haven't been a passenger."

"Just think of yourself as you are now." I sighed.

Lucien closed his eyes and soon he looked just like he had the last time I saw him in the real world. My Lucien was a whole man, not a boy still growing into who and what he was. He opened his eyes. I smiled at him and he smiled back. His eyes slid beside me and the smile fell.

Right.

My father.

"So, would you like to tell me what the hell is going on?" Papa said, crossing his arms and settling a stern expression on his face. "How did you find my daughter, Lucien? Who the hell do you think you are to take her future by marking her?"

"Papa, stop. I offered for him. He's not the same boy who banished you. You and Mama both said you forgave everyone," I replied.

"Just because I forgave him, doesn't mean I would approve of *my* daughter being *his* mate! The damage is already done; you're having his pups. I don't even know what to tell your mother. How could you be okay with this? He's old enough to be your father! I should know! We were only born a few weeks apart!" he shouted.

My stomach twisted. I always thought my parents could see me, but it seemed they couldn't. I thought they would be happy I found someone to accept me.

He couldn't understand why I loved Lucien, because pack wolves didn't know what it was to be rogue. Not even ex-packs truly understood. I was even more alone than I thought.

Remus growled at my father when a tear fell from my eye and landed near his snout. I hated crying. This hurt worse than when Lucien kept trying to get me to accept his apologies for what he did to my parents. To my father, the man I'd always looked up to, my mate, my pups, and the happiness they brought were blemishes, 'damage' to his vision of his daughter's life.

"Don't say things like that, Jean-Luc. I don't mind that you point out how much older I am than her. You didn't see how I changed after you left. You didn't see how she grew after you died. And you have no idea what we actually mean to each other," Lucien said in a low, angry voice. "If I could go back and apologize I would. If I could change this, I would. I would give up the only true happiness I've known in years if I could've saved Bellamy from the life she had to lead."

I didn't like when Lucien said things like that, but I was afraid of what would happen if I said anything. My papa might hate me. I didn't want him to hate me. He was already upset because of who I loved.

"Leave them alone, Jean-Luc! You haven't been out there with us. When I found out who she was, I was worried, too. Lucien dotes on Bellamy. He supports her collective. She's made the pack so much better," Robert told my papa.

"Bellamy believes the moon goddess *didn't* make a mistake when she paired Angelique and Lucien. Everything had to happen like it did so they could be together," Thierry stressed.

"If you feel the need to keep harassing my pheata, I will take her back to her body and you will have to wait until the end of her life to apologize," Talia growled.

"Why are vampires involved in this? What have you gotten my daughter into, Lucien?" Papa sneered.

"Talia took care of me after you died. She's my friend. She taught me how to fight like a vampire. If not for her, and people like her, I don't think I would've been able to kill the men who killed you and Mama," I admitted softly.

He froze and stared at me. Papa looked at Talia and around the room before focusing on me again. I didn't know what he was trying to find.

"*You* killed them?" He looked at me like he was shaken.

I didn't understand.

"Yes. I trained with every creature I met, I hunted them, I found them, and I killed them. It took me five years, but I avenged you like I promised I would." I nodded.

"You were eleven? Oh, Goddess, what did I do?" he whispered.

I started panicking. That was wrong? How was that wrong? Those men were responsible for so many deaths. They didn't deserve to live. It wasn't just for my parents; it was for everyone.

Lucien sat forward, his eyes intense, and reached for my hand, swiftly pulling me from the chair and into his lap, then holding me tightly against him. It was like he could sense I was on the verge of a breakdown. I snuggled into his arms.

He smelled like our pups and like home. My forever home, Lune Rouge, our quarters, our bed. He was mine. The only person who knew my dark side and loved me still.

I wanted my mama to come take Papa back. I didn't think telling him to leave would make it happen. He may not have been an Alpha, but he hated people telling him what to do.

Despite my distracting thoughts, I heard someone enter the room. Thierry gasped. I looked up to see my mama. She was just as beautiful as I remembered. She looked like an actual angel, with her golden waves of hair cascading over her shoulders and a peaceful, loving look on her face.

"Hello, princesse. I see you found your mate." She smiled at me and turned to her brother. "Bonjour, Thierry. I've missed you."

"Je suis désolé, Angelique," Thierry whispered.

"I know you're sorry, Thierry. You've always been like that. I forgave you a long time ago. I know my Bellamy told you." Mama winked.

"Why aren't you upset, Angie? She and Lucien are mated! She killed people as a child! Her friends are vampires! I left her alone and she became this… thing!" Papa stood and growled.

Lucien's chest rumbled as he held me. Remus was growling as well. I knew Talia would be furious, but nothing could have predicted the unexpected sound of many people growling at my father at once.

"You will not call our Luna a 'thing'! She did more for our pack than *you* ever did!" Jean-Claude snarled.

"Rogues fear our Luna. She's making our pack safer," Richard said angrily.

"Aunt Angelique, would you take your mate out of here? He's been insulting our Alpha, Luna, and allies. We appreciate his assistance in saving our Luna and future Alpha, but he needs to leave," Caleb requested in a cool, diplomatic tone.

My mama giggled. "He sounds just like you, Thierry. Another perfect Petit Beta."

She walked past my papa and stroked Remus' ears before kneeling before me and Lucien. I didn't want to look at her and see what I saw when I looked into my papa's eyes. Mama caressed my cheek and wiped away a tear.

"You are exactly the person the moon goddess told me you'd be. An ally to all beings, a dedicated Queen and Luna, and a salve to the soul of our Lucien," she whispered.

"What do you mean?" I asked.

"When I was pregnant with you, I worried about your future. The rogue life is not one we're taught much about. One night I had a dream. The goddess told me you would be born an Alpha. As strong as Lucien, but more in control of your emotions because of your rogue nature. She said you would be part of the healing of our people and that healing would start with the heart she made me break," she explained.

"He really was for me?"

"Yes, Lucien was always your intended mate. Everything happened as it needed to in order to make you the Queen you were meant to be, and him the Alpha he was meant to be. But, Lucien, you need to trust that Bellamy isn't a typical Alpha or teenager. She's a tactician, a warrior, and smart as hell. You can't just command her with a 'because I said so', and making a decree like you did in front of other members of the Association." She tsked at him.

"Let's talk about it when we get up in the morning, chouchoutte. Maybe we can come to a compromise that will work for both of us. I should've thought of that earlier. This is all my fault," Lucien murmured.

"No. It's Marion's fault. He told me he formed a blood-bond with you. Being able to seed a small part of himself into your subconscious was one of the benefits for him. You don't have to agree to have a blood bond form," I told him. "Marion turned your worry into doubt and fear."

He needed to understand that I wasn't mad at him. I blamed him for my getting lost, not for what Marion did. I would never blame him for what that undead bastard did or tried to do to our pups.

"You knew about this, Angelique?! Were you planning to tell me our daughter had changed into… this?" Papa growled.

"Shut up, Jean-Luc. I love you, but if Bellamy were a boy, you would've been proud of what she accomplished. Your lack of support is surprising considering she gets all of the things you are grumpy about, from you. *I* wasn't the one who started teaching her to fight before she learned to eat solid food." Mama rolled her eyes.

He sputtered, but then looked thoughtful and sat down. She did this to him all the time when I was little. My mama was flighty, but she was great at seeing things others overlooked in their own actions and reactions.

They were a good team. He was really down to earth, normally, and she was eccentric and dramatic. He was more by the book on things, and she felt that both rules and morals were flexible. They made up for each other's weaknesses.

"I'll take my mate back where we belong. You should be careful not to call spirits in the future, Lucien. Not all of them are young enough to remember their humanity."

"Will you forgive me for hurting you, Angie?" Lucien asked.

"I forgave you a long time ago. It had to happen so my baby would be happy when she grew up. You just have to stay healthy so you can be with her for as long as possible. Werewolves live a long time, but you're still at least nineteen years older than her." She reached up and tousled his hair before getting up to retrieve Papa.

"I am proud of you, Belle. And… I'm sorry I overreacted. I'll beat him up when he gets to where we are and be all better by the time you join us. Okay?" Papa winked.

"I don't know if it will go how you plan, but sure, Papa. Mama, how did you know everything?"

"We're not allowed to watch the people we left behind, but I was given special permission because of the weight of your existence. I, honestly, am so proud of you and everything you've done. I'll fill him in on what's happened since we left." She smiled and led my father to the door.

She ushered him through, then turned back to the room. The look on her face was disturbing. Her grin was huge and her eyes held a light like demon fire. It wasn't because of being dead…. Mama was about to do something she knew would embarrass someone.

"Just remember that we love all of you and forgive you for everything. We want you to move forward. Please, try to be happy." She turned back to the door.

I was confused. I knew that look. She would get it when she was about to embarrass or antagonize the neighbors. Was she messing with us? I looked around and saw my uncles looking relieved. They'd been expecting it, too.

"Oh, and Lucien, I am proud of the man you've become. So caring and… brave. I never would have… mmm… pegged… you for the adventurous spirit you've shown in recent weeks." She giggled and walked through the doorway.

Remus started laughing, and I couldn't resist joining. I had never seen a wolf laugh, and it was odd to hear such a human sound coming from an animal. He told Aurora about his warning to Lucien. We both thought it was hilarious.

Lucien blushed a dark red. No one else seemed to get the joke, and I appreciated that more than anything.

"Everyone go back to your own dreams. I don't think I've had a night this exhausting in years," Lucien groaned.

When they were all gone, Remus climbed onto the couch with us and put his head in my lap again. It was nice to have both halves of my mate where I could see them and touch them. This was a new nightmare to add to my list. I wasn't looking forward to what my brain would do with it.

"I want to go to the hospital first thing tomorrow, then we can talk about the Kyle situation," Lucien said.

"I like that plan. Just hold onto me for a while longer. I need you both right now. Thank you for coming to save me," I whispered.

"Never doubt that I will come for you, chouchoutte. You are my everything. I love you," he murmured, kissing the side of my head.

"I love you, too, mon saucisson. Forever." I sighed and relaxed in the warmth of my mate and his wolf.

Chapter 106: Reassurance and Progress

[Bellamy]

The next morning, we went to the hospital to ensure the pups were okay. Lucien and I were relieved when Dr. Mellette said they were healthy and on track for growth. When we heard their little hearts beating strongly inside me, I nearly cried.

After returning to the packhouse, Lucien and I went to his office. We would meet with everyone who was in the dream later. Right then, we needed to be together. I was still shaky from having almost lost everything.

We laid out on the couch, Lucien on the bottom and me on my back so he could hold me and the pups together. I leaned my head against his jaw and breathed him in while his warm arms surrounded me. It was peaceful and calming.

After a while, he sighed deeply. I hadn't been thinking of much, but it seemed like he had a lot on his mind.

"What is it, saucisson?" I asked.

"We need to figure out the Kyle thing and I just remembered we're getting married at the end of next week," he said.

"I didn't realize it was that close. All of the ranked females from Lune Rouge and Daylight Moon have been working on it. They only bring me things here and there so I have more time to deal with everything else," I replied.

"Well, I was thinking, there is this little bed and breakfast that would be perfect for our honeymoon. It's halfway between here and the Swift River Pack," he told me in a leading tone.

Swift River was the pack I had told him about. Not too far from their territory was the Hollowed Rib Collective. It would be the right size expansion that I wouldn't have to do mass intakes after I beat their King.

I chuckled. "You want to meet with their Alpha about the merger. That sounds like a fun way to spend our time off. We could add a few extra days without feeling guilty if we were preparing for our expansions."

"A few extra days without our people getting in the way or any responsibilities would be nice. Would you like me to book the room?" Lucien murmured into my ear, sending chills down my spine.

"Mmm, yes, that sounds lovely," I purred.

He pulled out his phone and went to their website to book the room. Lucien selected one that had a big jetted tub and a king-size bed. It was a beautiful room, from the pictures. I was excited.

"All done. Now, to the Kyle issue," he said.

"I will text him asking to meet in neutral territory. One of the covens in my collective should be able to mix up some pack scent. It will make you smell like an ex-pack. We should buy you some clothes and have Julio keep them at his house. They will pick up the ex-pack scent and make it even less discernable from a real ex-pack," I explained.

"What about my face? Should we get a fake beard?"

"No. Stanton can use makeup and silicone to give your face a different structure. We'll get him on that as soon as we can. We should contact the Association so they don't send their investigators. I can get the number for the King of Hollowed Rib, too. If I issue the challenge now, I can take the territory while we're there instead of posturing and setting the date. I can't risk him setting it for a date when I'd be too pregnant to fight," I answered.

"Let's do that now. It will feel like we're moving forward and maybe it will help us get past what happened last night. I still can't believe you called the Vampire High Council into my head." He chuckled.

"It's probably because of my standing with the Association. I was putting everything I had into my call for help," I said softly. "I was so scared Lucien."

"Well, Marius destroyed the bond. We don't have to worry about that leech coming for you or our pups ever again. Let's get these calls over with. I will schedule a meeting with Alpha Ennis Raymond, you will challenge...."

"I think it's King Sergio Sorrento. I'm not as familiar with the lesser Kings. He's third gen and they've held that territory ever since the first King in their line came of age. They were never a threat on any level, so I didn't put a lot of work into getting to know about him." I grimaced.

It was lazy, and I regretted it now, but it was what it was and I just had to go from there. I sent a text to Quinn. He was the keeper of all the contact information for the Association.

I also had him send me the info for Kyle and let him know we'd hammered out our issue. He was more than happy to comply. Quinn wanted Kyle gone and hoped we'd gather enough information for a challenge.

He messaged that the Association looked into what I said about my time in the collective by calling other Kings and Queens in the surrounding region and asking after anyone who may have moved collectives. We didn't have a paper trail like pack wolves. I only kept records because it made it easier to have Kieran accept ex-packs if they had documentation.

None of the chairs of the Association were happy about the reports they got on Kyle or Kingston. It would make it easier if I needed to kill him. They wouldn't oppose it.

After I sent off the message to Kyle to schedule our meeting, I relaxed against Lucien. His phone was in one hand, and his other hand rested on my stomach. I turned my head and kissed his jaw.

"I'm going to call Alpha Ennis now. Is that alright with you?" he asked.

"Sure. I'll find some way to entertain myself." I giggled.

He dialed the phone, and I settled in to listen to my Alpha be an Alpha. It was hot as hell knowing he was strengthening his pack and allowing me to help. I turned in the crevasse between the back of the couch and the curve of his side.

"Hello, Alpha Ennis, this is Alpha Lucien of Lune Rouge. I've heard you're having a hard time finding an heir," Lucien said magnanimously.

I heard the muffled Alpha on the other end explaining his losses and his pack situation. My hand settled on Lucien's chest and I traced little shapes over the broad expanse. He silently rumbled at my touch and I stopped moving my hand after he gave me a warning glance.

"I was wondering if you might be interested in a merger. My Luna and I will be near your pack in a little over a week for our honeymoon. We could get it settled then and you could retire with your mate, knowing your people are cared for," Lucien told him.

Carefully, I slid my hand down his body and started unzipping his pants. His left arm was trapped by my body and the couch; his right was busy holding his phone up. He was completely defenseless.

Reaching in his pants, I grasped him in a firm, but gentle, hold. I started stroking him slowly, just enough to feel good, but not enough to make him noisy. He tried to swat at me with his trapped arm, and I squeezed a little tighter.

He made the most adorable face as he worked to hold in a groan. I kept stroking with the firmer grip. Lucien bit his lips together and worked to continue his conversation.

"I'm glad to hear it…. Great…. I'll see you then. Goddess watch over you…. Thanks. Bye," he said and hung up the phone.

I picked up my pace and bit his nipple through his shirt, making him growl. He tossed his phone onto the coffee table and stopped my hand.

"You are a very naughty girl, chouchoutte." He chuckled.

"I can't help it, Lucien. You're so sexy when you're working," I purred.

"I expected more from you," Lucien sighed.

"Oh? I guess I'll do more to you next time." I giggled.

Using his trapped arm, he gripped me against him and rolled off the couch. I was careful to let go of him when I realized what he was doing. Lucien pulled me to the side of the couch and bent me over the arm. His hands slid down my hips to my legs, and he pulled my skirt up, then slipped my panties down.

"Make your call," he commanded with a deep rumble.

Goddess, that made me wet as hell. I reached forward to pick up my phone where it had dropped onto the cushion with our movement. He would make me suffer, and I couldn't wait.

Chapter 107: Punishment

[Bellamy]

I felt Lucien start to kiss and rub my bottom, his fingers slipping between my legs to spread my lower lips. He stroked over me, manipulating the sensitive flesh there. Lucien spread my legs further to grant him better access.

As I dialed the number, even though I could've texted, I felt his tongue slide along my crease and start teasing my clit with several firm licks followed by some lighter ones. The feeling of it made my breath catch as the phone started ringing. This was totally unfair.

"This is Sergio," an older male answered.

"Hello, this is Queen Bellamy," I replied.

"Ah, the young queen. I've been following news of you. I would ask how I can help you, but I have an idea of why you'd be calling me." He chuckled.

I bit my lip as Lucien slid a finger inside of me and started rubbing my g-spot while flicking my clit furiously with his tongue. Only stopping occasionally to give it slow, firm licks or gentle suckling. He was making this so much harder than what I did to him.

"Really? I wasn't aware I was so transparent."

"Ambition is rare in rogue born wolves, even Alpha rogues. You started your collective before you even got your wolf. Are you aware of how rare that is? You had no wolf to force the submission of those under you. And you took an entire pack. I took notice back then. When you started your expansions, I thought it would show your true abilities and it did. A successful expansion with *actual* rogues before you had your wolf!" Sergio laughed. "And the stories of your battle abilities…. Magnificent. I decided then and there that I would talk to you when I was getting ready to die."

"Talk to me? You don't have an heir?" I asked.

Lucien stopped his assault on my lower parts. I was both relieved and terribly sad about that. It would help me focus on what exactly was happening here.

"I fell in love with a human. Kept it a pretty good secret, but none of our kids were Alphas because of it. I loved her from the moment I met her until the moment she closed her eyes forever. I wouldn't give up that time for all the Alpha pups in the world. My collective will dissolve when I die unless someone takes over. I would like to offer it to you. I think you'll make the lives of my kids, grandkids, and great-grandkids better than any other Alpha could."

"Umm…. That's a little…."

"Suspicious?" He laughed again. "I know. But you don't realize what I've gone through. You're just a pup yourself. I've lived for ninety-four years. Unless I retire to some Goddess-forsaken wilderness, I expect to live for about thirty more years. I'd rather play with the little ones than hunt until something kills me," Sergio scoffed.

"I could use a lieutenant for that part of the territory. It's not a ton of work I have a website for disputes, you just resolve the minor issues. There would be plenty of time to spend with your grandkids and you would have an income," I offered.

He was thinking about it. I knew it was a good offer. Most of my lieutenants volunteered in the community or worked as teachers in my schools. They had enough free time to pursue what they loved. But none of them were Alphas.

Lucien stood and started rubbing himself against me. I was too short for that to line up properly. He pulled me up so my hips were on the arm of the couch and the decorative pillow cradled my stomach.

I needed to get off the phone before he entered me. I could hold back earlier, but I lost all control once Lucien was inside of me.

"Think about it and call or text me back. This is my cell, so you can reach me any time," I told him.

"I'll accept. When can I expect you?" Sergio asked.

"The week after next. I'll contact you once I'm in the area," I stated.

"Great. Thanks for giving me the chance to stay with my family. Not a lot of Kings or Queens would do that."

"Family is important to me. I trust you'll behave so I don't have to do something regrettable."

"I'll let you go. It sounds like your mate is getting a little more passionate than when I answered." He chuckled.

I blushed a deep red. Rogue hearing was more sensitive than pack wolf hearing. As fairly sexual creatures, things like this could be common. It didn't stop me from being embarrassed.

"Thanks. Don't die," I said.

"Same to you," he replied and hung up.

Lucien put a hand in my hair and pulled my head back while his other hand gripped my hip and he drove into me. I arched and squealed at the sensation of his firm length deep inside of me. There was nothing I could do as he pounded into my body.

His thick cock rubbed every good place. I moaned and whimpered at the brutal assault on my body. Lucien's fingers dug into my hip with delicious strength. I would definitely have a few minor bruises for an hour or so.

"You were a very bad girl, chouchoutte. I don't appreciate being distracted when dealing with other Alphas," he growled and moved his hand to deliver a firm slap to my ass.

I yipped. "Sorry, Alpha."

He paused for a second. I could feel his pleasure through our bond. His Alpha aura filled the room, pushing me over the edge of my climax. There is nothing hotter than a powerful male in charge, unless it's a powerful male submitting.

"Shit, chouchoutte. You know exactly what I want to hear, don't you?" He slapped my ass again.

"Yes, Alpha!" I squealed.

He groaned and rubbed where he slapped, still stroking in and out of me at a furious speed. Wave after wave of pleasure was amping up into something more potent. I reached between my body and the arm of the couch and started rubbing my clit. It was so close.

We came together explosively. The spasming of his cock inside me as I felt my body grasping at him was electric. Every twitch sent a spark through me. I silently thanked the goddess for making us for each other.

A powerful mate, a family of my own, a safe home, earth-shattering sex; it was all I'd ever wanted. The way he took care of me after was amazing. Lucien carefully carried me to the bathroom and gently helped me clean up. He laid soft kisses on my red and bruised skin.

"You were perfect, as usual, chouchoutte," he purred.

"Having a perfect partner helps. You aren't really mad at me, are you?" I asked with a little pout.

"I'm pretty sure the arousal I felt when watching you on the phone was what you felt when I was on the phone. I didn't realize negotiations could be so sexy," Lucien chuckled.

"Just wait until you see the takeover, saucisson," I replied, biting my lip.

"I look forward to that more than anything," he whispered and kissed me passionately.

Chapter 108: The King of Limb Torn

[Bellamy]

It took a couple of days to set up a meeting with Kyle. I tried repeatedly to convince him to meet outside of his territory, but he refused every suggestion. Lucien wasn't happy.

I showed him every text, and he understood I was trying to get what he wanted for this meeting. Sometimes, you can't get what you want. I planned to take two of my most trusted allies. Kyle insisted on wolves only.

Dilly and I picked up Henry at his home, and we all rode together to Kyle's territory. It was a long drive, about five hours, and none of us enjoyed being cooped up that long. It was tense. Werewolves and road trips don't mix.

A town bordering King Kyle's lands was where we stopped for the night at a hotel. With the agitation I knew I'd feel after dealing with him, that long drive home was out of the question.

It was just after two in the afternoon when we arrived at the seat of the Limb Torn Collective. The family had passed down the land for many generations. There were houses there and a training ground along with the large farmhouse where Kyle lived.

There was an arch at the entrance to the property. It was different from what I remembered. Large letters bore the words "LTC Ranch" and two crossed bones at the end of the letters accented the sign. We paused when I grabbed Dilly's arm.

"What is it, Bellamy?" he asked.

"Those are human tibia. What the fuck is going on?" I growled.

"Let's be on our guard. I don't like where this is going," Henry replied.

I nodded, and we drove on. My plan changed instantly. I'd heard he was crazy, but this was insane. I needed to know who he'd killed to make that warning. Those bones were different sizes. At least two people had died or been seriously maimed.

As we drove toward the farmhouse, I saw people walking patrols. They looked exhausted. Kingston had a solid patrol schedule that ensured no one was too tired to be effective. I made Dilly pull over near some men and rolled down my window.

"When did you start your patrol?" I asked.

They looked wary of me. I let out my Alpha aura, and they seemed to relax. That was a worse sign than their haggard appearance. No rogue should find comfort in the presence of an unfamiliar Alpha; their instincts should put them on edge and make them ready to protect their land unless otherwise planned.

"Thank the goddess. We've been on since early yesterday morning. Most of the collective has fled. Not enough live on the land for a good rotation. King Kyle only wants males patrolling," one man reported. "Please, tell us you're here to challenge him. He took one child from each family that remained and is keeping them in the old training rooms. We can't leave our pups, but we don't want to stay in this collective."

Anger flowed through me. I put my hand over my stomach. I would do anything to save my pups. After what happened with Marion, I could imagine what these people had been through.

Though my original plan hadn't involved challenging, it did now. I couldn't let this stand. Even if Kyle had nothing to do with the attacks on Lucien, he needed to be stopped.

"I'm High Queen Bellamy Carrington of the Eaten Heart Collective. I accept your request for assistance. Continue your patrol while I deal with King Kyle," I stated.

The men looked dismayed when I said my name. I didn't understand. There must be something I was missing.

"What's going on? Why are you looking defeated?" I demanded.

"You're his mate. He said you would be coming soon to take your place as his Queen. Please, don't tell him what I said!" the man pled.

"I am *not* his mate. I rejected his offers. My mate is at my collective seat, waiting for me to be done with this," I growled.

Their gazes locked on me for a moment before shifting to each other, a silent communication passing between them. It was pretty obvious something was wrong. Aurora went on guard.

"We need to tell you some things. This is not going to make you happy. I hope you won't decide to take it out on us," the second man said.

I motioned for them to go on, and they started telling me about the last couple of years in the collective. Kyle's mental health deteriorated. He killed anyone who criticized him. He refused offers from rogue females and sent them away. No one had seen any of the 'Shades' in the last couple weeks. The men thought they'd abandoned the collective.

Everything they told me grew my concern. Maybe Brown wasn't lying. I was in the territory of my enemy, who had, apparently, been preparing for a mating celebration. This wasn't the meeting I was hoping for.

We got to the farmhouse, and two big guys were on the porch. They looked healthier than the patrol wolves. Getting out of the car, we felt their eyes on us, tense and ready for a fight.

Dilly and Henry were about the same size in a lot of ways, trim builds with tight muscles and long bodies that made my shortness stand out. I selected them because I knew they had complementary fighting styles and I wanted to have a pack wolf and a rogue born with me. It showed the values of my collective. None of us were particularly imposing, but all of us were skilled fighters.

They stayed a couple of steps behind me as I approached the porch. The two men tensed. They were roughly Galen's size, maybe a couple inches taller. Both had close-cropped dark hair and dark eyes. If not for the difference in their scents, I would have sworn they were twins.

"Your King is expecting me," I announced.

"The pack wolf can't enter," the man on the right stated.

"Okay. Let's go home," I said and turned around. "Have fun explaining that to Kyle."

We headed back to the car. I'm sure the men thought I was bluffing, but I'm willing to take a bluff to the furthest extreme. I'd actually leave and just come back in the middle of the night to take care of them.

Once we were buckling our seatbelts and Dilly started the car, the men seemed to realize I wasn't kidding about leaving. They rushed to block our escape. One stood in front of the car and the other behind it. I smirked at Dilly and rolled down the window.

"We don't have a problem with running you over. Move, or be seriously injured," I warned.

"You can take the pack wolf. Just… don't go. He'll be pissed," the one at the front of the car said.

I nodded to Dilly, and he turned off the car. We got out and the bulge boys led us into the house.

It was exactly how I remembered it. The entryway opened up to a living room on one side and a dining room on the other. Both were massive, built to accommodate a small collective back when they were still starting. The whole collective worked together to build it before the winter came the first year after Limb Torn settled the area.

A long hallway led to the office, library, kitchen, storage rooms, and the old assembly room. Kingston built an assembly hall sometime before I first visited the collective. He partitioned off parts of the old room for his entertainment and little harems. Kingston sectioned them off by age and whether they would remain with him or rejoin their families.

The old cellars in the basement were the training rooms. Girls were kept there until their will to escape was completely broken. The second floor held bedrooms and guest rooms. I hated the place just from the memories alone.

They guided us down the hall to the office. When we reached the door, the men stood on either side and crossed their arms over their chests. It was so fucking stereotypical. I rolled my eyes.

Stepping forward, I put my hand on the old doorknob and took a deep breath. The last time I was in this office, it was because Kingston was pressing me about having been in his collective for a year without deciding. I was a little terrified he would send me to the training rooms if I was anything less than confident.

'You can do this, Bems. It's just a talk,' Dilly linked me.

'How can I hear that?' I heard Henry on the link.

There was no time to unpack that. Somehow, my lieutenant could hear and speak in the link. We could play with it more after I dealt with Kyle and took care of his people.

'I'll explain later. Let's get this over with,' I replied.

The door opened easily into the brightly lit room. Kyle was sitting at the desk with the back of the chair directed at the door. He turned when I entered. That time, I did roll my eyes.

Chapter 109: Not Okay

Kyle stood and smiled warmly. He'd grown up quite handsome. Unfathomably blue eyes complemented his dark blond hair. Kyle's face was aristocratic, but not in the regal way Lucien's was, mostly like those snooty, asshole rich people. The ones who believe they're better than everyone who has less than they did. He seemed as if he was looking down his nose at Dilly and Henry.

His clothes made him look more muscular than I knew he was. Werewolves had a sturdier musculature. Alphas didn't have to do as much to maintain them. I knew he didn't do much at all, at least, when my spies infiltrated the collective he wasn't. Maybe that had changed.

Circling the desk, he gestured towards a pair of large wingback chairs flanking a small table. Excitement and happiness shone on Kyle's face. It was rather unnerving.

"Bella, please, have a seat." He grinned.

"My name is Bellamy and you haven't permission to call me anything but High Queen Bellamy," I replied coldly.

Kyle chuckled. "I hadn't realized you were High Queen. When did that happen?"

I was confused. My expansion was common knowledge across the region; there wasn't a soul who hadn't heard the news. Was he so disconnected that he really didn't know? Or had his mind told him it couldn't be true?

"A couple weeks ago. I'm here investigating some allegations made by a rogue," I answered.

"Have a seat. You can't feel comfortable with all these tall males around you. I remember how nervous it used to make you," he said, taking a seat in one of the chairs.

I sighed and went to sit across from him. This was getting annoying.

"What are these allegations?" Kyle asked.

"That you have an issue with a pack Alpha and have hired people to kill him and his family," I responded.

"Oh. That. His ancestors and my ancestors had an issue. In the past, my family worked against his pack, sending rogues and hunters to knock them back down when they got too prosperous. I'm taking the initiative. Plus, it's a gift to you. To apologize for my past behavior and show you that I'm still thinking of you and value you," he said with an eager smile.

Kyle admitted the Fullers had been weakening Lune Rouge. Not just the rogue attacks, but the hunter attacks, too. There was no curse.

"Killing an Alpha is a gift to me? How?

"He's the one who banished your parents! The one you were afraid of when you were little. I found the information in my father's files. Once he's dead, you will don't need to fear him and can focus on being happy with me," Kyle stated magnanimously.

Rage washed over me. Even if I *hadn't* mated with Lucien, I would *never* have approved of this. Killing him wouldn't have made me love Kyle. I needed to keep my calm. The Association chairs were expecting a full report, and I wanted to tell Lucien everything I could.

"And trying to kill his pups?"

"If there's no one to avenge him, the fight is over and once his line is gone, I can take his pack into my collective and end that pack forever. His Luna must have some decent guards, or the man I paid wasn't very good. She got away." He sighed and shook his head.

"I've heard you kill any who criticize you and banish females who offer for you. Why didn't you accept their offers? I'd refused you enough, you should have moved on instead of hurting your collective with your stubbornness," I said.

"You were meant to be mine! The strength you have, the drive and motivation, is exactly what I need to bring my unruly collective back in order. A few had to die to keep them in line. They need to learn their place and respect their King." He shrugged. "Together, you and I will hold the entire region. The two largest collectives, with the two strongest Alphas."

He *was* delusional. I wasn't covering my mark in any way. *I smelled pregnant, for Goddess' sake!* My expression was hard, my body tense, communicating an unmistakable hostility. Kyle was so consumed by his own fantasies about us that he couldn't see any hint of malice.

"Now that's out of the way, let me offer for you one more time. Once you accept, we can be marked and mated. You'll be the most beautiful and perfect queen to sit beside me. We'll make gorgeous pups together and rule with an iron fist. None will oppose us or say my father was better," Kyle sneered.

Shock was clear on my face as I looked at him. Mr. Brown was right. I didn't need to hear Kyle's rambling; the crazed look in his eyes said it all. He was insane.

"I already have a mate, King Fuller. I *never* intended to accept you. The thought of having children with you disgusts me. Your father *never* had the right to promise me to you and *you* don't have the right to kill for the position of my mate," I replied sternly.

"But…. You were finally here to see me! I've been petitioning to see you for years and was always turned away. You never gave me the chance to win you!" he growled.

That was news to me, but Aurora wasn't upset. At least, not as upset as she should've been. She could see this wolf wasn't right as clearly as I could. My family did the right thing when they didn't let him come, but they should've told me.

"I'm not *required* to give you a chance. I am *not* a prize to be won. Obviously, I didn't want to see you. That *should* have been a hint."

"Where's your mate? I'll challenge him, then you'll *have* to be mine!" Kyle shouted in anger, standing and glaring down at me.

"I will *never* be yours! Even if you *had* succeeded at killing Lucien Deveraux, I wouldn't have accepted you. The crimes you've committed are enough to strip you of your collective. Instead, I'll challenge you for it. You've harmed your people and you tried to kill my family," I growled.

"No! That was my father who killed your family!" he yelled, red-faced. "I didn't even know who they were!"

My raging anger abruptly died down, replaced by a hollow, icy calm. Kingston killed my family? I couldn't believe it, but I could all at the same time.

He must have hired hunters to kill my family because rogues didn't attack other rogues unless it was for resources. Oh, Goddess. Stanton delivered me right to the man who took my life from me. Giving me to Kyle was his plan all along.

"Prepare for our fight, Kyle. You're going to die for what you've done to me and my family," I whispered.

"I told you, it was him! I never hurt your family!"

"*You* hired someone to kill my pups! If I were a pack wolf, I could've miscarried from the stress! Instead, I beat your assassin's ass and *my mate* killed him," I said, standing. "I am the Luna of Lune Rouge! You will die for trying to harm my children, my mate, and my pack!"

Kyle's jaw dropped, eyes wide, as he was stunned into silence. He inhaled sharply, his face paling as the gravity of the situation hit him. As I was walking away, getting ready to fight, I saw Dilly's eyes widen. Kyle was an idiot.

Turning quickly, I blocked the punch aimed at my head, the force of it jarring my arm, and countered with a sharp blow to his chin. Kyle reacted quickly, pulling back just in time to dodge before launching himself forward in an aggressive lunge toward me. I jumped backward, avoiding his grasp.

'We've got the meathead twins. Kick his ass, Bemmy,' Dilly linked me.

Kyle landed a couple of good hits, but not as many as I did. He didn't know how to defend and walked right into a couple fakes. Though he *could* take a hit. It was pretty impressive. I landed a difficult stomach shot, followed by an uppercut, and finished with a solid groin kick.

He fell to the floor, coughing and retching. I grew out my claws, preparing to strike, when there was a yelp behind me. One twin had Henry held by his neck and was jerking his arm out of the socket. Dilly had his hands full with the other.

I had to save my lieutenant. Kyle would be on the ground for a bit yet. I made an executive decision and aimed myself at the man who was hurting my friend.

A snap and thud made me glance at Dilly. He'd killed one and was going for the same one I was aiming at. We arrived at the same time. Dilly distracted the wolf while I tore his heart out.

Dilly looked after Henry as I turned to finish off Kyle. He was gone. The window next to the chairs was open.

The bastard ran away! Fucking coward!

I handed the heart to Henry and worked to put his arm back where it belonged. He ate the heart. It would help him heal a little faster.

Within twenty minutes, I felt a surge of power, the feeling of around one hundred wolves being attached to me and my collective. Kyle abandoned his collective. The loyalty of his wolves now belonged to me. All of his territory now belonged to me. I could have my people map it later. There was no way I could run the whole thing.

"We need to get those pups returned to their parents and have someone clean this mess," I ordered.

"How are we going to get everyone together?" Henry asked.

I thought about it. Henry could hear me linking with Dilly. It was worth a shot. I took a deep breath and focused on the closest connections in my collective.

'All rogues who had children taken by King Fuller, report to the main house to retrieve your pups. Welcome, to the Eaten Heart Collective,' I linked.

Henry's eyes widened in amazement. I knew he could hear me, but I was hopeful the other wolves would as well. I would know soon.

"I'm heading to the basement. There's a small clinic three doors down on the right. There should be shoulder slings available. Take care of Henry for me, Dilly," I said.

"Yes, High Queen Bellamy," he replied with a bow, and helped Henry from the room.

Chapter 110: Good News/Bad News

[Bellamy]

I headed to the back hall, to the door down to the basement. Several wolves were arriving. They looked at me with wide eyes.

"Thank you for coming," I said.

"How did you do that?" a female ex-pack asked. "I didn't think rogues could mind-link."

"I'm stronger than the average rogue Alpha. Come on. Let's get these pups. I need a shower," I sighed. "Once you've collected your pups, I want you to go gather anyone else in your home, and call other members who are settled off the grounds. Head to the Assembly Hall afterward. I want everyone ready to hear me in two hours."

I opened the door and turned on the light at the top of the stairs. It would illuminate the hall between the rooms, but the rooms themselves had no light. It was part of how Kingston and Mr. Brown broke the girls. No light, no other people, no clean water, no heat, no clothing. It was appalling.

A wide path extended to the back wall, and bolted doors were positioned every three feet. The cells were small and would normally house one teen to adult size female in each. I was worried about the children, given how poorly the hall looked.

When I opened the first door, I was relieved to see three warmly dressed pups in the room. A stack of thick blankets sat atop a lumpy mattress, next to several heavy gallon jugs of fresh water. At least Kyle wasn't all bad. It wouldn't take much to get these kids healthy again.

Parents flooded into the basement. They started opening doors and sniffing out their children. I was happy to see so many reunions. They were joyful and teary.

It made me miss my parents, Daniel and Olive. I would have to see if he wanted to come visit for a while before the wedding. She was still at Lune Rouge, but went home from time-to-time because she missed her mate.

It gave Lucien and me time to practice taking care of twins. Not that I was out of practice, but it wasn't an experience I'd had much of a partner on. I had to learn when to give him control. It was helping us test the rules and boundaries for raising our own pups.

There was a little boy looking for his parents still, even though most had left the basement already. I was getting worried as I noticed a few more, but I would stay there as long as it took. I sent out another link that there were still children in the basement.

Henry was at the top of the stairs, smelling each family as they came up to be sure no one was taking a child that wasn't theirs. Dilly reminded them to meet in the Assembly Hall. It shouldn't be all that difficult.

***

In the end, there were four children whose parents didn't come for them. I sent a link to the entirety of the ex-Limb Torn members ordering them to the Hall. I would find their parents, or I would find out what happened to them and get them fostered with a family that would fit their needs and background.

Henry and I took the pups to the living room and sat them down. They were scared and curled up together on a couch. We tried our best to soothe them, but they really wanted their parents.

Dilly entered the room. He looked at the kids sadly as he came over to where we were. I knew that feeling and hoped their family was based nearby and couldn't make it as quickly as the ones living on the ranch.

"What are our next moves, Queen Bellamy?" Henry asked.

"I need to put a kill order on Kyle via the Association. We have to get intake done on these wolves. Since they were already in a collective, their bond transferred over to me after Kyle abandoned them. I just need their stats, names, and plans. I need to know how many will stay in the collective, and how many will leave.

"We can suss out the ex-packs who want a pack instead and let them choose between Rose Moon and Lune Rouge. It shouldn't be too difficult. The collective was always more territory than population. We can decide what to do with the ranch and everything after," I explained.

"Sounds good. Families with smartphones can go to the website and fill in the form, and then we can have them help those who don't have one. Henry and I can take the pups into the kitchen for a snack while you contact the Association," Dilly replied.

Henry nodded. They gathered up the children and followed my directions to the kitchen. I hoped we would find their parents. It was a hard enough life being rogue.

One of the pups was rogue born, and the others were ex-pack. I should be able to find families for all of them if they need them. I would talk to Lucien about taking the rogue born. He was an Alpha and would need to be raised right. The boy would need extra attention.

I hoped he wasn't one of Kyle's. Since he was the one who hired the people to kill Lucien, that meant he had impregnated the maid. Brown told Lucien that Kyle was saving himself for me, apparently *not* in the way pack wolves save themselves.

Once they were gone, I pulled out my phone and called Jonas. After getting him on the line, we worked to conference in the other Alphas and Lucien. They'd all made sure their schedule was cleared so I could report in after the meeting. Lucien needed to know he was in danger.

"What happened, Bellamy?" Lucien asked.

"I spoke with Kyle and he admitted to being behind the attacks. He also admitted his family has been weakening Lune Rouge for centuries. I challenged him and he attacked me as I turned to leave and prepare," I told them.

There were several growls from the men. Pack Alphas were protective of females, but the rogue Alphas were pissed he'd attacked dishonorably. Some people like to believe honor didn't exist among rogues. For the most part, it didn't, but, when a challenge was issued, we believed in fair fights for dominance.

"Did you kill him?" Quinn asked.

"No. I was about to, but he had these big-ass guards who attacked my men. Dillon did fine, but one of them managed to get ahold of Henry and started trying to pull his limbs off. I couldn't let that happen and went to save my lieutenant. It didn't take long, but it was apparently long enough for Kyle to flee through a window. He abandoned his collective. I need a kill order on him," I answered.

"Why a kill order? Won't he just run off?" Brett asked.

"No. I have confirmation of what Jared Brown said. He's insane. The reason he wanted to kill Alpha Lucien, was to impress me enough that I'd accept him. When I told him I was already mated, he demanded the name of my mate so he could challenge him, with me as the prize," I explained.

"If this caused some sort of mental break, he might think killing you and Lucien is the only answer for the insult," Brett stated.

"I'm more inclined to believe this will throw him in the other direction. He knows Lucien is my mate. His original motives made sense to him. I think he's going to try to challenge him anyway or try to kill him. On some level, Kyle thinks he's going to win and I'll fall in love with him when he does." I sighed.

"We'll let all packs and collectives know. Can you text us a picture of him?" Jonas asked.

"Yeah. There are some around. I'll send one off as soon as I can," I replied.

"Do you want me to come down there?" Lucien inquired.

"I just have to get things coordinated and get my files updated. We'll stay at the hotel we booked and head home in the morning. I'll assign people to come out and get things settled here. I'm texting Charles, my other lieutenant, to have him send four teams of warriors to watch over this place until I can get a lieutenant installed and start the process of organizing," I told him.

I really wanted to go home, but that wasn't an option now. I had to get this territory settled. Soon, I could be back with my Lucien.

This was the first time we'd been apart when we weren't having an issue, and it was killing me. I bet it was killing him, too. He was asking because he didn't want to spend the night without me.

"Alright, Bellamy. I'll wait and have our patrols stepped up," he replied.

"Great. I'll talk to all of you later. Don't die." I signed off cheerily.

I couldn't let him know how hard it was to tell him to stay home. I'd call him before I went to sleep. The other Association chairs didn't need to hear our relationship stuff.

Before I headed into the kitchen to join Dilly, Henry, and the pups, I sent a text off to Chuck and waited for his response. He was thrilled about the newest expansion. His partner in the town he covered came from Limb Torn.

Derick was ex-pack and loved being a rogue, but hated being in a collective. When he applied to mine, it was because his mate was already a member. He sent me a box of really nice steaks after a month in my collective with a note that said my leadership was a thousand times better than Kingston's.

I still had that note. When I was feeling any sort of doubt, I would pull it out and feel better. Alphas don't doubt themselves often, but I was a little different.

Sliding my phone in my pocket, I turned to head to the kitchen. Suddenly, I got the feeling I wasn't alone. Someone was hiding nearby. With luck, it was Kyle.

I slipped off my shoes and focused on erasing my scent and quieting my body. I'd kill him before he had the chance to touch my Lucien.

Chapter 111: A New Collective

The scent was very faint. Whoever it was, they could function in hiding mode like I could. It was actually a fairly rare ability, but we let pack wolves think most rogue born wolves could do it.

That narrowed it down and told me I wasn't dealing with Kyle. He could never calm his mind enough to slow his heart and breathing to get into the zone.

But one of the perks about being a rogue Alpha was that my senses were stronger than the average rogue. It was faint, but there was a scent that didn't match the rest of the house. The familiar scent sparked memories.

"I can smell you, Sy. What are you doing here? I heard you and Tim took off like Brown did," I said softly, leaning against the wall and leaning my head back.

A deep, bass voice chuckled from above me. He'd never been able to control his scent when he jumped like that. It was one thing very few people knew about Silas Greene since only an Alpha would've smelled him.

He dropped to his feet and grinned. "Hey, Amy. You're looking good. How's your mate? Is he recovering well from the vampires?"

"Lucien's fine. Thanks for asking," I answered, not even a little surprised that he knew what was going on in my life.

Silas was the only one who actually called me Amy, but he only did it when he was sure we were alone. Otherwise, he called me Bella. It was part of how Kingston tried to dominate me. He tried to take part of my identity from me.

"We were just escorting Jared out of the territory and heading back. Tim got hurt by some boys who thought they were badass. There were six of them and they attacked while we were sleeping." Silas scoffed.

"Did you leave a witness or just kill them all? Is Tim okay?" I asked.

"I killed them all. No one hurts my mate," he growled. "Tim's fine, we took some time at a motel so he could recover more, but he doesn't heal as easily as I do. He's resting at home, now. We heard your mind-link. Interesting trick. So, you killed Kyle?"

"No. The big guys he had guarding him got involved and one of them got ahold of one of my guys and tried to pull off his fucking arms. When I turned, he ran out the window and abandoned the collective," I said with a grimace.

"The only good enemy is a dead one. What do you want to do? We're your weapons now, Queen Bellamy."

"Where do you and Tim want to live? I'd love to have you two serve as lieutenants here. You have to be the age to retire. Maybe adopt some pups. Take care of our people in a different way than you did before," I offered.

He looked wistfully out the nearby window where a couple were walking by with their kids. Silas was good to me. He wasn't supposed to teach me to fight, but did anyway. Tim taught me to inflict damage on people without straining myself. His lessons were more valuable than he probably ever knew.

The Shades were terrifying to everyone except me.... At least two out of three weren't terrifying. The memory of Jared Brown's hands on me made me sick.

"I always thought we'd retire like Jerry, some wilderness somewhere. We'd just fuck up a kid. Tim and I weren't made to be parents," Silas answered softly.

"I would've loved to have had you as my dads. It wasn't safe for me to stay and I couldn't risk the chance you'd side with Kyle and Kingston," I told him.

"You were an exception. We fought against Kingston's plans for you every step. We were going to sneak you out before Jerry started your training. I can make people disappear in more than one way. They wouldn't have found us."

"I love the family that adopted me. We can find that for you and Tim. Will you stay in the Eaten Heart, Sy?" I asked.

He looked down at me with a soft smile. Some part of me wondered what it would have been like to be raised by two rogue born wolves. Never having to hide what I was, but he was lying. They wouldn't have opposed Kingston. No matter how much he disagreed. Tim and Sy were always loyal to their leader.

"Yeah, we'll stay. This is our home," Silas said.

"Good. No more lying to me." I glared and stepped forward.

Releasing my Alpha aura, I directed the full force of it at him. His eyes widened, and a growl slipped from his mouth. Slowly, he lowered to his knees, but I could tell his wolf was trying to fight it.

"Submit," I snarled, lashing out with my power.

A whimper came from him as he prostrated himself on the floor. Once Lucien and I combined our power, it became permanent. The dominance of two powerful Alphas was bearing down on him.

'Bemmy, you're scaring the pups. Do you need help?'

'I'm almost done,' I responded.

I pulled my aura back and allowed him to stand again. There was a respectful gleam in his eye. Silas understood that I wasn't the little girl he'd known ten years ago.

"What can I tell you, Queen Bellamy?" he asked with a bow.

"Did you know Kingston hired the hunters who killed my family?"

Silas looked a little shocked. "How did you find out?"

"Kyle told me. I'm guessing that's a yes. Why? What did they do that he would involve hunters?" I pressed.

"They made you. One ranked blood ex-pack parent means a fifty percent chance. Two is one hundred percent. An Alpha female is rare since ranked blood wolves rarely end up being banished together, and males are more common from ranked stock.

"Kingston wanted you for Kyle. He even tried to offer them a place in the collective without his usual requirements after you were born, but your parents were suspicious and refused," Silas explained.

If I'd been a boy, they'd still be alive. Kingston wouldn't have killed to get another Alpha male. My birth was the catalyst for their death. My heart shattered.

I closed my eyes. Damned hormones. Holding back the tears was hard. That shook me more than anything before. I was the reason they died.

The front door of the farmhouse slammed open. Soon, strong arms engulfed me. The scent of my favorite ice cream flooded my senses. I didn't know how Lucien got there so quickly, but I didn't really care. He was exactly what I needed.

"Where can I take her?" he asked.

"Up the stairs. Turn left, third door on the right. It's a guest room. I'll go work on organizing everyone and getting my mate to the Assembly Hall," Silas said in a low voice.

"Good. I better not find out you hurt her, or I'll skin you alive," Lucien growled as he carried me off.

"No, sir, King Lucien. We're loyal to our Queen," he replied and left.

"Why did he call me 'King'?" Lucien asked.

I sniffled and managed to control my tears. "B-because you smelled like a rogue when you threatened him."

"We'll get into that later. Let's get you somewhere private, chouchoutte, then you can tell me what upset you so much. I felt like my heart was being torn out," he whispered and took me to the guest room.

***

We were lying on the bed in the guest room. I curled up next to Lucien with my head resting on his chest. He was processing what Kyle and Silas told me.

Lucien had always carried a lot of guilt about my parents' death, but now he knew it was actually my fault. I hoped he wouldn't hate me for it. Before, I'd felt bad about not being able to help them fight, but now, I felt the pain of knowing I was the reason they died. I couldn't bear thinking of it.

"I'm so sorry, chouchoutte. You don't deserve the pressure of this revelation. It wasn't your fault. I know that's why you hurt so badly. I felt it, too," he murmured and rubbed my back.

"How did you get here so fast?" I asked, wanting to think of anything else.

"I was talking to Talia when I felt the pain. She called Marius. Did you know he has the ability to appear anywhere as long as he's spoken to a person in that place within twenty-four hours? I called Dillon and put him on the phone. Marius brought me here and left," Lucien told me.

I nodded. As a child, I asked Marius why Talia was called 'The Traveler' when he could travel in the blink of an eye. He told me it was because she could travel on various plains of existence and didn't need permission to enter anyone's home or territory.

"Are you starting to feel a little better, Bellamy?"

"No. I think it will be a long time before I do. I need to go take care of this stuff. Did you want to call Talia and see if she can have Marius take you home?" I asked.

"He was pissed and said I was on my own before he left. I'll let Thierry know and stay with you until you're ready to leave. If we're together, everything will go more smoothly," he said confidently.

"I should've had you waiting for me at the hotel instead of leaving you at home. The hormones are making me more emotional. Thank you for coming, Lucien."

"I told you. I will always come for you, chouchoutte. Always," Lucien promised.

Goddess, I loved how he cared for me. I hummed and slid my hand down his chest and stomach, then into his pants. He groaned as I gripped him tightly and started stroking.

"Will you, saucisson? Will you *always* come for me?" I giggled.

"Now, you're going to be late for your meeting. I hope you're happy," he growled as he pulled me on top of him.

"Not yet, but I will be," I purred as I started working to lower my pants under his lusty gaze.

This wouldn't be the best start with the collective, but they had to learn. It was simply how their new collective worked. Their Queen loved her mate and would find time for both the collective and lovemaking.

Chapter 112: Collective Resources

[Bellamy]

We actually made it to the Assembly Hall on time. Of course, Dilly was teasing us in the link. Henry was laughing the whole time.

It seemed he was connected to my team, Lucien, and myself. And, like me, he could hear people who mind-linked to each other in those connections. Dilly and Lucien couldn't, though.

When we reached the Assembly Hall, Lucien paused for a moment and squeezed my hand. I turned to him. He was concerned about something; I could feel it.

"How are we playing this? Will the whole smelling like a rogue Alpha thing cause any issue?" he asked.

"You do still smell like a rogue King…. For now, we'll just pretend we were already aware. It will make us look more powerful and powerful leaders make all wolves happy," I said. "My only concern is that they may look to you as the leader of the collective."

"You go in ahead of me, we will tell them I'm your consort and I have my own people to care for. The Eaten Heart is the property of Queen Bellamy. Not King Lucien. If they have a problem, they can leave," Lucien replied.

I smiled. That was roughly what I was thinking of suggesting. I wasn't surprised that he was thinking what I was. He was smart and a good leader. The perfect Alpha.

We organized ourselves with Henry bringing up the rear and the pups walking between Lucien and Dilly. I warned the pups not to run off, even if they saw their parents. They feared me; it was a first for me. Normally, little ones liked me. They nodded and held each other's hands.

Opening the doors, I was a little shocked. There were close to a hundred wolves here, not counting all the children milling about. Kingston wouldn't have let the collective get this big. He believed strongly in keeping collectives to a maximum of eighty adults to avoid resource limitations and attracting hunters.

Keeping my head high, I marched to the stairs leading to the stage. As I progressed through the room, the chatting wolves all became quiet. Braden was right about one thing; I am fairly well-known. As the shortest known adult rogue wolf and as a deadly Queen.

When we reached the podium at the front, I saw a step-stool standing behind it. Looking at the crowd, I saw Sy sitting next to a well-beaten Tim. He smiled a little and nodded. I nodded back in appreciation. He had the forethought to add the stool. It would help me not look like a floundering child.

I stepped up behind the podium. A glance at the crowd told me many were excited about what was happening. The power of my collective had to be spreading through them. It was why some looked frightened. I was betting those were ex-packs.

Whispers about the pups scattered through the crowd. Speculation seemed to be out of my favor. Many people thought I was like Kyle and would make an example of the ones left behind. It annoyed me.

"Attention! Your Queen is about to speak," Henry announced forcefully.

"If anyone sees their pup up here, please come forward. You will be checked and then granted the child if they belong to you. If you know something unfortunate about the wolves I am looking for, please discreetly come forward and let me know," I stated.

Females started scooting through the crowd. The pups looked excited. Their mothers seemed to all be there. I was relieved. Trying to explain that their parents weren't coming for them wasn't a job I was looking forward to.

I kept the little King by me. His parents were important. I wanted to give them a place near me so I could oversee his growth. If his father was Kyle, I really wanted him nearby.

Dilly guided the other pups offstage to be reunited with their mothers. Henry sniffed them and verified the parentage. He led a woman up to the stage once he'd finished with the others.

She was about 5'9" with short, copper-colored hair and pale blue eyes. Her figure was trim and graceful. There was an aura of power coming from her, and she smelled like an ex-pack.

"Please," she said softly. "Let me have my son. I haven't seen him in months. We'll leave and he'll never challenge you. I promise."

"What did King Fuller tell you about the boy?" I asked.

"That he was an Alpha and King Fuller would keep him until he had a son of his own."

"So, he's not Kyle's child?"

"No. My mate died when our pack was wiped out. He was making sure I could get out. I had Ryan a week later. He's all I have left," she replied with tears in her eyes.

"What's your name?"

"Antonia Graves. I was the Gamma of the Midnight Whisper Pack in Montana," she answered.

My eyes widened. Everyone knew about the Midnight Whisper Pack.

A neighboring pack who refused to make an alliance with them since they were female-run wiped them out. I had a few of their people in my collective who I'd filtered to Daylight Moon quickly; a few female warriors and their families who'd made it out.

"I know a pack looking for a Gamma." I grinned, winking at Lucien.

He pulled out his phone and dialed. This would be the best way to keep the boy near enough for me to train while showing the new members of my collective how I worked for their wellbeing. Thomas answered after a few rings.

"Alpha Lucien, what can I do for you?" he asked.

"You're on speaker. Have you selected a Gamma yet, Thomas?" Lucien inquired.

"No. We have some ranked blood wolves that could be okay, but I was hoping to find an actual ranked wolf, like me and Julio," Thomas responded.

"Thomas, we found you a Gamma. She was the Gamma at Midnight Whisper. Will you accept her?" I asked.

"You better say yes, Thomas Lorrie, or I will whup your ass," I heard Charlie growl.

Several of the Dark Angels were from Midnight Whisper. They were amazing fighters and almost as stealthy as a well-trained rogue. I knew she'd want her.

"Of course I will, princess. Everyone knows how impressive the warriors of Midnight Whisper were. She will be a perfect addition to our… quirky… pack." Thomas chuckled. "Besides, the ranked wolves in female-run packs are amazing tacticians, planners, and creators. What is her name, Queen Bellamy?"

"Antonia Graves. What do you think, Antonia? It's a brand-new pack. You won't be stepping on anyone's toes by taking over," I told her.

"I never thought I would have that again. Oh, goddess. Yes! Please!" She smiled.

"It's done. When we leave, you and King Ryan will come with us. We will take you to your Alpha and I will release you from this collective," I replied.

"King Ryan?" Thomas asked.

"Her son. I'll take on training him to be a good King when he grows up. For now, we will see if we can make him a pack rogue," I explained.

"Sounds good. We'll work it out later. Goddess watch over you, Queen Bellamy."

"And you. Don't die," I responded.

"Same to you," he said as he hung up the phone.

I let Ryan go to his mother and Lucien pulled them aside, telling them what to expect for travel and what they would need to bring. Turning back to the crowd, I returned to my stepstool and addressed the collective again.

"Any ex-pack who doesn't have issues with violence and authority can be filtered into one of the packs in my collective. Either Alpha Thomas' new pack, Rose Moon, or Alpha Lucien's pack, Lune Rouge. It'll depend on what you want in a pack. No rogue has to stay in my collective.

"If you want to leave speak with Silas Greene or Tim Scarlet about it and they'll let me know. I'll process disconnections tomorrow morning. Just remember, I'm not only the Queen of the largest and most prosperous collective in the region, but I'm also the High Queen of the Werewolf Association. I can protect you," I stated.

Murmurs went through the crowd. Most of the ex-packs were talking excitedly about joining a pack again. The rogue borns were in awe. I'd secured a larger territory and had a plan to remove excess drains on collective resources.

'Very sexy, chouchoutte,' Lucien linked me.

I turned bright red from the embarrassment as a chuckle came from Henry. Of course, my mate forgot Henry could hear our links. I looked at the crowd to see if they had heard him. None of them seemed to. For that simple thing, I was immensely grateful.

"I'm turning this meeting over to my tech guy, Dillon, and my lieutenant, Henry. They'll walk you through getting registered in the collective. I will not process you until I know who you are, so don't skip it. Tim, Silas, please come with my consort and me to the office at the main house. I need to speak with you about the process of taking over this position," I said coolly.

They nodded and Lucien guided me back down the aisle and out into the late afternoon heat. We headed to the house, and I started accepting that I held the second most frightening collective in our region. Thanks to Kyle's laziness and cowardice.

Chapter 113: Feral Family

I closed the door to the office after we were all inside. The bodies and blood were gone and the smell of pine-scented cleaner was fading. They had it cleaned while Lucien and I were resting.

Tim and Silas stood by the chairs in front of the desk and Lucien stood beside the chair behind it. I walked around the desk and pulled him to sit in the chair, seating myself in his lap. It was always my favorite seat in the house.

Gesturing to the chairs across from me, I smiled at my guests. Preparing new lieutenants was a pretty simple job, but I had another important issue to cover. An issue I felt these two were perfect for.

"Thank you for coming and for accepting the lieutenant position. I usually like to have two people in charge of an area," I stated, as I opened the profile with my name on the computer.

Dilly had gone in and done his techie stuff, so I would have access to everything. He set up my profile so it would look like the one at home and on my laptop. I was a fan of consistency in simple things. It made it easier to handle the bigger problems.

"We're happy to take the positions. Sy and I are too old to do the jobs Kingston and Kyle had us on. We're loyal, but that stuff changes you after too long. We were planning to leave after things calmed down from Jared's departure. There are too many years, but too little time to keep being the torturer and assassin." Tim sighed.

"I understand. It's time to experience a different sort of life. Do you have smartphones?" I asked.

They nodded and pulled out their phones. I turned the screen to them so they could get the web address I had for enrolling lieutenants into my collective. While they focused on their phone applications, I turned the screen back and went to the part of the site for adoptions.

My collective had orphanages and foster homes for children left behind after pack massacres and resource conflicts. I wouldn't let other children suffer and fear being hurt by other wolves or humans like I did when I was a child. None of them would ever find themselves at the mercy of bad adults.

Sy was right about one thing; he and Tim lacked the skills to handle a normal rogue born child. Luckily for them, I had an option that would fit perfectly. It was the role of a leader to ensure the health and happiness of their people. Happy people were loyal people.

Lucien watched quietly from behind me. His hand rested low on my belly, over our pups. He seemed at peace and content to be my furniture. It was calming for me to have him there.

"All done." Sy smiled.

"Great," I responded and flipped back to the intake tab.

Their information showed up quickly, and I completed my end to get them set up, with the main farm house's address as their address. The house was perfect for them. It was perfect for everyone involved.

"Since this house is most central to this part of the territory, I would like you to move here. I will be taking the books back to Lune Rouge, but will make sure to get you copies as soon as possible," I told them.

They nodded again, seemingly pleased with the news of their new home.

"I want you to get the harem rooms torn down, install a hall, and put in more offices. One of them will be mine after it's complete. It needs to be soundproofed, windowless, and have biometric locks. Dillon will send what you need. It will already be keyed to me. Let me know when the office is complete and I'll come to set it up inside," I commanded.

"Yes, Queen Bellamy," they answered in unison.

"Call me Amy unless it's something in front of other rogues," I groaned.

They chuckled. "Yes, Amy."

"This is the farthest point from the seat of my territory. You're more than lieutenants. You're basically… Counts? Or something. A lesser royal title. You'll check in with me weekly via video chat. There's a site for minor disputes and you're expected to check it daily to resolve minor issues. Larger ones will be brought to you. If it's big enough to be brought to me, I want it immediately."

There wasn't a lot for lieutenants to handle. I had civil engineers to help with the other stuff. They were just busy this month. I had a few big projects going, so I was more than willing to pick up the slack. They would need to hire a few more people so I could manage this expansion and the next.

"I also have a special assignment for you. I have three ferals, one male and two females. They're six years old. Their mom pupped, but she and their father didn't want to be human to raise them. She abandoned them in my territory when they were almost five. We've gotten them potty-trained and speaking a little, but the rogues I have them with aren't equipped to deal with ferals," I told them.

"Ferals?" Lucien asked.

"They were raised by wolves as wolves, but are werewolf children. Their parents don't like being human. It happens with some rogues. You'll even find rogue ferals who breed with natural wolves. The pups of these unions will be born wolves and have their first shift at two years old. They'll be fully formed human adults at the first shift, knowing they're werewolves and essentially being wolves with human sides, like if Remus were in charge of everything and you were in his place.

"We call these people "wolf-weres" when we discover them, which is not often. Normally, wolf-weres just find another wolf-were or a feral to breed with. Mating with a wolf is similar to mating with a human, but your wolf mate only has a wolf's lifespan. Max of eight years in many cases. They don't understand why you don't age or anything about the human half of you," I explained.

"I always wondered what would happen if we mated with natural wolves," he murmured in a thoughtful tone. Pack wolves often had little experience with wolf-weres or feral rogues.

"You weren't thinking of mating with a natural, were you?" I teased.

"…. Maybe," Lucien mumbled.

I snorted. That would've gotten him his heir a lot sooner. The only problem was; that naturals were afraid of Alpha werewolves. We were bigger than them and powerful in a way their minds couldn't understand. Normal rogues and pack wolves had more luck if they looked that way for a mate.

Sy and Tim were quiet while I talked to Lucien. I knew they were consulting with each other and that was why I took the time to explain things, to lessen the pressure.

Kingston had Sy and Tim take care of any feral adults that came to the territory. These pups would be at least as civilized as the worst of the ferals they'd trained.

"We've wanted pups for a while, Amy," Tim said softly.

"Are you sure you want to give them to us?" Sy asked.

"More than anything. They need parents who will understand. Like you, Sy. You're proof that ferals can be just like everyone else." I smiled, gently.

"Have they accepted names?"

Ferals would only accept names once they had given up their wild nature. He was trying to see how far along they were. They would have a chance that a lot of adoptive parents didn't get often.

"No. We've tried a lot. They recognize me as their Alpha, but nothing else about the collective is important to them. I tried naming them, but they wouldn't answer to the names." I sighed.

"We'll pick some out," Tim said, squeezing Sy's hand. "Silas is amazing at getting ferals to accept names."

"Is there anything else? We need to pack to move in here and start getting ready for the pups. Do you know how soon we can get them?" Sy grinned.

"As soon as you want them, you can text Charles. Once Dillon has your accounts set up on the computer, you will have access to the numbers for me and all of my lieutenants," I answered.

They stood, and I shook their hands before they left. That had gone perfectly. Lucien wrapped his arms around me and held me close.

"You need to eat something, chouchoutte," he murmured in my ear.

I nodded. The pups were making me queasy. It was a long time since the fast-food cheeseburgers we'd grabbed on the way down.

Lucien and I headed to the kitchen. I looked through the fridge and freezer before deciding on grilling a couple of chicken breasts and having a salad. It would hold me over until dinner.

Kyle had obviously been planning a feast. There were some beautiful roasts in the fridge. I pulled them out with a few other things and started the oven preheating to cook them. Luckily, they just had to be warm all the way through and not cooked all the way through to make them edible for us.

Once my chicken and salad were all put together, I sat at the table. Lucien had turned down food, saying he could wait for dinner. I knew I needed a lot more right then. Our pups were starting another growth spurt.

"I'm going to go call Thierry and Robert. They need to know what's going on. I'm sure they're worried," Lucien said.

"Use the office for your call. Make sure the blinds are closed and the door is locked. I don't want Kyle coming for you again," I told him.

"Of course, my Queen. You eat and rest. I'll send Dillon to hang out with you, so you don't get lonely."

"You mean watch me so I don't get taken…." I sighed.

"I mean whichever doesn't get me sent to the couch tonight." He laughed.

I giggled. "That will never happen, mon saucisson. I need you too much."

"Don't say things like that too often, chouchoutte. I might become too prideful. You eat. I'll see you in a little while." Lucien grinned as he left the room.

I settled in and started eating my meal. After a little while, Dilly came in and grabbed a glass of water before sitting across from me. It had been hard to find time to talk to him with the Luna stuff and the investigation. I realized I was behind on everything in his life.

Guilt washed over me. We were so busy with our mates. There had been no time to sit with him and Cara to hear about their lives and issues.

"You okay, Bems?" he asked.

"I was just thinking about how busy we've been. I barely see you and Cara outside of training in the morning."

"You're Luna and High Queen, Bemmy. We don't want to bother you." Dilly smiled.

"You are *never* a bother. You're my best friend. Now, tell me all about your sexy mate while I have my snack." I winked.

He looked disgusted for a moment. "He's your cousin! Aren't you weirded out?"

I laughed. "I barely know him. Now, spill about your gorgeous warrior."

There was no lie there. Jean-Claude may practically be my half-brother, but I didn't feel about him like I felt about my adoptive brothers. I certainly never wanted to hear about any of *them* from their mates. Gross.

"Bellamy," he sighed. "Come on."

"Now it sounds good! Cum on what, where, when?" I giggled.

He turned red. "You fucking pervert."

"Please…. I'll tell you about Lucien and his current… fixations," I offered.

No matter how much Dilly changed, one thing stayed the same. He loved other people's secrets and hearing about sexy men. His look of defiance turned to resignation. I loved winning.

"From the beginning." I grinned, turning back to my food.

"The beginning? Seriously?" Dilly whined.

"We haven't had time to talk about the whole thing. While we were dress shopping you were all quiet. From the beginning, Dillon Metz. Now," I insisted.

"Fine…."

Chapter 114: When Dilly Met Jean-Claude

[Dillon]

Lune Rouge had the most perfect little town I'd ever seen. Everyone laughed when I said it was fucking adorable, but it was. I could see Bellamy at the front of the bus. Her eyes were enormous as she took in the town. She deserved this so much.

Movement out the back window caught my eye. I turned, tapping Drake on the shoulder. He looked at me and I pointed out the window. Others turned, too. Children we'd driven past were chasing the bus and popping into buildings, dragging people out to follow us as well.

They'd sometimes come out of a building with no one and sometimes with a whole family. More than half of the pack had to be following us. I almost laughed. Bellamy hated crowds.

When we stopped in the packhouse's courtyard, we discreetly turned and sat. We wouldn't get in as much trouble if she thought we didn't know. I wondered what was up, though. Crowds never gathered like that for Kieran.

Lucien stood up. Goddess, that man was hot as hell. I was glad he was going to let me join his pack. Not only would I be able to spend my life with Bellamy and Cara, I would get to look at that gorgeous ass of his. Serious yum.

Griff growled in my head. He was normally chiding, but relaxed at my attitude. I wondered if I'd done anything to make him mad.

'Everything alright, buddy?' I asked my wolf.

'He is our Qu… Captain's mate! Stop looking at him like he's a piece of meat! What if we find our mate and he finds out about what you've been doing?'

'You haven't worried about a mate since we were seventeen. Why's this coming up now?'

'I just… feel something. It keeps telling me he's nearby. Maybe he's in this pack! That would be perfect. We could be with our Queen and our mate. It would confirm that the goddess meant it to be.' Griff sighed.

He always had trouble with not seeing Bellamy as his queen. I'd been thinking of going rogue when I grew up before she came to the pack. She changed my whole life, and Griff loved her from the moment he saw her.

A cheer from outside the bus pulled me back to the present. Did they really just cheer for their Alpha?

I looked at Bellamy. She looked shocked. I could clearly see the beautiful dark honey brown of her eyes, wide and sparkling like warm honey in the sun.

A strange magnetism drew me to her; I couldn't explain the pull. She was more than my best friend. I had weird feelings for her. Even Griff did for Aurora. He insisted it was because she was such a powerful Queen. Nothing about her screamed power unless you fought her.

She glanced at us and shrugged before joining Lucien outside. There was another cheer and a chuckle from the crowd. They must have startled her. Bellamy was cute and great at playing sweet, weak roles. The pack must be eating it up.

"Everyone, let's get lined up in order. When Bellamy's finished we won't take as long doing our part. I want to get settled and call my mate," Jason ordered.

He pulled Bruce to the front of the bus and had him sit in the first seat. Jason was next to him, near the window. Todd slipped into the second seat, followed by Galen. I sat in the third seat, with Drake next to me.

As everyone else got seated, I looked out the window. Bellamy and Lucien were getting ready to greet the line of ranked wolves. I glanced over at them quickly and turned to talk to Drake about the rogue assignment when Griff started going insane.

'Mate! Mate! He's there! Look you fucking idiot! Look at him!' Griff shouted in my head.

I turned back to the tinted bus window quickly and pressed my face against the glass. My mate? He had a thick, toned build. His copper-colored hair was a little long on top, but shorn on the sides. I could just make out brown eyes, like Bellamy's. Bellamy! She would know who he was!

'Bemmy! My mate! I see him! He's so hot!' I linked her.

'Where, Dilly?' she asked.

How could she not see that glorious man? He practically glowed in the sunlight. He was a god of war and love and poetry. My heart sang ancient love songs in honor of his beauty. Holy fuck, I was getting weird.

I shook my head and noticed the man next to him. Almost identical, but not. Slimmer than my mate. They looked really similar in the face. She would know who I was talking about.

'Standing in the line, next to a not-as-hot guy who looks like him.'

Bellamy looked down the line. A small smile played on her face. I knew how excited she was for Cara, and now she was excited for me, too.

'The one with muscles and light brownish-red hair?' she asked.

How could she reduce him to such a boring description? Right, she had Lucien. He was almost as hot as my mate, so I could understand her not seeing what I did.

'Yes! You got it. Who is he?' I pressed.

'The head of the warriors, if I'm thinking correctly. His name is Jean-Claude.'

Oh, dear goddess, it was perfect. I wondered if he would call me by a cute French endearment like Lucien did Bellamy. I would have to figure one out for him!

'Goddess, a sexy name for a sexy man,' I replied.

'Chill. You'll get to meet him soon.' She giggled in our link.

"What's…? Get off me Galen! What the fuck!?" Todd shouted.

I looked over and saw Galen trying to press against the window, too. He had the same expression I'd seen a hundred times before, probably the same one I wore. His mate was there. That would be a relief. His little crush on Bellamy was really getting awkward.

"My mate's in the line. Bellamy knew his name," I said to Drake, loud enough to let Galen hear. "His name is Jean-Claude. Head of the warriors. Look, Dray-Dray. He's the last man in the line. Isn't he perfect?" I sighed.

"The Gamma's second son? Not my type, Dil, but congrats. He looks like a powerful warrior," Drake said.

He was right. Head of the warriors! I had to impress him. If he was even half as good as Bellamy, he was five times better than Drake.

"How will I impress him?" I muttered.

"Use your vampire tricks. If my mate could do what you can do, I'd be carrying her off to my room to show her the tricks *I* can do." Drake chuckled.

I grinned. It was perfect and made all the pain of Talia's training worthwhile. I heard Bellamy link us, asking if anyone else saw their mates and every unmated man looked around before responding with a sullen *'no'*.

"Salomé." Galen sighed.

"Which one?" I asked.

"The one next to Cara." He smiled.

Glancing over the line, I saw her and started laughing. It was perfect.

"Why are you laughing?"

"She looks like Bellamy! Different hair and eyes, same chin, nose, jaw, and mouth." I snickered. "Shrink her down, dye her hair, and give her color contacts, and she's practically a perfect match!"

"Does this mean we don't have to deal with Galen lusting after our little sister anymore?" Porter snorted.

"It was getting pretty awkward." Bruce cringed. "Mom and Dad were going to stage an intervention."

"Shut up! It doesn't matter anymore. My mate's right there. I didn't think I had one. It'll still be a few weeks before it's confirmed, but Bran says she's ours and I'll be here first thing in the morning of her birthday to claim her," Galen insisted.

We teased him a little longer about his underage mate, his crush on Bellamy, and anything we'd wanted to tease him about for years. Galen was usually pretty calm, so his reactions were hilarious as he got mad, embarrassed, or flustered.

Bruce stood. "Bellamy says it's time."

We scooted out of the seats. My stomach twisted with nerves. I had never been nervous about a boy before. I wondered if he'd like me, but shook it off. Of course he would. He was my mate. We were made for each other.

"Dillon! Go!" Porter growled, prodding me.

I hadn't even realized the others had left. It was my turn. I swallowed my nerves and headed off the bus. Time to show my mate how lucky he was.

"Dillon Metz. Sixth rank of the Elite Ten," I announced in a commanding tone.

Somehow, I kept a straight face and strode to my place in line. Out of the corner of my eye, I saw Jean-Claude grip the hand of the boy next to him. I knew it was his brother, but I didn't like it. Griff wanted to growl and warn him away from our mate, but I held back.

Standing between Porter and Drake for the few minutes it took for everyone else to file out and introduce themselves was pure torture. I was in agony. The scent of my mate wafted over with the breeze, and I was trying not to get turned on by the heady mixture of lavender and eucalyptus.

His fresh, sweet, tangy scent was driving Griff mad. I maintained my stance and didn't falter. I was stronger than my urges.

When Bruce dismissed us, I looked over at Bellamy. A small smile played on her face. I thanked the goddess for giving me a best friend who loved and supported me. I probably wouldn't have made it through my teen years without her. There was a brief nod from her and I leapt into action. Literally.

Quickly judging the distance, I sprung across the courtyard to land in front of my mate. He was just a little shorter than me, but big in so many other ways. His arms and chest were thick. I had to fight to keep Griff under control. I didn't realize he'd become such a horn-dog once we found our mate, but he was making me a little uncomfortable with all the things he was suggesting.

I placated him by reaching out and running my fingertips from Jean-Claude's temple, down his cheek and jaw, resting them below his chin. He looked even better up close. I wanted to kiss him so badly, but I was keenly aware of our immense audience.

"Hello, gorgeous. I've been looking for you," I purred.

"Our new Luna brings many blessings," Jean-Claude breathed.

He had no idea. I looked into his beautiful caramel-colored eyes. The eyes of my best friend, the eyes of my soulmate. The eyes I fell in love with when I saw Bellamy six years ago.

"She really does. I'll talk to you later. First, I have to get settled." I winked and rushed back to the bus to grab my bag.

I had to get away, or I wouldn't be able to control myself. The old Dillon was gone. I would love and cherish my mate for the rest of my life. There was no other man in the world who could tear me away. Faintly, I heard my mate and his father talking.

"I knew he was out there," his dad told him.

"He's a warrior. He's an elite warrior. Thank the goddess," Jean-Claude said in a happy voice.

Thank the goddess, indeed.

Chapter 115: A Lot to Unpack

[Dillon]

An omega led me through the packhouse and up to the guest rooms. My room was charming. The walls were a soft moss green with white wainscoting and light hardwood floors. My bed was a queen size with a beautiful quilted duvet that mimicked the colors of the room.

A glass-paneled door led to a small balcony. I opened it up for some fresh air and stepped out. It overlooked the garden behind the house. I loved everything about it.

Going back into the room, I unzipped my large bag and pulled out the body pillow I'd packed. Until I could cuddle my mate every night, it would have to do. I wondered if I could get one of his shirts to put over it so it would smell like him.

Shaking my head at the girlish idea, I started putting my clothes away and my toiletries in the bathroom. Working to put my mind to something else. Anything other than the feeling of Jean-Claude's skin under my fingertips.

The room was finally perfect after about thirty minutes. I started looking myself over to make sure I didn't go out looking a mess. I wanted to be perfect the next time I saw him. Griff was eager to get back out there and find our mate.

There was a knock at the door. Drake must have been ready to go hunting for the rogues that would be hiding in the pack. He and I were the best for tracking them, and we were honestly kind to the rogues we found.

Even though we both lost our parents to rogues, we were really close to Bellamy. It gave us a different perspective. It was hard to hate them, knowing that not all rogues were violent monsters.

I opened the door, and the warm, inviting glow of my mate's caramel eyes met mine. I found Jean-Claude's eyes, a rich, golden color with flecks of deep chocolate brown, were slightly more golden than Bellamy's. They were the most amazing eyes in the world.

Griffin whimpered in my head. He wanted me to grab Jean-Claude and kiss him so hard he would forget how to breathe. With a languid slowness, those breathtaking brown eyes scanned my body, making my heart pound. His desire for me increased his scent tenfold.

My wolf wanted to do even more than just kiss when Jean-Claude's eyes ate up every inch of my body. I could practically feel his gaze, as if his hands were all over me. He looked at me like I was everything he loved to eat. And the feeling was mutual, as my own eyes explored every curve and bulge under his clothes.

A slight blush graced his cheeks when his gaze stopped about halfway down my body. His tongue slipped over his lips as he stared directly at my package. I had such a dirty mate. It made me feel a little shy. I didn't know what to do about the feeling, so I took charge of the situation and reached out to pull him into the room.

Closing the door quickly, I used the vampire speed Talia taught me to press him against the wall with his arms above his head before he could even blink. I slid my hands down, feeling all the muscles of his arms until I reached his shoulders and pinned them to the wall.

He focused his eyes on my lips. Leaning in, I traced my nose along the curve of his jaw and down his neck. I found the spot I would mark one day and gently kissed it.

His low, guttural moan ignited a fire within me. It was all I could do to keep Griff from taking over. He wanted to take Jean-Claude to bed and mark him right then.

I kissed his neck again and nibbled it a little. He was panting and moaning in that gruff, growling way. The sounds my mate made were the most erotic I had ever heard. I could listen to him all day.

Pulling back, I moved my lips just above his. He was whimpering with need. I wanted to play a little. Sadly, I didn't have time to indulge in my need for him, though, because I needed to get to work. Instead, I'd tease him a little. Just until

"How can I help you, Mr…?" I left it open.

"Dubois. Jean-Claude Dubois," he murmured.

Goddess, that was a gorgeous name. It was like something I wanted to eat or bathe in. And the way his voice sounded when he said it was like velvet wrapping around my heart… and my other parts.

"Dillon Metz, but you already knew that," I purred.

Jean-Claude nodded. He leaned in, wanting to get closer, but I teased him by pulling back, still holding him against the wall. The desire in his eyes gave me a thrill I'd never had before.

"What do you want, Mr. Dubois?"

"You're my mate. I want *you*," he whispered with a blush.

I chuckled. I loved how straightforward he was, but I'd jumped into bed with a lot of guys in the past and that wouldn't be how I treated my mate. He was more than a lay or a minor entertainment. He was my forever.

"There's a lot we don't know about each other yet. Let's take it slow, gorgeous."

"Please, mon rêve. Just one kiss. To hold me over until we know each other better," he coaxed, with an intense gaze focused on my lips.

I leaned in and he closed his eyes, waiting to feel my lips against his for the first time. Griff was jumping and dancing in my head. He was almost more excited than I was.

'I need whoever's closest to the hospital to come collect an orderly who attacked me. Someone else find out where prisoners are kept and meet them there,' Bellamy ordered in our link.

Sam, Harrison, Freddy, and Porter were already at the borders checking patrols. Galen and Jason said they would go. Drake linked that he would head to the cells.

'Wait for me,' I linked back. *'I want to make sure the fucker gets locked up properly and I need to check out the security system there.'*

'I'll wait outside your room,' Drake replied.

I sighed. "Sorry, handsome. I have to go. Someone tried to attack Bellamy. I'll see you when I'm off work. We can talk for a while."

"A kiss won't take long," Jean-Claude stated.

"A kiss will turn into making out, handsome. She's my best friend and I'm here to watch out for her. Don't worry. We'll get there," I told him, caressing his face.

"You don't want me as much as I want you," he pouted and pushed away from the wall.

I pushed him back. "You are my mate. It's taking everything I have not to lock the door, throw you on that bed, and spend the next week learning every spot on your body that produces that sexy moan. I have responsibilities as a warrior, as a security expert, *and* as a friend to *your* Luna. Never *ever* think I don't want you. You. Are. *Mine!*"

My lips crashed against his in an intense, deep kiss, the taste of him lingering as the moment ended too soon. There was an adorable confusion in his eyes. If I didn't have so much to do, I really would've taken him to bed.

"I need to go, Jean-Claude. I'll see you tonight, then we can go a little slower and I can get more of those little growls from you," I said as I opened the door.

"Okay," he replied breathily, and left.

Drake was in the hall and gave me a look when I came out. It was half smirking. I knew what he was thinking and, given my reputation and past, I didn't blame him.

"Wow, cousin. Already got him in your room. That was faster than I expected." He chuckled.

"Shut it. Nothing happened. Let's go. I want to see this fucker that tried to off my bestie," I growled, and we headed to the cells.

Chapter 116: The Ball-Breaker

[Dillon]

—Several days later—

The ball-breaker had been great. Bellamy and I were the last ones standing… well, limping. We'd run off to assess our injuries and prepare for another attack. It was pretty common for us to be the last ones standing. The fight normally lasted so long because of us. Although neither of us was defeated, we needed breaks in fights like this.

Taking out my frustration about Jean-Claude marking me without permission, that bastard Pavel insulting my mate, and the overall powerlessness I felt about the situation was wonderful. I fought harder and more violently than in the past. Bellamy actually started grinning that deadly smile she got when fighting rogues. I knew she wasn't holding back, finally.

'Dilly, are you ready for the next round?' she asked in our link.

Attempting to move my left arm, I discovered it was partially dislocated. Nothing was broken, but the fight had left me. I felt my rage break, and the aching sadness of what happened remained.

When Richard and I ran the borders, he would talk while we were in human form and tell me more about the relationship between Pavel and Jean-Claude. For the first six months of their relationship, Pavel told him to hide that they were dating. Like my lovers would hide our relationships. When they let people know, it was just before the first time Pavel tried to get Jean-Claude to sleep with him.

Unlike me, Jean-Claude *actually* thought he was important to Pavel. He thought they were in love even though Pavel would guilt trip him into almost everything he wanted from Jean-Claude. Richard told him to break it off, but he was as realistic about his chances of finding his mate as I was.

Gay werewolves were rare. Bisexual werewolves were more common, but never had a same-gender mate. Few gay werewolves found their fated mates.

I wished I could've come here after my parents had died. I would've known he was my mate when I turned seventeen. Pavel wouldn't have gotten the chance to hurt him like he did, but I wouldn't have been there for Bellamy when she needed someone to understand her.

'Can we just lie and tell everyone you won?' I asked.

'You over your anger then?'

'Yeah. I just want to rest. I'll surrender.'

'Are you going to forgive him?'

'Probably. Eventually. I wanted him to trust me. I partially blame Bruce for this. Jean-Claude said something about how I used to date a lot of guys when we were arguing. He said he didn't know anything about me and he couldn't trust that I wasn't attracted to Randy and Stan,' I told her.

'I understand. Lucien thought I was attracted to Ricky and Galen. Even though I was marked, he was jealous. Jean-Claude loves you and was afraid of losing you. His trust was destroyed by that little snake. Now your anger is gone, please, give him a chance to talk to you. Don't reject him. It'll be more painful than you can imagine since he's marked you,' Bellamy replied.

'I'll give him a chance. Later…. I'm still not ready.'

'Don't let the anger live longer than it has to. I love you and I want you to be happy. I'll call Lucien out. You rest, someone will be there for you shortly,' she said.

I laid back against the dirt wall of the gully I hid in. With a little work and a lot of pain, I popped my partially dislocated shoulder back in. I would be at fault if something attacked me while injured. It would be a little while before someone found me, so I closed my eyes for a minute.

Sometime later, I opened my eyes and saw Jean-Claude's concerned face above me, his muscular arms carrying me effortlessly. I fought the urge to snuggle into his massive arms. No wonder Bellamy always let Lucien carry her around and hold her. It felt so amazing and safe.

Griffin wanted me to give in to the feelings we still had for our mate. He wanted me to forgive Jean-Claude and mark him, too. He wanted to be whole.

"Put me down and call another warrior," I growled.

"No."

"I don't want you to carry me. I don't want you to touch me. And I don't want you to talk to me. Leave me *alone*, Jean-Claude."

"Do you remember what you said to me when you carried me home after training that first time?" he asked.

I was stubborn and didn't want to even think about that time. Back when I was still stupid enough to think I could have something other than being used to make someone else feel good. I pursed my lips together and turned my face from him.

"You're *my* mate. I take care of what's mine. No other man will carry you *anywhere*. Do you understand?" he growled softly.

I felt tears well up in my eyes and my throat tightened. Since I first started thinking about what it would be like to have a mate, I wanted to hear a man say that to me, hear *my mate* say that to me. It was bittersweet coming from someone who had stolen something special from me.

"Don't cry, mon rêve. I know I messed up. I'll spend the rest of my life making it up to you, I swear. I'll never do anything to harm you ever again. Please, please forgive me," Jean-Claude whispered.

"Take me to my room and leave me alone," I answered.

He sighed dejectedly and kept going. An omega met us in my room and helped me clean up after Jean-Claude left.

She was really nice and very gentle, which I appreciated more than anything. All the omegas at Lune Rouge were caring and happy people. It spoke to Lucien's skill as an Alpha more than any other success.

"Can I ask you a question?" I asked.

"You seem to be quite capable, sir." She smiled softly as she helped me into my bed.

I chuckled. She was funny, her badge said Francesca. I liked it.

"What does 'mon rêve' mean?" I asked.

For the last few days, I'd meant to ask Bellamy or Lucien and kept forgetting. I could've looked it up on the computer or my phone, but I didn't know how to spell it. I felt a little stupid for asking, but I had to know what he kept calling me.

"It means 'my dream'. It's where the word reverie comes from," she explained.

"I need to figure out what to call him when I forgive him. I wish Bellamy could help me, or I could steal hers," I muttered.

"What do you mean?" Francesca asked, sitting on the bed.

"You haven't heard her talking to Lucien?"

She looked confused. "I've heard her call him her love in English and French. Otherwise, she calls him by his name or mon cœur. My heart. Is there another name she uses?"

I didn't know why she wouldn't call him by that name in front of people. She sounded adorable when she said it. I wanted something like that.

"Saucisson?" I said questioningly.

"Oh…. Some men might take it as sexual, so I can see her not saying it around here much. It means 'sausage'. She calls him her sausage. That's so cute." She giggled.

I chuckled a little, but it made my ribs hurt and turned into a groan. It sounded more like something I would've called my mate.

"You could call him anything and it would make Claude happy. We've known each other since we were pups. He seems fierce on the outside, but he's really soft and cuddly. Maybe mon nounours? My teddy bear. It might make him blush. I can help with more if you don't like that one," Francesca offered.

Maybe a playful reminder of the bear issue and that he is my only teddy bear. Griff liked it. We loved seeing him blush.

"Perhaps. Thank you, Francesca. I'm feeling a little tired."

"The Luna arranged food for everyone. I'll go check on it. Please, call me Frankie. All my friends do. Claude's my friend and you're his mate, so my friend by association." She smiled.

"You can call me Dillon. A lot of my friends call me Dil, but only Bellamy can call me Dilly. She'll get mad if she hears other people doing it," I told her.

"I don't want to make her mad. Thank you, Dillon. You rest, I'll come right back," she said and headed for the door.

I closed my eyes and sighed. Maybe I could talk to him later. He wasn't going anywhere, and I didn't want to reject him. I needed him.

'He should be here with us. We'll heal faster with our mate by our side, especially now we're marked,' Griff reminded me.

'Maybe. I don't know where he is. I don't know how I'd get him here.'

The door opened quietly, and suddenly, I smelled Jean-Claude. He stood outside my door, rigid, a silent sentinel as close as I allowed. The corner of my mouth lifted into a slight smile.

"Claude, you shouldn't be here," she whispered, not quite closing the door.

"Where should I be, Frankie? My mate is in there. He's hurt. Arnou refuses to leave. He wants to make sure our mate heals and even being this close is helping him," he admitted.

"He's still mad and he has every right to it. I *told* you not to compare him to your ex. You messed this up. You need to give him space. It was only yesterday. He'll let you know when it's time to talk. You're only encouraging him to reject you by pushing it!" she hissed.

"I won't let this drive us apart. He's mine. I may be an ass, but I'm a stubborn one and I refuse to let him stew. He doesn't have to forgive me; he only has to let me be near enough to show him how much I love him. Go get him something to eat. I'll be here," he responded.

"Stay out of the room, or I'll tell Alpha Lucien. I'm sure the Luna won't be happy with you," Frankie growled and the door gently clicked shut.

Chapter 117: A Conclusive Decision

After I ate, I fell asleep. Even having Jean-Claude outside the door was making my healing go so much faster. Almost as fast as Bellamy before she had a mate. I never realized how powerful the mate bond could be in things other than our feelings for each other.

After a while, a familiar voice in the hall woke me up…. Cara. She was talking like herself though, not like the sugary little Beta's mate she'd been playing since she got to Lune Rouge or the good little Alpha's daughter she pretended to be.

This was our sarcastic, haughty, snide, little princess. Cara was sharp and never pulled punches. She was as blunt as Bellamy. Before Bellamy came, they were worried about me because I wasn't bonding with the pack, but they were worried about Cara because she was 'too sweet' and they thought someone would take advantage of her. I knew her, though. It was all an act.

"You don't understand. They thought they'd be alone forever. No matter how badass you are, they'll worry about you seeing that side and leaving. Whatever you think you need to hide from them, isn't nearly as bad as what they'll be hiding from you," Cara was saying.

"Eventually, they'll feel like they can tell us and show us who they are," Lucien replied. "I learned my lesson about keeping secrets. I'm never keeping anything from her again."

I hoped she had Bellamy's permission to say something like that. I had no clue what she'd been saying before I was fully conscious. Bellamy wouldn't mind too much, but she was sensitive to interference from others because of her parents.

Why were Lucien and Cara talking in front of my room?

"I'm going to tell Dillon everything. I want him to tell me everything. That's never going to be me again. I've learned, too. I'm never keeping another secret from him," Jean-Claude said with conviction.

Cara was in so much more trouble than she had imagined. I didn't know what she said before, but I would kick her ass if she messed things up for me. Dangerous to my enemies? What did she tell them?

'You bitch. Stop telling tales.'

'No. You stop being whiny. So you got marked earlier than planned. He loves you and is basically everything you ever said you wanted. A powerful warrior, a confident man, with eyes like Amy's, big muscles, and part of a loving family. That mark made you part of the family you always wanted. Caleb and Richard have been giving him no end of shit over marking you. Randy and Stanton gave him one hell of a talking-to last night. EVERYONE is on your side. Imagine how alone he feels,' she answered.

'He hurt me, Cara.'

'And you've milked it for a full day longer than you should have. I know you've been fighting Griffin on this. If he's like my wolf, he wanted to forgive Jean-Claude that same day. I have to fight Ace every time Caleb starts to get all lovey.'

'Why, though? I know you didn't date because you wanted to save yourself for your mate, but you have him now. Why aren't you going to town on that man like Bellamy does with Lucien?' I asked.

'You had this whole thing about waiting for a few weeks and getting to know each other. I loved the idea. I want to be with him the first time as his legal wife, hearing him vow to love and keep me forever in front of our parents, our pack, and the moon goddess is the biggest turn-on I can imagine.' Cara sighed in our link.

She was right about Griff and about how much I wanted a mate just like Jean-Claude. His failure to live up to my dream hurt my feelings, but no one's perfect, so I should've accepted that and made a new plan. He wasn't just saying he was sorry. I could tell how much my anger was hurting him.

'Send Jean-Claude in. I'm ready. I need to let him fix this. Stewing isn't going to make it better. I have to take a page from Bellamy. I had space, it's time to move forward,' I told her.

From the other side of the door, I heard Cara go back to her chirpy 'Alpha's perfect daughter' voice. "Good! Dillon says you can go in, Jean-Claude. He's ready to talk and work this out. Lucien, Olive, and your mother want us back at your place. We're going over the last few things for the Luna ceremony and we wanted to have your opinions on what Bellamy's dress should look like. C'mon."

I prepared myself for my mate to come in. I really needed to move on, and it was really the only way. He was made for me. I wouldn't find anyone else who was as perfect as him. I just had to make sure he understood, really understood, why I was so upset.

Frankie got up from the chair. "I heard that. I'll head out so you two have some privacy. One of your friends is making Liddy uncomfortable. She isn't the flirting type and that's all he does."

"Probably Drake. Sorry, my cousin is all business until he's around pretty girls." I chuckled.

"Then, I'll take over for her. I hope he's ready for Flirty Frankie." She winked. "I've stunned a few playboys into silence."

She patted my head and left as Jean-Claude entered the room. He looked concerned. I knew I still didn't look great and tried to sit up, but my arm was still sore. I winced and he rushed over, scooping me up and settling my back against the headboard.

Heat spread over my face. I was one of the strongest warriors in my pack, and my mate was treating me like I was a delicate flower. It was embarrassing and endearing all at the same time.

Jean-Claude pulled the chair closer to the bed and sat, leaning near me and taking my hand in his. He was gazing at me hopefully. His thumb stroked the back of my hand and I felt tingles across my skin.

"Thank you for listening to me. I'm sorry I broke your trust. With what I heard Bruce say about your dating habits at Daylight Moon, I just... I was afraid you would choose someone else instead of staying. I don't know why. The thought of losing you when I'd only just found you... it was too much to bear," he said earnestly.

"You don't understand me and we haven't had enough time for you to know me…. My first boyfriend wanted our relationship kept quiet. He was seventeen and I was sixteen. I wasn't his mate and he made sure I knew that. He didn't want me to get my hopes up. We hung out like friends and would sneak off to fool around," I started.

His expression was a mix of anger and sadness. He could see the connection we shared and the pain we both felt. I had two years on him for being treated as a time waster and toy. But I never thought I loved them. That was where we differed.

"It never got serious, he wouldn't let it. He found his mate and left the pack, but not before introducing me to his other friend. That's how it went. I met a new friend or two, snuck around, and knew I would never be loved unless I found my mate. I only had my friends to love me. Amy and Cara didn't scold me or chide me, they were there for me and let me know I was important to them," I said. "I didn't need men to love me. I had my girls."

"I really hurt you. You never loved any man before and the first one you gave your heart to betrayed your trust," Jean-Claude murmured.

"I always hoped I would find my mate and feel what it was to be loved and cherished. Not treated like a whore or a secret. You didn't trust me because of what Pavel did, even though I'm not Pavel. In all the times we talked, you never said anything about him or your worries. We weren't to that point yet, I guess. When you marked me without my consent, it didn't feel like you loved me. It felt like you wanted to own me," I admitted.

His face dropped into an ashamed frown. I'd wanted to yell and scream at him at the time. I wanted to punch him, break him, make him hurt for taking my fantasy from me. There was some pleasure in knowing he'd been hurt yesterday, but now I didn't like how it felt.

"I was never hung up on him. I was realistic. If he or I found our mates, I knew it would be over and I would let him go. The way he did it…. The things he said…. Dillon, I'm still seventeen for a couple months. I know I seem more mature because I'm big and in charge of so many warriors, but I'm not. I'm a stupid boy sometimes. That's not an excuse, just an explanation," Jean-Claude replied.

We were silent for a while. I hadn't thought about that. He was younger than me. This was his first relationship after his first breakup. I was expecting more than he was capable of because I lived such a different life.

"Will you wait here for me, mon rêve?" he asked.

"I don't really have anywhere else to go for a while." I scoffed.

"Let me show you what I wanted this to be like. Let me start over. No pressure to mark me. You do it in your own time. I'll wait forever if I have to. Will you give me that chance? Please?" Jean-Claude begged with the same puppy-dog pout Bellamy used.

"That pout is cheating…. Fine. This is your only chance. I'm not doing this again," I told him.

His face lit up with a grin, and he ran out of the room. I had to laugh. My mate was just an excited pup who wanted to be loved and praised. I would have to do better for him, too.

***

I didn't realize I'd fallen asleep until the bedroom door opened and the omega from the first day came in. She was carrying a large tray and set it on the dresser. Someone else came in behind a vase with a massive bouquet in it.

What the hell?

"Thanks, Liddy. You can go, close the door behind you." Jean-Claude's voice came from behind the floral monstrosity.

She giggled and headed out the door, closing it behind her. Jean-Claude set the vase down on the nightstand next to my bed. He smiled brightly and winked when he came out from behind the flowers.

"What's on the tray?" I asked.

"Our dinner. I wanted you to have more time to rest. We'll eat in here and talk. I want you to tell me about your past relationships, what you want in our relationship, and what concerns you have. I'll do the same. We'll spend every minute we have free getting to know each other. No more misunderstandings. No more secrets. Sound good?" he said, scooping me up and carrying me to the table in the corner of the room.

"That sounds perfect."

"Then, let's get started with our first date. The next one will be a lot better. We'll go to my favorite spot for a picnic and let our wolves run. Arnou wants to meet Griffin since we missed our chance yesterday," Jean-Claude told me as he settled me in a chair.

"Griff loves the idea. I can't wait." I grinned.

Chapter 118: Matters at Hand

"So, yeah. We've been dating properly and he's just been perfect. Even after your reveal at the Luna ceremony, he waited and listened while I told him everything. He really wants to have you and Lucien over for a meal so he can get to know you better," Dilly said.

I had finished my snack and started dinner cooking while he told me everything. I was so happy they'd worked things out. Without Cara and me to talk to, Dilly bottled things up. It was what made him lash out as a teen. He needed to be relieved of some of his stress.

"And as of this morning?" I asked.

"I think we're well on our way to a matching mark for him. Maybe around the time of Cara's wedding. I need time still. He may be doing better, but I still have this reminder of when he didn't trust me enough to talk. It might take a while to trust him again," he admitted.

"You'll get there. If my cousin is anything like me, he'll keep working until you are entirely his again. At least he doesn't have to deal with the Alpha bullshit like I do."

"Wow, chouchoutte, I didn't realize you weren't a fan of the 'Alpha bullshit'. It's certainly not what came across when you started groping me while I was on an important call with another Alpha," Lucien said from the doorway with a laugh.

"I had to entertain myself while listening to you be so boring." I stuck out my tongue and rolled my eyes.

"Get that tongue back in your mouth before I bite it, chouchoutte," he warned.

I laughed and returned to cooking. It felt like we were back home, cooking and teasing in our kitchen. My worry about Kyle came back. I wanted to hunt him, but the shock of finding out I was the reason for my parents' death had given enough time for his scent to dissipate.

The biggest positive was that Kyle and Kingston didn't trust banks. He would have only created accounts to pay for the services he needed. Odds were good he hired a middleman for it. Otherwise, all of his collective's funds were in a safe onsite. He had nothing to help him hire anyone or pay anyone off.

An hour later, we were having dinner. Sy and Tim joined us so we could go over more about the transition. It was a decent meal. The food was perfect, and the company was distracting. I almost forgot about the Kyle issue.

That night, we went back to the hotel in the town that was now part of my territory. I could feel more and more wolves becoming attached to my collective as the borders solidified. I knew it would be weird for it to be automatic, but it was a little off-putting.

I could feel the refusal to submit, the acceptance of my dominance, and the fear many people had at being connected to an unknown Alpha. I decided I would do a mass mind-link in the morning before I submitted to my own Alpha and his delicious dominance.

***

After my mind-link, Dilly reported a flood of registrations on the collective's website. The success of the link thrilled me for a lot of reasons, not the least of which was making my ex-packs feel more comfortable. Sy and Tim fully accepted their roles as my lieutenants and, after we shared blood, they reported they could also hear people mind-link each other if they were in the same room.

It seemed the added connection to me and my power gave my lieutenants something extra. I mind-linked Katie and she could respond, and so could Derick, but none of my rogue born lieutenants could answer, except Sy and Tim. I would try renewing the bonds. Being able to communicate with them without a phone would be immensely helpful.

We packed the books; patrols arrived and took up their positions; everything was perfectly on track for our departure. The way everything was working out made me nervous. Whenever things lined up, something always seemed to happen.

***

The days seemed to fly past, and I was twitchy as hell. As if always waiting for the other shoe to drop and for the next big bad thing to come at me.

The clearing of the land for Rose Moon was uneventful. No other Alphas could be on the land when it happened, but Lucien let me read a book about how an Alpha claims territory. I loved the chance to learn how the other half did it.

First, he would mark the borders of the land he was claiming, then go to the center. At that point, he would do a little ritual to commune with the goddess and ask her blessing over the pack. He would vow to honor her, protect his pack, and grow his community.

When Thomas called us to come in, I was relieved. The land held the slight scent of him. It was his. That would fade by the time the next generation was ready to take over, but it was enough for a rogue to smell. Lucien said he didn't smell anything and that he only knew it belonged to Thomas because he'd felt his power before.

The necessary demolitions were completed quickly. My contractors and construction guys who were ex-packs took their personal time to come help. They saw it as an opportunity to show off how useful they were to Thomas and Lucien.

Both Lune Rouge and Rose Moon were getting a *lot* of ex-pack applicants. We were heading toward emptying my collective of nearly all the ex-packs who wanted to rejoin pack life. I was very happy for them. We even had a few rogues who volunteered to be pack rogues.

It seemed like the entire world was barreling along while I was trying to keep up. We had a checkup for the pups four days before the wedding. They were strong and healthy. Lucien got more pictures so he could show off. I loved how adorable he was. He showed them to anyone who paused long enough.

Two days before the wedding, I got a phone call while I was overseeing the removal of all the furniture from my office. While we were on our honeymoon, workers would outfit my room with new double-paned, tinted windows. They would soundproof the walls and hang a thicker door.

My furniture was being replaced or reupholstered. Dilly was getting me a new desktop computer and setting up everything I needed. Shelves to hold the books from Limb Torn were being added. When I got back, it would be all ready for me to move in.

The call was from Quinn. He had updates from other rogues and a couple Kings, including Ash.

"Bellamy, Kyle has been spotted in the westernmost area of the region. The rumors are that he's trying to hire someone to take out a pack Alpha. It seems like your assumption is correct. His request is that they kill Lucien, but not you, and he is promising to give them the Lune Rouge pack land plus a million dollars to do it. Nothing upfront. Just the promise of a displaced rogue King," Quinn told me.

"That idiot. Are we getting close to catching him?" I asked.

"No. He's using several different intermediaries. No one speaks to him, he is only glimpsed. King Ashley said his warriors are hunting him since he was last seen near some caves by his territory. We'll let you know. I just wanted you to know he was far from you and your mate. I know that weddings are important to females," he said.

"Several packs and collectives, along with my own are coming to patrol the area around Lune Rouge. I trust your information, but I never underestimate my opponent when my life or the lives of my family are on the line. Thank you for the call. It helped with my nerves." I chuckled.

"Not getting cold feet, right? He's your mate. This is just a legal thing."

"Honestly, I would rather do a justice of the peace or courthouse wedding. I hate this sort of thing, but now my biological grandparents know I'm their granddaughter and they want to be at the wedding since they didn't see my parents get married. It's a whole big deal that I don't really want to be a part of if I'm being honest," I sighed.

"So it's the ceremony, not the marriage itself, that you have a problem with?" he asked.

"Pretty much, but I'll do it for them. Lucien is getting really into it too. I better go. They want me to do a last-minute fitting. The seamstresses here are ready to do what needs to be done."

"Well, good luck on the wedding, my mate and I got the invite and looking forward to it. Don't die, High Queen," he replied.

"Same to you, High King," I answered and hung up.

That was yesterday. Now I was sitting in the library, reading one of the handwritten books Mr. Brown gave me, and trying to figure out exactly what the deal was with my Collective and these new abilities.

The door flew open, and I jumped almost a foot. Cara and Dilly entered with big grins.

"What?" I asked suspiciously.

"It's the night before your wedding, Bemmy. You know what that means?" Dilly said in a sing-song voice.

"No…."

"Yes! Sleepover/Bachelorette party!!!" Cara squealed as they both pounced and dragged me from my comfy armchair.

As much as I loved them, sometimes I really hated them.

Chapter 119: Party Time

[Bellamy]

I followed my friends out of the library once they let me go. Cara and I had agreed to a sleepover the night before our weddings, just like the ones we used to have back home. Dilly would do his when he was ready to marry Jean-Claude. It was the way we were planning to stay connected in the way we were as kids.

We headed from the packhouse to my quarters so I could pack a bag. Lucien already knew this was the plan, but I had kind of been hoping they would forget. Lucien liked the idea. He thought it would be luckier if we didn't see each other until the wedding.

My hormones disagreed with him. It really was all I could do to stay in the library while he was dealing with his work, so he would be done with it before we left. We'd scheduled two weeks away, with one of them mostly being our expansions.

People were really excited about the upcoming changes. Pack members at Lune Rouge loved how many new members they were getting, and they were doing a lot to be accepting. The level of conflict had drastically reduced since we started.

We'd already had twenty newly mated couples made of an ex-pack rogue and a member of the pack. People who had given up on the mate gatherings, both regional and national, were finally finding their fated mates. It made the pack more at ease as time went on, but it also made for a lot more work for Lucien.

If not for the fact that I spent most of my day in his office working, I would never see him. I struggled some days to focus on my work when he was right there, smelling delicious and looking damn near edible. I ached for the feeling of him.

Every day was intense. He was reacting to my hormones as badly as I was. We were gaining a little bit of a reputation…. Not that I minded. It's hard to shame a rogue.

***

Cara, Dilly, and I arrived at the head warrior's cottage shortly after leaving the house. It was about halfway between the packhouse and the north field where the warriors practiced. Because he wasn't eighteen yet, Jean-Claude couldn't move out of his parents' home.

Dilly took over decorating and getting it ready. He was a wonderful multitasker. No one moved into the house after my father left his post. The ranked members had taken over the work of training the warriors when my granduncle was too old to continue. He was the one who trained Jean-Claude.

I met him once in the last week. Jean-Paul took me out for a walk in the garden. I learned some interesting stuff.

"You know, Bellamy, in our family, your father was the only straight second son. None of us had ever created a child. Only our older brothers did that. You and your father are rare children." He chuckled.

All the men on that side of the family were some variation on the same design. One thick, one thin, hair that varied from coppery auburn to the red-tinged bronze of my hair, the Dubois eyes that everyone born into the family had, and, it seemed, one who would be straight and the other gay.

"I wonder at that," I replied. "Did the goddess arrange it so there would never be a power struggle? Or was it just an odd quirk of hormones? Did it affect other things? My papa was loving, you're really kind, and Jean-Claude seems so sweet. Were the older brothers all rude and judgmental like René? Robert doesn't seem like his father and neither does Richard."

He laughed so hard. It wasn't until a few moments later, when I heard the angry muttering and heavy footsteps of my grandfather René and uncle Robert, that I understood. I started laughing with Jean-Paul. I couldn't help it. He was as much my grandfather as René was, and we connected more.

As we walked, he told me about his mate, who he lost in an attack fifteen years ago. He showed me their cottage, but Dilly was already there and shooed us away. Dilly wanted it to be a surprise to everyone when they saw it.

Jean-Paul smiled at my friend's insistence that we leave. He put an arm around my shoulders and hugged me briefly. I knew how much the members of our family were grateful for Dilly, Cara, and me. We gave them hope for healing and the future.

Just the day before my bachelorette sleepover, Dilly took Jean-Claude to see inside. He said his mate should see it before anyone else. We didn't see either of them at dinner, but did see them for a run this morning. No training on your wedding day, apparently.

***

As we approached the cottage, I could see some changes already. All the trim and the front door were pale green, and the color glowed against the tan and red of the bricks. A few feet in from the main walkway, on either side, was a raised planter with posts and wires above some sprouts.

"Blackberries?" I asked.

"On the left. Raspberries on the right. My favorite and his." Dilly grinned.

"That's so precious. You should do something like that, Bellamy." Cara sighed in lovey tones.

"I never have time for gardening and I can't see it getting much better. Plus, I can prepare the foods my mate likes to eat with the things in the kitchen. Why don't you do it, Cara?" I asked, laughing.

She growled. Everyone knew Cara couldn't keep a dandelion alive, let alone any other plant. Not for lack of trying. She was just a natural plant killer.

Dilly opened the door for us and made a sweeping bow, indicating we were to go ahead of him. The entry led to a large, open floor layout. It was really lovely and bright.

He'd had the wood floors refinished in a pale golden color that mimicked the color of fresh wheat. The walls were white and all the wooden furniture was just a hint darker than the floor.

The colors he'd used in much of the decoration were reminiscent of the pale green of his eyes and the golden brown that ran in my family. The couches were a darker shade of Dilly's green and the chairs were leather the same color as Jean-Claude's.

Over the fireplace, there were three picture frames hung in a pyramid. The one on the left was the only one with a picture in it. I smiled as I examined it.

Someone had been taking photos the first day we were here. They caught a perfect shot of Dilly when he caressed my cousin's cheek upon their first meeting. I wished Lucien, and I had pictures like that. It was sweet and romantic.

"Where did you get that?" I asked.

"From the family that does the pack newsletter. It was in the eleven-page newsletter they sent with information about us and our pictures. You know… the one that let everyone know who we were and why we were here…. I compiled most of the bios."

"I totally forgot. A lot was going on over the last few weeks." I laughed.

"I get it. You ready for junk food and super secrets?" He grinned.

"So ready. I can't wait to hear the dirt you dug up."

"And you have to tell us *all* about your mate. Those are the rules tonight," Cara insisted.

"Then you both have to tell me everything about your mates. All in full detail."

"Don't try to tell her it's gross because they're her cousins. She doesn't care." Dilly sighed.

"Nope. Don't care. I want to know ev-er-y-thing." I laughed.

"You are so weird, Amy." Cara giggled.

"If I weren't we wouldn't have met. I can't imagine my life without my princesses," I teased.

"My voice dropped, I'm not a princess anymore, Bems," Dilly pouted.

"You will always be my princess, Dilly, no matter what. I love you both so much."

"Don't go from silly to sappy. It throws Cara off." He snickered.

"It's hard not to. So much has been happening and I didn't think just three weeks ago, that I would end up where I am. I'm only eighteen and responsible for the third largest territory in the country, pregnant with twins, about to be married, *actually* mated, and Luna of a whole pack. How did this happen?" I started panicking.

"Let's get her to the couch. She's freaking," Cara whispered.

They pulled me to a couch and sat on either side, wrapping their arms around me. Only Cara and Dilly could ever calm me with a hug until I met Lucien. Aurora and I felt safe with them. Their wolves had even felt drawn to us when they came.

It was like everything was falling apart while it was all coming together. I didn't know what would happen next, and that made me nervous as hell.

What would happen when I made these vows before everyone? How would it change our relationship? Would Lucien think he could own me more now?

In the past few days, I'd become less into his dominance. Was that going to become a trend? Or would it go away when everything settled?

There were so many questions swarming my mind. The biggest one terrified me.

What if everything was actually a mistake, and I'd just managed to fool everyone into thinking I was strong enough to handle it all? What if that wasn't my mother in the dream and I really wasn't meant to be the one handling all of this? Why didn't I ever question everything before? How full of myself was I?

There was a knock at the door. I remembered what happened when I started panicking at the Limb Torn house.

"I'll get it," Dilly said.

"No. Please don't he's going to hate me," I whimpered.

"What the hell is wrong with you, Bellamy?" Cara asked. "This isn't you."

"I… I don't know."

"Then we need to get it resolved. We can't have you acting like a scared pup. You need to pull it together. I know this isn't you. It's weird as hell," Dilly replied.

He got up and opened the door. Lucien walked in and saw me on the couch. The angry look he'd been wearing smoothed into one of concern. He smelled like a Rogue King again. Was I becoming weaker and was he taking my power? How?

"Stop. I can hear what you're thinking, I have been for a few minutes, and every time you've started to panic about this." He crossed the room and sat, pulling me into his lap. "I'm not taking anything. You're just worrying because you don't have anything to distract you. It's alright. We can sign the papers now with a witness and leave. Someone will take care of the notary. Everyone can have their party. We're not a mistake, *you* are not a mistake. If this wedding thing is stressing you out, I don't want it. Let's just go."

Lucien held me tight and rocked me back and forth. He was right. And after I'd made such a big deal about him regretting me just a few weeks ago. This was so stupid.

"You are my strong, beautiful, Alpha mate. You can do anything and I'll be there to back you up while you do. Believe in us, if you can't believe in yourself. Trust us, if you can't trust me. We're more powerful than just you and just me," Lucien murmured into my hair. "Now, start acting like an Alpha."

Right. I needed to get my shit together. Doubt like this would put me in a dangerous place. I couldn't risk it.

"Okay. I'll marry you tomorrow. Now, get out of here unless you want bad luck, stupid Alpha," I muttered.

Lucien laughed and settled me next to Cara again before leaving. I really needed to talk to him more. My terrible thoughts consumed me, and I didn't consider who I might affect.

Chapter 120: Bachelor Party…?

[Lucien]

I left the head warrior's cottage, feeling relieved. Ever since Bellamy went to Limb Torn, I started feeling her strong emotions. Recently, it was worry. A truly disturbing amount of fear consumed her mind.

When I started hearing her thoughts, I had to take some time to myself. I told her it would be best if we didn't see each other until the wedding, for luck. The truth was, I needed time to process some things she'd been thinking.

The horny thoughts were amazing. I don't know how much of it was the pregnancy hormones and how much was my mate, but I was hoping it was hormones. I might not be old, but I wasn't exactly young either.

Frankly, I was eager for a night where I could sleep. I only had a few things to deal with, then I could go to bed. If anyone told me a month ago that I'd long to go to bed alone instead of with a beautiful woman who desired me, I would've laughed my ass off.

Entering my office, Thierry and Robert looked at me with concern. I'd cut them off while we were talking and jumped off the balcony so I could get to Bellamy as quickly as possible. I didn't want her worries to make her run away or affect the pups. She wouldn't be kind to herself if something happened to them.

"Is she okay?" Thierry asked.

"Yeah. She was having some pretty intense thoughts and feelings. I don't know what's wrong with her. I talked to Maple, she's a couple weeks further along than Bellamy. She said she doesn't have any doubts about herself or her mate. All she feels is the increased libido I've heard about," I confided.

Thierry and Robert winced. They'd gotten used to Bellamy and my relationship in a lot of ways, just not the physical aspects of it. I didn't blame them. I wouldn't want to know about that with either of my nieces.

"I'm talking to you as my friends, not her uncles. Please. I need help. Her doubts weaken her collective. They will hurt her in the end. Rogues don't sympathize like we do. If they pick up on this… it would be bad."

"What can we do? What did the doctor say? Did you talk to any of the pack therapists?"

"The doctors have nothing. The therapists say it's probably all of the recent changes. Even Cara and Dillon noticed the change. They're both worried." I sighed.

"Maybe the vampires will know," Robert offered.

The Vampire High Council was expected soon. Talia told me to invite them to the wedding as a thank-you for helping out with the pups. It would keep our relationship with them sound. They wouldn't be insulted.

All of them accepted the invitation, and Marius was bringing them soon. Maybe the Angel could help. He put the pups back, and Talia told me he was a healer.

I needed something to bring my mate back from this void. It was much more than the problems I'd noticed in the beginning. This wasn't part of her normal worry.

There was a knock at the door sometime later. Robert answered. It was Talia and the other members of the High Council. I was relieved and motioned for them to sit.

Talia sat on Thierry's lap. He and Celesta had already gotten used to the fact that she was drawn to Thierry and Caleb. Cara didn't like when Talia flirted with Caleb, but she didn't get violent about it as a lot of unmarked-mated females would have.

Marius, Felix, and Phoebe sat on the couch. I took my seat and Robert followed. The smell of vampire was intense, but I was much better than I was when Talia first came to stay with us.

"Thank you for inviting us to your wedding," Phoebe said politely.

"It's rare for wolves to invite vampires into their territory. Your trust will not be shunned," Felix stated.

"Once Talia told us Bellamy held a chair in the Werewolf Association, we were more than happy to have helped. The growth of human knowledge about both our species has caused hunters to appear more often in all our territories. A friendship would be beneficial to both of our people." Phoebe smiled.

She was fantastic with diplomacy. Everyone felt at ease when she spoke. Marius watched everything with a sardonic smirk. He wasn't my worry right now.

"Actually, I was hoping to ask a favor. I know it's not generally done, but I need your help. I can't ask any rogues or I risk undermining Bellamy's collective and her Association seat," I told them.

Marius scoffed. "Ah, the real reason we were invited. The wolves want something."

"No. I asked you as a thank you before I realized something was wrong with my mate. I'm worried about what else Marion did to her in the dream. She won't talk about it. Maybe it wasn't any more than what we saw, but she's not herself. Bellamy is doubting herself and me."

"And you think that has something to do with Marion?" he pressed.

"I *know* THAT isn't my Bellamy. You knew her. You have to see that," I insisted.

"I didn't know her. She amused me. I trained her a little. We barely spoke." Marius snickered. "Did she say she knew me?"

I felt rage flood through me. What the hell was wrong with him? She was a little girl when they met. How could he not have talked to her?

"Alpha, remember. She said she only knew one vampire. Talia," Thierry said softly.

"That's correct. She traveled and trained with me for a while, that doesn't mean she knew me or I knew her. She was just a stubborn pup that wandered into my life and away one day. It happens a lot."

"No one can stand to be around Marius for very long. He bothers everyone. I have no idea how Nerys can stay with him as long as she has." Talia giggled.

"Because without me, she would die. I am her master. She is my human servant. It is her great pleasure to serve me," Marius huffed.

"Bullshit. I bet she draws things on him while he sleeps." Phoebe chuckled.

"Stop picking on Mari. If I can examine the Luna Queen, I can tell you if there's anything I can do," Felix said.

I snorted. "Mari."

"Do not call me that again, wolf, or we will have issues," he warned with a hiss.

"Fuck off, Mari. These are my allies and attacking them will mean war with me, my Solus Amor, our children, and all of their territories. You *definitely* don't want that," Talia growled.

I was a little confused. They were broodmates, strong enough to be peers. Why would her threat be enough that he actually looked stricken? He was *Death*.

"You've confused your friends, Talia. Alpha, Marius has a territory, but no children and no Solus Amor. He is Death, but cannot take on that many vampires at once. It wouldn't be a war; it would be a slaughter," Phoebe clarified.

A deadly smile crept over Talia's face. "None of these people are a match for my army. I have almost one hundred children, grandchildren, and such. As does my Solus Amor. She was a tactician and leader of one of the strongest countries of her time when she was alive. We do not lose."

"I won't call you that again, Marius. We needn't be enemies. I want my mate to be herself again. You don't know what she was like, but she was strong and confident. That was one of the first things I noticed about her. I want *that* Bellamy back," I told him.

"Let's figure out a plan. Your mate is important to us. She is the only inroad we have to the Association. She cannot lose her seat," Felix said.

***

It was a few hours later when we were approached the head warrior's cottage again. Dillon linked me when Bellamy fell asleep. It would be the best time to fix her.

The only reason the High Council could get into my dream was because Bellamy called them there. They connected with her and she carried them into the dream realm through her blood bond with Talia. If she wasn't calling them, they couldn't go.

Felix said if something happened during her sleep, her subconscious was holding it and keeping her from getting help like she did last time. He wanted to use Talia to travel into the dream realm again and free Bellamy from what was hurting her. I wouldn't be able to travel with them.

Talia told me she needed me holding Bellamy in case she woke up. My presence would keep her calm while they worked and might put her into a deeper sleep. I would do anything for my little chouchoutte.

We entered the house and went to the master bedroom. Dillon had carried Cara to the guest room. Bellamy was alone in the large bed.

Her nightgown tangled between her thighs, revealing one leg up to her hip. The vampires looked on appreciatively. I fought back my growl as I crossed the room and straightened her out before laying with her in my arms.

Talia and Felix sat on the little loveseat. I watched them twine their fingers together as their bodies relaxed. They looked like they were sleeping.

"We will guard our comrades' bodies. Your wolf can help guard your mate. This shouldn't take long. Time passes faster in the dream realm than it does here," Phoebe stated.

"Of course. Thank you for your consideration." I nodded.

Dillon came to stand near the bed and faced away, toward the door. I was grateful to have him. It made me relax more, and that helped Bellamy relax in her sleep. I kissed her forehead and focused on her breathing and heartbeat, praying to the moon goddess to help my mate heal.

Chapter 121: The Mark

I laid in bed with Bellamy in my arms. The wait was excruciating. I needed a distraction from the gnawing anxiety of what might be happening. I knew Dillon talked to Bellamy about everything with him and Jean-Claude back at Limb Torn, but I was still in the dark on a couple of things.

Namely, what happened with the forced marking on the day we ran Bellamy's borders. I let the boys deal with it on their own, but my curious nature got the better of me while I was trying to think of anything other than what was happening in Bellamy's dreams.

My marking of Bellamy had almost been a forced one because of the demon dust. What must it have been like to be on the other side of that? To have your choice taken from you in that way?

Dillon wouldn't have had any option but to accept what was going on. What was going through his mind? I wanted a distraction while waiting for Bellamy to heal.

"Dillon?"

"Yes, Alpha?" he asked.

"I wanted to talk to you about what happened with Jean-Claude. The marking."

"I don't want to talk about it in front of strangers. Can we wait?" Dillon requested quietly.

"Pretend we're not here. Marius isn't even paying attention. He's talking to his people in his head. I am more interested in my friends than I am in your werewolf drama. Trust that your lives aren't anything near interesting to us," Phoebe scoffed.

"You were a lot nicer before." I chuckled.

"I am nice around pretty girls when they're awake. Talia and Bellamy aren't here to see how wonderful I am." She winked.

Dillon snorted. "You're just like Tali said."

"Thank you."

"I just need a distraction, Dillon. Please. Let me think about something other than my mate suffering," I pled.

"You're as bad as she is. Damned nosy Alphas," Dillon grumbled.

I grinned. Bellamy was right. He couldn't resist trying to make people feel better. He would tell me his story and I would gain a diversion from the tears forming in Bellamy's closed eyes.

***

—The morning of the border run—

[Dillon]

It was earlier than I normally woke up when I turned off my alarm and growled at it. I really shouldn't have stayed up sparring with Randy and Stan. It was nice to really throw myself into a fight, though. Only Bellamy was a challenge for me anymore.

I realized it had been a few minutes and checked my phone. Shit! How had I lost fifteen minutes!? Now I didn't have time for a shower. I would have to take one when we got back.

Quickly, I pulled on a black undershirt and some basketball shorts, grabbed my backpack, and ran out the door. I stopped when I saw Jean-Claude. He was just a few feet from my door.

How sweet. He came to meet me.

Griffin growled in my head. He wanted to drag our mate back to our bedroom and link Bellamy that we were sick or something. We hadn't had any real time to get to know each other beyond the day he was laid up from training.

'Come on, he's yearning for us as much as we are for him.'

'No. You get to spend the entire run with his wolf. Don't try to force him into something he isn't ready for. We barely know him. Jean-Claude is important. We can't treat him like the others,' I chided.

'Like YOU treated the others. I was never involved in that. I told you to wait in the beginning, but you were already fucking like it was going out of style,' Griff growled.

'It'll be okay. He's fine with waiting. It'll be better that way, special. A palate cleansing couple of weeks, then we can go to town on that boy.'

'Let's go. I want to see what his wolf looks like!'

I smiled at Jean-Claude. He smiled back as he was slowly devouring my body with his eyes. Goddess, I couldn't wait to get him to bed.

Jean-Claude moved like he was going to kiss me, then froze. His face set in an angry expression. I didn't get it, but this wasn't the place to get loud.

He turned without a word and started walking away. I had to hurry to keep up. That was rare. Normally, I was the fastest walker in a group.

When we finally reached the front door, he paused long enough for me to reach him. We got outside, and I grabbed his arm. He jerked away.

Griff whimpered in my head.

"Don't fucking touch me!" Jean-Claude growled.

"Stop running away from me and tell me why you're mad, Claude. I can't fix it if I don't know what needs to be fixed!" I replied.

"You smell like the bears. Did you fuck them one at a time, or let them share you? You're my mate! How could you cheat?!" he shouted.

"Whoa! What the hell are you talking about? I sparred with them last night! They taught me how to get out of the holds most bears use! I didn't have sex with them! And for your information, I'm a fucking top!" I growled.

How could he think I would cheat on him? He was my mate. My perfect match. Created by the goddess to be my only love.

"Good to know you fucked them instead of the other way around! Bruce told me you slept with any man who crooked his finger at you. I can't believe I was so *stupid!* You never really loved me. Was I too small this time?" Jean-Claude yelled.

This time? Too small? What was he talking about?

I couldn't believe Bruce said something like that. I was pissed. He had no right to tell my mate about my past relationships. That was my job, and I planned to do it properly, not yelling on the front lawn like trash!

"I have no idea what you're talking about, but you need to take it down by about fifty percent. This isn't anyone else's business right now," I whispered harshly.

He looked away, and I saw he was breathing hard. His arms crossed his stomach, and he held himself like he was trying to keep from falling apart. My chest tightened. Was he going to reject me over something he thought?

"You keep pushing me away. You want to get to know each other better, but you're never around. I know you like big, muscular men, but I'm shorter than you are. They're more your type than I am. Just because we have a bond, doesn't mean you'll love me. Just look at…. Never mind," he strained.

"Just look at Lucien and his first mate? She rejected him because she loved someone else," I finished.

"How did you know?"

"How did you? He kept it quiet. No one outside his inner circle knew."

"Uncle Jean-Paul told me. He wanted to remind me that our first duty is to our pack. Forgetting that is what made… the man steal Alpha Lucien's mate," he replied nervously.

I knew it was Bellamy's family he was talking about. His family. They'd kept the secret well. I wondered why Jean-Paul would share it when it was obvious Lucien didn't want anyone else to know. That wasn't important now. What was important was making sure he didn't leave me.

"Claude, I love big men because the goddess made me to love you. You were meant to be as gorgeous as you are and I was meant to be attracted to that. I'm not into bears and I'm not into men who are taller than me. I'm only into Jean-Claude. Yes, I slept around when I was young, I'll gladly explain that later, but I would *never* cheat on you."

Stepping closer, I was relieved when he didn't move away. His breathing calmed, and he was looking at me from the corner of his eye. I moved slowly, not wanting to upset him.

"Don't reject me without talking to them. It's all a misunderstanding, Claude. I'm not cheating. I would never cheat on you. Please, listen. I don't want to lose you," I pled gently.

He nodded to himself and turned toward me. My heart leapt into my throat. Jean-Claude looked so serious. Please, don't let him leave me. I prayed to the goddess.

"I'll believe you. We can talk about it later. I don't like that you smell like them. Maybe I could hug you for a little while and you could smell like me instead?" he suggested.

It filled me with hope. He was willing to listen. He wouldn't let his mind ruin us. I nodded and closed the distance, wrapping my arms around his thick waist.

The warmth of his hold made me calm even more. My mate was really going to give me the benefit of the doubt now. I rested my cheek on his shoulder and kissed his neck gently.

His head dipped down and he started kissing down my neck softly until he made it to the curve where my neck met my shoulder. He began kissing, licking, and nibbling at my marking spot, making me moan. Sparks danced over my skin where he teased.

A hickey wouldn't be the worst thing in the world. I knew Cara sported one to make Caleb feel less hostile toward other males. It was a concession I was willing to give.

My arms tightened around him, and I rubbed along his hard muscles. None of my make-out sessions had ever been as delicious as this. His grip tightened, and I felt a rumbling in his chest.

"Mine," he growled.

"Yes," I whispered.

The pain was sudden and sharp. It took me a moment to realize what was happening. Marks wouldn't hurt when both parties agreed, but a forced mark would. Before I could even start fighting back, it was done, and he was licking the mark he gave me.

Anger flooded through me. I couldn't believe he marked me without consent. How could he do that?! I pushed him away as hard as I could.

Claude stumbled backward and looked confused. Did he think me saying yes to being his was me saying yes to a mark? Why would he think marking me after a fight was a good idea?

"What the hell did you do that for?" I asked angrily.

He blushed. "You're mine. Now no one can take you from me and I will know you didn't cheat the next time you come to me smelling like another male. I had to, mon rêve. I won't ever doubt you again because I'll always know you're faithful."

My rage boiled. "Always know I'm faithful!? Because of the hundreds of times I've cheated on you? The millions of lies I've told?! All the men I flirt with daily?! Because I'm a weak little slut who isn't capable of behaving without a fucking collar?! You asshole!" I shouted and punched him in the face.

I didn't feel bad when he fell. I just headed off to where Bellamy and Lucien were waiting. We had work to do and Griff was pissed off, too. Griff would forgive faster than I would, but it was nice to agree with my wolf for once in this relationship.

"Wait! Dillon! Stop! I'm sorry! I didn't mean it like that!" He grabbed the back of my shirt.

Twisting, I tried to pull away, but his grip tore my shirt. I decided I didn't need the shirt and started tearing the rest of it away. Grabbing him, I spun and tossed him a few feet back the way we came before heading off again.

Jean-Claude tried to mind-link me, but I blocked him. I wasn't going to let him into my head. If he had something to say, he'd have to wait until I wanted to hear it.

Every time he got close, I tossed him back. Eventually, he took off his shirt to stop me from doing it again. I didn't listen to his pleas and was relieved when I saw Bellamy. I was even more relieved when she knocked him on his ass.

***

[Lucien]

"And that was it. I just didn't want to hear him, talk to him, or see him until I dealt with him not trusting me," Dillon finished.

I couldn't believe Jean-Claude had basically called his mate a serial cheater. He was a kind and understanding boy growing up. I couldn't fault Dillon for his actions at all. Bellamy would have killed me.

"Wow, Wolfie. Your boyfriend seriously acted like a dick. This is why I don't deal with men. Too jealous and possessive." Phoebe sneered a little.

"I thought you weren't interested enough to listen," he pouted a little.

"Talia likes you, Bellamy likes you, I think maybe you're less like a man than most men. Would you have done the same if he smelled of another male?" she asked.

"No. I didn't feel like that when he came home smelling like the bears. I trusted him, but he didn't trust me. Once I knew why. Once I knew what Pavel did to my mate. I understood, but I didn't want to let it go. He stole my marking from me. That's why it'll be a while before I mark him. I may have forgiven, but I'll never really forget," he replied sadly.

Bellamy whimpered in her sleep, pulling my attention back to her. I would trust that she wouldn't fight the healing she needed. Soon my perfect mate would be back to the strong, confident woman I fell in love with.

Chapter 122: The Dream Realm

[Bellamy]

I stared out of the wooden bars that separated me from my family. Why couldn't I stop having this nightmare? Time and time again, I had to watch those men slaughter my family.

There was a new aspect to the torturous scene, though. Now, they didn't shoot my mama; they knocked her down. My papa went to help her up, not to mourn her death. And the lead hunter wasn't the one who laughed at them.

It was Kingston.

My parents crouched on the ground, glaring at Kingston as he strutted into the room. He looked like a broader version of adult Kyle. It was fairly well-known that Kingston's mother was an ex-pack. That was why he was almost as broad as a pack wolf.

Rogue born wolves tended to be leaner. Bulk wouldn't help us survive as much as the lithe muscles and more compact bodies did. It was an easy way to tell an ex-pack from a rogue born. It wasn't a hard and fast rule, just a generalization I'd seen as true more often than not. There were always exceptions.

"Where is the little princess, Luc? If I have to sniff her out, this won't be nearly as painless for you," Kingston growled.

"I don't know why you want my daughter, but I will *never* let you have her," my papa snarled back.

One of the hunters hit him in the head with the butt of his gun. My mama growled at him and tended my papa's head. I stayed still and kept my presence muted like they told me to. Was my brain mingling the new information with the old?

"Your daughter is meant to be a Queen, Luc. She deserves a mate like Kyle. The heir to the strongest collective in the region. Imagine the power the two of them could have." Kingston grinned before turning to the hunters. "You two, search the bedrooms, closets, cupboards, and basement. I want the little girl alive."

"She should be allowed to choose her mate. If Kyle is a good man, she'll see it and accept him. Is this why you wanted us in your collective?" Papa asked.

"Yes. Your daughter is more valuable than either of you. If you choose to come to my collective and betroth your daughter to my son, in a vow to the moon goddess, then you may live. I require the vow. I won't be tricked."

"No," Mama said. "I will *not* let you take the future our goddess promised my daughter. She's meant to be more than a broodmare to a minor King." She glared directly into Kingston's eyes, challenging him. "My Bellamy is meant to be a great Queen. My Bellamy will be the most feared Queen in the country. The most powerful woman in the supernatural world. She'll never be mate to your weak little son. If you kill us, you'll never get her. I will gladly die for her future."

"Angel, don't..." Papa started.

"Luc, you don't understand. I will *never* dedicate my daughter to your son, Kingston. I will *never* give her to you. We will *never* submit," Mama stated in a deadly tone that was so opposite her sweet voice, it was frightening.

Kingston scoffed. "I would've fucked that fire right out of you... Angel. You should have taught your mate to be more subservient to a male, Luc. It's the only thing I actually admire about you pack wolves. Women who know their place. Bella will learn the same. We'll keep her on a tight leash."

"My mate is right. Our daughter wasn't meant for your son. She's like her mother, like me. We despise tyrants and we always talk back. If we knew our place, we certainly wouldn't be rogues now." Papa chuckled.

Why were they doing this? It was like they were trying to get killed. I knew Mama had that dream when she was pregnant with me, but the baby. And me. She was trying to leave me all alone.

"*Don't* call her 'Bella'. You have no right and no permission to speak in friendly terms about our Queen. She will *never* be on the end of your leash. I vow to the moon goddess; that I will do everything in my power to stop you from stealing my Queen's future," Mama growled.

"You'll be dead soon, little wolf. You can't stop me. In fact, just to ensure you suffer the most, your little declaration has earned your *Queen* membership to my harem when she's old enough. I'll break her in properly and give her to the boy once she realizes a Queen is only meant to strengthen her King," he threatened.

Papa looked enraged and tried to lunge for him, only to be met with hunters armed with silver. The pain of his roar when the silver touched him was visceral. I choked back a whimper as Kingston continued.

"No male will want her for anything other than the power she can lend. Every rogue King who sees her, who feels that Alpha aura she used two weeks ago, will only want her for that power. I don't know what future you *think* the goddess promised, but there is only one. She'll never be loved, only used. I'll make sure my son knows how to love her. And I'll take my time teaching her all the different ways to accept his love." Kingston laughed in a way that made my stomach twist.

The front door slammed open, and something attacked. It was small and vicious. Blood sprayed from the hunters. A second, larger thing attacked afterward. Soon, the only living things in the house were me, my parents, and whatever was holding Kingston to the ground.

"Vampires?" Mama gasped.

"Talia!" I shouted.

"Hold him here while I get my pheata," Talia told Felix.

"Please, don't hurt my daughter," Mama pled.

"Even in a dream, you are a good mother. I would never hurt her. I love her as if she were truly my childe. Do not worry," Talia assured her.

She sniffed and followed her nose to me. Part of my training with her had been learning to make my scent almost imperceptible to vampires. I performed well until my attention slipped.

Pulling the top off of the large wicker vase and peering inside, Talia looked relieved. I stared up at her. The thing felt massive, but I knew it was because I was experiencing it as my younger self.

Talia reached in and helped me out of the vase. I wrapped my arms around her waist and hugged her tightly. She stroked my hair like she did when I was small.

"You look as you did when I first met you, pheata. Just a little chubbier." She chuckled.

"What's going on, Talia?" I asked. "I don't remember calling for help. I'm used to this dream."

"Lucien asked me for help, pheata. You aren't acting like yourself. We all noticed. Felix came with me to heal you," she answered.

My parents gasped. "Lucien?"

"You've tried fighting back before, haven't you?"

"I used to be able to. I was as strong and as skilled as I normally am, but this one. This started after I learned Kingston ordered them killed. I tried fighting back. I still watched them die. Instead of my original fate, I was taken back to Limb Torn. The dream got so much worse. I stopped a few days ago. I just couldn't take another night of going through torture, training, and being used. They made me kill Lucien. It was proof I was fully compliant and ready to be Queen," I sobbed.

"Belle, please don't cry. Everything will be fine," my mama said.

"He didn't get you. He won't get you," my papa promised.

"You need to kill him, pheata. He's the cause of your fears. We were right outside, we heard what he told your parents. All the fears Lucien told me you were having were in his words. He stole your life; he stole their lives. You need to kill Kingston Fuller, then I will bring your mate to you," Talia murmured. "Time to grow up and destroy him."

I closed my eyes and took a deep breath, remembering my eighteen-year-old self. Thinking about what clothing I would wear for this event. When I opened them, I was taller than Talia and wearing my comfortable workout clothes, topped with my Eaten Heart shirt. My parents gasped a little.

"What's going on?" Kingston asked.

"I've imbued this dream body with his soul. The best way for you to heal is to strike out at the one person you can't reach," Felix told me.

"The Angel is the only one who can create ghouls. We didn't know if this would work, but I am pleased to see my comrade is as powerful as I thought he'd be." Talia smiled.

"Bella, what the hell is going on? They're vampires, your parents are dead. I don't understand." Kingston strained, trying to pull away from Felix's vice-like grip.

"My name is *not* Bella!" I growled. "I am High Queen Bellamy Deveraux. Luna of Lune Rouge, Queen of the Eaten Heart. There is a kill order on your son. I have taken your collective. After he's dead, your line will end."

"Deveraux? Lucien had a son?" Papa asked.

"No. Bellamy is Lucien's mate. I dreamed it when I was pregnant with her. That's why I insisted on calling her 'Bellamy'. In honor of our lost beautiful friend who had to be broken in order to be made whole," Mama said, wrapping her arms around him. "Hush now. This is her time. Ours has passed."

Felix looked confused.

"This isn't a normal dream; this is part of a repressed memory. Kingston was there when Bellamy's parents died. He said all the things we heard. The actual dream only starts once she tries to change the memory," Talia responded.

"You can't kill what's already dead," Kingston chided with a smirk.

"No? Do you remember what it felt like when Kyle killed you?" I asked.

His face fell. "I'm punished with it. I'm never without the pain of my son's cowardice. He didn't even challenge me. He ripped my head off as I slept."

"You'll be awake for this. You know my threat. I will eat the heart of my enemies. That's you. Since *you* made *this* decision, you've been my enemy, Kingston. Release him, Master Felix. I'm fully prepared," I commanded.

"Of course, High Queen. Have fun." He grinned darkly and let go of the man who killed my family.

"I don't fear death and have no reason to fight for my life." Kingston snarled.

"No, but you have every reason to fight for my death. I'm the prize that escaped you, mated to your familial enemy, carrying his pups. Even if I die, I'll be the reason your son dies. No matter his cowardice, he's still your child," I answered with a laugh.

"Always laughing." He sighed. "Kill me, Bella. I spend every moment of my eternity suffering for what I did. Not only to you and your family. To everyone. To my family. To my collective. I don't deserve to live. Not even this false life. You were expecting an enemy who would fight? That's Kyle. I have no clue how long I've been suffering, but it feels like centuries. I have far more to go before I'm considered reformed."

I smiled and nodded. A new thing I learned, there is a form of Hell for werewolves. I would be even more careful to be a good person now.

He knelt on the floor in front of me. I looked for any sign this was a trap, but saw nothing. Better safe than sorry. I used the speed Talia taught me to quickly bust through his chest and pluck out his heart.

His face became a little peaceful. "I'm sorry, Amy," Kingston whispered as his soul left the dream body.

Looking down at my hand, I saw the heart. This wasn't a time to be bitchy about eating. Even if it wasn't real, it was real enough, and I had to end this nightmare.

Glancing at Talia, I winked and started eating. It was a good thing it was a dream. I just wished it tasted like cake, and it happened. I ate the whole thing and felt myself becoming stronger and more solid than I was before, at peace with my past, for once.

Chapter 123: Wedding Belles

[Bellamy]

Sitting at the vanity, I had my eyes closed as Cara applied the last of my makeup. She insisted on doing it instead of letting someone else, like Liddy the staff member who did my hair. I was just relieved everything worked out and was happy to let someone else be in charge for a while.

After my dream last night, I was more confident about my relationship with Lucien. Kingston was wrong. I found a mate who was an Alpha and wanted me for everything that made me who I was. Lucien wasn't taking my power. He was sharing it, just like I was sharing his.

We hadn't talked after he said good night to me when I woke, but I could feel his excitement and relief. Before today, I was only getting spotty feelings. Our connection was weak from my doubt and fear.

That wouldn't happen again. I was always going to trust that my Lucien loved me. I could feel his love for me coming through our bond. When I thought of him, my feelings of love got stronger, so I assumed that meant he was thinking of me.

It was, honestly, setting my hormones on fire. It had been over twenty-four hours since we were physical and I missed the feeling of him. I couldn't wait for our wedding night.

We would spend it here, then leaving for the inn in the morning after training. We had an entire week and a half away. All we had to do was facilitate our takeovers of the other pack and collective, then the rest of the time was ours.

Thierry and Robert were quite proud of how we were changing everything. They were excited about the pack growing, especially now they knew we wouldn't have as many hunter attacks with Kyle being out of power and Limb Torn belonging to me. Our future was looking bright.

"Bems, I have all the cameras set up and working. I'll set it to a live feed a little closer to time. The last of the Association has just arrived. They're being seated," Dilly said, the sound of his voice getting closer.

"Just a little bit more and you can look at what he wants to show you," Cara told me, the pace of her voice matching the pace she was swiping the little brush over my closed lids.

The preparation room was pretty full. My mom, Genevieve, Daisy, Janya, Celesta, Simone, Regan, Cara, and Dilly were there. A knock at the door brought two more voices I was starting to recognize. My grandmothers, Annette and Margot.

"Almost ready?" Annette asked.

"Nearly done… and… there. All finished, Amy," Cara sang cheerfully.

I opened my eyes and looked in the mirror on the vanity. My makeup was perfect, just enough to know I was wearing it, but not so much that it made me feel claustrophobic.

"You look beautiful, Amy," my mom said as I turned to everyone else.

"Lucien ended up with the prettiest bride I've seen in ages." Regan winked.

It was a little awkward. Mom, Daisy, Genevieve, and I all knew Regan was Lucien's second chance, but she was really trying to just be a good aunt to me. I appreciated it, nonetheless.

"Thank you, Aunt Regan," I said softly.

"OH! Dear Goddess!" Dilly exclaimed.

We turned to look at him, shocked. He was staring at the screen in his hands. Looking up, he pulled out the earbuds he was using to monitor the sound.

"You guys have to see this!" He bounced over to where we could all see and pulled out the connection, letting the sound from the screen fill the room.

On the screen, I could see the decorated aisle. My brother, Bruce, gaped at a woman whose back was to the camera. Cara gripped my hand. Everyone knew that look.

"What's your name, sweetheart?" Bruce asked gently after he collected himself.

"A-Antonia," a familiar voice said.

"Who's Antonia?" my mom questioned.

"She's the Gamma for the Rose Moon Pack. Her first mate died," I answered.

"This will be perfect. Being a Gamma's mate will suit him well," Mom replied.

"Shush! I want to hear what's going on," Cara hissed.

We returned our focus to the screen. It was so cute. He took her hand and kissed it.

"You are the most beautiful woman in the world. I would love to paint you. I can't believe I thought I knew what beauty was before I saw you. No star's glow can compare, no flower could be as vibrant. I can't imagine how jealous the goddess was when she saw she'd created someone so perfect," he murmured, kissing her hand over and over while looking into her eyes.

All of my brothers were like that. Hopeless romantic sorts. I was sure he'd been practicing that speech for years.

"Oh. Umm. Th-thank you? We should talk soon. I… I have something I need to tell you," Antonia said.

Bruce looked concerned. "You're not rejecting me, right?"

"No! I just… I have a son from my first mate. I wanted it to be something we could talk about alone. In case… you didn't want to stay with me," she murmured.

My heart ached for her. She really wanted a mate, but having a child could often lead to rejection. Some males would rather have no mate than raise someone else's child. My brother was from parents as caring as Olive and Daniel. He wouldn't reject her over that.

"Then I guess that means, I beat my brothers and sisters to giving my parents a grandchild. I hope you want to have more." Bruce winked and offered his arm. "I'll take care of everything you need. I'm not an elite warrior, but I am one of the best regular warriors of my pack."

Antonia took his arm and held it tight. "What's your name? You never told me."

"Oh, sorry, I was so taken with you, it totally slipped my mind. Bruce Carrington of the Daylight Moon Pack."

"Antonia Graves, Gamma of Rose Moon. I hope you don't mind that," she said shyly.

"It's as perfect as you are. I get to stay close to my family and I can raise the pups while you take care of the pack. I may be a Beta's son, but my little sister taught me not to accept the gender roles we're taught. Strong women are my weakness, you know," Bruce answered, caressing her cheek with his other hand.

"Carrington? Like Queen Bellamy? She's your sister?" Antonia gaped at him.

"Yes. Now, let's get you seated and we'll talk after the wedding," Bruce purred and led her down the aisle to her seat.

"All of my boys have their mates now. Thank the goddess. Now I only have to focus on the babies and all my grandchildren." Mom sighed in relief. "Bruce wouldn't have found her without you, Amy. You've blessed us again."

I blushed. They talked about how I'd blessed them by being a good daughter, by facilitating the heat that conceived the twins, and by bringing Galen to meet Salomé before he gave up and took a chosen mate. It was horribly embarrassing to me.

We got back to the preparations. Genevieve gave me the diamond-spangled combs she'd worn when she married Lucien's father. They had hooks for attaching the veil and it looked beautiful, with the way Liddy styled my hair. I wore the sapphire tennis bracelet my parents gave me for what we thought was my sixteenth birthday.

Cara lent me a necklace with a sapphire pendant for my 'something borrowed,' and my dress was new, so I felt prepared. I was slipping on my shoes when Annette and Margot stopped me.

"There are a couple traditional items that come from our family. You wear them for the wedding then hold onto them until the next female in the family is ready to use them," Margot said. "This, you will hang onto until the twins are old enough to find their mates."

She clasped another bracelet on my wrist. It was made of thicker white gold and held a ruby surrounded by little pearls. It was gorgeous and obviously very old. I wondered how many women in my family had worn it before me.

"This, you will turn over to Cara before she marries Caleb," Annette said, attaching a diamond brooch to the center bust of my dress.

It looked like it was made to go with the dress. I smiled at how perfectly it all seemed to be. Looking in the tall mirror, I hoped this was one of the moments the goddess would let my mama and papa watch.

"Thierry is linking me. Everyone is here and seated. We need to go. Your father will be here for you soon. He and Robert were still bickering over who has more right to walk you down the aisle." Simone chuckled.

"Come on everyone. Let's get set. We'll see you later, Amy," Olive said, kissing me on the cheek.

"Thank you, Mommy. And everyone. Thank you all for helping out with this and for accepting Lucien and me. We're going to make the region at peace. Our people are important, and so are our allies. We love all of you and want to see you living safely," I told them.

"We know you will, Amy. Collect yourself, and get your vows ready. It's time for you to take another step toward the Queen you're meant to be," Dilly murmured, giving me a hug.

They all left me alone in the preparation room. I breathed deeply and focused on my goal. My family. My mate. Our future together. I wanted more time, more everything, and I was going to savor every moment from now on.

There was a knock on the door, and I called out for them to enter. My dad's smiling face appeared as he opened the door. It broadened as he looked me over.

"Amy, you look like a true Queen. Like a fairytale princess. Lucien's very lucky. He better never forget it, or your brothers and I will make sure he regrets it."

"Daddy, stop. Lucien would never hurt me. He loves me more than anything." I smiled.

"He better. I'm your father. I will end him if he hurts you."

"Alright, Daddy, I've got it. I feel very protected now. Can I get married?" I chuckled.

"Yes. You can get married, princess. Just remember, you can always come home if you need space. We love you as if you were our natural daughter. We will always be there, even if we mess up sometimes." He winked.

I shook my head and took the arm he offered. It was finally time to make Lucien mine in the final way possible. I called myself Bellamy Deveraux in my dream last night. It was time to make it fact.

Chapter 124: Wedding

I stood in the covered area behind everyone. I couldn't see far down the aisle. After a few minutes, I saw Anise and Blossom in little puffy red dresses.

They had handbaskets with flower petals in them. Blossom dumped hers out as soon as there wasn't an adult beside her, then picked up the pile of flower petals and tossed them in the air. Anise was handing petals to the people sitting along the aisle.

We shuffled forward. Next was little King Ryan. They'd wrangled him into being the ring bearer since we didn't have any boys of the right age. I tried to tell them when they had an idea, what a bad choice it could be.

I saw Bruce staring at Antonia from the side of the seating area. He was so in love already; I was happy for him. He deserved to find his mate.

'Bruce, the ring bearer is your new son,' I linked.

His stare shifted to the aisle. Ryan was glowering at the people near the aisle. He was protecting the rings as if they were his own treasure. Rogue Alphas were a little more aggressive than pack Alphas, even when they were young. He would fight to the death to protect those rings.

'Look at my son, Amy. He's so strong. He'll be a powerful warrior.... Wait. How did you know?'

'The cameras were on. Congrats on finding your mate, big brother.'

'Focus on getting married, Amy. I love you.'

'I love you, too, Bruce.'

Once Ryan was down the aisle, out of sight for me, Dilly and Richard started forward. Robert and Thierry weren't part of the wedding, since they were my uncles. It was more appropriate for the future Gamma and future Beta to be in the wedding than the head warrior.

Jean-Claude wasn't happy but understood. He would sit by Dilly at the reception. It was the only way he stopped fighting it.

Once Cara and Caleb started down the aisle, I could see Lucien. He was in a simple black tuxedo. His shirt was white, but all of his accessories were blood red. A perfect mix of our colors. The white and scarlet red of Lune Rouge reflected in my side of the party, blood red and black on his side.

My dad patted my hand on his arm. I looked up at him. He was smiling just like he did when I joined the Daylight Moon Pack. A few more lines around his eyes and a little gray dotting his dark hair. It was a bit of a surreal moment.

"Ready, Bellamy?" he whispered.

"Ready, Daddy." I nodded.

He guided me down the aisle. Lucien's eyes slowly took me in. His smile was growing as he stared at me. My own eyes started tearing up. Damned baby hormones. I took a deep breath and worked to collect myself. Thankfully, everything was under control once I reached the end.

It was the longest walk of my life. I turned to my dad, and he kissed my cheek. There would be no asking who was giving me. No one gave away a sitting Alpha.

I climbed the short stairs up to the altar. When I reached the top, Lucien reached for my hand. I wanted to fling myself into his arms. I missed him so much, even if it wasn't a whole day.

We turned to face Pastor Blood. He'd been thrilled when I asked him to officiate my wedding. It made him feel important, and I felt it would help our relationship.

"Friends, family, Pack, and Collective. We are gathered for the rarest and most precious of reasons. Today, we witness the joining of two powerful Alphas, two caring souls, and two loving rulers under the watchful eye of the moon goddess. We are here to see High Queen Bellamy Petit-Dubois Carrington wed Alpha Lucien Leander Deveraux. The couple has prepared their own vows." He smiled. "Alpha Lucien, if you please."

Lucien turned to me. He looked into my eyes and smiled. I nearly melted at the pure pleasure in his face.

"Bellamy, you changed my life in more ways than I could even think of. I love you more than anything I have ever loved. When you decided to save my life, you decided to save so much more. I feared you wouldn't truly accept me. Learning that you were the daughter of my best friend, made me happy and sad at the same time. I wish he were here to see what a strong, beautiful woman you've become.

"Thank you for choosing me. Thank you for loving me. I will never let you regret it. I vow to keep you grounded, to listen to you when you try to keep me grounded, to let you keep growing as a queen and warrior. My love, I plan to make you the happiest woman in the world for as long as I live."

Tears started forming in his eyes. I reached up, standing on my toes to reach, and wiped them. Lucien took my hand and kissed it.

"Queen Bellamy?" Pastor Blood nodded to me.

"I've lost a lot in my life. I've also gained a lot. Friends and family surrounded me, but I was alone. I wanted someone to love me the way I saw everyone else falling in love. My heart grew cold, only warming enough to take care of my people and those who were important to me.

"When I saw your stubbornness and the strength of your convictions, I knew you would never give up on whoever you loved. Before you, I never told people I loved them. You made me see that I deserved to let love in and I wouldn't lose anyone for saying how I felt. You have become my heart, my reason, and my life.

"I promise to care for you, guide you, listen to you, and keep you safe for the rest of the time the goddess permits us. I love you more than reason and I will kill any who try to harm you or our family."

Lucien's hand cupped my cheek gently, and I rubbed my cheek against it. I wanted this to be over soon. I wanted my mate.

"The goddess has bestowed her blessing upon this couple. Those who oppose their union would do well to keep their opinions silent in even the darkest night, lest she hear your heart and decide to quiet it herself. No Queen has ever had a King so capable, no Alpha has ever had a Luna so powerful. Our goddess gives much to a match made as perfectly as these," Pastor Blood announced intensely.

I couldn't keep the smile hidden as whispers erupted from the crowd. They should've realized this would be more of a rogue wedding. We don't ask for objections; we threaten people into keeping their objections quiet.

"Please exchange your rings," he told us.

We did as he instructed. The rings were finally back where they belonged. Pastor Blood smiled.

"You are now joined in the eyes of our goddess, your people, and human law. You may seal this bond with a kiss," he said.

Lucien and I had debated this moment for the last few days. He believed we should have a chaste kiss. Rogues tended to be more ardent. I agreed to a lot of things to make this more pack-friendly.

He leaned down and kissed me gently, letting a little heat into the kiss. I wasn't going to let him get away with that. It wasn't enough.

Reaching behind his head, I gripped his hair and pulled him more tightly into the kiss. I locked my elbows over his shoulders and he lifted me up when he realized I wouldn't let go. His arms wrapped around me and he returned the passion of my kiss.

I barely registered the sounds of the rogues in the audience cheering and howling. I wouldn't let people say I was giving in to the role of Luna by letting him win this bout and started sucking and nibbling his lips until he granted me entrance.

When he could finally pull me away, I wiped the lipstick from around his mouth and winked. Lucien laughed and leaned in next to my ear.

"Fine, you won that one, Mrs. Deveraux, but I'll win the next one," he rumbled.

"I look forward to the fight, Mr. Deveraux," I purred.

He set me down and looped my arm around his, guiding me back up the aisle, followed by my two best friends and my cousins. I finally owned him in every way. I would never let him go.

Chapter 125: Reception

[Bellamy]

We stood at the arched area and shook hands with everyone who attended. It was polite with all the Alphas, Kings, and vampires we'd invited. This would be a perfect time to create alliances and strengthen the ones we had.

I made sure Lucien told the vampires their presence was an honor to us. I didn't want to be indebted to them. This put us at a return of the original favor. It was best to avoid owing anything to a vampire.

My family and Lucien's were the last to come through the line. My dad actually gave Lucien a hug. I was pretty pleased. I'd worried Daniel wouldn't accept Lucien, but he didn't hug people unless he cared for them.

Lucien's mother hugged me.

"That was the most… unique… ceremony I've ever seen." She smiled.

"It was a mix of rogue and pack tradition. Threats are common in rogue ceremonies. I felt it would be the best option for making my ex-pack and rogue born people all more comfortable. It showed a positive combination of both and how harmonious they could be," I replied.

"I loved it. I know Lucien's father would have as well." Genevieve told me and kissed my cheek.

She moved aside, and Lucien's sister stepped forward. She was tall, like 5'10" with her mother's hair and father's eyes. Like Simone, she looked regal, and she was as beautiful as Lucien. My pups were going to inherit some wonderful genetics.

"Bellamy, sorry we didn't get a chance to meet. Someone thought he read the time right, and wouldn't listen. You are so beautiful. Thank you for loving my brother. You look so much like Jean-Luc and Angelique, it's almost like having them back," Liana gushed.

That sort of acceptance surprised me, and I wasn't ready for it. Lucien said his sister was friends with my mama, but I thought she might still be miffed about the rejection. It was basically a rejection of her whole family.

"Thank you, Liana. I appreciate it. And thank you for coming," I answered.

"I'll return with the kids when your pups come and help out for a few weeks. Then we'll take Maman back home with us. She likes the warmer weather in the winter and autumn. These are my children!" She bounced. "Gabrielle and Nadia."

She pointed out two girls who, even without heels, were three inches taller than me and resembled their mother. In the four-inch-high heels I was wearing, I was about an inch shorter than a short adult female werewolf would normally get.

"And my little Julian."

Liana pulled a boy who was also about three inches taller than me to the front. He was darker with black hair and golden skin, but he had Lucien's silver eyes.

"It's a pleasure to meet you all." I smiled.

"Thank you, Tante Bellamy," they chorused.

I was an aunt to children who were less than ten years younger than me. It was shocking, to say the least.

Liana moved the children along, and I saw how much Lucien lit up. He really loved them a lot. I wondered how often he got to see them. I never asked and I probably should have.

"This is my mate, Alpha Gregory Diaz." Liana pulled a man who was taller than Lucien to stand beside her.

I could see where Julian got his looks. Gregory had the same dark golden skin, black hair, and a charming smile. He had very dark, almost black eyes, and a thick build. His suit seemed to have a hard time fitting his muscles.

Gregory put out his hand, and I took it. Alphas were all the same. He squeezed my hand tightly, and I returned his strength to him with little effort. Although annoyed, I accepted the test. He wanted to see if he was stronger than me. He was, but I wouldn't give in.

He pushed out his Alpha aura. Lucien growled a little and Liana looked embarrassed. I smiled and let mine out. If he wanted to see whose dick was bigger, I'd let him know I wasn't anything to scoff at.

I looked up into his eyes while my aura pushed at him. His wolf whined. The sound came from him and I fought not to laugh. It only took one more push to get him on his knees, where I didn't need to look up.

"*I* am High Queen. *You* are a standard Alpha. I appreciate your… position… but you are not at my level," I whispered.

"I didn't realize rogues could be so powerful," he strained.

"You didn't realize a woman could be so powerful." Liana snorted. "I told you things were different out here. And that's Jean-Luc's daughter. If she's even half the fighter her dad was, you're lucky she didn't kick your ass, too."

"Please, let him up, chouchoutte. I'm sure he's sorry now," Lucien chuckled.

"We should have all the Alphas come train with us in the morning, I know the rest of the Association would love to see the training I put my boys through," I told Lucien.

"I thought tomorrow was a light day since we were leaving," he groaned.

"We'll do a medium day. The same thing you started out with, my love," I replied.

"I'm sure Gregory will be happy to join," Liana stated.

"Sure. I can do that." He winced a small smile.

"You try to dominate me again and we'll have issues, Alpha Gregory. Do you understand?" I asked.

"Yes, ma'am." He nodded, and I released him.

Gregory moved to Lucien, who squeezed his hand so hard, just the pain had him back on his knees. I snorted and Liana shook her head.

"You try to dominate my mate again and there will be problems with more than just her," Lucien growled.

"Y-you're a lot stronger than you used to be, Lucy," Gregory grumbled.

"Because of my mate's training. Three weeks of elite training and two weeks of training with bears. Nothing like it," Lucien replied.

"Let him go, we need to get to the reception." I sighed.

Lucien let Gregory go and we followed everyone to the area that was set up for the reception. Gregory quietly complained to Liana the whole way, and she teased him relentlessly. Nadia walked next to me and asked questions about rogues. She was interested in the physiological differences and why we were so different.

I loved her curiosity. She told me she wanted to be a doctor and study the differences between all supernatural creatures. More than anything, she wanted to know what made us so different from humans, but still similar. I would have to talk to Lucien about having her come for the summers to intern at the pack hospital or one of my clinics. I was sure she would learn a lot there.

***

We'd had to set up the reception outdoors because everyone who lived in the packhouse and all our guests were just too many people to fit in the ballroom. It was really lovely, decorated with the blended colors of my collective and Lucien's pack.

I felt it was perfect how our colors were similar enough to harmonize with each other. It was a symbol of how we complemented each other in our strengths and abilities. The meaning in it made me happy.

It was traditional for the Alpha and Luna to have a waltz as their first dance when they were presented. Lucien took my hand and guided me to the floor. It was lucky that Daisy's lessons included formal dancing.

Lucien smiled down at me as he swept me around the dancefloor. He looked as joyful as I felt. My mate, my husband, was perfect in every way.

"Chouchoutte, I think tonight I will mark you again. It would be the perfect end to this day," he murmured.

I felt the heat of my arousal at that statement. The idea of him marking me a second time was exciting as hell. A smile that was too strong to hold back came out.

"Where?" I asked.

"That is a surprise. Something to look forward to, so you don't spend the entire night dancing with your friends," Lucien chuckled.

"Let's go home now. They can have their party. We can have ours," I purred.

"Non. We'll stay and fulfill our obligations. You will get no reward for pushing us along. Remember the traditions we still have to observe?" he asked.

I groaned and pouted.

"Bellamy," he warned.

With a sigh, I nodded. "Toast, meals, required formal dancing with the Alphas and Lunas, after your dance with your mother and mine with my father, then dessert and informal dancing."

"Very good. We can be back before midnight," Lucien promised.

"We better, or I'm going to be pissed." I hissed at him.

"I wouldn't waste the chance to mark my wife for the first time," he whispered, squeezing my waist gently.

That was a promise I would hold him to. I wanted to have a second mark like he did, to be more his than I was now. To know my mate wanted me so much that he had to mark me twice. Goddess, that would be divine.

***

Dinner was lovely. The kitchen really outdid themselves. My plates all had very rare meat on them. I made sure the other High Kings and their mates had rare meat. We served blood foods to the vampires and placed two bottles of blood-infused wine on their table.

When we were done, my first dance was with my father. He gushed over how I looked and the vows we said. I had only danced with him once before. It was at the party they threw on my seventeenth birthday.

Even though I'd found out my actual birthday and shifted a few months before the day we thought was my birthday, they had been working on the party for an entire year. I told them I still wanted to do it and would wait until then to get my presents. It was a beautiful evening that ended in my first pack run.

"Congratulations, Amy," he said softly as our dance ended. "You were the best daughter, and I can't wait to see those grandchildren."

"Thank you, Daddy. Just about three more months. I can't wait as well." I smiled.

My next partner came up alongside us. He was as big as his voice sounded. Jonas Harper was as thick as a bear. Rare for a pureblood rogue. I could smell that he wasn't half. He must have had really large ex-pack ancestors.

His smile was warm and his bright blue eyes sparkled with amusement. Jonas had white blond hair and a natural tan rather than the ruddy look you expect with a lot of people with that coloring. He was intensely warm as I grasped his hand and he pulled me into his arms.

"Queen Bellamy, I was surprised to see you. You're much smaller than I expected." He chuckled.

"Oh, I'm even smaller than this, King Jonas. I'm wearing four-inch heels!" I laughed.

"You're smaller than my ten-year-old son!"

"There are a lot of pups who are taller than me. That doesn't mean you should underestimate me, though. I'm as deadly as rumored."

Jonas twirled me as he grinned. It seemed like he didn't get to have much fun up in his territory and he planned to have as much as possible while he was at Lune Rouge. His mate was having a good time dancing with Lucien.

"We're still tracking Kyle. He's left the region. There was a report of him heading further north. If he ends up in Alaska, I'll have my people take care of him," Jonas intimated.

"Thank you. I'll keep an eye out in case it's a false lead."

"Always cautious, always alive," he whispered.

It was a common enough saying for rogues. We often lived our lives in danger from packs, other supernaturals, hunters, and the wildernesses we called home. Our violence was not the only thing we used to protect ourselves. Our intelligence, wits, and instincts helped us a great deal.

The night followed its schedule as intended. The cake was amazing; Yuri came to give me a hug once everyone could move freely. He was in tears. His long-suffering mate shook her head and handed him tissues. She was one of the warriors who protected Daylight Moon and wasn't nearly as squishy as our Yuri.

Overall, the atmosphere was one of happiness and sadness. It was my goodbye to the phase of my life when I was a child. Even though I had been a queen and protector in that time, it wasn't as intense as one would imagine. There was a bit of the carefree happiness of childhood that I would miss.

At the end of the evening, Lucien pulled me from where I was dancing with Cara and Dilly. We'd been going nonstop for six songs. Our stamina was higher because of our training. Most people had given up.

"Come, chouchoutte. Time for bed, my little love," he purred in my ear.

I wrapped my arms around his neck and kissed him gently. "I can't wait."

Chapter 126: A Remarkable Night

[Lucien]

I carried Bellamy up to our room and locked the door behind me. She snuggled in my arms. I loved holding and carrying her.

She sighed happily as I kissed her. I never thought I would have this, a mate, a wife, a family of my own. It was like a dream, one I hoped I would never wake up from.

"What are we going to do, mon saucisson?" Bellamy asked.

"First, we're getting you out of that dress. I don't want it to get messed up. I want you to keep only your shoes, stockings, and jewelry on. You look like a princess and I want to make love to my tiny princess," I replied.

She bit her lips together as a smile crossed her face. I knew she felt a little awkward about all the sparkly little things. Bellamy was a really down-to-earth sort of woman. She enjoyed dressing up a bit, but these trappings were outside her comfort zone.

I loved everything about her. Especially the way she blushed when I called her my tiny princess. I was planning to savor her, savor this first time together as a married and mated couple.

Bellamy slid down to the floor and turned so I could unzip her dress. I started taking off my suit while she worked to undress to the specifics I'd told her. I knew she was growing uncomfortable with my dominance in the last week, but she didn't mind my gentler commands.

"Is this what you wanted, Lucien?" she asked softly.

I turned and saw her. Her hair was down, but the tiara was still on. The jewelry glittered in the dim lights of the lamps I'd had our maid turn on before she retired for the night.

"You look perfect, chouchoutte." I smiled.

She winked and went to sit on our bed, crossing one knee over the other and leaning back a little. I was still mostly dressed, and her intense stare made me a little nervous.

"Keep going, Alpha. I want to watch you strip," Bellamy purred.

I chuckled and slowly started undoing my buttons, taking off my shirt, shoes, pants, and underclothes. Bellamy watched intently the whole time. She bit her bottom lip and stared without commenting.

"That's sexy as hell, Alpha. I could watch you undress all day," she said with heat in her voice.

"And I could look at my tiny, nearly naked, princess all day," I murmured as I crossed the room to her.

Kneeling on the floor in front of her, I took her heeled foot in my hand and started kissing where the shoe didn't cover. I made my way up to her knee, feeling the texture of silken stockings and the heat of her skin underneath my lips.

When I reached her knee, I nibbled her kneecap. She moaned low, relaxing her position. I slid my fingers between her legs and spread them, caressing her knees and kissing her thighs. My tongue traced along the edge of her thigh-high stockings, making her whimper.

I sat back and looked at her. The memory of the night I marked her for the first time came back to me. The food she made, the plans we were working on, and my embarrassment at her knowing about my curse all flooded back.

The memory of that little red dress and how it clung to her curves aroused me. I remembered thinking about wanting to taste every inch of her. By now, I already had a couple times over.

"I have a question, chouchoutte. It's a bit of an odd question, but I hope you'll indulge me." I smiled and traced along the edges of her stockings with my fingers.

"What is it?" she asked breathily.

"The demon dust Marion and Clea used on us. My desire to have a mate and my attraction to you was magnified. I asked what it magnified for you if not that, and you just gave me a look before I blundered and made you angry. What was it? I want to know," I requested.

"Seriously? Lucien. You're killing me here and you want to pause everything to talk about a false feeling from weeks ago!?" Bellamy was incredulous.

"Please?" I pouted, making her laugh.

"I was thinking about needing to make you calm down, jumping out the window, running around the house, and tearing apart the vampires. I was fighting my urge to destroy them for what they'd done to us. Like I said before, I wouldn't have won that fight, and I needed to stop myself. Focusing on you helped. Sorry, I wasn't thinking of the same things as you." She giggled. "I am now, though."

Her hands slid up my arms, and her fingers tangled in my hair. She pulled herself up to kiss me intensely. I held her closer, feeling her breasts pressed against my chest.

As I moved away from the kiss, I gazed into her beautiful honey-brown eyes. The eyes that had once looked on me as someone to be saved, and now looked as if they could devour me. Less than a month and she had given me everything I ever wanted.

"Lie back, chouchoutte. Let me worship my warrior queen as she deserves," I purred.

Bellamy did as I told her. I ran my hands up her thighs and began caressing her, manipulating her sweet spot inside and out while she moaned and writhed. I could feel her beginning to grasp at my fingers from inside, and pulled them out. Bellamy whimpered as I licked them clean and used that hand to pull her leg closer.

I began kissing and sucking the bare skin of her inner thigh, just above the line of her stocking. My finger stroked over her firm clit and she shuddered as she got even closer to that peak I was waiting for.

She tensed as the climax finally took her, and I extended my canines, marking her right where I'd been licking. Bellamy arched and screamed in pleasure. I cleaned the new mark and sucked the healed skin as I stroked her further. She came again quickly.

Tears were in her eyes as I watched the mixture of my manipulations and licking her mark bring her a third time. This was the best decision ever. I finally let her have a few moments to breathe.

"Holy hell, Lucien! The goddess will punish you for that one. It's going to get rubbed every time I walk! I can't believe you've done this!" she panted angrily.

"You think that training, walking, and sitting have been easy with a mark on my ass, Bellamy? No, I won't be punished. This is your punishment for putting me in a position where I got hard every training session for a week before I got used to it. It's your punishment for every time I had to stifle a moan while sitting down and for making me keenly aware of how often people touch my ass," I growled playfully.

She started laughing. I knew she'd find it funny. I did, too. At least… now that I was used to it. She'd get there, too.

"I hadn't considered that when I marked you. My poor Lucien turned on by sitting down," Bellamy gasped while trying to catch her breath from the hilarity.

"Just think of how much fun you're going to have when your thighs brush together as you walk." I snorted.

I climbed up on the bed and pulled her to straddle me. She slid to rub against me and cried out. Her thigh had rubbed on my hip.

"You are an evil man, Alpha," she pouted.

"I *am* an evil man. It's too bad you love me so much." I laughed manically.

"You're silly. I do love you, though. More than I thought I would when I first let you mark me. You're my whole world, Lucien. You and these pups we made. I would give up everything for you, but I'm glad I don't have to. You made good on your promise to make me your partner and not your princess. Thank you for being exactly the man I needed you to be," Bellamy murmured as she settled herself on my firm length.

"You gave me everything I wanted when you agreed to be mine, Bellamy. I will always do everything I can to give you what you need. I promise," I told her, reaching up to caress her face.

And I would, for the rest of my life, forever. She was my world, too. I couldn't imagine what my life would be like if I hadn't convinced her to be mine. I never wanted to find out.

Chapter 127: Training

[Lucien]

The next morning, we dressed for training. Bellamy grumbled about the feeling of putting on her exercise pants. It would be a long week for her. Apt punishment for the long week I had after the Luna ceremony.

We made our way to the training field. She gripped my hand tightly as the feeling of walking stimulated her. I chuckled the entire way to the south field.

When we arrived, I was pleased to see all the Alphas, Daniel, Thierry, Robert, the boys, the bears, and the vampires were there to join Bellamy and her team in training. The more people we had, the more fun it was.

I never thought I would believe training was fun, but Bellamy's games always made everyone smile. We all found our favorites over the past weeks. I wondered what game we'd play with the recent additions.

Bellamy walked to the head of the crowd, and everyone turned to give her their attention. She stood with a wider stance than normal. With the whispers, I knew that stance wasn't lost on the members of her team. Luckily, they didn't know exactly why she was standing differently.

"For all those who are new to our training, we're only doing a medium workout to accommodate all training levels. The kitchens are working to make sure meals are ready immediately after, then you can head back to your rooms to shower and sleep. Don't try to push yourselves too hard," she announced.

There were a few chuckles from the Chief Alphas. Of course, they thought they worked harder than anyone else. I was that sort of disillusioned. More chuckles rose from everyone who knew how wrong they were. The High Kings were shaking their heads. They didn't seem to underestimate my mate.

"The schedule will include a fifteen-mile run at our top, human form, speed. We ask that the vampires don't hold back on the run. Go as fast as you can or the exercise is pointless. We'll do three and threes. That's a form of sparring where three people attack one person at the same time. You only have three hits to an out, no matter your position.

"We'll wrap up with a game. Vampire Attack. There will be two teams, Vampires and Werewolves. This is not decided by species but by speed. I'll assess who will be on what team. If our vampire guests would like to play a werewolf, they are more than welcome. I'll explain the rules before we start. Let's get moving!" Bellamy shouted.

Jason outlined the path we would run, and we all got into position to start. The beginning of the run was called, and the vampires disappeared. Bellamy and Dillon were already in the distance. She looked like she was slower than normal. I grinned as I ran after them.

Halfway through the run, the vampires lapped us. Talia and Phoebe were laughing as they ran. The other two seemed to take it more seriously. I stayed solidly in the lead of the older men, ranking somewhere in the middle of the Elite Ten's pack.

When we reached the field again, Bellamy looked like she wanted to either punch me or jump me and couldn't decide which. Though it didn't take her long to decide I would be on her team for three and threes. Each team had a non-wolf in it. Ours was Talia. The fourth on our team was Jonas Harper.

"Our people are learning to deal with three attackers at once. Try to take yourself down to the level of the best of the other attackers. The last thing we want is someone saying it wasn't fair because they had to fight full-power Master vampires or Alpha werewolves. You will defend at your full strength and speed. All teams, decide who will be attacked first," Bellamy announced.

Talia chose to be attacked first. A Master vampire against three Alpha wolves. She only had one hit left when she tagged the last of Bellamy's hit points. We fared better than the others who were fighting vampires.

Once I was in the single position, I grasped exactly how upset Bellamy was with me. She whispered something in a very low tone to Talia, who started laughing. Bellamy nudged Jonas and nodded while making some facial expressions I couldn't quite make out and some hand gestures I didn't understand.

He started laughing, too, and got into position. I hadn't been nervous until I saw the dark smile on her face. She called for the next fight to start.

Jonas attacked from my left and I worked to defend myself while trying to use my senses to track the others. Talia came at me from the other side and I was blocking both of them while trying to figure out where Bellamy was. Suddenly, there was a smack directly on the mark on my ass.

I knew it was Bellamy because the mark had a more intense reaction to my mate touching it, even through my clothing. For a moment, I lost my focus. Soon, my three hits were gone.

"That was cheating," I growled in a low tone as she leaned over me.

"No. You said you were used to it. I just took you at your word and decided to grope my mate while I had an opening. I had no clue you'd lied to me," Bellamy teased.

"I'm never used to you touching my mark. That's the whole point of the marks. Focal points for our bond. You know that."

"Mmm. I suppose." She grinned. "But how are you going to try to use mine against me? You know I'll be defending even harder."

"So now Jonas and Talia know about my second mark," I whispered.

"And me!" Dillon called out.

"Pretty much everyone in the group next to us, who isn't distracted, knows. You seem to have forgotten to use your link when keeping secrets from other supernaturals," Bellamy giggled.

Heat flooded my face as I looked over. Jean-Claude was trying to hide a smile and Marius was sneering a little. I got up and prepared for our next fight.

"Such carnal beings," he muttered.

Jonas was up next to defend. He was good and fought with a smile like the one Bellamy had while fighting the 'Rogue Kings' at the intake. Rogues really loved a good fight.

He lasted a decent amount of time. Of course, he didn't have his mate attacking his ass like I did. I was still a little grumpy about the loss.

When he lost, he laughed. "That was the best fight I've ever had in training! I need to implement this into my practice. Amazing regimen, Queen Bellamy."

"Thank you, King Jonas."

We prepared for the last fight. It was time to make my little mate pay for embarrassing me. I would use my knowledge of her second mark, her movements, and all the previous fights we'd been in to beat her.

The fight began. Bellamy's small size made for a hard target for Jonas. She dodged and struck, tagging both Talia and Jonas within the first few moments. I landed a kick to her side, but she used my leg to swing me into Jonas. It cost us each points.

A little more dodging and striking knocked Jonas out of the fight and got Bellamy into a position where she tried to kick at me. I quickly grabbed her leg. The one I'd marked and reached up to pinch her mark. If it were like mine, it would drive her to her knees.

Instead, she used my grasp as leverage and kicked me in the face, knocking me down and using the last of my points. I watched from the ground as she faced off with Talia. The fight sped up as they blocked and struck.

They were the same height and fairly evenly matched when Talia was fighting at a lower speed and strength. Bellamy stumbled back after a hit, and Talia came to help her up. It was a move she'd watched me do enough.

I smiled a little as Bellamy attacked when Talia was in range and knocked out her remaining two points. Talia lay on the grass, laughing as Bellamy jumped up and cheered. It was probably the first time she'd ever beaten Talia.

After a brief rest, we lined up for team choices. Marius, Phoebe, and Talia elected to play vampires. Dillon and Bellamy were also on the vampire team. We took our position and Bellamy had Dillon hand out the blindfolds.

"Alright. Last section of training. My favorite game, Vampire Attack. Werewolves will be blindfolded and the start will be announced. The vampire team will attempt to land hits on the werewolves. Wolves must defend using any other sense than sight. This can be difficult. Don't be upset if you get out in the first round. We'll play twice. Five rounds max. Not everyone will make it to the later rounds. Sit off to the side when you're out," Bellamy explained.

We put on our blindfolds. I focused on the sounds around me, soft breathing, the beating of hearts, and the slight breeze that whispered through the grass. It was peaceful. I smelled sweat, wolf, bear, vampire, and the damp, torn-up earth from our sparring.

"Start!" she announced, and I was on guard.

I heard people grunting and felt a disturbance nearby. I leapt away from it. Carefully, I stood, prepared to move if I felt something like that again.

"Round one over! If you're out, please move off the field. Prepare for round two!" Bellamy called out.

It went on like that for a while. I was out in the third round. The only one left standing was Felix in the end.

"You three have to try this. It was actually fun," Felix told the other vampires.

Bellamy bit her lips together while she smiled. I knew she was always happy when people liked her training. She had a way of making it a mix of grueling and entertaining.

***

After training was over, we went back to the house to have breakfast and clean up. To my surprise, I wasn't nearly as tired as I had been after my first medium-level training with her team. She was bouncing and chattering in a very un-Bellamy-like way.

"I can't believe how much more fun that was with actual vampires. I actually got to play on the werewolf team! Did you see how I did, Lucien? Fourth round! With an actual vampire! Felix was so sweet. I have to remember that move Jonas did. It would be great to incorporate into our repetitive motion training. The elites here will really benefit from some fresh moves." She giggled.

"I'm glad you had fun, chouchoutte. Let's finish our morning and get ready to go. We've got our meetings with King Sergio and Alpha Ennis this afternoon. Are you alright to drive?" I asked.

"Yep. That was fun, but not overly tiring. I can't wait to get these takeovers wrapped up. Then we can have the next week and a half to explore everything and enjoy each other. There is a beautiful forest outside the bed and breakfast where we can go run our wolves," Bellamy smiled brightly.

"That sounds wonderful, chouchoutte. I can't wait," I replied.

"Neither can I, mon saucisson." She winked. "It's going to be amazing."

Chapter 128: Honeymoon Part 1

[Lucien]

We arrived at the bed-and-breakfast after noon that day. It was a colonial-style house painted pale blue, with white columns. The 'C' shaped drive had a parking pad off to the left. Bellamy pulled in and we grabbed our bags from the trunk.

She smiled happily as we held hands and walked up to the oak doors. There was a little sign that read 'Please come in' on the door, so we walked in. The entry was grand, with a high ceiling and a chandelier above a medium-sized, round table. A sign-in book sat beneath a floral arrangement along with a tiny bell.

We put our names in the book, as directed by a laminated sign on the table, and rang the bell. A few moments later, a cheerful-looking blonde woman walked into the entryway holding a tablet. She smelled like a rogue born.

"Welcome to the Romance Inn!" The girl grinned. "I'm Melinda. Can I get your names?"

"Lucien and Bellamy Deveraux," I replied.

Bellamy squeezed my hand. It was the first time I'd said our names together. I was a little amused by the joy that came through our bond.

"Right, I have you for a week and a half in our Honeymoon Suite. Now, we encourage no violence here. I can smell that you're a pack wolf, Mr. Deveraux, but your wife is a rogue. I'm sure you both will contain yourselves around our guests and family. We currently have two human couples staying with us. Runs are permitted in the early morning and after dark," she explained.

"This is the territory of the Hollowed Rib Collective, right?" Bellamy asked.

"Yes, my grandfather is the King." Melinda nodded.

"Then you're aware he's relinquishing his territory today?"

"Yes…. Are you the Queen of the Eaten Heart?" Melinda inquired with wide eyes.

"I am."

"You were serious that you aren't going to kill him or force him out, right?"

"I was. I'd like him to take on a smaller role in the collective, essentially that of a ranked wolf in a pack. He takes care of small things, I take care of bigger ones," Bellamy told her.

"That's wonderful news! I'm having my second litter and I want him to spend more time with the pups." Melinda smiled.

"Second litter?" I asked.

"Rogues rarely have singletons. We just say litter, it's easier." Melinda chuckled.

"We're only on our first," I said.

Bellamy sighed. "Congratulations on your pups. I'm sure your grandfather will love spending time with everyone."

"Let me take you to your room. I'll get you the list of restaurants in town that are pack and rogue-friendly. We have a fairly good relationship with our nearest pack neighbor." She started leading us up the stairs.

"The Swift River Pack?" I questioned.

"Yes. Alpha Ennis and my grandfather signed a peace agreement before I was born. I'm the youngest of my mom's last litter. They signed when my oldest siblings were born," Melinda answered.

"How many siblings do you have?" I asked.

"Ten. Only seven are living. Our collective is strong, but our threat isn't always upheld. We have few warriors left. Three of my siblings died fighting enemy ex-packs," she replied sadly.

"I'm sorry for your loss, I'll send a contingent to move into the area and help secure it. You won't have to worry about your children," Bellamy promised.

"Good. I hate the idea of my pups being killed. I was already thinking of applying to your collective, it would keep me close to my family, but also keep my mate and babies safe," Melinda said. "Oh, here's your room!"

She unlocked the door and stood aside so we could enter. It was just as big and beautiful as it looked in the pictures online. The quaint paintings and handstitched quilt added to the ambiance of the room.

"We have soaps and stuff in the bathroom there. Let me know if you need more towels. Try not to break the furniture, Queen Bellamy, I know how Alphas can be." Melinda giggled.

"I'll do my best, but my sweet little mate just loves it when I toss him on the bed and have my way with him," Bellamy told her with a wink.

I released some of my Alpha aura and Melinda's eyes grew wide again. I wasn't going to allow my silly mate to paint me as a weak wolf. My treatment by others was based on their perception of me.

"Another Alpha. That hasn't happened in centuries! My oldest brother is going to want to talk to you. He's been collecting rogue lore to put into books. Another rogue/pack pairing will have him in a tizzy!" Melinda bounced.

"We have an extensive collection of books he may be interested in, then. If he'd be willing to move to Lune Rouge, he can work on adding those stories to his archive," Bellamy offered.

"He'd love that! I'll call him now!" Melinda squealed and ran out the door.

Bellamy laughed. "Feeling challenged, my love?"

"No tossing me onto the bed, but you can always have your way with me." I chuckled.

Melinda came back to the open door and grabbed the knob to close it. "Sorry, I got excited. I'm billing you for any damages to the room. Any of the restaurants with a little half-moon are good for wolves of all affiliations, the ones with none are human-run, and the ones with a wolf are rogue only. Have fun!"

She closed the door behind her. It made Bellamy laugh even harder. The quirky innkeeper was definitely one of the friendliest rogues I'd ever met. It boded well for our stay and, hopefully, for our takeovers.

***

A few hours later, we were rested and ready to head to the collective seat. I drove, and Bellamy was meditating. She was doing the rogue hiding thing again, staring at the scenery as it passed outside the passenger side window.

We arrived at a large log cabin-style home. There was a deep porch with log rocking chairs and a heavy-duty porch swing on it. The forest wrapped around the house.

I touched Bellamy's hand and her scent filled the car as she came out of her trancelike state. She looked at me and I saw her features go from my soft mate to the cool, imperious Queen she needed to be.

We walked to the front door. I was a little behind her. Mates always walked a step behind in formal matters. I was doing my best to keep up the tradition.

"Lucien, stand beside me. You need to get in the rogue mindset so you give off the right scent. The comfort of giving his collective to a strong Queen will be doubled if there's also a strong King. His wolf will submit faster. I don't want to be here all night. Once we have these territories settled, we can have fun," she instructed.

"I didn't want to take any of your power from you, chouchoutte. So I was standing behind you as support."

"We aren't pack wolves. You're my mate. Your commands are *my* commands. We don't keep our mates in a hierarchy when they're the same level as us. Since you started randomly smelling like a rogue, I need you to act like a King. Remember, you're my partner, not my ruler. I take the lead, but you're by my side," Bellamy murmured as she knocked on the door.

"I'll remember that," I said softly.

"Don't worry, I know the rules for pack wolves. I can play ornament." She chuckled.

The door opened before I could respond and revealed an older man. He was a little shorter than me and had the wiry musculature that I recognized as a typical roguish build. His hair was white and his eyes were the same blue as Melinda's.

"High Queen Bellamy and…?"

"Alpha King Lucien," Bellamy responded.

"Seriously? There hasn't been an Alpha King in centuries," another male voice came from inside.

A younger man who looked like a slightly darker, male, version of Melinda appeared behind Sergio. He was taller and able to peer over his grandfather easily. His face was a mix of awe and pleasure.

"Then the Queen's title is 'High Queen Luna Bellamy,'" the man told the King.

"This is my grandson, David. He's excited to meet you," Sergio said, rolling his eyes. "Please, come in. I hope you'll forgive the crowd. My family's a little wary. They want to make sure this transfer goes as you've promised."

"No worries. They're well within their rights," Bellamy stated.

Sergio guided us into a large room filled with people. Four older couples sat on couches. Surrounding the room were men and women ranging from my age to Bellamy's. I could hear younger children playing somewhere in the house. There were at least forty people in the room.

"Are these all your children and grandchildren?" I asked.

"The ones who could make it back home. A couple of my great-grandchildren and their mates are here, too."

I nodded. I couldn't imagine having a family so large. Bellamy smiled softly as King Sergio introduced everyone. It was a lot to remember, but I knew Bellamy would be able to. She seemed to remember everyone we met.

"Hello, everyone. I'm High Queen Bellamy Deveraux of the Eaten Heart Collective. This is my mate, Alpha King Lucien of Lune Rouge." She put up her hand as David started to correct her. "The Luna part is implied by the fact that I'm mated to a pack Alpha."

"Would you like a cookie? It's my mate's recipe. I worked on perfecting it when she couldn't bake anymore." King Sergio picked up a plate of cookies. He looked at them with love and sadness in his eyes. "She would've approved of this transfer. She wanted me to take care of our family in any way possible."

"Thank you," Bellamy said and took one. "Normally, I wouldn't trust any food or drink while in someone else's territory, but I'll set that aside as a show of faith."

"Please, have a seat," he said, placing the cookies on a coffee table and indicating a large leather recliner.

It was almost as tall as Bellamy. She would look like a child in it. I watched to see what she planned to do.

Bellamy took me by the hand and made me sit in the chair before sitting on my lap. I pulled her closer so she could rest against my chest if she wanted. It reminded me of the situation during our counseling session with Warrick and Janya.

I listened intently as Bellamy went over the plan for the territory and the collective. The family listened as closely as I did. I watched them nod their heads and try not to smile as she went over the private, wolf-only schools and home-buying plans.

"I've been informed there was a peace agreement with the Swift River Pack. Their children go to school in town as well, it would be better to keep all the wolves together," Bellamy explained. "Plus, Swift River is merging with Lune Rouge. The school will care for my mate's pack and my collective."

I was proud she was thinking of this part of my pack. It wasn't large enough for a little school and there weren't many children left to warrant building one. The kids attending the mixed school would have a much better idea of rogue and pack dynamics.

"Everything seems to be in order. Shall we begin?" Sergio asked.

"Certainly." She nodded and slipped out of my lap.

Bellamy and Sergio stood facing each other. She took his hand in hers and they looked into each other's eyes. The faintest growl rose from each of them.

As if taking their cue from a count, both commanded the other to submit. Bellamy's Alpha aura flowed out. The other wolves started falling to their knees as the power level increased. I could sense Sergio's aura, but it wasn't nearly as strong.

He lowered himself to his knees and bared his neck after another couple of minutes. Bellamy leaned in and kissed over the pulse in his throat. A knife was on the table and she used it to share blood with him.

I felt her aura intensify as the territory transferred to her. There was a wave of strength that went through me. Suddenly, I felt a lot more powerful.

"All the ex-packs…" she whispered.

"What?" I asked.

"When the change of power went through… they didn't submit to me. They submitted to you. They're members of Lune Rouge," Bellamy gasped.

"I didn't realize that could happen," I said.

"It's written that when the territory of the first High King became large enough, ex-pack rogues in any collective he assimilated became his mate's wolves. We had thirty ex-packs. They're yours now, Alpha King," David explained.

"That makes it a lot easier," Bellamy chuckled. "You can transfer out anyone you don't want. At least I don't have to deal with the pain of releasing them."

"David, would you and your mate be willing to move to Lune Rouge? We have a collection of handwritten texts and we'll need your expertise regarding this Alpha King/High Queen Luna thing," I requested.

"Sure, my mate would love to live in a pack again. I have a ton of stuff already! I'll be ready to leave when you are, Alpha," he said with a bow.

"Great. We need to get going soon. Is there anything else?" I asked Bellamy.

"Nope. That's it for me. I'll have my people send out the welcome packet with all the information. Make sure everyone gets the contact info and website. I want intake forms finished before I get home," she stated firmly.

"Yes, Queen Bellamy," the Sorrento family chorused.

I stood and took her hand, guiding her back to the car. She seemed a little tired, but we still had dinner and the merger at Swift River. I hoped she'd be okay until we could get back to our room.

Chapter 129: Honeymoon Part 2

[Lucien]

It didn't take long to get to the pack lands for the Swift River Pack. Their pact with the nearby collective made sense. They were so close to each other that it was beneficial for both groups to team up. I had a lot of hope because of that relationship.

On the road, the warriors signaled us to proceed; we then headed for the packhouse. It was a fairly typical building, built like a mansion with several floors that were probably sectioned like other packs.

Our packhouse was rare in its construction. My some-odd-great-grandfather wanted that privacy for the ranked families. He felt it was important that their lives off of work got to be their own. It was why we had a separate exit and entrance from each house, along with the door to the attached hallway.

After we parked, two younger wolves, in their early twenties, met us outside. One was taller, with light brown hair, darker skin, and green-gray eyes. The other was on the short end for a werewolf. He had blond hair with blue eyes, and a cheerful-looking face.

"Hello, Alpha Lucien, I'm Ray," the brunet said.

"I'm Manny," the blond introduced himself. "We were the future Beta and Gamma for the pack. We look forward to hearing what you have planned for us."

I smiled and nodded. "This is my mate, Bellamy Deveraux. Thank you for meeting us. Where is your Alpha, though?"

"He and his mate are caught wrapping things up for the merger. They'll be along shortly. We're to take you to the Alpha's office and settle you in." Manny smiled.

"Thank you," I replied.

They guided us up to the second floor. The internal layout was similar to Daylight Moon's. They explained it as we went. I listened and mentally created a floor plan.

I would give Manny the top floor, and I would remodel the fourth floor into a single apartment for Ray. They would be my captains for this part of the pack land. I needed them comfortable so they could focus on the pack.

Once we settled into the Alpha's office, they began discussing the pack's excitement about the merger. I was happy to hear there wasn't much pushback. It wasn't entirely unexpected, though. A merger could bring life back to the dying pack.

"We have almost everything in line as per your instructions. That blue file is all our alliances with packs. The red file is our alliance with the local rogue collective. The yellow file is internal incidences from the last year. As you can see, it's pretty small. Our pack is caring and friendly. We rarely have infighting. The gray file is the one with incidences of attacks. Unfriendly rogues, hunters, vampires, and things like that," Manny explained.

I picked up the files and started looking through them. They had fewer alliances than Lune Rouge did. I wondered at that. There wasn't one for Daylight Moon, even though they were close enough to warrant one.

"Why aren't you allied with Daylight Moon?" I asked.

The boys looked uncomfortable, then their eyes darted to Bellamy as if they were worried. I had a sinking feeling in my stomach. My alliance with them began before I was out of diapers. Ennis' father brokered it with my own. Ennis and I were about fifteen years apart in age.

I knew these boys weren't the firstborn in their families. A serious hunter attack claimed the lives of a sizeable chunk of the young warriors a decade or more ago. These were the third or fourth sons of their families.

"Alpha, Manny, and I have nothing but respect for the Daylight Moon Pack. We did the rogue classes in school and learned a lot about how rogues were different and the same as us. Unfortunately, those lessons never touched Alpha Ennis. He holds his father's prejudice. They fraternize with rogues. He'd never ally with them," Ray said quietly.

"Maybe I shouldn't be here for this," Bellamy whispered.

"This is all but a done deal. We've already filed the merger with the Association. This is a formality. He's just handing over control. If he backs out now, I can challenge him," I stated.

"The transfer will go better if he doesn't know about me."

"This transfer *will* happen whether he wants it or not. Once we hold this territory, your collective will expand to cover this pack. He'd find out anyway. There's no reason to hide you, chouchoutte. You're my mate," I told her firmly.

"Goddess, it's hot when you're all commanding like that," she purred.

"Later, chouchoutte," I replied huskily.

"Anyway… he's very anti-rogue. He only created the pact as a way of getting relief for our warriors. Because the collective's Alpha is so old, none of the ex-packs have really taken it seriously in a few years. The last one we caught said he felt the King's power, but it was too weak to be a concern," Manny said with a sigh. "You may see the same problems."

"I just absorbed his collective. Are you two loyal to your pack, or your Alpha. You may want to say both, but that's not possible. You're either for your people or for the man who's led them into the ground," Bellamy growled.

"We're for our people. No other Alpha wanted us. This merger lets us keep our pack and our homes. Our fathers are retiring once the power transfer takes place. The Alpha found a pack in California to take him and his mate. They don't want to stay here, and we don't really want them here," Manny told us.

"I'm Queen Bellamy of the Eaten Heart. Your pack will be safe. I promise." She smiled.

"I heard about the Eaten Heart!" Ray grinned. "No one fucks with you."

Bellamy chuckled darkly. "The ones who do, don't live long."

Goddess, that was hot. I loved when she was cool and confident. She knew she was powerful, and she didn't care what anyone else thought.

"The Alpha is on his way now," Manny informed us.

I steeled myself. If this man insulted my mate, I'd have a few lessons to teach him. Ever since I mated with Bellamy, I'd found my tolerance for anti-rogue bullshit was extremely low.

The door opened and Alpha Ennis came in. He was about my height and build. Even though he was only fifteen years older than me, and werewolves aged slower than humans, he looked much older. The stress of maintaining his pack and losing his children must have aged him prematurely. I couldn't imagine losing so much.

"Alpha Lucien!" he said cheerfully. "And this must be your new wife, what a... lovely girl. Ought to get quite a few pups outta her."

Ray and Manny winced. Ennis' Luna entered behind him. She didn't seem affected by his declaration. I narrowed my eyes at him.

"I would appreciate it if you didn't talk about my Luna as if she were a broodmare," I told him coolly.

"No offense meant." He scoffed, waving away my statement. "I just meant that mating with a younger woman would give you more time to make pups. My mate and I got a late start because she was in another country for most of her life. We only got the two…. Now they're gone. But a strong Alpha with a big pack like yours shouldn't have any trouble protecting your pups."

The way he went back and forth from insulting to guilt-inducing was annoying. I used to have no problem brushing it off. Backhanded comments and quiet, snide remarks were common in pack situations.

"Let's get to the transfer," I said with a smile. The sooner we were done with this, the better.

"I'm gonna crack a window or two. I know you're staying at that rogue inn, but the stench is overwhelming," he snorted and headed for the windows.

I looked at Bellamy. She was stroking my hand and shaking her head. I wanted to punch him, and she was trying to calm me.

"Not worth it, saucisson," she murmured.

Ennis came and sat across from me, his Luna standing behind the chair. I hated that tradition. I knew it was to keep the Luna safe, but my mate belonged at my side, not behind me. It reminded me of what Bellamy said when I tried to walk behind her earlier.

She was more than my Luna. She was my warrior queen. I would never hide her behind me. We would face things together, side by side.

"That's a little better. What, did you roll around on one?" Ennis laughed.

Bellamy blushed. There was a sparkle of laughter in her eye. It was something like that.

"We met with King Sergio on our way here," I said. "His family was visiting at the time. Shall we get on with this?"

"Why would you meet with Sergio? Was it to ensure he didn't attack once you were in power? He's an old coward. Don't worry about him. I would worry about the rogue Alpha he's giving his collective to. I heard she's a real ball buster and an evil little shrew." He shuddered. "Never learn to be proper women, those rogue bitches."

My hands balled into fists. I was going to tear his head off. Bellamy gripped my arm.

'Lucien, he's not worth the trouble. A lot of pack wolves think like this. I'm not hurt or offended. Let's get this over with,' she linked me.

I took another calming breath and worked to control my rage. He was glaring at Bellamy. I knew he had to have scented that she was a rogue and a pack wolf by now. Was he trying to make me angry so I would do something rash?

"They're only good for a tumble anyway. I would indulge with the ones we caught sometimes before I found my beautiful mate. Those girls were a real wild ride if you know what I mean," Ennis laughed.

"This isn't important to the reason we're here," I growled.

"I think it's pretty important, Alpha! I can't believe this. I heard you had no mate, but to be so desperate as to marry one? Fuck all the rogue bitches you can nail, but you never marry one. Is she pregnant? Are you sure it's yours? You know she can lie without smelling like it, right? They all can. No rogue will *ever* be Luna of my pack!" Ennis shouted, his face turning red.

Bellamy gripped my arm harder. She wouldn't let me beat the sense into, or out of, the old man. I wanted to so badly.

"Your father would be ashamed of this, Lucien. He hated rogues even more than I did. I thought you were the same. A little rogue shakes her tail in your face, and suddenly you're sleeping with the enemy."

"You have a pact with a collective. How can you think like that after knowing King Sergio for so long? We share many similarities with rogues. You're looking for reasons to hate. This transfer was already approved. You can't back out now," I rumbled.

Ennis chuckled. "Those rogues send their warriors out whenever there is a rogue attack. Better their lives than ours. I haven't lost more than a couple of warriors to ex-packs in years, but he loses more each time."

I looked at Bellamy. That had to have affected her. She couldn't honestly expect me to stand by while he admitted to sacrificing rogue born wolves in fights.

"You should really know better, Alpha Lucien. You sleep with rogue women, not mate with them. No one will respect you with a rogue by your side. I refuse to give my pack to a disgusting, useless, rogue-loving, Alpha. You can leave," he said with a scowl.

"The deal is done. Give me your pack or I'll challenge you for it. I can't promise my patience will hold long enough to ensure you live through it," I responded with the same intensity.

"I'm not afraid of you, you jumped up pup. I accept your challenge. Manny, take him to the training field. Ray, keep an eye on the bitch so she doesn't go bite someone and give them rabies," Ennis snarled and swept out of the room, dragging his Luna behind him.

Chapter 130: Fighting for the Pack

[Bellamy]

I went with Ray while Manny took Lucien to find clothes to fight in. This was more like what I expected from the rogues. Strange how perception changes based on a title.

Lucien was pissed. I could feel it in our bond. He always forgot how we met and the things he said to me. I could easily forgive his reactions. Most pack wolves were like that and very few Alphas were as accepting of rogues as Kieran and Warrick.

This man was no different from all the pack wolves I'd dealt with in the past. All the ones who hated because of a title and lack of understanding. Wasn't happy with the rabies crack, though.

"How old are you?" I asked Ray as we walked.

"Twenty-one. I found my mate when I was seventeen. I was lucky. She was a pack member. Poor Manny has to live off pack lands because his mate is an ex-pack who lives in the nearby town. Ennis doesn't accept rogues, no matter the reason they are rogues." He sighed.

"Why is she a rogue?"

"Her family was in Ivory Moon. They left before the massacre. Manny talks about her all the time. They have a pup on the way, so he was hopeful for the takeover."

"Lune Rouge accepted before and was more sympathetic to those who lost their pack. Ennis was a fool. Lucien accepted anyone who was displaced if they were useful to the pack. He may not have been friends with rogues, like Kieran, but he wasn't as opposed." I scoffed.

"Will Alpha Lucien be a good Alpha for us? Our pack is getting smaller by the day. Most of the houses are empty and falling into disrepair."

"He accepted about thirty ex-packs from the local collective. We'll move them onto this pack land. I'm betting Manny's mate and her family are among them." I smiled.

He winced. "I'm sorry, Queen Bellamy. The Alpha gave an order and I have to follow it. Until your mate is officially our Alpha…. I'm sorry."

"Did he order you to kill me?" I asked.

I wouldn't put it past him, but I would only subdue Ray if I had to save myself from death. He had to follow his Alpha's orders. There was no other option for him.

"No. He ordered me to put you in the cage we keep on the field. He likes to show off enemies who've been defeated. It's silver, will you be okay?" Ray whispered.

"The pact made with the Hollowed Rib Collective was accompanied by a blood oath. That transferred to me. Alpha Ennis doesn't know, but this is my territory now. A silver cage will be fine," I assured him.

The field came into view and I was relieved to see it was as unimposing as I'd thought. Enough silver to keep a wolf subdued, but narrow enough bars a human couldn't slip through. The top had bars instead of a solid sheet of silver coated metal.

I would have to borrow some strength from my collective, but it wouldn't hurt me as much as the cells in Lune Rouge. The idea of going into the cage was a little frightening, but it was a show of good faith. I'd prove I wouldn't interfere with the fight and the pack would trust me more once we took over.

The decision not to tell Lucien was based on what would be best in this situation. He was upset about the pushback on the takeover and the things Alpha Ennis said about me, but this would piss him off. Lucien needed to be angry. He needed the added fuel to make him fight harder.

"Can I have a chair, at least?" I asked.

"Yes, Queen Bellamy. I'm having an omega bring one now." Ray answered.

A minute or so later, a young man came out carrying a wooden chair. One of the warriors placed it in the center of the cage and tried to grab at me. I slipped aside.

"I'm doing this voluntarily. If you try to touch me again, you'll pull back a bloody stump," I growled, releasing my Alpha aura.

The warrior moved away from me and looked at the ground. I glared at the others. They all looked away. None were strong enough to challenge me. No wonder he needed rogues to fight for him. His warriors were cowardly.

I entered the cage and sat, crossing one knee over the other and leaning back nonchalantly. I wouldn't show signs of distress. That wasn't how an Alpha acted.

Warriors surrounded the field. Lucien would be on his own, but I hoped this wasn't a trap of some sort. If all those men and the Alpha attacked, I wouldn't be able to save him. Once I was in the cage, I was essentially powerless.

Lucien entered the field ten minutes later. When he saw me in the cage, he turned red with anger and stormed over. To their credit, the warriors tried to stay calm and emotionless.

The weight of his aura was crushing. A couple men whimpered as Lucien neared. He stood in front of the cage and seethed.

"What's going on, Bellamy?" Lucien growled.

"Ennis ordered me caged until you beat him," I replied.

"Alpha Lucien, my Alpha is worried your mate will be more inclined to cheat based on her being a rogue. Please, we have to follow orders," Ray said softly.

"They have to, my love. I'm not mad. Go kick his ass. I'll be right here." I smiled. "But don't take too long. The pups will be affected if it goes on too long."

"Pups? I didn't know she was pregnant, Alpha, or I would've refused. I would've taken the punishment. Now that she's in there… only the Alpha of our pack can order it opened." Ray's voice quivered.

"Then I'll kill him," Lucien answered in a cold, deadly voice.

The scent of rogue increased. It was a turn-on when mixed with his normal scent. He was thinking like a rogue Alpha. A living enemy was an enemy for life. Until one of the two of you was dead, neither could have a safe life.

"If you kill him, you have to kill his mate," I told him. "Or she'll work to undermine or destroy you. Remember your old family curse. We have enough to deal with."

That seemed to snap him out of it. He looked a little appalled. The safety of females is paramount in pack society. I knew it would pull him out of the roguish thought pattern. His scent went back to normal.

"I can't kill her. She's done nothing wrong, except being mated to that asshole," he grumbled.

"Go fight to get me out of here. Do what you have to. Don't let me stay here too long, mon saucisson," I told him in a slightly pleading tone.

I really needed to make sure he was in the right headspace for the fight. If Ennis tried to kill him, I needed to be sure Lucien wouldn't let him live. That man wouldn't stop trying to hurt my family. His hate was palpable as we'd sat with him.

"Stay away from the bars, Bellamy. I'll be back in a little while," Lucien promised.

"I'll hold you to that, Lucien," I whispered.

He went to the center of the field. While we'd been talking, Ennis had arrived and had a shit-eating grin on his face. I wanted to punch him myself.

"If you win, she can go. If not, she's a rogue trespassing in my territory. I invited you and your Luna, not your whore," Ennis scoffed.

I took a deep breath and let that one flow over me. Not the worst I'd ever been called. Even Rhys called me far worse. I kept my face impassive.

The Luna scowled when she looked over at me. So, he was in charge of psyching out my mate and she was to report my feelings. I yawned and picked at some imaginary thing on the knee of my jeans. They wouldn't get a rise out of me.

Unfortunately, Lucien wasn't thinking the same way. His fists clenched and all of his muscles tensed. Ennis was digging his own grave. I couldn't calm Lucien if I was in here. I needed to do something.

"Keep your head, Lucien. He's just trying to rile you up. I'll be fine. You're going to kick his ass!" I called out.

"Shut your mouth, rogue bitch!" the Luna snarled.

"Fucking worthless pack bitch! Why don't you go sit down and look pretty? That's all you're good for, isn't it?" I shouted.

She growled and started toward me. Ennis grabbed her arm and shook his head at her.

"She's not worth it, Linda," he told her. At least I knew her name now.

Linda glared and returned to her spot behind him. I stuck my tongue out at her.

"Let's get on with this challenge, Alpha Lucien. Your mate is disgracing you in more ways than just being a rogue." Ennis snorted.

"Fuck you," Lucien growled and walked to his starting spot.

The fight began shortly after. I wasn't really worried. With all the training Lucien had been through in the last few weeks, he was better than his best elites and almost as good as Harrison, our weakest teammate.

Their claws were out, and they circled each other. There were a few swipes and punches. Ennis charged Lucien, knocking him back. Lucien shouted in pain.

Slashes appeared on his side. I hadn't seen a move that could create that mark. I stood and looked around. Linda was smirking, her hands behind her back.

I watched as another grapple ended with Lucien being driven back. He punched Alpha Ennis, knocking him to the ground. Ennis jumped up and tackled Lucien, slashing at his chest. Lucien kicked him off and took no time going after him in the same way.

He was bleeding a lot more than Ennis was, weeping slashes were on his chest and side. I knew Lucien could beat him. It was just a more difficult fight than we'd figured.

Ennis attacked Lucien's back, raking his claws over one of the few unmarked areas of my mate. Lucien turned and grappled with him again. That's when I saw Luna Linda move. It was subtle, but she moved her arm quickly behind Lucien.

Suddenly, a searing pain ripped through my marks. She was attacking Lucien with silver-tipped claws. I screamed from the pain, having little tolerance when surrounded by silver.

I was on the ground with my eyes closed, trying to get myself under control. A female shriek rang out over the field, then a sickening crack and squelching sound. I looked up to see Lucien drop Ennis' heart on the ground and turn to Linda, who was charging toward him with her claws extended.

Lucien moved quickly and gripped her throat as she missed her rush. A simple twist ended her life. He dropped her body next to her mate's and turned to me.

The look of shock on his face broke my heart. I wanted out of the cage. He needed me.

"Let your Luna out of that fucking cage!" he roared.

The warriors rushed to unlock and open the cage. In their fumbling haste, no one noticed Lucien fall to his knees. No one except me.

As soon as the door opened, I burst through and ran as fast as I could to catch my mate before he hit the ground. I got there as he was lurching forward and caught him before he could try to catch himself. I pulled his head into my lap.

The wounds were a lot worse up close. I know I yelled for someone to help him, but I didn't know if those words were in my head or if they were out loud. Whatever it was, someone showed up with a stretcher and took my mate from me.

I followed the march to the clinic. Someone held me back when they took him into a room. I didn't fight as hard as I could have. I didn't need to.

"If my mate dies, I will wipe this entire pack off the face of the earth," I growled to the men holding me.

And I would.

Chapter 131: A Critical Time

[Bellamy]

I alternated between pacing and sitting for a while. I needed to focus. There was a little discomfort when the doctors were stitching the scratches that went through Lucien's second mark, but no other pain.

Normally, I would feel his pain when he was hurt. It was a duller version of what he was feeling, but it let me know he was there and I knew it took some of the sting away. This painless sensation was too much like when I was unmated.

During the fight it made sense, but now it just hurt that he wouldn't lean on me a little. If it relieved his suffering, I wanted the pain. Remus had to be blocking it. There was no way Lucien was conscious enough to do it himself. I really needed a distraction.

"Who's taking care of explaining this to the pack? Who's taking care of the bodies? What's the general feeling in the pack?" I asked.

Ray and Manny were sitting with me and jumped a little at the sudden shift. I needed to be an Alpha in this situation. I just didn't know a lot about how packs worked in this particular situation.

"Our fathers are still in charge of their positions. My father is taking care of the late Alpha and Luna. Manny's father is dealing with the pack. He's making sure they understand what happened. Everyone already accepted the merger, this shames us more than it angers us. Our Alpha and Luna cheated in a challenge. It's not something *any* pack wants to have associated with them," Ray said.

I nodded. "I get it. No one likes a cheater. What else can I do? This is driving me crazy."

"Right now, just being in the same building helps the Alpha. We can take care of the pack for you," Ray told me.

"I need something to do. You have no idea how hard I'm fighting to stay in this room instead of busting into the procedure room. You may not have ever experienced it, or maybe it's stronger for Alpha wolves than it is for others. I need to be with him," I growled.

"Luna?" A doctor appeared in the doorway.

I rushed to him quickly. He looked a little scared, but I was sure it was because my Alpha aura had been fully out since I got out of the cage. I couldn't help it. Aurora wouldn't let anyone forget our threat or position while they were caring for our mate.

"How is he?" I asked.

"There was a silver claw tip lodged in his side. We got that out. Every time Alpha Ennis struck Alpha Lucien's chest, he struck in the same place. He was trying to do in several motions, what Alpha Lucien did in one.

"All of the silver scratches were on his back and right side. They were deep. He lost a lot of blood, but we have a transfusion going. He's all stitched up and propped onto his less injured side. His wolf has a lot to heal. The Alpha is unconscious and may not wake up for a day or two," the doctor explained, a little nervously.

I closed my eyes to process everything. Two days' unconsciousness meant he lost a lot more blood than I thought. It weakened Remus. He was wasting energy by trying to protect me from the pain.

"I want him on painkillers. His wolf is trying to protect me and it's not helping either of us. I doubt his wolf will listen to me if I tell him to stop," I insisted.

"We'll get him on some. We wanted to talk to you first. Some Alphas don't like that and you would know what he wanted more than we would," the doctor replied.

"I don't *care* what he wants. He *needs* to heal as fast as possible. No Alpha wants to be weak for long. Take me to him," I ordered.

The doctor bowed and led me to Lucien's room. Outside the room, I paused to take a deep breath and prepare for what was on the other side. He opened the door, and I pushed past.

Only the dim lights over the headboard and the monitors lit the room. I reached over and raised the level of the lights. My eyes filled with tears.

"Leave us," I commanded without looking at them.

The door sighed closed as the doctor scurried away. I needed to be alone. My nerves were on edge. My mate was injured. If he were a rogue, this would be a very dangerous time. My instincts told me I needed to guard him and keep someone from trying to kill him while he healed.

I moved toward the bed. The blankets covered his body and he looked like he was sleeping.

Reaching out, I pulled the blankets down to inspect his injuries. The bandages were thick on his chest. They'd had to shave his chest hair off to get them to stick. I touched the bare skin around the edges of the gauze and tape.

A whining sound filled the room and when I realized I was the source it surprised me. I got a grip on myself. Lucien looked distressed when I made the sound.

"I'm alright, saucisson. Just hurting for you. The doctor's bringing you medicine to take away your pain. Focus on healing, not on protecting me," I whispered to him. "I get to protect you now. I'm going to make sure you're safe and that your pack does what it should."

I stroked his arm as I talked. The sound of my voice and my touch made him relax. I wanted to crawl into the hospital bed with him, but I needed to wait until he'd healed more. The idea of causing him more pain made me sick.

The doctor returned with the medicine and injected it into the IV that hung from a metal post on the bed. Soon, Lucien relaxed more. I was relieved.

"We're getting a dinner plate for you. Ray said you were pregnant. We want to make sure both of our Alphas are healthy," he said.

"I need a lot of protein because I'm a rogue. I want minimal interruptions. How often can he have that medicine?" I asked.

"Every six hours. I'll send mated nurses. You're an Alpha, your wolf will be more overprotective and any potential threat we can reduce will help both of you," he replied.

I nodded, and he left. I wanted to be home with the doctors and warriors we knew. This would have to do. The car wasn't big enough to drive him home, and I didn't want to move him too much. Taking care of Lucien was my main priority.

Carefully, I made myself familiar with every wound. Odds were good the silver scratches could scar. I hoped not. I loved how he looked. Of course, I would love how he looked, even with the scars.

Suddenly, it hit me. There was no Alpha to oversee the early part of the merger. I couldn't leave Lucien or his healing would slow and he would become agitated. I wanted to keep any potential rival Alpha away from my injured mate.

The only option was Jason. I started forming a plan for everything I would need from Lune Rouge. It was only a two-hour car ride from there to here. Faster as wolves, but I thought of a way to make Lucien more comfortable and it would require things wolves couldn't carry.

Pulling out my phone, I thought about who to call. I knew I should call Thierry. As Lucien's Beta, he was the one in power when Lucien was unavailable. The thing was, I wanted to be comforted. Robert sounded like my papa. They were together often enough; I could just say I assumed.

It wouldn't do. I would have to call someone else. Not a potential enemy. The only person in the world I trusted as much as I trusted Lucien. I called Warrick. He picked up after a few rings.

"Ames, is everything okay?" he asked.

That was, apparently, all I needed to let go. I started crying and telling him what happened, as I sat down on the floor and hugged my knees. I really hated crying, but sometimes you have to let it out or it will eat at your heart.

When I was finished, I wept and sniffled as I waited to see what he would say, if he could help. Warrick had been my hero once, and I needed one again. I needed someone to guide me through the pack things I didn't understand. Someone to organize the things I couldn't reach.

"I'm putting Janya on the line. She's gonna help with what you need to do on your end. I'll organize things and get a team out to you. I think Jason is a good option, but you'll want someone familiar with how Lune Rouge runs. Caleb's been training for that. I'll have Jean-Claude gather a dozen warriors and come with. I can have them ready in less than an hour. Stay calm, Ames. We've got you," Warrick promised.

There were some muffled voices on the other line, and then Janya's frustrated growl. Exactly what I needed. An Alpha female to get me back on track.

"Stop crying, Amy. Your scent is becoming distressed. It's upsetting your mate. Listen to the heart monitor," she ordered.

I did. The pace of his heart had picked up a lot. I needed to control myself. Lucien needed me to control myself.

"Working on it," I replied in a clipped tone.

"Good. What you need to do is have someone get you a towel and washcloth that have never been used by anyone else. Take off your shirt and place it near his head, so he won't get anxious while you're gone, and go take a shower. Only use soap that smells like your bond scent. Get the smell of anyone else off of you.

"Use the towel to dry off and put it near his pillow until your things get there. The scent will calm him. Keep the room free of visitors. People should link you instead of coming in to see you. Only the doctor and two nurses should come in. All of them should be mated. No unmated people allowed. Got it?" Janya asked.

"Got it," I answered, and quickly linked Ray with what I needed.

"Good. The boys are almost ready. Dillon's coming with everyone. He's worried and we can't send his mate away without him getting more upset. Everything will be fine. This isn't a rogue collective. No one will try to kill your mate and take his pack while he recovers. I promise. I'm going to let you go and help Rick get everything ready," she told me.

"Thank you, Janie. I appreciate your help," I said softly.

"If not for your training, my mate wouldn't have survived his second challenge and I wouldn't have found him. This is the way I express my gratitude. Bye." She hung up.

I put my phone away and went to sit in the chair next to Lucien's bed. I had to be better than this. It wasn't his first challenge, and it wouldn't be his last either.

Chapter 132: Wake-Up Call

When I heard Bellamy scream, I lost it a little. I hadn't intended to kill Ennis. I *really* hadn't intended to kill Linda, either. On some level, I understood her anger and distress. Losing a mate is painful and can drive a wolf to madness.

Back when my father died, my mother went into a deep depression. My sister and I were the only people she could bear to see. If not for us, I knew she would've tried to kill as many of the hunters as she could, and wouldn't have put much effort into surviving.

Stepping up into his role had been hard for me. I was only *just* seventeen and still only had a basic knowledge of how to be an Alpha. If not for René and Gerard, I wouldn't have done well. They took me under their wing and guided me. Since my grandfather had died a long time ago, I had no other Alpha to turn to.

The work was grueling and losing Angelique made it difficult, but not as difficult as losing my head warrior. If not for Jean-Paul, I don't know what would've happened to our pack. All of it had changed the man I was sure I should've been. The kind of man who wouldn't kill an innocent woman.

Linda's attack was understandable. She was distraught over losing her mate, but I just killed her. It was monstrous. There had to be another way. I could have subdued her. Knocked her out. Ordered her to stop. Anything but killing her.

In the moments before I blacked out, I saw Bellamy in the cage and ordered her release. At least I did one thing right; I saved her from being caged.

The fuzziness in my head grew once she was free, and I didn't feel the strain on our bond from the silver anymore. She went from looking worried to looking frightened as she ran to me.

Feeling her little hands cradling me and guiding me to the ground made me relax. I was safe with her. She would kill anyone who tried to hurt me. The only time I felt like myself was with her, but the new rogue-like behaviors and attitudes were jarring.

The pain from my injuries was unbearable. I could tell when I was being carried away. I was stuck in a valley between waking and unconsciousness. Like a black veil was pinning me down. I didn't really deserve to wake up. I was a murderer.

"Lucien? You doing okay? Like mentally? I've got the physical part. Me and the docs are getting you right, but you're all melancholy," Remus said.

"I killed her. Like I was an uncaring monster," I replied. "How could I kill an innocent woman?"

"She was wearing silver tips, Lucien! She would've killed you! Here I thought you were finally being a man about your life. You're still hiding like a scared child! That's why you're staying down here!" he shouted.

"I lost a lot of blood. I'm just unconscious," I told him.

"No…. You *were* unconscious. Now, you're *choosing* to stay that way! Our mate is out there worrying over us, and you're pouting about killing some bitch who wanted to kill *you*. Did you forget how they hurt our mate? How exactly do you think Alpha Ennis knew what it was like to be with a female rogue if he didn't accept them into the pack? What do you think he would've let the unmated warriors do to Bellamy if you lost?!" Remus growled.

I hadn't thought of that. I felt anger boil inside of me. The idea of him letting his men touch *my* mate made me want to rip his heart out all over again.

The thought made me excited and sick at the same time. I'd never done that before. Watching Bellamy rip out the gang member's heart a couple weeks ago hadn't prepared me for the feeling of the ribcage shattering and the visceral texture of the muscle as I yanked it from its home.

Some part of me was thrilled. Aside from Remus, there was something else in me that enjoyed destroying my enemies. I'd always felt it. The bond with Bellamy was just bringing it more to the forefront.

That scared me, the idea that this monster was inside me and willing to kill other pack wolves…. People attacking my pack, my home, or my family, fine, but this wasn't the kind of fighting I did. I never killed a challenger in my life.

"Are we turning into a rogue?" I asked him.

"That's what this is about, isn't it? The fear you've had that she's turning you into a man you don't know. She's not doing anything, except freeing you from the man you were forced to be. You've pushed to be gentler since you banished her parents. You over-corrected and I let you weaken yourself."

"I'm not weak. I've been killing rogues and hunters. Fighting with enemies. Leading my people. Bellamy says I'm strong, too," I grumped.

Remus scoffed. "You threw yourself into caring for the pack. In addition to your other tasks, you babysit, construct houses, perform wedding ceremonies, and lay roads. You may not let the entire pack to treat you as an equal, like Warrick does with his pack, but you find a way to do anything they ask.

"Why the hell do you think Pavel felt he could be so fucking cavalier when he talked about hurting Jean-Claude?! The younger generation doesn't see you as a leader, they see you as a parent. Someone to make rules they can break, manipulate as they see fit, and who will go easier on them because of love. YOU ARE TOO SOFT WITH YOUR PACK!"

My pack depended on me to be a good leader. There was no real Luna to help out, and they needed more from me because of it. He only understood the wolf side that wanted to be more animalistic.

"How do I stop hurting people? How do I undo the turn I'm taking? Why aren't you more worried about turning rogue?" I questioned.

"Because you're the only one fighting this part of the bond. You refuse to give yourself over entirely to our mate and her wolf. I already gave in. Bellamy's changing, too. She's more ambitious now. She's more caring and soft. Our pack loves her and they love that she's making a real Alpha out of you, not the broody, moody, hungry-for-love, pup you've been for the last nineteen years!" he grumbled.

"I don't really need the lecture," I told him.

"Yes, you fucking do. *You* are meant for *more*, not for huddling in a corner protecting the pack like it's a newly hatched chick in a fox den. You have to be stronger, more ruthless to your enemies, less soft and squishy to other packs, and revel in the rogue she's given you. If you're going to help her keep expanding, she needs you to be more like her. If we're going to hold all these new wolves, you need to stop being a nanny to your pack and start being a leader," Remus stated.

I knew he had a point, but I didn't want to acknowledge it. He was a wolf and didn't understand the human side of our life. An Alpha wolf was an animal, not a man. I couldn't let go of the worried look in Bellamy's eyes. She saw what I did and wasn't happy. She was concerned.

There was a whimpering, whining sound. I couldn't see what caused it, but it sounded like Bellamy. I heard her comforting me and relaxed. Her gentle words and caring touch were soothing. I wanted to take care of her, but I didn't want to see her. The idea of her being disappointed in me, or worse, proud of me, was troubling.

"We're not the man she fell in love with. The bond will start weakening if we change too much," I replied sadly.

"No. Our bond is solid. Her love for us is just as strong as it's always been. She's not the one who keeps running from the future, she's the one who runs toward it. You need to learn from her. Accept the changes and move forward…. Do you smell that?" he asked.

The smell of distress was becoming overpowering. I focused and could hear Bellamy talking, sobbing. Why was she so upset? I was alive. She was with me. I heard her say Janya's name and realized she called Warrick.

"She went running to that other Alpha, again," Remus said with a growl. "This is all your fault. You could wake up nearly twenty minutes ago, and chose to stay here instead! The longer you wait to come to your senses, the harder it is on our mate and our pups.

"I'm tired of you doing this. If you want to pout, you pout. I'm going out there. You take over healing, I'll take over healing our mate. She got hurt too, you selfish asshole. Nothing I could do could protect her from feeling the injury to our mark," he growled.

I felt myself being pulled back further into the darkness. Further from my Bellamy. Deeper into my pain. It was what I deserved after what I'd done. I hadn't earned the life given to me. The mate I'd been given. The pack I'd cared for. None of it was meant to be mine in the first place.

Chapter 133: Wolf's Awakening

[Remus]

It took me a while to really take over Lucien's body. We'd trained like this for a while when we were seventeen, but he'd left it by the wayside when his father died. He did that for a lot of things.

For all that he ignored and left behind, Lucien gave the outward appearance of growth. This depression shit had been following him around since he lost his dad. It was worse when Angelique rejected him. I hated watching him give his body to any female who batted her lashes at him. Thank the goddess for the curse after he rejected Regan.

He didn't deserve Regan. I didn't think he really deserved Bellamy, either, but Aurora wanted us for her. I loved every single change I saw in him since then. He grew so much more as a man and leader in the little time we'd had her.

Even though I felt he didn't really deserve her, it wasn't my place to question the will of the goddess. She wouldn't have put us in that situation if she hadn't meant for this. In Angelique's dream, the moon goddess revealed Bellamy was destined to be with us.

I would trust Angelique. I knew Lucien didn't entirely. She hurt him, hurt us, but it was meant to be. So we could have our perfect mate, and I wasn't going to let him ruin it for us.

Our bond with Bellamy was solid now. She was ours forever, and he needed to get over this or it would hurt her. Weakening the bond can make an Alpha go crazy. We need the stabilization our mate gives us.

The takeover was complete when I could finally control Lucien's body. It felt like a weight was holding my eyelids closed and took a lot of effort just to open them. When I did, I saw a towel folded up next to my head. It smelled like Bellamy and made me smile.

My precious mate had done what she could to comfort us without risking harm. She was thoughtful and sweet. I wanted to hold her and comfort her as well.

Bellamy was curled up in an armchair next to the bed. I noticed her scent was filling the little room. No other scents were invading the space. I relaxed further and realized my muscles were stiff, making me groan.

"Fuck," I muttered as I tried to get comfortable.

Her eyelids flew open and tears started forming in her eyes. She sat up and reached for my hand, gripping it in both of hers. I loved how she looked at me. Concern, happiness, and relief flooded her face.

"Don't try to move, my love. You might pull your stitches," she murmured.

"I forgot about them for a moment, little one. Are you alright? I heard you crying."

"The feelings I'd been keeping back came out while I was arranging for someone to come help with the transfer. I'm fine. I'll blame it on the hormones if anyone else asks, though." She giggled gently.

"Thank you for being honest with me, and for helping keep me calm. Though, I was hoping it would be my cute little mate and not a damp towel lying beside me." I chuckled and groaned at the twinges.

"Do you want me to lick your wounds, Remus?" Bellamy asked.

"That would help a lot. Not the ones with silver, but…. Did you just call me Remus?" I was shocked.

"Of course. You smell more like a wolf than like a man. I figured you took over. I can feel what Lucien is feeling. He's been pretty upset. It made for some interesting little dreams. Will he be okay? Why doesn't he want to see me?" she questioned.

This was the thing that worried me. I needed to be gentle about the information, but it was hard. Wolves don't beat around the bush. We're straightforward, just like a natural wolf would be.

"He's… um… dealing with stuff. He loves you, like I do. Don't worry, he'll come back as soon as he's done pouting," I replied.

She sighed. "So he *is* upset about killing Linda. I thought he might be. He's softer than most Alphas. It's nice sometimes, but, right now, it's bothersome. You must not be terribly pleased either."

"No. Not really. But, at least, I get to talk to you like this. He hasn't let me take over since he was seventeen or eighteen. We only practiced sharing bodies a little before he shut it down."

"You two need to deal with your issues. You're functioning like two different beings in one body. I've never known a werewolf who argues as much as you two do. He never fully accepted you and that made you less willing to accept him. Hell, you accepted me before accepting him. That's not healthy, my love," Bellamy said softly, standing and moving closer to the bed.

With gentle skill, she removed the bandages, minimizing any pulling on my skin. I appreciated her gentle care. She seemed at peace as she pulled them away.

"I love you," I whispered.

Bellamy chuckled and looked into my eyes. "Of course you do. I love you, too, my handsome wolf. Now, let me focus on this."

I waited patiently for her to finish pulling off the bandages from the wounds that hadn't been made by the silver. She threw the gauze and tape into the trash, then went to a cupboard and pulled out some pillows.

She crossed back to me and situated the pillows behind me before pulling me gently to lie back on them. There was a feeling of relief on my right side as the weight of my body rolled off it. Bellamy walked around to the other side of the bed and put down the rail.

Bending toward my chest, her breath tickled along my skin. I watched as her tongue came out and started tracing over the thinner ends of the claw marks. The feeling of it was a mixture of pleasure and pain.

Her hand gently gripped my side, over my ribs, and she held me still as she worked over the larger wounds. I hadn't considered how the human body would register the feeling of my mate's healing. I blushed as I felt myself firming between my legs.

Bellamy pulled back and smiled. "Don't worry about me getting ideas. Until you're healed, we're celibate."

I laughed softly. "I appreciate that. You're the most beautiful woman in the world, you know. It makes Lucien a little nervous sometimes. I'm grateful Aurora picked us for you. You're both perfect for us. I always trusted you, and I loved you from the start."

"Always?" she asked, lifting an eyebrow.

My eyes widened. I was forgetting something. What was it, though?

Even when Lucien hadn't trusted her with the vampires, I told him to stop being rude and give her a chance. She *couldn't* have been bad. The way her personality changed when the vampire was there and when he left let me know she was telling the truth about being there to help.

"I'm pretty sure," I said cautiously.

"Even around my brothers?" Bellamy prodded.

I closed my eyes tight and pinched the bridge of my nose. "That was because you were in heat. I trusted you, I was just worried another male might steal you because we hadn't mated or even truly bonded before Lucien messed up."

She moved to some other scratches and started licking. It must have been the answer or she would have glared at me more. I relaxed under her soft attention.

"Remus, you're snoring. Your body is tired. You need more rest," Bellamy whispered.

"I want you to feel safe and happy," I murmured.

"I would rather see you heal quickly and be able to hold me than wait even longer and sit next to you. Get some rest. Take this time to connect with Lucien. You two need to have a stronger relationship with each other. Like Aurora and I have.

"It'll be easier for him to accept the more violent side of his nature if he accepts you for the being you are, instead of the one he wants you to be. Let him know I love him, no matter what. I know he can probably hear, but he might be more focused on his thoughts than what's going on out here," she replied.

"You're so smart. We're lucky to have a mate who is so in tune with us and so selfless."

Bellamy laughed. "Oh, I'm not being selfless here. You're my mate as much as he is, but Lucien's my husband. I want him back. I want my Lucien in his body and you in yours. Maybe this will encourage him to let you out more often. Aurora is tired of doing our daily runs without you over half the time. She misses you, too."

It was true Lucien rarely let me out. Just a couple times a week and whenever we were being attacked by wolves in wolf form. I'd asked about going when they did and he gave me some bullshit about having too much work to do.

"Alright. I'll go back to sleep and deal with him. I don't know how I'm going to get him to listen. He gave up on us years ago, I'm just a tool to him." I sighed.

"I know. Just keep talking to him, don't let it turn into a fight. You might have to get mushy and go on about your feelings, but it'll give him the chance to see how similar you two are. *You* are his other half, I'm just his mate. Go to sleep. Get better. I'll be right here, watching over you," she promised.

I let my eyelids close. A nap sounded perfect. Maybe I could get him to accept me. Then we could be the mate Bellamy and Aurora truly deserved. I wasn't lying when I said we were lucky. She was the most perfect she-wolf I'd ever seen.

She was brave, bold, and caring. Her people were happy, which was rare for ex-packs, but they really were. Bellamy was a perfect example of what a pack wolf leader should be, even though she was a rogue. I hoped Lucien would learn from her. Our pack needed someone like that to lead.

Sinking into myself, I found Lucien mumbling to himself. If this worked, we'd have a much better chance of being a stronger leader. I just had to figure out how to get him over the squeamishness he had about being who we were, who he was born to be.

"Lucien… we have to talk…" I began.

Chapter 134: When I Get That Feeling…

[Bellamy]

I knew Lucien needed to work on his issues with Remus, but I missed my mate and my husband. It was frustrating as hell when he didn't wake up again. I was not a patient woman, no matter how much I pretended to be.

Any distraction that presented itself to me, I took. I had notebooks where I would work out plans using my phone or the pack connection to reach the people I needed. Sometimes, I would have to leave the room.

Whenever I had to go deal with the pack or talk to the boys, I would put the towel by his head. It kept him calm and let me get out of the room instead of having to sit and stare at him. I just hoped he could learn to accept his wolf before Kyle found a way to use it against us.

Caleb and Jason worked well together. I was a little surprised. They'd been pushing at each other ever since we got to Lune Rouge. Jason loved Cara a lot and didn't think she should be a Beta female. He thought the goddess made a mistake and that she should be a Luna.

Seeing his sister so happy made him open to the idea of listening to what Caleb had to say. Jason seemed impressed by Caleb's diligence and foresight. When we talked the night they arrived, they explained their plan coolly and efficiently.

Once they got up the next day, they had the new pack all in order in a matter of hours. Every new report they gave me amazed me. Cara would be happy about the change, because Jason was looking at Caleb with the same respect he had for Galen. By the end of this, I was hoping they would be friends.

Jean-Claude and Dilly, on the other hand, weren't working together as smoothly. I met with them separately from Jason and Caleb. Dilly wanted to get the rogues organized and start bringing the ex-packs, who were now members of Lune Rouge, into the pack lands.

"If we get them settled in, it will restart growth in this corner of the pack. The info Sergio sent me last week says many of the ex-packs in his collective were families and some younger couples. There are a few empty houses that would be perfect," he told me.

"I'll go with you," Jean-Claude offered.

"No. I'm not imposing and I've talked with Sergio over the last week. He'll have an easier time trusting me and will be more comfortable helping me out," Dilly said, waving him off.

"Then, you're not going. I don't want you running around, alone, with strange rogues."

"He's like ninety! Even if he tried anything, I'm an elite warrior. You aren't in danger of me running off with some guy and I'm not in danger of being hurt. Don't worry," Dilly assured him.

"You're not going. Don't fight me on this. I made a decision and that's final," Jean-Claude growled.

"*You've* made a decision? *You!?* No! You don't make decisions for me, Jean-Claude! You never get to make another decision for me again. Not after the last one you made! You either accept that or leave. I don't need *you* to think for *me!*" Dilly shouted and stormed off.

Jean-Claude stared after him and clenched his hand over his heart. "I thought we were over that," he whispered.

I sighed. I would need another shower. Walking up beside him, I took Jean-Claude's hand and hugged his arm.

"You can't do things like that. Dilly isn't a normal wolf or a normal warrior. You've been training with him. By now, you should've realized he's self-sufficient and doesn't require that level of care," I told him gently.

"I don't know how else to take care of him. I made a mistake and now it's going to follow us forever."

"It won't follow you forever. Take care of Dilly by being there for him without being his shield. He's like me. You can't take his power from him. You have to support him," I explained. "I'll contact Sergio about you going with, but you have to figure out how to make up with Dilly. This isn't my place, cousin."

"I'm sorry to drag you into it. I just don't know what to do."

"Love him, hold him, give him space to be himself. He wants to be yours, but he also wants to live his life. You can't take away part of him and expect for him to act like his usual, lovey, self," I said. "I could go talk to him, but it's your job to make up with your mate. If you two depend on me too much, you'll never feel in charge of your relationship."

"Right. Thank you, Luna."

"Call me Amy." I sighed.

"I'll try… Amy." He bowed with a blush and took off after Dilly.

It must have gone well. They came back with smiles and a container of Sergio's cookies. I was glad.

All that remained was my mate waking up. I was sleeping in the hospital bed with him once the claw marks had faded. Licking wounds stimulates healing for werewolves. I was more than happy to help him heal and gave them a lick every five hours.

On the third day, I woke to my mate nibbling the mark on my neck while stroking the mark on my thigh. I'd been acting as the small spoon, giving him easy access to both as his arm draped over me. His fingers were a little rough against the soft skin of my thigh. I moaned and reveled in the feeling of his touch. He was *very* excited to be awake.

"So, did you work everything out with your other half?" I asked breathily.

"Yes. Am I all healed, or are we still celibate?" he murmured against my skin.

"You know the answer to that. I've just been hanging out here waiting for you to wake up, lazy Alpha." I giggled.

He growled and slid his hand under my skirt, grasping my panties and ripping them off. The sudden, sharp pain of it made me gasp and squeal. Lucien silenced me by putting his hand over my mouth.

"Hush, chouchoutte. We don't want any unexpected company while I take you," Lucien rumbled.

Goddess, that made me wet as hell. I whimpered and nodded. He was a fully functioning Alpha now. The power of his two sides combined made Aurora and me shiver with anticipation.

Lucien drew my leg up on his. After a little maneuvering, he was inside me. He kissed my shoulder and massaged my breast with his free hand.

I moved with him. Running his teeth along the line of my neck and over my mark, Lucien manipulated a nipple between his fingers. I hissed sharply and whimpered with a chirping squeak.

'Did I hurt you, chouchoutte?'

My body gripped his, and he felt the slickness of my first small orgasm. I blushed at having come so fast, but he was glorious and I'd missed him so much. He chuckled.

'Were you trying to be quiet, ma belle? That's the cutest fucking sound I've ever heard, Bellamy. I want you to make it more,' he growled in our link.

He wrapped his arm around my knee and started pounding into me as hard as he could. Every muscle in my body screamed for release, making it incredibly difficult to remain silent. I wanted to scream from the mixture of pleasure and pain as he ravaged me.

Lucien had been aggressive and dominant before, but this was a whole other level. I loved the strength and power coming from him. It was a window into all he'd been holding back.

My squeaks became moans as waves of pure fiery pleasure started ripping through me with every hard thrust of Lucien's hips. His hand still covered my mouth, muting me to the world. Only the rhythmic slapping of his skin against mine and the primal, guttural grunts of his exertion filled the room.

A few more orgasms and powerful strokes finally brought him to his end. Lucien drove himself into me and bit down on my mark, making me lose control, and I screamed into the hand covering my mouth as he poured into me. The twitching of his cock as it spurted hot cum inside of me reignited the flames as my body grasped him, milking him desperately.

We ended up sweaty, panting, and tangled in each other. The small hospital bed seemed even smaller, but in a cozy way. Lucien took his hand from my mouth as he withdrew from me, and I turned in his arms, letting them enfold me.

"You are mine, Bellamy. My mate. My Queen. My Luna. My wife. I'm going to hunt Kyle down and kill him for trying to take what belongs to me. What the goddess *gave* to me. I don't want to hear anything about not protecting you. This is my vengeance. I should have vowed it sooner. I wasn't thinking right, but now I am. I'll kill him," Lucien growled.

"I know you will, saucisson. Unless I get to him first."

"No matter what, that fucking mutt will die for messing with our family, chouchoutte. Now. We need to get out of here so I can see how things are going. Thank you for taking care of the merger, I've got it from here," he replied confidently.

'Our mate is acting more like an Alpha now. It's incredibly sexy,' Aurora purred.

'I'm glad they took that time to work out their issues. I didn't want to have to try to force him to see a therapist.'

'Have you finished with the building him up now? Can we get on with our lives and get rid of that bitch, Kyle, before he really fucks up our life?' she asked.

'Now that Lucien's whole, I know he's going to take care of his pack properly. He's going to support us properly, and he's going to help raise these pups properly. No more squeamishness.'

"Are you finished talking with Aurora about me?" Lucien whispered, kissing the top of my head.

"Pretty much. We were just saying how much better you seem now," I answered.

"Mmm. Let's get things wrapped up here. I have a few dozen more things I want to do to you before we let our wolves run this evening."

"And I have a few I've been thinking about while you were sleeping. I'm happy to have you back, saucisson. Don't ever stay away like that again, or I'll have to punish you," I threatened.

"A sexy punishment?" he asked.

"It will depend on how forgiving I'm feeling." I laughed.

"All punishments are sexy punishments when they come from you," he whispered huskily into my ear, sending a shiver down my spine.

"If you keep talking we're never getting out of here," I warned him.

"Better stop me, then. I can't seem to shut up," Lucien replied.

I tilted my head up and captured his lips with mine. There was a struggle for dominance, which I won once my arms were free. This was a new turn for us.

We were finally on the same page, and I loved where we were headed. It was time to embark on our shared future. The future we were meant to have.

Chapter 135: Afternoon at the Museum

[Bellamy]

It only took another day to get the pack and all the new ex-packs fully squared away. Lucien accepted the gifts and compliments from people in the pack. He was acting less embarrassed by it.

Before we sent the boys back home, he gave Caleb a list of things he'd been taking care of that someone else needed to be put in charge of. He was giving up all the extras that were taking up his time. I was relieved. It would mean more time for our family and our wolves.

When we finally got back to the inn, I was ravenous for him again. We lost a lot of clothes and had to pay for the entire room to be refurnished. We stopped trying to control ourselves after the headboard splintered and one of the bed knobs got kicked into the wall.

It went on like that for several days. We only left our room for food and to let our wolves run. When they were out, they would hunt, play, and spend time doing the wolf-y version of what we were doing every day.

Every morning, other guests would give us angry or impressed looks. The longer they stayed, the less impressed they were. We could only laugh and focus on not touching each other in public, which was easier said than done.

We managed it fine in the first half of the remaining week. Mostly, we secluded ourselves. During the second half, when we ventured out, it became more difficult.

Melinda suggested we go out and see the town a bit. She gave a few options, including the tiny history museum by the park near the center of town. We decided we'd walk over, check it out, look in a few of the shops for souvenirs, and have dinner at one of the restaurants in town.

When we reached the museum, I commented to Lucien about how cute it was. It was like a mini version of the museum from one of the larger cities nearby. I thought it was just adorable.

"You know, everything is cuter in miniature," he said in a low voice, making my skin prickle with desire.

I giggled and pulled him in. The old wooden floors were creaky as we entered and there was a little gift shop to the left. It mostly seemed staffed by people who looked like they had lived through the history of the town. All human. We paid the donation/entrance fee and started looking around.

In the back, they had a warehouse-style room filled with old vehicles and farming equipment. The little plaques described each item, its use, and its donor. Very educational and boring, which made Lucien whine.

We made our way up the stairs, to the second floor that had clothing and shoes from different eras along with the same descriptive plaques. I found Sergio's family name on a few things and Ennis's on others. Their families had been in the area since the mid-1800s, if the plaques were correct.

"Why are we doing this? I'm bored," Lucien grumbled.

"Because we should do something other than have sex all day," I whispered to him.

"At least *that's* interesting. I like all the little sounds you make, chouchoutte," he purred, getting close and wrapping his arms around me.

"Lucien! Behave!" I hissed.

"No, I'm tired of behaving," Lucien stated as he groped my chest and ran his hand between my thighs, tickling my second mark.

I elbowed him in the ribs, making him grunt and whimper. Extracting myself from his hold, I turned to him. He looked confused and sad while he was holding his side.

"I said no. No is the answer. We're going to walk around and be bored for a while."

"Fine." He sighed.

It made me laugh. He was adorable when he got all pouty. I wanted it as much as he did, but my body needed a break for more than just food and wolf-y activities. It took a lot more energy than I had to spend a week in bed with my husband.

We made our way back down to the natural history portion of the museum. There were displays about the flora and fauna of the area around the town, the different geology of the region, and how it benefitted early settlers. It was very useful to me.

The environment and its contents held significance for our collective. I carefully documented the area's edible plants, noting their species and abundance, alongside the local animals and suitable terrain for small, secluded houses for lone wolves. It was finally becoming a little fun.

Lucien wandered off at some point and made it back to me as I was just wrapping up my notes on the surrounding area. He tapped me on the shoulder and pointed to a doorway with a heavy curtain hanging on it. I was wary.

"You want to see something pretty?" Lucien asked.

"It's not your cock again, is it? I make a one-off comment, and you keep using it to trick me," I grumped jokingly.

"You love it. No, it's some rocks. I think you'll like it," he urged and pulled me to the room.

The room was about the size of our walk-in closet at home. A little bench sat in the center of the room, and displays of different rocks featured plaques describing their type and region of origin. I had no idea what Lucien thought I would find interesting until he closed the curtain and reached for some switches on the wall.

Darkness surrounded me as he turned off the light. Just as I was about to yell at him, he switched on another light. All the rocks glowed in different shades under the black light.

Frozen in place, I was captivated by the vibrant colors around me. It was beautiful. Like the night sky surrounding me.

Lucien came close and wrapped his arms around me. His body was behind mine, holding me close as we wandered the room a second time, looking at all the glowing rocks. It was terribly romantic.

"They're so pretty, Lucien," I whispered.

"Beauty is sometimes hidden in plain things, chouchoutte. They only need the right sort of light to bring it out. Our pasts were ordinary and ugly, but we are the light the other needed to make our lives beautiful," he replied.

"That's sweet, saucisson. I'm still not having sex with you in here."

"Oh, come on! I was romantic and everything!" Lucien said, pulling me to sit on his lap on the bench.

"You were very romantic, mon cœur. And I loved it, but this is a museum. I don't want to do it in a museum," I told him.

"How about a kiss then?" he asked.

I turned in his lap and began kissing him softly. His arms tightened around me and he deepened the kiss, making me moan a little. I wrapped my arms around his neck and attacked his mouth passionately. I didn't know how much of it was the baby hormones and how much was the honeymoon high, but it made me feel a lot more affectionate than I was prepared for.

After a few minutes of making out, I had my hands under his shirt and his hand had found the mark on my thigh. He was tracing over it, sending little shocks of pleasure through me. We barely noticed when someone drew back the curtain.

"Alright, you two," an older man in a guard uniform growled. "You need to leave the museum. This is inappropriate."

I blushed and got off Lucien's lap. Being reprimanded by a human guard was embarrassing. He continued his scolding as we walked toward the entrance.

"I know you kids are young and in love, but this is a place for learning and absorbing history. Not a place to go at it like a couple animals in heat. Respect yourselves and each other. Take your lady to a nice hotel or something. Not a bench in a museum," he lectured.

I bit my lips together and looked at Lucien, who seemed like he was trying not to laugh. Once we were outside, and the guard closed the door on us, we couldn't hold back any longer and started laughing. Getting caught making out with my mate was thrilling.

"You want to head back to the inn?" Lucien asked in a voice thick with desire.

I bit my bottom lip and shook my head. It had been embarrassing, but also fun and hot as hell. I craved more. Rogues rarely cared if someone saw them being intimate out in the wild, but they didn't seek it out. Here I was, the odd wolf out, craving some exhibitionism.

"What do you want to do, then?" he inquired.

"I want to go to the bookstore on the other side of the park, that Melinda talked about. Maybe they have something cool there." I smiled.

"A bookstore? I suppose. I expect a lot of sex tonight, for giving up the afternoon. Soon we'll be heading home, chouchoutte, and I just want to be with you as much as possible."

"Then be with me at the bookstore and the little shops on Main Street," I told him.

He didn't catch my double meaning and looked disappointed. I decided not to clarify. He'd figure it out in due time. This was going to be a lot of fun.

Chapter 136: Window Shopping

Walking through the park with Bellamy was reminiscent of the walks we had at home. Maybe she was right. We needed a break from the physical stuff. Making out with her in the rock room felt like being a teenager again. Especially with the scolding we got from the guard.

Bellamy seemed happier than I'd seen her in a while. She was always so focused on her work, and seemed almost obsessed at times. Now that I'd fully accepted Remus I saw her relaxing more. I was now more aware of potential dangers than in the past.

We made it out of the park and crossed the street to the used bookstore. It was in an old house on the corner, right before the 'downtown' area with all the little shops. The building was in good repair, painted a cheerful yellow with white trim. The porch and stairs were white as well.

Sunshine Books was written on banners that fluttered in the wind. There were butterfly and frog ornaments in front. Bellamy squeezed my arm. Her excitement was palpable. I never realized Bellamy was a fan of older books. I'd have to save that knowledge for later.

Upon entering, we saw floor-to-ceiling bookshelves with little alcoves made by backing one large shelf against another. Signs hung from the ceiling, listing which book genres were in each cove. The smell of ink, paper, and a little dust filled the air.

I wasn't into that sort of thing, but it was exactly what I imagined the place smelling like. It was nice to have something be what I expected. That was becoming rare lately.

In the corner of the main room was an L-shaped counter with a woman behind it and a cash register on top. I could see some stairs heading up and an arrow sign that said '*Science and Nature*'. It had a unique style.

'I'm going to wander. Why don't you see if there's anything that interests you here?' she told me in our link.

I nodded and started looking around at the different books and genres. After a while, I decided I'd see what human fiction writers were putting out there about werewolves. It was a good idea to keep abreast of any new theories. In case something they dreamed up could be dangerous.

Approaching the desk, I saw the young woman behind it stiffen. She was human, but seemed to feel my power.

"Pardon me. Where might I find books about werewolves?" I asked quietly, not wanting the handful of people milling around to hear.

The girl looked shocked. "Umm…. There are a few places. We have werewolves in horror, urban fantasy, and science and nature. Would you like me to show you?"

She took me to the horror section first. Many of the books had been out for years. I grabbed the newer ones.

Returning to the desk, I asked about the urban fantasy books. The girl, who'd introduced herself as Betty, led me to a section in the opposite corner. She turned to me.

"We have them in alphabetical order by author, but broken up by subject to make it easier on our patrons. That part is fairies, then general supernatural, vampires, werewolves, and witches," Betty said, pointing to each section as she did.

"Thank you," I told her and started looking through the books.

There was a wide range, much more than the vampires had. I tried to figure out where to start. I scanned over the titles and found a familiar name. Fernsby.

Louis Fernsby was a fairly well-known werewolf who wrote books for our kind and compiled collections of legends. He was reclusive, and no one had ever met him. I wondered how one of his books had ended up here. I had never seen this one before.

The title read *The Hunter's Mate*. I opened it up and immediately understood why I had never heard of this one. It was pure fiction. Not the kind humans assumed was fiction, but real fiction. I read a little further after going back to the cover and seeing that the author's name wasn't Louis, but Lou-Ann Fernsby.

The main character was a she-wolf who hunted the humans that preyed on supernatural beings. She was part of a pack called Hunter's Moon, which made me smirk. Warrick's pack.

Had the author known that, or was it just an odd coincidence? Either way, I doubted Warrick would appreciate his pack being turned into a band of human-hunting vigilantes.

I flipped a few more pages and found myself impressed. The opening scene threw the heroine into action immediately. She stalked her prey across a dark alley, waiting for the moment to strike. When the hunter turned to check his surroundings, she was already moving, silent and swift, taking him down before he even knew what hit him. I had to admit, that was a hell of a way to start a story.

Then I hit something that made me chuckle. According to this book, werewolves had an uncontrollable urge to arrange their dens by scent, organizing everything to ensure their territory was properly marked. Supposedly, a werewolf's home would be in perfect olfactory order, with the most comforting scents placed closest to their bed. I had no idea where people got these ideas, but it was entertaining.

An entire pack dedicated to hunting human hunters might interest Bellamy. Yes… I would buy it for her, but I would need to read it first just to be sure she would like it.

A few minutes later, I was reading about Maya preparing to kill a hunter until his scent hit her and it matched a jacket given to her by a man who saved her life when her pack was attacked. It was enthralling to think about what she would do. He was her enemy, but also her savior.

Then Bellamy linked me, *'Saucisson, I need you to come upstairs. There's something you have to see.'*

Remembering what Betty said about werewolf books being in science and nature, I was sure Bellamy stumbled across something important. I set the book down with the others at Betty's desk and headed up the stairs.

They didn't design the second floor for people over six feet tall. I had to duck a little to get through the arch at the top of the stairs. The area seemed pretty empty, aside from all the books. I guess few people were fans of science and nature; I thought as I wandered around.

Someone suddenly grabbed me and pushed me against a wall. I recognized quickly that it was Bellamy. Her hands swiftly went to work with the zipper of my pants.

As soon as I realized what was happening, I nearly laughed. She soon had me free from my jeans and was stroking me firmly. I leaned against the wall and enjoyed the sensation of her small hands teasing and grasping me.

I felt her lips slide over my tip and groaned softly. I didn't want to get caught again. Her hands and mouth worked at me, sucking, licking, tugging, and massaging. The thrill of being in public drew me ever closer to my end.

Bellamy pulled away and dragged me to an armchair, pointing at it, indicating I should sit. I shook my head and pushed her into the chair, spreading her legs up over the arms, and kneeling between them.

My fingers slid over the thin cloth of her damp, satiny panties. I slipped my fingers around the side of them and into the sweet, wet heat of my mate. Her body tensed and she moaned lightly while I curled my fingers inside of her.

"Oh, my god! Stop! Stop, right now!" a voice shrieked from behind me.

I pulled my fingers from Bellamy and crammed my hardened cock back into my pants before turning. Betty stood there with her hand over her eyes. Her face was beet red.

"Get out! Get out of this shop and don't come back!" she shouted, pointing back toward the stairs.

Taking Bellamy's hand, I rushed past the mortified shop girl. She was still shouting at us all the way out to the porch, where she slammed the door behind us. So much for my books.

Bellamy started laughing. "Goddess! I didn't think we'd get caught. I was up there alone for nearly thirty minutes and no one came up!"

"We should head back to the inn," I said.

"Or… we could go find another shop to finish in…" she suggested.

I surged at the idea. Here I thought she didn't like the idea of having sex in public. I needed her badly and nodded my consent.

Chapter 137: Another Man's Treasure

We visited several more shops, but they were either small, with no places that weren't visible, or heavily monitored by security cameras. Although there were some areas in the craft store we visited that weren't visible, several of the employees were werewolves. They'd smell us before we got very far.

In each store, we purchased something. We were trying hard not to look suspicious. If we didn't find somewhere soon, I was going to drag her into an alley.

Bellamy stopped in front of a shop that looked ideal. It was called *Another Man's Treasure Antiques*. Through the window, we could see the older lady behind the counter, cane by her seat. She was working on knitting something.

Walking in, I could tell by scent that the woman was human. Wonderful. Her cane would be audible regardless of our distraction, and she would be less likely to follow us. A quick scan of the shop revealed no mirrors around corners or cameras.

Bellamy squeezed my hand. This was it.

We greeted the woman behind the counter and started wandering around the shop. On the way, I picked up a peacock feather from a vase. Bellamy was looking at some silk scarves and I grabbed a few of them as well.

The store was bigger than it looked. Displays overflowed with items, creating a labyrinth of concealed areas behind towering stacks. Toward the back of the shop, we found the perfect spot. Partially obscured by several antique armoires and folding screens, a massive oak desk sat in the shadows.

With a surge of longing, I pulled Bellamy to me and kissed her deeply, the heat of her body igniting a fire within me. She threw her arms around my neck, her lips pressing against mine with a fiery intensity that mirrored my own. The bell in the doorway rang, making us stop.

"Hey, Harry, how are you doing today?" the woman at the counter asked.

"Pretty good, Maggie. And you?"

"Got some looky-lous in. Nice couple. I hope they buy something," she whispered.

"You got time to chat, then?"

"Are you two finding everything okay?" Maggie called out.

"Yes, ma'am. You have some beautiful things in here!" Bellamy replied with a smile.

"Did you have any questions?" she asked back.

"You just rest, ma'am. We'll come up to ask if we have any," I responded.

"Such a sweet couple. So respectful," Maggie said quietly to Harry.

I felt a little awkward, but decided we would buy anything we used, plus a few things. I'd outfit every office in my packhouse if it relieved some of the guilt of desecrating the elderly woman's shop. Bellamy raised her eyebrows, and I smiled darkly.

Slipping my hands under her skirt, I pulled off her panties and settled her on the table. Bellamy's hands slid under my shirt and she started tracing up my stomach to my chest. Her fingers teased my nipples, and I pulled her shirt up to reveal her beautiful breasts.

Gently, I removed them from her bra and stilled her hands. With a little maneuvering, I got her hands behind her back, and then I secured them with one of the scarves, the silk cool against my fingers. She started to protest, but my hand swiftly covered her mouth, silencing her before a sound could escape.

'Hush now, chouchoutte. Trust me.'

'Fine, but if we have to run away I'll be pissed,' Bellamy growled in our link.

'I'll take any punishment.'

I kissed her breasts, paying close attention to her nipples. I ran the feather over one while suckling on the other. She moaned softly, and I pulled back to reprimand her with a look. Bellamy bit her lips together.

As I moved to the other nipple, I ticked down to her second mark with the feather. She gasped. I couldn't keep her quiet. Pulling her panties from my pocket, I popped them into her mouth.

Bellamy's muffled growl vibrated against the makeshift gag. A low, dangerous sound. I knew I'd pay for that later. It didn't matter. I kissed down her body and began licking and sucking between her legs as she let out a muffled moan.

What she couldn't see was that I'd abandoned the feather and grabbed two of the scarves. I had a plan, and it needed to be a surprise or she'd make me stop. I put her feet on the desk and carefully tied scarves around her ankles, all while focusing on her sweet center.

This was where my new connection with Remus helped. He took control of our mouth so I could focus entirely on tying up our little mate. He kept her on the verge of orgasm, distracting her from the feeling of the scarves on her.

When we were done, her ankles were tied to her thighs with the scarves. As she attempted to move her legs, the silk cloth grazed her second mark, leading her to arch her back and let out another moan. Every move her body made slid the silk scarf over her mark. The scent of her arousal was thick in the air.

'Goddess, Lucien! Untie me!'

'Non, chouchoutte. I want you just like this,' I said, growling a little.

She let out a little whimper as her legs moved again, and she got another rub. I chuckled as I quietly took down my pants and scooted her body closer to the edge of the desk. Pressing into her was glorious. She was so hot and wet. I nearly groaned myself, but remembered to be quiet.

Carefully, I started moving in her. My movements were slow and deliberate, careful to avoid any noise, our breath mingling softly in the quiet. Bellamy made a lot of muffled sounds as her body writhed. Her eyes welled up, the golden brown irises shining with unshed tears. Goddess, she was perfect.

With great care, I powered toward my end. Bellamy's muffled cries drove me insane with desire. The desire to flip her over and drive into her consumed me, but I concentrated on keeping the noise to a minimum. As my climax rose, I pulled out and spun Bellamy to face me. Her eyes lit up with understanding.

I pulled the panties out of her mouth and gave her a moment before replacing them with my cock. Drawing in and out, I felt my peak coming. My hands massaged and manipulated Bellamy's breasts as she sucked me to my climax.

Finally, my end came. It was hard to stay quiet, but I managed it as I poured into her mouth and she swallowed everything I gave. Pleasure built up in my chest at the sound of her little moaning whimpers. I loved her so much.

Once we finished, I got her untied and rubbed her arms to help with circulation. I hugged her to me and she snuggled into my arms. I kissed the top of her head.

"I need this desk in my office," she purred.

I chuckled. "Anything you want, chouchoutte."

We made our way back to the front to make our purchases. Maggie, the owner, rang up the items, including the desk, with a friendly smile. I arranged to have the desk delivered to Lune Rouge and paid for our items.

Maggie handed me the bag of scarves and feather with a wistful glint in her eye.

"You know my Leon and I could never keep our hands off each other either." She winked.

I felt my face heat with a blush. Bellamy started giggling.

"Don't feel ashamed. Harry's the guard at the museum. He told me about you while you were busy," Maggie chortled.

I pulled Bellamy out after apologizing to Maggie.

"Oh, Lucien! That was hilarious!" Bellamy laughed, her arms crossed over her stomach as she walked beside me.

"Let's just get back to the inn," I growled.

"Aw, poor Alpha. Shamed by a little old human. Come on, Lucien. Let's race. Loser gets tied up," Bellamy said and started running before I registered what she said.

I took off after her, my feet pounding on the pavement as I chased her through the city streets. I wasn't going to lose. The thrill of competition coursed through my veins. When I won, I wanted her trussed up again and completely at my mercy with nothing muffling her screams and moans.

Chapter 138: Getting Back to Work

[Bellamy]

The week after we returned to Lune Rouge was Salomé's seventeenth birthday. Everyone in the packhouse was excited about it. Galen and Salomé had been one of the couples everyone was talking about in the pack. Jean-Claude and Dilly were the other.

People would remark on what a nice couple Galen and Salomé were or how good they looked together. I had to admit, when I would see them walking in the garden, they seemed like the happiest two people in the world. It was nice to see a couple with no issues around.

Dilly and Claude were doing much better after the trip to Swift River. They'd had a few bickering times before, but now we knew it was because of his residual anger. I arranged for them to meet with a counselor; they'd already had their first session. Even the bond couldn't overcome everything, but I was happy they were willing to get help.

My family was finally coming together and settling themselves. More than anything, I wanted to have them all close. Salomé moving to Daylight Moon would mean she was a close drive and I could see her when I visited my parents. It meant my adoptive family was my actual family in more than just my feelings.

Adding our own pups to the mix would create a family I could hold and care for the rest of the time. It may not be perfect for everyone else, but it was perfect for me. I'd heard Salomé and Galen talking about when they wanted pups. They were waiting for five more years.

Cara told me I needed to wait a year before my next pregnancy so we could have our pups together. She wanted at least a year of being the most important person in Caleb's life. It made sense for them.

My pregnancy made sense for me. I loved my little sisters and my baby elites. I played house a lot before my parents died. Whenever I found lost children, I loved caring for them until I found their home. I knew I was an effective warrior and queen, but I wanted a new challenge.

That didn't matter right now. What mattered now was my nervous big brother standing on my right, my oddly worried husband on my left, and my young cousin who had yet to appear in the packed dining hall. Maybe it reminded Lucien of the day my mother rejected him.

I reached over and squeezed his hand. Lucien jumped a little and chuckled. He'd been like this ever since Salomé's changing ceremony at midnight.

Normally, it was family only, but since he was her cousin by marriage, Lucien was with me. Her wolf was the same golden red as her hair. She came up and bowed to Lucien, then turned and bowed to me, accepting us both as her Alphas. I was thrilled.

'Why are you nervous, saucisson?' I asked.

'I don't really know. To me, she's like a daughter, as are all of Thierry and Robert's children. I want Galen to be right, but there were times when that didn't happen. It was some sort of mistake by their wolf. Those ones are the hardest to deal with as Alpha. I have to take care of my pack.'

'That's what the counselors and Gammas are for, my love. Galen has never had a miscommunication with Bran. If he says Salomé is his mate, then she is.'

'I hope you're right.'

Even if I had any doubts, the next few minutes showed I didn't need them. Salomé entered the dining hall. She was wearing a light blue sundress and had her hair tied back in a braid.

I was sure the reason she was so late was because she was looking for the right thing to wear and getting her hair and makeup perfect. Pack born werewolves traditionally dressed up on their seventeenth birthday, in anticipation of meeting their mate. She looked lovely.

Galen started toward her. I could see her look at him. A delighted bounce accompanied the bright sparkle in her eyes. He moved faster, and soon she was in his arms.

It was perfect. If they hadn't been mates, he would've apologized and left the room. I knew my brother; he would've gone off for a run to deal with his disappointment. He wouldn't be holding her like she might disappear.

Lucien slipped his hand from mine and wrapped his arm around my shoulders. His body relaxed more. I was happy Bran wasn't wrong. Galen deserved to have his mate and Jason deserved to be his pack's Alpha. I looked at Jason and he nodded at me.

'Galen, Todd, and I discussed it. She has one more year of high school. No one should be expected to take on their duties while trying to finish their senior year. We'll hold off on stepping up until she graduates,' Jason linked me.

'Good. I'm glad you guys worked it out ahead of time,' I replied.

We went to our seats, and breakfast was served. Galen and Salomé held hands through most of it. My mom and Celesta watched them and whispered to each other about how cute their grandpups would be when the time came.

They'd basically already started planning the wedding. All they needed was a time and a place. The mood in the room was happy and high. I enjoyed the shared joy everyone was experiencing. It took my mind off of my troubles for a while.

No one had seen Kyle since the last sighting on my wedding day. I hoped he was dead in some northern wilderness, but I couldn't feel comfortable until some part of his remains were found. Until then, I was tense and my people were still on guard.

***

After breakfast, Lucien and I headed to his office with Thierry, Robert, Dilly, and my new right-hand woman, Evan. She was one of the few rogue born wolves in my collective who became a pack rogue. When I was looking for a secretary, she applied and proved herself to be skilled at everything I needed her for. She was even a half-decent fighter.

We settled in and started our meeting. Dilly had new security features ready to launch and a new patrol pattern he wanted to try out with it. Though Jean-Claude was our head warrior, it was the Beta's duty to set patrols. Thierry looked over the pattern with the new information and approved it for a one-week trial.

I sat in Lucien's lap with my computer open. My office was finished, but I normally started my day in Lucien's office and then moved to my office after lunch. We would work on our separate jobs in the afternoon and focus on combined pack and collective interests in the morning.

It took everyone a few days to get used to it, but we were finally comfortable. Next, we covered the new ex-packs who were arriving in droves. Word had gotten out that Lune Rouge was accepting families and ex-packs who lost their pack.

We were shunting a lot of new members, especially the families, off to the Swift River site. There wasn't much room for them in the main pack land. Our main focus was on warriors from dissolved packs.

They were bringing in more knowledge of fighting styles, newer attack plans, and most importantly, more warriors to guard our borders. The ones who left for the safety of their family. The ones who couldn't stay behind in their pack once their Alphas were lost. All of them wanted a place to protect and settle.

I was planning a little gathering for unmated wolves in my territory. We'd taken in so many ex-packs, I was sure we'd find some mates for our singles. Every time we brought new people into the pack, single males and females would come to see if their mate was among them.

One part of what I was working on for the pack was training some wolves who had a sensitivity to magic on how to do the calming spell. It would lead to finding mates for rogues and make both the pack and collective happier. Not many had the ability, though.

"It looks like this latest addition to the pack has added thirty more wolves and bumped us up to the tenth largest pack on the west coast. Fifteenth in the entire country. If we keep moving like this, you'll have that Association seat before the end of the year, Lucy," Thierry said with a proud grin.

I rubbed Lucien's chest before getting back to what I was working on. We had a few new membership requests in the collective, and some of them were looking to move into a pack. I needed to focus on those while they were updating him on the growth of the pack.

"If not for Bellamy, we wouldn't be anywhere near this large. Do we have the resources for this sort of growth?" Lucien asked.

"I have the old Limb Torn area focusing on farming half that land they're on. The other half is set up for ranching. I was thinking mostly sheep. It would give us meat and wool. I have a few farms already, a ranch for chickens and one for cows. I have a pig farm, too.

"Our agricultural businesses are staffed by rogues. I have contractors and workmen who will give us a discount on buildings. My civil engineer group can have a look at the towns in each pack area and let us know how best to expand. Don't worry about this part. Rogues are good at resources." I smiled, working on my new email to get someone out to both pack sites.

Lucien's hand slipped between my thighs and stroked my second mark through my jeans. I slapped his shoulder.

"No. Work."

He sighed and moved his hand away. Dilly and Evan hid their smiles. This was fairly common for us. Lucien loved it when I was in control of situations. Even my uncles were getting used to it.

The rest of the meeting went smoothly, and we got everything accomplished that we wanted to before lunch. I had Evan take my computer and other things to my office and dismissed her for lunch at the end. Lucien and I were left alone at last.

"Just a few weeks until your team heads back to Daylight Moon. How are you feeling?" Lucien asked.

"My new team is coming together. I've hand-selected a team of elites in your pack who show promise in other areas and will get better with training. How is Jean-Claude dealing with Dilly leaving, though?" I replied.

"I don't think he's realized it yet. We can let him go with to help Dillon get his things packed. It should only take a few days. We'll have you lead the warriors training until he comes back," he said.

I turned and looked at him with a grin. "Really?!"

Lucien chuckled. "I thought you might like that. Don't kill them, but you can do whatever you like with them."

That was a wonderful gift. I loved training my men and it would be sad to not have that experience anymore. Plus, this would give me a chance to really see what the warriors of this pack could handle. I couldn't wait to have my chance.

"Thank you, saucisson. I'm excited. I'll talk with Jean-Claude and watch a few training sessions to hammer something out."

"How are the plans for Cara's wedding coming?" he asked.

"Dunno. Not my deal. I had a last fitting for the bridesmaid dress. They made some changes in case I'm showing when the wedding happens. Since I'm the matron of honor, it's fine if my dress is different. Pretty much everyone who's attending knows I'm pregnant." I shrugged.

"And how are the pups behaving? You sounded pretty bad this morning."

"That's not their fault. They don't like it when their mama's hungry. We really need to keep snacks in the bedroom when I'm pregnant. Mom used to have peppermints to suck on in her room when she was pregnant with the girls. It might be a good idea," I suggested.

"I'll have Felicity get some set up on the nightstand for you, chouchoutte. Maybe some jerky would be a good idea," Lucien offered.

I nodded. I was craving more and more meat the further I got into the pregnancy.

"How about a run after lunch? It won't be long before Aurora can't come out anymore." I smiled.

"That sounds fantastic, chouchoutte. Let's get going. I don't want you getting hungry again," Lucien said as he set me on my feet and stood.

I linked my arm in his and leaned against him while we went to the dining room. I really wanted them to find Kyle before the pups arrived. It disturbed me to have someone out there who might attack my family. For now, I would focus on Cara's wedding and fortifying our territory. It was all I could really do.

Chapter 139: Cara's Sleepover

[Bellamy]

In the last few weeks, we hadn't had a lot happening. My civil engineering group had sent assessors to Lune Rouge, Swift River, and Rose Moon. We had a solid plan for expansion and my contracting companies were already bidding on what they could do.

With the larger intakes, I had appointed people to apply for positions in the different contracting companies and with the engineers. We had more than enough people for all the work that would start in the next few months. There was a lot to get done in the surrounding area for my collective and in all three of the packs.

Jean-Claude and Richard had their eighteenth birthday just a few days ago. Jean-Claude wanted his mark, and hoped things were good enough with Dilly for it to happen, but no luck. I hoped they were doing well in counseling. I was planning to grill Dilly at Cara's sleepover.

The boys loved their gifts from me, though. I gave Jean-Claude a book of my workouts and different games. Richard got a book on rules and diplomacy for dealing with other supernatural beings. I had David help with it. He typed really fast. We printed a second copy for the archives of Lune Rouge.

Now, I was packing an overnight bag for Cara's sleepover. We were having it at Dilly's house again. Jean-Claude told him to live there and he would stay with his parents until they were ready to move in together.

I approved. It gave Dilly space and time to work on himself. It gave Jean-Claude an excuse to work harder. And it gave me a place to escape to when things got overwhelming.

"Chouchoutte, do you really have to go?" Lucien pouted.

"Cara was at mine. I'll be at hers. We decided on sleepovers instead of wild bachelorette parties. You should be happy. No gyrating, half-naked, men were dancing about the night before I married you, now we're giving the same consideration to your future Beta." I chuckled.

Lucien growled. "Fine. I still don't like the idea of not having you with me."

"You don't have to like it. You just have to deal with it," I replied and finished putting my things away.

"I'll do what I can to accept the torment of not having my wife with me tonight. Perhaps I could go see what the boys are doing. They were talking about a game night. I could have them teach me their video games." Lucien winked.

I laughed. "That sounds like an excellent use of your time, saucisson. I bet they will love beating their Alpha at some games. No tantrums when you lose."

"I would never! I can't believe you would assume I would lose, though."

"You haven't played a video game since you were how old again?" I asked.

"It's been at least fifteen years, but I can remember. I just need to get used to the controls. I can probably even beat you once I get back in the swing of it," he insisted.

That made me laugh even harder. Thierry and Robert told me he barely played when they were younger and he wasn't very good when he did. This would be an enlightening night for him, to say the least.

After I finished packing up, I kissed Lucien good night and headed out to the head warrior's cottage. The berry bush starts were coming in well. I was happy they'd taken well to their planter boxes.

Once I was inside, I went to put my bag in Dilly's room and joined him and Cara in the kitchen. She couldn't cook, but she was great with a knife and was doing the prep work. We were making one of her favorite dishes and would all work together just like when we were young.

"Hey, guys. Ready to start cooking?" I asked with a smile.

"You're finally here! I thought I was going to have to go after you and Lucien with a bucket of cold water and a pry-bar." Cara laughed. "Seriously, how are you two always going at it like that? Don't you have better things to do?"

"Nothing better than that." I chuckled.

Dilly snorted. "At least one of the three of us is getting some. I kinda miss when it used to be me, though."

"Yeah," I said, popping a bit of tomato in my mouth. "What's going on with that. It's been about two months and nothing. I understand you wanted to hold back a little after the marking thing, but this is a little long."

"Stop eating the ingredients," Dilly scolded. "Start making the pesto. You're better at it than I am."

I pulled together my ingredients and started making the sauce. Since rogues have a more heightened sense of taste than pack wolves, Dilly and Cara preferred when I cooked. They said it tasted better than when anyone else did it. I appreciated the praise but wasn't a fan of all the work that went with it.

Soon, we had a chicken pesto with marinated tomatoes and parmesan-roasted brussels sprouts settled on the table. A very high protein meal that hit all the marks for my pregnancy, and was one of Cara's top three favorite dinners. We settled in for our meal.

"So, is Caleb super excited for tomorrow then?" I asked.

"He was a lot more hands-y over the last couple of days. I almost gave in this morning. He pinned me against a wall and started kissing my neck, calling me 'ma colombe', and grinding against me in the most heavenly way. Goddess, the things he did with his hands…. It was more intense than any other time. Maybe it was because we're getting married tomorrow. Maybe it's because of how intensely I knew I would miss seeing him for the next twenty-four hours." Cara sighed.

"They all use French endearments. It's so cute. What does that one mean?" Dilly asked.

"My dove," I replied. "It's very cute."

"Jean-Claude calls me 'mon rêve', Frankie told me it means 'my dream.'" Dilly smiled.

"Lucien calls me his little cabbage. Really not fair. He insisted it was referring to the creampuff. The one I had the kitchen make the first time we had dinner with Lucien at Daylight Moon." I blushed a little.

They were my best friends. I would tell them everything. I always did.

"You're a little naughty, though. Frankie told me what you call Lucien," Dilly laughed. "You stole the best one."

"You don't have to give them French nicknames too, you know. I took French as my second language in school. You two picked Spanish because you thought it was easier." I chided.

"Wait, what does she call him?" Cara asked.

"Mon saucisson, my sausage." Dilly snorted.

"Dirty Amy. I can't believe that. No wonder you can't keep him off of you." Cara giggled.

"That isn't the reason, and you'll figure that out soon enough. Once you're marked and make that physical connection with your mate, there's not going to be a lot more that you want to do."

Dilly nodded emphatically. This time, Cara blushed. We laughed and continued our meal. At the last sleepover, we didn't get a chance for much fun because I wasn't feeling myself. Now we'd have more time to talk about everything.

I missed talking with my friends. Since everything was simmering down, we would have a lot more time to talk. It was the best part about their mates being here. I would never have to be without friends again.

***

Later, we were lying in Dilly's bed. Cara had fallen asleep and curled on her side away from us. My head was on Dilly's chest, and I was listening to his heartbeat. It was one of the things we'd done since we were young.

He used to joke that any male in the pack would give anything to be in his position. I admit, cuddling with my friends was an intimate feeling, but nothing like cuddling with my mate. I was missing his arms right now, but I knew we'd be together again soon.

"Dilly?" I whispered.

"Yeah, Bemmy?"

"Are you really doing better with Jean-Claude? I know you told Cara you were, but it felt like you were holding back," I said softly.

"It's the night before her wedding. You know Cara's a fixer. She would've pushed herself to try to fix us plus doing all her wedding stuff. I wasn't going to be responsible for that," he replied.

"What's going on? Is the counseling not helping?" I asked.

"That's going fine. It's really just me. I changed a lot from who I'm supposed to be."

"Says who?"

"Me. Your training and friendship made me act and think more like a dominant wolf. Maybe I'm not the man I was supposed to be. Maybe that's why we keep having problems. I was supposed to submit more to my mate and I can't." Dilly sighed.

"Bullshit. Don't pin that on me. You were a troublemaker who didn't take no for an answer before I ever got to Daylight Moon. I just focused your energy on something constructive. Your entire issue is that you expect Claude to trust you completely after only knowing you for a short while, and he expects you're going to see he's not worth the love you're offering. You make him show he loves you, but what have you done to show you love him as much?" I told him.

Dilly was silent for a while. I could hear his heart beating faster as I scolded him. He had to see this from another perspective or he would keep on with the same behaviors.

"I… I just love him as much as I can. I spend time with him, kiss him, cuddle him. What else should I do, Bemmy? I can't think of another way to show him."

"Mark him. He's yours. You don't plan to reject him. He's been doing everything he can think of to make up for what he did. When he talks to me, when he sees how Lucien treats me, he changes how he treats you. He's doing all this work to be a better mate to a powerful warrior. All he wanted for his birthday was to get a mark from you."

"He said he wouldn't pressure me about this, that I could take my time."

"Sure, he won't pressure you, but I'm not my cousin. Tomorrow night, Cara will get her mark from Caleb. Salomé and Galen marked each other on her birthday. It's got to be frustrating. He's been working so hard to change himself for you and you aren't doing anything but accepting his changes and keeping a wary eye," I replied fiercely.

"I want to mark him. I just don't know that he trusts me. Maybe when I come back from Daylight Moon," he said.

"Why don't you take him to our place and mark him? It's beautiful. Have Yuri make a picnic and take your time with each other."

His heart beat a little faster. "You're right. I want to get closer, but I keep pushing him away. Are you really okay with using our place?"

"At least one of us should have a memory there that wasn't us needing to get away from the assholes in the pack. That would be the ultimate ending to our time in Daylight Moon. Take him to the place that heard your fears about never finding love, and mark your mate there."

"Thanks for always pushing me. I think I would've done the same thing over and over. You know I'm a bit of a self-saboteur." He chuckled.

"I know. Once you feel attacked, it's hard for you to trust again. Work that shit out in counseling. For now, plan how you're going to become my family for real. Like Cara is."

"I forgot I'll be your cousin. That's definitely another positive to marking my mate as soon as possible. You and Cara will be my real family, not just my heart sisters."

"You were always more than a heart brother, Dilly. I just never had a word for it; like I've never had a word for how I felt about Cara. We're meant to be family. It's so much more than a feeling. It's fact. Now, we need to sleep or we won't be as pretty as our cousin in the morning."

"Goddess, I never had to worry about that before. Shut up so I can get my beauty rest. Now I have to compete with both of you," he hissed jokingly.

Luckily, our chatter didn't wake Cara. For all that I joked about there being any chance of being prettier than Cara on her wedding day, I knew she'd be the most gorgeous woman in the pack. Happiness increased beauty, and she was already beginning to glow with it.

Chapter 140: Wedding Preparations

The next day was full of bustle. Everything was perfect, but the whole thing took so many hands that there were people everywhere. All the tall wolves made me lose my bearings in the crowd. I had to link Lucien to come to save me a couple of hours after breakfast.

Trying to help with the final preparations was a hassle. One I really didn't like. I had always done badly at Daisy's party planning stuff.

I was a person with simple tastes, and that didn't translate well to extravagant parties. That was one of the many reasons I was glad that Cara would be my Beta female. She could take on the Luna's job of party planning. I warned Lucien that I wasn't a party planner in the beginning.

Luckily, Lucien believed me and was entirely prepared to let me off the hook. I was glad he didn't decide to tease me about it. It wouldn't have ended well for him.

When rogues party, there are no canapés and glasses of champagne, or whatever. It was more like a biker party mixed with a frat party. Lots of alcohol, very few good choices, and, eventually, police. Our barbecues were enough to stock the city coffers with all the fines they issued.

That never stopped them from approving our permits for another one, though. I'd replaced park equipment twice because of how crazy our kids could get. Blossom and Anise would fit in well with rogue children.

They were ahead of most pack wolf children their age. We saw that in a lot of the babies born in Daylight Moon over the last six years. I figured it might have something to do with my connection to the pack. It was why I'd started the baby elites.

Pack children were often slightly more advanced than human children. Rogue children were more than that. Those kids were advancing somewhere in between. They would be a benefit to their packs in the long run. Still pack, but just roguish enough to be better.

That was all beside the point. My mind had been wandering a lot since I woke up. It was probably from all the craziness going on. When Lucien appeared to take me to his office, I almost cried with relief.

Cara laughed through our link when I told her I had Alpha stuff to attend to. Apparently, she didn't think I'd last as long as I did. My friends knew me so well.

'I'll link you when to meet up to get ready. Don't be late. And no sex. I don't want you and Lucien wearing those goofy grins you get. Only serious expressions. You can maul him after the reception,' Cara demanded.

She was the bride, after all. I could manage to keep my hands off my husband until after the wedding. All I had to do was make sure he kept his hands off of me.

'I'll do my best.'

'You'll do it or Charlie will be my maid of honor and you'll have to walk with Richard instead of Lucien,' she threatened.

That was just plain mean. I said I'd do my best. Just because she could resist her mate....

'Fine. I won't do anything. I don't know why you're always so mean to me.'

'I'm as mean as you need me to be and you love it. Go spend time with your mate. Remember my warning.'

'Yes, mistress,' I replied jokingly.

I explained what was going on to Lucien. He was not pleased, but agreed to do what he could to avoid touching me.

"The positive is that Thierry, Robert, and the boys are in my office, so we won't be alone. I think that is what gets us most of the time."

"Alright, let's go."

We entered the office, and everyone looked at us. Thierry and Robert smiled like they always did when they saw me now. The boys still had a harder time. Jean-Claude warmed up because of his connection with Dilly and how much fun we had when we would spar.

"Luna, how are you today?" Caleb asked, standing.

"My name is Amy, Caleb. Once you're the Beta here, you'll be calling me Amy in non-formal settings. This is non-formal. I'm just your cousin right now."

"Sorry, Amy. Still having trouble getting used to it. You're my Luna and I didn't exactly grow up with you."

"I know. Hopefully, in a while, you'll feel more at ease with me. Like you do with Jean-Claude and Richard."

"Hey, Amy, have a seat. Are you hungry? I can have the kitchen round up a little snack," Robert offered.

"Thank you, Uncle Robert, but I don't need a snack, but a seat would be nice. I had a lot of walking and rushing around. I'm tired as hell."

They moved aside so Lucien and I could get to the large armchair we normally sat in. He settled in and I climbed onto his lap. My ankles were aching. I was grateful for the rest.

"So, how was your game night?" I asked as the boys got settled.

"Umm…. Pretty good. I can't believe you got Alpha Lucien to come play with us. Our dads joined in, too. Honestly, it was the first time we'd ever had a chance to play video games with them. Lucien says you're pretty good, too. I hope you'll play sometime," Caleb answered with a smile.

I smiled back. "That sounds like fun. Maybe after you and Cara return from your honeymoon."

He nodded. Most guys didn't believe I was good and wouldn't have invited me, so I was surprised. Maybe he was just trying to be nice.

"How hard did Lucien get his ass kicked last night?" I asked Thierry.

The boys looked shocked. They would have to learn that their Alpha was going to be their peer soon. It was one thing to see their fathers treating the man they'd grown up around like a friend. It was another to learn to treat him the same.

Thierry laughed. "They let him win the first few rounds. When he figured it out he ordered them to stop letting him win. He didn't win a single round after. Once the game started, he ended up shot in the head."

"It was a lot harder than I thought to make the little man do what I wanted him to," Lucien said softly.

"I'll avenge you." I giggled.

We chatted for a while. Caleb was excited and a little nervous about the wedding. He didn't know what living with Cara would be like. For all that they'd been together for about six months, her pushing away made him worry she didn't really want him.

"If it helps, Cara said she has to fight to not give in. You almost got her yesterday morning." I chuckled. "Don't worry. She wants you. She just wanted to have a relationship without all the physical stuff before marriage."

"Really? She didn't seem like she was fighting anything. I thought she was just letting me have a little more leeway because we were getting married today."

"Nah. She's friends with me and Dilly, you can trust that she's not some sweet little flower who will gasp and faint once you start getting physical. She is knowledgeable, but grasping onto an ideal. You'll be surprised." I winked.

'You aren't telling your friends what we do, are you?' Lucien asked.

'Of course I am. They're my best friends and we've been listening to Dilly's stories for years. I know all about what they've been doing with their mates, too.'

'I didn't tell my friends. That's not fair,' he said in a pouty tone.

'Your friends are my uncles. I bet they're grateful.'

'I have friends who aren't Robert and Thierry. I could tell them.'

'Go for it. I'm a rogue, saucisson. We're not easily shamed,' I replied.

I patted him on the chest, effectively ending the discussion. This would be something he'd have to deal with. I told my friends everything, and they told me everything. From the blush on Jean-Claude's face, he realized the same thing Lucien did.

"Don't worry, boys. I can keep secrets when I need to. I only revealed a little one to make Caleb feel more at ease. Don't worry about me revealing your intimate secrets." I laughed.

Richard laughed, too. He had no idea. Once he found his mate, I was going to become one of her best friends. I couldn't have someone directly under me who felt like an outcast. I'd let him laugh for now.

***

A staff member brought us lunch. I squeezed onto the couch between Richard and Jean-Claude. I didn't want to smell like Caleb when I went back to Cara. She'd be emotional and it wouldn't be great for her wolf's patience.

We ate and talked about the honeymoon. They were heading to the bed-and-breakfast we stayed at. Caleb liked it when he came to see us for something. Cara loved little places like that.

She wanted to see the places I told her about in town. I knew it was just the picturesque sort of town she'd love. There was a place in the woods with a secluded, spring-fed pond. The perfect place for a little tryst with her mate.

Soon, I got the link from Cara, letting me know it was time to get ready. I said goodbye to everyone and headed out. They were dressing in the Beta's quarters.

When I walked in, April and Charlie pulled me over to the vanity and started working on my hair and makeup. It looked like I was the last of the bridesmaids to get changed and done up. Cara was in the center of the room, getting her dress arranged.

It was a lot of poking, pulling, and tugging, but they got me looking like a little copy of them in short order. Once my dress was on, I pulled the little box with the brooch out and pinned it onto Cara's dress. It was as perfect as it had been on mine.

"You keep that until Salomé marries my brother," I told her.

She smiled. "Thank you, Amy. I'll take care of it until then."

"You look beautiful, Cara. My cousin is very excited and nervous. I bet he'll swoon as soon as he sees you looking even more like a princess than before."

"My big brother is so lucky to have such a beautiful mate." Salomé sighed. "I hope I look that beautiful when I marry my Galen."

"You will," I said. "Every woman is beautiful on her wedding day. It's the happiness."

"Are you ready for this, Cara?" April asked.

"More than ready. I've been waiting for this my whole life," Cara replied.

"No crying. It's only an hour until we start. We can't have you all red-eyed when you get to the altar. Caleb might die thinking you're regretting marrying him." I chuckled.

"Never. I will never regret it or make him think I do," she said, taking a calming breath. "Never ever."

That almost made me tear up. Damned baby hormones. It made me remember my wedding and the feeling I had when I married Lucien. It was all perfect. I hoped this would be, too.

Chapter 141: Healer of the Pack

[Bellamy]

We paired up to walk down the aisle ahead of Cara. Lucien was my partner, but would officiate the wedding. I appreciated them letting him walk me. Jean-Claude was actually Caleb's best man, so he would have been walking with me. This way, he got to walk with Dilly.

Once everyone was down the aisle, we turned and watched Kieran walk Cara. I glanced at my cousin. He was looking at her like she was the goddess come to Earth. Looking at her, she was just as entranced.

When they arrived at the altar, Kieran gave her away and Caleb grasped her hands like she would disappear if he let her go. We all turned to Lucien, who was looking at them with love and pride. I remembered how he told me Thierry and Robert's children were like his own.

"Pack, friends, and family; we are gathered here in the sight of our goddess, and nature, to seal the bond of Caleb Thierry Petit and Cara Isabelle Moore. In the past months, we have seen their love grow. We have witnessed their acceptance of each other and of their duties to their pack. Now, they will create a bond by human tradition and vow to love each other until the end of their lives. Caleb, your vows," Lucien stated in a powerful voice.

"Cara, the moment I saw you, I found the thing I was always waiting for to make me feel whole. I thought an angel had been released on earth and found her way to me. My heart filled with love from the first moment I saw you.

"More than making me complete, you made my family complete. Not just by adding yourself to it, but by bringing my cousin and Luna home. If not for our wedding planning, Alpha Lucien wouldn't have left early to go on his sabbatical and wouldn't have met your best friend. If you hadn't been my mate, she would've never had a reason to come here. You healed my family, my pack, and my Alpha by being the perfect, wonderful woman you are.

"I have so much pride in the fact that you're an elite warrior and a strong woman. You can count on my support in whatever you wish to do. I've learned a lot by watching the dynamic of our friends. You're the absolute love of my life and I couldn't imagine loving anyone as much as I love you. Thank you for being mine," Caleb said tearfully.

I looked at Lucien. He was right. Cara's mating with Caleb had been the catalyst for our entire relationship. I smiled.

My friends were loving and caring people. Cara was one of the humblest women I knew. She would've never made that connection if Caleb hadn't pointed it out. She was the one who created the chance for me to find my mate and family.

"Cara, your vows," Lucien smiled gently at her.

"Wow. I hadn't even thought of that. Caleb, I waited a long time for my mate. Not as long as some, but I had been thinking of you ever since I was old enough to realize the bond mates had. I prayed to the goddess to watch over you every night until I could find you.

"When I first saw you, I nearly fainted. You are the most handsome man I've ever met. In the past six months, I have seen what a noble, dedicated, and loving man you are. This has made me love you all the more. You will be the most amazing Beta when you take on the role because you are the most amazing man I know. All of this is made even sweeter by the joining of our families. My friends are now my cousins because of you.

"You may think I'm the reason for all of this, but you are, too. And the goddess is. She brought us together. One thing we have in common is our desire to help and heal those closest to us. She saw that and brought us together to heal our pack. I will do everything in my power to care for you and make you happy. I swear this to the goddess and everyone here. You are mine, forever." Cara blushed as she vowed.

Caleb's face lit up. His eyes drawn to her mouth. She was probably biting her lip. She did that when she was nervous.

"As our future Beta couple, the safety of our pack is in your hands. You are strong and capable, you are loving and kind, and you are the future of our pack. Your guidance and experience will help our pack grow. As much as they depend on you, you will depend on them. Elders are here to advise you, youth to support you, and your leaders to shelter you.

"If there is anyone who knows good reason these two should not be wed in the eyes of human law, speak now or forever hold your peace," Lucien commanded.

We stood in silence for a while. I was prepared to kick the ass of anyone who opposed it. I would fight for my friend and my cousin if I had to. Luckily, no one did.

"As none have spoken, no opposition holds. The goddess has blessed you with your mate and you have blessed your mate with your heart. Caleb and Cara have elected to have a marking ceremony. First, the rings," Lucien said.

I handed Cara the ring I held. She grinned at me and turned back to Caleb. I was so happy for her, for them. This was a beautiful start and a beautiful ceremony.

"These rings symbolize the connection of your hearts and souls. Though they are a human tradition, we honor their meaning. Exchange rings."

We watched them put the rings on. It was a simple action with a powerful meaning. I felt myself tearing up.

"Now, the marking. The giving of a mark is an honored tradition among all supernatural beings. Fae leave a magic mark with their kiss, witches give a magical seal to their mate, and the rest of us mark with a bite, which is the only physical scar we ever carry. A physical combination of our bodies that can only be taken by death. One that we wear on our souls for eternity. Please, mark your mates," Lucien instructed.

Cara reached up and loosened Caleb's tie, then unbuttoned his shirt. They came together tenderly. I could clearly see my cousin kissing Cara's neck before he bit her. If the ring bit hadn't started making me cry, the marking would have. It was such a tender, loving moment that my heart swelled.

When they pulled back, Lucien continued, "You are now bound in the eyes of your pack, your family, your friends, and your goddess. May this bond remain unsevered until the end of your natural lives. You may kiss."

They kissed each other gently, but amorously. Nothing like my kiss with Lucien, but it didn't need to be. It was precisely as it should have been. The sealing of their relationship.

We followed them up the aisle and set up the receiving line. There weren't as many people at her wedding as were at mine, so it wouldn't take nearly as long. Becky and Randy were there, along with Stanton and Talia. Several of Cara's other friends and all of her old team were there with dates or mates.

Once we were all settled in the ballroom, Caleb and Cara had their first dance. I had never seen my friend glow like she did. She was truly the most beautiful woman in the room. Probably the world.

Soon, it was time for toasts. I listened to Kieran and Thierry talk about Cara and Caleb. They said how glad they were for their family to grow with them and how proud they were of the people they'd grown into. Then Jean-Claude gave his speech, with a story about how Caleb mooned over Cara and his excitement over every new thing he learned about his mate.

It was finally my turn, as matron of honor, to give my speech. I was glad I hadn't decided to wing it. My mind was whirling with so many things I wanted to say. I was glad for the pre-planned speech I wrote.

"When Cara first left to go with her father on the journey that brought her to Caleb, I almost didn't want to encourage it. I didn't want her to find her mate and leave me and Dilly behind. We should've known she would find some way to drag us with her.

"She called me the first night she was here. Before I ever even saw him, I could describe Caleb to you in great detail. Every night for weeks, she called and told me every new thing she learned about him. He was her new favorite subject. All I can remember thinking at the time was how in love she sounded and how I was going to kick his ass if he ever hurt her," I stated with a little growl.

A chuckle came from the crowd. They mostly knew me and that this was completely normal for me. Caleb smiled warmly at me.

"I was happy to learn what a good man he was. Especially when I learned he didn't inherit his father's temper." There was another chuckle, and Thierry turned red. "Cara always told me how much she looked forward to finding her mate. I know Caleb will do everything in his power to take care of her. If nothing else, I can make his Alpha command it," I threatened with a wink, raising my glass. "To Cara and Caleb. I wish you many happy years fulfilling each other's dreams."

We all toasted the couple and spent the rest of the reception having a great time. There was even more fun and dancing than at my wedding, and not as many Alphas growling at each other.

Tomorrow would be when everyone left. Cara and Caleb wanted to be most of the way through their honeymoon before her heat hit. They'd seen the pack doctors about protection, so there wouldn't be any baby Betas for a while.

My men would all be leaving, along with my parents. Bruce was going to Daylight Moon and afterward Rose Moon to meet his mate. Salomé would go along, since school would start soon.

Jean-Claude was excited to go with them to Daylight Moon. He really wanted to see where Dilly grew up and stake his claim like Dilly had on his first day at Lune Rouge. I really hoped he took my advice and marked Claude. It was all up to him now.

Chapter 142: His Teddy Bear

Jean-Claude and Salomé sat next to the windows on the way to Daylight Moon. It didn't surprise me that neither had ever visited another pack's territory. The closest Jean-Claude had gotten was going to Swift River. He'd been amazed at the difference.

For most of the trip, I kept his hand in mine. I was a little nervous. Taking Bellamy's advice, I decided to mark him. I couldn't wait, or I'd mess things up again.

When we reached the town in the pack land, I pointed things out to him. My favorite café, the restaurant Bellamy, Cara, and I liked to go to when we were out, and the little dance club we would go to so we could blow off steam. It had an all-ages night on Fridays.

We pulled up in front of the packhouse, behind Kieran and Daniel's cars. Families were waiting patiently for their warriors to return. Porter's mate was looking pretty big. I was expecting she was more than ready to have her pup out.

Bellamy would probably be bigger when we got back in a week. I'd seen it when visiting some of the rogue born families. One visit the woman would look completely normal, and a week later, she would have a little round tummy like Bellamy did when we left. Then the next visit it was twice the size.

It was the first day of September. She was about half done with the pregnancy. The plus about rogue babies was that they grew quickly in their first year. Faster than pack babies. It would be cool to see.

After disembarking the bus, we grabbed our small bags, and then we went to see Aunt Bren and Uncle Toby. He hadn't met Claude yet. Someone had to lead the pack while Kieran and Daniel were away.

Aunt Bren grinned, hugging me. "Dillon! Oh, you look so happy."

"Thanks, Aunt Bren. You remember my mate, Jean-Claude, right?" I asked.

"Of course I do. Give me a hug, Jean-Claude!" she insisted, releasing me and opening her arms for him.

Aunt Bren was my mom's sister. They were very close, and she used to babysit me a lot when I was little. It was why Todd was so kind to me. We played a lot as kids.

She couldn't have any more pups after Todd. He was a miracle baby. She always said she didn't want a big family the way she got Drake and me, but she was happy we were her boys, too.

Bren hugged Claude tight and rocked him a little. She had always been really accepting of me. The most accepting adult in the pack, next to Yuri.

Toby tried, like he tried being more accepting of Bellamy, but it wasn't always easy. There were a few times he tried to convince me to take her as my chosen mate. Bellamy refused when he suggested it to her after I'd told him no for the tenth time.

According to her, I was meant to be with someone else, and the goddess would be furious if she interfered. Bellamy told me later that she didn't check, but also didn't want a mate who wouldn't want her outside of her heats.

I often joked about going straight for her, but the only part of her I found actually attractive was her eyes. The same eyes my Claude had. She was pretty, just not what I was into.

"Uncle Toby, this is my mate, Jean-Claude Dubois. He's the head warrior for Lune Rouge," I said.

Toby stuck out his hand and gave Claude a firm handshake. He had a big smile. I was betting he was a little glad to be rid of me. Not in an entirely bad way, just because he was never really comfortable with me.

"Nice to meet you," Toby told Jean-Claude.

"Thank you, sir. It's nice to meet you as well," he answered politely.

"Aunt Bren, could you take Jean-Claude to my room? I have to check in at the office and see what Lachlan has done with my system," I requested.

"I'd be happy to, Dillon. Come with me, Jean-Claude. I'll give you a quick tour after you're settled. He's like Bellamy with his work. A few minutes turns into a few hours. Have you eaten? I'll make you some lunch," she said as she started pulling him along.

Jean-Claude looked a little helplessly at me. She wasn't wrong. I'd left my network in the care of someone else for two months. I needed to make sure he was running it right. It would be his by the end of the week, but, for now, it was still my baby.

I followed them into the house and handed my bag off to Jean-Claude to take to my room, then headed to my office on the second floor. On the way, I linked Yuri and asked him to put together a picnic dinner for me and my mate. He was more than happy to help.

***

In my office, Lachlan was sitting at the desk and grinned when I came in. He was really the best option to take over. He had almost as much tech knowledge as I did and was taking online classes to get better.

Lachlan was handsome. He was about as tall as me, with a thick build, dark hair and eyes, and a devilish smile. His cheerful nature made him ideal for this position, and his ability to get serious quickly ensured the ranked members would respect him.

"Dillon! Welcome home!" he said sunnily.

"Thanks, Lach. How's my baby doing?"

"Everything is nominal. Security is running as it should and nothing's attacked in a while. On the external attack front, no vampire sightings since you left, no hunters, no rogues. Everything's green. I haven't been able to beat Bellamy's high score on that game yet, but I managed fifth place on the leaderboard." Lachlan chuckled.

"Sounds great. Let me at it. I need to check on my special projects." I shooed him out of the chair.

As I scooted past his large frame, he wrapped his arms around my waist and tried to kiss me. I pushed away quickly and stepped back. He looked confused.

I'd been seeing Lachlan for a few months before I left for Lune Rouge. I told him I was planning on moving there. He must have thought we would hook up while I was still at Daylight Moon.

"I found my mate, sorry," I told him. "We're done, Lach. I hope that won't affect you taking on this position permanently."

"Oh…. I didn't know. You got marked and everything? No chance for a one-off?" he asked hopefully.

"No. Marked and everything. I'm not that guy anymore, Lachlan. I need to get my work done, my mate is waiting for me to finish."

Lachlan sighed. "Lucky boy. I hope I find my mate soon."

"You will. You're a good guy. They're out there, waiting for you to find them, too," I promised as I settled in my chair.

We worked diligently for a couple hours before Jean-Claude linked me, asking if I was running away or if I'd be back soon. I shook my head and pulled out my phone to respond.

Since Bellamy was so far away, we'd lost our pass-through for my link. Since I was the only one marked, he could talk to me, but I couldn't respond. I would text my answers.

I told him I was busy working but would finish in an hour or two. I was setting up remote access to our servers so I could get into them if need be. Until the tech group got a few more people, I would be offsite support for Daylight Moon.

It was nearly seven when I was finally done with everything. I ensured I wouldn't have any more pack work while we were there. That meant I could get everything taken care of for the transfer and packing all of my things.

I owned everything my parents left behind. Settling everything would take the entire week; much of it remained packed in storage. I would send most of my things in a moving truck, then pack up my room and drive my dad's old truck back to Lune Rouge.

My life was moving forward at such an amazing pace. I couldn't wait to mark Jean-Claude and seal our future together. I had big plans for us, and the kick Bellamy gave me was what I needed to think of that instead of the past.

***

We met outside the kitchen, where I was picking up the picnic basket from Yuri. He had gotten one of the soft blankets from the closet for us. I appreciated it. Aside from Aunt Bren, Yuri was the best adult in the pack when I was young. He just wanted to take care of everyone.

I pulled Jean-Claude from the house and we walked, with our fingers entwined, out past the cabin Bellamy used to use for her heats. There was a rocky cliff wall spread for a mile or two. The bulk of the wall was in our territory. If you didn't know the right spot, you couldn't get up without walking for over an hour.

At the top, though, there was a beautiful grassy area with a pond just deep enough for swimming. There were trees near the edge that could hide us, and they were big enough that we could still enjoy the view of the pack lands and surrounding forest.

I found the rope with a hook we attached to a pulley and hooked the basket onto it before pulling it to the top. Then I tied the rope around the bush that hid the start of our entrance. It was a small area Bellamy found when we were goofing off about six years ago.

The climb was steep, but I was happy to see Jean-Claude keeping up with me. It took a little time to get to the top. I used the handhold we'd carved out of the ground to pull myself up and turned to help Jean-Claude.

Once at the top, he turned to look over the valley below. He was smiling happily.

"It's beautiful here," he said.

"We used to come up here to get away from the pack. No one really ever comes to the top," I explained.

"Did… did you used to bring men here?" Jean-Claude asked with a nervous tone.

I should've realized he'd think something like that. I tamped down my anger at his implication that I would take him to the same place I took *them*. He didn't know there were some places I would never have gone with them.

"No. This was just for me, Bellamy, and Cara. And now, you."

"I didn't mean… I mean… It's just a pretty romantic spot," he replied with a blush.

"Only when you're here," I told him and took his hand. "Let's get everything settled down. We can talk more later."

We gathered the basket from where it dangled in the tree at the top of the pulley. I spread the blanket in a spot that was far enough from the edge to be safe, but close enough to see the forest and pack land. Seeing the view with my mate was magical.

He helped me pull the food from the basket and we sat quietly eating while looking out over the dimming landscape. Stars began to shine, and people turned on the lights in the pack land. I loved watching everything from there.

When we were finished, we put the containers in the basket and laid out on the blanket, staring at the stars. I was nervous about how I would mark him. I wanted it to feel natural. Telling him I was marking him now felt too blunt.

"Mon rêve? What are you so worried about? Is it because of what I asked earlier?" Jean-Claude asked softly.

"No," I said and rolled on my side to face him.

He was more gorgeous than the first time I saw him. His head turned to me and he searched my face for some clue. I traced my fingers over the curve of his face until they reached his chin. His bowed lips looked soft and inviting.

I moved down and kissed him lightly. He sighed and pressed against my mouth, opening his and licking my lips. I opened to the request and deepened the kiss, our tongues playing together as his arms encircled me, pulling me onto him a little more.

My hand slipped behind his neck and I pressed our mouths tighter together. A moan slipped from me as I felt myself harden against him. Goddess, I wanted him so badly.

All other thoughts fled my head as he pulled me to straddle him, feeling he was as hard as I was. By the time I got my mind back, we were both shirtless, and I was kissing down his chest. His fly was open, and I was stroking him firmly while he moaned under my attentions.

Changing direction quickly, I headed back to his neck. To that spot in the curve where I'd been giving him hickeys to show my ownership of him until I could mark him. He didn't seem to think anything of the change in course.

"Dillon, mon rêve, mon amour. Goddess, please," he panted as I started kissing, nibbling, and licking his neck.

"You're mine, Jean-Claude. No one will take me from you. No one will take you from me. Do you understand, mon nounours?" I growled and extended my canines, marking him as mine officially and forever.

He groaned and arched as I licked and stroked him. "Yes, I'm yours forever. I promise."

I kept stroking as I headed back to my original destination. I wouldn't take my mate right here. Our first time together would be in *our* bed, in *our* house. But there were a lot of other things we could do, and I wanted to coax all those sexy sounds out of him.

I wanted to taste him. I wanted every drop of him, every morsel. He was perfection, and I finally owned him as much as he owned me.

Chapter 143: Associated Travel

[Bellamy]

It had been two weeks since Cara and Caleb's wedding. When they came back, Caleb went to stay in the Gamma's quarters and Cara holed up in the Beta's quarters. They planned to do that every month. At least they'd had experience with resisting each other during her heats over the last six months. I knew they could do it.

One good thing about the heat was its limitation to only your mate after the first mating. A female's hormones wouldn't affect any male other than her marked mate. But if a mated female was around another female in heat, the pheromones could stick and mix with her scent.

This led to a lot of times when I would come home after visiting Cara and Lucien would be insatiable, as if I was the one in heat. I made a point of visiting as often as possible. My hormones made me pretty horny, too, and this was the perfect way to make sure he didn't tap out because he was tired.

When Dilly and Jean-Claude eventually returned, I saw they were both wearing marks. I was so happy for them. Both looked more relaxed and content than I had ever seen them before.

They immediately started moving into their house. I helped with arranging some things Dilly had from his parents. It was a nice mixture of both boys. I did accidentally walk in on them getting busy. They knew I was there and still tried to be sneaky about it.

I loved that my friends were so happy.

When Cara's heat ended, we went out to a little restaurant in town for updates. It was important that everyone saw Cara and me out and about. She was the future Beta female and her role with the people in the pack was as important as my own.

We sat near the front of the restaurant. They both knew we had to code or our business would be all over the pack. The positive about our positions in our last pack was that we were fairly adept at saying anything we needed to in any situation. We couldn't simply have a mental conversation.

"Everything all settled at the house?" I asked Dilly as we glanced over the menu.

He nodded. "Everything's in its place. Perfect in every way."

"And you, Cara? Everything going well?" I asked.

"Very well. Also perfect. What about you and Lucien?" She smiled.

We noted how many ears perked up as we had this boring start. It seemed most of the restaurant was listening. I knew that would happen.

"Same as you two. He's an amazing man and I'm very lucky to have him." I winked.

The waitress came up beaming. We were definitely the focus of the staff. Giving her our orders, we waited for our drinks before speaking again. Once we had them, I smiled, and they nodded.

At the last sleepover, we worked out a few new codes. We couldn't go out in public and have linked conversations. To gain the pack's trust, we needed to show them we trusted them, but we also didn't want them discussing our bedroom habits.

"Have you had any issues with your sleep lately, Dilly?" I asked.

"Mmm. My sleep has been better than ever before. I tend to have several pleasant dreams each night. This is the best sleep I've ever had. Being mated is very beneficial." He grinned.

"Same sleep position as before, or have you changed position?" I asked cheekily.

He blushed. "Same as before. It's the only way I sleep. What about you, Cara, how are you sleeping now?"

"Much more restful than before, thank you. It's hard not having Caleb to cuddle with some nights, but I stand by my decision to wait a year for a pup. Sure, there'll be a few sleepless nights, but, in the end, I think this is better for us." She smiled happily.

"I'm glad you're adapting well to sleeping next to someone else." I nodded.

"We don't need to ask how you're sleeping, of course." Cara chuckled.

"You *know* I sleep very well." I winked.

'It seems like none of them are picking up that we're talking about sex,' Cara linked.

'A few are, but they don't know about everything we just said, only that it has nothing to do with actually sleeping,' I replied.

'Good. Now let me tell you two about this thing Jean-Claude does….'

The rest of the meal was informative and fun. People would come up and talk to us from time-to-time. Some women asked Cara about babies and she told them she wanted a year to settle in before she even thought about it. People asked Dilly about a wedding for himself and Jean-Claude, and he replied that they hadn't discussed it yet.

That wasn't true. They were talking about getting married in spring or summer, but it wasn't something they'd told anyone else about yet. I was excited. Cara and I promised to be in his wedding party since he was in ours. I hated the wedding stuff, but I loved seeing my friends happy. With luck, Richard would find his mate soon.

"So, you and Lucien are heading out tomorrow, right?" Cara asked.

"Yeah. Three days for the meeting of the Association, then back home. I really don't like the idea of flying, but they said I have to be there in person. No conference call." I sighed.

"I heard he booked a private plane. You're not a little excited about potentially joining the mile-high club?" Dilly chuckled.

I laughed. An amused murmur swept through the restaurant. He did that on purpose, probably to give them something other than our very boring conversation to talk about.

"I don't like being in high places where I can't control my descent. There is no way I'm getting frisky with Lucien on a plane." I shook my head. "Not happening."

"That's a shame. It might be your last chance," he said in a coaxing tone.

"Never," I replied sternly.

Cara and Dilly laughed as we finished our meal, paid, and left. We didn't have to pay. A lot of the businesses believed serving the ranked members was enough payment, but I refused to let the bill go unpaid and even tipped. We supported our pack in every way we could.

We headed up to the packhouse and split up. I had packing to do and everyone else had their jobs. Cara was shadowing Celesta for the week, learning the ins and outs of being the Beta female.

The rule for ranked members inheriting their roles changed from pack to pack. At Lune Rouge, they inherited if needed or when they turned twenty-one. No mating rules like Daylight Moon and they didn't ascend at the same time.

It was designed to give them time to adjust if there was spacing in their ages and the old ranked members were there to help if needed. They didn't just retire and leave the new members on their own.

Given all that, Caleb would take Thierry's position in a year and a half. It would be three years before Richard took over for Robert. Now that he was eighteen, and finished with school, Jean-Claude would start taking on more of the duties of the head warrior.

He was already leading some of the warrior groups. Soon, he would learn about all the other roles the head warrior played. It would get some work off Lucien, Thierry, and Robert's plate.

I wandered into my quarters and pulled out a duffle bag. I didn't need much for the trip. The trip was only three days long, and I would spend most of that time meeting with the other Alphas.

They didn't paint a terribly fun-looking week when I'd discussed the meeting with them earlier. Policy discussions, rulings on pack/rogue conflicts that needed mediation instead of jumping into a fight, and areas that needed attention. I was going to press for local investigation teams in each region that would report to us.

While I was working on packing, Lucien came in and wrapped his arms around me, caressing the firm roundness in my middle. He loved rubbing my stomach, and it was actually soothing to have him do it. The aches and pains seemed to go away when my mate was touching me so tenderly.

"Did you have a pleasant lunch with your friends?" he asked.

"Of course, Lucien. The restaurant you suggested was lovely," I replied as I leaned against him.

"Mmm. I heard you aren't planning to enjoy our flight to the meeting, chouchoutte," he pouted.

"I will enjoy being on the ground, saucisson," I told him.

"But flying is safe, Bellamy. You should trust that I wouldn't put you in a dangerous situation," Lucien chided gently.

"Just because I gave in on the treehouse last week, doesn't mean I'm giving in on this." I laughed. "You'll just have to suffer."

"You'll change your mind on the flight back. I'm not worried."

I turned and trailed my hands over his stomach. The truth was, I had never been on a plane before and I was a little scared. There was no way to save us if it crashed.

"Can't we just drive? I'll do naughty things to you on the trip if we drive," I offered.

"It's too late for driving and this will ensure we get there and back quickly. Everyone flew out to our wedding, so I know this isn't a rogue thing. Are you afraid of flying, chouchoutte?" Lucien asked, tucking a stray hair behind my ear.

"Yes. I don't like the idea of it. What if something happens?"

"Nothing will happen. I don't want you out of your territory too long. It isn't good for you or the pups. I've flown with this company several times. They're safe and keep all of their equipment in good working order. There's nothing to worry about," he assured me.

"Alright. I'll do it, but I'm petitioning them to move the meetings here. Our territory is more conducive to the meetings and we won't have to leave the pups behind."

"I'm fine with that. I would rather stay home anyway." He chuckled. "We leave first thing in the morning. I need to finish packing my things, too."

We went about getting our things ready and had a calm evening at home. Genevieve was visiting with my grandmothers and planning to stay with them so Lucien and I could have the place to ourselves. It was very nice of her to give us this time alone before the pups came.

There was still no word about Kyle. It was getting frustrating. Teams of wolves in the north were all looking for him or his remains. I didn't feel entirely comfortable leaving my territory, while no one knew if he was dead or alive.

***

The next morning, I dressed in a flowy skirt and a loose top. There was no real point in buying too many maternity clothes. I would just grow out of them with how rapidly I was changing. I grabbed my bag and headed for the door.

"What do you think you're doing?" Lucien asked.

"Going to the car so we can leave…" I answered.

"Give me your bag," he ordered.

"I swear to the goddess, Lucien, if you try to coddle me because I'm pregnant, I *will* kick your ass and leave you here," I growled.

"It's heavy," he replied.

"No, it's not. Stop."

"I still have a couple 'unreasonable' requests. This is one of them. I always carry your bags when you're visibly pregnant," Lucien stated.

"I regret giving you so many," I grumbled and handed him my bag.

He chuckled like he'd won something. I shook my head, and we left our quarters. Robert and Thierry met us at the main doors to say goodbye. Their pleasure was clear when they saw Lucien carrying my bag. Pack wolves pissed me off sometimes.

They gave me hugs and told me to be safe and take care of Lucien.

"He's going to be too busy with all of the other mates of the Association. I think they're all going to be knitting something. I'll have him make you some scarves."

My uncles laughed, and it was Lucien's turn to grumble. He pouted all the way to the airport. I thought it was cute as hell. He stopped pouting once we boarded the plane, though.

It was small and had a couple of seats on each side. There were no other passengers, just the pilots and us. They introduced themselves and got us seated.

Lucien had requested no other crew since he had been planning to do dirty things on the flight. That meant he was to get anything we needed from the cabinets near the front of the plane. I laughed as he fumbled with the little handles while trying to get me something to drink.

He sat in the seat across the narrow aisle and handed me a bottle of juice. I gratefully sipped it. My mouth had gone dry with anticipation. I to have this over with.

When we started moving, I grasped Lucien's hand. He stroked my knuckles and whispered soothingly in French as we started leaving the ground. All I wanted was to survive this whole trip somehow. I prayed to the goddess that we would get back home safely. It was the only thing I could think to do.

Chapter 144: An Unexpected Sight

It was the second day since Bellamy and Lucien left. They would be back after another two. The pack was doing well. Celesta was teaching me more about being the Beta female. It was a lot more work than it ever seemed when I saw Olive doing it.

A skilled Beta female never looks like she's working, but she's the support to the Luna. We would walk around the pack land, checking in with families and individual wolves to see if there was anything they needed. We handled minor issues that didn't involve conflicts. The Beta was in charge of pack security and working with the head warrior to schedule warriors for guard duties.

I was getting my makeup on while Caleb finished taking his shower. I'd foregone training that morning. It was tiring, and I needed to be alert and on the ball if I was going to learn everything I needed to know in the next couple of years. Goddess knows Bellamy wouldn't let me skip training for at least another year.

She would probably stay on me until I had a good excuse not to train anymore, and being exhausted from bedroom activities wasn't a good enough excuse. She was still making most of the training sessions even while pregnant, being Luna, ruling her territory, and entertaining her mate at night. I have no idea where she found the energy.

Bellamy was always like that, though. She pushed herself hard and expected Dillon and me to keep up. We were the only ones she seemed to think should work as hard as she did. It was flattering and annoying all at the same time.

Dillon didn't seem to mind as much as I did, but he wasn't a spoiled little girl when we started being friends with her. Not like I was. My position as the Alpha's daughter allowed me many privileges, and people didn't expect much from me. All I had to do was be sweet and pretend to be nice.

She pulled me out of my self-involved ways. If not for Bellamy, I wouldn't have been as strong as I was, and I wouldn't have ever been an elite warrior. My team back home wouldn't have existed. And I wouldn't have been the person Caleb and Lune Rouge needed me to be. I was actually grateful for everything she'd given me.

I couldn't imagine what taking on this position as a spoiled brat would've been like. Because of Bellamy, I was well-trained and could protect myself. My mate wouldn't have to worry about me nearly as much. It was a relief to Caleb when he saw me training with the group for the first time.

For all that I told Dillon and Bellamy I hadn't been as tempted to give in to my mate, Caleb had become much more aggressively amorous after the first time we'd trained together. Caleb told me seeing me that way was sexy as hell.

Taking care of him after that first training session was hard. He kept trying to grope me and grab me. Caleb begged me to lie next to him while he recovered, then seemed to be made of hands when I allowed it.

I chuckled thinking of it. If I'd known then what I knew now, I wouldn't have pushed away. Sure, it felt lovely when he kissed and nibbled, but I didn't realize exactly how lovely it would be when I let him keep going.

On our wedding night, I'd almost pushed him away out of habit. The urge embarrassed me. Giving in to him was the best decision I'd ever made. I was right, knowing he was entirely mine and would never give me up was one hell of an aphrodisiac.

I'd been so deep in my thoughts that I hadn't seen him exit the bathroom. It wasn't until he was looming behind me at the vanity that I actually realized he was there.

Caleb licked his lips and ran his fingers through my hair. I closed my eyes and felt him kiss the top of my head. His hand slid from my hair and he caressed my breast as his lips came down on my mark, making me moan a little.

"You know we don't have time this morning," I pouted.

"I just needed a little to keep me going. I won't see my beautiful mate until dinnertime. Until then, I'll hold your whimpers and sighs close to my heart," he purred.

"Very smooth." I giggled. "I'll miss you, but I'm excited about going to the city with your mom."

"She normally takes my dad. When you do trips to the city, I'll go with you in the future. It's a lot safer now that Bellamy claimed it, but I want to have that time with you. Just a day to ourselves in the city. No work or pups, or anything to stop us from having fun." Caleb chuckled.

"It's still a while off for pups. Don't get ahead of yourself," I chided.

'Cara, are you about ready?' Celesta linked me.

'On my way in a minute. I just have to pry your son off of me,' I replied.

"Your mom's ready to leave. Let me go, you cheeky pup." I snickered.

He rubbed his face on my mark, making me squeal. His fingers worked to tickle and grope everything they could reach. I was a giggling mess when he finally stopped.

"Don't get lost. Stay with my mom at all times. If anything happens to you, I will tear that city apart," he growled into the curve of my neck.

I loved how protective he was of me. It made me feel safe and cared for. I knew Bellamy didn't like that sort of stuff from her mate. She would've probably gone right off and gotten into trouble if Lucien said something like that.

Bellamy would never really understand what it was like to be a pack wolf. I felt for her. She'd never experienced a connection as strong as Caleb and mine. She would never really know what it was like to feel entirely safe.

After kissing my mate goodbye, I went down to meet his mother. She was looking cheerful in a pale blue dress with little yellow flowers on it. I smiled as she waved me over and linked our arms together.

"Are you ready for our big day out? I can't wait to take you to my favorite little café in the city!" She grinned.

"Sounds awesome. I'm so glad we get time off."

"Of course we do. Our Alpha would never make all the ranked wolves, and their mates, work so long without breaks. Lucien cares about our health, both physical and mental. He'll even cut back your workload when you're pregnant," Celesta said.

I nodded. I'd heard that about Lucien. Everyone in the pack just loved him to pieces. They were all very excited when Bellamy came. Especially when they learned she was pregnant.

Many considered it a blessing of the goddess that they got a Luna and an heir so quickly. When they found out she was a rogue, a lot of them questioned me about her. I told them all the awesome and amazing things Bellamy did for Daylight Moon.

I was more than happy to sing my friend's praises. She saved my life and my father's pack. It would only benefit Lune Rouge to have her there.

When we arrived in the city, we picked up the things we needed quickly and put them in the car. Then we wandered downtown looking in little shops and boutiques. If we found something we liked, we would buy it and drop our packages off before heading to lunch.

Celesta reminded me of my mother a lot. She was chipper and friendly. People smiled when they interacted with her because she was so outgoing and kind.

After we finished our shopping and dropped everything off, we went to the café. It was human-owned and operated. When we entered, I could smell there were at least two rogues in the place.

Because we were in Bellamy's territory, I wasn't worried. None of them would mess with the pack and risk her anger. She was terrifying when angry.

You wouldn't expect someone so tiny to be so frightening. I'd witnessed her callous attitude toward those who attacked our pack. I wasn't lying when I'd told Jean-Claude and Lucien how scary she and Dillon were. They were as deadly as they were loving. Which was probably even worse to anyone who saw how much they cared.

We sat in a booth with low backs. Humans sat behind me and a man who smelled like a rogue sat behind Celesta. He was reading a paper and seemed fairly relaxed.

Once we ordered and had our drinks, Celesta smiled in a way I had gotten used to. She'd get this smile right before the questions started. I almost shook my head, knowing what was coming next.

"So…. Are you absolutely certain You won't be giving me a grandchild any time soon?" she asked with big innocent eyes.

"I told you, I want at least a year. Maybe a couple months less. It would be nice to have time to really get to know my mate and my work before adding children," I told her.

"I just want a little baby to play with. Spending time with Olive's girls made me miss when mine were that young."

"You're still young enough to have more if you really wanted," I offered.

"It's not the same," she pouted.

"It's not the same because you want to spoil some little pups and then hand them back to someone else to take care of." I snickered.

Celesta laughed. "You got me."

"If nothing else, you have Bellamy's babies to spoil. She and Lucien would love to have as much family around them as possible."

The man behind Celesta stiffened. I didn't like that. He was listening to our conversation. Most wolves would at least try to pretend they couldn't hear what others were talking about.

"That's true. Lucien is so excited. You should hear him talking with Thierry and Robert about the future. He seems to believe he and Bellamy are going to have a whole dozen pups, if not more." She chuckled.

I could see the man gripping the paper firmly. His knuckles were white, and he turned his head slightly. I still couldn't see a face, but it was making me nervous.

"Bellamy loves children. I have no doubt that she was the one who first said a dozen. I can't see her with any less than six," I answered, watching the man behind her intently.

He relaxed when the conversation only had to do with Bellamy. I started taking in more about him. His clothes weren't exactly clean, but he didn't smell as if he weren't bathing. His hair was dark blond and hung just below his ears. I was going to have to prod him to get him to turn more, but I was already pretty sure of who it was.

Quietly, I pulled out my phone and typed in a text to Caleb with our location and the description I didn't want to risk a picture or Celesta might blow our chance. If we could catch Kyle, Bellamy would be over the moon. She would feel safer and I wouldn't have to see that worried look she gets when she thinks no one is looking.

"It's a good thing they found each other. No man could be more perfect for Bellamy than Lucien. As her best friend, I should know," I tittered, hopefully not sounding as nervous as I felt.

It worked. He turned, and I could see it was definitely him. Now I had to make sure he didn't know I knew who he was. I smiled at Celesta, pretending I didn't notice him.

"Either way. It worked out. Oh! I think that's our food," I said and pointed to our waitress as she approached.

We settled in with our food and chatted a little about things in the pack. People we were helping, new pack members, things like that. Whenever it looked like he was going to leave, I would throw in something about Bellamy and he would settle back in.

I prayed to the goddess that our warriors would be there soon. I didn't think I could pick at my plate much longer. They had to be there soon.

Suddenly, there was the squeal of tires and I turned to look out the window in front of the café. Caleb, Jean-Claude, and Dillon were getting out of the car. I was relieved as I turned back.

Then I realized he was gone. I took my eyes off him for only a moment and he'd run. I jumped up and grabbed our waitress.

"The man that was seated behind us! Where did he go?" I asked urgently.

"He took off through the kitchen like a bat out of hell."

'He ran out the back!' I linked Caleb and watched as they quickly changed direction.

'Stay where you are. I'll come back for you,' Caleb replied.

"Thank you. Can I get a refill on my drink and a dessert menu?" I asked.

"I guess." She shrugged.

I'd have to remember to leave a generous tip. While we waited, I let Celesta know what happened. She was pretty shaken up.

I clasped her hand, and we had a little dessert. It cheered her up a bit. I realized I should've been as upset as Celesta was. It was just one of the many ways knowing Bellamy had changed me. She gave me a calm head in the face of danger.

Soon the boys came in. I looked at them hopefully, but Dillon shook his head. Now I started shaking too. Kyle knew what I looked like and that I was Bellamy's best friend. He might try to use that against her.

"The warriors out back weren't able to catch him. They said he fought like a demon," Dillon said when they got to the table.

"Let's get back to the packhouse and call Bellamy. She and Lucien need to know he was here in her territory. Dillon, can you get his picture out to the police force and the supernatural police force? I want them to keep an eye out for him," Caleb stated. I loved seeing him in action.

"Got it, Beta. Celesta, take me and Jean-Claude to your car. We'll drive you home," Dillon told her.

Celesta nodded and left the café quietly. I paid the bill and left a healthy tip before leaving with Caleb. Before we got into the car, he wrapped me in his arms.

"Don't you *ever* do something like that again, ma colombe. Next time something like that happens, contact me then leave. You endangered yourself and my mother. What in the goddess' name were you thinking? What if he'd hurt one or both of you? It was reckless, Cara," he scolded, gripping me tighter and tighter.

"Caleb, I just wanted to make sure you caught him. I wanted to keep our family safe. I'm sorry," I whimpered.

"Don't ever do that again. Never ever," he whispered as his grip relaxed and he started rocking me gently. "I'd die if anything happened to you, mon ange. My precious angel."

I nodded. "I'll never do it again, I promise."

"Good. Let's go home. We need a full report." Caleb said, giving me a kiss on the head and guiding me into the passenger seat of the car.

I looked out the window as we drove. My heart was in my throat. I hadn't even fully registered how dangerous that was until he said it.

I hoped Thierry wouldn't be mad at me for risking his wife. I hoped they would all understand. With time to cool down, I hoped Caleb would see. I needed to save my friend. I needed to save my Luna.

Chapter 145: A Very Happy Birthday

When I found out Caleb scolded Cara, I was a little upset. I knew it was the nature of male wolves to be overprotective of their mates, especially pack wolves. That didn't change the fact that she was doing what she was trained to do.

We ended up getting so much more information than any of them even realized. The other rogue at the café was working in the kitchen. When he saw Kyle bolt through, he gave chase and ended up seeing the fight between the warriors and the exiled king.

That was more informative than anything else. The way he described and mimicked Kyle's stances and movements told me exactly what had happened when he disappeared up north. He was training.

Not just any training, either. After I left Limb Torn at eight, I ran into some rogue born adults who were heading north. They carried me with them after I found out they were going to train with an elite collective called the Goddess' Tears. The things they'd do to their enemies would make even the goddess weep.

I'd trained there for a year. It was where I'd met Ash. He was about ten years older than me, but he was also a quick friend and a wonderful sparring partner. We'd secured our alliance over that bond of spending a year together in hell.

For all that humans joke and talk about Canadians being super nice and friendly, they can also be aggressive and violent. This collective was like the concentrated negative traits of the entire country. They were fighters, and they didn't answer to the Werewolf Association in the US. They were under the purview of the Canadian Werewolf Association.

That was why they didn't report Kyle, kill him, or even know who he was. Once I realized he'd trained with the collective, I made a call to them. As a past member, they were more willing to talk to me than if I'd just been High Queen.

The new King of the territory was one of the children I'd trained with. People might think it odd for a collective to take in so many Alphas, but it was their safety plan. They had alliances with every collective around them and formed alliances with others from further away.

It made for a decent exchange of resources for fighters or trainers. That alone enabled them to have almost all of their members be fighters. They'd trained me on the promise of a future alliance.

My call revealed they'd trained Kyle for almost the whole time he'd been missing. As an Alpha wolf, he would've adapted to the training more quickly than others. It wasn't anything near what I'd learned over the year I was with them, but even a couple of months was enough to make him stronger than the standard warriors the boys had brought with them.

The boys weren't prepared for the reaming I gave them about not taking elite warriors when trying to capture an Alpha and their shortsightedness at the potential danger to their men. I couldn't believe Dilly hadn't thought about it.

He looked ashamed when I pointed out that they had no idea *how* Kyle could have changed. He'd endangered his mate, along with everyone else. What if Kyle had used weapons?

It's easy to get them as a werewolf. Especially an Alpha, even if they're not as well-trained as me. Humans are no match for an Alpha. We can take anything we need.

I was mad for a couple of weeks and made sure they felt it in training. They were going to see exactly what Kyle had been through in the last two months. No naps, no breaks, no quitting.

One thing I really pushed was harsher training for warriors and elites. As an apology, King Gnosis sent two of his best fighters from Goddess' Tears to train my men. It had been a month since they arrived and I was seeing a steady improvement.

Now, I was busy with another project. Today was Lucien's birthday. I was making him a special dinner with a dessert I knew he would love. Jasmine and honeysuckle cake.

The biggest problem with my plan was how often I needed to sit. People often joked that I was as big around as I was tall. I hadn't been in training for two weeks, because I could barely handle light days with the extra weight.

Because multiples usually arrived early, I was surprised to go past my projected due date. My due date was three days before Lucien's birthday. These pups were determined to stay in as long as possible. As long as they were healthy, we were going to let them.

The pain in my back had been a little intense for the last couple of days, and it seemed like the pups were constantly fighting. They moved around a lot and sometimes would hit me so hard that I would need to lie down for a while. It would make my muscles tighten terribly.

I pulled the steaks out of the marinade and got them onto the grill on the stovetop, then pulled the brussels sprouts out of the oven. They were a vegetable high in protein, so they were appearing in almost all of our meals. They also paired well with the garlic mashed potatoes and marinade I'd prepared for the meat.

As I turned back to the stove, I felt Lucien come into the kitchen. He slipped his arms around me and stroked my stomach. I flipped the steaks as he rubbed himself on my backside.

"Chouchoutte, we could have had the kitchen make this for us," he said.

"I couldn't get out to buy you a present. You locked down the whole border. So I get to make you a meal for your birthday and you're not going to change that," I chided.

"There's only one thing I want to eat for my birthday and it doesn't need to be cooked," Lucien purred. "It's even sweeter than that cake you baked."

I sighed. He was as bad as a pregnant rogue himself. The bigger I got, the more he seemed to want me. My hormones definitely approved.

"Let me at least get the steaks off the grill. We'll need fuel when we're done." I chuckled.

"If you must," he whispered, nibbling my ear while I pulled them off and sat them under tented foil.

I only just had time to turn off the stove before he swept me into his arms and carried me to the dining room, sitting me on the table. He slipped my panties off and seated himself in front of me.

The heavenly feeling of his tongue caressing me drove my need for him as he sucked and lapped at me. I felt his finger slide inside and curl up, tickling at my G-spot. I moaned and gripped the tablecloth under me as he pulled his finger out and started swirling his tongue around before entering me with it.

His growls vibrated through me. Goddess, he was amazing with his mouth, but I needed more. I wiggled my hips and pressed against him. Lucien moved back up and slipped two fingers into me, stroking firmly as he gently suckled at my clit. His other hand trailed up my thigh until it reached my other mark.

The feeling of him touching me in so many glorious ways threw me over the edge. I cried out as my back arched. He pulled back and stood, looking down at me while his fingers continued their work.

"Please, Lucien. I need you. Please," I begged.

"I need you too, chouchoutte. I've always needed you in so many more ways than this. You changed my whole life and made this the best birthday I've ever had," Lucien murmured as he withdrew his hand from me and soon replaced it with his hardened length.

I moaned with pleasure as I felt him filling me slowly. He pushed in and out languorously, his hands rubbing over my stomach and down my arms until he clasped my hands in his. I bit my lip as I watched him look at me with such love and happiness.

My heart soared at his words and the way he held my hands tenderly before he moved them back to my hips. He was everything to me. My whole heart, my whole world.

"I love you, so much, Lucien. You've given me everything I always wanted and never knew I needed," I replied breathily as he started stroking more forcefully.

He brought my hips to meet him, and I yipped with the impacts. Lucien started growling, and his eyes darkened. I'd never seen him like that before. His hands gripped me harder, and he started whispering something I couldn't quite make out.

As he kept going, pushing through the strain of my muscles tightening around him as the change in demeanor, and the rubbing of his body against my second mark, combined with the wonderful sparks that came every time he touched me bringing me to my peak over and over. It was too much to bear, but then he started getting louder and I could finally hear what he'd been whispering.

"Mine. My mate. My Bellamy. Mine," Lucien murmured over and over with a low growl.

Tears were forming in my eyes for two reasons now. The overwhelming feeling of my mate claiming me, and the adorable way he voiced his claim to the universe. He was mine, and I was his. Forever.

He struck finally, and a howl escaped him. Remus must have been close to the surface. Our wolves usually were on our birthdays, since it was the time we first connected with them at seventeen.

Lucien pulled me up and kissed me passionately. He pulled back and kissed my cheeks, my nose, and my forehead. I giggled at his silliness.

"Wait right here, I'll help you clean up and get you down from the table," he whispered huskily.

"Alright, my love. I'll be here." I smiled.

It was his birthday. I could be more dependent on him to make him happy. He looked shocked at the lack of argument, but cheerfully headed off to get things.

Once I was all cleaned up and off the table, we cleaned it and went to get our plates settled. I wasn't as hungry as I normally was. It was weird, but I was fine with it. It would mean more time with my mate. I had a few plans for the night that he would really enjoy.

During the meal, we kept the conversation lighthearted. We'd spent too much of our relationship worrying about what was coming or talking about Kyle. Instead, we talked about our plans for our pack and collective.

Our growth impressed the Association, and the third-ranking Alpha complained about missing the meeting next year because Lucien would have his seat by then. Lucien and I shared a look and said nothing, while the others speculated about our plans.

We cleaned the kitchen and dining room after finishing our meal and dessert. Genevieve was spending more time with my grandparents to give Lucien and me some time alone before the pups came. There was a standing order to contact her immediately if something happened.

"Are you ready to head to our room for a long bath and a massage, chouchoutte?" Lucien asked.

"You want a massage?"

He chuckled. "No, for you. I know your back was hurting a lot today, but you stood for so long while you were cooking and cleaning. I thought you might like one. For my birthday, I just want to take care of my precious mate and our pups."

I smiled and took his hand. "I would love that, saucisson."

We headed to the elevator. I didn't use it often, but Lucien wanted to take care of me and felt it was the best way. Safer than him carrying my chunky-self up the stairs.

Halfway down the hall, I stopped. Lucien turned as my eyes widened. I felt a strong contraction like the ones from when I was in Lucien's dream. Then, something wet started rolling down my leg.

"We need to go to the hospital, Lucien." I gasped.

His eyes widened this time, as he realized what was happening. He scooped me up in his arms and rushed out through the packhouse and into town. I'd thought a car was slightly more appropriate, but I wasn't going to try to tell him. It would only confuse him.

I focused on my breathing while I linked everyone to what was going on. We made it to the hospital in record time. The way he was panicking was a little cute. Smooth, strong Alpha couldn't seem to string more than two words together. It made me laugh in between the contractions.

Rogues didn't have long labors. I hadn't really expected it to be progressing as fast as it was, though. As soon as I was in the delivery room, Genevieve and my grandmothers appeared, along with Dilly and Cara.

"Nope! Too many people. Lucien, Cara, and Dilly stay. The rest of you will have to go to the waiting room," I said.

"But! Those are my grandchildren and their great-grandchildren! You can't kick us out!"

"Can, will, am. You saw your first grandchildren born already. My grandmothers saw theirs. This is for us. You all can come to the next one. Trust me. We're long from done. Now, go hate on me from the waiting room. This conversation is over," I managed to say before the next contraction hit.

I felt guilty about sending the older ladies away, but I didn't want too many people around and they would've been upset if I had kept one but sent the others off.

It was better this way. I had the three people I was closest to with me. Olive would be there as soon as she could, but would probably miss the birth. And I would have my pups soon.

Chapter 146: Best Birthday Presents Ever

[Bellamy]

My labor was intense, but not long. The babies were born just before midnight, giving them the same birthday as their papa. Lunette came first, followed by Étienne. They were precious little ones with black hair and chubby cheeks.

They didn't have their permanent eye color yet, but we knew from the dream that the dominant Dubois eyes wouldn't win out over the silvery gray color of Lucien's eyes. He was in love with them from the first moment he saw them.

"The best birthday presents ever, chouchoutte," he murmured as he cuddled both babies closely in his arms.

I chuckled. "I aim to please. Sorry about the things I said. I'm pretty sure there's no spell to make you feel what I was feeling. Even if there was, I think it's against the rules for witches to make one."

"I would take any number of spells or potions if it relieved your pain, ma choupinette." Lucien smiled.

The look of contentment on his face filled me with joy. My mate, my family, everything I wanted, finally in my grasp. Now, I just had to get rid of Kyle, and my life would be perfect.

"Luna, we're going to move you to the Luna's maternity suite," a nurse said. "Everyone has already been directed to that floor. Once you're ready, we'll let them in. Until then, it's only the people you allowed in for the birth. Let's get you cleaned up and get that bedding changed. Some of the staff is already lining the hall to catch a glimpse of the new Alpha."

"Thank you."

The nurse took me to the little bathroom where there was a shower and my soaps and stuff laid out. I was thrilled to see them there. I really wanted to get the sweat and ick off of me quickly and get back out to my family.

After a fast, yet thorough, shower, I brushed my hair and put on the nightgown that was set out. The nightgown was the one I packed. I'd had Dilly grab my bag while we were on the way to the hospital. I hoped he grabbed the other thing I asked for.

Lucien was next to the door as I returned to the room and swept me up in his arms, nuzzling my neck. He carried me to the bed and settled me there before pulling the blanket up and tucking it around me. I didn't fight it. I felt exhausted from the birth.

"Alright, let's get moving. Our Luna needs her sleep," the nurse directed.

"Alpha, the babies need to go into their bassinets now. You can't carry them in the halls. It's against hospital policy," she told Lucien.

"Of course. For the safety of the pups. I understand." He stood and Dilly came to help put them down.

An orderly pushed me out ahead of everyone, followed by Lucien pushing Lunette's bassinet and Cara pushing Étienne. Dilly was bringing up the rear with my bag.

She hadn't been lying. People were lining the hallway. Phones were out so they could take pictures of the babies as they passed.

We loaded into the elevator and headed up to the floor where the maternity rooms were. When the door opened, there were more people. Dilly led the way, and it was the reverse of the way to the elevator.

This time, I heard the whispers. People wondering about Lucien pushing Lunette. She was the next Alpha. Étienne was rogue born. Both were Alphas, but only one was a pack Alpha.

Lucien and I already knew it from the dream with the vampires. They said the rogue would be easier to put back first. Étienne was my little King. Though Alpha females rarely took over packs, Lucien and I talked about it.

She was the firstborn and a pack wolf. The odds of one of our future children also being Alpha was high, but it was her birthright to inherit the title of Lune Rouge's next Alpha. We would raise her for the position. If she was Alpha, her mate likely wouldn't be an Alpha as well. Until then, we would give her proper training for the position.

We ended up in a large room with a living room set in it, a queen-sized bed, and two very nice bassinets. It was decadent. Little touches all over made the room less like a hospital room and more like a medically enhanced hotel suite.

They moved me to bed. The sheets were soft, and the blanket was thick. The mattress was incredibly comfortable; sinking into it felt like melting into a cloud, instantly washing over me with tiredness. It was about midnight and I needed sleep.

"Are you ready for everyone, chouchoutte?" Lucien asked.

"No, but we need to do this or I won't get any sleep. This wasn't the physical activity I'd been planning for tonight," I groaned.

He chuckled and linked our families to come in. Olive was first through the door. She came over and kissed me on the head. Daniel stood behind her.

"You did great, baby. Are you happy?" she asked.

"Yes, Mommy. I'm very happy." I smiled. "Go on and see your grandbabies. I see you eyeing them."

She bounced a little like the first day I'd seen her. I was really grateful for Daniel and Olive taking me in. They didn't know exactly what they were agreeing to, but they'd taken everything in stride. I loved them as if they were my own parents.

Daniel patted my arm and followed Olive over to the bassinets. Genevieve and my grandparents all came in to see me before going to see the pups, followed by my aunts and uncles and my male cousins. The girls would see them in the morning. No one wanted to wake them.

"Let's get a picture of our two Alphas," Genevieve said.

No one said anything when he picked up Lunette instead of Étienne. They cooed and aww-ed over the two of them. Olive brought Étienne over to me.

"And one of our little King and Queen." She smiled.

I held my son in my arms and kissed his head. She took a few pictures. Then we did more, with Lucien holding both babies and all of us in the hospital bed.

When they finally finished, everyone left the room. I fed the babies and Lucien helped get them into their bassinets again. He stripped off everything but his boxers and crawled into the bed with me again, then wrapped me in his arms. I was so tired. I fell asleep immediately.

***

[Lucien]

I looked at my tired mate and kissed the top of her head. We finally started our family. I couldn't wait for the next years of our lives. She was as perfect as I'd imagined she'd be back when I first thought of making her my Luna. The goddess really had blessed me and I was immeasurably grateful.

Soon, my excitement gave way to my own exhaustion. I'd been up early for training the day before. Then I had shooting and blade practice with Stanton.

I wouldn't let Kyle catch me off guard if he tried cheating. Not when I finally had everything I wanted. I wasn't going down without one hell of a fight.

Falling asleep with my mate in my arms, while our pups rested nearby, was everything I'd dreamed of my whole life. I would do anything to protect the gift the goddess had given me. Anything to protect my family.

***

The feeling of Bellamy kissing down my chest woke me up sometime later. I chuckled at the feeling of her little hands rubbing all over me. Then I remembered the pups and my eyes flew open. Their bassinets were gone.

"Where are the pups?" I asked urgently.

"They went for some tests and I asked the nurses to keep them from the room for a while after," Bellamy purred. "There was something I wanted to do last night before we were interrupted."

She pushed me onto my back and continued her path lower. Her eagerness amused me. Bellamy nipped and licked her way to the waistband of my boxers. Her fingers slipped under the band and she worked them off of me.

"Now, I want you to relax and trust me," she said.

That didn't exactly leave me feeling relaxed. She settled herself between my legs and began licking and sucking my cock and balls. Her mouth was heavenly.

Bellamy pushed my legs until my feet were flat on the bed, then started tracing over the second mark on my ass as her tongue caressed around and under my balls. Her other hand stroked me firmly.

My body started relaxing under her attention. We'd done this countless times, but each time was better than the last. She added something to it every time.

Remus was going insane. We were still firmly connected because it was so close to my birthday. He'd never been this entwined with me while she was doing things. He'd loved having her on the table. This was a treat he never experienced before.

He panicked a little when the hand that had been stroking me dropped down and started rubbing around my backdoor. I moaned at the feeling while she was still licking and sucking my balls.

She hadn't touched me there since that night, months ago, when we'd first met Thomas. I'd wondered when she was going to again. It felt so good, yet taboo.

Bellamy pulled back, and I felt something warm dribble between my body and her finger. Slowly, she pressed in and I reflexively tightened. She pinched my second mark, sending a flood of pleasure throughout my body, and I relaxed again.

Soon, she was inside me and I could feel her finger make contact with something in me that made me feel like I actually had to pee. It wasn't until she stroked it a few times, in a 'come hither' motion, that I realized her true goal. The other feeling passed and the pleasure that grew was amazing.

I groaned with need. Her other hand came up from my mark and she started stroking me again while her tongue teased my balls. I'd never felt anything so intense. Remus was whimpering in my head.

As my end grew closer, Bellamy picked up the pace. She looked up at me with a glassy, desirous look in her eyes. It would take her a couple of days to recover, but I planned to make her feel as good as she made me feel.

"I want you to come for me, Alpha," she purred.

Coherent words weren't a possibility. I was already dribbling cum down her hand, but I wasn't there yet. It was so close. I could feel my whole body shaking subtly.

"Come on, Lucien. Come for your Queen," Bellamy murmured her gentle encouragement.

That did it for me. I felt a rush through my entire body. The shaking increased, and I experienced the most powerful orgasm of my life. I roared my completion, my hands grasping for something that didn't exist as I bucked and streams of my seed poured from me. It seemed endless.

When it finally was over, and the last of the shakes were done. Bellamy withdrew from me, making me shiver at the feeling. She got up and went to the connecting bathroom. I heard the water running, and she soon returned with a damp washcloth and a dry washcloth.

Carefully, she cleaned me up. Both above and below. Then picked something up off the bed and went back to the bathroom.

After Bellamy returned, she pulled the blankets over us and cuddled close. She curled up in the curve of my side and put her head on my chest. I was only just getting my breath back.

"What on earth was that?" I whispered.

"Prostate massage. Dilly told me about it and he made sure to grab my lube when he got my bag. I was planning it for last night. Everything is more intense when your wolf is at the surface." She giggled.

"Good goddess. I don't know if I could handle that again… but I really want to try." I chuckled.

"You always make me feel so good. I wanted to find something else I could do for you. And you take my directions so well," Bellamy murmured.

"You are my Queen, after all," I whispered, kissing her forehead.

"And you are my Alpha. I'll always do whatever I can to make you happy."

"You're all I need to be happy, Bellamy. You and our family," I told her.

And I truly meant it. Everything else was just icing. Having my family was the most important thing in my whole life.

Chapter 147: Little Messenger

[Lucien]

It was three weeks after the pups were born. Bellamy and I had gotten into a certain sort of groove. She and the pups would stay in my office in the morning. Once they'd had their afternoon feeding, Maman would take the pups back to our quarters and Bellamy would work on things in her office.

Bellamy was pumping milk, so the pups wouldn't need her in the afternoon. It was important that her work not lapse. She had many people depending on her as Queen, High Queen, and Luna.

Liana couldn't come to help out like she planned and my mother stayed longer. I didn't want any of my family at risk while Kyle was nearby. Bellamy agreed with the decision.

There had been a few more brief sightings of Kyle in the territory, but nothing came of it. We were just waiting to see what he did while sending out teams to track him. Although Bellamy said Kyle was shit at concealing his scent, he evidently fooled everyone I sent out. It was like he wasn't leaving any trace at all.

As the days grew cold and wet, we expected to see him sooner or later. There were whispers he was working on getting people to join him to attack our territory. I didn't care as long as he did something soon. The wait was killing me. Bellamy wasn't much better.

She was currently sitting in one of the office chairs across from me. She had her laptop on her knees and was working away. Since she didn't have much rogue or Luna business at the moment, she stayed in my office to help me with my workload this afternoon.

Dillon linked me while I was reading through some paperwork about permits for new construction.

'Alpha, there's someone at the main entrance with a message for you.'

'What does it say?' I asked.

'She won't give it to me. Her King said only you could accept it. The thing is, she's hurt and looks terrified. The first thing she said to me was 'Please, don't kill me'. I think she's from Kyle,' Dillon replied.

'Tell her the Alpha won't accept the message until she's been seen by the doctor and cleared medically. I'll get some food sent up and let Bellamy know.'

'Yes, sir. I'll be there as soon as I can. Could I have permission to tell her you ordered me to carry her? Her feet are cut up and the ground is cold.'

'Permission granted.'

I linked the admitting nurse at the hospital to let her know there was a priority case on its way to her. We needed this woman looked at immediately. Then I linked to the kitchen to have food delivered as soon as possible.

"Bellamy, Dillon says there's a messenger here and he thinks she's from Kyle. She's injured so I'm having her treated first. Then I'll have her brought here."

"Does he say she's not a threat?"

"He didn't say one way or the other. Only that she was hurt and she asked him not to kill her."

"Okay. Let's make sure we're ready for her then. We want to present our best face to her. You stay seated, you're a little imposing and we don't want to scare her." Bellamy smiled.

I nodded, and we worked to straighten up. When the food was ready, someone brought it up and placed it on the coffee table. The foods were healthy and high in protein. It would, hopefully, make her feel more at ease.

About an hour later, Dillon knocked on my door, and I told him to enter. I wasn't as prepared for the messenger as I thought I was.

He stepped in the door and a little girl peeked out from behind him. She had dark blonde hair and chocolate brown eyes. She couldn't have been over nine.

My gaze dropped to her feet, which were covered in bandages. I worked not to growl. Hurting a child really pissed me off.

Bellamy stood and crossed the room. She bent down and talked to the girl. It was mostly light murmuring that the girl either nodded her head to or shook her head to. Then Bellamy turned to me and shrugged.

"What's your name?" I asked her.

"E-Emily. My name is Emily, Alpha."

"And who is your message from, Emily."

"My King sent me with this letter that I can only give to you, sir," she replied quietly.

She limped over and handed me the letter. I looked at the thick envelope. It was barely closed and popped open easily when I tried opening it.

"Have a seat over there and get some food. We take care of messengers here," I said.

"Thank you, sir." Emily bowed a little and Dillon helped her over to the couch.

"I've linked Celesta to come take care of the girl. Dilly needs to return to his station," Bellamy whispered.

I nodded and pulled the folded paper out of the stuffed envelope. It was six sheets with handwriting on the front and back. As I read it, I grew more and more astonished at the crazy and outlandish claims in the pages.

It was from Kyle. He accused me of ensnaring Bellamy with a love potion as revenge against his family. He stated she was his destined mate and she would've fallen in love with him if I hadn't interfered.

He called me a liar, murderer, thief, and coward. I would've been angry about it, but some claims were so outlandish that I was confused about how it even connected.

Every page would end up rambling. He never called Bellamy by her name, only 'my Bella'.

Kyle said he could only sleep with other women if he thought of Bellamy. According to him, the goddess came to him in a dream and promised her to him. Bellamy was the only female he would ever love. And he had *proof* I used a potion on her when I found out she was his mate.

Every time I finished a sheet and set it down, Bellamy picked it up and started reading it. She was growing angrier as she read. Not seeming to care that this man had obviously gone mad at some point.

In the end, he challenged me to a fight. He called it a cor acie triplici and described it as a battle to the death with the winner getting Bellamy and the other's territory. He literally had nothing and was issuing this challenge as if he were still a powerful King.

I handed the last page to Bellamy and looked up. Celesta was fawning over Emily and encouraging her to eat more. The girl seemed to be happy and was eating as if she hadn't in a while.

"Emily, are your parents with your King?" I asked.

She looked startled and quickly swallowed the food in her mouth. "No. No, sir. They died. He killed them and said he'd kill me too if I didn't do as he said."

"He didn't make you take a blood oath?" Bellamy questioned.

"No, ma'am. I was too scared of him. He said I'd join his collective after he won his mate. That I would be his personal servant until that happened and he would reward me by picking a mate for me. When I tried to tell him I have a destined mate, like my mom and dad did, he beat me. I don't want to go back. I don't know what to do," Emily said tearfully.

"How long have you been with him?" I asked.

"Since summertime," Emily whispered.

'That means she was with him at Goddess' Tears. They didn't say he had a child,' I told Bellamy.

'He probably kept her somewhere else. They wouldn't have stood for that bullshit,' she practically growled.

"Can she join the pack, Alpha? Thierry and I have extra space since Salomé moved to be with her mate. We could adopt her. I already linked him about it," Celesta told me.

'I thought you didn't want any more children,' I said in our link.

'No more babies. She's not a baby, Lucien. She's a hurt, orphaned child. Like Bellamy was. I'm just spreading the love the Carringtons gave Bellamy to a child like her,' Celesta insisted.

According to Bellamy, Kingston was with the hunters when they killed Angelique and Jean-Luc. Like father, like son. He'd wanted a little girl that didn't belong to him and he damaged her to get what he wanted.

"Emily, would you like to join my pack and live with Miss Celesta?" I asked gently.

"C-can I? I'll be good. I swear."

"I believe you. We'll protect you from that nasty King. Once you're healthy again, we'll do an acceptance ceremony for you. When you turn twelve, you'll be able to link with the rest of the pack, until then, you'll be able to link with your adoptive family like with your own parents," I explained.

"Thank you. Thank you, Alpha," Emily wept.

"Take her to Thierry's office and have your maid grab some staff to help get her room set up. We'll have dinner in the Alpha's dining room tonight so she can meet everyone," I told Celesta.

"Yes, Alpha. Come on, Emily. I'll give you a piggyback ride across the hall," she said with a smile, and they left.

Bellamy climbed into my lap and put her arms around my neck. I held her tightly. We'd been hoping for something to break the tension of waiting. I was almost relieved.

"Three days, saucisson," she murmured.

"In three days, it'll be over. I don't understand the type of challenge he issued. That's not a challenge we have in packs," I said. "What's a cor acie triplici?"

"Triple heart battle. A triple heart battle is what happens when two males or two females want the same mate. If that mate can't decide for any reason, the challenge is issued. The thing is, it's never to the death. Adding in the territory made it an Alpha battle.

"He's trying to get back what he lost, but this territory, in rogue terms, is mine not yours. The wolves belong to you; the land belongs to me. If he won, he would get nothing. I could kill him for killing my mate and trying to challenge for my territory. He's already targeted for death," Bellamy sighed. "Kyle's really gone off the deep end."

"We need to prepare for this fight. I'm accepting his challenge. If nothing else, it gets him here. I'm not worried. He hasn't trained as long as I have," I murmured and kissed her temple.

"I'm worried. He's crazy and may resort to cheating if it looks like he might lose. I can't lose you, Lucien. You need to be prepared for anything. You aren't allowed to die."

"I won't, chouchoutte. I'm not just accepting some random challenge. Because of Kyle and his family, I lost my father and a lot of other family members. You lost your parents. I was taken by vampires to be fed on and used as a breeding stud. My mother almost died and that orderly attacked you, trying to kill our pups. I'm fighting for my pack and everyone they lost to the Fullers. I'm fighting for Lunette and Étienne," I said. "This mad wolf needs to be put down."

"I agree with that. Thank the goddess it's almost over. I don't think I could've handled it much longer. I was about to go hunt him myself." She chuckled.

"At least it didn't have to come to that. I wouldn't have done well knowing you were out there without me. You want to lock the door so I can show you how much I would have worried, chouchoutte?"

Bellamy giggled. "Of course I do, saucisson. You should always share these concerns with me in every possible way."

She climbed out of my lap and swayed her hips seductively as she went to lock the door. If Kyle thought for one moment he was going to beat me, he was dead wrong. Not when I finally had everything I wanted. Not when I had my Bellamy.

Chapter 148: The Challenge

Three days went by fast. We didn't train that morning. Instead, we made love. The scent of me on Lucien would make Kyle angry and angry fighters were impulsive fighters. I wanted to give Lucien every advantage.

We had breakfast in our quarters and my grandmothers came to help Genevieve with the pups while we were gone. There was enough milk for the day, so I wasn't too worried about leaving them behind. I trusted them to make sure the pups were safe.

Lucien imposed a lockdown order on the entire pack until the next day or until he gave the all-clear. We only allowed the ranked members, the warriors patrolling the borders, Dilly, and Evan out of their homes until we dealt with this.

Kyle arrived close to noon. Dilly and Jean-Claude escorted him to the north field. It was the one that had bleachers since the younger kids would play field games like football there.

We arrived just as Kyle emerged from the far side of the field, the sound of his footsteps audible even from a distance. Evan was behind me, Robert and Thierry were behind Lucien. Aside from me, Evan was the only other female on the field.

The two warriors from Goddess' Tears were also there. They'd insisted. We needed outside witnesses anyway. Neither Lucien nor I had a problem with them being there.

When Kyle saw me, he lit up and started making his way over. His eyes were entirely on me and didn't even glance at Lucien. Like he didn't exist. Once he reached us, in the center of the field, Kyle grinned at me.

"Bella, you look beautiful today. Don't worry about a thing. I'm going to kill him and break the spell he put on you; I promise. Then we'll deal with those two mutts he bred on you. You'll never ha…."

My foot in his junk cut him short.

"Never, *ever* speak of my pups like that! I'll kill you if you even breathe in their direction!" I shouted and nailed him again.

With a grunt of pain, Kyle crumpled to the earth, his hand clamped tightly over his injured groin. The urge to keep stomping on him was overwhelming; a primal need to crush him pulsed in my veins, but I restrained myself. I felt good after finally hurting the bastard who had been dodging me for months.

I stood over him and glared down. "My name *isn't* Bella! Call me that again and I'll rip out your tongue."

"E-everything will be okay once I break the spell," he coughed. "I'll even forgive you for that outburst."

"There is no spell you fucking idiot."

"He made the vampires put a spell on you to make you love him. I figured it out."

"The vampires were getting information from the assassin *you* hired, dumbass. They didn't want me in love with him. Werewolves in love are dangerous. I fell in love with him, I was not bespelled to love him. I *never* loved you and I *will never* love you. Even if you win this fight, I'm going to kill you," I growled.

"The vampires were working for me until he paid them off. I had them tie you up with your territory so I could finish your present. I honestly thought the Alpha's mysterious mate was the assassin I hired. You always hear about women assassins falling for their targets. I wasn't about to take that chance. That's why I hired the bears to find her," he explained proudly.

I saw red. "Innocent wolves were attacked! Children could've been hurt! You and your *fucking* father have *never* cared about anyone but yourselves! You deserve what's waiting for you after death, Kyle. It certainly won't be pleasant."

Turning to Lucien, I rubbed his knuckles, feeling the tension in his grip as he silently squeezed my hand while I spoke. More than anything else at that moment, I felt so grateful for it.

I released my mate, and as I stood free of the men, I faced the bleachers, hearing the hushed whispers of those watching. Robert, Thierry, and Evan, had grabbed their seats while I was dealing with Kyle.

"This is a challenge by King Kyle Fuller to Alpha Lucien Deveraux. Witness this fact before it begins. Although this challenge is in the name of a cor acie triplici, my heart is settled. I chose my mate and love only him. This is not a match to help me decide, because King Fuller was never even in the running to be my mate.

"Alpha Lucien accepts this challenge in the name of all who have suffered because of an ancient grudge held by the Fuller family. It has been decided that this will be a fight to the death. The goddess will aid whoever is in the right. This battle will begin after I have been seated. Premature start will indicate forfeit and the one who initiated it will be killed by the witnesses," I announced loudly.

I spun back to the men, who were now standing beside each other. Both looked confident. They were both exuding their Alpha auras. Lucien's was stronger, but it wasn't making Kyle back down.

"You may strip to your underwear once I head to the bleachers. There is no rule on form, so fight however you fight best. May the goddess bless the man in the right," I told them and went to sit down.

My stomach was twisting as I approached the benches. Evan watched the scene behind me intently. I wasn't having that.

"You better be ogling King Fuller and not my mate," I growled at her.

"Absolutely, Queen Bellamy. It's a shame he's ten pounds of crazy in a five-pound bag. That man is hot," she replied, licking her lips.

Politeness dictated that Evan, as an unmated female, give Kyle, an unmated male, attention. I turned back to the field. It was a rather nice view. I saw the stark contrast between the man who thought he owned me and the man who cherished and respected me.

Lucien was the same height as Kyle, but thicker with larger muscles. Kyle's more defined muscles were probably because of dehydration. The sun had worked its magic on my Lucien; he was darker, his skin a deeper, almost bronze shade. Blond men had never been my type; I'd always envisioned a tall, dark, handsome man as my perfect match. Lucien encompassed all of those characteristics.

"Stop drooling over your mate so he can kick that bitch's ass," Dilly whispered with a chuckle.

"You stop drooling over my mate so yours will stop smelling so jealous," I replied and sat between him and Evan.

Once I sat down, they began circling each other. I watched, trying to remain impassive, but the flurry of hits, swipes, kicks, and dodges had me mirroring the fight, my body mimicking the fighters' movements. A wave of frustration wash over me, leaving me irritable and helpless. I wanted to be out there, fighting for myself.

We'd contacted the other Association chairs, and they agreed this was a matter between the Alphas. Both had more claim than I did. If it had been Kingston, I would've had cause to step in. It pissed me off, but I wasn't going to let that hurt my relationship. We had boundaries, and I was going to abide by them.

Despite the tough competition, Kyle showed skill and determination, effectively holding his own throughout the intense fight. If he weren't trying to kill my husband, I'd be proud of the deadly efficiency with which he moved, a testament to his rigorous training. He would've made an amazing King… if he weren't fucking insane.

With a quick sidestep, Lucien evaded Kyle's attack, his fist connecting solidly with Kyle's gut, throwing him backward. Kyle transformed mid-air and landed as a brown and blond wolf. Lucien stood up straighter and stayed on guard.

It was rare to see two wolves battle while in different forms. It was generally believed the wolf form, with its sharp teeth and feral instincts, was far deadlier. That's why most of our training was in human form; it strengthened our weaker human bodies.

I knew Lucien had been spending countless hours with Stanton and Randy, pushing his physical limits in extra training sessions. Bears often fought wolves in human form; it improved their chances of winning.

With a ferocious roar, Kyle charged and leapt at Lucien, the ground trembling beneath his powerful strides. I saw Kyle's body slam into Lucien, a thud resonating through the air, but Lucien remained standing.

His jaws clamped down on Lucien's neck with a sickening snap, and I saw blood welling up and trailing down his back. I wasn't worried. I smirked as a sense of calm washed over me.

I'd seen Stanton use this on an unstable ex-pack once. There was a little jerk as he'd hit. I could see the stark terror reflected in the eyes of Kyle's wolf, a look that spoke volumes of its fear. Lucien had locked Kyle's front legs. This was the messy part.

Sitting forward, tense and breathless, I watched as Lucien jerked Kyle's forelegs apart, the sound of straining muscles and snapping tendons echoing. A thrill ran through me as I heard the sickening pops and crunches of dislocated joints and the rib cage tearing apart. It made Jean-Claude look queasy.

A sudden eruption of blood and entrails sprayed between the two, staining the brown tinged grass beneath them. Lucien tore Kyle in half. His mouth lost its grip on Lucien's neck. The wolf's corpse twitched, then shuddered, its fur rippling and parting and shifting back into his human form.

Lucien let the body fall heavily to the ground before bending over to begin a thorough search for a specific object. He pulled back and turned to run toward the bleachers. He was a mess of blood and cuts, but he wore a determined expression as he focused on reaching me.

As he neared, I stood waiting, feeling the tension in the air until he came to a stop. Lucien held out his hand, offering me Kyle's heart; still faintly warm, it pulsed weakly in his palm. I looked up into his eyes. I grew to hate eating hearts, but I looked forward to this one.

Before I could take it from him, Lucien put it up to his mouth and took a bite. That was hot as hell. He held it up for me to bite, as well. We shared the heart of our enemy. By eating our enemy's heart, we showed the other rogues and our pack that we were Alphas who took our oaths seriously.

When we finished, Lucien looked at the people behind me. He appeared cool and commanding. I wanted to climb him like a tree.

"This feud is over. My mate is mine. This region will be at peace," Lucien announced.

He glared at the assembled party as if daring them to say anything against it. The rogues bowed slightly, acknowledging his dominance. The pack wolves followed suit.

It was only then that the blood loss seemed to catch up with him and he swayed on his feet. I scooped him, a little clumsily, into my arms.

"I know you don't like it, but Remus won't want anyone else touching you while you're injured. Let me carry you home from battle like you've carried me. Let me be your strength, mon saucisson."

"Just this once, chouchoutte. Just this once," he sighed.

As I turned to head back to our home. I heard Evan propositioning Richard. That much blood was enough to make any rogue a little horny.

"No, Evie!" I called back.

"Fine. John, Caden, how about we go have some fun then, since the pack boys are off limits?" She giggled.

"I don't share," John growled.

"You'll learn, sweetheart," she purred.

I rolled my eyes. She was so bad sometimes. I was betting she wouldn't settle down even after she had a mate.

That was all I had time for. Lucien was bleeding pretty badly in some places, and I had to get him cleaned and bandaged. Damage from another werewolf would take longer to heal, even as an Alpha, and I was happy he didn't get as hurt as he did when he fought Ennis.

I headed back to the packhouse, my husband in my arms and my children safe with their grandmother and great-grandmothers. I finally had everything I ever wanted. My territory was safe, my mate was healthy, my children were perfect, the men responsible for my suffering were all dead, and I had more family than I knew what to do with.

I couldn't imagine my life without Lucien. With luck, I wouldn't have to for a very long time. For now, I could focus on the strong, smart, experienced Alpha who needed me to baby him and tend his wounds.

The true King to my Queen.

My mate.

Epilogue: Dilly and Jean-Claude

On Christmas Day, Jean-Claude proposed. It was the sweetest proposal. He gave me a large package. Inside was a big fuzzy robe. Wrapped in that, was a beautiful scarf and I could feel something heavy inside of it. While I tried to unravel it, the box fell out.

He got down on one knee and picked it up, opening it to reveal a white gold band with a golden brown topaz cut like a heart. It was almost the same shade as his gorgeous eyes. Jean-Claude smiled softly at me as I realized what was going on.

"I love you more than anything in existence, Dillon Metz. I have your mark, but I'd also like your hand. Will you marry me?" he asked with his heart in his eyes.

I could see the honesty in his words right there in his face. I was fine with not getting married at all if he hadn't wanted to, but we'd been talking about it being a possibility next summer. At that moment, I didn't really care about that. He was stepping up and showing his love for me.

"Yes, I'll marry you." I grinned.

He pulled the ring from the box and kissed me after putting it on my finger. I couldn't believe it was really happening and had to pinch myself. We made love all that morning and Bellamy was thrilled when I told her at dinner.

We decided on a brief engagement and a Valentine's Day wedding, even though we had previously talked about getting married in June. Bellamy, Evan, Cara, Celesta, and Simone helped pull everything together. It would be indoors because winters were often snowy here.

Aunt Bren came to stay and help with everything after the new year. She was so happy for me that she cried. I was grateful for her.

Things got super calm and comfortable in the pack after Kyle died. Lucien and Bellamy were working hard on taking in more ex-pack rogues and making more rogue born pack wolves. We had an elite team of rogues and they worked really well with my own elite team. Bellamy's top teams in her collective moved to town after she got married and the town was getting more settled.

Bellamy, Cara, and I had our final sleepover the night before the wedding. It was just as much fun as theirs had been. I loved spending time with my girls, especially without their mates and Bellamy's pups around. I loved those pups, but I didn't think they were old enough to hear the things I wanted to talk about.

We talked late into the night about our mates and our futures. Claude and I were thinking we'd adopt an older child after a year or two. Out of diapers, but young enough to be fun. We'd wait until Jean-Claude was twenty-one. We wanted to have a few years of fun and just being together, but who knows where life would lead us.

The wedding would happen at four in the afternoon. Since the sun went down at around six, and the wedding was inside, it would still enable Talia to be there. She was in my wedding party. We all thought it would be hilarious to have her walk next to Stan since he was 6'5" and she was just 4'10".

Our colors were those of the pack. It was typical for most of the ranked members to have the colors as their base and add something to it, but we loved the white and crimson for a Valentine's Day wedding. Especially since we had a Christmas engagement.

Some packs celebrated human holidays because of the influence of human mates. Christmas and Valentine's Day were ones I enjoyed a lot. And now I had even more reason to like them.

As I stood in front of our friends and family, gazing at my soon-to-be husband in his perfect white tuxedo, I felt the most joy I'd felt in a long time. It was like I'd been waiting my whole life to be here, even though marriage wasn't something many gay wolves did.

We went through all of Alpha Lucien's stuff and got to our vows. It was the part I was most excited about. Jean-Claude worked on his for weeks and wouldn't let me see them at all. I was dying from curiosity.

"Dillon, when I first saw you, I thanked the goddess for giving me such a handsome and capable mate. I'd always dreamed there was a man, a warrior, out there who I could love and who would love me. My granduncle, Jean-Paul, told me not to give up on the idea of finding my mate. He said if I gave up, I wouldn't see the love my mate had for me. I'm sad to say he was right. Because I'd given up, I didn't trust your love and I took something precious from you.

"I forgot you were as much a boy in love as I was and you were looking forward to this as much as I was. But you worked through your disappointment and forgave me. You still loved me. You helped me to understand you and the love you had to give.

"My cousin may have made me a better warrior, but you've made me a better man. I want to continue learning to be the kind of man you deserve and I promise to never doubt you again. You are my love and my entire life. Thank you for agreeing to be mine," he said, gazing lovingly into my eyes.

Our rough start had been a bit of a topic of conversation for everyone in the pack and all our friends. That he addressed it and how much he grew from it was endearing. I nearly kissed him right then, but remembered I needed to say mine.

"Eight years ago, I lost my parents and started a downward spiral. I became distant from my family and my pack. Pulling away because I lost the two people who meant the most to me. Then I met your cousin. She lost everything too, but instead of letting it drag her down, she worked to become a better person. When she looked at me it wasn't with pity, disdain, or fear, but with hope for love. The same hope I saw in your eyes the first time we spoke.

"You may have given up on finding love, but you never gave up hope it existed for you. I made a lot of mistakes in my past, ones I would love to take back, but you'll never have to worry, because that Dillon died the first time I laid eyes on you. All I ever want to do is care for you, and love you like you deserve.

"We had a… rocky start, but I think the extra work we had to put into our relationship only helped make up for both of us being a little broken still. Every inch, every ounce of my heart and soul belong to you. I promise to cherish you for the rest of our lives," I told him.

We exchanged our rings and had our first kiss as a married couple. It was magical. Knowing our friends and family were there supporting us, that this was the first of many married kisses, that this was the beginning of everything. A new beginning, a fresh start.

Right after the wedding ceremony finished, we were on our way to the main dining hall for our cocktail hour when Talia got a phone call from someone. She was more serious than I'd ever seen her.

I heard her say, "That's wonderful news, Victor. You have my permission."

I had no clue what it was about, then remembered the childe of hers that was hunting one of his children. She told me his name was Victor. He must've found him and been asking permission for a *final* punishment. He would have to run that by the Vampire Council.

Despite Lucien's threatening growls at any unmated male who dared approach Bellamy on the dance floor, the reception was otherwise a success. He was extremely possessive as she was getting ready to start her heat. Though it was hilarious, the sheer absurdity of it all still didn't top the funniest part of the night.

Pavel was the recipient of that specific award. Everyone who knew the truth of the Pavel situation wanted to know why would we invite that prick to our wedding. It was simple.

He got down on his knees and begged with tears in his eyes. He apologized profusely for everything he'd done and said. Pavel desperately wanted us to invite him and his fated mate to the wedding and seat them together.

Apparently, at Bellamy's Luna ceremony, Pavel found his mate. I saw the whole thing go down, but kept it to myself. Pavel got the scent of his mate and walked over, all confident and proud. It was like watching a train wreck; sad, gruesome, and too fascinating to look away.

His mate was Rhys, Warrick's little brother. The massive asshole who told my Bemmy that, as a female rogue, she was only good for one thing and was otherwise worthless. I got to know him over the times we would go to Hunter's Moon. I had no idea he was gay, not that I was interested.

Rhys turned, saw Pavel, and started shaking his head. I thought he was going to reject him, but he just walked away. I talked to Tyson later. The brothers were really close and Rhys told him he was bisexual and thought, like most other bisexual wolves, his mate would be female.

He refused to reject Pavel and lose the chance at a goddess-chosen mate, but Pavel refused to reject him, too. He told Rhys that, like it or not, he was his mate and he would win him. Tyson said he had a hard time not laughing at his brother. There were plenty of unmated females to choose from, but he didn't want to have to make the choice for himself.

So Pavel got ahold of his contact info and had been calling, texting, emailing, writing letters, and even visiting Hunter's Moon to get Rhys' attention. Pavel sent him gifts, flowers, love notes, everything he could think of. He was pulling out all the stops. He was desperate to make his mate accept him.

He hoped that a wedding on Valentine's Day would be the sort of romantic thing to make Rhys more open to his mate. Pavel chased after him for the entire reception. Jean-Claude felt sorry for him, but I didn't.

I felt it was the goddess' justice for my mate being hurt by the bastard. My friends also got a lot of pleasure from it and Bellamy alternated helping Rhys hide and Pavel find him. It was hilarious.

In the end, we were just happy to have people we cared for there. We were happy to belong to each other entirely. Mostly, we were happy that we were healing together.

Our pack and our family would stand up for us and to us, to ensure we were on the right path for our future. And we would do the same for them.

I loved Lune Rouge as much as I loved my Jean-Claude. It was the pack of my dreams, and not just because my best friends were the Luna and Beta. I was going to protect it until my last breath, no matter what.

Bonus Chapter:

The Vampire's Servant – The Watcher Witch

Greta mixed herbs and essences into the viewing dish she used for calling visions. A premonition told her the vampire she would feed that night was going to need it. That was rare for her.

Normally, her premonitions were about small things that had little to nothing to do with her gifts. They would be things like if a storm would be worse than the forecasters said, or if traffic was going to hinder her errands. That meant there was some powerful intention by the spirits and the goddess.

On a whim, she pulled out her scrying crystal and a map of the United States. Greta didn't know why she had the urge, but her instincts were never wrong. It seemed important to have this on the table.

She moved around the small, open living space. Her home was one of the newer houses in her neighborhood. An open floor plan with two bedrooms and two bathrooms.

She set up the second room as a mix of sewing room and guest room. Not that she had guests often. She remodeled the large pantry into her spell room. She filled the pantry with the spell ingredients she needed instead of canned and dry goods and used it to perform magic needing darkness or candlelight there.

"Please…. Please…. Help me…. Please…" a voice whispered.

Greta nearly jumped out of her skin. She started searching for the source of the voice until she got to her dinner table, where everything was laid out. She stared in disbelief as the whisper came from the viewing bowl.

That wasn't possible. She needed the blood of the person the viewing was for to activate her spell. The spirits were sending her this vision for a reason.

She looked into the still water with little herbs floating. As if something had dropped in, the flecks of plant leaves ran to the edge of the bowl. A room came into view.

A young man with dark hair, hazel eyes, and a healthy tan was sitting in front of a cereal bowl full of water with flecks in it. He was trying viewing magic? His parents should've taught him male witches rarely had an affinity with water and weren't seers if they did. She shook her head.

He was burning a black votive candle and had a magic circle drawn in chalk on the hardwood floor. His choices made no sense to her. It was like he was using as many types of magic as possible. The conflicting energies should've stopped anything from happening, but she could see the flame in the candle reacting.

"Please… help me…. Please, help me save my sister. Help me save Echo," his voice strained.

Greta put her hand over her heart. That poor boy. She wondered why his sister needed saving.

The boy pricked his finger and dropped blood into the water of the cereal bowl. Greta looked closely to see if it did anything. She gasped. The drop of blood took the shape of a moon with a spike through it.

Quickly, she ran to her bookshelf and found her book of symbols. That wasn't one she was familiar with. A male witch with a water seer specialty was so rare. She was excited to see what it could mean.

After a search, she found nothing. Unless it was a mixture of two symbols. Her doorbell rang. It was after dark. She'd almost forgotten about the vampire.

With a heavy sigh, she put the book away and answered the door. In front of her stood a tall man with beautifully high cheekbones, broad shoulders, a narrow waist, and a somber expression. His eyes looked violet in the porch light.

"Hello, I'm Victor. I was sent by the broker." He smiled and bowed a little.

"I need the code word," Greta replied softly.

"Of course. The code word is magical," Victor said.

"Please come in, Victor," she told him, waving him into her home.

"Thank you."

He entered the house and glanced around with a polite and cool expression. This was the vampire from her premonition. Treasure, the blood broker, only gave that code word if someone was probably willing to pay for her other services.

"Have you ever had witch's blood?" Greta asked.

"On occasion. I'm hoping it will help me in my search."

"I'm a water witch with a seer specialty. I normally charge extra for my services, but I get the feeling I'm supposed to help you. So I'll waive my usual fee," she said, leading him to the table.

"I appreciate that, but I'll gladly pay for any assistance. Shall we do the feeding first? I want to be sure you have the energy for both," Victor answered politely.

Greta found him to be a pleasant man. Most vampires were a little brusque when talking to her about feeding. The idea of another supernatural creature donating often bothered them. For all that witches looked human, they were as 'other' as werewolves and fae.

"We can do the feeding first. I can handle both. I appreciate your consideration."

She sat in a chair and bared her neck. Victor leaned in close. He was gentle and careful in preparing the area for the bite, and she felt nothing. It was like he was softly kissing her neck. Greta worked to suppress a moan that tried to work its way out. He was so careful with her that it made her heart flutter.

The feeding took only a couple of minutes. Victor stood up and smiled.

"Thank you for the meal. Your blood was quite wonderful."

A blush stained Greta's cheeks. She was more than happy to help someone who acted like a gentleman, even in a situation like a feeding. It was refreshing to meet someone like Victor.

"Please, have a seat," Greta said.

Victor sat in the seat near hers and looked at her expectantly. Greta was concerned about using the water that had given her the vision of the boy, but it seemed to be back to normal. The boy was gone, and the leaves floated haphazardly in the mixture as if it had never happened.

"Tell me about your quest, and then we'll use a drop of your blood to search for your answers," she instructed.

"Fifteen years ago, one of my children stole fifteen million dollars from me and fled my territory. I sent out word I would forgive him if he returned it within a year. A year passed, and I heard nothing from him. Again, I sent word that his punishment would be light if he returned within three months with whatever money he had left. If he didn't, I would kill him. The response I received was: 'You'll have to find me first.'

"I was livid. I've been hunting him since then. About five years ago, I discovered his route to America. The trail was spotty in Europe but disappeared completely when I arrived in New York. I've been checking all of the major cities, but I haven't been able to find any trace of him. That was how I ended up here.

"I've given up everything for this chase. He insulted me, his own sire, and rubbed my face in the insult. It was the last straw in a mountain of issues the boy has caused," Victor growled.

While he was explaining everything, Greta got a premonition of his search. He didn't highlight any of the difficulties he'd gone through. Sleeping in the ground at times, being robbed while sleeping in a vampire boarding house, being tricked and trapped by fae for months, and nearly dying several times over. Her heart hurt for him.

This wasn't a matter of pride, but a matter of respect and honor. Victor's other children would lose respect for him if he showed even more favoritism to the man he was tracking. They were already wary because of him allowing it to go on as long as he did. He lost his territory, his name, and his reputation over this.

"Give me your hand," she told him.

Victor held out his hand to her, and she pricked him with a needle, allowing the sluggish blood to fall into the water in the viewing bowl. She released his hand and gazed into the water. He looked too, but he wouldn't see or hear anything. Only a water witch could see and hear the visions held there.

She saw the water clear and glow. The bowl now held the workroom of another witch. Greta saw the woman pulling together herbs, grinding them into a powder, and adding some liquid essences. The woman poured them into a bottle and turned to a man with white-blond hair, an extremely pale complexion, and the same violet eyes as Victor.

"Now, Mr. Springer, you'll run a tub of water. Room temperature is best. Shake this bottle well and empty it entirely into the water. State the name of the person you don't want to find you and submerge yourself in the tub. The longer you're in the water, the better the spell will work. I suggest bathing for about an hour and submerging for as long as you can," the witch in the vision told him.

"Anything I need to know about this? Any warnings? It's not going to make me actually invisible or something, right?" he asked.

"Only to the person you don't want to find you. You must never speak of the obscuring spell. If he finds out about it, the spell will be broken. If you do as I told you, you could walk right past him and he wouldn't recognize you," she explained.

"That's amazing. How much?"

"Three hundred dollars," she answered.

Greta scoffed. That was an outrageous sum for an obscuring spell.

"What?" Victor asked.

"She overcharged him," Greta responded.

As she was about to settle the dish back down, another flash came from it. That was strange, but the water had been acting strangely, so she looked to see what it would show this time.

A room appeared. It was a study with book-lined shelves, a desk with a big chair, and a couch right across from it.

There was a frail-looking, pretty girl with black hair, pale skin, and hazel eyes, with a hint of forest green around the edges sitting on the couch. She was in a nice dress and looked nervous as a man sat next to her. It was Mr. Springer.

"I missed you," he purred.

"I'm sorry," she whispered.

"Don't be sorry," Mr. Springer responded, placing a hand on her knee. "Show me that pretty neck, sweetness. I'm so hungry."

The girl bared her neck and he barely even numbed it before biting her. She whimpered. Greta felt her heart clench.

Mr. Springer slid his hand under the girl's skirt while tears formed in her eyes. He fed greedily. Completely uncaring for the girl's obvious distress.

A movement at the window caught Greta's eye. She looked over and saw the boy who'd been asking for help in the vision earlier staring into the window. Anger and pain showed in his face before he disappeared back down to where he'd come from.

"Mmm, Echo. You taste perfect every time. I can't wait for next time, sweetness. Give me a little kiss, sugar. I want to taste those pretty lips."

"Please, Mr. Springer. Please, don't," Echo pled gently.

"Do as I say, Echo, or I'll have to tell your parents and you'll be punished. I don't want that…. Do you?" he asked.

"No, sir," she whispered and kissed him.

Greta set the dish down. She couldn't watch anymore of what he was going to do to the girl. There was no way that girl was old enough to feed vampires. There were rules in place against people under eighteen feeding them.

"He's using an obscuring spell. Now that you know about it the spell is broken. Let me scry for him now we know what spell he's using. I should be able to give you a general area to search. You'll find him more quickly that way," Greta said urgently.

"What did you see? You were fine, but then something else happened. What was it?" Victor pressed.

"He's hurting someone. I have the feeling he's going to hurt her worse if you don't find him. This is free. Completely. You have to kill him. You have to save her," she replied with a sniffle.

Greta could feel that girl's fear. She could see the red tinges in Mr. Springer's eyes. Even after the feeding, they were red. He was starving himself in between feedings. That girl was in serious danger of being drained.

After dipping the crystal into the vision water, Greta started swinging it over the map. It didn't take long before it landed in Oregon. Even after she released the chain, the crystal stood straight up. The boy's power must have attracted it. He was a powerful witch.

"There. That's where he is. The spirits want him gone, too. Witches normally against killing, but there's something about what I saw that made me feel sick. Go quickly," she pled.

"I'll take care of it. He won't hurt anyone ever again," Victor vowed and stood to leave.

Once he was gone, Greta breathed a sigh of relief. She had answered the request of the witch boy. The evil vampire would die.

She cleaned her dining room and went to make herself supper. It was a good feeling knowing that she helped someone. She only hoped that he would get there in time.

Something bad was coming for that girl. Greta could feel it in her bones.

About the Author:

Rory McCauley-Hayman is an author from Idaho with a degree in literature and experience in technical writing and creative non-fiction. Rory once hoped to become a research librarian and still takes great joy in exploring information for the sake of discovery.

After years spent as a reader rather than a writer, the stories that once appeared and vanished finally stayed long enough to be written in 2019. Rory published the first book in 2020 and continues to build new fantasy worlds inspired by a love of learning and storytelling.

ALSO BY RORY MCCAULEY-HAYMAN

The Twisted Design Series

The Rogue Queen
The Warrior and the Bouncer
The Vampire's Servant
The Rogue's Initiation
The Healing Souls
The Witch's Temptation
The Feral Heart

Short Story Collections from Twisted Design

A Twisted Collection, Book One
A Twisted Collection, Book Two

The Vasilia Series

The Demon Queen's Desire
The Demon Queen's Duty
The Demon Queen's Destiny

The Dark Hearts Series

Daughter of the Darkest Moon
Eclipsed Hearts

The Twisted Future Series

The Doctor's Dilemma
Insecurity

The Galaxies and Stars Series

Noncorporeal
Corporeal

Standalone Novel

A Hidden Truth